Sisters *of the* Quilt

∽§∾ THE COMPLETE TRILOGY ∾§∽

Cindy Woodsmall

WATERBROOK
PRESS

SISTERS OF THE QUILT
PUBLISHED BY WATERBROOK PRESS
12265 Oracle Boulevard, Suite 200
Colorado Springs, Colorado 80921

When the Heart Cries—All Scripture quotations or paraphrases are taken from the Holy Bible, New International Version®. NIV®. Copyright © 1973, 1978, 1984 by International Bible Society. Used by permission of Zondervan Publishing House. All rights reserved. *When the Morning Comes*—The Scripture quotations on pages 587, 589, and 639 are taken from The Holy Bible: International Standard Version. Copyright © 1994–2007 by The ISV Foundation of Fullerton, California. All rights reserved internationally. The quotation of Galatians 6:7 on page 639 is taken from the King James Version. *When the Soul Mends*—All Scripture quotations are taken from the Holy Bible: International Standard Version®. Copyright © 1996–2008 by The ISV Foundation of Fullerton, California. All rights reserved internationally. Used by permission.

ISBN 978-0-307-72995-8

Published in the United States by WaterBrook Multnomah, an imprint of the Crown Publishing Group, a division of Random House Inc., New York.

WATERBROOK and its deer colophon are registered trademarks of Random House Inc.

Library of Congress Cataloging-in-Publication Data
Woodsmall, Cindy.
    When the heart cries : a novel / Cindy Woodsmall. — 1st ed.
        p. cm. — (Sisters of the quilt ; bk. 1)
    ISBN-13: 978-1-4000-7292-7
    1. Amish—Fiction. I. Title. II. Series: Woodsmall, Cindy. Sisters of the quilt ; bk. 1.
    PS3623.O678W47 2006
    813'.6—dc22
                                    2006011000

Woodsmall, Cindy.
    When the morning comes : a novel / Cindy Woodsmall. — 1st ed.
        p. cm. — (Sisters of the quilt ; bk. 2)
    ISBN 978-1-4000-7293-4 (alk. paper)
    1. Amish women—Fiction. 2. Amish—Fiction. I. Title.
    PS3623.O678W475 2007
    813'.6—dc22
                                    2007015366

Woodsmall, Cindy.
    When the soul mends : a novel / Cindy Woodsmall. — 1st ed.
        p. cm. — (Sisters of the quilt ; bk. 3)
    ISBN 978-1-4000-7294-1
    1. Amish women—Fiction. 2. Amish—Fiction. I. Title.
    PS3623.O678W477 2008
    813'.6—dc22
                                    2008021380

Printed in the United States of America
2010—First Edition

10 9 8 7 6 5 4 3 2 1

New York Times BESTSELLING
AUTHOR OF *When the Soul Mends*

≈§ A NOVEL §≈

When the Heart Cries

Cindy Woodsmall

SISTERS OF THE QUILT, BOOK ONE

To the one man I never wanted to live my life without,
my staunchest supporter, my closest friend: my husband.
With you, life is more than I ever thought possible. Thank you.

To my two oldest sons, who believed in me.
You sacrificed your personal time to help with the needs of the household
and took great care of your younger brother so I could write. Thank you.
You also have my gratitude for keeping my computers and Internet in good
running order in spite of my best attempts at sabotage.

To my youngest son, the radiant energy to each day.
You never doubted I could do this.
When I needed humor in this story, your imagination came to the rescue.
May you one day write the stories of your heart.

To my new daughter-in-law, who has helped in hundreds of various ways.
I'm so thankful you're now a permanent part of our lives.

And above all, to God,
whose patience, love, and forgiveness make
every relationship in my life possible.
May I hear and respond to You and no other.

In loving memory of my mother,
whose inner character always strengthens me
and continues to make its mark on her descendants.

And to all daughters who navigate this ever-changing world,
trying to find who they really are as a child of the King.

Hannah Lapp covered the basket of freshly gathered eggs with her hand, glanced behind her, and bolted down the dirt road. Early morning light filtered through the broad leaves of the great oaks as she ran toward her hopes...and her fears.

A mixed fragrance of light fog, soil, garden vegetables, and jasmine drifted through the air. Hannah adored nature's varying scents. When she topped the knoll and was far enough away that her father couldn't spot her, she turned, taking in the view behind her. Her family's gray stone farmhouse was perched amid rolling acreage. Seventeen years ago she'd been born in that house.

She closed her eyes, breaking the visual connection to home. Her Amish heritage was hundreds of years old, but her heart yearned to be as modern as personal computers and the Internet. Freedom beckoned to her, but so did her relatives.

Some days the desire to break from her family's confinements sneaked up on her. There was a life out there—one that had elbowroom—and it called to her. She took another long look at her homestead before traipsing onward. Paul would be at the end of her one-mile jaunt. Joy quickened her pace. Her journey passed rapidly as she listened to birds singing their morning songs and counted fence posts.

As she topped the hill, a baritone voice sang an unfamiliar tune. The melody was coming from the barn. She headed for the cattle gate at the back of the pastureland that was lined by the dirt road. Beyond the barn sat Paul's grandmother's house, and past that was the paved road used by the English in their cars.

Paul used the cars of the English. Hannah's lips curved into a smile. More accurately, he drove a rattletrap of an old truck. Even though his order of Mennonites was very conservative, much more so than many of the Mennonite groups, they didn't hesitate to use electricity and vehicles. Still, his sect believed in cape dresses and prayer *Kapps* for the women. Surely there was nothing wrong with her caring for Paul since the Amish didn't consider anyone from his order as being an *Englischer* or fancy.

As Hannah opened the cattle gate, Paul appeared in the double-wide doorway to the barn. His head was hatless, a condition frowned upon by her bishop, revealing hair the color of ripe hay glistening under the sun. His blue eyes showed up in Hannah's dreams regularly.

He came toward her, carrying a pitchfork, a frown creasing his brow. "Hannah Lapp, what are you doing, stealing away at this time of day? The whole of Perry County will hear thunder roar when your father finds out." He stopped, jammed the pitchfork into the ground, and stared at her.

The seriousness in his features made Hannah's heart pound in her chest. She wondered if she'd overstepped her boundaries. "It's your last day here for the summer." She held up the basket of eggs. "I thought you and your grandmother might like a special breakfast."

He wiped his brow, his stern gaze never leaving her face. "Gram's awful mean this morning."

"Worse than yesterday?"

He nodded. "*Ya.*" A hint of a smile touched his lips. He often teased her about the word she used so much, threatening to tell everyone at the university about that word and the girl who used it. He knew her Pennsylvania Dutch pronunciation of the word as "jah" was correct, but that didn't stop him from ribbing her about it. As the slight smile turned into a broad grin, it erased all seriousness from his face.

Hannah clutched an egg, reared back, and mimicked throwing it at him.

A deep chuckle rumbled through the air. "Can't hit anything if you don't release it...or in your case, even if you do."

His laughter warmed Hannah's insides. She placed the egg back in the basket, huffed mockingly, and turned to cross the lawn toward the house.

This would be Paul's fourth year to return to college. Once again he'd be leaving her throughout fall, winter, and spring—with letters being their sole communication. Even that limited connection had to come through his grandmother's mailbox. Hannah's father would end their friendship with no apologies if he ever learned of it.

Paul covered the space between them, lifted the basket from her hands, and smiled down at her. "So, won't your family be missing you this morning? Or should I expect your father's horse and buggy to come charging into my grandmother's drive at any moment?"

"My *Daed* would not cause a spectacle like that." Hannah licked her lips, thirsty after hurrying the mile to get there. "I arranged with my sister to do my chores this morning."

"Then who will do her chores?"

"Sarah's off this morning 'cause it's her afternoon to sell produce at Miller's Roadside Stand. I paid her to do my chores. So it all works out, *ya*?"

"You paid her. Was that necessary?"

Hannah shrugged. "I'm not her favorite person. But let's not talk about that. She was willing to work out a deal, and here I am."

Paul opened the screen door to his grandmother's back porch. "I just hope Sarah doesn't say anything to your father."

"There's nothing for her to say. As far as she knows, Gram told me to be here to work." Hannah paused, grasping one side of the basket Paul held. "Besides, even *Daed* tries to remember it's my *rumschpringe*."

He released the basket to her. "But extra freedoms don't hold a lot of meaning for your father, do they?"

She refused the disrespectful sigh that begged to be let loose. Her father could be exasperating at times. "The traditional rules keep him a bit subdued. It wouldn't do to have the bishop discover he's not following our traditions."

Hannah opened the door to the house; but Paul placed his arm across the doorframe in front of her, stopping her in her tracks.

He bent close. Hannah kept her focus straight ahead.

"Look at me, Hannah." The soft rumble of his words against her ear made a tingle run through her. The aroma that she'd come to recognize as easily as the man himself filled her. His scent had come to make her think of integrity, and it made her long to draw closer to him.

Several seconds passed before she managed to lift her gaze to meet his. His lips were pressed together in a smile, but his blue eyes held a look she didn't understand.

"I've been aching to talk to you before I return to college. There are some things I just can't write in a letter. If you hadn't come today, I was planning to knock on your door this afternoon." A light sigh escaped his lips. "But the problems that would have caused would have prevented us from getting to speak."

"Paul!" a shaky voice screeched out. The slow thump of a cane against the wooden floor announced that his grandmother was only a few steps from seeing them.

Hannah took a step backward, thinking she'd die of embarrassment if anyone saw her this close to Paul.

He straightened, putting even more distance between them. "Promise me we'll get time alone today. I need to talk with you before I leave."

Hannah stared into his eyes, promising him anything. "I give you my word," she breathed.

He lowered his hand from the doorframe. "Gram, Hannah's here."

From the berry patch, Paul heard the familiar chime of the sitting room's clock. It rang out five times, but Paul needed no reminder of the hour. He was more than ready to see Hannah for a second time today and before he left for the fall semester.

He dumped the handful of blueberries into the half-full galvanized bucket. He straightened the kinks out of his back and studied the horizon for a glimpse of Hannah. The moment they had washed the last breakfast dish, Hannah had scurried home, hoping no one had missed her. So they hadn't managed to find a moment for private conversation. He turned his attention back to the almost-bare bushes, glad he'd bought two pints of blueberries from Lee McNabb's Farmers' Market yesterday.

He'd had more than enough of treating Hannah as if she were only a friend when he was in love with her. If she were a few years older, he'd have shared how he felt long before now. But even if he told her and she felt the same way, she wasn't the only one who would have to continue keeping their relationship hidden. If he wanted to keep her out of trouble with her father and even her community, he couldn't afford to tell anyone about her. He had too many distant relatives in Owl's Perch who could ruin their future by getting talk started.

Assuming she was interested in a future with him.

As Paul stood at the picnic table, adding the purchased berries to those he'd picked, he saw Hannah topping the hillock of the dirt road. The sight of her caused his pulse to race.

Most of her beautiful chestnut-colored hair was hidden by the prayer *Kapp*. Her brown dress, thick with pleats, came far below her knees and was covered by a full-length black apron. The Amish aimed to be plain in every possible way, from their eighth-grade education to the strict codes of their clothing. A smile tugged at his lips. Hannah had the heart of a lioness and the gentleness of a kitten. Keeping her ordinary was a feat that couldn't be accomplished by a set of rules—even the laws of the *Ordnung*.

She spotted him and waved. He returned her greeting and set down the bucket. His entire being reacted to her: his heart pounded, his palms sweated, and his thoughts became jumbled. But what kept him returning to Owl's Perch each summer wasn't his physical attraction to her. There was something between them that he didn't understand, but he knew it was hard to come by in a guy-girl relationship. With her as his wife and his degree in social work, there was no telling what the two of them could accomplish. He and Hannah both wanted to make a difference in the lives of others—especially children. What better way than to become a lifelong team, even though Hannah was just now learning how to pray and trust God. Until recently, for her everything had been a matter of adherence to rules.

Paul watched her every move as she opened the back gate and crossed the field. As he unlatched the cattle opening to the front of the pasture, loving words rose in his throat and all but forced their way out of his mouth. But, as always, his lack of confidence and his respect for her more stoic ways kept the words unspoken.

"Hi." She handed him the cloth-covered bundle she'd been carrying.

He raised the bundle to his face and breathed in the aroma of fresh-baked bread. "Mmm."

She gave him a challenging grin. "So, who do you think made that bread?"

"You." He spoke with absolute confidence.

Her hands settled on her hips. "There are four bread makers in my home. How can you tell whether I made it?"

"When you've made the dough, the loaf has a hint of blaze within it, as if you put part of your soul in it."

Hannah laughed. "You talk foolishness, no?"

"I'm serious, Hannah." He inhaled the scent of the cloth-wrapped loaf again. "If you breathe deeply, you'll smell the heat." He held the bread toward her face. "Just like the fire in you, Lion-heart."

She clicked her tongue, warning him he was edging toward impropriety. He lowered the loaf and gazed into her eyes, not wanting to disrupt the power of the feelings that ran between them. To him, Hannah possessed all the courage, control, and nobility associated with lions. The term fit perfectly, even if its use did embarrass her.

"Wait here." Paul strode to the back door, grasping the handle to the bucket of blueberries on the way. He marched across the porch and into the kitchen. After setting the pail and the loaf of bread on the table, he hollered, "Gram."

Finding her in the living room reading her Bible, he stepped to the round mahogany end table next to her. "Hannah's here. We're going for a walk." He took one of the walkie-talkie radios off the table and turned it on. "If you need anything, just push this button." He pointed to the knob with the musical note on it. "If you buzz us, we'll come back pronto." He set the radio on the table and attached the matching one to his belt loop.

His grandmother's eyes searched his face.

Paul raised an eyebrow. "Please try not to need anything." He kissed her on the head.

"I'll give you fifteen minutes, young man. Then I'm pushing that button. Young people don't require any more time than that."

"Come on, Gram. Hannah and I need some uninterrupted time to talk."

Soft wrinkles creased her face as she studied him. "I'll give you twenty. After that, whatever needs to be said can be said on the back porch or in the kitchen. And no back talk or I'll drive to her parents' place myself."

Paul sighed. "Yes ma'am." He hurried to the back door. Gram never allowed him to feel like an adult. When he was with his parents in Maryland, they gave him a lot more freedom than his gram did, and at the university he had freedom galore. He didn't need it there.

He checked his pocket for the gift box and bounded out the back door.

Hannah stood on a knoll, staring across the green pastures at the grazing herd as the breeze fluttered through her skirts and played with the strings of the *Kapp* on her head. He'd love to have a photo of that. Any photo of Hannah would be nice.

He came up to her and held out his hand. For the first time, she placed her hand in his.

They jogged across the field and into the shade of the woods. When they came to a bridge that stretched across the creek, they slowed. Hannah peeled off her slip-on shoes and sat on the edge of the wooden planks. Her feet dangled high above the water.

Paul shook off his sandals and sat beside her.

For a moment no words were spoken. The sounds of the water babbling, some birds chirping, and an occasional cow mooing filled the air.

Ignoring the nervousness that clawed at his gut, Paul covered her hand with his. "It gets harder to leave every year." He drew her hand to his lips and kissed it.

She gawked at him, as if she hadn't ever expected him to kiss her. He leaned in closer, hoping to kiss her cheek.

Clearing her throat, she pulled away from him. "I think it would be best if we go back now." She stood.

"But…" Paul jumped up. "I…I'm not finished with what I wanted to say. I want to talk about us."

She picked up her shoes. "Don't ask to see my heart and then return to your girls on campus." Without looking at him, she stuffed a foot into each shoe. "I may not be educated like them, but I'm nobody's fool, Paul

Waddell. I've heard stories of what it's like out there, and I don't appreciate this. We're better friends than this." Brushing her hands against her apron, she lifted her gaze to him.

Uncertainty roiled inside him, making his stomach hurt. He slid his feet into his sandals. Was he ruining the very friendship he cherished above everything else in his life? "I do not have a girl on campus, and I never have. There's no one for me but you…if you'd care to be called my girl."

She stared at him for a moment. "What are you saying?" Her hoarse whisper etched itself into his soul.

Paul moved in closer. "I'm saying I want us to have a future…together." He reached into his pocket and pulled out a long, thin, gold-colored box. "This is for you."

Hannah shook her head. "I can't take that."

"All this time we've been friends, and you can't take a simple gift?" He held it out for her, hoping she'd accept it. "It's what we've done together, working for Gram along with making goods to sell at McNabb's Farmers' Market."

She lifted the box from his hands and held it while questions remained in her eyes.

Paul dared to touch her cheek with his fingers. "Hannah, you are all my thoughts and hopes."

She stared at him, her breathing rapid.

"We'll have to wait at least a year, but…" Paul stared at his feet, kicked a patch of moss, and tried not to mumble. "Hannah Lapp, will you marry me?"

She didn't utter a sound or even twitch a foot. He raised his eyes. Her face had disbelief written across it. "But…my family… I…I… It'll be hard enough on *Mamm* if I don't join the faith, but her heart will break if I move out of Owl's Perch."

Paul rubbed the back of his neck. Winning the approval of her family was an uphill battle, one he had to win or her heart would rend in two. He gazed into her eyes, hoping to assure her that he'd do his best.

They both knew that if she married him, it would affect her relationship with her family for the rest of her life. Since she hadn't been baptized into the Amish faith, she wouldn't be shunned if she chose to marry a Mennonite. But her father wouldn't allow an outside influence to enter his home any more than he would allow electricity. When she was permitted to have a rare visit, she would not be allowed to enter the house. Things weren't that way in every Amish family, but that didn't help Hannah's situation.

The key to winning over her father, Paul hoped, was patience and timing. As much as he wished for the right words to soothe Hannah's concerns, he didn't have all the answers.

As if absorbing and accepting the truth of his feelings for her, a slow smile erased her distress. She managed a nod.

"Is that a yes?" He clasped his hands over hers, which were still holding the unopened box.

"Yes," she whispered.

"Hannah, I can't believe this. I mean...I didn't think... You keep a man guessing, that's for sure."

She angled her head. "Would you have me be bold, like those girls I hear about among the English?"

Paul squeezed her hands. "I'll never be interested in anyone but you." He reached for her face. His fingers lightly trailed down the sides of her cheeks. "You're so beautiful."

Hannah backed away, sputtering. "Beauty is vanity, and I'll thank you not to put any stock in it."

Paul laughed. "Oh, you are beautiful, but that's not why I'm interested. Why, I could find lots of beautiful girls if that's what mattered to me."

She studied him for a moment before she chuckled. "Listen to your boldness. Why, I should have thrown that egg at you this morning."

Paul laughed. "Too late." He pointed to the gift. "Open the present."

With her cheeks covered in a blush, Hannah removed the golden ribbon wrapped around the small box. She lifted the lid and pulled out a thin book, about two inches by three inches. Her brows knitted slightly as she opened the book to a page of columns and numbers.

"The card I had you sign last week wasn't for Gram's tax purposes. It was for our savings account." He pointed to the bottom number in one of the columns. "With all our work over the summers, this is what we've earned so far to sponsor that little girl in Thailand."

The joy-filled surprise in her eyes made every drop of sweat worth it. "You've saved that much?"

"*We've* saved it. We planted that huge garden beside Gram's every spring for three years. We sold the vegetables and bought the supplies for canning. I may be the one who got stuck with the handyman jobs of roofing and such, but you sewed all those doodads—from dolls to comforters. It took both of us to earn this money. Thanks to our efforts, some young Thai girl will go to live at House of Grace instead of being sold into slavery. She'll get clothes, food, and an education."

Hannah ran her fingers over the columns of numbers. "Who would have thought that with a little hard work we could do so much for someone?"

"God, I suspect." He desperately wanted to kiss her. Instead, he held his hand out for the book. "I want to show you something else."

Hannah gave him the book, and he flipped the page. "This section shows a portion of money I've set aside in a separate account." He pointed to the right spot. "This is for our living expenses."

Hannah's attention moved from the book to him. "But you're the only one who's been putting money into the living expenses part, right?"

Paul nodded, unsure what she was getting at.

She scrunched her brows. "Then how do you have so much already?"

"I've been aiming at this for years."

She seemed too surprised to respond. He kissed her on the forehead and was taken aback by the softness of her skin. The longer he stood so close to her, the stronger the need to kiss her lips became. But he was afraid she might not appreciate that move. "As soon as I graduate, I'll work for your father all summer without charging him. During that time, I hope to get his blessing to marry you."

Hannah rubbed her throat, concern flashing in her eyes. "And if he doesn't approve?"

"He will, Hannah, even if we need to wait an extra year or two." Paul bent and planted a kiss on her cheek. Her soft skin smelled sweet, like honey and cinnamon. "Your folks will come around."

A shadow seemed to cross her features. She picked up the side of her apron and tucked the gift box, ribbon, and book into the hidden pocket inside her pinafore. "If anyone can win over my family and community, it'll be you." Lifting her chin and squaring her shoulders, she giggled. "*Ya?*"

"*Ya.*" Paul nodded and smiled.

The two-way radio beeped at him, and Gram's voice muttered his name.

"Come on." He held out his hand. "We'd better get back before Gram ruins my plans to win your father's approval."

Hannah put her hand in his, and they hurried toward his grandmother's house. "My heart is fluttering."

Paul paused, tightening his hand around hers. "I love you, Hannah Lapp."

She lowered her head, staring at their clasped hands. "I love you too."

Carrying the bucket of blueberries, Hannah locked the back cattle gate and waved her last farewell to Paul. As she headed for home, her heart was soaring higher than the jets she'd seen streak across the sky. Wherever those people were going couldn't be as exciting as where her dreams were taking her.

What a remarkable man, to be willing to work for her father in order to win his approval, to wait patiently to win her family over. Her heart thumped with excitement, and laughter welled up within her.

She moved the thin metal handle on the bucket of blueberries to her other hand and wiped a bead of sweat off her neck. Paul had spent time on a hot August afternoon picking berries for her family, and he'd get no credit for the kind deed. It was just like him to work hard for others and be thankful if he'd managed to be of help. She couldn't believe such a wonderful man considered it a privilege to marry her.

Since his dream was to become a social worker and for them to be foster parents, perhaps she could do him justice even though she had only an eighth-grade education. She loved children. And she knew how to run a household and how to turn a profit doing ordinary things like canning, sewing, and cleaning. The English girls at his college might have their education, but Hannah was determined to outshine all of them when it came to being a perfect wife for Paul and a wonderful mother to their children.

She touched her *Kapp,* proud that Paul found her ways pleasing. Oh, there were so many things she wanted to ask him, so many conversations they could have now that she knew he loved her. She looked forward to his letters more than ever. This time, there was no question that the sea of girls out there held no interest for him.

At the sound of car tires crunching against the pebbles on the dirt road behind her, she stepped to the far shoulder. Was it really possible that Paul had asked her to marry him? The tiny bubble of doubt burst as she slid her hand under her apron and felt the leather book in the hidden pocket. He'd put her name on all his hard-earned money. He trusted her with his heart, his dreams, and his earnings. He'd win her parents' approval. She knew he would.

Realizing the car she'd heard hadn't passed her yet and assuming the driver wanted more space, she stepped farther to the side of the road. It was just a one-lane country road, used mainly by horses and buggies. She refrained from looking over her shoulder, even though the smell of the acrid fumes from the growling engine grew stronger.

The car pulled up beside her. "Excuse me," a man said.

Hannah stopped and turned. She saw a sleek car that looked different from anything she'd ever seen. Shifting her gaze to the driver, she supposed he wasn't even as old as Paul, although she couldn't see much of his face. He had a beard that looked a couple of days old, and he wore a baseball cap and sunglasses.

"Can you tell me how to get to Duncannon?"

Studying the countryside, she thought of the route the hired drivers always took when chauffeuring her and her family toward Duncannon. Hannah pointed down the road in the direction his car was headed. "Keep going until you come to a four-way stop. Take a left. You'll go quite a piece until you come to another stop sign. Turn left again. Then keep going, and you'll start seeing signs that show how to get to Duncannon."

The man frowned and shook his head. After turning off the car engine, he opened the door. As he got out, he looked behind him at the long dirt road. Then he turned back. "How far until I reach a paved road?"

"About a mile."

The man smiled and eyed her from head to toe. "Right after that one farmhouse?"

Feeling pinpricks of discomfort, Hannah smoothed her skirt with her free hand and swallowed hard. He wasn't as unfamiliar with these roads as he'd made himself sound at first. Hoping he'd get in his car and leave, she started walking.

The man grabbed her arm. "No need to run off."

She fought against the sense of panic, jerked her arm free of his grip, and ran.

Two large hands hit her back, pushing her hard. She went sprawling across the gravel road. Her blueberries tumbled in every direction as the bucket flew from her hand. Hannah tried to stand up, but another forceful push to her back sent her careening again. She pulled herself to her knees, trying to gain her balance. As she scrambled to her feet, she realized her palms were bleeding.

She glanced back at the stranger. Although most of his face was hidden behind his sunglasses, beard, and hat, she saw him smirk as he reached for her. *Run, Hannah! Run!* her mind screamed, but she couldn't move.

The man grabbed her by the thick apron straps that crisscrossed her back. He lifted her body slightly, dragged her to his car, spun her around to face him, and tossed her across the seat like a rag doll. Grabbing her by the pinafore, he shoved her farther into the car. The back of her head hit the door on the other side. Her vision blurred.

The man climbed on top of her. Hannah pushed against his face and body, but he didn't budge. She flailed at him, but he didn't flinch. He repositioned his body, jerking at her skirts.

What was happening?

Tears streamed down Hannah's cheeks. Shadows swirled from within, as if she were being buried under layers of suffocating soil. Fear and anger joined forces within her, altering, shifting who she was, how she thought about life.

When she no longer felt like Hannah Lapp, his weight lifted, and he pulled her out of the car. He dragged her several feet in front of the vehicle, then flung her to the road like a filthy rag.

Only vaguely aware of her surroundings, she heard his car engine roar. Confusion lifted. She knew he intended to run over her. Crawling on her hands and knees, she moved out from in front of his car. Her dress tangled around her knees, and she couldn't move any farther. She pulled herself upright. Gravel spewed from the tires. As he passed her, he flung the car door open, hitting her with it. She flew forward and landed hard on the ground as his car sped off.

Gasping for air, she spotted the shiny silver pail lying near the ditch. On her hands and knees, she grabbed the bucket and tried to gather its spilled contents. Her body screamed out in pain with every movement, but *Daed* would be furious if she wasted the produce. She swiped at her tears, desperate to find all the berries. Clawing at the road, sifting through dirt and pebbles, she searched for the fruit, dropping each berry into the bucket. Dragging her apron across her eyes, she cleared the tears away. She looked in the pail. It contained mostly gravel and clods of earth with a few bruised and torn berries.

After staggering to her feet, she turned in one direction and then the other. Confused, she stood in the middle of the familiar road. Which way was home? She had to get home.

Her *Mamm* would know what to do.

The scent of freshly baked bread wafted through the evening air, guiding her in the right direction.

fraid the man might return, Hannah hurried along the road toward home, faltering with every step. When her house came into sight, a bit of relief nipped at the corners of her panicked soul. She stumbled across a patch of grass, dropping the bucket of ravaged blueberries.

As she ran across the dirt driveway, the heel of her shoe caught on the ripped hem of her long brown skirt. She went sprawling across dirt and gravel, scraping more flesh off her palms and forearms. Getting to her feet, she reached to adjust her *Kapp* and realized it was missing. Bands of hair had fallen loose from the regulated bun.

Forbidden.

A painful shudder ran through her. She placed her bleeding palms over her skirts, bent over, and threw up. Shaking so hard it frightened her, she wiped her mouth with her apron. The scorching sun and miserable August heat made staying on her feet even harder.

Surely her mother would make sense of this nightmare. Hannah's eyes searched from one end of the property to the other, covering the yard, barns, and garden. She finally spotted her, carrying an armful of sweet corn.

Mamm's smile faded when she caught sight of Hannah. The husked corn fell to the ground, rolling in every direction. She gathered her long skirts and ran to her daughter. The odd sight of *Mamm* letting go of everything and running added to Hannah's nausea.

Mamm wrapped a consoling arm around her.

"Oh, *Mamm*, there was this horrible man." The words stammered from her lips in Pennsylvania Dutch. "He…he pulled me into his car."

She stepped back, resisting her daughter's embrace. Pulling Hannah's chin level with her own, she gazed into her face. Her mother's eyes, which had always embodied gentleness and control, grew strange and unfamiliar. The color drained from her face, like apple cider spilling out of an upturned Mason jar. *Mamm* shrieked at the top of her lungs.

Horror ripped through Hannah. Confusion once again churned inside her soul. She had never heard her mother scream before. Ever.

"Zeb!" *Mamm's* high-pitched voice rang throughout the farm. "Zeb!" She elongated the word, sending it once again across the peaceful grounds.

Her father sprinted from the garden, dropping the hoe from his hand.

Chills ran up and down Hannah's body. The familiar sight of her father in his black trousers, brown shirt, suspenders, and straw hat looked real enough. Then why did she feel so detached from her body? Her siblings seemed to float from the corners of the property to see what was going on.

Her father waved a hand at them without slowing his pace. "Tend to your chores." They slid out of sight.

Daed didn't slow until his hand was under his wife's forearm, supporting her. *"Was iss letz?"* he asked, using the only language they spoke among themselves. Hannah was relieved they had their own language. If that horrid man was lurking in the woods, he wouldn't know what was being said. Her father looked at her fallen hair and torn clothing.

"My Hannah." *Mamm's* ruddy hand pointed a shaky finger in her daughter's face. "She's been attacked!" A moan escaped her lips.

Nausea churned in the pit of Hannah's stomach at the guttural sound. Suddenly she wished she hadn't told. Her mother clung to her father, screaming in agony as if God Himself had pronounced a curse upon the Lapp family. *Mamm* released her grip, doubled over in pain, and collapsed. *Daed* clutched her, keeping her from falling to the ground. He lifted her and carried her in his arms.

He looked at both of the females with equal concern and confusion in his gray blue eyes. "Are you in need of a doctor?"

Hannah stared at the limp body in her father's arms. That couldn't really be her mother. This woman seemed too tired to walk, and yet she continued to tug at her father's shirt, mumbling nonsense about Hannah's future.

"I'm speaking to you, child." *Daed's* tone remained even. His calmness seemed out of place.

He shifted the woman in his arms while keeping his focus on Hannah. "Luke and Levi are gone for the evening. Do ya need your sister to go to Mrs. Waddell's for help?" His words came out slow and purposeful.

Hannah looked toward the road. That man might be out there, creeping around. If everything happening was real and her sister did go for help… "No. I…I don't need a doctor." She stared at her palms, wondering how she'd ever heal from such gashes. Lowering her hands, she focused on her father.

The taut lines in his face showed more stress than his voice. "Can you get some water for you and your mother?"

Hannah nodded and then watched her father stride toward the wooden bench that sat a stone's throw behind their home, under the broad, heavily leafed limbs of the beech tree.

Disoriented and dreamlike, Hannah moved to the pump and wrapped a corner of her apron over her right hand so she could cushion the cuts from the pump handle. She took the tin cup from the wooden bucket. Lifting and lowering the pump handle soon produced a trickle of water. When the cup was filled, she trudged up the slope to her mother, who was being held upright on the seat by her father. He was patting her hand and telling her to trust God. Hannah thrust the cup toward her parents. Her father took the drink and held it to *Mamm's* lips, insisting she swallow.

Hannah turned away and gazed at the scenes playing out across the yard as if she were watching life in slow motion. Her fifteen-year-old sister, Sarah, appeared to be purposely distracting their younger siblings by taking them to the pond. Lifting Rebecca onto her hip, Sarah carried the three-year-old across the road. Samuel ran ahead and grabbed a fishing pole that was propped against a tree. Twelve-year-old Esther opened the gate and waited for the brood to enter the pasture before fastening the lock.

Hannah turned her focus back to her parents. Her father was still holding the cup of water to *Mamm's* lips. Hannah waited, feeling nearly invisible, wishing she truly were.

Daed talked in soft tones, assuring his wife everything was fine. When her mother stopped mumbling gibberish, his attention moved to Hannah. "Have you caused more trouble than you should have, child?"

"I…I…" The pain in her chest grew. It was an unfamiliar, sickening feeling. Unlike the times when she'd skinned her knee as a child or baked a bad batch of bread, this pain was being intensified by the very people who had comforted her through the other bad things.

The frustration on his face eased, and the gentleness she knew so well softened his features. "Tell me of this thing that's happened."

She tried to comply but found embarrassment so thick that it made speaking impossible.

"You can always tell your father what's going on. How else can I guide the household?" His slow, patient manner reminded her of the closeness they had shared—before she changed from being his little girl to a nearly grown woman.

Hannah swallowed hard and willed herself to obey. She managed to release pieces of information between her sobbing and stammering. Tears filled her father's eyes and burned a trail down his weathered face. He pulled his arm from her mother, making sure she was steady enough not to keel over.

He eased to his feet and placed his hands on her shoulders. " 'Tis not right, Hannah," he whispered. "What happened to you should happen to no one." Her father enfolded her in his arms. She could smell the familiar mixture of garden soil and hard work. But his embrace didn't carry the same warmth it had yesterday. Oddly, his touch, which had always held pleasant fellowship, disgusted her.

"The unmentionable has happened to you."

She pushed free of his embrace. "I don't understand."

The horrid noise of her father fighting to keep control of his emotions filled the air. "You were forced to do the unmentionable," he whispered hoarsely. "You were…raped. And that is illegal, even among the English."

She covered her face with her apron and wailed. Unable to keep herself upright any longer, she sank to her knees on the cool grass and rested her forehead against the earth.

Within moments, her mother's arms enfolded her. She nuzzled her chin against Hannah's shoulder, rocking back and forth. The two cried bitterly.

Guilt bore down on Hannah, blame so heavy that no amount of tears would ever wash it away. But she couldn't pinpoint why she felt in the wrong. As Hannah gained some control and sat up, anger burned even more than the guilt. "It's not right, *Mamm*. It's not right."

Her mother's swollen eyelids closed slowly as she nodded. "I know."

"Then let's do something about it." The words hurled out, vengeful and desperate.

A pair of strong hands wrapped around her upper arms and raised her to her feet. She found herself staring into her father's eyes.

"You're upset. You can't really mean that." He released her.

Hannah staggered backward.

His eyes misted. "You know we must let God take vengeance, not man."

The throbbing in her temples matched the ache in her abdomen and

the rending of her heart. "If we don't tell someone…maybe the police…"
—she searched for words amid the confusion that screamed inside her
head—"he could do this again to someone else, no?"

The shoulders of the stout man she'd always trusted slumped. "Ruth,
please try to talk some sense into her."

Rising from the ground, *Mamm* took hold of her husband's arm to
support her shaking body. "We live a simple life, Hannah, as God commanded." The quaking of her voice made her words hard to understand.
"You know our ways do not allow us to defend ourselves. Besides, without phones or cars, we would have no way to get help if we provoked this
man. What would we do if he…brought trouble? It is best to leave things
in the Lord's hands."

"But—"

"Look around you, daughter." Her father made a sweep with his hand
in the air. Hannah viewed the rolling landscape, cattle, outbuildings, and
her house. At the pond across the road, her brother and sisters sat on the
pier, dangling their bare feet in the water. "Peace reigns here. You cannot
destroy that just because you want vengeance. I understand how you feel.
I do. But we must leave this alone and move forward."

"*Daed,* please—"

"I'm sorry you don't understand, Hannah, but I must do what is best
for the family and the community." He patted *Mamm's* arm. "Ruth, you
must calm yourself. Your daughter is upset, and rightly so, but we will take
good care of her. She is safe, and we'll put this behind us. Now take her
inside and prepare a bath for her. Then she can go to bed for the evening.
Sarah will tend to the young children for tonight." When he folded his
arms across his chest, Hannah knew the conversation was over.

Hannah sat on the stool in the bathroom, struggling not to cry as *Mamm* connected a hose to fill the large tin tub. The hose ran from the window behind the kitchen sink—the only source of heated water—along the side of the house and through the bathroom window. Trying to block out the vision of what had taken place less than an hour before, Hannah watched her mother pour vinegar and Epsom salts under the running water.

"You'll be fine," *Mamm* cooed with a shaky voice. "Fervent prayers and a few days of time will get this behind you, *ya?*"

Unable to share her feelings, Hannah nodded.

Her mother stirred the water with her hand. "It's not in your father's ways to use a doctor, but if you need one after a few days of rest, he'll take you."

Hannah tried to stop herself from shaking. Her father had said she was safe. But she didn't feel safe.

Laying the hose in the galvanized tub, her mother's hands still trembled. She dried them on her apron. "I'll grind some lobelia seeds for your pain."

Hannah gasped for air. "Yes, I'm sure that will help." A sharp pain stabbed her throat. Had she not just lied? She shook her head, burying the guilt.

Mamm squirted some liquid soap under the hose. "I'll fetch your gown and a towel." She left the room.

Hannah sat on a stool beside the tub and stared at the bubbles as the horror of the attack played out in her mind. The suds burst and disappeared, much like the innocent life she'd known before today.

Her heart ached to talk to Paul. He was good at explaining things to her, at making life take on joy and hope. But what would he think of her now? Unable to imagine sharing such a horridly embarrassing thing with him, she pushed aside thoughts of getting comfort from him. Instead she tried to visualize him pleased with her—as he'd been when she had agreed to marry him. It was a vain effort, for every time she tried to see Paul smiling, all she saw was that man dragging her into his car.

"Hannah." Her father's deep voice rumbled through the washroom.

Unsure of which images flashing in front of her were real, she blinked. "Yes?" she whispered.

"Take this." He held out a small piece of brown paper folded in half with a powdery substance in the crease. Her mother thrust a mug in front of her. But Hannah's arms remained limp by her side, refusing to respond.

Mamm lowered the cup. "I told you she didn't hear me when I was talking to her. I tried for three or four minutes to get her to hear me. Look at her, Zeb. What are we going to do?"

Her father held the folded paper filled with crushed lobelia seeds between his thumb and forefinger. "Open your mouth, child." Hannah obeyed. Her father dumped the medicine on her tongue. Her mother held the cup to Hannah's lips. Hannah swallowed, her throat burning at the invasion.

"She'll be fine." *Daed* placed his hands firmly on Hannah's shoulders. "Won't you?"

Wondering if her father really believed that, she nodded.

Mamm broke into fresh tears and ran from the room. *Daed* stared after her. "Go ahead and take your bath." Without another glance in her direction, he pulled the door closed behind him.

Forcing her body to do as her father had told her, Hannah rose from the stool and locked the door. Her arms and legs felt heavy, as if each were carrying a bucket of feed. She pulled off her filthy, torn clothing. After she slid into the tub of warm water, she buried her face in a towel and sobbed quietly.

A tap on the door interrupted her weeping.

"Hannah?" *Mamm* called through the door. "Are you okay?"

Hannah lowered the thick towel from her face. She kept her eyes shut tight, afraid if she opened them, she might discover she was in that car again. *"Ya."* Her voice sounded feeble in her ears.

"You've been in there for two hours." Her voice sounded scratchy. "The water must be cold."

Hannah had only been in the bath for a few minutes. She forced her eyes open. The room was dark. How could that be?

She stood and wrapped her aching, dripping body in a towel. Climbing out of the tub, she realized how cool the water had become. She dried off, then grabbed the matches from the shelf to light the kerosene lamp. Her hands were still trembling as she lit a match and placed the flame against the wick. As the blaze lit the room, odd shapes took form. Everything looked unfamiliar. She'd helped do laundry in this room every winter since she was three, but the wooden shelves, pegs, and basket for dirty clothes appeared foreign.

Hannah slid into her nightgown and wrapped a shawl over her shoulders. Paul must be at his parents' place by now. Maybe *Daed* would let her go to Mrs. Waddell's and call him, just this once. She wouldn't tell Paul what had happened, but she was desperate to hear his voice. He'd tell her of his love and the wonderful future they would have together.

But if she asked permission to call him, her father would know of their friendship. If he learned of the relationship this way, it would be much harder for Paul to earn *Daed's* approval later on. And then the monster— that awful, nasty man—would have ruined everything.

An odd, prickly sensation ran through her chest, making breathing difficult. She removed the wooden peg lock and opened the door. Her mother stood just outside, in the small back entryway where boots and coats lined the walls. A shadowy glow from the lamp fell across *Mamm's* stricken face. Resisting the urge to fall into her mother's arms and cry, Hannah remained at a distance.

Her father entered from the kitchen, carrying a small jar of salve. His medium-sized frame appeared large when encircled by the shadows from the lamplight. "Your younger siblings are asleep. You will get some peace and quiet tonight." He smiled, obviously trying to sound like his normal self. "See, all is well," he assured her, though his confidence seemed forced. But there was something different in her father's voice, something suggesting an edgy coldness he'd never had before.

She handed her father the lamp and followed her mother into the kitchen. Stiff and shaky as a new colt, Hannah made her way to one of the benches that sat on each side of the kitchen table. The familiar rich wood brought no warmth to her tonight. Too weak and dizzy to talk, she sat in silence, hoping with every blink of her eyes that she would awaken from this horrible nightmare.

Her father set the lamp on a nearby shelf and paused in the doorway. "I've been thinking. It is best that you not speak of this to anyone, including your brothers and sisters. They only need to know that you fell on your way home and your mother thought you were more injured than you are." He paused. "Everything I just said is true, no?"

She didn't want anyone to know what had really happened, including herself. She silently begged God to let her die. She couldn't handle this. Incapable of responding, Hannah lowered her eyes.

Mamm shuffled to the gas stove and removed the lid of a simmering pot. "I prepared some broth and rice while you were in the bath. It'll make you feel better." Her mother's jerky movements and quivering voice made Hannah think *Mamm* might start screaming again.

Hannah glanced at her father, wordlessly asking permission to turn down the offer. The muscles in his face appeared taut as he stepped closer to her. Lifting the edge of the shawl that had fallen off her shoulder, he nuzzled it against her neck. The movement was comforting, causing Hannah to think she might survive the night yet. Then he leaned close and whispered, "Do as your mother says."

The shaking that had subsided returned with a vengeance.

Her father knelt in front of her. "She needs to know you'll be fine," he whispered before turning her hands over and gently rubbing some salve on her wounds.

Closing her eyes tight against the onslaught of nausea, Hannah realized her father's desire to prove to *Mamm* that Hannah was fine outweighed everything else.

She gulped. The hard, dry swallow was followed by an intense desire to flee the house and seek refuge at Mrs. Waddell's. Fear grew until it seemed to form its own silhouette. The thought of going to Mrs. Waddell's was ridiculous. Hannah couldn't go anywhere. *He* might be out there waiting for her.

Hannah hung the shawl on a wooden peg and silently padded to the foot of the bed. Moonbeams cast a silvery glow across the room, revealing the two double beds with her three younger sisters in them. The wonderful scent of air-dried sheets brought no comfort as she slid between them.

Sarah roused. "You okay?" Her slow speech and groggy voice felt like a slap across Hannah's bruised heart. How could she have been sleeping peacefully while Hannah's world was crashing down around her?

Loneliness filled Hannah, smothering her just as that man's body had. "*Ya*. Go back to sleep."

Sarah turned her back to Hannah and snuggled against the pillow beneath her head. Soon Hannah heard the deep breaths of her sisters sleeping all around her. *Mamm* was still downstairs, talking to *Daed*. The whispers of her mother's stress settled over the night. Her scratchy voice mingled with *Daed's* muted tones.

Hannah curled into a ball and buried her face in the pillow, afraid to make any noise.

*P*aul sat at the desk in his bedroom, writing a letter to Hannah. Yesterday evening when he got home, his parents had all seven of his high-school classmates waiting to see him. A huge meal had been spread out on picnic tables in his backyard, and his sister and her family were there. Since the parents of his graduating class had pulled their kids from the local public school in seventh grade and had begun their own school in a garage-turned-classroom, the eight of them stayed in contact with each other regularly. Marcus, his closest friend, was there too. He was the only one at the get-together who wasn't Mennonite, but Marcus wasn't one to ever feel out of place. He and Paul had been neighbors and good friends most of their lives, and now they were college roommates. Without Marcus's influence over Paul's parents, Paul might not have been allowed to further his education, since most of his sect didn't believe in going on to college.

The only disappointing part of the evening was that Hannah was not by his side. As he wrote to her about the party, he assured her there would be plenty more gatherings that she would be a part of. It was easier to write to her now that he knew how she felt about him, now that they had plans to marry.

A knock at the bedroom door made him lay down his pen and turn the top page of his letter facedown. "Come in."

The door eased open just enough to reveal Carol's upper body. Paul rocked back in his seat, facing the doorway. "I thought you and William had plans with your boys tonight."

His sister was seven years older than he, and her face seemed to be quickly becoming identical to their mother's. "I was hoping I could talk you into joining us for the evening. We're going to the Senators' game." She looked at the stack of papers on the desk.

Paul laid his hand on top of the letter. Hannah would love to see a minor-league baseball game. Snacks at the stadium and the entertainment between each inning would be treats for her. "I have some things I need to get done today, packing and such. I have to leave tomorrow afternoon since classes start on Tuesday. I need time to apply for jobs and get settled in before Tuesday."

Carol huffed. "You cut your time with us shorter every summer."

Paul rose from the desk, guilt nipping at him. "There's just not enough time to spread around. It's nothing personal."

She pushed the door open farther, and Paul saw Dorcas standing behind her. She was one of his seven classmates and the daughter of his mother's best friend.

Looking at the lace on her dress, he felt his face flush. His sister was up to something, and he didn't need his bachelor's degree to figure it out. He wanted to shoot an angry look toward Carol, but Dorcas would see it. He didn't want to hurt the girl's feelings. She was a nice-enough person, he guessed. But Paul had seen enough of her selfish side over the years to make him wonder if she was truly as manipulative as she sometimes appeared.

Carol's eyebrows rose, warning him to behave.

Paul willed himself to smile at Dorcas. "Did you sleep in after our late-night gathering?"

Dorcas's green eyes fastened on him as they'd done for as long as he could remember. "My sister piled on my head at eleven o'clock, calling me Rip Van Winkle. You?"

"I awoke before the sun rose."

An awkward silence fell between them. Every possible topic had been discussed at length last night as his company had talked and laughed until after two in the morning. The only subject that hadn't come up was Hannah. Every once in a while over the past few years, he had mentioned to Carol that he was interested in someone—usually whenever she started pushing Dorcas on him. His know-it-all sister had accused him of having his eye on Gram's Amish helper. Paul hadn't denied or confirmed her suspicions. But he trusted that Carol had never said a word to his parents about why he was willing to spend his summers helping Gram while doing odd jobs for her neighbors.

Carol edged to the side of his bed and took a T-shirt from a clean but crumpled pile. She shook it out and folded it. "We'll help you get ready and pack tomorrow if you'll go out with us tonight."

Paul shook his head. "I can handle it. You guys have fun."

After placing the folded shirt on the bed, Carol moved to his desk. "Are you making a list of things to do?" Her fingertips grasped the corner of Paul's letter.

Paul placed his palm over the paper. He gave a firm look to his sister, hoping she'd realize that he was an adult with a right to his privacy.

Concern shone in her eyes. "Please don't tell me you're still infatuated with that Amish girl." She said the words "Amish girl" as if Hannah were inferior.

Dorcas gasped. Paul looked back to the doorway where she was standing. She looked hurt. Was it possible she still hoped that Paul would take an interest in her? Her attention moved to the letter in his hand before she turned her head. But she remained there, listening.

"You're out of line, Carol. And I'd appreciate it if you wouldn't say the word *Amish* as though they're dirt."

Carol sighed. "Look, I have nothing against them. But if you're planning on courting one of them and bringing her out from her people, I'm warning you, it'll never work."

He stood and placed his hands on Carol's shoulders and forced a gentle tone. "She and I both hold to God's truth. He'll give our relation-ship strength to work through our differences."

Carol eased onto the bed, freeing herself from his tender grip. She grabbed the folded shirt and squeezed it to her chest. "Is it that Hannah something-or-other?"

Hoping he wasn't making a mistake in admitting it, Paul nodded.

"Paul, the Amish aren't like us. They're legalistic beyond reason. I mean, we live without television and radios, but that's nothing compared to the Old Order Amish restrictions. She'll continue in her ways, even if she's physically removed from her people."

Paul scoffed. "Hannah will find whatever freedoms she thinks are the right ones, given time."

Carol stood, facing him. "You're being naive. She could never be com-fortable outside the ways she's been taught. It's the same as you getting comfortable wearing a dress and a *Kapp*." She tossed the shirt on the bed. "Everything that girl's been taught she learned from the Amish, including her schoolteacher—someone with only an eighth-grade Amish education herself. Even those who leave almost always go back."

Paul crouched beside his bed and grabbed a duffel bag from under it. "You're exaggerating, and you know it."

Carol stepped back, giving him room to get the bag out. "Paul, for goodness sake, think this through. If she marries outside her faith, it'll break her parents' hearts, ruin all fellowship with her siblings, and bring embarrassment to her whole family."

He pulled the bag out and stood.

At the bedroom doorway, Dorcas tapped the wooden frame with her fingernails, drawing their attention. "I'm sure Paul knows what he's doing."

"But...," Carol sputtered.

Dorcas tilted her head and gave a slight shrug. "You've already shared your opinion, Carol. It's time to let it go."

Carol stood motionless, other than blinking a few times.

The right words were leaving Dorcas's mouth, and Paul appreciated it, but something about the way she looked hinted that she wasn't saying what she really thought. Putting an end to the game playing from both of them, Paul decided to disclose his secret. "I'm not going to change my mind about Hannah. I've already asked her to marry me."

Carol's eyes opened wide. "You what?"

Paul glanced at Dorcas's blank face, then returned his focus to Carol. "I need you both to keep this between us. I'm hoping I can win her family's approval before they find out."

Carol's eyes narrowed. "Marry her? You can't possibly believe you love this girl."

"Oh, Paul," Dorcas whispered, as if he'd just shared terrifying news.

"This is ridiculous." Carol grabbed several pages of the letter and shook them.

With a gentleness he didn't feel, he wrapped his fingers over the rumpled pages in Carol's hand. "Let go of it." His calm tone belied how much anger was rising within him. When she hesitated, Paul spoke slowly and purposefully. "Now, Carol."

She released her grip on the pages. "You have no idea what it takes to make a marriage work. It's like..." She paused, clearly trying to think of the perfect allegory. "It's like using your truck to carry a dozen people to a formal wedding."

"You're comparing Hannah to my truck?" In spite of his best effort, sarcasm oozed from his words.

"What I mean is that Hannah was built for one kind of life. Changing her will cause serious problems, not just to her but to her family. And you. Not to mention your children. Can't you see that?"

"I know this isn't what you want for me, Carol. But you're gonna have to trust me on this."

Her shoulders slumped. "This conversation isn't over."

Paul kissed her on the cheek. "Of course not." He smiled down at her. "I know what I'm asking of my family and friends—and hers. But the only life I want is with her." Paul laid the pages against his chest and smoothed some of the wrinkles from them.

Carol rolled her eyes. "You always were melodramatic."

He placed the letter back on his desk and chuckled. "Levelheadedness must make room for love, or we have no need of living sensibly. For without true affection, practicality has nothing to protect." He grabbed his bag and unzipped it.

An obviously forced but peacemaking smile crossed his sister's face. "Spare me your philosophical ramblings." She tapped the papers on Paul's desk. "So, can you pull yourself away long enough to watch a Senators' game with us? I'll still help you pack tomorrow."

Paul was glad he'd been so bold as to tell them of his plans. They'd both accepted the news better than he'd thought possible. Maybe now his sister would recognize that he would never be more than cordial friends with Dorcas.

From the doorway, Dorcas pointed to his clothes on the bed. "We might even swipe an iron over one or two things." She giggled. "You know my motto: putting off work until tomorrow can make today a ton of fun."

Paul tossed the travel bag onto the bed. "I guess a night at City Island would be a nice distraction."

ristly heat and sweat roused Hannah to consciousness. She pushed the sheet away from her face and half opened her eyes, checking the clock. Streams of sunlight filtered in around the green shades. The room was sweltering as the cool morning air gave way to the scorching heat of late summer. Unsure why she was still in bed, confusion swirled for a moment before the all-too-familiar images hurled against her. How many days had passed since the attack—two, maybe three?

She lay motionless, searching for a ray of hope that would bring comfort, but she couldn't find one.

Nausea rose. Desperate for some cooler air, she darted down the steps and out the front door. She hurried to the beech tree, hoping to go unnoticed by her family. A cool breeze stirred the air.

"Hannah."

The sound made her jolt. Looking in the direction of the voice, she saw her twenty-year-old brother, Luke, striding across the yard toward her. Her body tensed, making her injuries hurt even more. Standing in the yard in her nightgown, she could easily imagine what words of correction her eldest brother would have.

Luke came to a halt in front of her. He held a galvanized bucket in one hand; with the other, he hooked his thumb through a brown suspender. Compassion shone in his brown eyes. "Are you still feeling poorly this morning?" He gestured to her gown. "I suppose that's a foolish question. *Daed* said you lost a whole pail of berries the other day. He had me scavenging the countryside this morning to replace them, but it's so late in the season, I'm surprised you found a bucketful when you did." He set the almost-empty container on the ground.

Hannah tried to say something, but the words wouldn't come.

Luke smiled. "Cat got your tongue?"

Determined to give an answer, she found her voice. "It was a nice try." She stared at the pitiful pile of blueberries lying in the same bucket that had been brimming with them before…

Luke gently took her hands, facing the palms up. *"Ach, wie entsetzlich."* He raised his eyes to hers. "Are your knees this bad?"

She cleared her throat, surprised to find that the simple action helped her gain control of her emotions. "I'm fine, Luke."

Her brother tilted his head, a dozen questions reflected in his eyes. He nodded and released her hands. "I'm sorry you got hurt."

Knowing nothing else to say, she left without answering him. If she could see through the fog that covered her mind, maybe she could make some sense of what had happened and figure out how to fix it. But clear thought seemed impossible.

She walked barefoot across the thick grass, eased open the screen door, and stepped inside. Hoping to avoid seeing anyone else, she paused to listen. She heard her youngest sister, Rebecca, in the kitchen with their mother and Esther. By the sound of things, they were busy canning. Somehow Hannah's bolt outside had escaped her mother's notice.

Or maybe her mother was unwilling to face her.

Too weak and drained to work through any more thoughts, she tiptoed upstairs and crawled back into bed. She covered her head with the lightweight sheet.

The rumbling of an English vehicle startled Hannah from her sleep. A sense of panic rose within her as the engine noise grew louder and then stopped right outside her window. The acrid smell of exhaust fumes drifted through the open window and past the closed blind. Visions of her attacker loomed in her mind's eye.

Shaking, Hannah rose from the bed. Barely able to breathe, she forced herself to take a quick peek out the side of the drawn shade. Relief flooded her. It was only Mr. Carlisle in his refrigerated truck. He was here to get the milk. He always came between two and three in the afternoon.

He stepped out of his truck, talking to her father. As Mr. Carlisle leaned against his truck, he looked up at her bedroom window. She jumped back as if she'd touched a fire. Could he tell what had happened just by looking at her? She crawled between the sheets and buried her head again.

Moments later a rapping on the bedroom door seemed to shoot through Hannah's last nerve. She lay still, with her head under the covers. She heard the door open and tried not to budge so whoever it was would go away and leave her alone.

"Mr. Carlisle stopped by." Her mother's reassuring voice worked its way through Hannah's mind. *Mamm* sat on the side of the bed. "It's almost suppertime. You've got to eat. You can't hide forever."

Hannah squeezed her eyes tighter. It couldn't be suppertime. Hadn't Mr. Carlisle just left? Something odd was happening. Time kept jumping—as if it were no longer bound by any rules.

A clinking metallic sound, like an eating utensil against a plate, filled the silence. "You haven't eaten anything in two days, Hannah. I peeled and chopped the fruit for you." She patted Hannah's leg through the bed-covers. "Come on, child. Sit up and eat."

Hannah remained quiet, hoping her mother would give up and go away.

"Now." *Mamm* tugged at the covers over Hannah's head. At first Hannah resisted, but out of dread that her mother might call *Daed,* she let go of the sheets.

"That's my girl." *Mamm's* soft hands caressed Hannah's cheeks, brushing wisps of curly hair from her face. "I know this is hard. But it's time to push against how you feel and do what's necessary. Do you understand?"

Fresh tears slid from the corners of Hannah's eyes. She nodded.

"Good. Now, dry your eyes." Her mother lifted the bowl of fruit. "Sit up and eat."

Hannah sat up and took the plate of fruit her mother held toward her. *Mamm* rose and grabbed a hairbrush from the nightstand. With the fork, Hannah stabbed a piece of green fruit. *Mamm* ran the brush through Hannah's long curls. The soothing strokes of the brush and the delicious medley of fruits provided a welcome relief from the isolation of the last... She didn't know how much time had passed.

Her mother worked on Hannah's untamed curls without complaint. She twisted Hannah's hair into a bun and pinned it. She then placed the translucent white *Kapp* over her head and fastened it to her hair with straight pins.

Mamm laid the brush on the side table. "Slip into your clothes and sit with us in the yard. There's a cool breeze. It's enough to refresh anybody's soul."

Hannah didn't want to, but to refuse would cause more problems than it would solve. "What has *Daed* told everyone?"

Pushing the sheet off Hannah's legs, *Mamm* seemed unable to look her in the eyes. "As little as possible. They think a car hit you and the fall caused the gashes on your hands." She took a blue dress off its hook and laid it on the bed. "He wasn't going to say that much. But you've holed up in this room so long, they knew you hadn't just fallen on your way home. If you don't get out of bed and return to normal chores, they aren't going to accept that story either."

Her mother turned to leave. "We need you, Hannah." She faced

Hannah squarely this time, her brown eyes filled with sorrow. "The house never runs as well without you." She gave her daughter a forced smile.

When *Mamm* pulled the door closed behind her, Hannah sank back onto the bed. Is this what her life would be like from now on? Pretending she was fine in order to hide the truth of the unmentionable from her siblings, and hiding from her parents the fact that she was going insane? She stared at the floor, trying to gain enough strength to go downstairs and pretend.

Ten minutes later Hannah stood at the back door, running her hands around her waist to verify that she'd pinned her apron securely. She peered through the screen, watching her family. *Mamm* and *Daed* sat on the bench, watching the children. The younger ones were catching fireflies in the open field while the older ones helped them place the bugs in a jar. Hannah tried to take a breath, but a stabbing pain in her chest stopped it short.

As she pushed the door open, the squeaky noise drew her parents' attention. Willing herself to walk, she started across the lawn. Her chest ached. Her skin felt as if someone were peeling it off. But worse, here in the open she had no ability to silence her thoughts. She came to a halt in front of her father, her gaze fixed on the ground, her arms limp at her sides.

Mamm rose from the bench. Her fingers cupped Hannah's face, and she kissed her on the cheek. "I'll fetch us some lemonade."

"*Dankes,*" Hannah whispered.

Daed patted the empty spot beside him. "Come and we'll talk."

Hannah eased onto the far end of the bench.

With both feet planted on the soft earth, her father placed his hands on his knees and straightened his back. "God will get us through this, Hannah. Our ways are not easy, but they are right." Her father removed his straw hat and lowered his head. "I'm not yet sure what's the right thing to do between you and the bishop."

Hot pain shot through her chest. She lifted her head and stared into her father's eyes. "What do you mean?"

He turned toward the fields. "I should inform him of what happened so he can make a ruling of what needs to be done."

Swallowing hard, she willed herself not to cry. "*Daed,* no, please. No one can know."

His sigh assured her he understood her feelings. "I'm not saying I'm going to tell him. I haven't decided yet. To keep this from the bishop is wrong. He's our spiritual leader. He can't guide us properly if we keep secrets from him." His jaw clenched as he stood. "Because this is so uncommon, if we share it, he's likely to seek counsel from the church leaders, maybe even from the head of each household. Then it'll be impossible to keep it from spreading to our whole community and beyond. That'll mean the news will reach any prospective beaus." He glanced at her, sorrow filling his eyes. "And that will ruin your chance of ever having a family of your own. You've lost your virtue, child, and there's nothing anyone can do about it."

As she stared at the bend in the dirt road that led to Mrs. Waddell's, guilt threatened to swallow her. Maybe God had allowed this attack so she wouldn't leave the community He'd placed her in. Who was she to consider changing God's plan for her life?

Guilt gave way to anger at the injustice of her situation. How could she *not* want to get away from this place?

She stood. Like nectar to a bee, her bed called to her. But she couldn't continue to give in to the urge to bury herself in it. She had duties, responsibilities. "I should take a loaf of bread to Mrs. Waddell," she said, dreading even that chore.

"No," he said, his voice gruff. "You're not to return there for now.

Luke or Levi will take Sarah back and forth to help the elderly lady until she can hire someone else."

Hannah turned to look at her father. He seemed to expect her to plead for the right to work at Mrs. Waddell's, but she had no energy to walk on eggshells while she argued with him. The set of his jaw was a clear indication that his patience with her was used up.

He stared at her, as if reminding her of his rights as head of the household. "You must help out around here. Your family needs you."

Numb, she trudged toward the house.

*T*he round-faced clock that hung on the wall behind the professor's head showed that class should have been over ten minutes ago. Nonetheless, the man droned on, making Paul later for work by the minute.

School had been back in session for three weeks, and he missed Hannah so badly he couldn't sleep at night or concentrate during the day. If a letter would arrive, maybe that would take some of the edge off his misery. Letters from Hannah were always slow in coming, but it'd been weeks since he'd left.

Writing to him was problematic. She had to have time alone to secretly pen him a note. Then she had to get it to his gram's place so she could mail it without Hannah's family getting wind of it. Even though he often went up to six weeks without hearing from her, he'd never gotten used to it.

Scribbling notes as quickly as he could, Paul tried not to think about the interview he had coming up this afternoon. He was hoping to land an internship as a caseworker with social services. If he landed this position, he would get enough training so that he could find a job closer to Owl's Perch after he graduated. If he found a job near Owl's Perch, he could juggle working for Hannah's father and for social services.

His boss at the tire store wouldn't be too thrilled when he arrived late. He'd be even angrier when Paul requested time off during the middle of his shift to go on his interview.

His part-time job at the retail tire store came with long hours and unfriendly co-workers. But it was his own fault. Instead of putting in his job applications in May for the fall, he'd hightailed it to his gram's place the day school was out so he could see Hannah. And he hadn't returned to campus until the weekend before classes began. Now he'd spend the entire school year paying the price for his impatience.

Paul sighed and glanced at the clock again. As usual he was half paying attention to the teacher and half missing Hannah. A long-distance relationship was one thing, but no communication other than letters was almost unbearable, especially since it was so long between letters.

A few students slipped out the side door. Paul wanted to follow them, but he needed the details of the next project due for class, and this teacher didn't pass out info sheets, post assignments on the Web, or write lists on the white board. He gave all pertinent instruction orally, once, as if the students' presence at the end of class was part of the project itself. Paul drew a ragged breath and began to pack his book bag as he listened to the teacher's last few recommendations regarding the assignment. As more students slipped out, the professor glanced at his watch and dismissed the class.

Slinging the strap of his backpack over one shoulder, Paul merged into the flow of human traffic. The past month had dispelled any question of how crazy his senior year would be. He wished he'd known four years ago how to plan his required course hours. He should have taken extra classes early on to give himself more time for his most important classes now. He had to graduate this spring.

It would be easier if he could stay in school one extra semester. But he couldn't do that. He'd promised Hannah they'd be together by summer. Besides, his heart was set on being with her come mid-May. *Graduation.* What a liberating word. Right now, however, graduation seemed a decade away.

He ran through the corridors, out the main doorway, and across the parking lot. Jerking open the unlocked truck door, he tossed his backpack to the passenger side and dug into his jeans pocket for his keys.

They weren't there. He tapped the outside of the pockets in his jacket and on the back of his pants.

Couldn't *something* go right? One thing? Anything?

He stifled the urge to let an angry scream ring out across the parking lot. Leaning across the bench seat, he grabbed his backpack and searched its array of small pockets. Life had been like this since he'd arrived on campus. Murphy's Law was working overtime for him, and he wished it would just go to work for somebody else.

Unable to find his keys, Paul climbed into his truck. *God, am I off track? Is this not where I'm supposed to be? Or is this just a part of learning patience?*

Paul wrapped his fingers around the top of the steering wheel and leaned his forehead against the backs of his hands. Visions of Hannah flooded his thoughts. *I miss her so badly, Father. I...I didn't think it would be this tough.* How many times over the past month had he fought the desire to forget school and go be with her?

He lifted his head and squared his shoulders. This was no time to think about quitting school. If life wanted a battle, he'd fight. And he'd win. Because to lose would hurt his and Hannah's future, and there was no way he was going to allow that to happen. No way on earth.

His stomach grumbled, and suddenly he remembered where his keys were. He jumped out of his truck and ran across the parking lot, back inside the building, to the closest vending machine. He grabbed his keys off the top of the red appliance. All this trouble and he hadn't even gotten a pack of crackers from the antiquated junk-food source. It wouldn't take his crumpled dollar, and he had no change.

Running back across the parking lot, Paul was glad his job was only a few minutes away.

Soon he pulled into the parking lot of the tire store and ran inside.

"Waddell."

Paul stopped midstride. There was no denying that crotchety, booming voice bellowing out his last name as if it were a curse word. He turned. "Sir?"

"You're late. Again." Kyle Brown's face turned a deeper shade of purple than normal.

"Yes sir. I'm sorry. Class was—"

"Give it a rest, Waddell. I don't care what was going on at that place you call a learning institute. Seems to me you college boys can't even tell time."

Paul hated this place. But life was expensive. "I'll come in early and stay late on Saturday to make up for it."

"You better believe you will." The man wiped his hands on a filthy rag and shoved it back into his pocket. "But that don't change the fact that the guys in the pit can't begin lunch shifts until there's a fourth person here. Three men've been waiting on you so somebody can go eat." He glanced at his watch. "At two thirty in the afternoon."

"I'm sorry, sir."

Mr. Brown clapped his hands. "Well, what are you waitin' for? Get to work."

"Yes, I'll do that, sir. But first…I need to tell you that I have to be somewhere at four. I told Mr. Banks about it when—"

"Well, Mr. Banks ain't runnin' this department. I am. If you leave before the last customer is taken care of, don't bother coming back. We'll mail you your check along with an 'adios, amigo' card."

Paul nodded. He'd explained his scheduling issues to Mr. Banks. The owner had assured him it could all be worked out. But obviously Kyle Brown didn't care what his boss had agreed to.

If Paul got this internship, he'd be doing his dream job with child services part-time during the week, but he could work here on days he wasn't a caseworker and all day on Saturdays. Jobs with decent hours that didn't make him work on Sundays were hard to come by. He had to keep this one.

*L*uke clomped up the steps of the old farmhouse. He looked into his parents' bedroom and found what he was searching for: Hannah. She sat on a low-rise stool with her back to him, sewing. He tapped on the open door.

Hannah jerked as if he'd startled her, but she didn't turn to see who had knocked. *"Kumm uff rei."*

Doing as she bid, Luke entered the room.

He was still baffled as to why his mother had made him move the sewing machine out of the kitchen and into his parents' bedroom yesterday. Every Amish home in his community had the sewing machine in front of a set of windows in the main part of the house, either the kitchen or the sitting room. It was what the district leaders had agreed upon, long before either Luke or Hannah was born. The bishop's job was to help keep conformity inside and outside each home to squelch man's natural bent toward competition.

So why had his mother insisted that he move it upstairs? He wasn't at all sure the church leaders would approve. But when he had turned questioningly to his father, his *Daed* had waved a hand in the air and barked at him to do as his mother told him. It had cost Luke the better part of the afternoon to disconnect, move, and then reconnect the machine, the automobile battery, and the converter to the upstairs.

Realizing Hannah wasn't going to stop sewing, he spoke over the whir of the machine. "I'm not sure if you heard, but there's a singing tonight. The bishop's gonna be gone tomorrow, so he moved it to tonight instead of Sunday. Don't know if that's ever happened before. But I'd be glad to take you." He crossed the room to stand beside her.

Accelerating the speed of the machine, she continued to run a pair of broadcloth trousers under the needle. "You've talked me into all the singings I ever care to attend."

With his middle finger and thumb, Luke lightly thumped her shoulder—half joking and half in frustration. "You beat all. Everybody that's not married likes the singings. It's the only way to really get to know someone."

The machine stopped its annoying hum, leaving the soft ticking of the wall clock as the only sound in the room. His sister shifted her focus and stared up at him. The circles under her eyes and her pale skin revealed exhaustion, although she'd done very little work of late. For reasons that made no sense to him, she was being allowed to do nothing but sew clothes for the family in a private room. She wasn't even responsible for juggling any cooking and childcare duties while she sewed. That was even stranger than moving the old Singer.

Hannah scowled. "I have no desire to be driven home from the singing by some…man…in hopes of us finding interest in each other."

Luke grasped a straight pin out of an overstuffed, tomato-shaped cushion and plunged it in and out, over and over. His sister had always had a mind of her own, one that didn't follow all the beliefs of the Old Ways, but she'd never been rude before. He decided, for both their sakes, to keep his tongue in check with her.

"I didn't tell ya that the bishop said the singing won't last long tonight. If you don't come, Mary won't either. She'll think it's too brazen to be seen alone with me at my parents' place on a singin' night. Plus, she's afraid if we're together without you, it'll cause rumors to spread that we're a couple." Luke shrugged. "She's not ready for that. You know Mary gets miserably embarrassed if she thinks people are talking about her."

He picked up one of Samuel's newly made shirts and tried to poke his pinky through a fresh-sewn buttonhole. Hannah hadn't done a good job of cutting the hole inside her stitching. "I was hoping to take Mary for a walk across our land tonight after the singing. I want to show her where *Daed* and I are considering building me a harness shop. If you'll come too, no one will think anything about us all going to the pond and millin' about since the three of us are seen together all the time."

Surely his sister understood what he was unable to speak of freely. If he could get Mary to see how stable his future was and if she cared for him as he hoped, they would become promised to each other by the night's end.

Hannah, seeing the mistake with the buttonhole, held her hand out for the shirt. "If you want to walk the property with Mary, just do so."

He passed her the shirt, holding on to part of it to help keep her attention. He boldly stared into her eyes.

Hannah released the shirt, leaving it dangling from Luke's hand to the floor. Her head lowered as if she were too weary to continue holding it up. "I…I…can't."

Disappointment formed a knot in Luke's chest. He dropped the shirt on the floor and grabbed his suspenders, squeezing them tight. "Your company for the night doesn't have to include a guy from the singing. It can be just us three."

Hannah didn't answer. She left the shirt on the floor and began sewing on the trousers again, ignoring Luke altogether.

If he told their father about Hannah's disinterest in being courted by any Amish men, *Daed* would set her straight quick. A *rumschpringe* was for finding an Amish mate, nothing else. Luke had plenty of suspicions about why Hannah found such great joy in working for the elderly woman down the road. But he hadn't shared his thoughts with their father. *Daed* had a strong opinion about his kids not turning to the Mennonite ways.

Luke hoped his sister's desire to spend time at the Waddell place had nothing to do with any of the English farm hands or Mrs. Waddell's grandson, whatever his name was. The grandson was from a very conservative Mennonite family, but they weren't in fellowship with the Old Order Amish. "*Daed* still doesn't know that Mary and I have been bringing you home from the singings."

A look of defiance came over her face. She lifted her hand, showing an inch of space between her index finger and her thumb. "I have about this much freedom under our bishop, and only because it's my time of *rumschpringe*. Singings and buggy courting are a private thing. Don't take that away from me, Luke."

"But, Hannah, you ain't using your freedom to find a mate. You're just pretending to. It's not right."

Her eyes grew cold and hard. "It'd be best not to talk to me of what's right. Not now. Maybe not ever." She turned away from him and pressed the pedal on the old Singer.

Laying the trousers aside, Hannah rose from the stool and crossed to the far window. She watched Luke amble toward the barn to hitch the horse to the buggy. He and Mary would fritter the night away, laughing and having their mock arguments. Not long ago the three of them had delighted in playing board games and strolling in the cool of the evening. Now all she felt was indifference and bitterness. Where had her love for life and for her family gone?

Her dear friend Mary always listened whenever Hannah was chafing against the strict conformity demanded among the People. But even with Mary, Hannah didn't share too much. If Mary's parents knew Hannah questioned the authority of the bishop, preachers, and even the *Ordnung*, they'd never let Mary see her.

But those irritations didn't compare to the resentment and vengeance that warred in her soul of late. What seemed like years ago she used to dream of Mary and Luke remaining close to her even if she didn't join the faith. Now nothing seemed possible. Hannah no longer shared kindred thoughts with anyone—Luke, Mary, or even herself. Paul had loved her energy and sense of humor, but she didn't possess that now. She'd become an empty kerosene lamp, the outward part of no use without its fuel.

Yet, in spite of every gloomy thought moving within her, she felt a lingering trace of optimism that when she heard from Paul, her once-hopeful soul would return, and life would again have purpose. The haunting question of why Paul hadn't written made a shudder run through her body.

For several nights now, her father had been pacing the floors hours before the four o'clock milking. And she knew why. He still hadn't decided whether to tell the bishop what had happened to his daughter. If he did, all power to have final say over her life would be removed from him. If the bishop chose to tell certain ones in the community about the incident, the news would eventually get back to Paul since he had distant cousins who lived in Owl's Perch.

Glancing at the shiny, gold-trimmed clock, Hannah took a deep, miserable breath. Paul had promised to send her a letter within two days after he left. Although she couldn't manage to keep track of the days, *Mamm* had told her it had been more than three weeks since that day on the road.

Sarah had ridden the mile to Mrs. Waddell's with their brother Levi. Surely Sarah would bring a letter for her today. Hannah had spent quite a bit of time patiently reasoning with Sarah to convince her to bring home any letters without telling *Mamm* or *Daed.* Her sister had finally agreed.

Hannah sighed and shuffled to the machine. Bending to grab the shirt off the floor, she spotted several folded papers sticking out from between the bottom of the dresser and the last drawer—as if someone had hidden them under a drawer and they had worked their way out. A closer look said it was probably a letter. Without hesitation, she eased the papers out of their half-hidden spot.

Paul sat in his apartment with his open books spread across the small desk as he studied for another psychology test. The place was quiet since his roommates were all out enjoying the evening with a group of girls. The alarm on his watch sent out an elf-sized rendition of reveille. He pushed a button, silencing the tinny music. It was four o'clock and finally past all chance that his grandmother was still down for a nap. Now he could call her. Of course his true goal was to speak with Hannah.

If they could instant message each other, e-mail, or talk on the phone, their separation would be much easier to deal with. Conversing only through letters in this day and age felt like trying to send for help by carrier pigeon. His chance of catching Hannah was minimal since her scheduled time at Gram's was a bit irregular, shifting as the needs of the Lapp household altered. But it was worth trying, repeatedly.

He picked up the cordless and punched in Gram's number.

The phone was on its tenth ring when the slow, rustling noise told him his grandmother had picked up.

"Hi, Gram. It's Paul. How are you feeling today?"

They spoke of the weather, her aching joints, and how often she'd walked to the pond to feed the fish. Paul had to ease into the subject of

Hannah, or his gram might get defensive. In the past she'd minced no words explaining her feelings about him and Hannah. She wavered between accepting the ever-growing friendship between her Mennonite grandson and her favorite Amish girl and detesting the heartache that lay ahead for both of them—whether the relationship lasted or not.

"Gram, I haven't gotten any letters from you."

"More to the point, no letters from Hannah." Her tone sounded cheerful. That was good. "Sarah's been comin' here in her stead. I'd like to say she's been doing Hannah's job, but that'd be a lie."

That piece of news bothered him. He hoped his extra time with Hannah the day he left hadn't caused her to get into trouble. Then again, whenever life became hectic at the Lapp household, they kept Hannah at home and sent Sarah in her place.

"I can let you talk to Sarah next time she comes," Gram said with a bit of mischief in her voice.

Paul chuckled. This was the grandmother he'd known growing up— before the aches and pains of old age made her irritable with life and everyone around her. "You offer that every time the Lapps send her. Why can't you do that when Hannah's there?"

"Because ya need no encouragement when it comes to her." Silence filled the line for a moment. "Paul, are ya sure you're doing the right thing…for Hannah's sake?"

The concern in her voice echoed his own anxiety. But his grandmother had no idea how far he'd let his feelings for Hannah take him. She only knew they cared for each other. There was no way she could miss that.

"She's of courting age, Paul. She needs to be going out with her own kind. Is she doing that? Or is she waiting for you?"

Jealousy and guilt nibbled at his conscience. He couldn't bear to think of her seeing anyone else. That was why he had asked her to marry him before he left—that and his concern that she might join the church this spring if he didn't give her another option.

"Paul." His grandmother's firm tone brought his thoughts up short.

"Yes ma'am."

The line fell silent again. He had no desire to try to answer her question. Fact was, he had no answer that she'd care to hear.

"There's no sense in you looking for letters from Hannah or sending any here for her, not for a while. Sarah says it'll be weeks before Hannah returns. In the meantime, you'd better think this through. Let this space clear your thoughts." She worded it as a suggestion, but her tone made it more of an order, one he'd better follow if he didn't want the wrong people to learn of this relationship.

"Were you able to give her the letter I sent?"

"I haven't received any mail from you since you left for school last."

"You must have. I sent a manila envelope with a letter to you and a thick white envelope inside it for Hannah."

"I'd remember a letter from you, Paul, and it ain't arrived. Just as well. I think it's best if you two stop conversing for a spell. I let things get out of hand over the summer."

Keeping his voice respectful, Paul said, "I'm not a child, Gram."

"No, you ain't. But she is."

"You and Grandpa were eighteen when you married."

"Our parents approved of us seeing each other from the get-go. If Hannah's father weren't so stubborn about his kids remainin' Amish and staying in his district..." Gram paused.

Paul wondered why Gram, who had nothing to do with the Amish community aside from Hannah working for her, seemed to think she knew how Zeb Lapp felt. "But—"

"But," Gram interrupted. "But Hannah's father will not spare the rod on her if he gets wind of this, and you know it. Now, no more talk. You'd best spend your time looking at the realistic aspects of this relationship instead of letter writin' and callin' and such."

Paul's temper threatened to get the best of him. "I need to go, Gram. I'll call you in a few days." He hung up the phone.

Irritation pulsed through him. Still, Gram had made some good points. Hannah was young. But she was mature enough to make lifelong decisions.

Wasn't she?

He glanced at the psychology books spread out over the desk. He was torn between his desperation to make a connection with Hannah and the nagging feeling that maybe his grandmother was right.

But where was the letter he'd written, the one in which he'd shared openly about his love for her? If a letter from him never arrived, what would she think of his commitment to her?

He could try to circumvent his grandmother's wishes and drive to Owl's Perch to see Hannah. But that could prove detrimental to their future relationship and get Hannah in a lot of trouble.

Paul's only option was to give his grandmother time to change her mind about allowing Hannah and him to communicate through her address.

<hr />

Her heart pounding, Hannah unfolded the letter. The top page had a watercolor painting of a sunset on a beach. She shifted to the second page, where large handwriting in the salutation said, "Dearest One." Refusing to give in to defeat just yet, she flipped to the last page. It was another beach scene but from a bird's-eye view. She flipped back to the second page to find the closing: "With all my love, Zabeth."

Disappointment drained what little strength Hannah had. She sat on the side of the bed, holding the letter in her lap. Her momentary hope that Paul had written to her and that somehow, through the mystical way of love, the letter had found its way to her was gone. It was a childish dream, without merit or good sense. As she adjusted to the fresh setback, a new thought worked its way to the front of her mind: who was Zabeth, and was that even an Amish name?

If it was, she'd never heard of it. Dozens of questions floated through her mind. She wondered who "Dearest One" was, why the letter had been stuffed under a drawer, and if the written words might hold any clues as to why she hadn't heard from Paul. As she sat there, the questions grew and so did a desire for answers.

Rising, Hannah hid the letter behind her. After bolting the door, she returned to the bed and unfolded the letter.

Dearest One,

It has been too long since we've seen, spoken to, or written to each other. I pray you will set aside your shame of me and find it within yourself to return a letter.

When we were but youth, I made my choices and you made yours. Now we are fast approaching old age, and I need no one's judgment—every day of my life I've paid the price for my decisions. But surely, as I deal with this horrid illness, our separation need not go any further.

I'm your twin. We shared our mother's womb. And once we shared a love so deep we could each feel what the other one felt before any words were spoken. Perhaps the need to break that connection is why you moved away from Ohio and joined the Amish in Pennsylvania.

The shunning of the past two and a half decades has been bitter. When it is my time to die, I do not wish to leave you behind with acrimony in your heart against me.

With all my love,
Zabeth

Like hornets buzzing in panic during late fall, Hannah's thoughts zipped around furiously without landing anywhere.

Who is "Dearest One"?

She flipped to the backside of each page, looking for a clue. There was none, not even a date anywhere on the letter, so it could be really old, although it didn't appear to be.

She glanced back to the closing of the letter. Zabeth sounded like a woman's name. Skimming the note for any hints of whom it was to, Hannah paused at the word *Ohio*. Her father had a few distant relatives in Ohio, but he didn't have a sister. Most of his brothers lived outside Lancaster, where his parents were buried.

She'd been told her grandparents *Daadi* John and *Mammi* Martha had moved to Lancaster several generations ago. So whoever Zabeth was, she—or he—had probably been a sibling to one of Hannah's grandparents.

In spite of her disappointment, the few moments of reading the letter had given Hannah's raging emotions a welcome distraction. But her attention wasn't drawn away for long, especially over something that went back to her grandparents' youth.

Deciding that the letter was none of her business and not of interest anyway, she put it back where she'd gotten it—careful to hide it better this time. But one nagging thought kept coming at her as she headed for bed. Would she one day send a letter begging her siblings to write to her?

$\mathcal{L}$uke positioned the harness over the gentle mare's muzzle, then slid the bit into her mouth before placing the bridle around her head. He connected metal fasteners, leather straps, and leads from the horse to the courting buggy. Blue skies and wispy clouds filled the late-September sky. It was perfect weather for an outing. Since there'd been church last Sunday, no services would be held tomorrow.

As he hooked the shafts from the buggy to the mare, he wiped his sweaty palms on his trousers, hoping he didn't look as nervous as he felt. He'd been courting Mary Yoder for nearly five months. Tonight, after the singing, he was going to ask her to marry him. He hoped she was willing to do all that it would take for them to wed.

He threw the leather straps across the horse's backside and pulled its tail through the loose restraints. He remembered the first time he had worked up the nerve to ask Mary if he could take her home after one of the singings. He'd spent hours that day polishing his buggy to a shine and grooming the mare in preparation. He grinned as he looked at the buggy and horse he'd readied for tonight. He didn't feel any less nervous now than he had then.

In spite of Hannah's attitude about the singings, he thought the ritual was a good setup. All those of courting age within the community gathered in a barn and sang a cappella for hours. One or two of the older singles would start the hymn at a faster pace than used during church times. And even though the bishop and some of the parents were always there, plenty of laughter and quick-witted humor rang out during the singings. Sometimes words were altered to make the serious lyrics come to life with youthful glee. As long as the songs stayed respectful, the bishop allowed it.

Young people could get to know each other better during a ride or two home, without anyone committing to a relationship. If they weren't compatible, no one's feelings got hurt. The man didn't have to take a girl home again if he didn't want to. The girls never had to accept a ride from anyone.

This was one area that parents didn't get involved in, not even with a suggestion. The bishop saw to that. He said God was responsible for putting young people together, not man.

In his years of going to singings, Luke had taken several girls home. But Mary was the only one he'd ever truly courted, the only one he made a point of seeing at times other than during a ride home from the gathering. Now they ducked her parents' eyes and went out every chance they got.

Her decision to marry him would mean she was ready to give up her time of extra freedoms and submit to the *Ordnung*, the written and unwritten rules of the People. Luke never doubted that she would give up those things. He just wasn't confident she was ready to do so now. If they planned to marry next fall, Mary would have to start going through instruction by springtime.

He'd chosen to be baptized into the church a year and a half ago. According to the *Ordnung*, he could only marry a baptized member.

Luke pulled his handkerchief from his pocket and gave the leather seats one last cleaning.

Sometimes, after an evening of a cappella hymns, Mary liked to try her hand at driving the buggy. He considered himself a liberal man, and he enjoyed occasionally letting her take the reins. His father would scowl at a woman driving when a man was in the buggy, but Luke saw things differently. When Mary grasped the reins, her greenish blue eyes reflected both excitement and insecurity. She even talked to the horse to get it to behave. Luke never conceded whether he thought the horse understood her. But Mary was awfully cute working her way through her fears and making the horse do her bidding. As the only girl among the ten siblings, Mary'd had little opportunity to drive a buggy at home.

After tucking the bandanna into his pocket, he climbed into the buggy and sat on the leather seat. He stared at the house and thought about Hannah. Something was wrong with her, seriously wrong. She hadn't been the same since the night she had fallen nearly a month ago. She barely ate, talked, or worked. *Daed* had even allowed her to stay home from church since the incident and to get out of the work gathering at the Millers' yesterday.

Worse than all that, Hannah had no spunk lately. Why, she hadn't baked him a cake or even fetched him some cool water when he was working in the fields. He flicked the reins and clicked his tongue. *Wunnerlich.* That's what it was. *Strange.*

Too tormented to do any more work and too anxious to sleep, Hannah lay on her bed, listening for the sound of a horse's hoofs, while daylight still streamed in her window. She felt a little sorry she hadn't gone to the singing with Luke. Some fun time with Mary might have helped Hannah's sanity return. But she was still waiting to hear from Paul. Her chest ached with worry that when Sarah returned, she might not have a letter with her.

Thoughts of the letter from Zabeth came and went. Asking her parents about it was not an option. When Hannah was very young, they'd made their position clear: if a topic was approachable, they'd bring it up during mealtime. If they didn't bring it up, their children weren't to do so.

But what if her parents had lost the letter and then forgotten it? Hannah sighed. That was silly. People didn't just forget such important—

She bolted upright.

Paul's gift! The small leather book. Hannah rubbed her forehead, desperate for a moment of clarity. Where was it? When had she last seen it?

Feeling dizzy, she sprinted down the stairs, grasping the handrail firmly. *"Mamm?"* She hurried through the living room and into the kitchen. *"Mamm?"*

"In the laundry room."

Barely recognizing her mother's scratchy and tired voice, Hannah came to an abrupt halt when she arrived at the doorway. Huge stacks of dirty clothes were shoved into a corner, covered with a sheet. Clean, wet clothes sat in a pile in the large galvanized tub. "Why are you doing laundry this close to nightfall?"

Her mother turned and smiled. "Oh, Hannah, it's good to see you downstairs again." *Mamm* looked about the room. "We aren't managing things very well without you." She whispered the words as if *Daed* wouldn't figure out how poorly Hannah was doing if *Mamm* didn't tell him.

"I had a small leather book in my apron—"

"Today?" *Mamm's* brows furrowed.

"No. When…" Hannah searched for the right words.

Her mother lifted an armful of dirty clothes and tossed them into one of the smaller galvanized tubs. "You mean the last day you worked for Mrs. Waddell?"

Blinking back her resentment, Hannah realized how comfortable her mother had become with that awful night. "Yes. I had a small book in the hidden pocket. Have you seen it?"

Studying her daughter, *Mamm* pushed the tub of dirty clothes into the corner. "I never saw it. But the clothes you had on were burned the next day."

Burned?

Hannah dashed out the side door and across the back field. Clawing through cold ashes and soot in the barrel where they burned trash, she found no shreds of clothing.

It was Esther's job to burn trash. Maybe she had found the book and put it away somewhere. Looking across the yards and gardens, Hannah soon spotted her sister picking lettuce in the garden.

"Esther, can you come here, please?"

Leaving the small basket, Esther strolled toward Hannah, wiping the dirt from her hands on her black apron. "Feeling better?"

Hannah shook her head. "My clothes you were told to burn, you know the ones?"

Esther nodded.

"There was a small leather book in the hidden pocket of my apron. Tell me you have it."

Esther shrugged. "I can't tell ya that. I would have brought it to ya had I found something." Still rubbing dirt off her hands, Esther huffed. "I can tell ya that I'm tired of doing my chores and yours. So is Sarah, and now she's having to work for Mrs. Waddell too. You ought not do us this way."

Ignoring her sister's irritation, Hannah got down on her hands and knees, searching the grassy grounds near the barrel. "Is there any way the book might have fallen out of the pocket?"

"Don't see how. *Daed* had your clothes all bundled up when he gave them to me. I unfolded them over the barrel so they'd burn more thoroughly. I know how to do my jobs, Hannah." Esther put her hands on her hips. "And yours too, now."

Unwilling to give up hope, Hannah continued hunting for the missing item until the newly healed skin from the gashes turned raw. It was no use. The book was nowhere to be found. Why had she stayed in bed like a fool and let the gift Paul had given her come to ruin?

Her bitter disappointment jolted to a halt when she heard hoof steps. Standing, she saw Levi and Sarah riding bareback together. The horse ambled toward the barn. Hannah sprinted in that direction.

Levi paused while his sister slid off the back of the chestnut horse. Sarah thrust an envelope toward Hannah. "I don't see how you put up with working for Mrs. Waddell. She's the crankiest woman I've ever dealt with. According to her, I didn't do one thing right all day."

Hannah took the envelope and pressed it to her chest. "Thank you, Sarah. Thank you." Feeling waves of joy, Hannah beelined to the side yard, ripping open the letter. But it wasn't a letter. It was a card with a scene of a white-steepled church sitting among autumn trees with leaves of gold, red, and yellow. That was odd. Since the People rotated homes for their services rather than use church buildings, it didn't seem likely Paul would send her a note like this. She flipped open the card.

Dear Hannah,

I'm sorry to hear you aren't well. I find it even more distressing that you won't be returning to work for me. We have an arrangement. I will be in especially deep need when the holidays come. You must speak to your father about this, or I will.

Sincerely,
Mrs. Waddell

Hannah ran inside, searching for Sarah. She found her in the laundry room with *Mamm*. "This is it?" She waved the card in her sister's face. "This is all you came back with?"

"It is." Sarah lifted a galvanized tub filled with clean, wet clothes. "Would you have me write the letter myself that you want so badly?"

Hannah stared at Sarah. Then she glanced at her mother, aware of how much she had just revealed.

Her mother sighed, seemingly unaware of the new piece of Hannah's life she'd just learned. "All right, girls. That's enough. You'd do well to remember your quiet upbringing and the teachings to hold your tongue, before your father uses his strap."

Sarah set the cumbersome tub on the floor. "I've been doing Hannah's chores for nigh on four weeks now. That Mrs. Waddell is as harsh as the cold winter's wind in January. And then my sister comes fussing at me about things I have no control over."

Nearly four weeks? Was that possible? Surely Sarah was exaggerating. There was no way nearly a month had passed.

"Silence." The thunderous voice filled the room. All three women turned, wide eyed, to face Zeb Lapp. "Sarah," he snapped, "are you complaining?" His voice was loud enough to be heard into tomorrow. "Has your older sister not always carried more than her fair share in this house? Yet now that she's been feeling poorly, you whine like a feeble cat."

He turned his focus on Hannah. "And you. Did I not tell you to start pulling your weight around here? Look at your mother. She's worn ragged. Life on this farm must have everyone's full strength for each and every day. Have you become lazy like the fancy folks who can't get meals on the table even when the expensive stores do most of the cooking for them?"

He raised a finger and pointed at Sarah. "Hannah's not the one who told you to do her chores. I am! How dare you grumble! If I hear one more word, I'll take you to the smokehouse and teach you a lesson you won't soon forget. Do you hear me?"

Hannah wondered how they could not hear him. His face was red, and his throat would hurt from screaming when his temper settled. But she refused to apologize. She was sorry for lots of things, but snipping at Sarah was not one of them. And she'd not lie about it, whether she was made to go to the smokehouse or not.

Sarah lowered her head, seemingly unable to look at anyone. She was trembling so hard Hannah thought she might pass out. "I was wrong. I beg your forgiveness."

Waving his hands in the air, their father continued. "When I see the fruit of your words, then we'll talk of forgiveness. Now, leave the clean laundry there. There's no sense in hanging it out to dry at nearly dusk. We're getting behind on more important things than laundry. We didn't harvest near enough potatoes for a full day's work."

He took a long, deep breath. "Sarah, gather your siblings. All of you go help Levi sort today's potatoes and get the bins cleaned out for tomorrow's digging."

"Yes, *Daed.*" Sarah headed for the door without lifting her head.

"And remember my warnings, Sarah." Her father's booming voice made *Mamm* jump. "Do not let the youngsters out of your sight. No one is to go near that road without one of your older brothers."

Sarah scurried off.

Hannah wondered what good a pacifist brother would do. What would Levi do if something awful happened to one of his sisters? Stand there and politely ask the person to go away? Panic roiled within her, but she held her tongue and started for the door.

Her father glowered at her. "Samuel's been out of pants that fit him for far too long. Have you finished sewing for the day?"

She'd been so distracted by the letter from Zabeth, the realization she'd lost the bankbook, and the disappointment of another day without a letter from Paul that she'd forgotten her goal for today. "No, *Daed.* I'll go do that."

"The three of us need to talk but not now. There's work to be done."

Dreading the idea of anything her father might say to her, Hannah nodded compliantly before she scurried through the living room and up the steps.

Luke watched all the young people making their way out of the Stoltz-fuses' barn and to the buggies. He felt sad for some of the young men who'd come to the singing hoping to find a girl but were leaving alone. Some twenty-odd years ago a slew of boys had been born into the community. That was a great blessing to all the men who needed strong hands to help run the family farms. But now, when it came time to find wives for them all, the gender imbalance was a problem. Having so many males in each household also made it difficult for parents to uphold the long-standing tradition of offering their sons housing and land when they married.

Mary climbed into Luke's buggy, not pausing a bit to see who was getting into the other buggies. Luke smiled at her and took hold of the reins with a wink.

She folded her hands in her lap. "The air is so refreshing tonight. The first comfortable evening for months, *ya?*"

Nodding to Mary, Luke mumbled softly to the horse. *"Kumm zerick."* The horse began backing up. *"Gut."* The mare stopped. Luke clicked his tongue, and the buggy lurched forward.

Only the silvery glow of the moon gave them light to see by. Looking at a sea of open buggies with single occupants, he mumbled, "So many of the young men go home alone."

Sighing, Mary stared at her folded hands. "I heard the Miller twins are going to Mennonite singings."

The horse's hoofs clopped against the paved road. "If word of that gets back to their *Mamm,* they won't be doing it for long."

The local parents preferred their children to stay within the district to marry, though they'd bend in that area if need be. However, flirting with the Mennonite ways was equal to treason in the hearts of lots of Amish folk. Many respected their Mennonite neighbors, but they didn't want to lose their children to them. Luke's own father was the most determined on the issue of any man he'd ever met. None of Zeb Lapp's children would turn from the Old Order ways. None.

Mary shook her head. "Those Mennonite girls would do well to catch one of the Miller twins. Can't say I like their sense of modesty, though. The lightweight material they use and the few pleats they put in show off their figures much more than we're allowed. Have you noticed?"

Luke pulled the left rein, causing the horse to turn onto Newberry Road. "I'd best not be admitting to noticing such a thing even if I did."

Mary laughed gently and shoved her elbow into his side. "Your cousin Elizabeth thinks we should make our clothing by their pattern and material. Though it doesn't much matter what any of us think. Bishop Eli said it's not the right way to dress, and he gets final say."

Coming to a stop sign, Luke pulled back the reins. "I was hoping not to take you straight home tonight. Do you mind if we ride slow and talk for a while?"

Mary shifted in her seat, facing him a little more. "I don't mind."

When they turned onto a gravel road, Luke slowed the horse. He would have liked to stop the buggy entirely so they could talk without having to speak above the clopping horse hoofs and the grinding gravel under the wheels. But if someone saw them parked, he wouldn't be abstaining from the appearance of evil as he'd agreed to do when he joined the church.

As the horse plodded along, Luke grasped both leads in one fist. Then he reached for Mary's hand. She jumped with a start and jerked from him. Luke's heart sank.

She giggled. "Ya caught me by surprise, Luke. I wasn't expecting..."

Luke took the reins with both hands again. Mary reached out and enfolded her soft, delicate fingers over his. They lowered their entwined hands onto the seat. Her touch made him think the horse and carriage would float through the sky like a hot-air balloon. "I care for you ever so much."

She gazed at the scenery to the right side of the buggy, away from him. A few agonizing moments later she turned and faced him. "I feel the same way."

"Does your father know who's bringing you home from the singings?"

"I don't think so. But he's in a much better mood since he knows I'm going to the singings regularly and not fritterin' my Saturday nights away among the English."

Heat ran up the back of Luke's neck. "He's just glad you're not using any more of your *rumschpringe* to slip into town and date English boys." His words came out angry, and he immediately regretted them.

"Like you didn't mix among those English girls while you were deciding where you'd spend your future. You even kissed one or two if the rumors have any truth to them." In spite of her words, Mary's face reflected peaceful acceptance of his running-around time.

Swallowing hard, Luke once again wished he'd never gone out with those English girls. He couldn't tell Mary that he had just used them to boost his ego. It was fun to cross the forbidden border and go out with a few English girls. But soon enough he'd realized he didn't like the non-Amish women, not one of them. They were nice enough and all, but he just didn't have enough in common with them. They wanted to talk about television, music, movies, and computer games. His idea of a good conversation was about last week's softball game in the Millers' mowed field, but the English girls never knew the people he was talking about. It wasn't just that; it was everything. There was a wall between him and those fancy girls, a wall he decided he didn't want to tear down.

His father would be furious if he learned that Luke hadn't used his *rumschpringe* for its real purpose of finding an Amish mate. Nonetheless, that time of being free from the usual constraints had caused him to know without any doubt that he'd rather live the strict, simple life of his forefathers.

The swift clomping of a faster buggy came up behind them, the driver clearly wanting to pass Luke's slow pace. Glad for the few minutes of distraction, Luke pulled the right lead, making the horse move as far off the shoulder as it could.

While waiting for the buggy to pass, he wondered about Mary's days of extra freedoms. Had she cared for some English boy before Luke had started bringing her home from the singings? Even now, with her beside him, annoyance ripped at his insides as he thought of his sweet Mary spending time with those conceited, worldly young men.

He knew Mary would eventually choose to join the church, but left on her own, she might wait a few more years. She, like Hannah, enjoyed having some freedoms from her parents' watchful eyes. Wondering what indiscretions Mary would confess to her mother before her baptism, he gripped the reins until his hands tingled with numbness. There were worse things than what could be expressed through a confession. What if she had given part of her heart away, a part he'd never own? That would haunt him the rest of his days, whether she was his wife or not.

Mary nudged him. When he glanced at her, she tilted her head toward the buggy that was beside them. He turned to look. Matthew Esh had slowed his carriage. He was riding alone, obviously milling about, wasting time. Luke had done a fair amount of that himself before he had a girl to spend time with.

Luke smiled back. "Fine evening for a buggy ride, *ya?*"

Matthew pulled back on the reins, keeping his horse at an even pace with Luke's. "'Tis that. I thought maybe your horse had gone lame you were goin' so slow."

Luke shook his head. "It's a good night for riding and talking." He winked at Mary, then turned back to Matthew. "But not to you."

Matthew's laughter filled the cool night air. "I'll not be insulted by honesty. Is Hannah not gonna come to any of the singings?"

Trying to think how to be honest and yet not say too much, Luke answered, "She's mostly staying around the house."

A look of concern flickered across Matthew's face. "That could be *gut* news, I s'pose."

"Could be." Luke shrugged.

"*Gut* evening to ya now." Matthew clicked his tongue, and the spirited horse took off.

The leather seat moaned as Mary leaned in close. "There aren't enough girls for all the men in our community as it is. Hannah shouldn't be holing up at home, making herself unavailable."

Slapping the reins against the horse's backside, Luke looked straight ahead. "Is that how you feel as well?"

In his peripheral vision he saw her chin tilt up, but she didn't respond. Sometimes she and Hannah were too alike for his tastes. He hated when Hannah pulled that chin-tilting silent routine. "Mary Yoder, if you want to drive this buggy, you'll answer me." He held the reins toward her.

She smiled victoriously and took them from his hand. Her body tensed with excitement and nervousness. "I can do this, right?"

Luke leaned back, enjoying her pleasure. "You always do, panicky as it makes you."

She moved her head from side to side. "It always makes my shoulders hurt."

Luke dared to place his hands on her shoulders and rub gently. "That's because you get so uptight. The mare is old and well mannered. Just relax."

Mary fidgeted with the reins, looking as if she might bolt from the buggy if the horse so much as swooshed its tail.

"All right, now you'd better start talking to me, or I'll take the reins away." As she briefly glanced his way, he smiled. "Spill it, Mary Yoder."

"*Druwwel,*" she muttered.

Luke leaned forward, feigning innocence. "Trouble? Me?"

"No, the horse," Mary teased.

Bending close to her ear, he whispered, "You made a deal."

"All right. Give a girl a chance to think." She turned the horse and buggy onto a small path.

He breathed in the fragrance of freshly cut hay, the last for the season. His nervousness evaporated under the spell of Mary Yoder. She had a wonderful way of making him fall in love with life all over again every time they were together.

She continued out the small path and stopped under a huge tree at the back of the Knepps' place. "Do you mind?"

Mind? She had to be kidding. "You did the stopping, not me. If someone sees us, I'm pleading innocent."

She shook her head at him, but her giggles let him know she wasn't the least bit put out. Wrapping the reins around the short metal post on the dash in front of them, she sat on the edge of the seat. She began looping the reins in her fingers. "When I was enjoying my freedoms, I learned things I didn't know and experienced things that will be forbidden when I join the church."

Feeling anxious, Luke pressed. "What have you experienced?"

"Well, one night I went out to eat at a restaurant with Ina, and I wore a silky red dress that showed my knees."

He could easily accept that she'd dressed that way once. And he wasn't surprised she considered it a great freedom to go to an eatery. If he had nine brothers to help cook and wash for, he'd have made eating out one of his first thrills too. Mary hadn't hidden the fact that she was fond of Ina, the English girl whose parents owned the music store where Mary worked. Being employed there would be forbidden when she joined the church.

Luke removed his hat and held it for a moment to help cover his fears. "That can't be all you've done with your freedom."

Brushing a gnat away from her face, she continued. "Another time I bought a bathing suit and went swimming in Ina's pool. It's in her backyard. We swam until past midnight. I'll never forget that."

Feeling naked without his hat, Luke placed it firmly on his head. "Just the two of you?"

"Oh no. There were a dozen girls there. We laughed about silly things until my sides hurt."

Luke raised an eyebrow. "Only girls?"

"Luke Lapp, are you edging toward asking if I went swimming with boys?"

He gazed into her eyes, determined to confront the things on his mind. "It crossed my mind."

"I would never…" She scowled at him. "You know, if I weren't so fond of you, I'd get out of this buggy and walk home."

A goofy smile etched itself on his face, and he was powerless to erase it. "How fond?"

"Luke!"

Confident this was the door he was looking for, he became serious. "Fond enough to be baptized into the church this spring, published next October, and married by early winter during the wedding season?"

Her face went blank. Luke couldn't tell what she was thinking. Soon her greenish blue eyes danced with laughter. "Are you asking 'cause you're curious or because you'd like to be the one I'm published with?"

"You got somebody else in mind?"

She giggled and huffed at the same time. "Answer my question before you go asking more things."

Doing his best not to lose his nerve, he took a deep breath. "I'm asking because I can't imagine there being a better wife in the whole world than you."

The words were barely out of his mouth when Mary flung her arms around his neck. "Oh, Luke, when you started taking me home from the singings, I was sure it was just because Hannah and I are such good friends. As I grew to love you, I was afraid you didn't return those feelings."

Joy turning flips within his chest, he held her tight. Slowly he backed away and bent to kiss her on the lips.

She put her hands against his chest and pushed against him. "There'll be no lip kissing until we're married."

His jaws ached from the huge smile on his face. "And is this a new rule?"

She planted a kiss on his cheek. "That's the first kiss I've given any young man who wasn't a brother."

"Ah, so you kiss *old* men, is that it?" The buggy shook as Luke laughed.

Mary lifted one of the dangling reins from its resting post and playfully smacked him with it. Luke wrapped her delicate face in the palms of his hands. "I'm so proud of who you are. I…I wish I could give you the same gift of not having kissed anyone else."

Her playfulness stopped cold. She released the leather strap. "Luke, I remember the day you joined the church. Although you didn't say the words, I knew your time among the English had brought you nothing but grief in your soul. I forgave you that very day, knowing even then that I'd marry you in a minute if you asked. Now, we'll talk no more of it. Ever."

Feeling warm and blessed, he kissed her on the cheek. Luke wanted to marry her immediately and not wait until harvest season was over next fall. But Amish life didn't work that way. He puffed out his chest, a silly move that might be deemed prideful and sinful if certain ones within the community saw it. "I didn't realize I was such a fine catch as to have Mary Yoder willing to marry me back when she was but fifteen years old."

She slapped his hat off.

"Mary!" Luke grabbed his hat off the floor of the buggy, wanting ever so much to tickle her rib cage. "That's not proper."

She clicked her tongue at him. The buggy jolted forward as the horse began walking. They broke into laughter.

"You'd better take the reins and drive, Mary."

"Not me. I've had enough driving for one night."

The horse kept plodding forward, though neither one took the reins. They laughed and joked, but each refused to be the one to give in. The horse continued onward, leaving the small path and ambling straight across the three-way, unpaved intersection. When the horse came to the edge of the ditch on the far side of the road, it stopped. Luke and Mary stared at each other, laughing.

Out of the pitch blackness, rays of car lights crossed the top of the hill. Luke grabbed for the reins, but they wouldn't loosen from the post. Standing, he reached for the reins closer to the horse's backside.

The lights blinded him.

Mary screamed.

*H*annah folded the clothes she'd sewn for Samuel and laid them on *Mamm's* dresser. Through the open windows, she heard people moving downstairs. The back screen door creaked open and then slammed. She recognized the heavy, paced footsteps that entered the home as her father's.

He'd been in the barn for well over two hours, and from the sounds of it, he'd returned without any of her siblings. He must be ready for that private talk he'd mentioned earlier. Hannah eased down the steps. Halfway down the stairs she heard a few whispery words from her mother, and Hannah stopped cold to listen.

"Zeb, I can't stand seeing you like this. I know I agreed to your terms when we married, but it's been twenty-four years, and I've changed my mind."

In an effort to hear the whispers of her parents, Hannah stilled her breathing.

"It's not *your* mind you want to change, Ruth. It's mine. You're not seein' how dangerous this is. Zabeth destroyed the roots of an entire family. I had to move hundreds of miles just to get some peace. She was the cause of an early grave for both my parents. If we aren't careful…"

His voice lowered, and Hannah couldn't hear his words for several long moments. Was it possible that her father and Zabeth were the twins she'd read about in that letter? Something about that idea tasted delicious—as if there was a depth to her father she hadn't known existed.

Even if *Daed* and Zabeth were just siblings and not twins, Hannah had an aunt on her father's side—an aunt none of *Daed's* brothers ever spoke of when they came to visit. Her uncles didn't come from Lancaster often, not even once every few years. Stranger than that, her family never, ever went to visit them. *Daed* said they couldn't leave the farm long enough to make the trip to his brothers' homes. The dairy cows had to be milked twice a day—no exceptions. But inwardly Hannah questioned that excuse. Other dairy farmers hired workers and went on trips.

Her mother's coarse whisper interrupted her thoughts. "Zeb, you don't think Zabeth would show up and try—"

"I don't know, Ruth." *Daed* sounded upset and confused. A wave of compassion ran through Hannah before her father's voice rose. "But I won't stand for Zabeth's rebellious influence coming into our home, especially with what's going on with Hannah. We've got to remain in unity."

His voice lowered, so Hannah couldn't hear anything else. Maybe the letter said more than she realized. She tiptoed back up the steps to her parents' bedroom. She eased the bottom dresser drawer out of its track and set it to the side. The gas-powered pole lamp cast more shadows than actual light. She ran her hands across the wooden runner. Feeling something made of paper that was thinner than the letter, she pulled it out. An empty envelope. Surely it went with the letter she'd read earlier. She held it up, allowing the lamplight to catch the letters so she could read what it said.

It was addressed to her father. The return address had only one name: Bender. That was an Amish last name. Still, she supposed it could belong to someone not Amish. The street address: 4201 Hanover Place, Winding Creek, Ohio. A warm, relaxing feeling ran through Hannah.

"Hannah?" *Daed* called from the foot of the steps, his voice void of the intensity of a few moments before.

Hannah hid the envelope behind her and hurried to the top of the steps. "Yes, *Daed.*" Her voice trembled, threatening to betray her.

He motioned for her to follow him.

"I'll be right there." Without waiting for him to order otherwise, she hurried back into her parents' room and put the envelope back in its hiding place. After she slid the drawer back in as quietly as possible, she turned off the gas pole lamp.

With her chest pounding, she made her way down the steps and into the kitchen.

Her father waved toward the refrigerator before taking his spot at the head of the table. In hurried movements, *Mamm* grabbed a glass and poured him some cold lemonade. Hannah walked to the far side of the table and took a seat. Once the drink was in her father's hand, her mother's motions slowed, and she eased into a chair adjacent to his. The women sat in silence while he sipped his cool drink, the furrow never leaving his brow.

The kerosene lamp sputtered, needing to be refilled. Even in the dim, wavering glow, her father looked weary. Another round of guilt assaulted Hannah. He, too, was getting behind because of the disruption she'd caused. Added to that, there was a stress in her home she'd never known before. She had no idea whether it was because of the new rules concerning the road and her younger siblings needing to be watched closely or because Hannah wasn't pulling her load or because of hidden stress brought on by her mystery aunt. But the whole family seemed to be suffering under some unspoken, unbearable burden.

Finally he placed the empty glass on the wooden table and removed his straw hat. "The bishop came by today when I was in the potato field. He was checking to see if we were doing all right."

Hannah's breath caught in her chest. The flame of the lamp spit and dimmed, barely staying lit as the last of the fuel on the wick burned. Bishop Eli checking on a family usually meant he had concerns that someone in the family was moving toward needing a correction. That could mean her father would be questioned in depth by the church leaders. She always thought the bishop's visits were nothing more than a spying mission, but her father considered them a worthy part of staying submissive and humble under a higher authority.

Mamm leaned toward her husband. *"Was denkscht?"*

Hannah also wondered what her father thought. They both waited on the head of the household to answer the burning question.

"He wants to know why Hannah missed two church services and the work frolic and why she wasn't in the field working with me."

A look of concern shrouded *Mamm.* "What did you say?"

"I told him the truth. I said that Hannah's behavior had nothing to do with rebellion and that all my children were obedient and respectful."

"Ya. Gut." Her mother breathed a sigh of relief. The ticktock of the living room clock kept a steady rhythm through the quiet house as the three of them sat in silence.

In spite of her upbringing, Hannah wanted to protest this game. Her father was always telling the truth and yet not. It was enough to drive her mad. Why couldn't he tell the bishop that it was none of his concern what Hannah was or wasn't doing with her time? She wasn't a baptized member of the church. The bishop had only a certain amount of say over the young adults who hadn't yet submitted to the *Ordnung.* So he used his power on the ones who had been baptized—the parents—knowing that few young people were willing to cause trouble for their *Mamm* or *Daed,* even if they disagreed with the views of the church on a particular matter.

Mamm rose and pulled a full kerosene lamp out of the pantry. She set it on the table and lit it just as the other lamp went out.

Her father folded his hands and rested them on the table. "I told him that if I had anything I thought needed sharing, I'd come to him right quick like. I just ain't decided whether this unmentionable should be told or not. It's not like there are rules concerning it. Still, I'm wonderin' if it might be best to go ahead and tell him and let him decide what the right thing is."

Hannah stood. *"Daed,* I think this needs to stay just with us three. You said so yourself the night I was…the night I came home."

His hand came down on the table hard. "Do not try to confuse me, Hannah. I am trying to do what's right. Have you no sense of respect for my position or the bishop's?"

Her chest tightened, and her heartbeat seemed to speed up something horrible. Breathing became difficult, and she bolted outside.

The cool night air brought no relief. She glanced toward the barn with its kerosene lights glowing through the windows. Her siblings were still working, trying to make up for her lack.

Somewhere in the not-too-far distance, a long, continuous car horn pierced the quietness of the night.

~~◦∫∂~~

An awful noise rang through the air, waking Luke. He tried to open his eyes. Piercing pain ran up Luke's right arm and down his back. Where was he? And why did he hurt so badly? Forcing his eyes open, he gazed at a dark sky filled with brilliant stars and a sliver of the new moon. He was lying on damp grass, but why? And what was that ear-piercing sound?

He rolled to his side and pushed against the dewy grass, but only one arm was able to help him; the other hung limp with excruciating pain. As he staggered to his feet, pieces of what had happened came to him. He spun, looking across the open field where he'd landed. He didn't see Mary. Blinking, he turned his attention to the buggy—some thirty feet away. Pain beyond anything he'd ever experienced throbbed through his head and down his right arm and back. He didn't care. He had to find her.

A car with its headlights on was smashed against the open-top carriage. The impact must have thrown him. Maybe it threw Mary too.

Cringing in agony, Luke strode toward the car. "Mary! Mary!" If he could stop that deafening noise, she might be able to hear him. Scanning the surrounding area through his blurred vision, he stumbled across the open field and toward the road. As he got closer, the car lights silhouetted his overturned buggy. Pain disappeared as panic struck him. With his long legs, he straddled the barbed-wire fence and then brought his back leg over. While trying to gain his balance, he fell into the ditch on the other side.

"Mary! Where are you?" He dragged himself to his feet. The horse was on its side, thrashing and whinnying. Even with the aid of the car lights, he couldn't find Mary. For the first time in his life he ached to lift a heartfelt prayer, a plea from his soul to God. Suddenly he realized he didn't know how to pray, other than the standard rote prayers from the *Christenpflicht.*

O Lord God, heavenly Father, bless us with these Thy gifts, which we shall... The memorized words flooded his thoughts. Pushing past the ceremonial jargon that filled his mind, he tried to think of a more-applicable prayer. He couldn't. Never in his life had he used anything but the rote prayers. He needed real help, and he needed a real God to hear him. Now.

Luke looked toward heaven. "God, please." Shame swallowed him. How dare he think he had the right to lift his head toward heaven and speak so honestly to the Lord of all?

He glanced at what was left of the upended carriage. His legs buckled. He landed on his knees. "Please, Father, if You will, help us."

Warm chills ran through his body, sort of like the ones he felt when Mary touched him, but these were stronger, more...

He looked at the deep purple sky with glittering white stars and a tiny, crescent-shaped moon.

A strong desire to release the mare flowed over him. With renewed strength, he stumbled to his feet and made his way to the horse. In the twin streams of light from the car, Luke witnessed terror in the animal's bulging eyes. Based on the stride marks in the soft dirt and torn-up grasses of the shallow ditch, she'd worked hard to try to stand. She had gashes where the shafts of the buggy had gouged her flanks when it was pushed forward by the impact of the car.

"Easy, Old Bess, easy. *Begreiflich, alt Gaul. Langsam un begreiflich.*" Luke murmured idle phrases as he used his able hand to unfasten the leather straps from the shafts. Gently pulling on the reins, Luke guided and cajoled her until she finally stood. Old Bess tossed her head toward the sky and took off.

Luke ran to the car. In the driver's seat he found a man slumped over the steering wheel. "Mister?" The man didn't answer. Luke reached in and eased the man off the wheel. The deafening noise stopped.

A moment later Luke thought he heard a soft moan coming from the other side of the buggy. "Mary?" He headed toward the sound. When he reached the far side of the carriage, which the car lights didn't illuminate, he saw Mary's body pinned under it. He realized the horse had been jerking the buggy back and forth while Mary was pinned under it. What a strange thing that he had felt so strongly about releasing the horse before doing anything else.

Luke grabbed the sides of the carriage. Pain seared through him, and he fell to his knees. His right arm had no strength. Furthermore, it seemed to be draining his whole being of its power.

Staggering to his feet, he tried to think. The overturned buggy was angled toward the downward slope of the ditch, causing leverage and gravity to work against him. He squatted, placing his left shoulder under the side of the coach, and pushed with all the strength he could muster. The carriage didn't budge. He was too weak to lift the weight off Mary.

Mary moaned. "Luke."

He turned to see her reaching for him. He knelt, brushing back the tall grasses around her face. "Hold on. I'll get help."

He studied the fields and roads. The accident had occurred so far away from any main streets, no one would have seen or heard the collision. And no one would miss them for hours.

A gentle brush against his leg jolted his attention back to Mary. "Listen to me." Her faint voice brought tears to his eyes. He bent closer, and she reached for his face. "I have loved you for as long as I can remember, Luke. We would have made a *gut* family, *ya*?"

"Mary, don't talk like that. We *will* make a *gut* family. You'll see. I..." Luke wanted to promise her she'd live and all would be set right, but he knew better than to cross that line. It wasn't within his power to make such things happen.

Caressing his face, she whispered, "Don't you ever forget, you're the best catch around. You'll find someone else."

"No. Do you hear me? I said no!"

Her hand fell from his face, and her eyes closed. He clasped her hand in his. It felt lifeless and cold.

"Mary?" He patted her cheek. She gave no response. He tried again. "Mary!"

He rested her hand across her chest. Swaying, he stood. After stumbling back to the car, he pushed on the steering wheel, hunting for the horn. When he shoved the silver metal piece, that awful noise blasted through the still night again. On the floorboard he spied a tiny blue telephone. After placing the man's limp body against the horn, Luke headed for the passenger side. As he rounded the back of the car, he wondered if he would be able to figure out how to use the device. He'd seen people use cell phones but had never tried one. He'd only used a corded touch-tone twice in his life.

After opening the car door, he grabbed the phone. He moved in front of the headlights and pressed the thing to his ear. No dial tone. He remembered the day a couple of local firefighters had come to his school and, among other things, said that in an emergency a person needed to get to a phone and dial 911. He pushed those numbers. Each time he pressed a button, an odd electronic sound chirped. But no sound came out of the earpiece.

He gazed across the field, screaming, "Somebody help us. Please."

Looking back at the cell phone, Luke saw the light on the screen go out. He put the device to his ear. Still no sound. He punched the buttons again. The numbers illuminated. Now the screen read 911911. He pressed every button, but nothing helped.

Luke tossed the phone onto the car seat. He stumbled back to Mary and sat on the dirt beside her. When he touched her face, it still held a bit of warmth. Stretching out his legs, he lifted her head and placed it on his lap. Feeling helpless, he brushed wisps of hair from her face. "I don't know what to do, Mary. I'm so sorry."

Drops of blood fell onto Mary's head from somewhere. Luke wiped them off with the palm of his hand. When he looked at his right arm, he saw blood dripping out of the cuff of his long-sleeved jacket. Leaning back, he lay down on the gravelly area. Darkness pulled in on him, and he was unable to resist it. As he closed his eyes, something resembling sleep took over. He could still hear the horn blasting. Maybe someone would come searching for the source of that awful racket.

Drifting into a place he couldn't pull out of, Luke heard sirens. Car doors slammed. Two voices—a man and a woman—began talking. Luke tried to rouse himself. He ached to yell, "Over here! Come help my beloved Mary!" But no matter how much desire welled up within him, something kept pulling him deeper into nothingness.

"We've got a bleeder," a woman shouted. He heard the sound of scissors working against fabric, then felt his jacket being pulled from his shoulder.

No. Not me. No.

"Male. Approximately twenty years of age."

My Mary. Please, save Mary. Can't you see her?

"It looks like a bone from a compound fracture has nicked the artery in the right arm."

An awesome feeling, which went beyond the rules of the *Ordnung,* called to him.

Through the silence that continued to envelop him, he heard the faint sound of the woman's voice.

"I can't find a pulse."

The Lapp house was silent, with everyone asleep, as Hannah crept to a straight-backed chair on the porch, next to the open front door. If she saw car lights, she'd be in the house with the door locked before the driver could spot her. In spite of her fears, the cool air and the night sky with its shiny jewels staring down ministered to her bruised heart.

For the second time that day, she listened for the sound of hoofbeats against the hard-packed dirt road. The sirens she'd heard earlier bothered her. She knew worry was a sin, but Luke didn't usually stay out this late. It was past eleven. He'd need to be up milking the cows before he knew it.

The cool air made her shiver. She wrapped the shawl tighter around her. No doubt she wasn't the only one in love. Luke probably fell just short of worshiping Mary. With love like that, he'd draw plenty of strength to sustain him through his workday tomorrow, no matter how little sleep he got.

In spite of not hearing from Paul, she had begun to feel her sanity trickling back. Although the moments were rare, they brought enough relief to comfort her. She had to find her way out of this embarrassing, angry, painful fog she was living in.

Having a shunned aunt in Ohio made her curious if her aunt ever felt some of the same things she did. Somehow that thought helped her, and she began to wonder what her aunt was like.

A single moving light on the road caught her attention, and she quickly dismissed her daydreams. The glow was coming from a kerosene lantern on an open buggy. A tiny laugh escaped her. The horse was trotting at an incredible gait. After whiling away the hours with Mary, Luke was trying to make double time coming home.

As the courting buggy came closer, Hannah could see it wasn't being pulled by their old mare. She stood and walked to the edge of the porch. When the carriage came into clear sight, she recognized its occupant.

Matthew Esh.

Concern slid up her spine. Why was he heading away from his home and at such a speed at this time of night?

Matthew stopped the buggy and gave his warm smile. "You're up awful late."

"I was hoping Luke would be home before now."

"Ah." Matthew propped his foot on the side of the cart. "I saw *Mr. Lapp* and *Miss Yoder* a good bit earlier. They were moseying 'round outside our district."

His jovial tone caught Hannah off guard, and she laughed. Only the English called each other by such titles. Amish students called even their teachers by their first names. But their relaxed ways about names didn't apply when they were talking to or about the English.

Matthew's horse snorted, drawing Hannah's attention to the gorgeous creature pulling the cart. "You got a new horse, *ya?*"

"I bought him at auction last week, thinkin' I could turn a profit. I already sold him to the wealthy folks in Virginia that my brother is building cabinets for. I'm gonna take him to the new owners as soon as the Sabbath is over."

Hannah couldn't remember ever seeing such a fine horse. Its body was lean and sinewy. The reddish brown color shimmered even under the cover of night. When Hannah touched its shoulder, she realized she'd come off the porch and was standing beside Matthew's buggy. She lowered her hand, wondering afresh about her sanity.

Matthew leaned forward. "He's mesmerizing, no?" The lilt in Matthew's whisper made her lift her gaze. He held his index finger to his lips. "But if ya say I boasted about the horse, I'll have to deny it."

Hannah bit her bottom lip and refused the smile that wanted to be expressed. "Does the new courting buggy go with the horse?"

"Yep. I refinished it myself. Those Virginia people want it as a treat for their fancy inn. The stallion was a racetrack runner, ran well for many years."

Moving to the front of the horse, Hannah caressed its muzzle. "He's gorgeous."

The horse whinnied and tossed his head high in the air.

Matthew chuckled. "I think he agrees with you. But I didn't know you cared anything for horses."

"Some things are too striking not to notice. What's his name?"

"Vento Delicato. It's Italian for 'gentle wind.' With a track record like his, I'd think they could have named him better."

Hannah murmured to the horse. "Gentle Wind's not such a bad name."

Vento Delicato lowered his head and allowed her to stroke his face.

Matthew propped his elbow on his knee. "If you don't mind me saying, you're looking a bit down in the mouth these days, Hannah."

She hated that "if you don't mind me saying" phrase. When someone said that, a body might as well brace itself to mind whatever was about to be said. Even so, it was wrong of her to carry her sadness for the world to see.

"I…I was…under the weather. I'm feeling better. Thanks."

Matthew slid forward on the seat. "He won't get your hands dirty. I spent too much time grooming him before the singing tonight. I got all the loose hair off him I could so it wouldn't fly off and cling to a girl's good dre—"

Hannah knew the rest of the sentence. He'd hoped to take a girl home from the singing. More than ever before, she realized the pain of Matthew's disappointment. Leaving the singings alone time after time had to hurt deeply, causing loneliness to grow unchecked.

Hannah looked down at her clothing. Surprise reverberated through her. She was in her nightgown! Modest as it was, going from her neck to her ankles and down to her elbows, it was still improper. She glanced up at Matthew.

His familiar lopsided grin brought back memories of their school days and softball games. He'd graduated two years before Hannah. But because he'd had to repeat a grade when he was very young, he was three years older than she.

He pointed at her and then the horse. "Obviously one of you is too gussied up for the occasion."

Suppressing a smile, Hannah mocked, "Are ya saying I'm not dressed well enough to be standing beside your horse?"

"If the brand-new horseshoe fits, Hannah Lapp…"

Quiet snickers erupted from both of them.

"Would you like to see how smooth his gait is? It's like riding on a fast-moving cloud."

Hannah glanced down at her attire. "I'd better not."

"If you're worried that I'll think this means something, don't be. It doesn't take a genius to figure out that you're more interested in my horse than any single guy around here."

She studied him.

He shrugged. "At least you picked the finest horse."

His relaxed posture and easy talk were refreshing after the misery of the past few weeks. She had a strong hankering to climb into the carriage and see what this horse could do. But first she'd need to change out of her nightgown.

"Can you wait a minute?"

Matthew held up his hand. "Just a dart down the private path on the other side of the barn. It'll take less than five minutes." He spread his fingers apart, signaling five. "If ya go change, you'll likely wake someone, and then you'll never get a chance to see how riding with this race-winning stallion feels."

The horse bobbed its head up and down. Matthew motioned toward Vento. "See, even he agrees."

Hannah glanced back at her lifeless house. Everyone was sound asleep, and they'd be back awful quick like. Vento stomped his foot and shook his mane as if telling her to give him a try. Eager to give life another chance, Hannah clutched her shawl with one hand. "Let's see how this gentle wind rides." Grabbing the buggy handle, Hannah pulled herself aboard.

Matthew gave the signal, and the stallion took off. The force of the forward movement made them fall back against the seat. Their laughter erupted, and the negative thoughts that had haunted her for a month finally gave way to positive ones.

Surely Paul would write her soon. He had to be terribly swamped at school. He'd told her they only had to get through this year, and then he'd work for her father until they had his blessing. She took a deep cleansing breath. Paul had no way of knowing her world had been shattered, and he couldn't be held responsible for being busy with his last year of schooling and… What did he call that other thing? Oh yes, internship. He was also busy doing that.

The wheels to the carriage left the ground as they rolled over an in-ground rock. Hannah grabbed the seat on each side of her. Both she and Matthew burst out laughing. Feeling exhilarated, she sensed faith in the future beginning to stir within her.

~ిౖ$\text{\textrm{ಐ}}$

Sarah stood on her tiptoes, peering out the bedroom window as her sister climbed into a buggy with a man. All Sarah could see of the driver was the top of his straw hat.

Hannah Lapp, you're a liar.

Hannah had everyone doing all her work because she was too tired. Sarah clenched her fists so tight her arms tingled with numbness. She'd spent all day at that awful Mrs. Waddell's, and for what? So Hannah could traipse around the countryside at all hours in her nightdress? The bishop would hear about this.

The congregation was told regularly not to cause trouble by confronting someone. If there was a questionable issue, it was to be brought to the bishop, and he'd sort things out. If need be, he'd do it without ever saying who told him. And he could approach people confidentially. If they repented, no one else even need know about the event.

Then again, maybe she didn't want to keep this quiet. It irked her to no end how Hannah always managed to sponge up everyone's admiration; *Daed, Mamm,* and even Luke seemed to think she was some kind of Amish superhero or something. Levi wasn't as bad about it as everyone else, but even he thought Hannah could bake, sew, and take care of the young'uns better than she could, which just plain out wasn't true.

It would serve her sister right if they all knew the real Hannah. Why, if *Daed* and *Mamm* knew their daughter was gadding about like this, Sarah would never again have to hear her father say that she needed to be more like Hannah.

A shudder of excitement ran through her. Maybe this was more than just a way to open her parents' eyes. Maybe it was what Sarah had been looking for ever since Jacob Yoder had taken to noticing Hannah over her. Why, Sarah'd had her eye on Jacob for more than a year, but of late the only Lapp he ever noticed at the meeting place was Hannah.

Sarah figured that whenever her sister went to Mary's house, she was warming herself up to Jacob. The very thought made Sarah so mad she sometimes thought she hated her own sister. She'd told Hannah a long time ago how she felt about Jacob. Hannah had given her word she wasn't interested in him. But Sarah wasn't a fool. Jacob hadn't shifted his attention to Hannah for no reason. His interest in her would end quickly if he knew about tonight.

Still, Sarah couldn't be the one to tell him. He might take offense, saying she was a tattletale. There had to be a way for her parents—and Jacob Yoder—to know about this without anyone thinking less of her for it.

Hearing the sound of buggy wheels against the road, Sarah realized they'd returned. Wanting accurate details, Sarah took notice of everything she could. She had never seen a horse like that within her community, nor had she seen that courting gig. It wasn't either Old Order Amish or Old Order Mennonite. As a matter of fact, it looked like some type of commercial rig, used for touristy stuff. If that was true, the driver probably wasn't Amish or Mennonite. He was more than likely English. Oh, this was getting better and better. But why would an English boy be out at this time of night?

She watched Hannah climb out of the buggy. Her sister must've made some English friends from the hired workers Mrs. Waddell took on during the summer months. This man probably drove a tourist buggy for a living and wore that straw hat to make himself look more authentic for his customers.

Sarah would bet this wasn't the first time Hannah had pulled such a stunt. No wonder her sister was always looking for mail to come to Mrs. Waddell's. She had an English beau she needed to hear from in order to make her sneaky plans. Sarah huffed. Hannah out taking rides and whooping it up with a man while pretending to be sick. Sarah would get her back just as soon as she could speak with the bishop without anyone else knowing. If telling the bishop didn't get this piece of news to her parents and Jacob Yoder, she would figure out another way. She was sick of playing second best to the likes of such a liar as her sister.

*M*orning light filtered through the bedroom windows as Hannah made her and Sarah's bed. Careful not to wake her two youngest sisters, Hannah slipped into her day clothes.

The aroma of bacon and sausage wafting through the house smelled inviting. In spite of the minor nausea that still clung to her these days, a bit of hunger gnawed at her stomach. Maybe, somehow, she'd survived the worst and things would get better from here.

She tiptoed down the stairs, hoping to find Luke before her mother realized she was up. Hannah had no doubts that if Luke had managed to propose, Mary had accepted.

Hannah also knew it was time to try to resume her full set of chores and make up for the difficulties she had caused her family. She scurried out the side door and headed for the barn. Sucking in a lungful of clean, brisk air, she resolved to hold on to those refreshing feelings that had come to her last night.

As she traipsed up the hill toward the milking barn, she spotted Old Bess, one of Luke's mares, standing outside the fence. *How did she get out?* Hoping that in his tired state Luke hadn't left the gate open, she sprinted across the yards to the pasture gate. It was latched securely.

She glanced across the meadows, looking for something that would make sense of this strange occurrence. Finding nothing out of the ordinary apart from the horse outside its fence, she grabbed a rope harness off the fence post and eased toward the mare. "Where's your master this fine morning?" As Hannah slid the rope around its neck, she noticed that the horse's left side was covered in dried mud. Puzzled, she led the limping mare toward the barn.

As she entered the open doorway into the barn, she saw her father toss a sack of feed onto his shoulder. But Luke was nowhere in sight. *Daed* glanced her way and paused. A smile worked its way across his weary face. "I'm glad to see you up and ready to help with chores. Do you know where Luke is?"

Hannah twisted the horse's lead rope as if she were wringing out wet laundry. "He's not here?"

He tossed the feed sack onto the ground and stood it on end. "He must be around here somewhere. He wouldn't leave before milking." He pulled a pocketknife from his trousers, opened it, and jabbed it into the feed sack.

Levi stepped out of a stall, looking more like his older brother as each day brought Levi closer to his nineteenth birthday. He hung the pitchfork in its place on the barn wall, and strolled to Hannah. "Where'd you find Old Bess?"

"She was outside the fence."

Levi's eyes skimmed over the horse. A frown knitted his brows as he rubbed the matted dirt that covered the mare's girth and belly. The horse whinnied and stepped back from him. "*Daed!* She's got gashes."

Dropping the knife and letting the sack of feed fall over, *Daed* tore out of the milking barn. Levi and Hannah followed him. He ran to the carriage house and flung open the door. When he turned back to face Levi and Hannah, the concern in his eyes made her cringe. "Luke's buggy is missing."

Quick, repetitive sounds of a horse's hoofs made the three of them turn toward the driveway. A horse and rider came sprinting toward the barn. Matthew Esh brought Vento up short a few feet from them. His hat was missing, and his face was rigid. "Zeb," he said in a breathless voice, "is Luke here?"

Daed shook his head. "His buggy ain't here either, but his horse is. And it's injured."

Matthew squirmed in his saddle. "Someone from the hospital came to Bishop Eli's place this morning. Said there are two unidentified young people in the hospital. They're sending out word to all the surrounding districts."

Daed lowered his head and moaned.

Matthew shielded his eyes from the first rays of the day. "I saw Luke and Mary last night. They were headin' toward the very area where the accident took place."

Daed grabbed Levi's arm, his eyes wide and his face drained of color. "Hitch up two horses and two buggies. I'll get your mother and the children."

Levi took off running toward the barn, and her father ran down the drive and into the house. Hannah stood there, frozen, unable to move or even think.

Matthew dug his heels into Vento's sides and charged to the back door of Hannah's house. He slid off the horse and knocked on the screen door. "Zeb, I got an idea that will save some time."

"Tell."

"If I ride straight to the bishop's house and have him send one van here and one to the Yoders, it'll save at least an hour, probably more."

"Yes. Yes. That's sound thinking. We'll get everyone ready. Hurry, young man, hurry."

Hannah held her baby brother Samuel's tender hand in hers, reassured by the comfort of it. All eight Lapps stood in their front yard, watching billows of dust follow a large car down the dirt road. *Mamm* had her wedding travel bag by her side, the closest thing to a suitcase she owned. If Luke was staying at the hospital, so would she.

The van slowed, then came to a stop. A petite woman in bright pink pants and a matching top stepped out of the vehicle. "I'm Kelsey Morgan." She held out her hand to *Daed.* "I'm Hank Carlisle's daughter and a nurse at Hershey Medical Center."

Daed released his suspender and held out his hand. "I'm Zeb Lapp. This is my family."

Ms. Morgan shook his hand. "You believe your son may have been in the accident last night?"

His cheeks flushed. "Our oldest did not come home last night. He's never done that before."

The woman pulled a picture out of her pocket and showed it to him. "Is this your son?"

He grimaced. "It is."

"He's in the intensive care unit at our hospital. It's not the closest hospital, but it's where he needed to be for the type of injuries he sustained. If you'll load your family members into the vehicle, I'll take you all there." She opened the passenger-side door and then climbed behind the wheel.

Without delay or questions, *Mamm* and *Daed* collected their brood. As he lifted the children into the van, she operated the seat belt buckles for them.

Hannah stood near the open van door, peering inside. The interior smelled of dyed leather and a sickeningly sweet air freshener. The odor caused her stomach to roil. At the sight of the long bench seat, she began to shake as visions of being thrown into her attacker's car pelted her. She stumbled backward. The day of the unmentionable flooded her mind in horrid, living color.

"Get in, Hannah." *Mamm* pointed to an empty seat.

Gasping for air, Hannah backed farther away. "I can't."

"You're safe, Hannah. Trust me and get in, please," her father reasoned.

Hannah shook her head. She could hear the sound of each breath that she forced through her lungs.

The nurse climbed out of the van and came around to their side of the vehicle. "Does she have asthma?"

Mamm reached for Hannah. "No, she's just a bit spooked at the car."

Avoiding her mother's grasp, Hannah turned away. The nurse stood directly in front of her, compassion in her eyes. "Honey, you'll be safe in the vehicle. I promise." Her golden voice washed over Hannah. "Normally this isn't how the hospital handles these situations. But my dad feels strong ties with the Amish in these parts. So when he heard that some local Amish were taken by helicopter to the hospital where I work, he asked me to come here personally and try to help. Surely after I've traveled all this way, you'll let me help, won't you?"

Hannah stared at the woman, unable to speak or even nod.

She gave a warm, endearing smile. "Your brother gained consciousness for a few minutes a couple of times. He was anxious and confused. He needs his family around him."

Hannah gazed into the woman's eyes and caught a glimpse of unspoken truth about Luke's situation. A different type of panic ran down Hannah's spine. "And Mary?"

The nurse took a deep breath. "I'm not at liberty to say anything about her except that she was brought to our facility by helicopter. Another van is taking her family to the hospital."

Nightmarish memories warred within Hannah. Setting her will against her emotions, she cleared her throat and forced herself to step into the van.

~~~∿✗

Ignoring her pounding heart and the nausea, Hannah gazed out the car window and tried to focus on the scenery. Gentle hills and farmlands whizzed by. After forty-five minutes of back roads, the view outside changed from rolling acreage to a wide, flat river. Brown rapids and white foam seemed to be racing the van. The sun's brilliance sparkled against the rippling water as if starlight had been captured and brought to earth. The first bit of fall color nipped at the leaves on some of the sprawling oaks along the riverbank. She closed her eyes, tuning out the ever-changing scenery and hoping the sick feeling would go away.

When the van pulled into a parking space and the engine cut off, Hannah exited as quickly as she could, the rest of her family following.

A noise ripped through the air as if it were destroying the vast parking area. The air around them seemed to vibrate from the sound. With Samuel holding Sarah's hand and Rebecca sitting on Hannah's hip, all nine of them made their way across the acrid-smelling lot. A few moments later Hannah saw the source of the racket: a helicopter landing near the far end of the hospital. The same helicopter, she guessed, that had brought Luke and Mary here.

Somewhere a siren shrieked and a car horn blasted. Those noises, mixed with the busyness of cars coming in and out of the lot, assaulted her nerves.

Rebecca wailed. Hannah hugged her close and snuggled against her soft neck. "Sh, little one. It's all right."

In spite of Samuel being seven years old, Sarah lifted him into her arms and kissed his cheek. "The English must search for ways to make noise. No?" Samuel bobbed his head in agreement, and his baby-fine, straight, blond hair moved with the wind.

The worst of the summer heat was over at home, but here it seemed to radiate from the blacktop.

They followed Ms. Morgan to a square, brownish building. Two large sliding-glass doors opened without so much as a touch.

The city smells disappeared along with the heat as they entered. The room they stepped into was three times as large as any barn Hannah had ever been in. She had visited the doctor near her home a few times in her life, but she'd never been to a hospital. She blinked, trying to take it all in. The lobby wasn't cold, menacing, or intimidating, as Hannah had expected. Dozens of beautiful chairs sat near small tables. Lamps and plant stands with various types of foliage were scattered throughout the room, giving the place a peaceful feeling.

They turned right, walking past a hexagon-shaped oak desk with a sign above it that said Information. *Daed's* focus stayed straight on where they were going, unlike his children, who gaped at everything around them. Regardless of the nice setting, Hannah was sure Luke and Mary ached to be home, where a breeze coming through an open window gave more refreshment than air from a machine.

Ms. Morgan took a sharp right. The Lapps followed her. After a couple of yards she turned right again and then stopped outside an elevator door. Ms. Morgan pushed a large button with an arrow pointing up on it. "After you speak with a doctor, you'll need to return to this floor and fill out some paperwork."

"I'd like to see Luke before we see the doctor," *Daed* said as the doors opened.

Once they all squeezed in, Ms. Morgan pushed another button, and the doors slid shut. "We'll find a quiet place on the second floor for you to talk with the doctor. After he explains things, you may see Luke."

Daed removed his hat and fidgeted with it. "We don't have insurance."

Ms. Morgan nodded. "Luke and Mary came in under emergency status. Care is guaranteed, but there are still forms to fill out."

~~ঔঌ~~

Hannah listened to the nervous murmuring of her family as they all waited in a conference room behind closed doors. Her mother paced the floor, bouncing a whimpering Rebecca on her hip. Her father appeared calm, sitting in a chair with his hands propped on the large table. But he kept squeezing his fists so tight they turned white. Then he'd release them and do it again. Tiny dots of sweat covered his forehead.

Levi and Sarah sat quietly with their hands folded in their laps. Samuel bounced on Esther's knee, eating peanuts that a hospital worker had bought for him from a vending machine.

The oversized wooden door opened. A man in his late twenties entered. He glanced about the room and gave a smile. "I'm Dr. Greenfield." He took a seat across from *Daed. Mamm* passed Rebecca to Hannah and sat in the chair next to her husband. The young doctor pulled an ink pen from his shirt pocket. "Mr. and Mrs. Lapp?"

Her parents nodded, looking too emotional to try to speak.

Dr. Greenfield slid his hands into the pockets of his lab coat. "Your son is in serious but stable condition. He has a concussion, but that is mild and temporary. Our main concern is the injury to his arm. We had to operate on it. There was a slight nick on an artery, and the blood flow wasn't sufficient to give the hand and lower arm the circulation they needed. We repaired the artery, and things look good right now. The next few days will let us know how well his lower arm and hand will heal. We'll need to watch him closely during that time. He's in ICU, so he'll get the medical care he needs."

Daed's eyes narrowed. "You said he had a concussion."

The doctor gave a slight nod. "We are closely monitoring his condition, but there's every indication that his head will be fine."

He squeezed his hands into fists again. "Is there a chance he could lose his arm?"

A grimace caused lines across the man's face. "Yes. But we hope that won't be necessary. Right now everything appears to be healing. There's no damage to any tendons or ligaments, which means if his arm and hand do well over the next twenty-four to forty-eight hours, he won't have any lingering issues to deal with—except needing as little stress as possible and getting plenty of rest for three to four weeks."

Swallowing hard and hoping she wasn't about to upset her family further, Hannah spoke. "What about Mary?"

The doctor gave her a friendly smile. "I'm sorry, but I can't tell you about a patient who isn't a family member. The Yoders arrived a few minutes after you, and they're currently meeting with Mary's doctor. They can share with you any information they wish."

He turned back to her father. "Two adults at a time are allowed in ICU, but no one under twelve is admitted unless circumstances dictate. With supervision, the younger children can stay in here or go to a waiting room. There's a cafeteria downstairs. If you'll go to the nurses' station, they'll show you to Luke's room."

Her mother took a deep breath. "Thank you."

Daed nodded. "Yes, thank you."

"Glad to help." Dr. Greenfield left.

Mamm straightened her pinafore. She turned, eying each of her children to make sure they were ready to cope with what faced them without drawing undue attention.

In a quiet, stoic manner they filed out of the room.

For the first time in months, maybe years, Hannah felt her own ideas and desires fade. All that mattered was that Luke and Mary get well.

H annah." Her father's voice cracked a bit as he called to her from the doorway of the hospital waiting room.

"Yes sir." Hannah rose and placed little Rebecca in Sarah's lap.

"You go in next. Then you can get Sarah, Esther, and Levi ready to see Luke. I'll find a pay phone and call the Bylers to let our community know how things stand."

"Yes sir." Hannah hoped the Bylers would be close enough to hear their phone. It was located in a shanty at the end of their long lane and used mainly for business purposes. They had an answering machine inside the shanty, but days passed without them remembering to check it. After thinking about it, Hannah was sure her father would call Mr. Carlisle if he couldn't reach the Bylers. Mr. Carlisle would see to it that the community was informed of what was going on.

Leaving Sarah to watch over their three youngest siblings, Hannah walked through the door and down the ICU corridor. As she made her way along the hallway, she saw Jacob Yoder leaving ICU and heading for the waiting room. The young man looked pale and shaken. But Sarah was here; she'd be pleased to keep him company. Hannah dipped her head low, avoiding eye contact just as she'd promised Sarah she'd do. But a quick glance up said he never even saw her.

Hannah nodded at a nurse who glanced up from her station. Coming to a halt outside Luke's room, she saw her brother through the sliding glass entryway. She froze.

He lay in the bed with his eyes closed. His right arm and hand were bandaged. Restraints held both arms to the metal sides of the bed. A bag containing some type of amber liquid and a bag of what had to be blood dripped into different tubes attached to his good arm by needles. Strange machines were connected to him and to various boxes she'd heard the nurse call *monitors.*

Her mother sat in an upright recliner beside the bed, staring at Luke. The expression on her face spoke of despair and hopelessness. Determined to help as best she could, Hannah stepped into the room and eased into the small chair beside her mother. "It's okay, *Mamm.* Luke and Mary are gonna be all right. You just wait and see."

Although Hannah hadn't gone in to see Mary yet, she'd overheard Becky Yoder tell all she knew of her daughter's injuries. Poor Mary. She'd suffered a right femur fracture, a right dislocated shoulder, and a left subdural hematoma. The doctors had said that with physical therapy Mary's leg and shoulder weren't a concern. But she could have problems with her memory, speech, and coordination because of the head injury that required surgery to relieve the buildup of blood against her brain. She might not remember her family or friends. She might need to learn how to brush her teeth, feed herself, walk, and get dressed all over again. She'd also need months of physical therapy for the injuries to her shoulder and leg.

Becky said her daughter's heartbeat had been so weak at the scene of the accident that the medic thought she didn't have a pulse. Hannah wondered just how close to dying Mary had come.

Guilt nibbled at Hannah, for even with the grief of this situation, she was finding this world of medicine fascinating.

~~∽§∽~~

Hours dragged by as Hannah and her family took turns watching Luke breathe. Various nurses and doctors came by and explained all sorts of medical issues that were hard to keep up with.

The younger kids were miserable camping out in the waiting room, and *Daed* was fed up with just waiting for Luke to awaken. He'd mumbled something a few hours earlier about the rest of the potatoes having to be harvested before the weather turned.

While Hannah sat in Luke's room, both sets of parents gathered in a conference room to discuss who would stay at the hospital and who would return to the farm. Hannah knew the heads of the households wanted to get as much of their families as possible back home. Not only was there plenty that needed to be done, but the contact with such worldliness through the televisions and some of the people was not something either man wanted his children exposed to. And meals at the cafeteria were expensive for an entire family. Besides, it made no sense for two entire families to hold a vigil here.

"Hannah." Her mother motioned for her to leave Luke's room and come with her. Hannah followed her out of the ICU area and into a secluded hallway. Her mother turned to her. "Your father came to me about this and then talked to Becky and John Yoder. We think the best place for you to be is here. Becky and I will stay as well."

The sadness in her mother's eyes and voice hurt, and Hannah couldn't answer.

Mamm glanced down the hallway. "John and Becky would like you here in case Mary wakes up. If you tell her she's safe and everything is okay, that will settle the matter." She smiled, but it never entered her eyes. "Won't it?"

Hannah nodded. Mary did trust her. There had been a time when Mary wouldn't believe she was safe from a storm or an imaginary monster unless Hannah told her so. But that was years ago, back when Mary was a child.

Hannah was also fairly sure of what her mother wasn't saying. If Mary never woke, or if she woke with some of the problems the doctor had mentioned, Hannah could be a comfort to Becky.

Mamm took Hannah by the hand. "The man driving the car that ran into Luke and Mary showed up here at the hospital."

Hannah hadn't expected this. "Why?"

"He's in the conference room with your *Daed*, John, and Becky. He's so sorry for the accident, Hannah." Her voice cracked, and she fought to control her emotions. "It ain't his fault. He wasn't speeding. He just topped the hill as the buggy was crossing the road. He and his wife have both offered to come work for us awhile. I think it'll do the poor man some good to know he's helping those he hurt, even if it wasn't on purpose. And with their help, we won't be short-handed if you stay here." She paused, searching her daughter's face. "Besides, your *Daed* says that you're doing better here than at the farm and that maybe you need some time away."

Hannah swallowed. "I'd be happy to stay here with Luke and Mary. I'm learning bits and pieces about medical stuff, and it's fascinating."

Their conversation paused as they waited on a man to pass them in the hallway. Hannah hated the reason they were at this place, but there was so much to learn around here. When no one saw her, she'd managed to read a few lines from a novel that someone had left in a waiting room and had flipped through a few psychology magazines.

Her mother smiled. "I've always said you'd make a good midwife one day, Hannah. Now, go on back in with Luke."

An hour later *Mamm* came into Luke's room, explaining that John Yoder and *Daed* had found lodging near the hospital for the three of them who were staying. Two drivers had arrived, and everyone else was downstairs loading up to leave.

Mamm, Becky, and Hannah went down to say good-bye to their families. Mary's father promised to return in a few days. In the meantime, Becky was to call him at the Bylers' house with updates at a preset time each evening. In what seemed like a blur, Hannah stood in front of the hospital waving good-bye to most of her family.

How did life change so quickly?

Luke couldn't manage to open his eyes, but he felt a peacefulness in his heart that he'd never known existed. The God who dictated the strict ways of the *Ordnung* had another side to Him. Based on what Luke's heart felt, it was a gentle, listening, loving side. One that was quick to warm Luke's being and build hope during desperate times.

He heard Hannah near him, singing a hymn from the *Ausbund*. He pushed against the weight that tried to force his eyes shut and caught a glimpse of his sister.

Hannah smiled. "Hi, Luke."

Where was he? His eyes closed and refused to open again, but he didn't give in to the pull of sleep.

An image of Mary broke through his murky thoughts. He tried to focus while his sister explained to him where he was, where Mary was, and why. Hannah's always gentle voice now irritated him. He wanted to get up and demand that someone take him to see Mary. Now! But no matter how hard he fought against the engulfing grogginess, he couldn't break free.

In addition to his sister's voice, he could hear other strange noises. There was a whooshing sound that reminded him of the diesel-powered milkers used on the dairy cows, rhythmic beeps like he'd never heard before, and the faint hum of some machine. Something under his nose was blowing cold air up his nostrils, but beyond that he detected a smell like the chemical his *Mamm* used to clean the floors. He ached from the top of his head down to his lower back, but his eyes refused to open, and his body occasionally jerked against its imprisonment. Unable to fight any longer, he allowed himself to sink back into that restful place.

Sitting in the recliner beside Luke's bed, Hannah hurt for both Luke and Mary. She closed her eyes. With them in such a bad way, it was only the beginning of difficult times.

In spite of her concerns, sleepiness nipped at her. While she relaxed, an idea flowed into her mind.

A quilt.

With Mary having months of recuperation ahead and Hannah intending to spend as many of those hours with her dear friend as she could, it seemed a good time to start a quilt for Luke and Mary. If her friend awoke with problems remembering her life, it could serve to tie Mary to her past and to her future as they worked on the squares together. Thoughts of gathering materials and designing a special pattern brought a sense of peace, causing Hannah to close her eyes and lean back in the recliner.

"Wh-where's Mary?" Luke's scratchy voice shot through her.

Hannah jumped to her feet, startled. Breathless, she grasped his hand. "Luke, you're awake."

He stared at her, confusion radiating from his eyes. "Is...Mary... alive?"

"Yes. She's in a room down the hall."

A nervous chill ran through her. A nurse had said that when Luke woke, no one was to tell him any more than Mary was alive and resting. Desperate not to utter the wrong thing, Hannah motioned toward the door. "I…I'll tell *Mamm* and the nurses that you're awake."

As nurses flitted in and out of Luke's room, *Mamm* sat in the cushioned chair, keeping her show of emotion to a minimum. But the light in her eyes helped to ease Hannah's heartache.

Luke was awake, absorbing his new surroundings with a mixture of thankfulness and frustration. In spite of his numerous attempts to see Mary, the staff had refused. Dr. Greenfield was concerned that the stress might slow Luke's progress. Sometime after she was removed from life support—if all went well—Luke would be allowed to see her.

On Mary's third day after her surgery, the doctor would run tests to see what was going on inside her skull. If there were signs of healing and no pools or clots of blood, the staff would begin the process of waking her and might remove the ventilator.

Hannah's heart turned a flip every time she thought about the doctor's words. They were so noncommittal. *If* Mary responded well, she *should* be able to breathe on her own. Recovery seemed so tentative, so faltering. The possibilities made Hannah feel panicky. But quiet misery seemed the only way to respond as the waiting went on and on.

Paul walked beside his supervisor as they strode down the corridor of the family-services department. Connie, a thirty-something mother of three children, was his mentor in this learning process. She had blond hair and wore slacks with tailored jackets whenever Paul saw her, which hadn't been often since he'd begun working here only a week ago. After this initial two-week training period, Paul would work here two days a week.

Thankfully, his immediate boss at the tire store hadn't had the last word about Paul getting fired if he left work early to go to the interview for this job. Mr. Banks stepped in and told Kyle that Paul having flexibility with his work schedule was part of the store's agreement when Paul was hired. Kyle seemed to quietly seethe over the reminder of that piece of news, but he'd stopped breathing threats at Paul.

"You studied my notes last night?" Connie flipped open the thick file and skimmed the first page, checking to see if Paul had initialed it.

"Yes ma'am." The case in question involved the Holmes family—mother, father, and four children, including a teenage daughter named Kirsten, who had shown a tendency to throw fits at her family while in the yard where neighbors could see her. She also had a penchant for hysteria while standing on her property. When Kirsten ran away from home, the police brought her back and contacted social services.

After the initial home visit, the caseworker determined the situation to be detrimental for all the children. An uncle who lived with the family had a history of alcohol abuse and violence. The parents had been ordered to attend counseling sessions, which, according to the report, they had been doing faithfully. Today's session would include Kirsten. *This should be interesting,* Paul thought.

"Any questions?" his supervisor asked.

"Yeah. What's the status on the uncle?"

Connie closed the file. "Both parents have sworn that he is not allowed back into their home."

"What will happen if Kirsten runs away again?"

"Well, there are a couple of ways this could be handled, but I'd suggest we do another in-home visit and interview the other kids to see if something is going on that shouldn't be."

Approaching a closed door, Connie put her hand on the doorknob and turned to Paul. "Now, Kirsten is dramatic. She's quite good at putting on a show. I can guarantee she's going to cry and try to throw blame on everyone but herself. Her dramatic ways are not necessarily an indicator of what's really taking place inside the home. There's plenty of blame to go around, but our job is to help this family function as a unit, not to take sides."

Paul nodded. "I'll do my best to remain objective."

~~✺~~

The third day after Mary's surgery finally arrived. Her test results had indicated that the area inside her skull where surgery had been performed was healing better than the doctors had expected. The medicines that were keeping her in a coma had been reduced a few hours ago. Mary's doctor, Dr. Hill—a man much older and rounder than Dr. Greenfield—predicted that Mary should be awake by nightfall.

Still feeling as if her mind and heart were shrouded in a thick fog, Hannah sat by Mary's bed on one side while Becky sat on the other. *Mamm* hadn't left Luke's room all day. He'd been moved out of ICU and onto the fifth floor. The hardest part of the last few days had been dealing with Luke, even though the doctor kept him mildly sedated. When Luke was awake, he was irritable and constantly demanded to see Mary. Then the sedatives would take over, and he'd drift back off to sleep.

Hannah believed Dr. Greenfield was right; Luke didn't need to see Mary like this. Becky had agreed to visit Luke here and there, knowing he'd come closer to believing Mary was doing well if her mother wasn't staying by her side every second. Hannah admired Becky for being willing to leave her daughter for periods of time to help Luke stay calm.

The past few days had taxed everyone's strength, although no physical work was required. Hannah, *Mamm,* and Becky took turns sitting with Luke and Mary, returning to the hotel for catnaps and grabbing quick bites of food in the cafeteria. A lot of Old Order Amish folk—some relatives, some not—had come from all over Pennsylvania, Ohio, and Indiana, many hiring drivers to bring them, to visit and offer support. Those who could donated money for the mounting hospital bills. Even though they wanted to return to the farm with the young ones, *Mamm,* Becky, and Hannah were far from feeling lonely with all the Amish folks who came. From what Hannah was told, only one of Mary's aunts didn't come to visit, the one who was expecting twins in February and lived in Ohio. Her husband came by train, traveling with relatives and friends.

In his phone calls with *Mamm, Daed* told her about the dozens of Amish men and boys who were pitching in with the farming. Several brought their wives to help with the cooking and such at both the Yoder and Lapp homes. The community support given during this time did Hannah's heart good. Her people were kind and generous. Somehow, because of her vehement desire to marry outside her community, she'd forgotten the many blessings of being Amish.

Her *Mamm* said that their English neighbors had been stopping by and offering to help too. People were putting their heads and money together to design a harness shop and an attached apartment as a surprise for Luke and Mary. Hannah hoped they could get that built. That would be a wonderful gift for her friend.

Singing a made-up song from their childhood, Hannah glanced at Becky, whose eyes were glued to her daughter. Mary's limp, lifeless body had been moved into what the nurse called a semi-Fowler's position, with the head of the hospital bed at a forty-five-degree angle.

The minutes droned into hours as Hannah sat beside Mary's bed, softly singing and rehashing old memories. For now, Becky was in Luke's room, trying to convince him that Mary was fine. Hannah squeezed

Mary's hand. "Remember the day we found that litter of abandoned kittens in your *Daed's* old tool shed?" A soft laugh escaped Hannah. "It took us days to convince our mothers those poor things really were abandoned." Hannah ran her fingers up and down Mary's arm. "When they finally believed us, they gave us milk for them and let us use eyedroppers to feed them. We held those tiny kittens and fed them every hour like we'd die if one of them didn't make it." Hannah clicked her tongue in disgust. "They aren't worth the milk we put into their stomachs. They turned out to be mean old rascals that killed every decent cat your *Daed* had in his barn. But they lived."

Hannah laughed. "How about when we were thirteen and worked all fall collecting and sewing comforters for the Mission House? Oh, Mary, we were such a determined pair of girls about everything, remember?"

Whenever there was an occasional slight shifting of Mary's fingers or toes, Hannah whispered to her friend where she was and why. The staff came in and out a lot, though they didn't seem to be particularly concerned.

The ventilator was set to breathe for Mary only when she didn't breathe for herself. Hopefully, Mary's own respiratory system would take over as soon as the medicine-induced paralysis had completely lifted. Hannah listened to the machine force air into Mary's lungs. It happened more times than she thought it should.

Come on, Mary, breathe. Just breathe.

A white form crossed the doorway. Hannah's gaze moved from Mary to see Dr. Greenfield.

"Patience." He smiled. "Her slowness to wake is well within normal."

Hannah forced a smile, glad that Dr. Greenfield was around. He stepped farther into the room and adjusted something on Mary's IV bag. Without saying a word, Becky slipped into the room and took a seat beside her daughter's bed. Mary's eyelids twitched, and her legs shifted. She turned her head, as if trying to free herself of the contraption that covered her mouth. She coughed and pulled against her restraints. A long, loud shrill began.

Dr. Greenfield pushed a button on the ventilator, turning off the alarm. He moved to the bedside and checked Mary's pupils. "This is all perfectly normal," he assured Hannah and Becky. "Dr. Hill began making his rounds a little while ago. He'll be in soon." He turned and walked out the door.

As the hours wore on, Mary looked less and less like a corpse, though Hannah would be hard pressed to say why.

Mary's legs shifted, and Hannah leaned near her ear. "Mary, you were in an accident. We're at the hospital, and you're safe. The odd feeling in your throat is a tube that's helping you breathe. A machine is breathing for you some of the time. Don't fight it. Just relax. Luke is down the hall, waiting to hear that you're awake. When he woke, he felt very much like you do, and he's doing really good now."

Hannah talked on, repeating herself over and over. It seemed that Becky found talking impossible right now. A few times she'd tried speaking to her daughter, but she had choked on the words and returned to silence. Whenever Hannah paused in singing or talking, Mary pulled her head to the side, trying to free herself of the tube attached to her face, pulling against the restraints and coughing.

Becky's face drained of all color before she motioned to the doorway and then left.

Tears spilled down Hannah's cheeks. "There are communities across several states pulling for you, Mary. Luke needs you." She lifted her friend's hand to her cheek and caressed it. "I need you." Hannah swallowed, determined to keep the conversation hopeful. "I...I have a plan for us to work on a special quilt. But it'll take both of us to make this patchwork come true."

When Dr. Hill and a nurse entered the room, Hannah stopped talking.

Mary turned her head, pulling against the tubing going down her throat. Her wrists tugged at the restraints. Hannah grasped her friend's hand. "Easy now, *Liewi*. I'm still here. The doctor is here too. Everything will be fine."

Reading over the chart in his hand, he said, "Her oxygen rate is good, and it's been stable for some time now. She hasn't relied on the ventilator for two hours." He passed the chart to the nurse and moved to the far side of the bed. "Mary, we're going to remove the machine that's breathing for you. It might feel like we've taken your breath away for a few seconds, but don't panic or be frightened. Just relax, and you'll soon be breathing on your own."

Wishing Becky hadn't just gone to see Luke, Hannah laid her hand over Mary's and repeated in Pennsylvania Dutch what the doctor had said. As Dr. Hill worked on Mary, making her cough, Hannah closed her eyes tight and kept talking to Mary, assuring her she was fine. Hannah shivered when she heard a suctioning noise, but she refused to open her eyes. She muttered and sang to Mary, hoping her voice didn't betray how scared she was.

Someone touched Hannah's shoulder. "She's breathing on her own," Dr. Hill said. "The tubes have been removed."

Hannah opened her eyes. The contraption that had been taped over Mary's mouth was gone. A nurse was placing a thin tube under Mary's nose. Mary managed to open her bleary eyes and focus on Hannah. Elation soared through Hannah's soul, and her lips parted in a wide grin.

"Ah, a smile," Dr. Greenfield teased her. "That alone was worth altering my rounds for."

Hannah beamed at him. Until this moment, she hadn't realized he'd come into the room too. "Thank you." She looked at Dr. Hill. "Thank both of you for everything. I should go tell her *Mamm*."

Dr. Hill grunted. "You stay here and help her remain calm. A nurse will see to that."

"Th-h-h-h," Mary barely got the sound out before she started coughing.

A nurse grabbed the container of ice water and a cup off the nightstand. She filled the cup and placed a straw in it. Hannah placed the straw in Mary's mouth and held the drink for her.

After several difficult swallows, Mary tried to speak again. "L-l-l-l-l...Luke?"

Chills ran over Hannah's body. Mary remembered!

As soon as the medical personnel left the room, Hannah started talking to Mary about Luke and their future and the beautiful children they would be blessed with. She told her about her plan for the two of them to make a special quilt together.

It wasn't always easy to understand Mary. Her words were a bit jumbled, her memory blank about some things, and her voice hoarse. But she appeared to remember all the important things in life: her childhood, her love for Luke, and her faith in God.

Hannah was thrilled.

 uke stifled a moan as he eased his body into the wheelchair his sister was holding steady. It was nearly midnight. *Mamm* and Becky
had gone to the hotel for the night.

He looked straight ahead as Hannah wheeled him onto the elevator,
off at the second floor, and toward Mary's room. He didn't care what the
doctor said; he had to see Mary. He heard Hannah take a nervous breath
as she pushed his wheelchair past the nurses' station on the way to Mary's
room.

A plump, dark-haired nurse glanced up from her work. "Fifteen minutes maximum."

Luke lifted his good hand in acknowledgment. "Thank you."

Hannah bent down to his ear. "I feel much better now that we have
permission." She stopped his chair outside Mary's room. "Luke, they've
shaved her head. They had to. She had a lot of gashes that needed tending to besides where they performed surgery."

"I'll be fine. Let's go on in."

Hannah opened the door and wheeled him inside.

Mary was white as a sheet and gaunt. How much weight had she lost
since Sunday night? She looked frail and helpless. Her bald head had a
huge white patch taped to the side and several smaller patches showing
through her white prayer *Kapp*.

Hannah wheeled him closer to the bed and squatted beside him. "Dr.
Hill said she will probably get to leave ICU within the next day or so."

Luke's hands began to shake. How had this happened to them?
They'd been so happy, laughing and teasing, and then...

Miserable guilt bore down on him until he thought he might pass out. His breath came in short, wheezing spurts. As he searched through his feelings for something that made this bearable, an idea came to him. Maybe it wasn't his fault. Finally he was able to catch a breath.

But then whose fault was it? He stared at poor Mary while he tumbled that thought around and around. He wouldn't have been near the Knepps' place if…

Not comfortable with where his thoughts were taking him, Luke resisted.

A few moments later the blame pointed its finger again, and this time he didn't resist. If Hannah had gone with them to the singing as he'd begged her to, they would have been at the farm, and this would have never happened. He sat there, staring at his sleeping fiancée, wondering why Hannah hadn't joined them that night.

"She's doing very well, Luke. Really," Hannah whispered.

Luke studied his girl. His throat constricted, and his eyes burned with threatening tears. Mary's best friend had put them out there on that road. Why did his sister have to be so stubborn?

A dark-haired nurse entered the room with a full IV bag. As she quietly changed the bag, Mary woke. When she saw him, excitement shone in her eyes for an instant before dread took over. She touched her bald head around the edges of her *Kapp,* looking painfully embarrassed.

The nurse lowered Mary's bed and then the rail between Luke and Mary.

He reached for her, and his fingers enveloped her fragile hand. He knew the anguish of having her head shaved would haunt her for years to come. "You're alive. Don't you dare think anything else matters." His voice broke as he fought to not cry.

Mary wept. "Oh, L-l-luke," she said in her faltering, broken speech, "I 'idn't want you to 'ee me like 'is."

How can she think that matters?

The nurse cleared her throat. "I'll be back in fifteen minutes."

"Me too." Hannah followed the nurse out of the room.

Luke lifted Mary's hand, caressing the smooth skin. "Your hair will grow back, sweetheart."

She cradled his hand in hers. "I 'on't 'emember what 'appened." Her voice sounded as if she had laryngitis.

"It's sort of hazy for me too."

Relief that he'd understood her reflected in her eyes.

He glanced at the machines still attached to her, pumping pure air and keeping track of her heart rate and such. "How are you feeling?"

"S-s-scared."

Luke kissed Mary's hand. The feel of her warm skin against his lips broke through his resolve. He choked on his tears. "I've been so worried." He buried his face against her shoulder.

She leaned her cheek against the top of his head. "I 'on't know what I'd do without Hannah. She…"

When he looked up, he realized Mary was trying to speak, but her thoughts wouldn't form into words. He began to see her need to keep Hannah close. If anyone could speak for Mary, understand her without words being spoken, it would be his sister.

But Mary didn't know what Luke knew.

Setting the blame aside, Luke reached for her. After awkward hugs and sputtering words of thankfulness that they were both alive, Luke lifted his head and touched her angelic face. "You do remember agreeing to marry me, right?"

"M–m–maybe." Playfulness entered her eyes, filling him with thankfulness. "I 'member you s-s-saying s-s-something about yard work not bein' w–w–women's w-w-work."

Luke laughed. "But yard work *is* women's work. You've known that since before you were born, I s'pect. There might even be an edict from the bishop on the matter."

Mary smiled. "Is n–n–not."

"So, in order to marry you, I have to agree to do what everyone in our community considers a woman's job?"

She nodded.

"Done," Luke quipped.

Mary laughed and then moaned from pain. "Should've m-m-made a harder 'argain."

Luke tried to clarify her sentence. "Oh, I think you drive a plenty hard bargain, don't you?"

She nodded.

Luke kissed her fingertips. "You can have anything I'm capable of giving. Just name it."

She eased her hand from his, placed her fingers over her lips, and kissed them. Then, shaking, she laid her fingers on Luke's lips. He kissed her fingers, reveling in how much that simple touch felt as if his lips had touched hers.

Mary smiled. "I…m–m-marry you n–n–no m-m-matter what."

His throat constricted, and he couldn't answer for several moments. She leaned back against the bed while he smothered her hand in kisses. Her eyes closed, and she drifted off to sleep.

Tomorrow he'd explain to her that he was being released from the hospital soon and had promised his mother he'd follow the doctor's orders by going home and resting. The doctor assured Luke if he didn't follow his advice, he'd be in no shape to help Mary in the months to come.

Hannah paced the corridor near Mary's room, basking in the joy of her friend's recovery as well as her brother's. There was no denying the light in Mary's eyes the moment she saw Luke.

Her heart fluttered a bit. There was something so precious, so strengthening about the kind of love that ran between a man and a woman who wanted to marry. Love that strong would endure a lot and come back even stronger. A fresh ache to see Paul stole some of her excitement for Luke and Mary.

Her thoughts jumped to the long road of recovery that lay before the two. Mary's journey would be a particularly difficult one, but Hannah intended to be by her side every minute that Mary needed her.

Determined to settle her emotions, Hannah stopped pacing and eased into a chair. She leaned her head back against the wall and tried to quiet her mind. If only there was some way she could communicate with Paul, some way to get a letter to him...

She gasped. *There is!*

Why hadn't she thought of this before? If she could get her hands on some paper, she could write Paul a letter and mail it from here. If he received the letter before Mary was discharged, maybe he could sneak in a visit with her at the hospital.

She jumped to her feet and glanced at the clock over the nurses' station. She had seven minutes before she'd have to take Luke back to his room. The gift shop would have paper and pens. Her mother had left her money for food. If she skipped breakfast, maybe lunch too, she'd have enough to buy paper, envelopes, and stamps.

She dashed for the elevators. Once inside she pushed the *L* for lobby. When the doors opened, she scurried to the gift shop. Disappointment filled her when she saw that it was closed. But the sign on the door said it would open again at nine the next morning.

For a moment she considered calling Paul. That thought faded as quickly as it came. His phone number at the apartment wasn't listed under his name. She knew his best friend's name was Marcus King, but the phone wasn't in Marcus's name either. She didn't know Ryan's or Taylor's last name. Paul had written down the number for her once, but it was taped to the underside of a drawer at home.

She'd just have to wait until tomorrow and mail him a letter.

The nagging question of why she hadn't heard from him ruffled her elation. Maybe he was sorry he'd asked her to marry him. He did wait until the last day to ask. That could mean it was a spur-of-the-moment idea. But no. The savings book proved he'd been planning this for years. Then again, maybe his years of planning referred simply to sponsoring a little Thai girl. She couldn't remember exactly how the conversation had gone.

She did remember two columns of figures in the book he'd given her. But since it had been burned along with her clothes from that day—

A bolt of excitement shot through her. Memories of that day were no longer a mass of confusion. She knew what had taken place between her and Paul. She could think.

Yes. She remembered.

She balled her hands into fists that hung by her side, refusing to show her emotions to anyone in the lobby.

Through the bars of the gift shop, she saw the selection of writing items. No stationery but plenty of greeting cards. In the morning, when the store opened, she would go in, make her purchase, and write to him. Her family had passed through Harrisburg, the city that shared part of the name of his college, on the drive to the hospital. If Paul got her note in time, it'd take him less than an hour to drive to Hershey. Then she would finally know what was really going on with him.

Doubts jerked her emotions. Part of her feared what the truth might be.

But determination won out over her concerns. Whatever was going on with Paul, it was time she found out.

*P*ushing her disappointment aside, Hannah tried not to think about the five days that had passed since she had written to Paul. She hadn't heard anything from him, and Mary would be discharged tomorrow. Hannah stepped inside the physical-therapy room, awed at the amount and variety of equipment. She was here to learn the workout routines her friend would need to do over the next weeks and months.

It was an interesting place. Three patients, all in different areas of the room, worked with their own personal physical therapists. A man dressed in shorts and a sleeveless shirt pushed against some type of cushioned arm-rest thing. The pulleys lifted a stack of thin, oblong items that, based on the strain on the man's arms, she assumed had to be weights. In the middle of the floor was a short set of stairs that had steps on each side so a person could walk up one side and down the other. Huge rubber balls, each taller than her youngest sister, rested against the walls. Scattered throughout the room were treadmills, stacks of towels, jump ropes, rods that looked like broom handles, and an array of things she didn't recognize.

Hannah waited by the door, hoping to spot Mary's physical therapist. Desiree, who looked barely old enough to be done with her schooling, had come to Mary's room daily and worked with her, lifting and rotating her limbs, even before she was brought out of the coma. She was energetic and friendly, but she gave Mary very little slack when it came to the workout.

Desiree came waltzing out of an office with her jet-black ponytail banded carelessly on her head. She had on a burgundy hospital uniform.

She spotted Hannah and headed toward her. "Hi. Glad to see you found the place." She held out her hand.

Hannah shook her hand. "Good morning."

Desiree glanced at her watch. "You're right on time. But I need to speak with someone before we get started. Okay?"

"Sure." Hannah waited at the entrance of the workout room while the physical therapist walked over to a middle-aged man wearing a similar uniform.

The young woman didn't seem miffed that John and Becky Yoder had decided that once their daughter was discharged from the hospital, she wouldn't return here or go anywhere else for physical therapy. One of the many discoveries Hannah had made while staying at the hospital was the rights of all Americans to certain health-related freedoms. Not only was health care provided for Luke and Mary before the hospital knew who they were or if the bill would ever be paid, but they also had the right to refuse medical help—no matter how a doctor, nurse, or the entire medical staff felt. Even the most educated had to yield to the individual's rights.

Desiree motioned for Hannah to follow her. "Let me grab Mary's chart, and we'll get started." She sauntered into a small office and over to a stack of clipboards that were lying on a well-organized desk.

Hannah waited by the office door, marveling at the many health-related books lining the shelves.

Sifting through the clipboards, Desiree picked one out. "I'll teach you what she needs to do on a daily basis. The routine will change as the days and weeks pass, but we'll cover that too. I'll send home all sorts of information you can use for reference."

She walked to the stack of towels. "Our first goal is to get a good range of motion back into Mary's injured shoulder." She grabbed a folded towel and passed it to Hannah. "Let's sit on the floor and work from there."

While showing Hannah the workout routine, Desiree shared her medical knowledge. Each thing she explained caused a sense of excitement in Hannah unlike anything she'd ever experienced. The young woman explained things about the muscular, pulmonary, cardiac, and vascular systems, as well as various symptoms to watch for. As their two-hour time slot drew to a close, Hannah had a long list of health-related facts. She knew more than she ever could have imagined, but her appetite for medical knowledge gnawed at her to learn more.

"Okay." Desiree gathered into one pile the workout routine charts that were spread over the floor. "Tomorrow I'll teach you about gait training, where she'll learn to use a walker for short periods of time. But she won't be ready for that for another month. I'll also show you how to use a rolling walker and a quad cane." She rose to her feet. "When we've covered everything, I'll attach my card to the stuff I'm sending home with you so you can call me if you have any questions."

Taking one last look at the chart in her hand, Hannah passed it to Desiree. "It's fascinating."

Desiree nodded. "I think so. And I think you'll do well with Mary. You picked up on everything quickly. Next on your to-do list is learning how to check Mary's blood pressure and heart rate. Someone will work with you on that later this afternoon."

Wow. Hannah wished she had more time to learn.

~~∿❦~~

Paul parked his car in the lot behind his apartment and headed up the curved sidewalk. Exhaustion covered him, just like the gloomy, starless canopy overhead. He needed sleep. So far today he'd accomplished getting through his classes, working all afternoon at the tire store, and studying for hours at the library—all on about four hours of sleep. His bed was calling to him.

As he passed the student mailboxes, he had a fleeting thought of picking up his mail. *I'll do it tomorrow…or the next day.*

He used to check his mailbox every day, eagerly anticipating a letter from Hannah. But since Gram had put her foot down on passing letters to him, there was no way he was going to hear from Hannah anytime soon. With that possibility gone, he felt no reason to check except to occasionally keep up with bills. Since he'd always intercepted the mail, his roommates never went to the mailbox.

He placed his key into the apartment lock and slipped inside. After pulling off his shoes, he shoved them against the wall. Using the only light on in the place, a dim one in the hallway, he made his way to his and Marcus's room. He dropped his heavy book bag in a corner and sprawled across his twin bed. He would get ready for bed in a few minutes. Right now he had no energy for anything but to lie there.

Paul dozed in and out but never really fell asleep. He eased his feet to the side of the bed and rubbed his face. Perhaps if he changed out of his street clothes, he'd sleep better. As he stood, his keys fell to the floor. In one slow swoop, he picked them up and tossed them onto the nightstand. The small, gold mailbox key on the chain reflected the hallway light. The desire to check his mailbox returned. Ignoring it, he shook his head and made his way into the bathroom.

He brushed his teeth and peeled down to his boxers. Then he crept back to his bed and pulled down the covers. As he slid between the sheets, the nagging desire to look in his mailbox persisted. Finally giving in to the craving, Paul pulled on a pair of jeans, grasped the key, and headed outside.

His bare feet tingled as he crossed the cold concrete sidewalk. Under the glow of a streetlamp, he opened his box and pulled out a few items. A green flier advertising a sale on tires made him snort. Beneath that, he noticed a couple of bills, a coupon ad, and a note-sized envelope. He tucked the miscellaneous items under his arm and turned the envelope address side up.

His heart lurched. The return address belonged to his grandmother, but the handwriting was Hannah's. He tore it open while dashing back to his apartment. In spite of the solitude of the campus this late at night, the privacy of his bedroom was the only place to read Hannah's letters.

After flipping on the reading lamp, he sat on the side of the bed.

Paul,

My brother Luke and my dear friend Mary have been in an accident. I'm staying at Hershey Medical Center. If you get this letter
in time and wish to speak with me, do come. Mary's room is on
the second floor.

Hannah

If he wished to speak to her? Of course he wanted to speak to her. He wanted it so badly he had to squelch his feelings of joy in light of her rea-son for being at Hershey. He said a prayer for Luke and Mary, and then he checked out the postmark on the letter. Hannah had mailed it five days ago. It had probably been in his mailbox for two or three days. In spite of hoping Luke and Mary were well on their way to being released, he also hoped they were still at HMC.

He skimmed the brief note again. Excited as he was at the prospect of seeing Hannah, the coolness of her note gave him pause. She was not one to indulge in giddy romantic nonsense, so her letters never contained words of endearment or had a flirtatious tone. But this one made him flinch. They were engaged, for Pete's sake, yet she mentioned nothing about missing him or wanting to see him. It was more like an invitation offered out of protocol, because she was now in the vicinity, rather than an opportunity she hoped he didn't miss.

Reading the message again, he decided he was being self-centered. She'd managed to mail him a note. What more should he expect in such a traumatic situation?

Scurrying around like a maniac, Paul wrote Marcus a brief note and headed out the door.

The thirty-minute ride to Hershey was not a pleasant one. His thoughts and desires pulled him in ten different directions for every minute he drove. He wished he didn't have to be separated from Hannah like this, but he had to get his bachelor's degree under his belt. Frustration with Gram hounded him. But what if she was right? His family wouldn't have as many qualms about Hannah as hers would about him, but they'd have plenty of reservations.

His thoughts zipped in every direction, but when he pulled into the parking lot of the hospital, he knew one thing for sure: he had no answers, only desire.

While jogging across the lot and through the main entrance, he formed a plan. He'd check each waiting room on the second floor and hopefully catch a glimpse of Hannah without being spotted by any of her family. That would be far preferable to asking at a nurses' station about Luke Lapp or Mary Yoder. The fewer people who knew of his visit, the safer his and Hannah's secret connection would be.

When the elevator doors opened at the second floor and he stepped into the hallway, Paul realized he was on the ICU floor. It must have been a bad accident. Striding down the long corridor, he checked the first waiting room. She wasn't there. After searching the last wing of the unit, he gave up and went to the nurses' station.

"Excuse me."

A plump, dark-haired nurse looked up from the papers on the desk in front of her. "Visiting hours are over, sir."

"I'm looking for Luke Lapp."

"He was removed from ICU four days ago. I heard he was released from the hospital two days later."

Paul rubbed his forehead, chastising himself for not checking his mailbox sooner.

A half smile graced her lips. "I take it that wasn't the answer you were looking for."

Paul tried to hide his mounting disappointment. "Is Mary Yoder still here?"

A buzzer went off, and the nurse jumped to her feet and hustled down the hallway. Without slowing, she turned toward Paul. "She's been released from ICU. If she's still a patient here, she'll be on the fifth floor. But their visiting hours are over too."

"Thank you," he called after her.

The woman waved as she disappeared inside a cubicle.

Paul strode to the elevators, clinging to a draining hope that Hannah might still be at the hospital.

Just as he'd done on the second floor, he walked the corridors, looking and listening for any sign of Hannah. When he heard a man's voice with a distinctly Amish way of turning a phrase, he slowed his pace. He peered into the waiting area from an angle that wouldn't catch the attention of whoever was in the room.

Excitement pumped through his veins. There she was, his beautiful Hannah, sitting and talking to an Amish man. She laughed in that friendly, shy way of hers. Leaning her head toward him, she spoke softly. "I wouldn't confess this to a relative, and you'd better not either. But as a friend, I'm telling you, I did."

Friend? This guy wasn't a relative?

In an instant, insecurity took over. Jealousy reared up. His Hannah was sitting directly beside some young man, talking nonchalantly and chuckling. Paul's view only gave him a profile of Hannah and her *friend.* Their legs were stretched out side by side, their feet propped in a chair across from them.

He'd never seen Hannah in her own world, but this was not how he'd always envisioned her. To him, she had seemed reserved. He'd assumed she would have a backward way about her when it came to men, even among her people.

The man, who looked to be about Paul's age, pushed against her feet with his. "Ya did not."

Hannah laughed. "Why, Matthew Esh, how would you know? Were you there?"

"Ya know I weren't. But I've knowed ya since before ya could walk. I know ya like nobody else, Hannah Lapp. If anyone could tell when you're lyin', it'd be me. So tell the truth. It ain't true, is it?"

Paul's breath shortened. Who was this Matthew fellow who claimed to know his Hannah unlike anyone else?

Hannah bit her bottom lip and tilted her head. "If you're so sure I'm lying, then you don't need me to tell you anything."

Matthew chuckled, plunking his feet onto the floor. "This round of the game ain't over, but I better be headin' out. The driver said he'd be leaving his party at twelve, and I'm to meet 'im out the main entrance at quarter after." He rose. "Tell Mary that when she's settled at home and up to havin' company, I'll pay her a visit."

Hannah stood. "I'll tell her. It was nice of you to go out of your way to come here."

Matthew straightened his hat. Paul darted quietly down the hallway and around a corner where he couldn't be seen by the two leaving the waiting room. From his hiding place, Paul watched Hannah and Matthew stroll to the elevator, where she bid him good-bye. As she turned to come back down the hallway, Paul stepped out from the corner and called her name.

She wheeled around so fast she almost lost her balance. Her face flushed. Her movements froze. Guilt and embarrassment seemed to flood her entire being. "Paul." Her voice was a hoarse whisper, but there was no smile, no sign that he was welcome.

He glanced down each hallway. They needed someplace where they could talk in private. "Let's go back to that waiting room you just came from."

Without any show of emotion, Hannah moved back to the quiet space. Paul followed. Something hung between them, but he had no idea what it was. They stood in the small room, staring at each other. The unspoken friction whispered words of disbelief in his heart. They'd been so close, so sure of things just a month ago.

Paul cleared his throat. "Are Luke and Mary going to be all right?"

She lowered her head and fidgeted with her apron. "Luke's been re-leased. It looks like he'll completely recover. Mary will be released tomor-row. The doctors suggested she stay a few days to a week longer, but she and her parents signed an AMA form."

"AMA?" Paul asked.

"Against Medical Advice. Her parents insist she's well enough to go home." Hannah shrugged. "I'm not sure she is, but they didn't ask me. She's got a long way to go—if she *ever* gets her full strength and agility back."

Hannah sounded as though she'd learned a lot during her stay here. Her speech patterns were even smoother, more scholarly than before. She'd always hungered to learn, and he'd shared books with her for years—books that had to stay at Gram's.

"What happened?"

Hannah wiped her palms down the front of her pinafore. "They were riding in a buggy when a car hit them. They both came close to dying. Mary can't talk very well. She has too many injuries to even try walking just yet."

"I'm so sorry."

Hannah cleared her throat. "They are mending."

"I'm glad."

Paul studied her, but she never looked at him. He knew the rigid upbringing that took place under Zeb Lapp. She fell into guilt far too effortlessly. The side effect was that she thought everything that went wrong was a direct result of her not handling something right. She probably considered herself at fault for Luke and Mary's accident, even though she had nothing to do with it. Her tendency toward guilt bothered him greatly. But he was confident that, given time and freedom, she'd overcome this trait.

Then again, perhaps what he was seeing written on her face had nothing to do with her oversensitivity to her self-accusing nature. Maybe it had more to do with Matthew. As much as he hated to ask her, they had to clear the air. He stared at the floor while shifting from one foot to the other. He shoved his hands into his pockets. "So, who is Matthew Esh?"

When Hannah didn't answer, he lifted his gaze. She stared at a blank television screen in the corner of the room. "He is the man you just saw leave."

"Yes, but…" Never in all their years as friends had he seen such a look in her eyes. It was an odd mixture of things, maybe embarrassment and… and…something else.

Father, help me. Help us. Please.

Her hands fluttered to her head, feeling for wisps of misplaced hair and making sure her *Kapp* was in place. "You sent no letter."

It was a statement that seemed to hold no irritation or worry. Was that supposed to explain who Matthew was?

"I did, but…" He stepped closer to her. She didn't look up at him. "I don't understand why, but it never arrived at Gram's. Before I could send another one, Gram decided we needed to think about our relationship for a while before she'd let us pass letters through her."

She lifted her gaze. To his surprise, anger blazed in her eyes. "So, now that you've had time to think about our relationship, what have you decided?"

"Hannah." Paul touched her arm. "What is going on with you?"

Her eyes clouded with tears. She gasped for air and backed away from him. As she lifted a hand to wipe a tear off her face, something on her palm caught Paul's attention.

He grasped her hand and turned it palm side up, seeing long, raised areas of pink tissue. "You have scars. What happened to you?"

Her face and lips grew pale. She eased into the closest chair.

She took a deep breath and straightened her back. With her shoulders squared with resolve, she gazed up into his eyes, her eyes brimming with tears. "Let me go." The hoarse whisper in her voice made Hannah sound old and tired.

Physical pain shot through him. "You're not making any sense, Hannah."

She grabbed some tissues out of a box on a coffee table. "Trust me. You don't want to wait…for the likes of me."

For the *likes* of her? Another inkling of suspicion concerning her faithfulness to him rose within his heart. "What are you talking about?"

"I…I…" Tears choked her, and she could say no more.

Paul sat beside her, determined to figure her out. "Hannah, close your eyes and take a deep breath." He gave her a moment to do so. "Now, let one thing come forward in your mind. Don't try to tie it all in. Just stick to one issue, and with your eyes closed, tell me."

She swiped a Kleenex over her cheeks and nodded, as if he'd given her a task she could manage. "The bankbook is missing." She opened her eyes, absent-mindedly tracing the scars on her right palm with her left forefinger. "I'm not sure what happened to it. I…I…" She turned ashen again.

He placed his hand on her back. "It's okay. The bank doesn't even use those kinds of books anymore. They haven't for decades. I got that one from a friend who works there and had a few books still stashed in his desk."

"It must've been in my pocket when *Daed* burned my clothes."

Paul removed his hand. "Burned them? Gram said you'd been sick. Were you so sick that they thought your clothes needed burning?"

Hannah's eyes carried uncertainty. She fled to the other side of the room and stared at the beige wall.

He understood a little more now. To Hannah, losing the gift was probably unforgivable. Still, her reaction seemed too much for just a lost bankbook. He sighed. Perhaps getting to the bottom of all that was on her mind wasn't possible with the time constraints they had to deal with.

She sniffled.

Walking up behind her, he grabbed some tissues and passed them over her shoulder. He longed to share consoling words with her, but one thing stood in his way. "Do you care for someone else?"

She turned to face him, indignation burning in her eyes. "No!" She sidestepped him and walked across the room, sobbing into the tissue. "Never!"

Her reaction worked the doubts and fears right out of him. He walked to the corner of the small room and placed his hands on her shoulders. "Then nothing else can stand in our way. I promise you that, Hannah."

She turned to face him. "You don't understand."

"Then tell me."

A look of terror came over her. Clearly she was fighting to gain control of her emotions. Coughing and gasping, she whispered, "The…the day…you left…"

Her face was white, humiliation carved in her features. Seeing her like this cut him to the core. All he wanted was to remove whatever was bothering her. But how?

He touched her *Kapp* and ran a finger along one of the ties. He did his best to smile. "Hannah Lapp, we can do this. But you have to trust me."

She studied him through teary eyes. "Oh, Paul." She lowered her forehead onto his chest. "The day you left…a car…with a man…he…it… knocked me…"

The power of her words hit him so hard he couldn't move. He heard her fighting for air. "You were sideswiped by a car?" He felt her head nod. He took her by the shoulders and put some space between them. "Did your father contact the police?"

She shook her head. "I…I asked him to."

Just then a nurse came into the waiting area. "Hannah, Mary's mother called. She was unable to sleep and is on her way back here. She said you can take the shuttle back to the hotel and get some sleep."

"Okay. Thank you." She sighed as the nurse left the room. "She'll be here within ten minutes."

He wasn't concerned with Mary's mother arriving. He wondered if the anxiety of that incident was what had made her so sick that her father had thought it best to burn her clothes. Rage at the idiot driver and anger that no one had stood up for Hannah made him understand a little better Hannah's wild emotions. She'd been traumatized that day. Obviously, that's where the scars on her hands had come from. He wrapped his arms around her, resigned that there was nothing he could do about the incident now.

Her body was stiff, yet he could feel her tremble.

"We need to look ahead, not behind." He kissed the top of her head through her *Kapp*. "I'll love you forever, Hannah."

A moment later he felt her take a deep breath. She wrapped her arms around him. Her embrace filled him with renewed commitment.

The frailty of her feminine frame became clear in that moment. She wasn't just a stalwart, stoic, good-natured worker. She was also a girl, overwhelmed by the odds against them.

She embraced him tighter. "It's been dreadful since the moment you left."

If Hannah, his queen of understatements, used the word *dreadful*, he knew things had been horrendous. He held her, not sure he'd ever know the full extent of what had gone wrong since he'd left. For now, it was enough to know that in eight months, he'd be finished with school and living within a mile of her. As soon as possible they'd get married, and no one would ever keep them apart again.

When her tears finally began to subside, Paul led Hannah to a chair and sat beside her.

He glanced at the clock. Their conversation, with all its patchwork exchanges, had taken over an hour. And he still felt she was keeping something from him, though he couldn't imagine what or why. Still, with their time running out, and since there was little chance they'd be able to communicate again in the near future, he had to bring their time to a close on a positive note.

"Hannah."

She looked up at him.

He opened her hand and kissed her scarred palm. "Conversations make a relationship strong. Unfortunately, they won't be a part of our relationship for a while. But we can clear away whatever weeds grow during this time if we hang tough and faithful"—he winked—"until May."

She offered a slight grin. "Don't you dare start that winking business with me, Paul Waddell."

He chuckled. He'd winked at her years ago and made her so angry she wouldn't speak to him for weeks. There was a scripture in the Old Testament about it, but he figured her real problem was that winks went hand in hand with flirting, and it seemed to unnerve her to think of him winking so easily at girls.

He squeezed her hand. "Eight months, Hannah. No problem for us, right?"

Hannah drew a ragged breath. "*Ya.* I'll be busy helping Mary with her physical therapy for that long at least." She finally gave him a little smile. "And Mary and I have plans to make a quilt I've been designing in my mind. I'm going to call it a 'Past and Future' quilt, and it's going to have a diamond-in-the-square design."

Paul brushed her cheek with the back of his fingers, glad to see a spark of pleasure in her eyes. "And in the meantime, I'll be busy working toward our future together."

For a brief moment she closed her eyes and leaned her cheek against his fingers. Then she stood. "I've got to get out front before Mary's mother arrives. After Mary is released, I'll be living at her grandmother's house for a while, helping Mary get her strength and agility back."

"At Mary's grandmother's? Why?"

"Her parents' house is narrow, with two large flights of steps and two single steps. She'll be in a wheelchair, so that won't do. Her grandmother's house has two stories, but everything we need is on one very wide level. Mary's mother has her other children to tend to. And her grandmother can't lift Mary, so she'll move in with Becky for a while, giving Mary and me a house to ourselves." Hannah smiled. "Besides, Mary wanted me to stay by her side, and she could ask for the moon right now, and her parents would find a way to get it for her."

Hannah stared at him. The look in her eyes said she loved him. "It was so good to see you."

Paul rose, wishing they had more time. "You must never forget how much I love you." He'd expected her to nod and turn to leave, but she put her hands on his waist and drew him close.

A nurse peeked into the room. "Mary's mother just stepped off the elevator." She sang the words like a friendly warning.

Hannah jolted and released him. Without another word, Paul disappeared down the hallway just as Becky rounded the corner.

A sigh escaped Hannah's lips. Darkness seemed to surround her like billows of toxic fumes. She hadn't come clean with Paul. What would happen if he figured out that she was keeping secrets from him?

If that unmentionable night wasn't so humiliating, she might find the courage to tell him. But which was worse—Paul knowing nothing, leaving her to pretend she was fine, or his knowing the truth? She ached for the peace and freedom that would come only if there were no secrets between them. But there was no way to know if he could handle finding out about the rape unless she told him about it.

I wish I could just vanish for a while and hide out while I think this through. Maybe go to Ohio. How hard would it be to find Aunt Zabeth?

But then Paul came back to mind, and the thought of fleeing to Ohio lost all its luster. He'd looked so good last night, his touch making life seem worth its troubles. She wished that she hadn't cried through most of his visit. The nightmare of her attack had to be put behind her, or it was going to ruin everything.

After being pulled one way and then the other, in a moment of clarity she realized a truth. Carrying the weight of silence was certainly not the worst thing that could happen. The worst tragedy of all would be to lose Paul.

Hannah leaned against the windowsill of Mary's fifth-floor room. The fresh rays of daylight filtered through the glass as Mary slept fitfully. Becky was down in billing, taking care of whatever it was that needed taking care of in order for Mary to leave the hospital today.

The door to the room opened. Dr. Greenfield stepped inside, holding two plastic foam cups on top of a large hardback book. Hannah had to smile. Their friendship was fleeting and sometimes awkward, but he seemed to be a truly genuine person.

He shoved the door closed with his foot. "I was hoping for a minute with you before Mary's release." He held the book toward her.

Hannah took the cup closest to her, surveying its steaming contents. "Hot chocolate?"

"You're too young for coffee." He smiled, lifting the cup of coffee to his lips with one hand and holding the book toward her with the other. "This is for you. It's about anatomy and how the body works. I think your family will allow you to have this since, among other things, it explains what to expect during a woman's recuperation from a subdural hematoma. I think you'll find it quite helpful as you work with Mary."

She grasped the book and opened it. An outline of a human body stared back at her. Dr. Greenfield reached across and turned a clear page, laying it on top of the nondescript image. The clear page revealed the vital organs and the veins and arteries running throughout the body. Beside the organs were lines with numbers.

"Ach, wie wunderbaar."

"Excuse me?"

Hannah looked up, embarrassed at her lack of manners. "Forgive me. I...I said it's wonderful."

He beamed at her. "It's an overlay. There are several of them." He turned to another page. "This one shows the respiratory system." He flipped a few more pages and then stopped at solid white ones covered in typed print. "This part explains what you're looking at."

Hannah slid her hand over the silky page. "This is amazing." She looked up. "Thank you."

Dr. Greenfield nodded. "You're welcome." He took a pen from his pocket and held his hand out for the book. She passed it to him. He wrote on the inside of the back cover. "I know getting to a phone is problematic for you. Nonetheless, if you ever need anything, this is the number for my answering service. Just tell them who you are, and they'll reach me. It might be a few hours before I get the message, depending on where I am and what I'm doing at the time. But I promise I'll return your call ASAP."

She watched him write in her new book and had to squelch the desire to tell him not to. Books were too special to be written in. "ASAP?"

"As soon as possible."

Hannah grinned. "Ah." She was going to miss talking with someone as good-humored and open-minded as Dr. Greenfield.

He closed the book and handed it to her. "The nurse will be in shortly to change Mary's bandage. Then she'll be released. You should already have all the instructions for her care, but if you have any questions, don't hesitate to call the number the nurse gave you." He strode out the door.

She opened her new book and began devouring the pages.

A crackling noise made her stop reading and look up. Edie Walls, one of the young nurses, stood there with a cup pressed against her lips. She lowered the cup, crunching on ice. "Sorry. Didn't mean to disturb you." She set the cup on the side table. "Ice chips. It's the best thing I've found for morning sickness." She opened a drawer in the table beside the bed and pulled out a roll of gauze and tape. "Morning sickness is a stupid thing to call it, though. When I was pregnant with my first child, I only felt nauseated in the evening. With this one, I'm sick all day every day. And then I'm so tired."

Nausea and tiredness. Hannah had felt that way for weeks. But there were so many odors around here, and she hadn't slept decently in forever, and—

"But that's not the worst part." Edie unrolled a long piece of gauze. "Why, my emotions are such a roller-coaster ride, they're driving me nuts."

Blood rushed to Hannah's temple. Was that the reason her feelings were going in every direction at once?

No, it couldn't be.

Pregnant? Surely that couldn't be the reason for the feelings of nausea and sickness. She was just stressed and—

Edie pulled a pair of scissors from her pocket. "The first time I was pregnant, I couldn't stand the idea of eating anything those first few weeks."

The book fell from Hannah's hand. Her arms and legs felt too heavy for her body.

From the outermost part of her peripheral vision, blackness closed in. It gradually blocked out the room as well as Edie.

Hannah felt Edie's hand under her forearm. Edie was saying something, but Hannah couldn't make out her words.

God! The words screamed inside her. *Please. Please. Noooooooo.* Her heart raced as the continual cry rang out in her soul.

It couldn't be.

It couldn't.

"Hannah? Can you hear me?" Edie took her by the shoulders and eased her to the floor. "Hannah, lie back. Help is on the way."

Edie held Hannah's ankles, keeping her feet and legs slightly elevated. Some sense of reality flowed back into her. Terror and chills ran throughout her body. Fighting to gain control, she jerked her feet loose and sat up.

"I…I'm fine." She wasn't. But no one could help her. Hannah turned, placing her hands on the seat of the chair behind her, and pushed herself upright. On wavering legs, she made her way to the door.

In the hallway a woman took her by the arm and spoke to her. Hannah couldn't make out what she said. Pulling free, she ran to the stairwell. The door closed behind her, thudding loudly. She flew down one flight of steps before stopping. She leaned against the wall, gasping for air.

A moment later the stairwell door above her burst open, and Edie barged in. When she spotted Hannah, she scurried down the steps. The blank look on her face said that she had no idea what to do or say.

Hannah's vision blurred as someone else clomped down the steps.

"What happened?"

With her back against the wall, Hannah slid to a sitting position on the cold tile floor. She wrapped her arms around her knees and buried her face. A pair of large hands took one of her arms and held it. Velcro ripped, her arm was covered with a band, and the strap was tightened. It loosened. Stayed loose for a while. Then tightened again.

"What happened right before she began blacking out?" The voice sounded like Dr. Greenfield's but different...sterner. She didn't want to see him.

Then again, who better? But how would she ever explain...

"We were talking," Edie said. "That's all."

"About?"

Hannah's chin was gently lifted and the back of her head pressed against the wall. She felt what had to be a stethoscope roam over her chest.

"Can't hear much of anything through all these layers of clothes," the man mumbled.

"Actually, now that I think about it, I was doing all the talking. I was telling her about being pregnant and how ice chips help me feel less nauseated."

Determined to get out of there, Hannah pushed the hand holding the stethoscope away from her. She ripped the Velcro loose from its grip and slid the cuff off her arm. Bracing herself against the wall, she tried to stand. A strong hand helped her to her feet.

"Let's get you to the ER, Hannah." Dr. Greenfield placed his hand under her forearm, steadying her.

She shook her head, desperate to get away. "I'm fine. I need air. That's all." She pulled away from his grip. "Leave me alone. Please."

With his hand under her arm, supporting her, Dr. Greenfield led Hannah outdoors like a child. The cool fall air, mixed with the smells of automobiles, whipped against her face. She eased her arm out of his grip and followed the sidewalk away from the hospital to a private nook between two wings of the building. Shaking, without any power to stop, Hannah sat on a gray stone bench that doubled as a retaining wall for plants.

Dr. Greenfield sat beside her and took her wrist, pressing his fingers against her pulse. "I'd really like you to be checked out."

She barely shook her head and managed a whisper. "No."

Patches of puffy clouds moved across the sky, transforming shapes as quickly and easily as life altered. If she really was pregnant, Paul must never find out. *Never.* Maybe she wasn't. Maybe what happened to her wasn't how women got pregnant. How would she know? The subject was forbidden.

She hated that man. Hated him. Images of slashing a knife across his belly flooded her. But the fury would do her no good. She was powerless on all sides. She didn't know who he was.

Dr. Greenfield placed his forearms on his legs and leaned forward, his gaze never leaving her face.

Hannah swallowed. She had to know if she might be pregnant. And she had no one better to ask. "The Amish don't talk about…certain things."

"I'll talk to you about anything you want to know."

She shifted, turning away slightly. There was no way she could ask him this. "Never mind."

"Hannah, Edie says she was telling you about her pregnancy. Is there something about that conversation that caused your reaction?"

Hannah shrugged and gave a slight nod.

"Is that a yes?"

She nodded.

"Are you pregnant?"

Hannah closed her eyes. "I...I don't know."

Dr. Greenfield's face didn't change a bit. "But there's a chance you're pregnant—is that it?"

"I...I don't know."

"You don't know if you're pregnant, or you don't know how someone gets that way?"

Hannah could feel her cheeks burning.

"I'm going to take a shot in the dark here and tell you how a woman conceives." With a voice as kind and gentle as she'd ever heard, he told her all she needed to know.

It made perfect sense. She lived on a farm, for heaven's sake, with livestock that were bred. But somehow understanding how women became pregnant had eluded her. Feelings of embarrassment were so thick she thought her heart would stop beating right then.

She cleared her throat. "And if...if someone is...overpowered... forced to...can she still get pregnant?"

"Hannah, if this happened to you, you need to see a doctor and the police."

"No." Her voice shook.

He drew a deep breath. "Yes, a woman can conceive a child even then."

She rose. "Mary's probably been released by now. Her mother will be searching for me. Thank you, Dr. Greenfield." She eased one foot in front of the other, taking several shaky steps.

"Hannah, wait." In one quick movement, he stood in front of her. "What can I do to help you? What will you let me do?"

The compassion in his voice touched a place deep inside her. She stared at the stethoscope dangling around his neck. "There's nothing to do." Her jaws ached. Her eyes burned. Why couldn't the earth just open and swallow her? "Who knows? Maybe I'm jumping to conclusions."

"It's possible. Trauma causes a woman's body to do odd things: feel nauseated, skip cycles, have panic attacks. It can even result in chemical changes in the brain that can send a person into severe depression. But if you're having those symptoms and pregnancy isn't the cause…"

She touched the sides of her *Kapp,* making sure it was in place.

"Hannah, I know a woman doctor who works exclusively with females. She's gentle and understanding. She can at least confirm whether or not you're—"

"Please don't," Hannah interrupted him. "I'm going home and pray for the best."

Dr. Greenfield put one hand on her shoulder, gazing into her eyes. "I'm so sorry."

"Hannah!" *Daed's* voice made her jump. Dr. Greenfield immediately removed his hand and pulled away from her.

She turned toward the voice and saw her father standing at the T in the sidewalk, the bishop right beside him. The looks on their faces were a mixture of bewilderment and accusation. Dr. Greenfield leaned in close behind her. "We aren't finished talking yet, Hannah."

Her father's brows knitted. "Come, child. Now."

Dr. Greenfield stepped forward, looking her in the face. "You don't have to, Hannah. You can stay here, and we can get you some help."

She knew the word *we* meant other doctors, the system, even the police. But she couldn't for one moment imagine them all examining her and asking questions. She needed to go home, to wait and find out if she truly was pregnant.

"Now, Hannah." Her father removed his hat and squeezed the brim, avoiding the doctor's eyes.

"Your daughter and I are in the middle of a private conversation," Dr. Greenfield retorted. "She has rights among the English."

She shook her head at him. He was only making things worse.

Her father and the bishop gave a nod of grudging acceptance and strode past them into the hospital. They weren't going to argue; to cause conflict was against their rules and their ways.

Dr. Greenfield turned to face her. "Are you sure going back is the right thing to do?"

She nodded. "My family will do more for me than your whole staff can."

"Hannah, please. We could—"

She held up her hand. "No more."

"If you'll work with me, we can find all sorts of ways to help you. There are programs for rape victims, homes for unwed mothers, adoption agencies, and clinics that can offer you other...options."

She closed her eyes, knowing that none of those things would help her if Paul found out. "I'm going home, Dr. Greenfield."

"But, Hannah, you must be seen by a physician."

She crossed her arms against the nip in the air.

He rubbed his forehead, looking resigned but not pleased. "You have my phone number in the book. If you need me for anything, Hannah, please call me." He pulled a card from his wallet and held it out to her. "This is my private cell phone number."

She studied his face. "I'm glad we met, and I'll always remember the nice English doctor at this hospital. But I won't be seeing you again."

*H*annah opened the potbellied stove and stirred the coals with the poker. Mary, sitting in her wheelchair by the window, kept a watchful eye on the driveway, waiting for Luke to arrive.

She and Mary were living in the Yoders' *Daadi Haus*—Mary's grandmother's home. *Mammi* Annie, Mary's grandmother, had moved into the main house, a stone's throw away, with Mary's parents and brothers. The *Daadi Haus* was small, but the rooms were able to accommodate Mary's wheelchair. The home had indoor plumbing and a bathroom off the bedroom that the two girls shared. It was a good setup, except that Hannah had to put forth extra effort to avoid Sarah's beloved Jacob. Mary's brother lived next door with his parents, so keeping her distance from him was a bit tricky, especially when he came to visit his sister. But Hannah thought she was managing that quite well and Sarah should be pleased.

Between working with Mary several times a day on her physical therapy and using the kitchen and laundry room of the *Daadi Haus* to help Becky with the laundry, baking, and canning needs of the main house, Hannah felt as if the three weeks since they'd left the hospital had flown by.

As time allowed, she and Mary worked on the "Past and Future" quilt. While Luke visited, Hannah made herself scarce by digging around in Mary's grandmother's attic for scraps of material from doll clothing she and Mary had sewn when they were young. She found the first apron they'd ever made and even pieces of a doll's blanket they'd sewn.

Luke.

He hadn't said anything unkind to Hannah, but he seemed a little angrier with her with each visit. Between Hannah disappearing to the attic when he came in and Luke keeping his visits short, they'd not talked about whatever was bothering him. She figured he was just grumpy from still being on certain medicines and from worrying about what Mary was going through.

But his visits did give her time to search for material. She didn't want just any fabric; it had to tie into Mary's or Luke's life. *Mammi* Annie had spread the word to the women of the community about what Hannah was doing. Pieces of material were coming to Hannah and Mary with notes on them as to how they were a part of Mary's or Luke's past.

At this rate, the past side of the quilt would not lack for fabric. Now if she could figure out how to acquire plenty of material for the future side, the rest of her plan would come together.

Neither her father nor the bishop had mentioned the incident with Dr. Greenfield. She was sure the event had looked lustful to them. Hannah refused to think about that day. She had become quite adept at tuning out things she didn't want to think about, but the change didn't feel like a victory.

She set the pressing iron facedown on the stove and removed the handle. Hopefully no one would catch her ironing on a Sunday. She grabbed a split log from the woodbin beside the stove and tossed it onto the glowing embers. After closing the small metal door, she placed a few bricks on the back part of the flat stove and dusted off her hands with her apron.

The house was especially quiet today. At nearly lunchtime, only she and Mary remained on the property. It was a no-church Sunday, so Mary's family would spend the day out visiting, repaying folks—through words and homemade goodies—for the kindness they'd shown during this ordeal. In addition to helping Mary's father with his farm during the weeks following the accident, their Amish neighbors had built a harness shop with attached living quarters for Luke and Mary after they were wed.

Placing Mary's cotton head scarf over the towel that lay on the ironing table, Hannah smoothed it as straight as possible with her fingers.
Today held the promise of rekindling some of life's joy. She would witness
Mary seeing the harness shop for the first time. Mary wasn't even aware
that a living area above the shop had been built for them. From what John
Yoder had told Hannah, Luke and Mary shouldn't outgrow the small
home until their third baby arrived. Hannah couldn't wait to see Mary's
face when she saw her future home.

After slipping the handle back onto the pressing iron, Hannah lifted
the iron from the stove and worked the wrinkles out of the scarf. In spite
of the nervous edge she felt concerning today's trip, Hannah was confident
that Mary had enough strength to endure the five-mile ride one way,
though she would probably need a nap before heading back. But Mary
needed to see firsthand the progress that had been made toward her future.
Besides, Luke would no doubt mollycoddle Mary every step of the way.

Hannah had to admit that her excitement wasn't entirely on Mary's
behalf. The way Luke described the location of the shop made it sound as
if it bordered Gram's property and was in clear sight of her house. If that
was true, surely Hannah could steal a visit to see her sometime today. She
missed the elderly woman more than she'd expected to, and the need to
see her grew with each passing day.

Shifting her wheelchair slightly, Mary turned from the window. "Has
Luke shown you this shop he's so excited about?"

"I haven't stepped foot off this farm since we arrived here from the
hospital," Hannah said. She hoped her voice didn't give away that there
were troubled waters between her and Luke. She didn't know what the
problems were, but with secrets to keep hidden, silence was Hannah's
safest harbor. When May came, Paul would begin trying to win the approval of her family. In the meantime she needed to keep as much peace
as possible between her and her family and the community.

When the wrinkles were gone, Hannah flapped the material in the air to cool it. She looked forward to seeing her home again and getting out of this place for a bit. Mary's progress had been better than Hannah could have imagined, but helping Mary maneuver to the bathroom at all hours of the night and day was taxing.

Hannah crossed the room to Mary and tied the purple scarf over her head, being careful to cover the blond peach fuzz but not to bind the cloth around her skull too tightly.

Mary was healing quickly. Hannah hadn't needed to call the doctor's office once, even though the bishop had approved the Yoders having a telephone installed only sixty feet from the house. Mary's father and brothers had built a phone shanty—a wooden booth with windows. The phone company had come out and installed a black, push-button wall phone.

Mary lifted her *Kapp* off her lap and handed it to Hannah. "Getting me ready would be easier if we didn't need to attach the prayer covering to the bald-head covering."

Hannah took several straight pins from her pinafore and clenched them between her teeth, removing one at a time as she attached the *Kapp* to the head wrap. "Even the community's most beloved princess must wear her prayer veil." Hannah kissed Mary on the forehead.

Mary ran her hands over her scarf and *Kapp*. "I'm going to do you a favor and not tell the bishop how cheeky you can get. Calling a dedicated Plain woman a princess…" She turned to face the window, keeping a sharp lookout for Luke.

Hannah sat on the arm of the couch right behind her. It felt good to hear Mary tease her. The fear that had threatened to take over Mary, the panic that wouldn't let Hannah out of her sight, had slowly been replaced by a fragile peace as the People surrounded Mary with love.

The sounds of horse's hoofs and grinding gravel drew Hannah out of her musings.

Mary's pale face lit up. "He's here. Grab the blankets and wheel me outside."

Hannah seized the stack of folded blankets off the couch and laid them in Mary's lap. Grabbing their shawls off the coatrack, she mentally ran through her to-do list for today's outing.

Mary pounded the arms of her wheelchair. "Come on. Come on. What's taking you so long?" Her jesting made Hannah's day.

She wheeled her friend toward the doorway. "If you had half this much enthusiasm for your therapy, I wouldn't have to argue with you about it every day."

Mary scrunched her shoulders. "It's a dreadful routine, and you know it."

Before Hannah reached the door, Luke tapped and then eased it open. He scanned Hannah disapprovingly before absorbing Mary like rain after a drought. "You're looking mighty healthy today." He strode inside. "Here, let me take those for you." He lifted the blankets from her lap. "She'll need some heated bricks for her feet."

Hannah wrapped the shawl around Mary's shoulders. Then, like a maid, she shuffled off to the kitchen to finish her chores. While Luke took the blankets and Mary to the buggy, Hannah packed the bricks in old towels and finished gathering the picnic items.

As she hurried through the house, she made a quick visual inspection of all the kerosene lamps, making sure they were out. Satisfied that everything was in order, Hannah pushed through the door.

Luke loomed in front of her. "I'll take that."

His voice was demanding, and Hannah knew that saying "thank you" was inappropriate. He lifted the basket from her.

Hannah drew a deep breath to steady her hurt feelings. "She hasn't heard one word about the apartment that's been built for both of you. I can't wait to see her face. Mary's been through so much, and I—"

Resentment entered Luke's eyes, startling Hannah. "I think you've done more than enough."

He spoke as if correcting a dog, but why?

Luke pointed his finger at her. "If it wasn't for you, she wouldn't have been through so much, now, would she?" He turned his back on her and marched to the waiting buggy.

Stunned, Hannah was unable to move. What could she have possibly done to make life harder on Mary? With her knees shaking, she stood on the porch watching Luke tenderly place the heated bricks under Mary's feet and wrap her in blanket after blanket.

When Luke began to shut the door on the buggy, Mary held up her hand, and Luke stopped. "Tell Hannah to come on. I'm eager to be on our way."

"Hannah will go another time. She needs to stay here." Luke's face became like granite as he faced her. "Isn't that right, Sister?"

How can Mary miss the venom in his voice?

With heaviness bearing down on her, Hannah slowly walked to Mary's side. "I think I'll rest while you're gone."

Compassion filled Mary's eyes. "You deserve time to rest. I keep you up all night, and then I sleep during the day while you help *Mamm*. But I'm disappointed you aren't coming. Are you sure you don't feel up to it?"

Hannah nodded. "I'm sure." She tucked a slipping blanket corner around Mary's back and closed the carriage door. As Luke made his way around the back, Hannah followed him. "What have I done?" she whispered.

He turned to face her. "It was your fault we were out near the Knepps' place."

"My fault?"

"Oh, don't act so innocent. I begged you to go with us to the singing so Mary would feel comfortable returning to our farm afterward. You knew she wouldn't come with just me. I needed you to go with us. But you didn't *feel* like it."

Hannah shook her head. "I…I remember you and I had some sharp words, but I…I don't recall… My mind was so cluttered from—"

"Yeah, you took a spill on the side of the road and cut your hands and knees. Somehow that stole your memory, your ability to work, and your loyalty to your family." He glared at her. "Yet look at all that's happened to Mary, and she's bounced back."

"Luke, I'm…I'm sorry. I never meant—"

He strode to the driver's side and climbed inside.

She watched the buggy pull away with the people she loved leaving her behind.

cold wind whipped through Hannah's skirts and shawl, but the temperature in her heart seemed even colder. Her jaws ached as tears threatened to form. Disappointment worked its way through her. She'd really wanted to see the harness shop and Luke and Mary's future home, not to mention the joy on Mary's face as she took it all in for the first time.

A calf in the barn bawled for its mother. Hannah trudged across the back field to the barn.

My fault? How could he think that? Was it true? She remembered so little of those dark times following the attack.

She pulled the barn door open just far enough to slip inside. The place was warm and smelled of sweet feed and calf starter. She took a few steps toward the calf pen, and another familiar scent filled her nostrils: fresh cow manure.

The calf stuck its head through the split-rail pen, begging to be touched. Hannah patted the cowlick in the center of its forehead. The calf's tongue looked like saltwater taffy being pulled and stretched as the calf lapped at her clothing. It butted its head against her arm as if she had milk for the needy thing. "Sorry, fella. You're plain outta luck."

Hannah stepped back and folded her arms across her chest, tucking her shawl around her. Streams of sunlight caused dancing dust particles from the hay to look like shiny flecks of gold. She and Luke used to pretend the floating bits of dirt were tiny people and that if they could catch them and immerse them in water, they'd grow into life-sized children. They'd spent hours trying to create people from suspended pieces of hay dust.

Now Luke hated her. And she couldn't fully remember what he was talking about. She didn't doubt his account of what had happened. She'd never had much desire to attend the singings for appearance' sake. She was sure that during those most confusing days of her life, she'd refused to go anywhere with anyone.

Desperate for a place to hide and think, she climbed the ladder to the hayloft. She clambered over the mounds of loose hay and opened the hayloft door. Another blast of cold air stung her cheeks. Brown leaves swirled in the wind, falling from the trees like rain. She wrapped the shawl around her and tried to find solace in the beauty of the earth. Most of the trees had lost their leaves, and they stood with gray branches reaching out and upward. Brown fields lay resting for the season. Brilliant blue skies carried such a variety of clouds—thick mounting ones, wispy ones, thin-lined ones.

She wondered if her Aunt Zabeth had once loved her father the way Hannah loved Luke. She bet Zabeth would understand how badly she hurt, how isolated her life had become. Hannah wondered what her aunt had done that caused her to be shunned. Whatever it was, she never repented, because the letter said she was still under the ban.

A flock of twelve or more purple finches gathered under the sweet gum tree, enjoying the seeds that had fallen.

She looked out at the land and drew a deep breath. God had done a magnificent job with creation. Warmth spread throughout her body, and in spite of the stabbing pains from Luke's accusation, peace flooded her.

I know the plans I have for you...

She'd heard this verse during a church service, and it had struck her as powerful even then. But today, as she stood in a hayloft alone and unsure of her future, it meant hope. Hannah knelt and closed her eyes. "God, I know so little... I understand almost nothing." Chills covered her body. "You are my God, whether I understand You or not. I choose You."

Thoughts from every corner of her life assailed her. She saw herself sitting in various homes, barns, and workshops for preaching services, hearing strong messages against sin. A snapshot of her father kissing her fingers the time they got mashed in the buggy door made her smile even now. It had amazed her that day how a tiny kiss truly made the pain disappear. Visions of Paul laughing with her over the years and aching with her when she cried on his shoulder at the hospital filled her with fresh turmoil.

Faster and faster, images flew through her mind—arguments with sisters, cooking in a hot kitchen, and respect for the Old Ways even though much about those ways stirred doubt within her. Then the puzzle pieces of her life took an ominous turn, and she could barely see a clear picture of anything in her mind's eye. Luke and Mary's buggy accident. Luke's anger.

The attack.

That was the real reason she'd had nothing to say to God for two months.

She shifted off of her knees and sat. Life didn't make sense. Parts of it were so beautiful, so touching, that a moment of it brought her strength that could last for years and could only have come from God. But what about the other part, the part that was so wretched with ugliness it stole her desire to live?

It didn't make sense that God willed both. Maybe it never would make sense.

Hannah struggled day in and day out with blind acceptance of everything that happened in life. If God put a person where he or she was supposed to stay, then how did the Pilgrims come to America? How did the Amish cross an ocean to get free of the Church of England?

If authority couldn't sometimes be ignored, there would be no Old Ways to cling to. So who got to decide when it was time to stand against authority and when it was time to submit?

She sighed, not knowing the answers to any of that.

The tugging question in her heart right now seemed to be if she trusted God to be her strength and guiding force, whether she understood things or not.

Pulling her knees to her chin, she wrapped the shawl around them and closed her eyes, sifting through more of her thoughts. "God, I...I can't accept that the attack was Your will. I can't." Oddly, fresh peace flooded her, as if God understood her feelings.

"Hannah!"

The shout startled her so badly she screamed. Her eyes flew open, and she jumped to her feet. On the ground, some fifteen feet below, Matthew stood, looking up at her.

"Matthew Esh, scare a girl to death, why don't ya!" But seeing his friendly face quickly removed her frustration.

The gleam in Matthew's eyes, which defined him more than any other trait, didn't falter for a moment. "Well, it's not like I weren't calling to ya," he said, pointing to the ridge where Esh land met Yoder ground, "from the moment I recognized it was you sittin' up here. I been wantin' to see how you're doin'. Everybody's so wrapped up in Luke and Mary, pampering them like—" He stopped cold. "I mean, they've had it rough and all, but..." Matthew grabbed his suspenders and kicked a rock.

He had a good heart, one that didn't want to say anything negative. Sometimes, in his honesty, things slipped out anyway. But with no one home, they needed to find a better time to visit.

"I think we'd better talk later, Matthew." She enjoyed his company. He often reminded her of Paul with his sense of humor and work ethic.

And he reminded her of the best parts of Luke, with his sincerity and dedication to the Old Ways and his family.

"Aw, come on. It's important."

Seeing the disappointment in his eyes, she relented. "Well, if you're needing to talk, come on up."

A wind gust zipped through the barn and right through Hannah's clothing. She pulled on the handles to the double doors of the hayloft and bolted them shut.

The ladder creaked, and soon Matthew's black winter hat peeked through the small entrance. "Can't say I ever climbed into a haymow to talk to a girl before."

"Did too." Hannah eased onto a mound of hay and stretched out her legs, thankful for a break from the seriousness of her life.

Matthew mocked a scowl at her as he finished climbing into the loft. "Liar."

Hannah laughed. They'd get in ever so much trouble if the adults knew how they threw such an ugly word around like it was nothing. His playfulness reminded her so much of Luke...before the buggy accident.

Wrapping her cloak tighter around herself, Hannah clenched her jaw in feigned annoyance. "You told me about it yourself."

Matthew slid off his jacket and threw it on her lap before he fell back on the hay beside her. She coughed at the spray of dust he caused, then realized he'd probably planned that little dust-scattering move. She waved her hand through the air, clearing it some so she could breathe. He stretched out his long legs, obviously unperturbed at her reaction.

Glad for the extra warmth, she spread his jacket over her lap.

"Prove it." Matthew picked up a long straw and stuck it between his teeth.

"Got to that point of the game already?" Hannah took the straw from his mouth and tossed it into his lap.

He shrugged and grabbed another straw. "I got somethin' I want to tell ya. But first, you have to prove your claim."

Curiosity grabbed her attention. "Motty Ball."

"Climbing a haymow to talk to a cat doesn't count."

Hannah buried her cold hands under the jacket. "Motty Ball is a female, and that's what you said. So, what's this news?"

Matthew's eyes danced with mischief. "I met somebody."

"Old Order Amish?" Her automatic question bothered her. Was she that much of a hypocrite that Matthew had to find an Amish girl but she could be engaged to a Mennonite?

Matthew laced his fingers together and tucked them behind his head, looking quite pleased with himself. "Of course."

A chorus of relief sang within her. "Who?"

"Won't say. Not yet."

"For tradition's sake—keeping the relationship a secret until you're published?" She was too excited to drop the subject easily.

"Nah. That's silly stuff for old women and childish girls. It's 'cause I don't know yet how she feels about me."

"Oh." Her excitement ended abruptly. She would hurt all over if Matthew fell for someone who didn't return his feelings.

Looking at courting from this viewpoint, she saw some of her father's concerns. Suddenly she couldn't find fault with him for taking it so seriously.

"Come on, Matthew. You gotta tell me."

Matthew picked up a straw and twirled it. "If you can figure out the riddle, you'll know. But you can't tell nobody." He placed the straw between his teeth. "Now, pay attention 'cause I'm only going to say it once." He shifted his feet and leaned back in a relaxed manner. "She comes and she goes almost daily…by driver. In thick snow, she'll stay. Her name is said like it's one letter. She's not yet been allowed to take her vows, but she's been old enough for several years."

Hannah shook her head. "Not allowed to take her vows yet? I never heard of such a thing. Matthew, are you playing games with me?"

He smiled. "It's the honest-to-heaven's truth. And if I told you more, you'd get more confused. She's as unique as an Amish community has ever knowed."

Hannah sat there, dumbfounded. "If she comes and goes by driver, then she's not from this district."

Matthew smiled broadly. "Not yet."

His confidence was disconcerting. He was missing a huge part of the chain of command: the girl's father. The bishop of each district would easily agree to let any Amish of good standing move to a different district. But a girl's father—well, that put a whole new spin on the issue.

Matthew squared his shoulders. "That's all I'm saying. Either you're as smart as I think you are and can figure it out, or you won't know."

"Well, I'll know when you get published."

Matthew laughed loud and strong. "She ain't even gone for a buggy ride with me yet." He shrugged, clearly having a moment of insecurity. "But when I met her, there was something between us, Hannah. Ya know?"

She wanted to argue that his feelings were too much too soon, but she of all people couldn't argue that point. She'd fallen for Paul as hard and as quickly as a tree felled for firewood. "Yeah, I know." The dreamy look in his eyes made Hannah ache to see this work out for him.

His riddle was quite a puzzle. A girl of age but not yet allowed to take her vows. Strange. Her name sounds like one letter. Hmm. This would take some considering.

Ready for a little childlike reprieve after weeks of hard labor, she reached for the straw dangling from his lips. He threw his hand up, deflecting hers. A scuffling match ensued as she tried to grab the straw and he tried to keep her from getting it.

"Schick dich, Hannah. *Schick dich."* He grabbed a fistful of hay and rubbed it on her head. *"Du bischt Druwwel."*

She stood and threw his jacket to the foot of the ladder.

"Dankes, Hannah."

Hannah curtsied. "You're welcome."

"What'd you do that for?"

Feigning innocence, she said, "It flew there all by itself."

"Aha! Proof! You are a liar!" He squared his shoulders in triumph, clearly certain he'd won this round of the game.

"Hello!" A deep voice boomed through the air.

Hannah stopped dead as if the breath had been knocked out of her. That was the bishop's voice.

Matthew tilted his head, studying her. "It's okay, Hannah. We've done nothing wrong." He put both feet on the ladder and began his descent. He stopped on the third rung. "Perhaps one day the lot will fall to me, and I'll become a bishop." The words came out but a whisper so the bishop could not hear him. "Maybe then you will behave around me, *ya?"* He smiled and straightened his hat before he climbed down the ladder.

His humor did nothing to settle the terror that ran through Hannah's body. There were so many levels on which she feared the bishop. She wanted to be all that he and her parents wanted. She really did. It just never seemed to work out that way, no matter how hard she tried. The bishop would call her mind-set sin. Dr. Greenfield would probably call it free will.

She called it utter confusion.

She peered through the hole to the ground floor. The bishop handed Matthew his jacket, then looked up into the loft. Her hands fluttered over her apron, trying to free it of loose hay. She reached for her *Kapp.* It was askew, one side nearly touching her shoulder and her hair pulling free of its restraints.

The bishop's austere glare bored into Hannah, and guilt hounded her—guilt for every ungodly thought she'd ever had. The bishop rubbed the palms of his hands together, making a noise like sandpaper against wood. "I came to see John Yoder. I take it no one is home but the two of you."

Matthew glanced up at her, and she knew he was just realizing that himself.

The bishop cleared his throat. "I think it's time you go home, Matthew. Hannah, I'm sure there are better ways to spend the Lord's Sabbath than this. Tell Mary's father I came by to see him and I'll catch up with him later in the week."

The two men disappeared from her tiny square view from the hayloft. With a heavy heart she made her way down the ladder.

*H*annah stirred the chocolate frosting with all the strength she could muster. An electric mixer would be awfully nice on days like this. Her arms were weary from having washed clothes all morning. She had always known that a lot of jobs fell to Mary as the only daughter among ten children, but she hadn't realized the full magnitude of her workload. Thankfully, four of Mary's brothers were married and had homes of their own now. So Becky, *Mammi* Annie, and Hannah had only six males to look after. The responsibilities had been minimal when Mary first returned from the hospital, but as more and more Amish women went back to their homes, both Hannah's and Becky's workloads increased.

Hannah placed a layer of cake on a plate and began frosting it with a dinner knife. She had done mounds of laundry today, including a full tub of towels. Of all the items that had to be run through the gas-powered agitator, worked through the hand-cranked dry wringer to squish the soap out, rinsed by hand in a tub of clear water, and worked through the wringer again, towels were the most tiring. They got quite heavy as she dunked them in the rinse water and lifted them in the air, repeating the process over and over until the soap was out. Of course, boys' and men's shirts, of which there was no shortage in the Yoder household, were no picnic. They weren't heavy to rinse, but the wringer broke the buttons easily. At least at this stage of Mary's recuperation, she was well enough to sew buttons back on.

Hannah positioned the second layer of cake on top of the frosted one and dropped a large dollop of icing on it. As she smoothed it around the top and over the sides, she let her mind wander. A few more weeks had swept by as she'd stayed busy helping Mary regain her strength and the Yoders run their household.

There was one benefit to all the jobs and concentration: it helped time pass as she dreamed of seeing Paul again. Going without letters had been harder than she'd imagined. But with a little less than six weeks until Christmas, she'd almost made it through the arctic wasteland of time. A sense of well-being washed over her. She had set her will, defied her emotions, and carried out her responsibilities.

But Hannah didn't understand Gram's ridiculous edict that she and Paul could not write to each other. For the thousandth time, she wondered if there was some other way to pass letters back and forth without her family finding out.

With the aid of her walker, Mary shuffled into the kitchen. A patchwork potholder she had been sewing was scrunched between her palm and the handle of the walker. "I'm afraid the entire wedding season will pass by before I'm strong enough to attend any of them."

Hannah set the frosting to the side. She pulled a golden brown loaf of bread from the gas stove and set the pan on a baker's rack to cool. She put another pan of unbaked bread in the oven and closed the door. "Every bride and groom has come to see you before the wedding, no?"

Pinching off a bit of a freshly iced cake, Mary nodded, then popped the chunk of cake into her mouth. "Mmm, *vat's* awful *goot.*"

"Molmumumpm," Hannah mocked jovially. "How can I understand that garbled talk? Neither English nor Pennsylvania Dutch. Shame on you." Hannah cut the cake where Mary had pinched off a piece and set the slice on a plate on the table. "You've had plenty of nutrition. It's time for some much-needed calories." She grabbed a fork out of a drawer and laid it beside the plate.

Mary eased into the chair. "I came out to help, but, as usual, I sit and take it easy while you work."

Hannah grabbed a glass and filled it with milk, then placed it in front of Mary. "You're doing just as you should."

Mary took several long gulps of milk before setting the glass on the table. "I'll make all this up to you someday, Hannah. You'll see."

Hannah lifted the kettle of boiling water off the stove and poured the steaming liquid into a cup that held a tea bag and the last of the honey they had from the Esh farm. "What I see is my friend being strong enough to want to do things but too weak to do them just yet, no?"

Mary sighed. "It's frustrating. I lie in bed dreaming of doing things, and as soon as I stand, all my strength is gone."

"It will return."

"But I slept for days after my outing with Luke."

"I know. When you start getting your strength, it'll come quick like." Hannah set the hot drink in front of Mary. "The womenfolk will be here soon with their quilting items in tow. I want all of us to work on your quilt, and they want to come and lift your spirits. But if you get tired during the gathering, you say so, and I'll cart you off to bed."

Mary frowned. "I'm to go to bed while everyone else gets to work on the quilt you designed for me?"

Hannah opened the stove, checking the next batch of bread. She closed the oven, then turned to dump the other loaf onto a rack so it could finish cooling without getting soggy. "You'll do as your body asks."

Mary took another bite of cake. "You've done a wonderful job planning and gathering fabric for our quilt." She paused, her eyes studying Hannah with a depth of caring that only Mary had for her. "Hannah, I'm not so weak or confused from the medicines that I haven't noticed how sad you've been. I vainly assumed my injuries were the reason. But something much deeper is going on with you. It haunts your sleep and brings tears to your eyes when you think no one sees. If everyone wasn't so concerned over me and Luke, they'd be sick with worry about you. Can you tell me what's going on?"

Hannah scraped the last of the frosting out of the bowl and swirled it onto the cake, wondering if Mary was strong enough to hear the full, horrendous story. Although Hannah had to keep her and Paul's relationship a secret even from her best friend, she had always shared everything else with Mary.

The explanation of her unhappiness would be a painful shock for Mary. On one hand, Hannah wanted to spare Mary the ugly truth; on the other, she ached to talk to her, was desperate to share with someone the burden that ate away at her night and day. With her living here, her parents seemed to have forgotten the whole thing had ever happened.

Hannah gave a smile that had to look fake in spite of her best effort.

Mary's eyes brimmed with pools of water. "Something awful is wrong, and I'm so sorry. I feel so selfish, beaming about the new apartment and shop." Using the table as support, Mary stood. Her cool, soft hands pressed against Hannah's arm. *"Mei liewe, liewe Bobbeli, was iss es?"*

Dear, dear baby. The term of endearment would have caused giggles if the situation weren't so filled with misery.

Dread swamped Hannah. How could she talk about the attack when Mary knew little to nothing about what Dr. Greenfield called sex? For Hannah, getting the explanation past her lips would be tough enough if Mary already fully understood the concepts.

Hannah placed the spreading knife on a plate. She turned and faced her friend. So much love and compassion shone in Mary's eyes.

She swallowed. *"Du kannscht net saage…"*

Mary shook her head. "I won't, dear Hannah. You know I'll not tell a soul."

Hannah's knees shook so hard that she plunked into a kitchen chair. Mary sat beside her, holding her hands. Hannah swallowed. "A few weeks before your accident—"

A swift rap at the door startled both of them. Mary engulfed Hannah in a hug. "It's probably just *Mamm* dropping some sewing stuff off early, and I forgot to unlock the door. I'll ask her to give us some more time."

Hannah squeezed Mary gingerly before letting her go. As Mary shuffled to the door using her walker, Hannah rinsed her face at the sink, still debating how much to share with Mary. She could just tell her about Paul and how hard it was being separated from him. Was it safe for her friend's health to tell her any more than that? Could she handle even that much? It had taken Mary a week of extra rest to recoup from her visit to the harness shop, and Luke hadn't even allowed her to climb the steps to get a gander at their future home. She was more frail than she knew.

Mary opened the front door, then turned to look at Hannah. The crestfallen expression on her face said it all; they'd lost track of time. The women had arrived for the quilting.

"Are you all right, Mary?" Naomi Esh looked past her, searching for Hannah. Behind Naomi stood Deborah Miller and Grace Hostetler, all of them looking concerned.

Hannah stepped forward, placing her hands on Mary's shoulders. "She's fine. *Kumm uff rei,*" Hannah added, showing them in. Hannah helped Mary take a few steps backward with the aid of the walker, making room for the women and all their sewing goods to enter the room. Maybe this interruption was for the best. Mary's sudden inquisitiveness had caught Hannah off guard. Hannah needed time to weigh her words, to decide what Mary could handle.

The women cleared the food off the kitchen table and scrubbed the surface clean before spreading the partially finished "Past and Future" quilt across the table.

Mary remained near the front door, leaning on Hannah. "It's always about me. I'm so sorry." Her body shook like a newborn calf.

"Sh, *Liewi*. Sh." Hannah forced a smile, hoping it looked genuine. "It's a day we've looked forward to, no?"

Mary laid her head on Hannah's shoulder and wept. Beyond any question, Hannah knew that her friend was not strong or well enough to deal with the truth of what had taken place in her life. Just the idea that Hannah was unhappy had caused Mary to tremble and quake.

More women arrived, including Mary's mother and grandmother. When they saw Mary weeping in Hannah's arms, anxiety filled Becky's eyes. *Mammi* Annie frowned in concern. Hannah nodded to assure both women that Mary would be fine in a few minutes. Becky helped *Mammi* Annie move into the room and get seated.

Sarah bounded through the door next, chattering as only fifteen-year-old girls can, with no regard to the somber mood of the room. Hannah's sister didn't even speak to her. Then again, maybe she was giving her and Mary some privacy.

A quick glance outside informed Hannah that her *Mamm* hadn't come. Sarah had apparently hitched a ride with Edna Smucker, their closest Amish neighbor, who was walking toward the house with a small stack of already-sewn quilt patches.

"*Kumm,*" Hannah whispered to Mary. Leaving the walker behind, she led Mary to the best seat at the table, the one near the wood stove, so she wouldn't need to shift out of the way as people milled about.

Mary wiped at her eyes, her hands still trembling. As she sank into the seat, she clung to Hannah's hand like a frightened child.

Hannah kissed her on the cheek and whispered, "Don't let my girl-hood silliness upset you. This season of life will change soon enough, no?"

"*Ehrlich?*" Mary asked, her hushed voice unheard by the babbling women busily spreading the quilt background over the table.

Hannah drew a deep breath. No, it wasn't honest, but it was the truth condensed into something Mary could handle. Hannah would move beyond this spell and be happy. All she needed was Paul close by. *"Ya."* Hannah patted Mary's shoulder. *"Ya."*

The women talked as they laid small pieces of fabric over the off-white background. Each one seemed keenly aware of Mary's fretfulness but acted nonchalant and oblivious.

Hannah lifted two pieces of cloth off the table, a deep purple and a gorgeous magenta. She held them in front of Mary. "Impatiens wait to be designed into this quilt by the best among us at sewing flowers." She lowered the material in front of Mary. It was well known that Mary could outdo any seamstress when it came to designing flowers into quilts. As Mary's hands went toward the material Hannah held, she withdrew the squares and held them toward Becky.

The whole room, including Mary, broke into laughter. Although Becky Yoder was good at sewing all sorts of items from nature, she had often complained that she couldn't sew a flower to save her life but her daughter could do it in her sleep.

Mary laughed. "I thought you wanted impatiens, not blobs."

Becky mockingly wagged her finger in her daughter's face. "Not one of my children has suffered yet due to my lack of skill."

Ah, the mantra of every mother alive: for her children not to suffer because of what she lacked. Hannah cleared her throat, drawing everyone's attention. "That might be taking it a bit far, don't you think?" She peered at Mary, whose face was brightening by the moment.

Mary nodded. "When Robert lay under that blanket you made for him, he thought one of your flowers was a monster about to smother him in his sleep."

As laughter filled the room, Hannah returned to the stove to check the loaf of bread she'd forgotten. Becky wasn't nearly as bad at sewing flowers as she took ribbing for. She loved the teasing, egged it on most times. She often said that she considered a sense of humor about oneself to be nourishing to the soul and to the souls of others as well.

Hannah pulled the bread pan from the oven and, with great theatrics, turned it toward the women. Their hoots and cackles made the room vibrate. Her loaf of bread was burned all around the edges and gave off a horrible aroma. "It seems one of you could have noticed the scent of burned bread before now."

Naomi, with splayed fingers, waved her hand like a Victorian lady, then placed it over her heart. "It's an aroma we didn't recognize, having never burned bread in our lives."

Fresh roars of laughter filled the home. Every woman had burned foods while baking. The day was too filled with juggling babies, food preparation, and side businesses to keep up with everything perfectly.

Hannah carried the pan toward the doorway. Becky hurried to open the door for her. As Hannah stepped outside, she whispered, "I may take a few moments for myself while Mary's distracted. Do you mind?"

"No, child." Becky looked lovingly at Hannah. "Annie and I will tend to lunch." Becky closed the door, keeping the brisk wind out of the house.

The cold air almost took Hannah's breath away. She should have thought to get her shawl. Hurrying to the edge of the yard, she dumped the pan over, emptying it of the smoldering bread.

She stood straight, gazing over the brown lands of late fall. The husbands of the lighthearted quilters were out hunting pheasant and quail today, hoping to bring home some good birds before Thanksgiving next week. A few of the menfolk had managed to kill wild turkeys a couple of weeks back, but that season was closed now, so the other men were aiming for something less weighty.

The strength and pleasure of the women who loved, laughed, gave birth, served their families as well as their community, and finally died having tried to fulfill God's call on their lives warmed Hannah like nothing else. The tenderness of those who had known her all her life—who knew her mother, grandmother, and even her great-grandmother—melted the edges of ice that had formed around her heart.

Hannah walked toward Becky Yoder's home. She could at least wash a few dishes for Becky while the women quilted.

$\mathcal{S}$arah's hopes of seeing Jacob had taken a hard blow the moment she learned that all the Yoder men had gone hunting today. She'd spent weeks looking forward to catching a few words with him today even if she had to mill about the property half the day to see him.

Chapter 18

What a miserable disappointment.

She wondered how many times Hannah had made ways to see Jacob without any of the Yoders realizing it. When the sewing needle pricked Sarah's index finger, she yelped. A few of the women tittered with laughter. Mary barely glanced up. Her reaction stung Sarah deeply. It didn't seem to matter at all to Mary that years ago, before Mary and Hannah began school, Mary had been Sarah's best friend, not Hannah's. Everyone in this room spoke highly of Hannah, even Grace Hostetler. Clearly Grace's husband, Bishop Eli, had not yet shared with her the information Sarah had given him about Hannah's midnight ride in her nightgown. If these women knew the truth about her sister's indiscretions, Hannah wouldn't be the queen bee around here. Sarah put her finger in her mouth to keep blood from staining the quilt.

Mary passed her a handkerchief, which Sarah quickly wrapped around her wound. When Mary rose from her chair, Grace bounded to fetch the walker.

"Dankes." Clutching the handgrips, Mary shuffled away from the table. "Come with me to the bathroom, Sarah. I've got just the thing for that finger."

Surprised and a bit honored, Sarah followed Mary, trying to think of something she could say that would impress the girl and make them close friends again.

Mary opened the mirrored medicine cabinet. She pulled out a box of Band-Aids and then turned on the faucet. "Hold it under the water for a minute."

Sarah removed the handkerchief and stuck her finger under the stream. "*Daed* finally got our plumbing all straight."

Mary squeezed Sarah's finger, expressing a few drops of blood. "I bet that makes life a lot easier, especially with Hannah here all the time."

Ire ignited in Sarah's chest. Why did everyone talk as if Hannah were everything and Sarah nothing? "Hannah's not all that great, you know."

Mary turned off the water. "That little prick should be all cleaned out now." She pointed to the cabinet under the sink. "Clean washrags are under there, but you'll have to get one yourself. I can't bend that low yet."

"I'll do it." Sarah grabbed a rag and dried her wet hand.

Mary's lack of response to her comment about Hannah was a clear indicator of her loyalties. If she only knew the truth. "Since you two are best friends and all, I'm sure Hannah's told you she's been running off with some *Englischer* during the night." Sarah gave her sweetest grin, hoping she'd worded that piece of news in a way that sounded upright and innocent.

Mary peeled the Band-Aid out of its paper wrapper. "This should keep your finger from bleeding on the fabric."

Sarah huffed. "I guess she didn't mention it to you after all. But it's true. I saw her myself." She glanced in the shaving mirror, pretending to make sure her blond locks were safely tucked inside her *Kapp*. "You know, *Daed* and the bishop saw her with an English doctor at the hospital. In his arms in broad daylight! I overheard *Daed* telling *Mamm* about it. He's fit to be tied."

Grasping the walker tightly, Mary shot Sarah an angry look in the mirror. "Why are you telling me this?"

"Since you're her best friend, I thought you'd want to help keep her on the straight and narrow. It'd be a shame if she—"

"Who else have you told these things to?"

Sarah bristled. "Look, you can keep secrets for her if you want, but I'm not going to. She can't pretend to be something she's not."

"Oh, really?" Mary's voice quavered like a pot of simmering stew. "Isn't that precisely what you're doing? Trying to make me think you're telling me something for Hannah's sake when you're simply doing it out of spite. Though why you would want to harm your own sister is beyond me." Trembling, Mary grasped the walker and shuffled out the door.

Sarah followed her to the bedroom. Concern for how badly Mary was shaking made Sarah fear for what she'd begun. She hadn't meant to upset Mary, but it was only right that the girl see Hannah for who she really was.

Mary sat on the side of the bed, her breathing labored. "Did you"— Mary took a quick breath, her speech coming in gasps—"approach Hannah…before spreading your version of…whatever it is you're talking about?"

Mary's accusation stung, but Sarah wasn't ready to give up. "Hannah has been far too preoccupied with herself to be approached about anything."

Mary glared at Sarah. "What a *deerich* girl you are. What a foolish, foolish girl." Her eyes rolled back, and she fell over limp on the bed.

"Mary!" Sarah screamed.

Within seconds, a herd of women raced into the bedroom.

Becky grabbed her daughter's head, obviously searching for signs of alertness. "Mary!" There was no response. "Go get Hannah. She's outside somewhere. Hurry."

Confused and frightened, Sarah ran out of the bedroom and through the front door. "Hannah! Hannah!" She dashed toward the road, skimming the lands for her sister. Oh, why had she tried to win Mary's approval by sharing her secret? She should have known it was a pointless venture. Mary was now Hannah's close friend, and nothing she could say would change that. Hearing the truth about her wouldn't easily dissuade the loyal girl.

When the women learned she was the reason Mary had gotten upset, they'd wag their tongues about Hannah's mean little sister for years to come. She searched her mind for ways to avoid the scolding she was in for.

As she ran past the Yoders' home, she saw Hannah coming out the front door, looking relaxed and carefree, wiping her hands on her apron.

"Hannah," she shrieked, "Mary's having a spell of some sort. She collapsed. *Dabber schpring!*"

Even before Sarah finished screaming, Hannah was bolting up the driveway toward the *Daadi Haus.*

~~~

Hannah barreled through the side door, out of breath after her short sprint.

Grace pointed to the bedroom. *"Kammer."*

Upon entering the small room, Hannah found the rest of the women hovering around the bed. "What happened?"

The terror in Becky's eyes made Hannah's knees nearly buckle. *"Ich kann net saage."*

She couldn't say?

Hannah grabbed the blood-pressure cuff and stethoscope out of the dresser in a far corner of the room. If Becky didn't know what was wrong, then Mary must have been more stressed by thoughts of the secret Hannah had never shared than she had realized.

As Hannah came to the edge of the bed, the women cleared the way for her. Mary's face was flushed, but she looked coherent, even a bit annoyed. Hannah passed the items in her hand to Grace.

"*Deerich,*" Mary mumbled.

"*Liewe* Mary, you're not foolish at all. Now just relax." Placing her hand behind Mary's back, Hannah eased her forward and removed the pillows that were propping her up. She helped Mary slide downward in the bed, the loving hands of several women easing her into a flat position.

Hannah placed the pillows under Mary's feet. "Close your eyes. Take slow, deep breaths. Everything will be just fine." She retrieved the blood-pressure cuff and stethoscope from Grace. Hannah cooed in her most consoling voice while wrapping the cuff around Mary's arm. Hannah pumped the rubber bulb on the blood-pressure cuff. After the appropriate number of pumps, she stopped to read the gauge; it said 112/71, normal for Mary. Hannah loosened the cuff and let it hang. She tossed the stethoscope onto the bed and took Mary's wrist, checking her pulse.

Mary motioned with one hand. "*Du muscht verschteh.*"

"I do understand. Shush now. I need to think." Counting the beats for thirty seconds and then doubling that number, she came up with 134 beats per minute. That was high, definitely worth calling about. "Sarah?"

Sarah edged forward. "*Ya?*"

"There's a little pamphlet in the top drawer of the dresser. Could you get it, please?"

She scurried to do Hannah's bidding.

"A nurse's direct line is written on there. Take the pamphlet to the phone shanty and dial that number. Tell whoever answers who you are and what's going on. I'll come to the shanty before the nurse gets on the line."

"*Deerich.*" Mary raised herself up on her elbows and glared at Sarah. "*Die entsetzlich Druwwel Du duscht.*"

"Mary," Hannah whispered, "lie back. You're talking nonsense. Sarah hasn't brought any awful trouble to me." Hannah glanced at Sarah. The girl looked stricken with worry. "It's okay, Sarah. Just go call that number. I'll be there in a few minutes. I want to check her blood pressure and pulse one more time first."

Sarah darted out of the room.

"Hannah." Mary pulled at her arm, nodding at the women in the room and then toward the door.

Clearly Mary wanted to speak to Hannah alone. It seemed rude and bold, but Hannah wasn't about to argue. "Becky, I think some homemade chicken soup would do her a world of good."

The women all filed out of the room with a new mission, to pull together a batch of soup as quickly as they could. As the last woman to leave, Edna closed the door behind her.

Hannah tightened the dangling blood-pressure cuff and put the stethoscope on Mary's antecubital as she'd been taught. "Mary, what happened to you?"

Mary's greenish blue eyes were wide open, her pupils dilated. "Sarah told me some things. Dreadful things. Hannah, I believe your sister is betraying you to the community, and you'll end up paying for it for years to come. You've got to stop her. You've got to."

Hannah's heart raced, battling between compassion for her younger sister, who often spoke first and thought second, and wrath at Sarah's lack of tongue control. But what had the girl told Mary about her? What did she know that could hurt her so badly? Had Mrs. Waddell told her about Hannah's relationship with Paul? Or had she overheard their parents talking about the unmentionable?

When she got another normal reading on Mary's blood pressure, she took off the stethoscope. "What did Sarah tell you?" she asked, her voice trembling.

"She said you were in the arms of some doctor and that she saw you in your nightgown taking a midnight ride with a man."

A slap across the face couldn't have hurt any worse. Hannah forced a smile. "Little sisters do that sometimes—tattle in hopes of causing trouble. Since you don't have any sisters, you just didn't know." Hannah patted her leg. "I need to get to that phone and see if the nurse agrees with my thoughts. Rest now. I'll be back soon."

When Hannah walked out of the bedroom, Becky met her. "Do you think she needs a doctor?"

Hannah fought against her indignation at Sarah and tried to find a gentle tone to answer her. "I'm not sure, but I think she's fine, just a bit weak."

Becky grasped Hannah's hand. "I'll go sit with her."

Hannah nodded and whisked out the side door and down the driveway toward the phone shanty. Thoughts of striking Sarah roiled through her. What had the girl been thinking, sharing such idle gossip? Their father must have said something about the doctor, probably not with the intention of Sarah or any other sibling hearing him. Hannah squeezed her fists.

Father God, help me see beyond my fury.

She glanced at the sky. Gray clouds hung low, and the scent of snow hung on the air. It would be Christmastime soon, and Hannah would see Paul. Thankful for that refreshing thought, she drew a deep breath.

As she watched the movement of wisps of clouds, she thought of Vento. Matthew had been right; the stallion's gait was as smooth as the clouds he'd compared the horse to.

Sudden concern lurched within her heart. *Matthew.* If Sarah's gossip got to the ears of Matthew's prospective girl, it would end things between them for sure.

Through the windows of the small shanty, Hannah saw Sarah holding the phone to her ear. Hannah opened the door.

Sarah lowered the mouthpiece. "I'm still on hold. How's Mary?"

"What did you say to her?" Hannah seethed.

"I-I…" Sarah stammered, looking like a frightened little girl.

"Out with it, Sarah. What did you tell Mary about the buggy ride?"

She gritted her teeth, making that "tcht" noise she was famous for. "I
told her the truth. That you were out with some *Englischer* in the middle
of the night in your nightgown."

An Englischer? Anger at her sister took a backseat to the relief that
poured over Hannah. Sarah had no idea the driver was Matthew. "We
were gone for five minutes. How much fuss have you caused over this?"

Sarah's right cheek twitched. "Five minutes, nothing! I saw you. You
were gone over half an hour."

Hannah glared at her. "Liar!"

A distant voice spoke through the earpiece. Sarah thrust the phone at
Hannah. As she skirted around Hannah to leave the shanty, their backs
raised like two cats in a fight.

The woman on the phone spoke again. Hannah raised the receiver to
her ear. "Yes, this is Hannah Lapp. I'm calling about Mary Yoder. She was
in ICU six weeks ago with a head injury."

"Hold, please."

She wasn't going to let any damage between her and Sarah distract her.
Only two things were important right now: making sure Mary was fine
and getting word to Matthew to tell no one that he was the driver of the
buggy that night. But how could she manage to speak to him privately?

*H*annah hung up the phone, relieved that the nurse believed Mary was probably fine, just too weak to deal with visitors and activity. She needed solitude, good meals, and lots of sleep.

Hannah finished jotting down the nurse's instructions so she wouldn't forget anything. She needed to keep tabs on Mary's blood pressure and heart rate over the next few days. Help her pace herself, allowing for physical therapy but no more sewingfests. Mary needed lots of water, and Hannah was to start pushing the extra calories, as she'd done earlier with the cake. A brisk wind could topple Mary right over these days.

As she left the phone shanty, Hannah's focus was on alleviating the concerns of everyone who was worried about Mary and then figuring out a way to talk to Matthew. But how? It wasn't like she had any real reason for visiting him.

She ran up the small hill to the *Daadi Haus*. Concerned faces met her as she entered. How had she managed to get this role of being the medically knowledgeable one? She was too young for all these mothers and grandmothers to look at her with such hopeful confidence. Hannah smiled as warmly as she could manage. "The nurse thinks she's fine, just a bit weak with so much going on. She's to sleep, eat, rest, and not have much company or excitement for a few more weeks, maybe longer."

Nods of agreement made a round through the room.

Becky came out of the bedroom. "She's asleep now, but she was asking for you." She pulled the door closed behind her. "What did the nurse say?"

"Basically that we're too wild of a group for a fragile young woman on the mend." Hannah flashed a broad smile, hoping no one saw past it to her anger at Sarah.

The women busied themselves putting all the sewing stuff that wasn't theirs back in its out-of-the-way spot in the living room. Then they streamed out the door, bidding good-bye to her, Becky, and Mary's grandmother Annie. Sarah passed her sister without a word.

Edna gave Hannah a quick hug. "We'll spread the word that Mary shouldn't have visitors. As soon as she's up to it, let everyone know."

Hannah patted Edna's back, assuring her that she'd keep the women informed of Mary's progress. As she watched her sister climb into Edna's buggy, Hannah wondered what meanspirited things Sarah would say about her on the ride home.

Naomi Esh paused in front of Hannah, carrying a large basket filled with sewing supplies. "I'm a stone's throw from here. If you think of anything I could do for Mary, the Yoders, or you, just holler."

Still trying to come up with a way to talk to Matthew, Hannah said, "That basket looks awful heavy."

Naomi let out a sigh. "Matthew drove me here. But since our get-together broke up earlier than expected, looks like I'll have to walk back home with this load."

Hannah glanced into the kitchen, where Mary's mother and grandmother were tidying up. "I'd be happy to walk with you while Mary sleeps." It would be considerably out of anyone's way to drive Naomi home following the roads that made a huge square to get to the Esh place. But it was a fairly short trip to march across the back fields where the two properties met.

"You have plenty to do here. I can manage."

Hannah's heart fell for an instant. Then she perked up. "I used the last of the honey in Mary's tea tonic this morning. If I walk with you now, I could bring some back with me."

Naomi held the basket out to her. *"Kumm."*

The two women walked in silence across the open fields from the Yoder place to Esh land. Unable to think of anything but what Sarah's gossip could do to Matthew's future, Hannah only managed nods and grunts at Naomi's attempts at conversation. Finally Naomi stopped talking, and they walked in silence.

As the chilly air whipped around her and her temper began to calm a bit, Hannah grew cold. She had, once again, forgotten to grab her shawl. Pulling the basket closer, she was struck so hard by a new thought that she had to fight for her footing.

If by some chance she was pregnant and Matthew's name got out to the community as the one Hannah was with in her nightgown, he might as well dig a grave for his chances of finding a wife anywhere in these parts. Her steps quickened as that worry took root.

"Give an older woman a break, Hannah. I can't go at that pace."

Chafing, Hannah slowed. She wasn't pregnant. She couldn't be. Conceiving that monster's child was more than she could cope with. It was all she could do to keep the rape a secret from Paul. How would she conceal a pregnancy? And what would she do with a baby? She shuddered.

Just don't think about that. It's not true. It's not.

The internal pep talk worked, as it had for well over a month, and her fears calmed to a bearable state.

Naomi and Hannah left the rough terrain of the fields and stepped onto a horse-trodden path. They crossed the driveway and soon were walking into the Esh home. Hannah had been there several times before, had sat on the front porch on many a no-church Sunday. Although the layout of the place was somewhat different from her own home, it was similar in many respects, such as the color of the sofa and the type of clock on the wall. If she weren't so livid with Sarah and so tired of Luke being angry with her, the scene might have made her homesick.

Hannah set the basket on the table as Naomi walked to the bottom of the stairs. "Peter? David?"

Loud, awkwardly rhythmic clomps echoed against the stairway. "They're at the Millers' place, *Mamm*, pluckin' feathers off today's hunt."

At the top of the twisting stairway, through the red cherry balusters, Hannah saw Matthew's feet, one with a sock on and one with both a sock and a shoe.

He hobbled down another step, gripping the rail, keeping his socked foot elevated. "Whatcha need?"

His legs came into full view as he hopped on one foot past the walled section of the winding stairwell. When he reached the midpoint landing, his face lit up. "Hannah. Hey."

She pointed to the foot he was keeping off the ground. "What happened?"

A corner of his mouth rose, and his eyes twinkled. "I fell…in more ways than one." He jerked his eyebrows up and down quickly.

Naomi waved her hand in the air. "I don't want to know about all this." She scurried up the steps and past her son. "Hannah needs honey. Go to the storage room and find her a couple of quart jars, will you?"

"Sure thing, *Mamm*." Using the railing, Matthew limped down the last ten steps.

Hannah pointed at his hurt foot. "When? Where?"

He motioned toward the corner. "Guess."

Hannah turned to see what he was pointing at and spotted a pair of crutches. "There's no time for games, Matthew. We need to talk." She grabbed the crutches and handed them to him.

"Aw, come on, Hannah." He paused, gripping the handles of the crutches and studying her. "Okay, short version. But you're ruinin' the fun." He clunked the props this way and that until he was finally headed in the right direction.

Hannah fell in behind Matthew as they maneuvered at a snail's pace through the house toward the storage room that had once been a small back porch. He angled his head, talking over his shoulder. "When I took Peter and David to school a week ago Monday, I saw smoke coming out of the windows and doors. The teacher was in a fit, tryin' to douse the fire she'd started in the wood stove to warm the room before any of the kids arrived. As soon as I saw the smoke, I remembered that some of the older boys had joked about stuffing the top of the chimney. So I dashed in to help, telling her that putting the fire out had only made more smoke. Then I told her the flue was probably stuffed. Using a ladder I climbed to the lowest branch of the red maple beside the school, and I managed to get the cloth out of the flue. But on the way back down the tree, I fell."

They stepped through the narrow entryway into the storage room. It was lined from ceiling to floor with shelves filled with various sizes of jars filled with honey.

"I stayed at the school while the teacher went to the Bylers' and got someone to substitute for her. She took me to the doc's, then brought me here and made me lunch."

"Really?" Hannah said, impressed with the personal attention this woman had shown. "Who is the teacher this year?"

Matthew shuffled around on his wooden supports until he was facing her. His eyes beamed. "The girl I told ya about. I told her this injury totally messed with my plan of going to the singing that next Sunday. She agreed to come get me if I didn't make her be the chauffeur and then invite some other girl to join us. Of course I agreed to that. So she came by and picked me up." Matthew laughed. "We had the most wonderful time you can imagine. We made the same arrangement for the next singing."

Hannah was so excited for him her skin tingled. "That's the best news I've heard in forever. I'm really happy for you, Matthew. But..." She closed the glass-and-wood door to the main house. "Matthew, we need to talk."

His smile faded slightly. *"Was iss es?"*

"Sarah saw us on the midnight ride."

Matthew chortled. "Ya take things too seriously, Hannah. The bishop won't eat ya, only admonish us for our own good. We did nothin' wrong during the world's shortest buggy ride."

Shaking her head, Hannah grabbed a plastic grocery bag from the shelf. *"Du muscht verschteh."*

Using his arms to balance his weight on the crutches, Matthew lifted both feet off the floor, showing off his stability. "Then explain it to me and maybe I'll understand."

Hannah took a large jar of honey off the shelf and put it in the bag. "She says we were gone a really long time."

He shrugged. "So, who cares?"

"Matthew, the bishop already thinks right poorly of me. My father doesn't know what to think of his eldest daughter lately. Luke blames me for his and Mary's accident."

Putting his uninjured foot on the ground, Matthew's brows scrunched. "That's not fair."

"Ach, it's ridiculous." The words came out bitter as resentment stirred a little deeper within her, each swirl eroding a bit more her desire to do what was right. "Sarah doesn't know it was you driving the buggy that night. Please, for your sake, don't tell anyone."

Matthew squeezed the handles of his crutches. "I can help get this straight, Hannah. We can go to your father and the bishop together and tell them the truth."

"No, Matthew. There's more to the gossip than what I just said."

"More?"

"Quite a bit more." Hannah placed another jar of honey into the bag.

"Has Sarah been saying other stuff too?"

"I…I don't think so."

Matthew held out his hand for the bag. As she hooked the handle of the heavy bag over his hand, he toppled forward. He grabbed on to the freestanding unit of shelves. It tilted forward. The jars rattled. Matthew tried to steady it while getting his balance. One of the crutches plunked to the floor, and the other fell against the shelf. "Whoa." Matthew wobbled on one foot. "If we knock over *Mamm's* whole shelf of honey, we'll never have to worry about another rumor—or anything else—ever again."

Hannah slid her shoulder under his arm and reached around him to take the bag from his hand. "The weight of the bag in the very hand that's trying to set the shelves steady is pulling them forward."

"You'll have to wriggle the handle loose. It's pinned between my hand and the shelf. If I move it, the shelves will topple."

With her shoulder steadying Matthew's left side and her trying to loosen the bag from his right hand, Hannah wondered if they'd get out of this mess without the shelves falling on top of them—or at least the jars of honey. When the doorknob rattled, Hannah was hopeful someone had arrived to help. Glancing in that direction, Hannah saw a beautiful young woman through the window. Her expression went from expectant to crestfallen within a split second.

"Elle," Matthew whispered.

Hearing the desperation in Matthew's voice, Hannah knew this was the young woman he so hoped to share a future with.

*P*aul paced to Mr. Yoder's barn again, watching for signs of Hannah. He'd spent days getting this trip all lined up, hoping, at the very least, to pass Hannah the letter that was in his pocket.

Chapter 20

Come on, Hannah.

His grandmother was inside with Mrs. Yoder, visiting while Mary slept. It had taken him weeks to talk Gram into coming here; she probably wouldn't stay long.

He jammed his hands into his pockets and sighed. This wasn't the way it was supposed to go. Not after all the planning and scheming he'd done to get here today. If he and Hannah stood a chance of seeing each other on the eve of Thanksgiving, he had to get this letter to her today.

Surprisingly, Gram had readily agreed to his plan, which included her asking Hannah to come to work for her the day before Thanksgiving while he was off from school. He wrote Hannah the letter, telling her how important it was for her to get her parents' permission to accept Gram's invitation to work that day so they could spend some time together. Determined to put the letter in Hannah's hands personally, he'd told Gram they should visit the Yoders to check on Mary, never for a second anticipating that Hannah might not be there when he arrived.

When they knocked on the door where Mary was living during her recuperation, Mary's mother, Mrs. Yoder, greeted Katie Waddell warmly, and Gram introduced her grandson to her. Gram asked about Hannah, and Mrs. Yoder informed them that she was at Naomi Esh's place getting some honey.

Paul had excused himself and gone outside. He'd been pacing out here ever since. Rubbing the back of his neck, Paul's attention never left the horizon. His muscles tightened more with every minute that passed. He couldn't leave the letter with Mrs. Yoder or even Mary for that matter. If he did, it would probably cause quite an uproar.

He picked up a rock and threw it as far as he could. He'd missed his last class today and his work shift tonight to get this visit in, and now she wasn't here. He scanned the ridge, fairly sure he was looking at the property Mrs. Yoder had said was Esh land.

He strode in that direction. Maybe she'd be right across the hill, dawdling time away while Mary slept.

~∞~

Through the window, Hannah saw the dejected young woman turn to go. Matthew let go of Hannah.

"Elle." He lurched for the door and stumbled. The shelves started tipping forward again. Hannah grabbed the shelf, and Matthew grabbed her. Several empty jars crashed to the floor.

The noise caused Elle to turn back, a look of concern in her eyes. She entered the room and grasped Matthew under his arm. He wavered awkwardly on one foot, still trying to get upright and balanced. Hannah put her strength under his other arm. Between the two females, they soon had Matthew balanced.

Hannah kicked the crutches out of their way. "Let's get him to a chair in the kitchen." Elle nodded, and together they escorted Matthew down the hall.

Except for her traditional clothing, Elle didn't look like any Amish person Hannah had ever seen. She had strawberry blond hair, some of which was dangling about her face in spite of the traditional bun and

Kapp. Her skin was as smooth and white as rich cream. Hannah could certainly see why Matthew was smitten with her.

When they reached the kitchen, he sat down. Elle shifted an adjacent chair and motioned for him to place his hurt foot on it. Then she whisked out of the kitchen and toward the living room. Matthew moaned and laughed as he placed his foot on the chair, calling out to her as she moved about. "It seems I'm destined to fall each time you're near."

"Oh, so it's my fault you're clumsy," Elle shot over her shoulder as she walked into the living room. "Just like it was my fault the flue at school was stuffed."

Matthew shrugged, but the playful delight had returned to his eyes. "She hasn't decided if I'm guilty of the wood-stove incident or not."

Hannah's interest moved from Matthew back to Elle as the girl re-entered the kitchen, carrying a pillow. She was mesmerizing in an unusual way, with dainty features, long brown lashes in spite of her hair color, and pale freckles across the bridge of her nose. Elle looked briefly at Hannah. Her eyes were a color Hannah had never seen before. A light lavender mixed with blue. Absolutely stunning.

She'd never heard of an Amish woman named Elle, but the newer generation challenged the older one on all fronts, and names were just one area that people were stepping out in. Not every child's name was biblical anymore.

"Hannah Lapp, this is Elle Leggett."

Leggett? That wasn't an Amish last name, was it?

The girl held out her hand. As Hannah shook it, she noted this girl had an air of confidence that Hannah could only dream of.

Elle paused beside Matthew's chair, waiting for him to raise his foot so she could place the pillow under it.

Hannah turned the knob on the kerosene lamp in the middle of the kitchen table, making the room a bit brighter.

Elle gave the pillow that held Matthew's leg one last dusting with the palm of her hand. "I...I didn't mean to interrupt you." Her eyes flicked over Hannah. "I saw Matthew's mother heading for the barn. She said he was in the storage room and I should go on in. She didn't say he had company."

The concern that registered in Matthew's eyes was distressing, and Hannah knew he was beginning to see what she had tried to explain. Hannah's reputation was being tarnished by her own sister, and Matthew's newfound friendship with Elle could be ripped up by the roots before it had time to grow strong.

Elle held out her hand. "Hannah, it was nice to meet you. Samuel is awful proud of his oldest sister. He speaks of you often at school." She smiled. Elle's features held no malice or petty jealousy but plenty of disappointment. She nodded at Matthew and turned to leave.

"No." Matthew lightly smacked the table. "Don't go."

Elle looked from him to Hannah.

"Please stay." Hannah eased into a kitchen chair and shoved one out for Elle. "So, you teach in our district?"

Matthew rolled his eyes, playfully mocking Hannah. "She's been out of touch, bein' at the hospital with Luke and Mary for weeks and now chained to the Yoder place while Mary mends."

Inquisitiveness crossed Elle's features. "And you're here now because..."

Hannah stole a glance at Matthew. She liked this girl. Her direct but polite approach left no doubt what she wanted to know. "I...I sort of came for honey." Her cheeks burned. *Sort of?* She hadn't meant to word it like that, and now there was no backing up.

Matthew leaned forward. "Her real reason for coming here was to see me and talk. We're friends, Elle."

Elle eased into the chair Hannah had pushed her way.

Hannah noticed the same high spirits in Elle's eyes that Matthew had, but there was something else, something harder, more assertive.

Elle leaned forward in her chair. "If someone doesn't either clear the air or let me leave with my pride intact, you're going to need another trip to the doc's, Matthew Esh, and I'll not be accompanying you this time."

Matthew cocked his head. "There's no more between Hannah and me than there is between you and her brother Samuel."

Elle studied her.

Hannah searched her mind for something friendly to say. "I've never heard the name Elle among our people before. It's beautiful."

The girl stole a look at Matthew. "I was born in Pennsylvania, but I wasn't born Amish."

Trying to hide her surprise, Hannah stammered. "B-but you're Amish now? How is that possible?"

Elle leaned back in the chair a bit and let her hands rest in her lap. "When I was ten, my mother became very ill. Abigail Zook, my mother's best friend and a very loving Amish woman, began taking care of me. Not long after my mother died, my father left...and has never returned. To keep me out of the foster-care system, Abigail and her husband, Hezekiah, took me in while a search was made for any relatives I might have. None were found." Elle dispensed the information like memorized lines from a book rather than a past filled with heartache and hope. She possessed an inner strength that Hannah found inspiring.

Matthew's eyes were glued to Elle as he spoke to Hannah. "Abigail and Hezekiah have been married about fifteen years, but they were never blessed with children of their own. They only have Elle, and now she plans on joining our faith when the bishop says she can."

The looks that ran between Elle and Matthew left little doubt that she was as interested in him as he was in her.

Matthew had told her right. It was the strangest thing she'd ever heard tell of among the Amish. But Hannah couldn't let this go without making sure the girl had thought this through. "It's hard to live without electricity once you've had it."

Elle's eyes widened as she nodded in agreement. "No doubt. But Kiah—that's what I call Hezekiah—allows for bending a few rules." She pulled a cell phone out of her hidden pocket. "What he's not willing to bend rules on, I can live without."

Hannah stared at her. "How can you be so sure?"

Elle laughed. "Life is filled with sacrifices of one type or another. I've seen both sides of life, the fancy way and the plain way. I choose plain. Not because it will save me, because it won't. Just because it's where my life is, with Kiah and Abigail. When I have kids, I'd like Abigail to get to hold my babies and know they're her grandchildren, although she'll still be young enough to have a baby of her own if she could have children."

Hannah gave a slight nod, as if she understood the deep connection Elle felt to Abigail and Hezekiah. But she wasn't sure she did.

Matthew ran the palms of his hands across the tabletop. "She drives a horse and buggy around the district to make visits to her students' homes and such, but because she lives so far from here, she leaves the horse and buggy at the Bylers', and a driver takes her home."

Elle laughed. "More like the horse and buggy drives me. Can't say I've gotten the hang of making the horse do my bidding."

"I think the Bylers need to own a better-trained horse. I got one I'm working with that'll be up for sale in a few weeks if they're interested." Matthew leaned forward, catching a glimpse of the clock. "Ya better go or the driver will leave, and you'll be sleeping at the Bylers' for the night."

Elle stood. "Yeah, I'd better go. Hannah, it was nice to meet you. Samuel will like that I finally met you."

"I'm glad we had this snippet of time, Elle." Hannah rose. "I need to get the honey and go too. But I'll clean up the mess in the storage room first." She grabbed the broom and dustpan and walked out of the kitchen, giving Matthew and Elle a moment alone.

As she picked up the fallen crutches, Hannah heard thunder rumble softly in the distance. She leaned the crutches against the shelf. Sweeping the broken glass into the pan, she dreaded walking home. She hadn't been on a walk alone since her attack, except from the house to the barn. Her palms were sweaty with the thought.

After putting the broom and dustpan in a corner, she grabbed the bag containing the jars of honey. The heavy jars could be used as a weapon if need be.

When she stepped onto the porch, Elle was in her gig, pulling out of the driveway.

Naomi came across the yard, leading a horse-drawn cart. "Someone needs to take Hannah home before the rains get here. Since you're useless around the house these days, I chose you."

Relief as well as humor washing over her, Hannah laughed.

Matthew growled playfully. "Thanks, *Mamm*." He made his slow descent down the porch stairs.

With a smile plastered on her face, Naomi motioned to the small rig. "I hitched the pony cart up for you so you can easily climb in and out of this low-to-the-ground thing." She winked at Hannah. "Now, go, Son. And if the rains catch you, stay at John Yoder's for the night."

"Gosh, *Mamm*, are you trying to get rid of me?"

Naomi chortled and turned to go inside.

Grateful for an escort, Hannah climbed into the weathered wooden rig. After settling on the bench, Matthew laid his crutches between him and Hannah. He took the reins and slapped them against the horse's back. Hannah set the bag of honey in the seat, feeling nervous about being gone so long.

The pony trotted across the top of the ridge and into the Yoders' barn-yard before Matthew brought the rig to a stop. "I'm glad you got to meet Elle."

Hannah climbed out of the cart. "Me too. But remember what I said about that midnight ride. Just don't tell anyone it was you, and your rela-tionship with Elle won't feel any strain from the rumors."

Matthew shrugged as he scanned the yards. "Looks like Mary had more *Englischers* come visit."

Paul was backing Gram's car out of the driveway.

Hannah's heart jerked inside her chest.

*P*aul pulled onto the paved road, disappointment so thick he couldn't think. Maybe it would be better if Gram drove, since he was almost blind with disappointment. All his weeks of planning ruined, and because he hadn't seen her today, he probably wouldn't have the chance to see her over Thanksgiving either. He doubted he could change his dad's mind about leaving the state for the Christmas holidays. After disappointing his father with how little he'd been home over the past few years, he couldn't refuse his father's gift of a family vacation at the beach. Besides being rude, it would cause a rift between them, and he needed his father on his side during the lengthy spell to win the approval of Hannah's family.

Paul sighed. He didn't know when he'd been more aggravated. Now he might not see Hannah until May. Would she continue to wait for him through all these unforeseen obstacles? Another angry sigh escaped his lips. May was too far away. Something had to be done.

He glanced at his grandmother. "Gram, you've got to help me get a letter to Hannah."

Gram's soft wrinkles seemed to droop more than normal these days. He figured she was missing Hannah as much as he was. Hannah was one of the few people who managed to ignore his grandmother's curtness and stubbornness. Gram could hire laborers left and right, but she couldn't pay someone to truly care. Hannah always cared.

Gram harrumphed. "I can't, Paul. I came here today. That will have to be enough."

He squeezed the steering wheel. "Please, Gram. Surely you can pass her one letter."

She shook her head. "I promised…" Gram dropped her sentence, squirming uncomfortably against the bucket seat.

Paul stopped the car, not caring that he was in the middle of the road. "Go on."

The lines on Gram's face stiffened. "You two will be fine…if you're supposed to be. That's all there is to it."

"Who did you promise that you wouldn't pass letters to Hannah?" Paul stage-whispered the words in an effort to remain gentle and respectful with his grandmother. There were only a few people who would ask for a promise like this from his grandmother: Hannah's father, her mother, or one of her older brothers. Paul decided to go with the most likely person. "Did her father come to see you?"

Gram didn't move a muscle. "She is his daughter, Paul. And whether you believe this or not, he has more rights over Hannah's life than you."

A deep disappointment stabbed him in the center of his chest. Mr. Lapp wasn't supposed to know, not yet. Not until Hannah was legally an adult so she couldn't get into too much trouble with her father. "What did he say?"

The sternness on her face softened as her eyes glistened with tears. Paul realized he'd been putting her in a tug of war for months by wanting one thing from her while Hannah's father demanded another.

She pulled a handkerchief out of her purse and dabbed at her eyes. "It came to his attention that Hannah had been waiting on letters to come to my house for her. Her father suspects there's an *Englischer* or Mennonite working for me who is tempting his daughter away from where God has placed her. He didn't ask for specific information, and I offered none. I did, however, agree not to allow any more letters." She shoved the hanky back into her purse. "Paul, I'm sorry, but the man has good points. She's his daughter, and by English laws she's a minor." She clapped her hands and motioned for Paul to get the car moving.

He eased his foot onto the gas pedal, driving without noticing much of anything. "How did he learn of the letters?"

"I think Sarah told him."

So even her sister was against him and Hannah being together. The magnitude of all that was against them settled heavily onto his shoulders.

Gram rubbed her forehead. "When Hannah got sick right after you left, Sarah started coming in her stead. She asked me if I had any letters for Hannah. My guess is that Hannah must have asked her to pick up anything that came to me for her."

Coming to a stop sign, Paul brought the car to a halt. "So her father is going behind her back to end things. This isn't good. I wanted a chance to earn his respect."

Gram glowered at him. "Kinda hard to earn respect when you're sneaking around behind the man's back."

Paul accelerated too quickly, causing the tires to squeal. "I don't know what else to do, Gram. Let her go when that's not what either of us wants? I mean, if God's Word said something against two people who love Him falling in love, then I'd back off."

~~∿§~~

Hannah stood by the side of the road, watching Gram's car disappear around a curve. She was so tired of life not being fair that she could crawl in a hole and stay there. She waited, hoping Paul would spot her in the rearview mirror. But as the car disappeared around a bend, her heart sank. She turned and trudged back up the driveway.

She heard a horse exhale and looked up. Matthew had ridden from the barnyard and down the driveway.

He stood beside the buggy, holding up the sack containing the honey jars. "You forgot the honey."

She reached for the bag. "Thanks." Holding the honey against her chest, she faced into the wind and took a deep breath, trying desperately to get a hold on her emotions.

Matthew motioned toward the paved road. "I take it whoever was in that car is the reason you don't mess with singings."

Hannah closed her eyes, weary of secrets, half truths, and slinking through life as if she was a sinner. Even Matthew didn't understand. She saw it in his eyes. In spite of Elle's background, he didn't understand that all she wanted was a life with Paul. That's all.

The wind thrashed against her cheeks as thunder rumbled and a streak of lightning shot across the sky. She wished it were possible for the wind to snatch her up and land her in a place where life wasn't a constant choosing of sides.

"You'd better go on in, Matthew. The rains will be here before you get to the edge of the field." Hannah took the pony by the harness. "Go on in. I'll put the rig in the barn and the pony in a stall. When the storm blows over, you can go home."

Matthew surveyed the skies while grabbing his crutches and getting out of the wagon.

Before he could say another word, Hannah led the pony into the barn. As she unhitched the animal from the carriage, a delicious new thought danced into her mind. Maybe, just maybe she could use the Yoders' phone to call Paul. She had no idea why she hadn't thought of it before. Maybe because using the phone for the first time earlier today had made her realize how easy it was to place a call. Excitement pulsed through her.

As she put the pony in a stall, another round of thunder clapped, vibrating the air around her. The fast-paced clops of a horse heading in her direction made her quickly fasten the stall gate and rush to the door of the barn.

Luke.

Looking pale with worry, he came to a halt just outside the barn and slid off the horse. Holding the reins, he sprinted into the shelter. "How is Mary?"

"Still asleep as far as I know." *Becky would be calling for me if she weren't.*

He thrust the reins toward her. "Edna said she had some sort of spell today."

"A tiny one." Hannah took the leather straps, knowing he intended for her to walk the horse until it was cool and to rub the sweat-soaked creature down. "We just need to make sure she has less excitement and no hint of discord with anyone." She patted the horse's neck, feeling the sweat on the beast. "She's never been one to cope well with gossip, and a quilting is not the place for her right now."

Between his concern for Mary and the brewing storm, Hannah knew her brother would be staying the night. With Luke there, hopes of sneaking out long enough to call Paul faded. She grabbed a sackcloth and started drying the horse's neck.

Luke struck a match and lit a kerosene lamp. "That's why she didn't want to come to the farm without you the night of the accident; she was afraid it'd stir unfounded gossip about us."

"She didn't want to be the target of speculation where you were concerned." She hung the damp sack on the rail and grabbed a dry one.

"Ach," he growled. "So it's my fault?"

"That's not what I was trying to say. Luke, I…I'm sorry I didn't go with you that night. Really I am." Hannah could only take his word for how her decision to stay home had resulted in their accident.

"Bein' sorry doesn't fix a thing, now does it? She's your best friend, Hannah. You knew how she felt about being seen with me on our property without you there to make it look like friends spending time together. You knew!" Luke turned his back on her and dashed for the house.

Large drops of rain pelted the tin roof. Hannah swiped the cloth over the other side of the horse. Luke's words could only hurt her so deep this time. His resentment against her was ridiculous. He had told Mary he forgave the man driving the car that hit them. So why couldn't Luke forgive his own sister? She was fast becoming weary of her brother. He was too much like her father—pleasant to those he agreed with, angry and demanding with those he didn't.

Longing to talk to someone who truly knew her welled in her heart. She had to call Paul, regardless of Luke's presence. Maybe now was the best time, while they thought she was tending to the animals. Hannah hurried to finish this chore so she could steal around the back way to the phone. If only she could hear his voice, she could endure until Christmas.

As she tossed feed into a trough, she noticed John Yoder's horse penned up for the night. The men and boys of the Yoder family must have returned from their hunt and from school while she was at the Esh place. Her stomach growled. It was past time for supper, and she hadn't had lunch.

She turned off the kerosene lamp and shut the barn door behind her. Standing under the eaves of the barn, she plotted the best route to the phone without anyone seeing her. Having settled on a course that went behind trees and bushes, she took off running.

Shaking from apprehension as well as the cold rain, Hannah yanked open the shanty door. She dialed 411 and asked for the phone number of Edgar Waddell, Gram's late husband. Using the paper and pen that lay beside the phone, Hannah soon had the number in hand. There was no way to deny that there were things about the modern world she liked. Feeling triumphant for the first time in forever, she dialed Gram's number.

When the phone was picked up quickly, she was sure it would be Paul.

"Hello," Gram said.

It was good to hear the woman's voice. "Hi, Gram. This is Hannah. The Yoders got a phone shanty, and...is...is Paul there?"

"No, dear. I guess Becky told you we came by her place, but he left as soon as he dropped me off. How are you feeling these days?"

Groping to find her voice, Hannah murmured a few niceties in order to answer her and hung up the phone.

She leaned her head against a wall of the tiny booth, aching to hear Paul's voice.

Between her miserable sorrow and the wet clothes that clung to her, Hannah shivered hard. She closed the shanty door behind her and headed around the back side of the house. The downpour had ceased, leaving only a light mist.

Her body ached from the day's events, and the hopelessness in her heart only added to her discomforts. As the wet clothes clung to her physical body, the aches and pains of the past few months clung to her soul, dragging her into ever-deeper waters.

She heard an automobile rumble on the paved road some twenty feet away. Hannah scurried into the shadows. A horn gave a short toot, and lights flashed. She turned. Through the misting night, she saw an old, midnight blue truck. The door opened, and Paul jumped out. He hustled toward her as if he'd caught a glimpse of her before she had retreated to the shadows. The sight of him in blue jeans and a button-down shirt running toward her was almost more than her knees could take. She ran down the hill and threw her arms around his neck. His strong grip lifted her off the ground and held her.

He nuzzled against her neck, even planting a kiss on her cold, damp skin. Her arms tightened. *Oh, please, tell me I'm not dreaming.*

He set her feet on the ground. His hands moved to her face, cradling it. She gazed at him intently, expecting him to speak. Slowly a smile eased his tense features, and she heard him draw a heavy breath. He lowered his face until his lips touched hers. Warmth and power swept through her. She had no idea a kiss felt like this. Desperate to bury all the pain her family had heaped on her, she reveled in the magnitude of Paul's touch. She kissed him, not wanting to ever stop.

Astonishment jolted her, and she pulled him closer, running her hand over the back of his head. His soft, warm, gentle lips moved over hers, and she returned the favor, until Hannah thought they might both take flight right then and there. Finally desperate for air, they parted.

Paul rested his hand on his chest. "Wow." He gulped in air. "I needed that so badly." His eyes bored into her. He smiled. "Hi."

Hannah bit her bottom lip, too thrilled and embarrassed to maintain eye contact. "I called Gram's. She said you were gone."

He reached into his back pocket. "I couldn't leave without trying one last time to get this to you." He passed her a letter. "It explains all sorts of things. I...I'm sorry, but I can't be here for Christmas. But I'll be at Gram's the day before Thanksgiving. It'd be our only time until this spring. Please tell me you can get away."

She took the letter from his hand, then tucked it inside the bib of her apron. She reached for Paul's hand. "I'll find a way."

His lips met hers again and again, and she finally understood the desire of a woman to yield herself to the marriage bed.

"I miss you so badly, Hannah. You can't imagine." He whispered the words as he kissed down her neck.

"Hannah?" a deep voice called through the low rumble of thunder.

Hannah jumped, turning her head toward the sound of Matthew's voice. She didn't see him, which probably meant he hadn't seen her. She cuddled against Paul's chest for a moment, then took a step back. "That's Matthew," she whispered. "Mary must be asking for me. I have to go."

Frustration seemed to pass through Paul's eyes.

"Hannah!" Matthew called again.

"Go," Paul whispered, nudging his head toward the *Daadi Haus*. "I love you."

"Always and forever, Paul," Hannah whispered. "Always and forever." She tilted her chin slightly as strength returned to her. Biting her bottom lip, she winked before trudging up the soggy hill.

~∽℘~

Paul climbed into the truck, damp but ecstatic. His heart thumped against his chest. All he wanted to do was close his eyes and enjoy the exhilaration of what had just taken place. He ran his thumb over his lips.

Wow.

That encounter was not something he would have ever dreamed possible, unless he was dreaming of their wedding night. But even then, he hadn't considered that kind of uninhibited passion from Hannah.

Refusing to pass in front of the Yoder house, he cranked the truck and put it in reverse. Finally all his weeks of planning had meant something. Just about the time he was ready to explode in frustration, the most amazing encounter of his life occurred. Paul drew in a deep breath, determined to remember those few moments anytime discouragement tried to eat away at his confidence in their future. Reveling in the incident, he backed the truck onto a road to his left, then pulled forward.

Whenever he'd thought about seeing Hannah over the Thanksgiving weekend, he'd hoped to at least get a kiss on the cheek, maybe even a brush of their lips. But what had just taken place— That reunion was a million times better than the teary, discombobulating scene at the hospital. Funny, he'd gone to the hospital expecting a warm welcome only to find her an overstressed, teary-eyed mess. Earlier today he'd looked forward to slipping her the letter and gazing into her eyes from across the room. He'd been bitterly disappointed then too. But tonight he'd come by simply hoping to find a way to pass her his note or get a glimpse of her through a window. What he got was far, far more than he'd known to hope for.

Life—it's strange.

Now, if Hannah could manage to come to Gram's next week, they could have all day together before they were separated until his spring break or maybe until he graduated.

Paul mulled over the situation with Hannah's father. No parent liked the idea of his child, especially his daughter, choosing something aside from what the father had in mind. But surely Mr. Lapp could adjust.

H annah stuck her sewing needle in the small tomato cushion and shook her hands, trying to get the blood flowing again. Laying Samuel's shirt on the finished pile, she mused over all the work she'd gotten done for her family while living at Mary's grandmother's place. She had worked extra hard since Paul had made his brief appearance. She'd baked goods and sent them home with Luke. He in turn had brought her mounds of mending, and she'd worked on it every spare moment. Getting up well before dawn, she'd done everything the Yoders needed before they needed it, determined to earn the right to go to Mrs. Waddell's for the eve of Thanksgiving.

Today was the day to ask permission to go. Her parents, with all the children in tow, were coming here to Mary's house after church.

With only the aid of a quad cane, Mary trekked into the room. Her gait was slow and a bit unsteady. Her eyes narrowed as she pointed to the sewing basket and stack of clothes. "On a Sunday?"

Hannah felt little remorse. "With everyone at church but us, it was a good time to get this done. My feet were propped up, and I was stress free."

Mary chuckled. "You, relaxed? Are you capable of taking things easy?"

The sounds of buggies and voices signaled that the families had arrived home from church. Hannah grabbed her scissors and pincushion and stuffed them into the sewing basket. She stacked the mended clothes on top and dashed for the bedroom, where she hid the evidence in a corner.

When her parents entered Annie Yoder's home, they told her that Sarah had ridden home from church with Edna. She was the only Lapp who hadn't come to Mary's today. At least the girl was showing some good sense. Unless she intended to apologize and take back the gossip she was spreading, Hannah knew Mary did not want anything to do with her.

After lunch had been eaten and the table cleared, Hannah found herself alone in the kitchen with her parents. This rare moment of solitude was the opportunity she'd been hoping for. *Daed* was lingering over a cup of coffee, *Mamm* watching him. The rest of the clan were playing board games in the living room. Hannah slid the last of the dishes into the warm, sudsy water, knowing her father wouldn't want her washing them until after sundown.

When she turned around, her parents had their heads together whispering back and forth. She wondered if they were discussing Aunt Zabeth. Maybe they thought Hannah was old enough to hear about the aunt she'd discovered months ago.

Their conversation stopped when they saw she was looking at them. They each gave a slight shake of the head, assuring her she was to ask no questions. Just as well. She had her own things she needed to talk about.

She dried her hands on a towel and drew a deep breath. "*Mamm, Daed,* I was wondering… See, I always help Mrs. Waddell cook before Thanksgiving. She packs everything in coolers and goes to her son's house in Maryland early Thanksgiving Day." She held her breath, waiting for their reaction. Hannah's explanation of Mrs. Waddell's Thanksgiving tradition wasn't the complete truth, but it was close enough. If they knew that for the past two Thanksgivings, Paul had worked beside her and then had driven his grandmother to his home in Maryland for the rest of the Thanksgiving weekend, they wouldn't consider this request.

A look of triumph and surprise crossed their eyes, giving Hannah the uneasy feeling that she'd just walked into a trap. Her mother gave a slight nod to her father. He turned the coffee cup in his hand, squeezing it firmly. "If…if you'll do something for your mother first, we'll allow it."

She moved to a chair. "*Was iss es?*"

Daed pushed the cup away from him. "We want you to come by the house on your way to Mrs. Waddell's." His eyes moved to his wife's. Uneasy looks in her parents' eyes replaced the victorious expressions of moments earlier.

"Okay." The word came out long and slow. "But why?"

Her father shrugged, his eyes focused on the table. "Could you do as we've asked without pestering us with questions?"

Hannah looked to her mother, who was staring a hole in the center of the table. What did they want? Whatever it was, they didn't desire to discuss it here with family and friends in the other room. By their responses, it was something they knew she would be against. Most likely they had heard about the rift between her and Sarah and intended to force her to put an end to it.

But it didn't really matter what their plan was. They were her parents, and she'd end up complying no matter what they wanted; otherwise, she wouldn't get a day at Gram's with Paul.

Samuel ran into the room with Mary's seven-year-old brother, Robert, hot on his trail. Nine-year-old Jesse followed, teasing them both by dangling a spit-up towel from their oldest brother's infant. The volume in the room grew by the moment.

Hannah rose from her chair, her parents watching her every move. The uneasiness of their request sat hard on her lungs. But no matter what they had in mind for her, no price was too high to pay to see Paul again.

Hannah's eyes bolted open. She tossed the covers back and jumped out of bed. Today she'd see Paul. Scurrying through the dark, cold room, she got ready for the day as quietly as possible. Leaving Mary asleep, Hannah slipped out the front door and headed for the barn.

The day before Thanksgiving dawned cold and cloudy. By the time the skies gave way to dreary light, Hannah had hitched John Yoder's horse to a buggy. After a quick stop at home, she would finally be on her way to Mrs. Waddell's. With her treasured anatomy book beside her so she could show it to Paul, she gave a light slap of the reins against the horse.

Before she'd even left the Yoders' barn, she spotted Matthew Esh rounding up stray cows. When she hollered, asking him what was going on, he said one of his brothers had left the gate open. Loose cows were a hazard for motorists. Hannah unhitched the buggy. She put the horse in its stall and then helped chase the roaming cows back toward Esh land.

Soon Mary's father, four of her brothers, and Matthew's two brothers joined them, and they managed to get the daft cows back where they belonged. After she and Matthew rounded up the last two cows, they stopped by his house for a drink. Matthew apologized for interrupting her morning, then he heated bricks for her feet while he hitched his warmest buggy to a horse for her. When she said she needed her book from the other buggy, he sent Peter to get it.

By the time Peter returned, Hannah was flustered at how much time had passed. But neither the late start nor the overcast sky could cool Hannah's spirits. She slapped the reins against the horse's back, spurring it to go faster. Though still unaware of what her parents wanted, Hannah was determined to do their bidding quickly—even if she had to apologize to Sarah for things that weren't her fault.

The horse's pace was entirely too slow for Hannah. She laid her hand on the cover of the anatomy book on the seat beside her, looking forward to studying it with Paul throughout the day as time allowed. She understood so much more now than last summer, when he had taught her a few things through his textbooks.

As Hannah neared her house, she was surprised to see her mother standing by the side of the road. She pulled the buggy to a stop and opened the carriage door. "A bit cold to be out here, no?"

Mamm patted something inside the bib of her apron and walked around to the passenger's side of the buggy without saying a word. Choosing not to give her mother any cause to begin a debate, Hannah slid the book under the seat of the carriage.

Mamm climbed in and wrapped her shawl more tightly around herself. "I need to ask you a question."

Hannah clicked her tongue, and the horse trudged forward. *"Was?"*

"Something's been weighing on my mind. I dreamed about it last week, and, well, Hannah, have you had a woman's time since the incident?"

Hannah's throat constricted. She didn't want to think about this, not ever, but especially not today. She shook her head. "But Mary hasn't had one since her accident. Dr. Greenfield said trauma can do that to a female."

Reaching into her bib, *Mamm* pulled out a small, rectangular-shaped box. "Follow the instructions on the back of the box."

"What is that?"

She drew a deep breath. "It's a pregnancy test."

Hannah's eyes blurred with tears as she pulled into the driveway. *"Mamm,* no. I'm not…I'm not."

"It's been three months, child. It's time to find out."

Feeling alarm at the very idea, Hannah said nothing.

Daed stepped out of the house, looking troubled. He walked to the buggy and opened Hannah's door. They had her cornered. She had to comply in order to see Paul today, but if the test was positive, she couldn't face him. No wonder their eyes had lit up at her request to go to Gram's. It meant she wouldn't argue about taking the test.

Powerlessness churned in her. Even if the test came back positive, she couldn't break her word to Gram and not show up for the workday. Her parents had to be banking on that.

Hannah folded her arms over her waist, rebellion rearing its ugly head. She wanted to rail against them, make them admit how calculating they were being.

"This is ridiculous," Hannah spat, not caring that she was talking back. But the frightening thing was, their request wasn't ridiculous at all. As much as she wanted to deny that she might be expecting, her body was changing in ways she'd never experienced. Her chin tilted upward, and her shoulders stiffened.

Mamm held the box toward her. "Take it."

Hannah obeyed. "I'm not pregnant."

Her father held the door open and motioned for Hannah to exit the carriage. "Come on. Let's go for a walk." His voice was the gentle, loving one she remembered from childhood.

Holding the rectangular box in her hand, Hannah followed him up the hill to the same bench they'd gone to after her attack. The same angry and confused feelings washed over her. *Daed* sat on the bench and patted the spot beside him. She sat. He took her hand. "Hannah, you're my daughter. No matter what comes, I'll take care of you."

Oh, God, I don't want to be pregnant. Please.

She chafed at the prayer. Either she was pregnant or she wasn't. Moaning to God wasn't going to change that. Neither would ignoring the possibility. But she didn't want to know, not today. Not on her last day with Paul until spring.

She blinked, trying to clear her vision and read the instructions on the home pregnancy test. "I'll do it," she said through gritted teeth. "But I'm not staying to read the outcome."

Pulling back on the reins, Hannah made the horse move at a snail's pace, biding her time so she could control her trembling. When Gram's farm came into view, Hannah spotted Paul's truck parked in the driveway.

She tugged at the right rein, pulling in behind it. Paul stepped outside before he could possibly have heard the buggy. He waved. His face beamed.

Inside her, a roar of determination exploded. She wasn't going to sink into a heap, not today. When she returned home, she was certain she would discover that the test proved she wasn't pregnant.

As she pulled the buggy closer to the barn, Paul fell in step beside it. Once inside, she pulled the reins and yanked the brake. Paul opened the buggy door and held out his hand. "I was getting worried that you couldn't get away."

She grabbed the book from under the seat and took his hand. "The Eshes' cows got out."

As soon as her feet landed on the ground, Paul engulfed her in a hug. "You're shaking." He released her, compassion in his eyes. "Go in and warm up. I'll tend to the horse. Maybe we'll get some time to talk alone if Gram takes a nap."

Hannah angled the book toward him. "A doctor at the hospital gave me this. I can't wait to show it to you."

Paul chuckled. "You and your love of science books."

She looked through the open barn door, studying the gray sky. "The air smells of snow, no?"

Paul loosened the leads on the horse from the buggy. "Hard to believe it'd snow this early in the season, but there's a chance of it today." He motioned toward the house. "Go on."

In spite of wanting to get out of the cold and into a warm house as quickly as possible, Hannah had no energy for hurrying across the yard.

She opened the back door to let herself in as she always did. Gram stood at the kitchen stove, stirring a pot of something. From the many wonderful aromas, Hannah could tell Gram had already begun cooking for tomorrow's feast.

"Hannah." Gram tapped the wooden spoon on the side of the pan, freeing it of dripping oatmeal before laying it on a small plate.

Hannah laid the anatomy book on the oak table, crossed the kitchen, and wrapped Gram in a hug. Hannah's arms hadn't felt this full in a long time. She'd missed Gram so badly—not as much as she'd missed Paul, but the emptiness had been painful.

Paul had always been so tied into Hannah's feelings about coming to Gram's that Hannah hadn't realized how much she loved this woman. Even in the long winters, when Paul couldn't visit very often, Hannah came to Gram's with the expectation of receiving and passing letters. But now, as she and Gram stood locked in an embrace that erased months of separation, Hannah realized her love for Gram stood on its own, regardless of Paul.

"You shake like a leaf, my girl." Gram released her. "Paul has built you a roaring fire, and I have fresh coffee."

Hannah turned toward the large stone fireplace. "No coffee for me, Gram, but thanks." The living room glowed in shifting amber and tawny colors from the reflection of dancing flames, dispelling the shadowy fears that made her shake. She loved a blazing fire in an open hearth. It warmed a home in so many more ways than a gas furnace, kerosene heater, or wood stove. Walking toward the dancing blaze, she remembered years of work, games, and bonding with Paul and Gram that had taken place in this very room.

Soon they'd begin a life together, and nothing would separate them. Perhaps after she and Paul married, they could build a small home right on this property. That way she could always be here for Gram.

Hearing a board creak, she turned. Her breath caught in her throat.

Paul.

With his shoulder against the doorframe, he smiled, looking relaxed and confident. She didn't know how long he'd been standing there while she reminisced over their past and dreamed of their future. As they stood across the room staring at each other, dreams of their future grew within her. A warm home, children, aromas of upcoming feasts, and love so strong it could give a backbone to a jellyfish—that was their future.

He held a steaming mug toward her. "Gram said you're not drinking coffee this morning."

"Dr. Greenfield, the man who gave me the book I brought, said I'm too young to be drinking coffee."

"Oh." Paul shrugged, taking a sip of the steaming drink. "I think if he knew how hard you always work and how good a cup of coffee is on cold mornings, he'd change his tune." He rubbed his chin. "There were bricks in the floorboard of the buggy. Am I missing something?"

Hannah untied her winter coat and slipped it off. "I thought you had Old Order Mennonite in your blood. How can ya not know what warming bricks are?" As she waltzed into the kitchen, Hannah playfully pushed against his shoulder.

Gram pulled a few green apples from the cupboard. "She's got a point, Paul."

Paul shook his head. "Any Old Order Mennonite in my blood is so far up the line it would take a genealogist to find the connection."

"The bricks hold heat and help keep the feet warm. Matthew put the bricks in the buggy when he hitched the horse for me." Hannah set a kettle of water on the stove. "Gram, you got a list of what all we're cooking today?"

Gram pulled a long, thin piece of paper from her apron pocket.

"Matthew?" Paul grumbled. "How come he fits into every conversation lately?"

Hannah took the list and read over it. "I didn't realize he had. Gram, is this a three or a five beside the butternut squash pies?"

Gram set a sack of flour on the table. "Five. Hazel, Paul's mom, is having extra family in for Thanksgiving. And the Millers too." Gram turned to stir a pot of broth on the stove. "I'm sure Paul's told you about the Millers. He and Dorcas are pretty close."

Hannah looked to Paul, and he rolled his eyes. "The Millers are close with my parents. Dorcas is one of their daughters."

The odd fluttery feeling around Hannah's heart returned but something else too. A burning sensation like resentment rose. It wasn't that he was friends with some girl that bothered her. What irked her was the realization that she never got to see him in his day-to-day life—while Dorcas did.

*P*aul flipped through the pages of the anatomy book Hannah had brought, not noticing much of anything but the long list of phone numbers the doctor had written on the inside cover. It seemed a bit odd, but the doctor must have figured the book was the best place to write numbers that Hannah would need if she ever had to make a call on Mary's behalf. He heard Hannah creeping down the steps. He closed the book. If his grandmother took that nap she'd agreed to, he and Hannah would have a couple of hours to themselves. Hannah tiptoed into the kitchen.

Paul stood. "Is she sleeping?"

Hannah moved to the stove to check on a pecan pie. "Close. She wanted to hear all about Luke and Mary's accident and recuperation. We talked for a long time before she felt sleepy."

He passed her a set of potholders. "Hannah, about Gram's remark. Dorcas is a friend of the family because her mother and my mother are best friends. End of story."

Placing the pie onto the cooling tray, Hannah's brown eyes gazed deeply into his. "I never thought otherwise. The girls at your campus have made me a bit jittery over the years but"—she grabbed cold cuts out of the refrigerator—"that's to be expected, I suppose." She opened a loaf of bread and began making two sandwiches.

Paul opened the game cabinet and pulled out Scrabble. He loved playing board games with her more than anything else…except the kisses they'd shared a week ago. That was amazing, and he wouldn't mind a repeat performance. But during games they talked about bits and pieces of everything until their connection was tighter than before and the bond between them had a sweetness that he craved when they weren't together.

He hated to admit it, but his need for long conversations was stronger than Hannah's. From what he understood, the desire for long, open talks didn't fit the household Hannah had been brought up in. Whether because of her upbringing or not, Hannah had a quiet restraint that buried life's events rather than shared them. Each time they got together, he had to patiently draw her out until she was sharing all the goings-on in her life and thoughts. An afternoon of talking heart to heart with her strengthened him for months.

She passed him a plate with a sandwich and a bowl of sliced bananas and strawberries. She set a can of pressurized whipped cream on the kitchen table near the Scrabble board. He squirted some fluffy cream onto his fruit. While lining up two letters, he briefly wondered if such a short word was allowed, but he decided it didn't matter since they played by their own rules anyway.

She frowned. "Yo?"

He took a bite of strawberries and whipped cream. After swallowing he answered, "It's a word." He leaned over to look at the numbers on the bottoms of the square wooden pieces. "Worth five points."

Her eyes danced with amusement. "Why, Paul Waddell. What's next? YoMama?"

Paul laughed. "That's not one word, and where did *you* hear such a saying?"

"At yohospital on yoTV." She looked at the seven letters he'd doled out to her. She sighed. "Are you rigging the game again?"

"Hannah," he chided.

She moved the letters around, frowning at them. "Yeah, I know, I know, you don't need to rig it to lose; you can lose all by yourself."

Paul burst into laughter. "I think you said that wrong."

Hannah cocked an eyebrow. "I think I said it perfectly right for the very first time, no?" She shook her head. "Now, let's see, H, E, E, A, E, A, P. What are the chances of me getting this many vowels on the first deal?"

"Obviously pretty good, or else you're just lucky."

She placed an A below the Y and her H after the A. "That's nine points, genius."

"That's not a word."

"*Yah.* It's a fine word."

He shook his head. "That's zero points for you, dear woman."

"You mean *liewe Fraa.*"

"Excuse me?"

" 'Dear woman' in Pennsylvania Dutch is *liewe Fraa.* Of course *Fraa* also means 'wife,' but…"

"Ah, so *yah* is a Pennsylvania Dutch word. But you pronounce it 'jah.' "

"If you'll cooperate, I'll start saying *yah.*"

"Oh, I see, my *liewe Fraa.*"

"*Ya, liewe Dummkopp Buhnesupp.*"

"Hey, I heard the word *dumb* in that phrase."

Hannah covered her mouth, laughter shining bright in her eyes. "It doesn't have to mean 'dumb.' It could mean 'blockhead' or 'dunce.' "

He tried to glare at her, but her eyes, holding such joy, made even mock anger impossible. "I have no idea why I think I can win at this game. So, what did the other word you said mean?"

"You mean *Buhnesupp?*"

"That'd be the one."

"Bean soup."

"So you called me your dear dumb bean soup?" He fought to keep a straight face while watching her laugh so hard she covered her face. He studied his letters, trying to think of something that might make her laugh even harder. He placed two O's after her *yah* word.

She frowned. "Yahoo?"

"It's a search engine, e-mail, chat room. Yahoo covers all sorts of things on the Internet."

She patted his hand condescendingly. "The Internet. Didn't we decide that's your make-believe friend that you say carries answers for research, mails letters with no paper, and can send pictures without film?"

He removed his hand from under hers and patted her hand in the same manner. "You're gonna have to trust me on this one."

"I know it's a word. I think you yelled it out into the evening sky about a week ago, no?"

He was surprised she brought up the kisses, even in a roundabout way. He was beginning to realize this girl had a lot of surprises in her.

Paul leaned forward. "I don't remember actually yelling...or even whispering it. But if you could oblige me again, I'll be glad to oblige you and shout *yahoo*."

Her cheeks turned a beautiful shade of pink. She lifted the pressurized can of whipped cream.

He chuckled. "First you threaten to pelt me with eggs and now with whipped cream. You may tease, but I know you won't follow—"

Cold whipped cream smacked him in the face. He gasped and reached across the table for her. She leaped up and ran out the back door. He grabbed the can and pursued her.

She bounded down the steps and across the side yard. When she turned, he saw surprise reflected on her face. "Snow!" She held her hands toward the skies as dainty white flakes drifted down.

"Whipped cream," Paul retorted. He took off after her.

She screamed and ran. He caught her around the waist from behind.

She laughed and squealed at the same time. Paul's heart thumped against his chest. They were made for each other. No doubt. "Apologize, Hannah."

She nodded. "Okay. Okay."

With her back against his chest, he lifted her off her feet and nuzzled her neck before planting a kiss.

"Paul, please." She squirmed against him.

He let her go, shook the can of whipped cream, and held the nozzle toward her. "Say it."

Her smile faded. She lowered her head while smoothing her skirts with the palms of her hands. Her demeanor was suddenly total meekness.

"Mock submissiveness is never a good thing, not for me." He grabbed her wrist.

Her face radiated innocence. "But I'm not mocking. I'm serious." She took a deep breath. *"Du kannscht net verschteh, Sitzschtupp Bobbeli."* She lifted her head, looking completely repentant.

Paul lowered the can, studying her. She meant her words, whatever they were. He passed her the can. "You win."

"Dankes." She curtsied.

"So, what did you say?"

She broke into laughter, squirted him with whipped cream, and took off running.

In less than ten seconds he grabbed her arm and stole the whipped cream. But he didn't dare squirt her. She didn't have a change of clothes here. "I can't believe I fell for that. You've become tricky since I left, no?" He used his best Amish accent.

She slipped on the snow and fell to her knees laughing.

He helped her stand, pulling her against him. "What did you say to me, Hannah Lapp?"

She gazed boldly into his eyes, once again surprising him. "I said, 'You can't understand, you living-room baby.'"

"You called me a living-room baby? And I thought you said, 'Forgive me.' No fair."

She smiled, a flame of desire shining in her eyes.

"Is that a common insult among the Amish?"

She grinned and raised one eyebrow up and down quickly. "I just made it up, because it fits."

Paul laughed. "Thanks."

He wrapped his arms around her, watching snow fall on her face. Slowly he bent and brushed her lips with a kiss. "You're incredible, Hannah. Every time I get to spend a smidgen of time with you, I'm reminded all over again how amazing you are." He coddled her face, gazing into her soul.

Her eyes grew distant. "I'd die without you, Paul."

He pulled her closer. "I feel the same way about you."

She ran her fingers behind his head, pulling his face to hers. Snow swirled around them as memories of this moment forged in his brain. They kissed until steam rose from their faces and formed a corona of vapor. This was the only woman for him. He'd never forget the joys of today—even when he was so sick of school he didn't think he could show up for class one more time.

They could make this work, whether they lived in Owl's Perch or Maryland. All they needed was each other and a chance. His lips moved over the cool skin of her cheeks, feeling the dampness from a few melted snowflakes.

Leaning back enough to look her in the eyes, Paul cradled a loose strand of wavy hair in his palm. "I didn't know your hair was this..."

She cocked an eyebrow. "*Uncontrollable* is the word you're searching for, and it's a hassle to keep confined."

Paul wound the soft curls around his finger. "Like the girl it belongs to?"

She shrugged, lowering her gaze, but not before Paul saw defiance spark in her eyes. She was an oxymoron in so many ways: yielding but defiant, caring but detached, belonging with him and yet…not. Sometimes, when the night was long and quiet, he worried that her undeniable beauty and deep naiveté would pull her into life with one of the young men in her community, leaving him empty ever after.

"Hannah." He released her hair and put his hands on her shoulders, looking her straight in the eye. "Be careful while I'm gone. There will be no end to the number of men wanting you." He ran his palms down her arms and clutched her hands. "Like this Matthew guy who keeps popping up everywhere you are."

She shook her head. "It's not like that with Matthew."

Paul squeezed her hands and forced a smile. He couldn't imagine any man not being drawn to her. "I trust your heart. That's not the problem. It's just…I'd go crazy if someone came between us. You need to be careful with the Matthews of your world. They hang around waiting for…" Paul drew her hands to his lips. By the look in her eyes, he could tell he was confusing her. "I don't want any part of you shared with someone else, not your heart, your dreams, or…your lips."

"Ach, Du bischt hatt."

Paul chuckled. "I know I've pushed too far when you fall into speaking your native tongue at me in frustration. I just want to shield you…us. And wisdom is the best protection against mistakes." He cocked his head, trying to read what she was thinking.

He saw deep pain reflected in her eyes, but why? They were clearing the air, making sure she understood the ways of men, preparing her for what was sure to come when she turned eighteen, confined in a way of life that pushed, like no other, for single people to find a mate quickly and among their own people. And he'd be months from returning to her.

He leaned to brush her lips with his, but she turned her head. "Tell me you understand what I'm saying."

"I understand." She cleared her throat. "You said you'll have nothing to do with me if I get tricked into sharing so much as a kiss with someone."

He kissed her forehead, ready to drop this subject before he ruined their time together. "Yeah, that about sums it up." He gave the line his best comedic voice.

She stiffened and pulled from his embrace, searching the horizon in every direction.

Paul followed her gaze. "What?"

Rubbing the back of her neck, she shook her head. "I...got the feeling we were being watched."

Concern ran hot through Paul. He looked across the vast fields. Gram's farm sat so far off from the main road in front of it and the dirt road behind it that it would be nearly impossible for anyone to see them. The only visible building was Luke's new harness shop, but no one was there today. He hoped. He studied the shop off in the distance. "It'd be hard for anyone to see through the swirling snow. But let's go inside. I need time to win this game of Scrabble, *ya*?"

Hannah searched the fields as she walked. *"Ya."*

Walking close behind her, with his hands on her shoulders, Paul gave her time to work through her thoughts and feelings. She'd been quite emotional since they'd become engaged. But he couldn't blame her. They were in a difficult position with all the time apart and the unknowns concerning how her family would take the news. He'd decided years ago, back when they were only friends, that he needed to do what he could to free her of the rigid repression by always giving her space to think and feel from deep within her soul. Hannah's becoming emotional so easily now was startling. Then again, a woman who had a tenacity for life like his Hannah had to feel intensely about many things. He was just glad she felt so strongly about him.

They climbed the short flight of steps leading to Gram's porch. When

Hannah took a deep breath and the muscles under his palms relaxed, he decided it was time to try to bring her some laughter. But how? They crossed the covered veranda, Paul right behind her with his hands still on her shoulders.

Yahoo.

That was it. Paul squeezed her shoulder, then spun out the porch door and onto the snowy steps. "Yahooooooo." He whispered it softly to the white flurried heavens.

He felt Hannah's boot on his backside. She pushed. With great theatrics, he stumbled down the few steps and landed on his knees. "Yahoo?"

She rolled her eyes and shook her head, but laughter erupted.

He sucked in a deep breath, as if he were about to scream at the top of his lungs. He saw Gram behind Hannah one second before the old woman called his name. He exhaled, pretending to choke. Hannah chortled.

Gram tapped her cane on the wooden porch. "Paul Waddell, what are you doing?"

He stood and bowed. "I'm sharing my great joy with the heavens, Gram."

"Well, stop it and get inside." She turned and, with her therapeutic shoes and walking stick, clunked her way into the kitchen.

Hannah was still snickering when she turned to follow Gram. Paul bolted up the steps, wrapped his fingers about Hannah's waist, and whispered against her neck, "Yahoo."

Hannah burst into giggles as they entered the kitchen. Paul moved to the counter and leaned against it. He shrugged innocently at Gram and winked at Hannah. Hannah bit her bottom lip and dipped her head.

Paul pulled out a straight-backed chair and turned it around, straddling it. "Gram, did you tell Hannah what we've discussed for my Christmas present this year?"

His grandmother took a glass from the cabinet and filled it with tap water. "I've agreed to give him the gift of talking to you. You'll come here the day after Christmas. Paul will be with his family in Florida, but I'll be home. I'll have a number where you can call him, and you two can talk for hours." She scrunched her face. "I hope I'm doing the right thing here. But I never promised not to allow phone calls, only letters."

Hannah's eyes narrowed, but she didn't ask who Gram had promised not to allow letters. Right then, Paul knew Hannah understood more than she voiced to him.

She drew Gram into an embrace. "A long conversation would be a wonderful Christmas present, Gram. Thank you."

He gave a nod toward the Scrabble board. "We have a game to finish."

Placing O-G-L-E after one of the O's in YAHOO, Paul straightened his shoulders in triumph. "If I had another G, I could do GOOGLE."

Hannah wagged her finger at him. "You know, these make-believe friends have got to go."

Paul shrugged. "We'll never know who won if we each keep using words and phrases the other one can't verify as real."

Hannah looked up at him through her lashes. "Winning the game isn't the point, is it?"

Paul winked and shook his head.

~~∿✺∾~~

He followed Hannah's buggy in his truck, staying some thirty feet behind her. He wasn't sure if Hannah's request for him to follow her was because of the maniac who'd run her off the road in his car or because she still thought someone was watching them. No doubt a buggy wasn't much protection against weather or mean people. But it was better than her being on foot. After the car incident, he didn't want her walking back and forth to Gram's ever again.

When they arrived at the last bend in the road before her house, he stopped the truck and watched her buggy disappear into a fog of white haze. Her driveway was only a few feet ahead of her.

What a fantastic day they'd had. He said a quick prayer over her and put the truck in reverse.

By the time he returned, Gram's car was packed, and she was ready to go to Maryland.

s Hannah pulled the buggy into the driveway, optimistic energy bounded through her. Paul was amazing, and by the end of May he'd be living just a mile from her home. She hopped out of the buggy and flung open the barn doors. If she'd ever doubted it before, she knew now that she could never tell Paul her secret. He couldn't handle it.

Tugging at the harness, she led the horse into the barn. She would return it to Matthew tomorrow. As she unhitched the buggy, movement near her home caught her eye. She glanced up and saw her parents walking up the driveway toward her. If they were both coming to see her…

Her heart screamed in pain.

She looked down and continued to loosen the leather bindings, her hands trembling. In an attempt to calm herself, she began singing a song she'd learned in church. *"Herr Jesu Christ, er führt mich."*

"Hannah." Her father's voice faltered.

Without looking up, she sang the same lyrics, louder and in English. "Lord Jesus Christ, He leads me. He leads me." She clung desperately to the hope that she wasn't pregnant, that she and Paul could marry and raise children, and—

"You must listen to us, child," her father said over her singing. He placed his hand on hers.

She jerked away from him and turned to face him squarely. "No. Do you hear me? I said no!"

He nodded. "It is what it is, Hannah. We will take care of you." His shoulders slumped, and he looked old and weak. "But you must go to the bishop right away and tell him you are with child and how it happened."

"No!" She stomped her foot. "I won't. You can't make me."

Grasping his suspenders, her father drew a deep breath. "This is hard. I know it is, Hannah. But from our best figuring, you have until the middle of May before the baby will be born. You'll adjust by then."

Confusing thoughts screamed at her to run. *May? Paul's coming to Owl's Perch to live starting in mid-May.*

Could she keep this a secret from him if she were still pregnant and he was living a mile down the road?

"Hannah?" Her mother's shaky voice interrupted her thoughts.

Hannah lifted her chin. "I'll not go to the bishop."

Her father's demeanor changed from one of compassion to one of fury. "I am still your father, and you'll do as I say."

"Then you do as you say and tell him yourself." Hannah couldn't believe the defiance that rose within her.

Her father's face drained of all emotion. "I'll not. We've waited too long for me to be the one who tells him. He'll accuse me of hiding your sins for you, and then our whole house will pay for the secret that's been kept." *Daed* began pacing. "I should have never let you go back and forth to Mrs. Waddell's. Then this would never have happened." He stopped pacing and turned to her. "I forbid you and your sister to go ever again."

"What?" Disbelief churned within her, making her feel too powerless to even breathe.

"I'll not take a black eye in our church over this, Hannah. You will go to the bishop with this, or you will not be welcomed back under my roof." He turned and walked out of the barn.

Hannah's mother stood near the barn entrance, her eyes filled with sadness. "This is difficult. Believe me, I understand."

Hannah snatched a harness off the barn wall, put it on Matthew's horse, and mounted it bareback. "You understand nothing!" Hannah spurred the horse and flew past her mother. Unsure where she was heading,

Hannah urged the horse to go faster and faster, hoping to somehow outrun the shroud of reality that chased her.

Pregnant.

Through the powdery dusting of snow, Hannah galloped through field after field. Crying too hard to care where she was going, she released the reins and allowed the horse to choose its own path. Her mind tortured her with thousands of questions as horrid thoughts of what might happen to her and Paul played out before her. How could she possibly keep this pregnancy concealed from him?

Purplish evening skies loomed overhead by the time the horse stopped. Wiping the tears from her face, she glanced about the property. The poor creature had gone home and taken her with him. She slid off the weary animal and removed its harness. It ambled into the barn.

Frantic for time alone, she looked around for somewhere she might hide. Through blurry eyes she spotted Matthew's buggy workshop a thousand feet away from any other building on Esh property.

She ran to it, entered through the narrow back door, and climbed the wooden ladder to the storage loft. She stumbled to the far corner. Huddling behind crates and broken buggy pieces, she sobbed.

It couldn't be true; it just couldn't.

Her father had said he'd take care of her, but she knew him. When her stomach started rising like bread dough, he wouldn't even be able to look her in the eyes. As horrid and lonely as that would feel, it didn't begin to compare to what would happen if Paul discovered she was carrying a child that belonged to someone else. She buried her face in her apron and cried until she could cry no more.

Her head throbbing, she closed her eyes. She imagined herself existing in another place and time, before the rape. If only she could find her way back there.

"Hannah!" In the distance a young man's voice called to her.

She jolted, realizing she'd fallen asleep. She rose, her joints aching and sore. As she peeked through the attic vent, she saw two people with lanterns plodding through the snow, calling for her.

Oh no.

Closing her eyes and wishing she could disappear, Hannah waited. When she opened her eyes, the soft glow of lanterns still dotted the otherwise dark fields. No amount of wishing altered her reality.

It had to be almost daylight. No wonder her father had sent people to look for her. As she worked her way through the dark room toward the ladder, beams of light came through the opening, followed by the top of an Amish man's black hat.

Hannah stood stock still.

The black hat tilted back, and she saw Jacob Yoder. "Hannah, do you have any idea how many people are searching for you? What are you doing up there?"

"I...I fell asleep."

He set the kerosene lamp on the floor, but he didn't climb the ladder any higher. "Well, I figured you had to be somewhere out of the cold. Since midnight a group of men have been checking every building we could think of." He picked up the lantern. "You best come on."

As she climbed down the wooden ladder, she tried to brace herself for the day ahead.

By the time she placed her feet on the floor, Jacob was sitting on a wooden crate. "What's going on with you, Hannah?"

She shook her head. "I just needed time alone to think and..."

"Yeah, you fell asleep. I heard." He shook his head, his eyes scanning her from head to toe. "You stayed out all night, and the whole community knows it. Don't you realize what that will do to your reputation? I mean, men like a little spunk, Hannah Lapp, but you sure know how to push every limit that's been set."

"I don't need your approval, Jacob."

He stood there with his arms folded, staring at her. "Sarah's right. Tornadoes are more predictable than you." He nodded toward the door. "We need to let others know you're safe."

Jacob walked to her and held out the lantern. "I wouldn't want to be in your position when you face your father. Rumors about you and last night are already running wild."

The shed door opened, and Matthew's younger brothers stepped inside, each carrying a lantern. David and Peter gawked at her and then looked at each other.

David lowered his lantern. "People are looking for you, Hannah." His attention shifted to Jacob. "Your *Mamm* and *Daed* said you'd been out since midnight and if we spotted you to say it's time you came on home."

Jacob opened his mouth to speak, but no words came out.

"He just found me... I came in here last night and fell asleep... and..." Hannah's words trailed off. She knew how children of David's and Peter's ages liked to tell stories at school, the more scandalous the better.

David rolled his eyes. "Save it for the bishop and your father..."

Hannah felt sick at how powerless she was to stop the tongue wagging that was about to bury her alive. Without any doubt, word would quickly spread about her being found with Jacob. And Sarah would hate her forever after this.

Suddenly Mary came to mind.

Hannah turned to Jacob. "Does Mary know I'm missing?"

"She thinks you spent the night at your house."

"I've got to get back to Mary. Tell the others you found me."

The ties to her *Kapp* blew in the wind, slapping her in the face as she scurried across the fields. She pulled out the pins that held her prayer bonnet in place, jerked it off, and shoved it into the pocket of her apron. She had no intention of ever praying again, so she would never need it.

*L*ying in bed, staring at the ceiling through the darkness, Hannah moved her hand to her slightly protruding stomach. A tiny ball formed under the warmth of her palm, as if the child inside were begging for a bit of love from her.

Since Thanksgiving Day and right on through Christmas and New Year's, revolting reports had circulated about Hannah, saying that she'd tried to win Matthew away from Elle and that she was out all night with Jacob. But worse were the rumors that Hannah had been a gadabout while staying at the hospital and had been seen in the arms of a doctor.

In his arms. How ridiculous.

Others whispered about some English man whose identity no one knew, but he had picked her up in a horse and buggy after midnight. But none of the rumors mentioned that she was with child. Thankfully that secret had been kept between her and her parents.

After a while, the rumors died down, though Hannah was certain that mistrust toward her remained locked in people's minds.

Because Hannah couldn't ask anyone without it sounding wrong, she didn't know how Elle and Matthew were faring. Worst of all, Christmas had come and gone without any contact with Paul. Since she'd been denied the right to return to his grandmother's house, she wasn't able to call Paul the day after Christmas. Torture over what Paul must be thinking about her absence was constant.

She'd tried to use the Yoders' phone to call him, aching to hear his voice telling her about his plans for their future. But John Yoder had put a padlock on the door of the phone shanty. He'd even boarded up the glass so no one could break in. Hannah didn't ask why. She figured either her father had requested that or John had heard the rumors about her and had taken it upon himself.

Hopes of a future with Paul were about all that kept her tied to this place—that and Mary. Throughout the day ideas of going to Ohio and finding the aunt she'd never met floated in and out of her daydreams. Zabeth would understand the misery of being looked down on by everyone.

Aside from the fantasies, Hannah lived in a fog of ache.

She pulled the covers off, careful not to wake Mary, who was sleeping beside her. Slowly she sat upright. Trying to shake the ever-tightening trapped feeling, Hannah stood and tucked the covers around Mary. At least Mary was none the wiser about her pregnancy. But how much longer could Hannah keep it a secret? Her stomach was growing at a remarkable rate these days.

With Mary almost recovered, their sabbatical from church gatherings was drawing to a close. Starting the first church Sunday of March, they were both to return. That meant she and Mary had a little more than two weeks to find the strength to return to the meetings.

Hannah trudged into the bathroom to change.

Paul was never far from her mind. She thought she'd seen him drive by one Monday afternoon in early January as she and Becky Yoder hung nearly frozen laundry on the line. If Hannah hadn't been pregnant, she'd have run to the truck, and if Paul really was inside it, she would have climbed into the passenger seat and never returned to Owl's Perch. Ever.

Considering the magnitude of the sins she was supposed to have committed, she found it surprising that the Yoders allowed her to stay with Mary. Undoubtedly she was being allowed to remain because Mary wanted her near, and she knew nothing of the night Hannah had disappeared into Matthew's workshop or of the rumors surrounding Hannah—except for the bits Sarah had shared.

Even with minimal contact, it was clear to Hannah that these days the community tolerated her, nothing more. She could see it in the faces and hear it in the tones of those who came to visit Mary.

The fact that she refused to wear a prayer *Kapp* only strengthened the force of the gossip. She couldn't say she didn't care about the ugliness going around about her. The gossip cut her to the quick. But that wasn't enough to force her to wear her *Kapp*. She pulled her hair into a bun and tried to secure it with hairpins.

On the positive side, Mary was doing remarkably well lately. The home-health provider had come to visit Mary on two occasions. But Hannah didn't need the nurse's confirmation to know Mary was gaining strength daily. A testament to the power of love and community support, Hannah figured.

She pinned her apron over her baggy dress, thankful the Amish garb hid her figure well, then slid her feet into the black stockings. Every visit her parents made to Mary's, they managed to needle Hannah behind Mary's back. They wanted Hannah to tell the bishop about her pregnancy before he found out on his own.

Over and over Hannah refused. Going to the bishop meant Paul would find out. Besides, that was too close to confessing, and Hannah had no sin to confess, except the hatred in her heart for the man who had done this to her.

But neither anger nor denial of what was happening carried any answers for her. Wriggling one foot and then the other into her boots, Hannah allowed thoughts to ramble around inside her head. What was she going to do with the baby once it was born?

Keeping it wasn't one of her choices; neither was giving it to anyone who lived in Owl's Perch, Amish or English. Elle came to mind, specifically the things she'd said about her guardians, Abigail and Hezekiah Zook. According to Elle, Abigail was young enough to be a new mother, but she was barren. Surely they'd cherish a newborn. They sounded balanced and lenient within the Old Ways. Abigail and Hezekiah were probably the best choice she could make even if she had a thousand couples to consider. And if she handled this with a little skill, no one would be the wiser concerning where the baby came from.

The baby was due in the middle of May. By the time Paul graduated and spent a few days at home, he'd probably be in Owl's Perch before June first. If she hadn't had the baby by the time he returned, she might need to spend a few weeks with the Zooks. Paul wouldn't be able to catch a glimpse of her in passing if she were there. Once the baby was no longer in her life, she intended to marry Paul, with or without her father's blessing. The community had nothing left for her but stoic politeness. Their behavior would remain that way unless she repented and joined the church. That wasn't going to happen. So she'd do just as well to leave and start fresh with Paul.

Hannah couldn't imagine moving back home anyway. Luke still believed the accident was her fault. Sarah had spread rumors all over the county, reaching far beyond their district.

Hannah stuck another hairpin into her bun. It was time to dry her eyes for the day.

A creak of floorboards let her know Mary was stirring. Hannah jumped up and rinsed her face. It was daylight, past time to be in control of her emotions.

Yesterday Luke had thrust three letters at her when Mary wasn't looking. To her deep disappointment, none were from Paul. The notes had come to her through the mail delivery at her parents' house. They were from various Amish families within the community, begging her to repent and join the faith. All of Owl's Perch seemed to think she was some kind of harlot. And her father wanted her to confess her pregnancy to them?

No way. Legal adulthood was hers the ninth of March. But she couldn't leave then. The baby wouldn't be born until mid-May, and then she'd be free to go to Paul.

"Hannah, *kumm uff.*" Mary's voice carried through the wooden door.

"I'm coming." Hannah splashed another handful of cool water on her face. Mary thought Hannah's sadness was due to the rumors Sarah had started. If only her problems were that small. Hannah plodded out of the bathroom and into the bedroom. "Sleep well?" She grabbed some hairpins and added them to her bun, trying to keep her hair under control.

"*Ya.* If we get all the laundry done early, we could take Luke a lunch at the shop." Mary's eyebrows jumped up and down conspiratorially.

Hannah had no desire to go to the harness shop, but she couldn't tell Mary that. She would continue to pretend she didn't mind and to hope Mary didn't notice. Hannah grabbed a basket of dirty clothes. "Oh, good, we get to do my favorite chore: laundry."

Mary laughed and grabbed her hand. "While you were in the bathroom, *Mammi* Annie came to tell us that my aunt called yesterday. The doctor thinks the babies will be born this week. So *Mamm* and *Daed* are making plans to take everyone but us to Ohio." Mary shrugged. "*Daed* says I can't go this time. He's afraid it'd be too much stress, but he says he'll make it up to me somehow. I like the sound of that." Mary gave Hannah a huge smile. "Why don't you come eat with the family today? It might be the last chance you get before their trip. After breakfast we'll collect their dirty clothes and get started."

Hannah crinkled her nose, trying to keep things lighthearted. "I'm not hungry. You go ahead, and I'll work on laundry." She hoped Mary didn't hear her growling stomach.

She hadn't sat at the Yoders' table in weeks, and there was no way she was going to start today. They didn't welcome her anymore. The love that once shone in Becky's eyes had faded and been replaced by skepticism. Luke seemed to have turned Mary's brothers Jacob and Gerald against

Hannah as well, although she didn't know exactly what he'd told them. None of the Yoders were ever rude, but the scorn in their eyes was more than she could bear. So time after time, when Mary asked her to eat with them, Hannah made excuses to stay in the *Daadi Haus* instead.

While Mary ate breakfast with her family, Hannah washed and wrung out three loads of laundry. While dunking a shirt into the rinse water again and again, she heard a rustling noise behind her that drew her attention. When she looked up, she saw Mary holding the three letters Hannah had received yesterday.

Concern flashed in Mary's eyes. "I found these when I was removing the sheets."

Hannah dunked the shirt again. "If I'd realized you were going to do sheets today—"

"Hannah, stop this. I'm not that weak girl of a few months ago. What's going on? I know you've been miserable lately." She shook the letters in Hannah's face. "Talk to me."

Hannah cleared her throat, trying to gain control over her emotions. No matter how badly she wanted to tell Mary, her friend simply wasn't capable of handling the whole ugly truth. But Hannah had to tell her something. "What do you want to know?"

"You could begin by telling me about this doctor you were caught with."

Hannah ran the shirt through the wringer. "I was with him in midday, having a conversation. Nothing more."

"And the *Englischer* the rumors say you've been seen running off with?"

She shook out the shirt and laid it in the pile to be hung out to dry. "One ride for five minutes. It was foolish, I know. I had on my nightgown while I was standing on the front porch waiting for Luke to come home. A…a friend came by with a fast-moving horse and buggy. I rode with him." Hannah grabbed a soapy dress that had been through the wringer and began dipping it into the rinse water.

"If it's all so innocent, let's set the record straight."

Hannah lowered the dress into the water, refusing to turn toward Mary. *If it's all innocent?* Hannah's heart sank. Did Mary believe the rumors too? "How do you suggest we do that?"

Mary ripped the letters in half. "For one thing, you need to be at church, showing them where your heart is by being faithful and upright. I may not be up to a full service yet, but I'm well enough to be left here alone while you're gone."

Hannah lifted the dress out of the water and dunked it again. "And why do you think I haven't set things straight already, Mary?"

"I…I'm not sure."

Hannah turned to face her. "The only reason a person wouldn't try to straighten out the gossip is if, buried under the lies, there was a truth that was more dreadful than any rumor." She wiped her hands on her apron, anger and bitterness rising to the surface so fast she couldn't stop them. "Put that in your pot of *if*s and let it stew for a while."

Mary took Hannah by the shoulders. Determination and love shone in her features. "I have no *if*s, Hannah. I'm strong enough to hear the truth. Are you strong enough to tell me?"

Hannah paused, considering what to do. Stepping around Mary, she walked to the laundry room door and closed it. "It's an awful nightmare, and there's no waking up from it. If I tell you, it'll be your nightmare too."

Mary's greenish blue eyes stared at Hannah, filled with earnestness. "I only pray that I may be as good to you in your trials as you've been to me. I promise you loyalty and silence, Hannah. I promise it even from Luke, if that's what you want."

A craving so severe it caught Hannah completely off guard gnawed at her insides. She was withering inside from keeping it all to herself. She motioned to the wringer. They turned it on, blocking out their voices if anyone came near the doorway. Then they sat on the floor in a far corner, and Hannah spoke the truth—the complete, hideous, unbelievable truth. For the first time since summer, the weight lifted off Hannah's shoulders as she told Mary of her deep love for Paul, her hopes, her fears, even her rape and pregnancy.

As the words poured forth, Hannah worried that Mary wouldn't understand, that she might even turn and walk away. She hungered for Mary to still love her. But no matter how she responded when it was all laid before her, Hannah felt relief. She had finally told someone.

~~~⁓⁓~~~

As breakfast ended, Sarah poured the last drops of coffee in her *Daed's* cup. In spite of the unbearable irritability that grated her insides, she kept her movements controlled. To let her father see an emotion outside the few he could cope with would be a huge mistake, one her big sister had taught her to avoid. Sarah coughed, hiding the sounds of disgust that naturally spewed from her at the very thought of Hannah. Her sister had crossed too many lines of late—even being seen with Jacob after staying out all night. But Jacob discounted that rumor right to Sarah's face. He said he'd had nothing to do with Hannah, and if he got his way, he'd never have to see her again. Sarah wasn't sure what to think about Hannah's motives toward Jacob. But Sarah longed to believe Jacob, to believe that everything between him and her sister was as innocent as he had made it sound.

After returning the pot to the stove, Sarah put the bacon and scrapple back in the refrigerator. As she began removing the breakfast plates from the table, her family went on to the next phase of their day, leaving Sarah in the kitchen alone. Except for the two youngest children, only a few mumbled words had been spoken all morning. Awkward silence had become a staple over the last few months, growing worse with each passing week. Sarah had no clue why her family moped around wordlessly. But the dark mood threatened to drive her mad.

After slipping into winter attire, *Daed*, Luke, and Levi headed outside to continue the endless chores of owning a small dairy herd. Samuel had to go to school in a little while, but first he needed to gather firewood from the lean-to and move it to the back porch. Esther, who would soon turn thirteen, wasn't going to school today. It was her last year to attend, and *Daed* had decided she could miss a few days here and there in order to help make up for Hannah's absence.

Mamm gave Esther and four-year-old Rebecca a few quiet instructions as they made their way upstairs to begin preparing their home for Sunday's meeting. It'd take the better part of the week to get their home as shiny clean as *Daed* and *Mamm* wanted it for a worship day. The rotation that scheduled church to be held on their property once a year had circled back to them.

She chucked another log into the potbellied stove and set the pressing iron facedown on top of it before turning to wash the last of the breakfast dishes. She'd been weary and cross of late. Both sleep and peace had seemed impossible. For months, a recurring nightmare had chased her. The unseen image tracked her, wreaking terror at night. And its memory haunted her during the day.

As her thoughts meandered in every direction, Sarah continued moving through the kitchen chores. She put jars of garden-canned kale and whole-kernel corn on the counter before placing the kettle on the back of the wood stove. In the five months that Hannah had been living under Annie Yoder's roof as Mary's nursemaid, the Lapp household had learned to run quite smoothly without her.

Sarah went to the cupboard, where freshly canned deer meat was stored. Things were better than just running smoothly. In spite of Hannah being trained in some medical knowledge, she no longer held a place of great respect within the community. Actually, due to a few rumors, Hannah's lofty position had plummeted. Her sister being on the outs with *Daed, Mamm,* and Luke felt even better than Sarah had imagined it would. When a snicker erupted from Sarah, guilt rose. She didn't mean to feel so giddy about Hannah's misfortune.

But the idea of spending another quiet, clammed-up day inside the house stole her fleeting delight in the dethroning of her sister. Sarah grabbed two Mason jars filled with meat. Setting both jars on the counter, Sarah sighed. What difference did it make if Sarah had told the bishop about that night? Sarah had kept tons of secrets for Hannah.

But her sister had done plenty of good deeds toward her too. Hannah had been a shield for her hundreds of times, like when *Daed* caught her dawdling away precious work time as she daydreamed. Hannah had stepped in between *Daed* and Sarah regularly, making all kinds of excuses until he stormed off without taking Sarah to the woodshed.

No matter. It was Hannah's own fault that rumors were ripping through the community. If she hadn't been doing something wrong to begin with, Sarah would have had nothing to tell. And if Hannah hadn't been so deceitful as to make herself look better than she really was to everyone, including Jacob, Sarah wouldn't have had cause to put Hannah in her rightful place by telling people what she was really like.

But Sarah's thoughts often stole her sense of time. Was it possible that Hannah had only been gone a few minutes that night?

If Hannah was telling the truth about that…

Stark terror ran down Sarah's spine. If *Daed* ever found out that she was the one who'd told the bishop about that ride, he might beat her until she had no tomorrow.

Fresh hatred for Hannah rose within her.

*P*aul turned out the last of the lights in the tire store and set the security system. His new title of assistant manager came with longer hours and more responsibilities, but it also came with a much-appreciated raise. The February wind slapped against him, sliding down the nape of his neck and back as he curved his body to lock the double glass doors. The lock clicked into place, and he shook the door to verify it was bolted. He stood straight, pulling his jacket tighter and shoving his paycheck deeper into his coat pocket. Paul waited by the door, making sure each employee's car started on this cold winter night.

Across the lot, he saw Jack climbing into his 2000 Honda Accord. The man should have received the promotion Paul had gotten, and he would get the position when Paul left in May...if Jack could pull his life together by then. Jack was in the middle of a divorce, and the word *depression* didn't begin to describe what he was going through. Jack's situation made Paul's blood boil.

Jack was a good and decent man who worked hard in every avenue of life. He'd had good reasons to be suspicious of his wife's faithfulness long before the ugly truth became clear. While he worked two jobs to support his family, Melanie was running around on him. Paul didn't know why it had taken Jack so long to see it. Having been around Melanie some, Paul had considered her capable of every bit of the buzz that was going around about her. But Jack, the poor sap, had refused to believe anything but what his wife said. He'd been a fool and had ignored all the signs while hoping for the best until the truth could no longer be denied.

While Jack was getting help from a therapist, Paul stepped into the position of temporary assistant manager so the company wouldn't hire a permanent employee in Jack's place. Paul had been so upset about Jack's situation that he ended up venting to Dorcas about it. Of course he'd also talked to her about his hopes and plans of a life with Hannah. He couldn't help but talk about that since Dorcas was one of only three people who knew about her.

Dorcas couldn't stop talking about a guy she'd begun dating a few weeks ago. Paul hoped the four of them could enjoy spending some time together, maybe playing board games at Gram's. His grandmother's place was Hannah's best chance of getting to be part of a double date.

As the last employee pulled out of the lot, Paul trotted around the back of the building, heading toward his car. In three months he would be in Owl's Perch with Hannah. Man, he was looking forward to that. As he came closer to his truck, he recognized the red Ford Taurus parked beside it. The driver's-side door opened, and Dorcas climbed out.

She batted her eyes against the strong wind. "We need to talk."

He stood motionless. He couldn't imagine what would make her drive all the way from Maryland to talk rather than using a phone.

She ran her fingers back and forth over her chin. "A few hours ago my mom and I got back from visiting Jeanie, my mother's cousin who lives in Owl's Perch."

Paul's heart lurched. "Is something wrong?"

She held up an envelope. "This is a duplicate of a letter that was sent to Hannah."

He closed the distance between them. "Sent by whom?"

She shrugged. "It's not signed." Dorcas stroked the edge of the envelope. "But Jeanie got it from the person who wrote it."

Paul studied the envelope in her hand. It was addressed to Hannah, but the seal had been ripped open. It had a stamp on it but no postmark across it, as if after preparing to mail the letter, someone changed their

WHEN THE HEART CRIES

mind—maybe had even snatched it back from the mailbox before the mailman had a chance to pick it up.

Dorcas tapped the envelope against the palm of her hand. "There are things in this letter you need to know about." She lowered her head. "I'm sorry."

Indignation ran through him. "What kind of things?"

Dorcas pointed to the passenger door of her car. "If you want to know all I've been told, get in."

Paul ducked into the car, slamming the door behind him. "Make it quick because I'm going there to check on her as soon as we're finished." He pounded his fists on the dashboard. "Regardless of her father's or anyone else's wishes."

Paul's old truck knocked along the back roads as he burned rubber getting to Owl's Perch. Forget studying, tomorrow's classes, and work. Him and all his plans, always putting Hannah second. He sighed. *Idiot.*

He raked his hands through his hair. The whole community was buzzing ugly things against Hannah because they'd shared a kiss. The poor girl.

No one had a right to say Hannah was a sinner and needed to repent. He sped down the road, fuming at the injustice of it all.

Matthew Esh. The name dug its way past his anger at Hannah's accusers. Was there something to all these rumors? Dorcas had said Matthew's name a dozen times in all the gossip. But surely the community wouldn't be angry with her and write letters of correction if being alone with Matthew was the only "misdeed" she was accused of. They wouldn't hold it against her to this degree even if she did stay out all night with him...or was it Jacob Yoder that she was supposed to have stayed out all night with? She might get some mean-looking frowns, even a few murmurs or cold shoulders, but not letters and the community wagging their tongues freely about her. Something more than Matthew…or Jacob…was going on.

Was it possible she'd gotten caught up in a relationship with that English guy at the hospital that Dorcas mentioned? The rumors said she had, and she'd acted weird the night he'd showed up.

"That's ridiculous!" Paul railed against himself, smacking the steering wheel with the palm of his hand. "Are you going to join in and accuse her?"

The rumors were based on lies. He had no doubts about his Hannah. The truck jolted as he hit a pothole.

Well, okay, he had a few doubts. He'd witnessed firsthand how friendly Hannah was with Matthew. No big surprise that half the rumors involved him. The other half involved some nameless English person and that doctor Hannah quoted from time to time. One or two of the rumors had Jacob Yoder's name attached to them. Dorcas said Jacob was one of Mary's brothers. Heat ran through his body.

She wasn't guilty. No way. He knew her. She was simply naive and didn't always think about how things might look.

Dorcas had told him that, according to her mother's cousin, Hannah was still living at the Yoders' *Daadi Haus* with Mary. He intended to knock on the door and insist he be allowed to talk to Hannah. He had to make sure she was okay.

She might even be willing to leave Owl's Perch and go with him. She would turn eighteen in a little over two weeks. They could hide out somewhere until then if need be.

If she wanted out, he'd get her out.

The letter Dorcas had shown him, which was a duplicate of one sent to Hannah, had quoted Scripture about dressing modestly and being honest. He growled. Ridiculous hyperbole. Hannah was no more capable of sneaking out to be with a man in her undergarments than Paul was of flying.

Let's see them send those letters when they don't know where you live, Hannah.

As Paul pulled into the Yoders' driveway, he noticed there were no lights on in the house. He drove farther into the driveway, stopping in front of the *Daadi Haus*. He saw a light on in the living room. Maybe Hannah and Mary were still awake.

Paul knocked on the door. He didn't care if the whole neighborhood heard him. He was tired of sneaking around as if he and Hannah were sinners.

A girl with greenish blue eyes and blond hair covered by a white prayer *Kapp* came to the door dressed in a flannel gown and housecoat. He assumed it was Mary, though he'd never met her, since she'd been asleep the day he came to her house for a visit with Hannah. "Mary?" he asked.

She nodded.

"I'm Paul Waddell. I need to speak to Hannah. Is she here?"

She nodded and opened the door. "Hannah went to bed with complaints of aches. She's asleep now, and I'd hate to wake her."

Physical pains brought on by the emotional weight of the rumors, Paul figured. "I'm not leaving until I speak with her, even if every member of this district learns that I'm here."

Mary tilted her head, considering his words. Finally a smile crossed her face. "I suppose I'll be the one in pain if I don't wake her. I'll be right back."

Paul paced, much as he'd done when he'd come to visit her in November. She'd been out that day, and by her own admission she'd been with Matthew.

Hannah came to the living room door, her long hair loosely pulled into a bun with wisps breaking free everywhere. She had a shawl wrapped over her day clothes, but she didn't have her *Kapp* on. She looked a bit addled, as if she'd been sound asleep.

Paul bolted to her, clasping his hands over hers. "Are you all right? I heard…"

She stared at him, but she didn't ask why he was here or suggest he hide his truck. He rubbed his head, feeling confused.

Mary came up behind Hannah and whispered something in her ear in Pennsylvania Dutch. She held Hannah's head covering out to her.

"Ich kann net." Hannah shook her head, refusing to take it.

Paul would have found Hannah's refusal to wear her prayer *Kapp* disturbing enough even without any rumors flying on the winds. Doubts concerning her began nibbling at him. All the women from his sect of Mennonites wore *Kapps*. Where was her submission to the ways they'd agreed on as right?

As he tried to decipher what the two were whispering about, he'd never felt so out of place. Mary said something about calling for a doctor. Hannah reacted angrily. Did Mary need a doctor? Surely Mary didn't think Hannah needed one just because she'd gone to bed achy.

Mary grabbed Hannah's coat and helped her put it on, still whispering. *"Grossmammi iss do. Du kannscht net im Haus schwetze."*

"Ya, gut." Hannah nodded.

Yes and *good*—that he understood.

Hannah fastened her coat. "Mary's grandmother has moved back into her bedroom upstairs. We need to find a quiet place outside to talk."

Without a word, Paul followed her out the door, up the hill, and past the barn. When they came to a huge oak, she stopped.

She played with the bark of the tree, barely turning to look at him. "I didn't expect to see you until May."

"Dorcas came to see me. She said you're being treated poorly, almost being shunned among your people. I came to see if you're okay."

Looking wearier than he could ever have imagined, she shrugged. "There are rumors and displeasure among the People. But any mention of shunning is absurd. That's not done lightly and never to an unbaptized member. There's some pressure, but I'm fine."

She didn't look fine. She looked miserable. Whatever else was going on, she didn't seem the least bit glad to see him. "Have we made a mistake, Hannah?"

She turned, mumbling something in Pennsylvania Dutch. Then she seemed to realize her lapse and repeated her words. "If you don't know, I can't tell you."

He studied her. She'd changed. In a thousand ways he couldn't even define. "Tell me what's going on, Hannah. I'm always gone, always trying to build a life for us. I don't understand what's happening."

She stepped away from him. "When you graduate, will you still want me?"

He jammed his hands into his pockets, feeling the letter in one and his paycheck in the other. "Yes, absolutely."

Clearing her throat, she lifted her chin and nodded. "Then I'll be here."

Paul clutched the letter in his hand, pulling it from his pocket. "But, Hannah, where have all these rumors come from? What's going on?"

She glanced at the paper in his hands, but she didn't ask about it. "I'm tired. That's all."

He stepped closer to her, trying to look her in the eye. "That answer doesn't address my question about the rumors. Were you out for a ride in your nightgown with some guy?"

She returned to playing with the bark on the tree. "I want to answer you, Paul, but you've got to hear me out. Okay?"

He shoved the letter back into his pocket. "All right."

She spoke without looking up from her fascination with the tree bark. "Almost every rumor you've heard has a piece of truth in it."

Doubts and questions came in on all sides. "Go on." He moved in closer until he was directly behind her as she faced the tree.

Hannah sidestepped, moving out into the open. "I did go for a ride in my nightgown. It was the night of Luke and Mary's accident. My family had gone to bed. I hadn't felt well for weeks and was restless. Luke and I had argued earlier that day. I wanted to talk to him as soon as he got home. So I waited on the porch in my gown. Matthew drove up with a new horse and buggy. When he offered me a ride, I took it. We were only gone for a few minutes."

Matthew Esh again. Paul simmered quietly.

She brushed wisps of curly hair from her face. "I've paid dearly for those five minutes, Paul."

"And is Matthew paying too?"

She shrugged. "As far as I know, we've kept his name out of that particular rumor mill."

Paul propped one hand against the tree and kicked at a patch of snow. "And the gossip about you and that doctor?"

Paul listened as she explained rumor after rumor. He was disappointed in his bride-to-be. She should have handled herself more carefully than to have been in the hayloft with Matthew. To Paul, the fact that the bishop caught them was beside the point. And there was no way she could justify staying out all night just because she was upset. The thing with the doctor didn't seem as inappropriate as the other issues. But the longer he listened, the angrier he became. Her carefully worded explanations were beginning to sound like fabricated stories.

The night he went to the hospital, he'd heard Matthew mockingly call her a liar, teasing her that he knew her better than anyone and that she lied really well but not well enough to trick him. Was she really a liar? According to what Dorcas said, even the church leaders thought she was being deceptive.

Had he allowed himself to be blind, like Jack? Paul was only in Owl's Perch sporadically, and even then he was confined to his world, waiting on her to come to him. Matthew had been with her the day Paul came to visit. Later that night Matthew had called her name, searching for her while she was secretly in Paul's arms. Matthew had warmed the bricks for Hannah's trip to Gram's, but he had no way of knowing Paul was waiting for her at the other end.

"You spent an entire night alone in Matthew's repair shop. And when you were found, Jacob Yoder was with you. But it's all perfectly innocent?"

"I fell asleep. When I woke up, Jacob had come into the shop looking for me." Tears rolled down her cheeks. "I'm telling you the truth, Paul."

Her crying addled him. "Okay, okay. But answer me this. Every piece of this puzzle is attached to one common thread." He paused, pity for her beginning to drain from him as indignation stirred. How many times had Melanie cried her way back into Jack's heart? "The common thread is you being too sick or too upset to go home. I understand why you were concerned about Luke not coming home the night of the accident. But why were you so upset that you ran to Matthew's repair shop? And what caused you to be so sick after I left that they burned your clothes and Sarah had to take your place at Gram's?"

She lowered her head. "You know enough about that day, Paul. There was the car...and..."

He grabbed her arm. "Hannah, what is it you're not telling me?"

She jerked against his hold. Determined to look into her eyes and finally understand, he pulled her toward him.

A firm, round belly pressed against him.

"No!" She placed a hand on his chest and pushed him away.

He held tight to her wrist, staring at her. As if in slow motion, he splayed his free hand and laid it on her stomach. It was as round and firm as if it held a basketball…or a baby.

His precious Hannah was pregnant.

Dear God, what a fool I've been.

A thousand thoughts ran through his mind within a few seconds. No wonder she'd been so evasive with him. She was carrying Matthew Esh's baby! Nothing but friends, indeed. But apparently he didn't want her and their child because Hannah had asked if he would still want her after graduation. Did she really expect him to raise another man's child as his own?

Great, racking sobs shook her body as she tried to pry his fingers off her stomach. "Paul, I-I can explain. I…"

He grabbed her by the shoulders. "You always have an explanation. Always! And I've always been fool enough to believe you. No more, Hannah. No more!" Pulling his keys from his pocket, he ran down the hill.

"Paul!" Her scream was haunting, but he refused to look back. "Paul, please! The unmentionable happened. Please don't leave me!"

He jumped in his truck and started the engine as her last words rang in his ears. "The unmentionable" meant either adultery or unmarried sex. How in the world could he forgive her?

He glanced up the hill. Hannah was on her knees, rocking back and forth and screaming for him to listen to her. Tears blurred his vision. He'd been such a fool. He threw the truck in reverse, with no intention of ever laying eyes on her again.

*B*arely aware of her surroundings, Hannah watched Paul back into the road, squealing his tires as he sped off. He was gone. It was over. The only thing she'd wanted out of life had just left, hating her. The cold, wet ground seeped through her clothing, making her shiver. The sobs jolting her body tore through the silence of the damp night air.

A pair of gentle hands covered Hannah's shoulders, helping her rise to her feet. "Sh, *Liewi*. It'll be okay. It'll all be okay." Mary steadied her as they walked back toward the *Daadi Haus*.

Human silhouettes formed in the driveway as Mary and Hannah made their way down the hill. Through her blurred vision, Hannah saw Mary's parents and two of her brothers. She had no idea how much they'd seen or heard. But what did it matter now? Paul knew the truth, and he'd made his choice. He thought she was a liar, and he'd left her. She knew he would never return.

~~∽§~~

A cool cloth pressed against Hannah's brow. She stirred, wondering how long she'd slept once she could weep no longer. Her pain had poured out as she huddled in the bed like a child, crying for hours. Each time she roused for a few moments, Mary had whispered reassuring words to her.

Drawing a deep breath, Hannah pulled her aching body to a sitting position. She hurt all over: her back, thighs, head, and across her stomach. Leaning back, Hannah rested against the headboard, waiting for some of the pains to subside. Her eyes closed; she took a few deep breaths. "What's the time?"

"It's ten in the morning."

The baby shifted. On impulse, Hannah reached for Mary's hand and placed it on her stomach.

Mary gasped. "That's so amazing."

Hannah hadn't ever thought so before, but maybe Mary was right. She opened her eyes and realized she still had on her day clothes from yesterday. The skirts were covered in mud, and to her horror she remembered kneeling on the ground begging Paul not to leave her. She groaned. A lot of good her begging had done.

Mary shifted her hand as the baby moved, following the slow, easy motion across Hannah's belly. "It's a *Bobbeli*, Hannah. A real *Bobbeli*."

It kicked and Mary jumped. She laughed, but Hannah couldn't find any humor in the incident. It was a real baby, all right. One that belonged to a creep.

Mary placed the cloth from Hannah's brow in the bowl and walked to the dresser, where she set the basin down.

Hannah put her feet on the floor, rubbing her rounded, aching sides.

"I'll do the laundry; you rest." Picking up Hannah's pair of mud-caked stockings, Mary gave an exaggerated roll of her eyes. "*Mamm* set the tub of dirty clothes on the back porch. But my aunt gave birth to her twins during the night. My whole family left for Ohio before sunrise, and they'll be gone for the week to help my aunt with her young brood and the newborns. They left us a key to the phone shanty, saying they'd be calling some here and there." Mary dunked the stockings into the bowl of water, dipping them up and down.

Twins. The word conjured up images of Hannah's aunt who had been shunned. It was hard to imagine what Zabeth's life must be like after all these years without any family around her. Hannah wondered if Zabeth regretted doing whatever it was she did that caused her to be put under the ban.

Hannah dismissed those thoughts and gazed at Mary. "It's not laundry day, is it?"

"No, but we didn't do laundry Monday. We talked and cried."

Hannah supposed it was a good thing she'd told Mary everything a few days ago, or last night would have been even worse, if that were possible.

She rose. The room spun, and she grabbed the headboard to steady herself. "I need to take a shower."

Mary came to her. When Hannah turned around, Mary untied and unpinned her pinafore. "I don't think my family heard much of anything last night. If they had, they wouldn't have kept their plans and gone to visit my aunt. *Daed* said something about us not milling about the property at night while they're gone."

"It doesn't matter what they heard, not anymore." But Hannah knew it did. In a world where conforming was paramount, her parents could pay a high price for Hannah's defiance of the Old Ways. If the bishop decided she had to do things a certain way, and she refused, he could do little to her. But his power over her parents was another matter. They wouldn't be shunned, but they'd be ostracized, however politely.

"Pacifists," Hannah mumbled. "Passive aggressive is more accurate."

Brushing wisps of hair off Hannah's neck, Mary whispered, "My family didn't come outside until they heard Paul's tires squeal."

It took a few moments for Mary's words to sink in. Hannah slid her apron off and faced Mary. "Then they don't know about…" She touched her protruding stomach.

Mary laid her hand on Hannah's belly. "They don't know." Mary's warm, gentle hand caressed Hannah's stomach, and her face crumpled with sympathy. "We could surround the little thing with love, no?"

As Mary spoke the words, the infant fluttered in a new way, as if it had been waiting to hear a caring word, causing Hannah's soul to stir with an inkling of an emotion that had never been a part of her before. Hannah felt sorry for the tiny being. It seemed so desperate to be loved.

As she headed for the shower, Hannah noticed their half-sewn "Past and Future" quilt on the side table. The women of Owl's Perch had donated so many scraps of material for the future side of the quilt, there'd been plenty left over to make baby blankets for the children Luke and Mary would have. Running her fingers across the basting that held the two sides together, Hannah dismissed the pity she'd felt moments earlier. "No, I can't love this child, but someone else can."

Mary grabbed a clean apron and dress off a peg and passed them to Hannah. Taking the clean clothes, Hannah padded into the bathroom. A vision of the monster who had fathered the baby jolted Hannah, and she bristled against Mary's suggestion.

Talking from the other room, Mary changed the topic. "You'll miss our shower when you move back home."

Tuning out Mary's effort at general niceties, Hannah closed the bathroom door and leaned her forehead against it. She and Mary were long overdue for returning to normal life. But when the news of her pregnancy spread, she would no longer be welcomed at the Yoders'. And her father wasn't going to let her move back home unless she set things right with the church leaders.

What am I going to do?

Her future with Paul was destroyed. The pain of that was so deep it hurt to breathe. She'd known all along if he knew the truth, it would end everything. Her best efforts at concealing the pregnancy had failed.

She finally moved to the tub and flicked on the water. The only thing left to do was to make plans for the baby. Hannah's life was over, but a new life was growing inside her, preparing to embark on its own journey on this planet.

She sat on the side of the tub, moving her hands over her swollen stomach. The baby was still now, quieted for a nap, she supposed. Pulling the lever on the faucet, Hannah started the shower running. Amid all the heartache and embarrassment clinging to her, a new desire sprang forth. She eased to the bathroom door and listened. Mary had left the bedroom. Tiptoeing through the room to the dresser, Hannah kept her eye on the bedroom door. She opened the drawer with the stethoscope, wanting to hear the infant's heartbeat. But she didn't want Mary to see her. It was a private thing, something between a mother and her child.

As she grabbed the stethoscope, she shuddered. *A mother?*

Hurrying, she slid out of her dress, put the stethoscope in her ears, and began searching for a heartbeat. Unable to find it, she flicked the water off and listened again. After a minute of moving the stethoscope around, she heard a whooshing noise. That had to be it. It was rhythmic, like Mary's heartbeat, but much faster.

Chills covered her. *Like Mary's heartbeat?*

Oh, dear God, it's a real baby.

She had known that, hadn't she?

Listening to its blood flow through the tiny chambers of its heart, she had to admit the truth. She'd realized it was alive, but she'd wished over and over it wasn't. She'd known it was growing and that it had the power to ruin her and Paul. But never, not once, had she had a suspicion that it was as precious as Mary's heartbeat. She took the stethoscope out of her ears and dropped it on the floor.

Placing her hand over her belly again, the baby balled up under it, as if responding to its mother. Remorse entered Hannah's heart. "I'm sorry. I'm so, so sorry."

She took a deep breath and stepped into the shower. As the warm water soothed her taut, sore muscles, she tried to ignore the awful grief of losing Paul. She put her face under the showerhead and let the pelting water rinse away her tears. As she leaned against the shower wall, visions of Paul's angry face haunted her. He'd had no mercy for her, only judgment. *God, help me, please.*

An image of a tan-skinned, young Jewish girl, about Hannah's age, formed a vision in her mind's eye. That girl had been pregnant before she was married too. The picture lasted less than a second, but suddenly Hannah didn't feel so alone. A sense that God had not abandoned her, and didn't intend to, strengthened her.

This sense of God was a welcomed one, and it wasn't completely new. She'd felt His closeness and acceptance after Luke had spewed his venom on her, before Matthew showed up at the Yoders' barn back in October. But within a month she learned she was pregnant, and from there most thoughts of God were far from her as she desperately tried to hide her pregnancy from Paul. Oddly, God didn't seem angry with her about it. He seemed more than willing to step in and comfort her. She propped her palms against the shower wall, muttering confessions of her weakness. Tears clouded her eyes, but they weren't from sorrow or self-pity. She'd tapped into joy, unbelievable as that was. As the thoughts gave her courage, she knew what had to be done. This infant and she were connected. It didn't belong to its father; it belonged to the Father. That's who Hannah would pray the child would take after: its heavenly Father.

As she got out of the shower and dressed, her thoughts spun with snippets of hope. But all traces of good feelings aside, her reality hadn't changed a bit. So now what? Pinning her wet hair into a bun, she searched for answers.

Although Mary wasn't in the room with her, the memory of her soft voice filtered through Hannah's soul. *We could surround the little thing with love, no?*

She ran her hand over her stomach. Suddenly another understanding poured into Hannah's mind. Love—real, God kind of love—gave the infant worthiness, because in life each being was both worthy and unworthy at the same time. A tiny bolt of laughter ran through Hannah. "Yes, Mary. Yes, we can surround this baby with love."

⁓⋘⋙

Mary listened without interrupting as Hannah paced the room, explaining her decision to keep the baby. Mary nodded. "We will cherish the babe because it is, simply because it is."

Going from one end of the room to the other, Hannah voiced her thoughts. "I have no money and a baby on the way. How will we do this?"

"*Ach,* Hannah, you'll have to get the support of your family and our community. I can see no other way. Our parents inherited their homes. Luke and I have a place because people donated money and their labor. You can't provide for a baby on your own."

A slow pain worked its way through Hannah's back and around her abdomen. It intensified, and she grabbed the back of the couch, waiting for it to ease. When the discomfort stopped, she took a breath.

Mary held up her index finger, telling Hannah to wait. She dashed into the bedroom and came back holding Hannah's *Kapp* in her hands. Mary had scrubbed it clean and, by the looks of it, had probably spent over an hour ironing it. "It's time for this, no?" Mary held it out to her.

Hannah closed her eyes, feeling the weight of joining the church bear down on her. She placed her hands under her round belly and stared at the ever-growing ball before she moved to the window. As she watched the barren trees sway in the winds, she wondered if she'd always feel this trapped.

"Hannah, I see no other choice. Your father will not help you if you don't come under the church's leadership, and he won't allow anyone else in the community to help you either…even if they would. Even my *Daed* is not going to allow us to remain close if your father is set against you."

Hannah leaned her forehead against the cold window. "Oh God, help me."

Mary placed her hand on Hannah's shoulder. "He is helping you, but to take the help He's provided, you must put this on."

Hannah turned and studied the sheer *Kapp*.

"I'll be behind you every step of the way."

Mary was right; it was the only way. "Yes, it's time to come under the leaders' say. But there isn't time to join the church before the baby is born."

Mary cupped her hand under Hannah's chin, tilting her face up. "The baby won't know it was born before instruction classes began or that it was several months old before you finished and then joined the church. The people won't tell, not once you're baptized. They will forget those things that are behind." Mary gave a sad but sweet smile. "And they won't speak of them again."

An undeniable need to settle the issue as soon as possible grew within Hannah. "I've dreamed for too long of a life that became impossible the moment I was attacked." Hannah took the *Kapp*. "Maybe before."

Mary wrapped Hannah in her arms. "Then we'll do this together."

Hannah hugged her, thankful for Mary and determined to be the kind of mother this child would be grateful for. "Make arrangements for the bishop, preachers, deacon, and *Daed* to all come here this afternoon, but I need to see Matthew first."

*P*aul pulled into the tire store, not quite sure how he'd gotten there. Although he'd shown up in class that morning, he didn't remember anything that was said and couldn't recall leaving campus. It was scary to be at work with no memory of having driven there.

Hannah wasn't going to win at this twisted game of hers. That's all there was to it. He'd keep to his routine and put every memory of her to rest. He sighed. It was going to be a long journey to healing. He hurt as if Hannah had gazed lovingly into his eyes while jamming his heart into a meat grinder. He was still so angry he couldn't quit shaking. Difficult as it was to understand, Hannah was just like Melanie. And he, just like Jack. He'd been a fool not to see it sooner. Finally he comprehended the unnamable thing that had stood between him and Hannah all these months. It was her unfaithfulness.

He clocked in and moved to his messy desk in a tiny, poorly lit back room. Sorting through papers that had been piled there while he was at school, he tried to think through the cloud of betrayal covering his mind. He pulled a new order from the stack and began jotting down information for a paper receipt.

"Hi." Carol's voice pulled him from the dozen different worlds colliding inside him.

He didn't look up. Undoubtedly, Dorcas had told her what was going on. Now she was here to check on him; he was sure of that. "I'm fine, Carol. Go home."

"I'm really sorry, Paul."

Paul crumpled the receipt he'd just messed up and grabbed another blank one from his desk drawer. "Yeah, I bet you are."

"Paul." She sounded wounded. "I never wanted you to get hurt."

He tossed his pen on the desk and looked at her, hoping she had some sort of answer for him. "How could I be so wrong?" His voice cracked, and he wished he hadn't started this conversation. Tears had choked him some during the night as he wrestled with memories and the realization of who Hannah really was, or rather who she'd become. But he wouldn't shed another tear over this. Not one.

Carol closed the door behind her and took a seat. "So I take it you confirmed the rumors about her…seeing other guys while you weren't around."

"Yeah." That was an understatement. But Paul wasn't going to tell anyone that Hannah was pregnant. If he'd only opened his eyes, it would have been obvious long before she conceived. When did she get pregnant anyway? Was it before or after she'd agreed to marry him? He huffed at himself. It didn't matter.

"Paul, I think it would help if you talked about things."

He picked up the pen, holding it in the middle and tapping each end back and forth on the desk. Talk? His sister probably couldn't handle hearing what he had to say right now. After studying the effects of drugs, alcohol, and unfaithfulness on families while dealing with Jack and Melanie, he'd grown quite cynical of people. He'd seen pessimism grow in him for a while, but he never thought he'd have cause to disrespect Hannah of all people.

Still, in the depth of his soul, he couldn't believe what was happening. He simply couldn't fathom Hannah giving herself like that to another man. He picked up a stack of folders and set them in front of him. There had always been things about Hannah that stunned him. Her ability to sneak off from home time after time without getting caught, the way she could hold secrets from everyone, her ability to attend church while planning to leave her faith, her warm openness with Matthew. Her friendliness must have included that doctor who gave her the really nice book with all his phone numbers in it. Hannah had become uncomfortable when Paul had mentioned the phone numbers.

If he'd been following the clues, this wouldn't have been such a shock. Flirting with Matthew at the hospital. Throwing herself into Paul's arms that night at the Yoder place. Kissing him like…like a woman who'd been kissed many, many times before.

He rose. "I've got work to do."

Carol gave him a hug that he didn't return. "At least no one knows about this but Dorcas and me. We won't tell anyone."

Paul eased out of her embrace and shuffled papers on his desk. "The silver lining: saving face." He opened his desk drawer, in search of what he didn't know. When Hannah's community learned of her pregnancy, there would be no saving of face for her, no place of refuge. What a mess she'd made, and what an awful price she would pay. In that moment he realized the heavy, unbearable grief that covered him was also for the suffering Hannah would go through. She'd been foolish, even deceitful, but the price she'd pay would cost her dearly for life.

~~∞~~

A sharp pain shot across Hannah's back, stealing her breath as she trod across the pasture toward Matthew's house. "I have much to do today, God. Grant me the strength and wisdom." She whispered the words, knowing there was no perfect answer for her situation. Nothing she could do would set everything right. She would take her time of instruction this summer and join the faith in the fall. That way her father would be calmed and allow her to live in his home and keep her baby.

As she drew closer to the Esh yard, she heard a rhythmic tapping coming from the repair shop. She knocked on the door and opened it.

Matthew sat at his workbench, hammering a tiny nail into a frame holding a piece of glass. He glanced up, then returned his focus to his bench. Dread shuddered through her as she remembered Paul's reaction. She rubbed her thumb against the palm of her hand. "Matthew, I'm going to talk to the bishop today." She drew a breath. "But I need to see Elle first."

Matthew tossed his hammer onto the bench. "You slept in this shop all night, causing rumors about me as well as Jacob. Haven't you caused enough trouble between me and Elle?"

Hannah walked closer to him. "I'm sorry, truly I am."

Lifting a broken wheel to a different section of his workbench, Matthew nodded. "She's still wavering a bit about believing that I never saw you that night. She's been pressing the brakes on our relationship. It'd be best if you stayed away from me...and her."

Her throat stinging from tears she wouldn't let flow, she leaned against an exposed beam. "Matthew, I don't know how to say this, but surely you of all people know I'm not guilty of all that's being said of me."

Matthew captured her gaze and held it. "Yeah, I know that. But I can't let nothing about you destroy me and Elle. She needs me right now. That's possibly the reason she's hanging on to the hope that I'm telling her the truth about us. Her real father has written her a letter. He's meetin' her tonight at Kiah's place for the first time since he ran off. I can't tell ya how much it means to her that I be by her side for this. She says she'll see him, but she won't let him change her mind about joinin' the Amish faith."

Hannah prayed for strength. "I never intended to join our faith, not since I fell for someone who wasn't Amish. For years, Mrs. Waddell's grandson and I have been seeing each other every summer, sometimes during the school year." Hannah cleared her throat. "Last summer, the day he was leaving for his last year of college, he asked me to marry him. Even on that day I never shared a kiss with him, Matthew. I promise."

Matthew waved his hand toward the couch. "Ya look awful, like you need to sit."

Glad to get off her feet and hopeful it would ease her back and leg pain, Hannah moved to the sofa. Matthew sat on the far end of it.

She stared at the scars on the palms of her hands. "You heard that I had an incident with a vehicle. Well, that's not the whole truth. Matthew, I...I was forced to...to be with a man."

"What?" He jumped up. "No." He shook his head and walked away from her.

Hannah closed her eyes, hoping Matthew believed her. When she opened her eyes, he was facing her with hurt and anger mingled on his face.

"I'm so sorry." He eased onto the couch and took her hand.

Another pain shot down her sides. She squeezed his hand. "Thank you. At first, *Mamm* and *Daed* wanted to keep it a secret so that maybe I could still get a husband. I wanted to keep it a secret so Paul wouldn't find out, so he would still marry me."

"The beginning of September is when you started hiding out at home more than normal."

She nodded. "Yes. The buggy ride we took was the first ray of hope that had entered my world since I was...since that night."

"Our ride began a hard time of rumors for you. It's time we tell everyone the truth. It'll make things go easier for you."

"No," she snapped. Closing her eyes, Hannah blurted out, "Matthew, I'm pregnant."

Matthew looked as if he might keel over from the shock of her words. Finally he drew a deep breath. "What can I do to help?"

His kindness made it impossible for her to speak.

Matthew leaned forward, propping his forearms on his knees. "You said you wanted to see Elle. Do you think telling her about your"—he pointed to her belly—"is going to help?"

"When she hears I'm pregnant, you know what she'll think—that either you or Jacob is the father." A sob jolted from her throat, but she forced herself to regain control. "I know you're sorry you ever spent a moment with me, and if I could change things to protect you, I would. But I can't. I'm sorry."

Matthew's hand covered hers. "No." He squeezed. "I'm the one who's sorry. I should have come to see you, to make sure you were okay, to learn why you'd slept in the shop that night." He patted her hand. "Don't worry. We'll try to set this right. If things go awry, it's not your fault."

Her mouth hung open. This wasn't what she'd expected. He had no repulsion that she was pregnant by some maniac *Englischer*? He had no accusations that somehow all this was her fault?

"What will you do to clear Jacob's name?"

Hannah shook her head. "I'm not going to do anything to try to make Sarah's life easier. Besides, she'll believe Jacob easy enough. You and Elle are innocent bystanders in all this. I've got to try to make her believe the truth."

He rose, looking at the clock that sat on his workbench. "School's been out for a bit. But the driver won't pick Elle up for another hour. She always stays and grades papers and such. We could catch her. But maybe we should wait until after the stress of this meeting with her father. I'm going to the Bylers' tonight, and a driver is picking me up there so I can join Elle about an hour before her father arrives."

Hannah remained on the couch, thinking. To push forward seemed selfish, yet to wait was dangerous. She had to tell the church leaders that she was pregnant as soon as they arrived at Mary's *Daadi Haus.* "If we wait, the news might reach her before we talk to her."

He jerked his hat off and thrust his hand through his hair. "What should we do then?"

The hinges on the front door of the shop creaked. Ten-year-old Peter burst through the door, laughing. "Tell him I didn't do it, Matthew." He hid behind his big brother beside the couch.

Thirteen-year-old David ran into the room. "Tell him I'll get him anyways." David lunged at Peter.

"Easy, boys." Matthew spread out his arms, keeping them at bay from each other.

The teasing in the boys' voices made Hannah miss Samuel and little Rebecca, who she hadn't seen the past few months. They wouldn't recognize their eldest sister if she didn't start seeing them more often.

The door popped open for a third time. Elle entered. The smile on her face faded at the sight of Hannah.

Matthew glanced at Hannah. The decision of whether to wait had just been jerked from their hands.

annah trod across the lumpy, pothole-filled pasture. Her thighs burned and throbbed. The increasing pains in her sides made taking a deep breath impossible. Surely the discomforts she'd been suffering wouldn't keep growing throughout the pregnancy.

Her foot landed in a brown, grassy hole, and she stumbled. She'd never noticed before how difficult this field was to cross. The aches in her sides turned into sharp pains as she plodded through the barnyard and onto the Yoders' lane.

When she opened the door to the *Daadi Haus,* she heard low tones of men muttering to one another. Before Hannah had fully entered the home, Mary hurried to her side. "They've come to talk to you."

The horses and buggies must have been pulled into one of the barns, meaning the leaders knew they'd be here a while. Hannah didn't know whether the bishop and preachers had responded to the news so quickly because they were willing servants of the people, or if they were simply vultures swooping down on a fresh carcass.

Needing a few moments to compose herself, she stepped inside the enclosed back porch, leaned against a canned-goods pantry, and took a deep breath.

Elle had been visibly shaken upon hearing what Hannah had to say. But she responded that she had too much going on with her father to know what she thought of Hannah's confession. She seemed to want to believe Hannah's account but needed a little time before making a stand.

Hannah understood Matthew's desire for Elle. Unusual beauty was the least of the girl's attributes. She was so open and kind as they talked that Hannah found herself wishing she was more like her. Before leaving, Elle had caressed Matthew's face and smiled, saying they could remain friends no matter what. To his credit, Matthew didn't beg her to believe him or become angry with Hannah over her part in all this.

In the face of this upcoming meeting, Hannah could only hope the men would be half as gracious as Elle had been.

"*Kumm.*" Mary put her arm around Hannah's shoulder and led her toward the living room, where the men waited. As they passed the bedroom, Hannah caught a glimpse of the "Past and Future" quilt, lying on the table beside the bed. Each half of the quilt was vital, that which had already happened and that which was yet to happen. A spark of hope danced across Hannah's heart. Soon enough what faced her today would be part of her yesterday.

The four men rose as she entered—not out of respect for her as a woman, she was certain, but because they thought she had summoned them in order to repent. She did intend to repent of any wrongdoing on her part, but she had no intention of repenting of things that weren't her fault. That's where things would get sticky.

She eased into a chair in front of the bishop. The men took their seats as tension mounted. Her father sat to her right, along with Preacher Nathaniel Miller. Preacher Ben Zook sat to her left. She'd known Nathaniel since before he became a preacher. Ben had been close to her grandfather when Hannah was just a girl and had spoken words over her grandfather when he died.

The deacon hadn't come. He was probably unable to drop everything and get here on the spur of the moment. There were organized ways of doing things—certain days and times set apart for such matters. But exceptions were always made to help those in need. Clearly, Hannah was in need.

The bishop laid his hat in his lap. "*Was iss letz?*" Bishop Eli Hostetler was the most intimidating man in the room. His weathered face and beady eyes made him look as old as Hannah imagined God to be—and just as displeased with her. Eli's knobby body was as thin as the rickety boards that were barely holding the old barn together.

Hannah tried to swallow, but her mouth was too dry. The bishop wanted her to get right to the point. But where should she begin?

She gazed at each man, wondering if she possessed the strength to say all that needed to be said. Nathaniel Miller was about her father's age, early forties, with small brown eyes and a large nose that didn't fit his face. Ben Zook was older than the bishop's fifty years by about a decade. He had deep scars over his face that Hannah had always assumed were from acne when he was younger. Slowly her eyes made their way to her father, who wouldn't even look at her.

She willed herself to begin. "At the beginning of this ordeal, my father asked me to come see you. He begged me over and over. But I didn't listen." She drew a ragged breath as another round of aches went through her back and thighs. If the ordeal was Hannah's pregnancy, then her statement was true.

From behind her, Mary passed her a glass of water and several handkerchiefs. As Hannah took a drink, she skimmed the men's faces. Her father's gray blue eyes had a sense of hesitancy about them, of what Hannah didn't know. Was he unsure of the bishop's reaction or unconvinced of his daughter's virtue? Had he fallen prey to the rumors?

She shifted her attention to the bishop.

Hannah started to lean forward to set the glass on the table, but Mary reached out and took it for her.

The bishop cleared his throat. "Mary, I think it would be best if you left us alone for a spell."

Mary nodded. "I'll be in my house if you need me."

As she rose to leave, the bishop glanced at Hannah's father. Hannah knew that what she'd begun might take weeks or even months to finish working out. No matter what the bishop decided, there would be families who disagreed. The families who believed the rumors would accept nothing but full disclosure and repentance on Hannah's part. The ones who chose to believe Hannah's confession today would be resentful until the one who began the gossip came clean.

If it weren't for Matthew and Elle's relationship, Hannah would welcome people learning all there was to know about the gossip. Matthew could probably set people straight, and Sarah would have to admit that she lied about how long Hannah was gone that night. Hannah would thoroughly enjoy seeing Sarah get put in her place.

When the back door closed behind Mary, Eli nodded at Hannah.

Averting her eyes so she didn't have to see the men, Hannah explained. "In the last days of August, I was on my way home from Mrs. Waddell's, our Mennonite neighbor…" With stammering and long pauses, Hannah described the attack the best way she knew how. When she finished, the room was silent for a long time.

The bishop turned to her father. "Zeb, do you believe this account?"

She would have been less startled if the men had held her at fault for walking along the road that day. She'd just revealed the most embarrassing event of her life to these men, and the response was to accuse her of being a liar?

Her father stared at the floor. "I…I was there when she came home. I have no doubt of the trauma that took place."

Eli arched an eyebrow at him, then turned his attention back to Hannah. "And the midnight ride in your nightgown?"

"It was only a few minutes. I never left sight of the house."

The bishop didn't look as though he believed her, but he said nothing.

Hannah's head throbbed, and her sides ached. Sarah's rumors had the bishop discounting everything Hannah said. But she didn't have the strength to drag her sister into this. Besides, it was quite clear that even if she tried to straighten things out by saying that Sarah was a liar, no one in this room was going to believe her.

The bishop continued. "Is it true that you exchanged letters with a Mennonite man against your father's wishes?"

She wished that was a lie, but she couldn't deny it. She nodded.

"Is it his child you carry?"

"No! I told you—"

The bishop interrupted her. "Is it true that the day before Thanksgiving you were in that man's arms, the one you were sending secret letters to, kissing him while your body carried another man's child?"

So, someone had been watching her that day, and they'd told the bishop. Or maybe he was the one who had seen her. She nodded.

"And is it true that Matthew Esh told you that you were a liar?"

Hannah covered her face with the handkerchief. She was buried too deep in mistakes to ever clear her name. What could she say? The bishop himself had heard Matthew say that. Hannah couldn't deny it. No wonder the man had kept silent about his discovery of them in the barn that day. He thought Matthew was correcting her, not playing. If she explained that it was a game, then the bishop's view of Matthew could change, causing even more rumors to run through the community about her and Matthew. If Sarah was ever going to be held accountable for the lies she'd told, Matthew had to be held in high esteem by the church leaders.

She nodded.

"Is it also true that you've snuck off from your home to be with this Mennonite man on many occasions over the years, using your work for Katie Waddell as an excuse?"

She lowered the handkerchief and stared at her lap. She couldn't look at her father. What must he think of her?

The bishop drilled Hannah over and over concerning the same rumors, trying to get her to expound on the reports. She could think of nothing that could open their eyes to the truth. Then again, almost every rumor was rooted in truth, only a twisted version of it. How could she untangle herself from it?

By the time the clock struck five, Hannah was so tired, so racked with physical and emotional exhaustion, she couldn't even lift her head.

"Look at me!" The bishop's voice thundered through the house.

Hannah lifted her face for the first time in over an hour.

"You will stay here alone tonight. Zeb, since Mary's family is visiting relatives quite a ways from here and can't easily return, I think the best place for Mary is with you. The community will accept our decision better if Mary stays with those who will become family members later this year." Bishop Eli folded his hands and stared at them for a spell before looking at Hannah. "Tomorrow we will return. I suggest you spend the night thinking on this account of 'rape.' Consider hard, Hannah, the path you are choosing. There can be no forgiveness without true repentance. We cannot allow you to join the church if you are covering your sin through lies." He rose, and the other men followed suit. "Perhaps a night alone will cause you to think more clearly. I'm concerned that Mary's devotion and her naiveté are serving your manipulation and lies, causing them to grow within you, but she won't be around tonight."

Without standing, Hannah looked up at her father. "Do you question me about the attack too, *Daed*?"

He stared at his daughter. "You have lied to me for years about Mrs. Waddell's grandson. What am I to think?"

Hannah was dumbfounded. How could he think that the brokenness he witnessed the night she came home with gashes in her hands and trauma to her body was somehow linked to her rebellious relationship with Paul?

In unison, the men turned their backs on her. It was a warning of what was to come if she kept to her story of rape. When the door slammed, Hannah buried her face in her hands, too drained to even cry.

The wall clock above the mantel ticked on persistently. An eeriness she had never experienced before filled the evening. She was truly alone for the first time in her life. This separation from human contact felt unruly—even boisterous. And the silence grew louder with each ticktock.

A howling wind interrupted the lull, pushing hard against the house and making it moan. Hannah rose and ambled to the window. Snow lay sparsely across the ground, but the heavy flakes that continued falling from the black sky said the land would be hidden under a blanket before long.

Thoughts of Ohio played across Hannah's mind. At the moment it sounded like a safe haven. She wondered if her aunt might appreciate getting a visit from her brother's eldest daughter.

She huffed at her silliness and placed her hand over her stomach. "We knew it would be a battle to get back in the good graces of *Daed* and the church, but it seems your mother has made things even worse than she realized." She patted her belly. "I'm sorry, little one."

Pulling the shade down, Hannah realized she'd drawn one thick curtain after another between her and her parents through years of deception concerning Paul. How foolish could she be?

Her stomach grumbled, reminding her she hadn't eaten since…dinner yesterday. Plodding into the kitchen, Hannah grabbed a kerosene lamp off a nearby table. As she struck a match and lit the wick, her hunger faded. She hurt all over, from her upper rib cage to her knees. She pulled a few ibuprofen tablets out of a bottle and swallowed them with a glass of water. The bottled medicine had to be better than the homegrown and ground lobelia her family used. On her way back into the living room, a muscle spasm forced her to grab on to a chair and wait.

While she took some deep, relaxing breaths, she wondered if these types of aches were normal. Another spasm hit her lower back and worked its way across her stomach. She moaned, long and low, waiting for the ache to stop. The odd, painful feeling lasted nearly a full minute. Something was wrong. It had to be. Panic jolted her. No one was around. The phone shanty was locked.

Stop worrying. You're fine. It's been a long, grueling day, and your body is weary, nothing more.

The terror leveled off as she assured herself the symptoms were due to the difficulty of the last twenty or so hours. Heartache over Paul lashed out at her. None of what was happening in her life was as painful as losing Paul. But he was gone, and right now her focus needed to be the infant inside her womb.

She shuffled into the bedroom and lay down, covering herself with a blanket. Surely a little rest, along with the pain reliever, would ease the tenseness across her lower back and stomach.

As soon as she laid her head down, sleep came. It was a restless, pain-filled sleep but ever so welcome. When a knock at the door thundered through the room, Hannah glanced at the clock. Eight. Surely the bishop's decree that she spend the night alone had made the rounds already. Who would dare come to her door?

Paul?

Hope stirred. Could it be possible that he came to believe her?

After tossing back the covers, Hannah waited for another long, hard spasm to abate.

The knock at the door came again. "Hannah? It's me, Matthew. Are you all right?"

She felt sick as her foolish anticipation fell to the floor with a thud.

Pushing against the bed, Hannah rose to her feet. She waddled through the rooms and opened the storm door. A blanket of snow covered the ground, and snowdrifts were stacked in various places as the wind danced across their cottony tops. "What are you doing here? Aren't you supposed to be with Elle?"

The wind slashed through the air, ripping the door out of Hannah's hand. Matthew grabbed the storm door, holding it tight. "Her father's plane ain't even landed in Baltimore yet, but I'm on my way to meet a driver just as soon as I make sure you're doin' all right."

Wishing they could enter the warm house, at least enough to close the door, Hannah grabbed a shawl off the nearby coatrack. "You heard about the bishop's edict?"

He nodded, pity showing in his eyes. "I wasn't going to come in. I just needed to check on you. His instructions didn't say someone couldn't check on you."

Hannah smiled in spite of herself. Matthew had always been one to obey while bending the rules when he disagreed with a decree. "I'll be fine, Matthew. I just need some rest." As she spoke the words, tightness sprang from nowhere, almost stealing her breath. Grabbing the doorframe, she panted. In response to his worried expression, she forced a laugh. "I'm fine. Really. I just overdid it today, and my body's having a fit about it."

Matthew stooped. "You sure?"

Determined to leave his life as uninterrupted as possible, Hannah pushed her fears aside and answered as lightheartedly as she could. "Yep. Go. Please, whatever you do, don't be late."

"I'll be back to check on you as soon as I can. It'll be after midnight for sure, maybe close to two before I return." He paused. "You don't look so good."

"*Dankes.*" Hannah managed a tiny curtsy.

Matthew didn't chuckle. He pulled his hat down low and headed for his buggy.

She locked the storm door, still panting. The only things she needed were her bed and some rest. Matthew should not miss being with Elle because of that, especially not tonight. As the carriage disappeared through the haze of powdery snow, she closed the wooden door and went back to bed.

Between shooting pains and aching tightness, Hannah dozed. Suddenly she bolted upright. Her skirts were wet. She pulled herself out of bed, lit a kerosene lamp, and headed for the bathroom. A sharp pain stopped her cold. Trembling, she set the lamp on the table. Like lightning momentarily illuminating a dark sky, suddenly reality dawned on her. Her aches and pains weren't from the difficulty of the past day. She was in labor. From the best she could remember, she had been for more than twenty-four hours.

But the baby's not due until the middle of May.

As that realization settled over her, she wanted to cry out to God, but a sense of betrayal stole her words before they could form.

It was the third week of February. If the baby came now, it might not survive.

Sinking to her knees, she moaned as a long, hard contraction pulled downward on her stomach. Her mind whirled in a hundred directions. Feelings of utter stupidity flooded her. She should have realized hours ago that these weren't normal aches and pains, even though she'd never been through so much turmoil in her life.

When the tightness eased, she rose, using the bed for support.

As she gained her footing and her breath, ideas popped into her head left and right. Mary kept the key to the phone shanty in her pocket. That meant Hannah would have to go to the barn, grab an ax, then make her way to the phone shanty and try to break into it. But did she have the strength to do all that? The answer had to be yes. But she could barely claw her way to her feet with the aid of the bed.

The anatomy book.

Holding her belly with one hand, she scoured the dresser drawers, searching for the book. It had a section on birthing babies. It was only a few pages, and she had read them several times, but… She tossed clean clothing from the drawers onto the floor. Where did she have it last?

Under the mattress! That's where she'd put it. She eased her way back to the bed and ran her hands between the mattress and the box springs. Her fingers touched the smooth, silky cover, and she pulled it out. Breathing with difficulty she flipped the book open to the section on home delivery and began reading. With each word she read, she shook harder. She couldn't do this.

A knock at the door made her jump. Hope sparked—someone had come. She shuffled across the floor to the back door. As she lifted the shade to look out, both relief and dread flooded her.

Matthew.

Fighting within herself, she opened the door. "Matthew," she whispered, "why are you back here?" Placing her arm under her belly, she lifted some of the weight. She could feel her wet, cold skirts against her legs. Her breath came in short puffs as stabbing pains worked their way down her back.

Matthew put his foot over the threshold, making her back up to allow him entrance. He angled his head, trying to read her face. "I had to return." He frowned. "Hannah, are you holdin' a secret?"

She hesitated. If she told him, he'd stay, and nothing about his quiet life would remain intact. Self-hatred covered her, but it held no answer. Fear of being left alone squelched her concerns. "I need help. I think the baby's coming." A sob racked her body, causing her to stumble forward.

Matthew tucked his hand under her forearm, steadying her. He helped her to the bedroom. "I knew somethin' wasn't right. I just had this feeling…" He eased her onto the bed. "I'll call for help."

"The shanty is locked and boarded," Hannah sputtered.

Anger ran through Matthew's eyes. "Don't worry. I'll get in. You stay put."

As he ran for the door, a deep pressure grew in Hannah's body. "Matthew, wait." Her voice came out a mixture of a desperate whisper and a scream.

In a second he was by her side. Hannah pointed to the book. "I need scissors and string from the sewing kit by the dresser. And I need some clean sheets, towels, and…and the nasal aspirator from the medicine cabinet. Hurry."

Almost throwing the stuff at her, Matthew fulfilled her requests, then darted out the door.

Settling herself against the pillows piled at the headboard, the desire to push became so strong she almost couldn't stop herself. She panted through the next few contractions, silently begging herself not to push.

Outside she heard glass breaking and boards being beaten and ripped.

The desire to push grew stronger than her will, more powerful than anything she'd ever experienced. She took a deep breath, and her body took over, ignoring her mental commands to stop. She pushed and moaned. Pushed and panted. Pushed. Pushed. Pushed. Her brow became drenched with sweat. She begged her body to stop pushing, to give Matthew time to get an ambulance. But it wouldn't.

The back door banged and clattered, sounding as if a herd of cows had come in out of the foul weather. A moment later Matthew stood at the door of the bedroom, his face taut with worry. "I got in, but the lines are down. I'm going to fetch *Mamm*."

Hannah raised her hand in the air, unable to speak. Matthew paused, rocking back and forth nervously on the balls of his feet. When the contraction eased, she relaxed against the pillow and drew a breath. "Don't leave me. Please."

"Hannah, you need help. I'll ride bareback across the fields and be back in less than ten minutes. My mother's no midwife, but she's helped deliver a few babies in her time. I...I can't keep you or the babe from dying."

Matthew was as pale as the sheets under her body. His legs carried him like a newborn calf trying to stand. Another contraction slowly built force. "Go," she whispered.

Matthew sprinted across the room, tripping over the sewing basket he'd left out earlier. She heard the back door slam shut.

Her body told her when to push, when to take deep breaths, when to rest. *Hurry, Matthew.* The minutes ticked by with only the sounds of the clock and the howling wind. Amid the pushing and resting, a small head appeared between her thighs.

It wailed in loud protest. Relief ran through Hannah, giving her fresh strength to take on the newest phase of this ordeal. Stacking pillows behind her for support, she leaned forward, holding the clean towels. The little body that issued from hers was tiny. Too tiny. She'd had baby dolls that fit inside her hidden apron pocket that were as large as this baby.

A closer look told her she had given birth to a girl. A daughter. Her child. She dried the infant, noticing even in the dim light of the kerosene lamp that the little one's coloring appeared more like that of a salamander than a baby. The skin was translucent, making the mapping of the veins evident.

Hannah drew the flailing girl into her arms. The book said warmth was paramount. Hannah wiped her off more and wrapped her in the soft sheet and then in the "Past and Future" quilt. The infant screamed, but her eyes didn't open.

Snuggling with her newborn, Hannah smiled down at her. Basking in the maternal feelings that were coursing through her, she cooed. "Rachel is a good name, no?" Her daughter opened her eyelids and seemed to focus on Hannah's face. Tears burned Hannah's eyes. "Hi," she whispered.

The infant blinked, then closed her eyes. Before Hannah drew her next breath, a catlike sound came from Rachel. A moment later a pitiful moan escaped her miniature body. Hannah pulled the wrappings away from the infant's chest, watching…for what, she wasn't sure.

Her daughter's chest caved inward. Hannah's heart thudded hard. Her baby was struggling for air.

The back door banged open, and Naomi rushed to Hannah's side, carrying a folded towel full of items. She laid the bundle on the bed and opened it.

Hannah broke into sobs. "She can't catch a breath. God, please, she's not breathing."

Naomi eased the quilt away from the infant's head and gasped. She met Hannah's stare and shook her head. Hannah didn't need words to know what Naomi was thinking. Rachel was too young, too premature to survive.

Naomi tied off the umbilical cord and cut it with the scissors she'd brought with her.

Sobbing, Hannah drew her convulsing daughter closer to her chest. "Forgive me."

Pitiful moans escaped the newborn as she fought for air. "Be stubborn, Rachel," Hannah cried. "Fight." Hannah hugged her close, willing her to live. She whispered to her in English, refusing the Pennsylvania Dutch of her forefathers.

Hannah sensed Naomi's movements about the bedside as she took care of her midwife tasks. But Hannah never once removed her focus from Rachel, even as the little girl's skin became deeper and deeper blue. After several minutes, her daughter stopped squirming, stopping moaning, stopped everything. Feeling the little girl's life slip away, Hannah wished she knew what those nurses at the hospital knew. Then she might be able to save her.

Rachel's body jerked and then stilled so completely that Hannah knew beyond a doubt her daughter had drifted into another world, one that Hannah probably wouldn't see for many decades. Guilt bore down on Hannah's soul, ripping her heart. She rocked her infant until she knew there was no way to revive her even if medics showed up in the next second.

Regret twisted her heart like a steel vise. If only she'd been up front with everyone about the rape from the start, maybe this wouldn't have happened. She studied the lifeless being in her arms as one word forced its way out of its hidden spot deep inside her. *Rape.* Chills ran up and down her body. "I was raped!" The words poured forth with strength she didn't possess. "If only I'd told…if I'd confessed that to begin with…" The words died in her throat.

What was so horrible about owning up to the rape? Hannah closed her eyes, tuning out Naomi's movements and everything around her.

Resentment at the injustice of the attack rose, demanding to be heard. But as she allowed that thought, a thousand others flooded her: reflections of the bishop's harshness, Luke's bitterness against her, Sarah's backstabbing, the district's thirst for gossip, her father's constant wavering on every subject except his dislike of Mennonites and the unquestioning obedience of his children to his strict ways.

Resentment took hold of her, and she nurtured it as strongly as she would have nurtured her child if she'd been given the chance.

*H*er body still aching from giving birth less than eight hours earlier, Hannah stood by her infant's half-dug grave. The sickening hole in the ground that would hold her infant was under the large beech tree on Matthew's property. The air was unbearably cold, even with the sun shining brightly at eight o'clock in the morning. The fields were covered in a thick layer of snow.

The lines and creases of Matthew's face hinted at a multitude of emotions. He jammed the blade of the shovel into the frozen ground and dumped icy dirt next to the undersized hole. The frozen flecks of the broken sod glittered like shards of glass under the morning rays.

Matthew drove the shovel into the earth again. Digging deep in frozen turf was an arduous task. But his act of kindness had relieved Hannah's father of the need to decide whether he would allow an illegitimate infant of an unbaptized mother to be buried on his land.

Matthew had proven again what Hannah had known about him since they were young: that he was stalwart in his decisions and able to bear the weight of the *Ordnung* while carrying out its truths in his heart. Hannah knew Elle hadn't left his thoughts for a moment. Her name seemed to be etched across his worried brow. But he hadn't once mentioned her or shirked from helping Hannah in any way he could throughout this ordeal.

He'd missed being there for Elle last night during what was probably the most difficult event the yet-to-be-Amish girl had endured. Elle had been forced to face her father, the man who had turned to alcohol and then abandoned his daughter not long after her mother died. And poor Elle had to do it without Matthew by her side. That had to be eating at Matthew.

Keeping him from Elle was another rock in the burlap bag that was tied around Hannah's neck and another incident she could do nothing about.

When the hole was dug, Matthew leaned the shovel against the nearby tree. The sounds of a horse and buggy made him turn and peer in that direction. Hannah didn't bother to look. She was too tired, too numb to care who'd come. But even through the haze of trauma and exhaustion, she understood that anyone's arrival at this secluded spot meant all of Owl's Perch knew of last night's events. She could only assume that Naomi Esh had gone home before sunrise and had spread news of the scandalous events to people desperate for Hannah's correction from God.

Hannah felt a gentle hand come under her forearm, steadying her.

"I'm so sorry, Hannah." Mary's voice cracked.

Mary's embrace was warm. But Hannah didn't speak. She didn't even weep. No amount of crying could change what had happened.

Mamm, Daed, and Luke filled in beside Mary. There they all stood, about to bury a child no one but Hannah knew the name of. Matthew stretched two long pieces of rope across the open hole. Luke stepped forward and grasped the two ropes on one end while Matthew trod to the buggy and easily lifted out the foot-long pine box that carried Rachel. He had done everything he could to help Hannah while possibly laying an ax to his own life in the process. Grabbing the ropes on the end opposite Luke, Matthew pinned them under his boots on his side of the grave and then leaned over to place the wooden box on top of the ropes. He stood.

Six grief-stricken faces stared at the handmade coffin and freshly dug grave. The chestnut horses stomped the cold, hard ground, causing the black buggies attached to them to rattle and creak. Luke and Matthew, positioned opposite each other, held the ropes that looped under the casket. They carefully lowered the wooden box into the ground.

Mamm wept quietly. Hannah's father spoke words of forgiveness. But Hannah couldn't accept his words. Her heart was being consumed with a brutal rage. How could her daughter be dead, without ever getting the chance to live? The tiny thing had never even felt her mother's love, because Hannah had never had any, not until it was too late. A sob broke from her throat, piercing the frigid air that surrounded the group.

Hannah thought of how much the Amish had given to support Luke and Mary in the wake of their accident. Yet those same people had devoured the rumors about her. The bishop and preachers had treated her worse than a leper. Her own father had wavered under the bishop's questioning and had abandoned his daughter in the process.

Matthew prayed aloud, but Hannah heard little of what he said.

A cold wind flapped against their bodies as Luke shoveled frozen soil over the wooden box. His face was as rigid as stone, his movements those of a detached gravedigger.

Mary tugged at Hannah's arm, trying to lead her to a buggy. Hannah's feet seemed rooted in place.

Her mother started walking toward her, but Hannah's father stepped forward and wrapped his hand around his wife's arm. He stared at the ground, mumbling, "Your daughter grieves severely for an infant conceived by rape, no?" His eyes lifted to meet Hannah's, accusing her of things she couldn't disprove. Her mother lowered her head and took her place beside her husband as they walked away from Hannah and back to their buggy.

Hannah's heart froze a little harder. Would this be her lot forever—to live among a people who condemned her for things she hadn't done?

She studied the white fields with barren trees lining the horizon and scattered in small patches around cleared pastures. Her vision blurred, and she couldn't see anything but gray light. Finally she turned to follow Mary's gentle nudging toward the buggy.

"Hannah."

She stopped. It was a whisper from somewhere. Scanning the fields, she looked for signs of mockers, but there were none.

Mary squeezed her arm. "What is it?"

"Did you hear that?"

Worry creased Mary's face. She shook her head. "I didn't hear anything."

Hannah stared at the faces of those who surrounded her. Obviously, no one else had heard the voice. She trudged toward the buggy, snow crunching beneath her feet.

"*Hannah.*" This time the two syllables of her name were drawn out, like the echoes inside an empty barn.

She stopped and turned. "I'm listening." She said it aloud, not caring what anyone thought.

"*Kumm raus.*"

"Come out to where?" She made a complete circle, listening for an answer, but she heard none. When her gaze landed upon Mary, she saw that the girl had gone pale.

Matthew came beside Hannah and led her into the buggy. "You need sleep. It's over now. It's time to rest."

That was it. She needed sleep. With the aid of the portable wooden steps that Matthew placed on the ground, Hannah climbed into the buggy.

"*Hannah.*" The familiar voice returned. Afraid of what responding to the voice would do to Mary, Hannah didn't dare answer.

As the buggy plodded across the field to the Yoders' *Daadi Haus,* the wind whispered her name over and over, begging her to *kumm raus.*

Hannah would be glad to go, if she only knew where.

Through the murky sleep of grief-filled nightmares, Paul's own groaning woke him. "Hannah, *kumm raus!*" The cry resonated in his head.

He sighed and sat upright, placing his feet on the floor and his head in his hands. Streams of sunlight poured in around the white shades hanging over the windows. He glanced at the clock. Eight o'clock. Just two and a half days ago he'd discovered Hannah's pregnancy. How would he ever get over that?

The door to his shared bedroom popped open. Paul leaned back, determined to act as if he were fine.

Marcus strode in with a towel tied around his hips and water covering his upper body. "Man, Waddell, you look like death warmed over. It's no wonder. You must've called for that Hannah girl a hundred times, whoever she is."

Paul grabbed his pants from the foot of the bed and jerked them on. *Yeah, whoever she is.*

Sifting through dirty clothes, Marcus picked out a pair of pants and a shirt. "The snowplows have cleaned up the mess from the storm night before last. But last night's winds knocked out the electricity to most of the campus. All classes are canceled."

Jerking open a drawer, Paul seized a fleece shirt and put it on. No matter how angry and hurt he was with Hannah, his heart kept calling to her, in Pennsylvania Dutch no less.

Marcus pulled on his baggy jeans. "So, I figure this Hannah girl must be what's kept you from dating anyone else or even looking, for that matter, right?"

Paul didn't answer. Hannah meant so much more than that to him. She was the lion that roared in his soul.

And the girl who's carrying another man's baby.

Pain thudded against his chest.

Marcus poked his still-damp arms through the sleeves of a dirty sweatshirt. "So, what does 'come ros' mean?"

Paul had heard Hannah use the phrase many times. "I'm pretty sure it means to come out."

In spite of the different worlds that sometimes made it hard to understand each other's lives, there was always a force within both of them that drew them together. Over the years her sweet innocence and wild sense of humor had clashed with her unwavering sense of propriety, and he'd always understood that.

Clouds of jealousy parted momentarily, and for the first time since he'd confronted her, Paul saw something besides the green-eyed monster. Was it possible that the wedge between them wasn't Matthew or Dr. Greenfield or any other man the rumors conjured up? Could the chasm he'd sensed from their first contact after they were engaged be caused by Hannah withholding some other secret?

"The unmentionable." He mumbled the words, pacing the undersized room.

Marcus's face registered confusion. "Uh, yeah, you've obviously spent years not mentioning her."

Paul frowned, refusing to get sidetracked. "No. She used the word *unmentionable*…" Paul raked his hands through the knots in his hair. "You know the Amish a little. One word often means several things. What do you think they would use that word for?"

Marcus sat on his unmade bed, smiling at Paul. "Ah, so she's Amish. That explains a lot. The way you've kept it under wraps, I thought maybe you'd fallen for an older divorcée with a passel of kids."

Paul scowled. "Stop joking around and stick to the subject. This is serious."

Marcus nodded, but the grin didn't leave his face. "Okay, okay. Let's see, I've heard my aunt use that word. She lives among the Amish in Lancaster. The only time I've heard it used is when they're talking about adultery."

"I know that." Paul shoved his hands into his pockets. There had to be something he was missing.

The smile disappeared from Marcus's face, and he sat up straighter. "I think they use that word to describe anything to do with sex. So I guess it would include premarital relations, probably even rape."

Dumbstruck, Paul couldn't respond. Rape? That wasn't the answer he was searching for. Wasn't there something between Hannah giving herself to someone and rape? Both ideas were incomprehensible. Totally unacceptable. Confusion and anger fought for control of his body.

Marcus broke through his thoughts. "For that matter, *unmentionable* would probably be used instead of adjectives like *pleasure, gratifying,* or *desire.*"

Paul bristled, looking at the floor. "Keep the unnecessary annotations to yourself, okay?"

Marcus leaned forward. "I didn't mean…"

Paul sighed. He had left the subject of sex out of every conversation with Hannah, telling himself it was inappropriate. Maybe it was, or maybe he wasn't any more comfortable discussing that subject than she would have been.

Paul opened his nightstand and looked in his bowl of change to see if he'd dropped his keys in there when emptying his pockets. If sex was a topic even he was uncomfortable talking about, there was no way Hannah would have brought it up with him. "Especially if she thought I'd think less of her."

"What?"

Paul sat on his bed and put his elbows on his thighs. He buried his head in his hands. "Never mind. Listen, you date different girls regularly. Have you ever thought one of them was seeing someone behind your back?"

"Hey, I spend my time with quality women—Bible-believing, God-honoring, denying-their-darker-side women. Besides, I think most girls would rather handle things relatively honestly."

Paul sighed, trying to remember the exact words Hannah had said. "Relatively?"

Marcus shifted on the bed, making it creak. "They'd rather dump a guy than cheat on him, even if it means fudging a little on why they don't want to be with him. So, is this Hannah the kind of girl who would be relatively honest, or would she be more likely to run around behind your back?"

Paul lowered his hands, making eye contact with Marcus. "She did make a few remarks recently about me not wanting to do all that it would take to wait for her. She never talked like that before we became engaged—"

"Engaged?" Marcus interrupted.

Paul stood. "I... We...were... I don't know." He paced the small room as his mind conjured up images from years of friendship with Hannah. His need to build a foundation that went deeper than just friendship had begun when he'd returned to Gram's two summers ago. Hannah's beauty had blossomed strikingly, and he knew she would attract every single man around. The night he went to the hospital to see her, her friendliness with Matthew watered the seeds of jealousy that had been planted long before. When her reaction to his visit was less than enthusiastic, his lack of confidence turned into festering envy.

"Paul?"

He stopped pacing and sat on the bed again. "I went to see her the night before the snowstorm. We argued and I left." Paul punched the mattress below him. "What happened to us?"

Marcus shrugged. "I have no idea, my friend. You haven't told me anything about this girl, you know."

Neither Paul nor Hannah had anything to lose at this point, so Paul told Marcus all about her. As he talked, he realized he should have done this with Marcus years ago. Just airing everything cleared his mind and made all sorts of things make sense. As he retraced their relationship, doubts he'd had about Hannah's faithfulness began to shrink.

Marcus's eyes shifted back and forth, studying Paul's face. "She's pregnant?"

He nodded, all doubt of Hannah's innocence completely gone. His insecurity and jealousy had blinded him for a few days. "You can't mutter a word of this to anyone."

"Come on, Waddell. You know I won't."

"It's just that I've spent years trying to protect her, not letting anyone know about us so her father wouldn't find out and punish her." Guilt at leaving her there, begging him to listen to her, hounded him. "Dear Father, what have I done?"

Paul grabbed his shoes and yanked them on. "I've got to go to her and make this right. She'll be eighteen in two weeks. I'll need to hide her until her birthday, but after that her father can't legally make her return home. I bet the reason she's not living under his roof anymore is because he won't let her." He lunged toward the door.

Marcus stepped in front of him. "Wait. Just take a few minutes and think about this. You're talking about some serious baggage. Maybe rape and a baby?"

Paul stopped, horrified at the words that had just come out of his friend's mouth. "And I can only hope she needs me enough to forgive me."

As Paul strode toward the door, Marcus followed him. "The winds have caused snowdrifts across some of the roads. I doubt if the snowplows have gotten to the back roads of Owl's Perch yet. Let me go with you. I might be able to help."

Paul grabbed his coat off a chair. "In spite of the complete idiot that I am, I'm fine on my own."

"Look, I'm sorry about the baggage comment. If this is what you want, I'll back you. But you need to give me a break here, not to mention yourself. Your reaction wasn't what you wish it was, but you got sideswiped. You can't hold it against yourself because you needed time to think and process. That's just part of being a human."

Paul's heart lurched. "Sideswiped!" What an idiot he'd been. He grabbed a kitchen chair and squeezed the wooden spindles as hard as he could, rage building inside him. "That's when she stopped going to Gram's. That's when she started acting weird. The unmentionable must have happened…" It all fell into place. He couldn't bear to think of what had happened to her…and what he'd done to make matters even worse.

Unable to take any more, he lifted the kitchen chair into the air and smacked it over the table, wishing he could find the man who had dared to hurt his sweet Hannah. He brought it down again and again until he held only spindles.

He turned to Marcus. "We waited years, were willing to wait years longer to win her father's approval, and some idiot took advantage of a girl weaker than himself." Paul's peripheral vision turned red and began closing in around him.

Marcus had backed away as Paul destroyed the chair, but now he stepped forward. "Paul, you're wasting time. Hannah needs you. Come on, I'll drive. My car has better traction in the snow than your truck."

Paul dropped the pieces of wood. How would he and Hannah ever find their way back to who they once were?

Marcus grabbed his keys off the hook beside the front door.

Climbing into the passenger seat of Marcus's Ford Escort, Paul wrestled with guilt and a sense of urgency.

As they traveled north on 283, Paul rapped his nervous fingers on his leg. "What's with all the brake lights?"

Marcus shifted into second gear. "I don't know, but it doesn't look good."

fter burying her daughter, Hannah slept fitfully for hours in Mary's *Daadi Haus*. But the high winds that screeched all night made rest nearly impossible.

When morning broke and she heard familiar voices, she almost felt sane. She sat up, listening to the Pennsylvania Dutch words fly back and forth between Luke and Mary. Since it was barely daylight, Hannah figured Luke must have stayed the night at the Yoders' main house. Hannah eased her body upright, every part of her painfully aware that she'd given birth just two nights ago.

"You can't believe she doesn't know who the father of her child is, Mary. That's ridiculous. If you want to forgive her, fine. But at least make her be honest about her situation."

"You're wrong to hold such bitterness against her, Luke. Why do you hate her so?"

"I've got my reasons. And you'd do well to take more stock in what Sarah says and less in what Hannah says."

Hannah swallowed. Part of her wanted to step out and not eavesdrop. The other part wanted to stay put.

"I want to know what you have against Hannah." Mary's voice was different than Hannah had ever heard it.

"Fine. I'll tell ya. If she'd agreed to go with us the night I was gonna propose, we wouldn't have been out at the Knepps' place."

"What? You think you would've proposed with Hannah around? Just who are you foolin'? And if you want to blame someone for that night, blame me. I'm the one who was supposed to be driving. I'm the one who twisted the horse's reins around the stob. I'm the one who didn't want Sarah blabbing to the whole community about us being a couple when I didn't know how you felt."

"I…I… Hannah's the one who's been running around seeing that Mennonite behind everyone's back."

"And just who did you see behind everyone's back during your *rumschpringe*, Luke Lapp?"

"You're…you're seeing this all from Hannah's side."

Luke sounded rattled, and Hannah was glad. She didn't possess the strength to step into the room and argue with Luke. Besides, Mary was making headway—opening Luke's eyes. Hannah was sure of it.

"This argument has gone on way too long," Mary said.

Through the open bedroom door, Hannah saw Mary cross from the kitchen into the living room. Shaking, Hannah hid behind the doorframe and watched.

Mary thrust Luke's coat and hat toward him. "If that's how you feel about your sister, it's time you left." She opened the front door. "And ya need not bother returning."

Luke scowled. "Will she fool you your whole life, Mary?"

Mary pointed out the door. Luke took his coat and hat and stormed out. Mary sat on the couch and started crying.

Hannah rested her head on the doorframe. Causing trouble seemed to be her gift, her destiny. She didn't mean to. Sarah was right; Hannah was a tornado. Hannah had caused divisions in her own household and between Matthew and Elle and probably in every home within her district and beyond. She couldn't take it any longer. There had to be something she could do.

"Hannah. Kumm raus."

Chills ran up her back. That whisper was calling to her again. The voice sounded familiar, but she couldn't place it. The tone was soft and pleading.

The cold floor made her sore, achy body hurt even more. She returned to her bed and crawled beneath the blankets. As she closed her eyes, her mind danced to a place where no one knew her, a place filled with people who accepted her as if she'd never worn a scarlet letter that she didn't deserve.

Ohio came to mind again, and a half smile tugged at Hannah's lips. Wouldn't that be something—to leave all this behind? She could look up her Aunt Zabeth and maybe begin life anew.

The idea of leaving brought more than just hope of finding respect outside Owl's Perch and of ending the wars that had begun between people she cared about. The dream seemed to open her heart to the possibility of forgiving those who'd wronged her and letting go of her bitterness. With each moment of reflection, the hateful anger that raged within her began to quiet.

If she left, Mary and Luke would come to a we-agree-to-disagree resolution of some type. They loved each other too much not to. Her father wouldn't have to decide what to do with or about Hannah. She wouldn't have to spend a lifetime facing people who believed the rumors or at least pondered the truth of them.

Some people in the district would disrespect Hannah for the rest of her life. From what she saw at the graveside, she had even come between *Mamm* and *Daed*—*Mamm* wanting to comfort her, *Daed* treating her like an unrepentant adulteress.

Mary and Luke, Matthew and Elle were paying a ridiculous price on her behalf, being divided because there was no proof of her innocence, only evidence of sin—the child she carried, the men she'd been seen with, the lies she'd told her parents over the years. Hannah sighed. That was only part of the problem she'd cause over the next few years.

But if she left... The thought pulled at her imagination.

Where would she get the cash to travel? She had very little money... except the funds she and Paul had in an account together. She didn't have the bankbook, but Paul said she didn't need it to make withdrawals or deposits. Nine hundred dollars of the money in that joint account was hers. That should be enough for all her needs until she found a job.

Maybe she could go to Ohio and find her Aunt Zabeth after all.

She would need to call the bank and see if she could withdraw money using her pictureless identification card. She only wanted to take what was hers. There was no way she'd ever touch Paul's money.

The fanciful idea grew quickly. Dreaming of the possibilities, but too sore and tired to think anymore, Hannah dozed off.

She woke less than an hour later, feeling a bit of physical strength in spite of the emotional agony. Even before she opened her eyes, thoughts of leaving sailed across her soul, leaving some hope in their wake. The desire to leave this disgusting mess behind was stronger than anything she'd felt in her life.

Ohio.

The compelling thought caused hope to stir within her.

She smelled coffee and eased out of bed.

As she took a shower and dressed, an even stronger thought entered her mind. The voice that had been whispering her name had carried a captivating message: *kumm raus.* Those words formed images of her packing and landing in a new place.

Was that really possible?

Titillating desire mixed with nervousness made her feel like the Hannah of old, the one she'd been before the attack. The world beyond Owl's Perch was a big one, filled with good and bad people, to be sure. But she'd already encountered the worst life had to dish out, hadn't she?

Maybe there was something better. Maybe there wasn't. Either way, she was tired of life in Owl's Perch. She'd tried to please everyone, especially Paul. Those nurses at Hershey Medical Center didn't hang on what men thought or wanted, not like she had.

She slipped out of the bathroom and tiptoed to the bedroom window and gazed across the snow-covered fields. As she watched the sun dance off the white blanket that covered the tree limbs, she saw some Amish children sledding in the distance. If only she were young… The whispers of yesteryear rang in her head. But even that didn't beckon to her like the dream of leaving.

Hannah closed the bedroom door and pulled a stack of paper from a drawer. Before she left, she had to do what she could do to repair some of the damage.

She wrote a long letter to Elle, praying she would accept her explanation and forgive Matthew for not being with her the night she'd had to face her father—the night Hannah needed Matthew. Elle would lose a good man who loved her dearly if she didn't forgive Matthew his only fault, which was an overriding loyalty to the needy. Hannah had needed him more that night than Elle. Matthew knew that, and he'd acted on it. Surely Elle could see that if the child had been Matthew's, he would never have begun a relationship with Elle. Elle was smart. She could see past the lies to the truth, especially if Hannah bared her heart on paper.

She wrote a letter of thanks to Matthew, the only male friend she had left and someone she would pray for the rest of her life. Pray for? Hannah smiled. Yes, she concluded as she shook the dust of this place off her feet. She would pray in her new life. She would.

She wrote to Luke, hoping he could find it in himself to stop blaming her for Mary's injuries.

Weaving words of hope and forgiveness into the letter to her parents was the most difficult. She begged her *Daed* to understand that she needed to leave. There was no doubt in her mind that her decision to depart the

CINDY WOODSMALL

Lapp household and separate herself from the community here was for the best. Then her shame would be counted as hers alone and not as a reflection on her family.

As she filled page after page with words of her new decision, the force of life slowly flowed back to her. The idea of leaving was terrifying. But staying would be slow death.

I'm not eighteen yet.

That bit of realization stole her breath. It was thirteen days before she turned eighteen. For a moment she considered staying until her birthday. Hope drained from her. A sensation of losing her mind washed over her, and she knew without any doubt she couldn't stay—not even until she became a legal adult.

The two people who would be the saddest would be her mother and her dear friend Mary. They would understand her plans, but Hannah wasn't naive enough to think that they'd agree with her decision. They were too afraid of angering God, of severing ties, of Hannah getting hurt.

Hannah closed her eyes, contemplating whether *Mamm's* and Mary's future concerns for her were well-founded or not. She had no desire to make things worse by leaving without giving thought to what their reservations would be.

Hannah played out conversations in her mind, careful to hear every bit of apprehension her mother and Mary would share. But after considering all possible arguments either one would present, she decided fear was the only sound reason they'd have—fear of the unknown, of what might happen, of what might not happen.

The imagined conversation had brought up valid points. She might run into danger, might not get a job, might…might…might. The torments of what could happen frightened her. As Hannah burrowed deeper into her own thoughts, looking for answers, a startling revelation sprang forth. Fear might be her traveling companion, but she didn't have to let it stop her. Perhaps she'd have to carry it with her, unable to get free of it. But she didn't have to become immobilized by it. *That* was within her power to decide.

Excitement at that understanding grew, and desire to move forward became a part of her. With stacks of triple-folded letters all around her, Hannah took pen in hand to write the last letter before making her final plans to leave.

Hannah stacked the letters together and laid them inside the book Dr. Greenfield had given her. With trepidation she eased out to the kitchen to tell Mary of her plans. Hannah was surprised to see Matthew sitting at the kitchen table with Mary.

They turned to look at her. Relieved smiles erased the misery on their faces.

Matthew rose and pulled out a chair for her. "Good morning. Come sit."

Glad to get off her feet, Hannah eased into the chair. "How are things with Elle?"

Matthew shrugged. "I heard from the Bylers that her father didn't arrive that night due to the weather. She hired a driver the next day and went to meet him in Baltimore and spend a few days there. Other than that, I don't know."

Matthew poured a cup of coffee and passed it to Hannah. Mary dished out a gigantic cinnamon bun from a pan in the center of the table and placed it beside the cup. Deciding she was no longer too young for coffee, Hannah took a sip of the warm, brown liquid. She played with the metal cup in her hand, praying that Mary and Matthew would support her resolution. "I'm glad you're both here," she said, her voice sounding even more resolved than she felt. "I need to talk to you about some decisions I've made."

The sun warmed the snow-covered earth as Hannah stood in John Yoder's beaten and damaged phone shanty, waiting for the woman at the bank to complete her verification. Mary and Matthew stood nearby, talking in low tones.

"I'm sorry," the woman said, coming back on the line, "but that account has been closed."

"What?" Hannah barely breathed.

"All the money has been withdrawn from it." The woman ended the conversation with another apology, and Hannah hung up the phone.

She couldn't believe this. How could the account be closed?

Hannah lowered her forehead against the receiver, which rested in its cradle on the wall. The disappointment and betrayal were too great for her to bear. Was Paul not at all the man she'd thought him to be?

Mary took the few steps to the shanty's doorway. "What'd you find out?"

Hannah closed her eyes and gave a long, slow shrug. "The account is empty. I…I guess Paul took the money."

Mary wrapped her arms around Hannah. "I'm sure he's just not thinking straight, Hannah. He'll come around. Maybe you should contact him."

As they walked to Mary's front porch, Hannah squelched that burning desire. She hated to admit it to herself, but she ached to call him, to hear his voice one last time, to at least say good-bye.

Hannah sat on the top step. "I've got a little money from the summer's produce. I guess it'll get me somewhere."

Matthew sat beside her. "I think—"

The phone rang, and Mary ran across the yard to answer it.

Hannah smiled. "Her strength is back, no?"

"*Ya.* She does well, thanks to you." Matthew leaned his forearm on his thighs. Neither of them spoke for several minutes. "Hannah, are you sure about leaving?"

Before Hannah had time to answer, Mary strode back to them, hurt showing in her face. "That was my parents. They are returning today and…"

Hannah didn't need to be told what that call was about. She patted the step beside her. "I'm to be off their property before they arrive."

Mary sat. "I'm sorry."

Hannah placed her arm around Mary and rubbed her shoulder. "I'm sure my own mother feels much the same way. I know *Daed* is angry and telling her not to come, but he couldn't keep her from coming to me if she had a mind to."

Matthew tugged his hat lower on his head. "I've got some money."

"That money is for you and Elle to start a home with."

He stood. "Don't deny me the right to do what I think is right. I've spent too many months trying to stay out of hot water when I should have been trying to be a friend." He shrugged. "Either Elle gets that or she doesn't."

Hannah reached out and clutched his fingers, overwhelmed with his generous spirit. "I'll send the money back as soon as I can, after I get a job and get settled."

Matthew gave her hand a warm, reassuring squeeze. "Don't worry about trying to pay me back. Just let us know you're okay every so often."

Mary hugged Hannah, tears brimming in her eyes. "*Ya*, write to us."

"I will." Laying her head on Mary's shoulder, Hannah said, "Let's call the train station and arrange for a driver."

Matthew helped her to her feet. "Call Russ Braden. He's the easiest driver to reach on such short notice. While you do that, I'll run over to the safe in my shop." He studied her. Then without a word he took off to fetch the money.

Paul was glad they'd taken Marcus's car since it had a radio. He flipped on a news station, listening for a traffic report. A minute later he heard about a bad accident somewhere ahead of them that would have traffic backed up for a long time.

Paul took a deep breath to keep himself from hitting the dashboard. "How could I do that to her?"

Marcus turned the radio to an instrumental music station. "Personally, I think you were justified in walking out on her. But let's just say you blew it by handling the whole thing wrong. We all blow it, Paul. Hannah's got some responsibility in this too. Right?"

Paul shook his head. "I should've known better. The ridiculous thing is, aside from my uncontrollable jealousy, I did know better. She's so amazing, Marcus. When you get to know her, you'll agree."

As they sat in stand-still traffic, Marcus had the car in neutral with the handle of the emergency brake raised. "She must be special to have grabbed your attention and kept it all this time. How'd you meet her?"

"She was Gram's helper when I went home to supervise those guys we hired to replace Gram's roof and repair the barn and fences. She was fascinating: quiet, a hard worker. But when she spoke, she had a dry sense of humor. Weeks later when I went back for a family gathering at Gram's, I was sure she'd be happy to see me. She didn't even seem to notice my presence. So I hung out in the kitchen, giving her time to realize I existed. She passed me a chef's apron. To her I was either helpful or in the way." He chuckled. "I was hooked right then. There's no figuring her out, but there's pure pleasure in being with her."

Marcus smiled wryly. "Okay, so maybe I should have been glad you weren't able to talk about her all this time."

"Get us out of this traffic, and I'll never bore you again."

"Promise?" Marcus revved his engine as if he could take off somewhere.

Paul leaned his head against the headrest and growled in frustration.

Hannah gazed at the prayer *Kapp* in her hand. Mary stood behind her, pinning Hannah's apron to her dress. Traveling regulations dictated that she either have a photo ID or wear full Amish garb with her pictureless ID. Though ready to be free of everything Amish, Hannah placed the covering on her head and attached it to her hair using straight pins. She turned and faced Mary.

Mary brushed a piece of lint from Hannah's dress. "Are you sure about this?"

She nodded, unable to speak. She took Mary by the hand, and they walked outside, where the driver was waiting.

Matthew loaded Hannah's bag into the trunk of the hired car. As he shut the trunk, a buggy pulled into the driveway. Matthew turned. "Elle."

The cool nod she gave him could have come from an aristocrat sitting in a fine carriage rather than an Amish girl in an open wagon.

"I thought you were in Baltimore." He stepped toward her buggy. "I'm sorry about the other night. Are you—"

Elle interrupted him. "You don't seem to ever lack for info about what's happening in Hannah's life." Her eyes moved to Hannah. "What's going on?"

Hannah stepped off the porch. "I'm leaving."

Elle's jaw was set, her cheeks flaming red from the cold wind. "Then at least some of what I've heard is true."

"Very little, I'm sure." Mary's voice wavered.

Elle shot an angry look at Matthew. "Did you disobey the bishop's decree concerning Hannah? Did you go to her when I asked you to be with me that night?"

"It's a long story, Elle, but now isn't the time."

Hannah pulled Mary into a hug. After a long, teary embrace, Hannah released her. Then she stood there, fidgeting with her apron, wanting to clutch Matthew and tell him how thankful she was for his kind, understanding spirit. But to do so might cause even more trouble between him and Elle.

A look of determination passed through Matthew's eyes. "I'm goin' with ya. When you're settled on the train, I'll return to Owl's Perch."

"That's ridiculous." Elle raised her body slightly off the bench seat, making the horse step forward. "What do you expect me to think of this?"

Matthew took Elle's horse by the harness, stopping it from moving any farther. "Her train don't leave until early afternoon tomorrow. Mary can't go; her parents have made their stand clear. Hannah's my friend, Elle. I won't leave her in Harrisburg to stay overnight at some hotel by herself."

Elle scowled, clearly getting angrier by the second. "If you don't care at all what I think, why don't you just say it outright, Matthew Esh? You've pretty much just told me you plan to stay at a hotel with her. If you do that, you're sure to get in trouble with the church leaders. You'll be disciplined by the bishop. You know you will."

Matthew released his grip on the horse and walked closer to the buggy. He placed a foot on the spindle of the front wheel. "I know. But they're wrong about Hannah. And friends should stick by each other, even when it costs them."

Elle cocked an eyebrow. She stared at Matthew for nearly a full minute. He watched her face, looking neither worried nor apologetic. Hannah struggled to breathe, guilt heavy on her heart.

Tugging the reins low, Elle caused the horse to back up. Matthew removed his foot, acceptance in his features. Elle's beautiful eyes never left his face as the horse continued backing up.

She stopped the buggy, her brows knitted, her gaze still fixed on Matthew. "Regardless of where we end up in all this, it still seems best that someone go with you, Matthew, to keep things looking respectable before the People and the church leaders." She looked to Hannah. "You have to know that's true."

"Yeah, absolutely. But there's no one else."

"I'll go."

Hannah was startled by the woman's voice behind them. She turned and saw Naomi Esh standing near the car with her hands on her hips.

"I was there the night Hannah's baby died." Naomi gave a weak and humble smile at Hannah, then turned to face Elle. "I believe her account of how she came to be with child. But I'll not have my son's reputation ruined, and clearly he's determined to go with her."

Elle shrugged. "I guess your mother chaperoning will count for something when the church leaders hear of what you've done."

Matthew pulled a letter from his pocket. "Hannah wrote this to you. Maybe it'll help ya understand." He gave a nod to Hannah and motioned for her to get in the car.

Hannah turned to embrace Mary one more time. Her friend broke into sobs.

"It's okay, Mary. I'm going to be fine." Hannah placed her hands on

Mary's shoulders and put some distance between them. "You'll be fine too. Make amends with Luke. He'll come around concerning me as time goes by."

"Mary," Elle said.

Hannah paused as Matthew held the car door open for her.

Elle smiled at Mary. "I'm staying with the Bylers tonight. Esther Byler is helping me with some projects for the kids at the school where I teach. Would you care to join us? We certainly could use your help."

The grief in Mary's face, as well as the lost look in her eyes, faded a bit.

Remorse as well as thankfulness entered Hannah as she considered that if she left, Elle would likely become Mary's closest friend.

"Hannah." The whispery voice floated across the fields, seemingly coming from all directions.

Instantly Hannah's resolve was renewed. She climbed into the backseat of the waiting car. Hope in the future lifted her spirits.

bout the time Paul couldn't take one more minute of waiting, traffic finally started moving again. He drummed his fingers on the dashboard. He had to get to Hannah and offer to take care of her and her baby. Maybe, eventually, she'd come to trust and love him again and they could marry.

As they finally entered Owl's Perch, he gave Marcus directions to the Yoder place.

Marcus pulled into the driveway. Paul jumped out of the car and banged on the front door of the *Daadi Haus*.

Come on, Hannah. Answer.

No sound came from inside; he saw no flickers of light from a kerosene lamp. He knocked longer and louder. Still no response. Disappointment and concern threatened to swallow him.

Paul climbed into the car. "We're going to the Lapp place." He gave Marcus directions.

As they pulled into the driveway, Mr. Lapp stepped out of his house. Paul got out and spoke to Mr. Lapp from across the roof of the car. "I'm looking for Hannah."

He waved Paul away and marched off toward the barn.

Paul caught up to him. "Mr. Lapp, please. I need to speak with her."

Mr. Lapp sighed. "She doesn't live here anymore. I did my best to protect her. But her sneaking around did more damage than a father can stop." He paused and looked at Paul. "It's you, isn't it? You're the one she wrote letters to and snuck out to visit."

There was no easy way to explain his relationship with Hannah. He loved her, to be sure. But that wasn't what Mr. Lapp wanted to hear. "I'm Katie Waddell's grandson, Paul."

Mr. Lapp studied him. "It didn't have to end this way. If she hadn't been so stubborn about going to the bishop—"

"Where can I find her?"

He frowned. "She's staying at the Yoder place."

"I went there. No one's home."

The look on Mr. Lapp's face told Paul that was news to him. "It seems I've spent far too much time not knowing where my daughter was or what she was up to." Mr. Lapp stalked off, grumbling as he went. "Please leave. Just go, and let me forget for a while the devastation you've brought to us."

Paul hated the way Mr. Lapp perceived the events, but it would take a lifetime to change the man's opinions, if it could be done at all. Paul climbed in the car and slammed the door. "How can he just turn his back on his own daughter like that?" Guilt rose within Paul, choking him. He had turned his back on Hannah too.

Marcus shrugged. "Where to now?" He backed down the driveway and stopped where the road met the lane.

"Let's go back to the Yoder farm. From there we'll try to find the Esh place. She and Matthew were friends. He should know where she is—not that he'll tell me." He looked at Marcus, desperate for some answers. "We have to find her."

"We will. Even if we have to cruise her district all day and night. But first, can we go by your grandmother's and get some food? I missed breakfast."

That was a brilliant idea. Maybe Gram knew where Hannah was. Maybe Hannah was even there. "Yes. Go there first."

Marcus pulled onto the main road.

"Do you have your cell with you?" Paul asked.

Marcus pulled the phone from his jeans pocket.

"If Gram doesn't know where Hannah is, I'll call my mother and tell her what to do if Hannah calls. Then I'll call Carol and Dorcas. One of them should be willing to go to our apartment and man the phone. Ryan or Taylor will let them in, but I don't trust our roommates not to leave for a food run or something, even if I ask them to stay by the phone for me. I'll make sure Gram stays near her phone too. If Hannah calls any of those places, I'll get the message right away." He held up Marcus's phone and waggled it.

Hannah lay on the bed, staring at the soft lighting of the electric floor lamp at the far end of the hotel room. The sun had gone down, but there was no need for matches or kerosene lamps.

She clutched her train tickets to her chest. Buying them was the first thing she and Matthew had done when they'd arrived in Harrisburg. He gave her the money for the one-way tickets, but he hadn't joined her when she talked to the man at the ticket window. The man patiently helped her decide what train she needed to take and where she needed to get off. Her final destination would be a little depot in Alliance, Ohio. That was the closest depot to where her aunt lived in Winding Creek.

Matthew and his mother were out getting supper. Hannah remained behind, desperate for some time alone. Matthew said he'd bring her back some food.

A phone sat on the table beside her, begging to be used. She desperately wanted to call Paul and have some type of friendly ending to their longstanding relationship. She sat upright and lifted the receiver from its cradle. At Thanksgiving Paul had given her the phone numbers for Gram, his parents, his apartment, and even his sister. She'd memorized them all.

Following the directions taped on the tabletop next to the phone, she pressed the button to get an outside line and then punched in the number to his apartment. Leaning back on the bed, she drew a deep breath. Her stomach ached with nervousness.

"Hello?" a young female voice answered.

"Uh, yes, this is Hannah Lapp. I'm trying to reach Paul Waddell."

~~∽~~

Daylight peeped over the horizon as Paul continued to cruise Owl's Perch in Marcus's car. Gram had been no help, saying she hadn't heard from Hannah in months.

He'd left Marcus at his gram's house, thinking Marcus'd be better suited for reaching him than Gram if Hannah did call. He'd contacted his parents, his sister, and Dorcas, making sure every place Hannah might call was covered. His mother was baffled and stressed to learn of Paul's relationship with Zeb Lapp's daughter, but she said they'd do as he asked.

When he drove back to the Yoder place, he discovered that Mary's parents had arrived home at some point while he was riding around the district. When Paul knocked on the door and asked about Hannah, he learned that they didn't know where she was. The looks on their faces said they didn't much care either. When he asked to see Mary, he was told she wasn't at home, and they weren't going to reveal where she was. But he did learn that Mary's mother had gone to see Mary, wherever she was, and Hannah was not with her. They wanted it to stay that way.

As he continued driving, Paul studied the homes and yards of every Amish place, hoping for a glimpse of Hannah or Mary. Using Marcus's cell, Paul called his parents and Gram; no one had heard from her.

He dialed his apartment and waited for someone to pick up. After what he thought were too many rings, Dorcas answered.

"Hello."

"Hey, any news?" Paul expected a quick answer, but instead the line went silent. "Dorcas, did Hannah call?"

Dorcas stammered and stuttered, infuriating Paul. "Uh, well, there was a call...but, uh, it...well..."

"This is no time for incompetence, Dorcas. It's an easy question. Did Hannah call?"

There was a shuffling sound, and his sister came on the line. "Easy, Paul. You made her cry. This is a pretty miserable place to spend the night with Ryan and Taylor in and out at all hours. We've had to argue with them twice in order to keep them off the phone, and the best we've been able to do is doze on these horrid things you call couches. I was outside, getting something from the car, when the call she's talking about came in. Dorcas said a young woman called, saying something about a party coming up next Friday."

Disappointment flooded him. "That call would have been for Ryan or Taylor. Did anyone else call?"

"Not unless it came while I wasn't within earshot. Dorcas, did anyone else call?" There was a short pause. "No, no one else called."

"Carol, please stay close enough to hear the phones, okay?"

"Sure. I can do that."

He disconnected the call, concern growing with each passing moment. "Hannah, my Lion-heart, where are you?"

The argument Luke'd had with Mary yesterday kept repeating itself in his mind as he climbed into his buggy and took off down the road. He'd spent all night rehashing what she'd said. In the morning he woke feeling even more confused. He hadn't been able to shake the feeling even though he'd dared to spend this Sunday morning at his harness shop.

So he decided a good, brisk ride would clear his head. He flicked the whip, making the horse pick up speed. His sister had managed to come between him and Mary without so much as opening her mouth.

How was that possible?

He knew the answer. She'd done things she shouldn't, really bad things, and the rumors had caught up to her. Of course Mary thought she was innocent. Mary loved her. And he was sure his girl never saw or knew the things Hannah had done that caused the rumors. If Hannah ended up ruining him and Mary, he'd…he'd… Luke sighed. He didn't know what he'd do.

With thoughts of who was right and who was lying swirling through his mind, he rode farther and farther, ignoring the cold temperatures. It did seem odd for Hannah to have this many rumors about her when her worst behavior seemed to be her love of working for Mrs. Waddell. Hannah saw that grandson of Mrs. Waddell's during her visits, but he didn't hold that against her. As Mary had pointed out, he'd done similar stuff way back when.

Luke tugged on the right rein, guiding the horse onto the dirt road near the Knepps' place. The need to see the place where the accident took place had nagged at him long enough. Since Mary wasn't speaking to him, he had a little time for getting this ghost behind him. A tremor of nervousness made his chest constrict. Old Bess jerked her head into the air and whinnied.

"It's okay, ol' girl. It's okay."

He didn't find his words a bit comforting. He squeezed the reins in his hands as memories of that horrid night rushed at him. Bess became flighty as they approached the spot where she'd been injured. Luke pulled back on the reins and jumped out of the buggy. "Easy, Old Bess." He patted her neck and led her onto the small path that went by the old tree where he'd proposed to Mary. Once off the main dirt road, the horse set-tled a bit.

Drawing a deep breath, Luke rehashed parts of his argument with Mary. Before yesterday, he'd had no idea the girl could argue like that. Why, she said if he had to blame someone for the accident to blame her. Okay, so maybe he had been looking to blame someone, and maybe it wasn't his sister's fault. But that didn't clear her of all those rumors.

Luke tucked the reins under a heavy rock, knowing Old Bess would stay wherever he put her without much fight. He ambled back out to where the accident took place. Absorbing how different the fields looked with their thick layer of snow and patches of tall brown grass sticking through, Luke climbed the fence on the far side of the road. The leaves had been green when he and Mary were here last. Somehow this past fall he'd missed autumn's changing colors and the trees going bare. Stomping through the high snow to the area where he'd landed after being thrown from the buggy, he realized he'd sailed through the air quite a ways. But he had no memory of that.

What did happen that night?

As if waiting to be asked that question, memories of crying out to God came to him. When he'd prayed for help that night, he'd been engulfed in...something. Maybe compassion? The nightmare of trying to find Mary washed over Luke. The awful realization that he didn't know how to use a cell phone and that Mary might die because of his helpless-ness had left him square in need of—

Chills ran up Luke's arms. He looked skyward, watching billowy gray clouds roll and slide east.

Square in need of...

What was it that he needed so badly that night, the very thing that seemed to cover him with acceptance and strength at the same time?

He'd been injured and too weak to do anything on his own. What had taken place between him and God that night?

With questions churning inside him, Luke headed back to the buggy.

What was it, God?

Like an unexpected peal of thunder ripping across the sky, Luke knew. It hadn't been one understanding. It was a lot of things, all parts of God, which had forgiveness, strength, and hope rolled into it. Once the feeling touched him, things he shouldn't have been able to know, he knew. How to find Mary dawned on him instantly after he prayed. Strength he hadn't had before entered him. He never figured out how to use the cell phone, but the car horn idea came to him, and he knew how to do that. He'd been told that constant noise had caused someone to call the police.

A bolt of energy ran through him.

Oh, God, I see.

"There's a part of You that talks to people sometimes. That tells us something that isn't passed down by the church leaders...or *Daed*."

Luke knelt on the cold snow, bowing his head. "Dear Father, thank You for saving Mary and me that night." He saw Hannah in his mind's eye. He lifted his face toward heaven. "God, what am I to think of her?"

No instantaneous ideas came to him. Luke remained on his knees, hoping wisdom would pour from heaven onto him. It didn't. He started to shake as the snow melted under him, causing his pants to soak up cold water.

He rose and made his way back to the buggy. As the horse plodded toward his harness shop, thoughts of his sister over the past six months ran through his mind. When his harness shop came into view, Luke saw a car parked in front of it.

A customer on a Sunday?

As Luke pulled the buggy to a stop, their milkman, Mr. Carlisle, stepped out of his car. "Luke,"—Mr. Carlisle closed his car door—"Russ Braden came to see me about an hour ago. Something was weighing on his mind, and now it's weighing on mine."

Luke couldn't imagine why Mr. Carlisle was telling him about Mr. Braden. "Yeah? What's that?"

—◌◦◌—

Hannah sat in the train station clutching her tickets and ID, feeling as if she held her future in her hands. She'd had a restless night, hoping Paul would return her call. He hadn't. With fading hopes, she'd stayed at the hotel as long as possible, giving him time to change his mind and contact her.

Perhaps it was best that she not tell him good-bye. Temptation to reveal where she was going might have been too much if she'd spoken to him. It was important that no one know where she was heading. She wanted a fresh start, with no worry that someone might show up or send another horrid letter warning her of the wages of sin.

Drawing a deep breath, she gazed around the train depot. It wasn't particularly large. But the building was interesting and looked to be centuries old. She couldn't help but wonder how many people over the years had come through here to begin a new life elsewhere.

A thousand emotions vied for her attention: guilt over leaving, hope at what lay ahead, longing to find peace, desire to succeed, and overwhelming grief. She took a seat on a long wooden bench, waiting for Matthew to return. He'd gone to the ticket window to ask a few more questions concerning arrival times and such, but he'd promised that he wouldn't pry about her destination.

The overriding emotion seemed to be the misery of feeling that her body, mind, and spirit were disconnected from one another. As if her body was here but her mind and heart were suspended in some distant, fog-covered world. Perhaps if she took her body to a new place, a clear mind and a mended heart would join her…someday.

Matthew put her lone suitcase on the floor beside her and sat down. "I upgraded your accommodations. The train from here to Pittsburgh is coach only. But once you get on the train in Pittsburgh to wherever your final destination is, you'll ride first class in a roomette. Meals are free, and you'll have a berth to sleep in, private bathroom facilities, and a door that can lock."

Hannah crossed her arms over her waist. He shouldn't have paid extra money to upgrade; riding coach all the way would have been fine. "Matthew…"

"You need the rest, Hannah." Matthew was resolved, and he wasn't going to apologize. "In a few minutes a redcap will come by. He'll take you to the train platform by elevator to save you from clomping down a couple dozen fairly steep stairs." Since Matthew had traveled by train a few times, he explained to her about tipping the redcaps and the basics of life on a passenger train. When he finished, they sat in silence.

To Hannah's chagrin, he'd given her nearly two thousand dollars in cash, in addition to paying for her train tickets and everything else since they'd left Owl's Perch. If he could work things out with Elle, he'd need that money to set up a home. It would take him years to recover.

Matthew removed his hat and set it on the bench beside him. He rubbed his forehead. "Hannah, promise me you'll take care of yourself." He sighed. "You'll have no one to make sure you're eating or anything."

Hannah wrapped her hand over his. "I promise, Matthew. I'll eat whether I'm hungry or not. I'll rest and take good care of myself."

Mr. Carlisle turned down another narrow street. "When we get to the train station, you want me to wait in the truck or go with you?"

"I don't know." Luke's laced fingers tightened. "What if she's gone already?"

Stopping at a red light, Mr. Carlisle turned to his passenger, concern clouding his eyes. "We're cutting it close. Russ wasn't sure what time her train was leaving. He only knows what he overheard in the car after the train tickets had been purchased."

Luke tried to remember what Mr. Carlisle had told him less than an hour ago. All he could recall was that Carlisle's friend Russ, who worked as a driver for many of the Amish, had taken Matthew, his mother, and Hannah to the train station late yesterday, waited for them while they went inside, and then taken them to a hotel. Russ had heard them say that Hannah had purchased a one-way ticket, but he didn't know her destination. He did hear them plan to use the hotel's shuttle service to get Hannah back to the depot today around twelve thirty.

Mr. Carlisle checked his watch. "It's one fifteen now, so that was forty-five minutes ago. Russ thought they were planning to get to the station about an hour before their train leaves." He tapped the steering wheel. "If I got it figured right, that gives us a ten- to fifteen-minute window to catch her."

"If I hadn't been out riding this morning..."

The light changed, and Mr. Carlisle made a right turn. "And if Russ had told me what was going on yesterday after he dropped them off at the hotel rather than waiting until this morning to come see me, we wouldn't be in this fix."

"I'm glad ya came to tell me. I just hope we get there in time."

"When your father finds out I kept this from him, well, it won't go over too well. But I figure Hannah got a bad shake in this deal, and I'm not tattling on her. I'm just givin' you a chance to intervene. Maybe you can talk her into not leaving."

"I hope so."

Shifting gears, Mr. Carlisle turned left. "I don't know what's really going on with Hannah, but I've been hearing stuff for months. One thing I do know: Hannah doesn't deserve what's been happening to her. I don't give a rip how many of those rumors are true."

Luke nodded, realizing the full truth. If Mr. Carlisle could see it, why, as Hannah's brother, couldn't he have seen it sooner? He just hoped he wasn't too late to talk her into staying. With a few people on her side, she could weather this storm. He had to convince her of that.

When Mr. Carlisle pulled up in front of the train station, he nodded toward the depot. "I'll park and meet you out front. You go find your sister. When you're ready to leave, just come outside."

Luke opened the truck door and climbed out. "Thank you, Mr. Carlisle."

"You're welcome. Now, hurry."

Walking through the two sets of doors, Luke took in the large open area in a single glance. Hannah wasn't there. To his left was a small store. Through the shop windows, he saw a few people milling about; none of them was Hannah. In the far corner to his right, a small line of people waited at the ticket window. She wasn't there either.

He jogged through the next set of open doors, which led to another large room with wooden benches sitting end to end and back to back. Still no sign of Hannah.

God, please let me find my sister and take her home.

Suddenly he saw her and Matthew sitting on one of the benches. A small suitcase sat at his sister's feet. "Hannah!"

When she turned and saw Luke, shock covered her face. She rose from the bench.

Luke rushed to her. He studied her pale face. Only one thought filled his mind. "I'm sorry. I'm so very sorry." Without waiting for her to respond, he hugged her tight. She didn't push him away, but she didn't return the hug. "Please come home, Hannah. What happened to you is awful, and you ain't been done right, but don't leave."

Hannah took a step back. "That's what you say today. What about tomorrow?"

Luke took her hands in his. "I've been mean and difficult, and I'm really sorry for all of it. Give me a chance to make it up to you."

She eased back onto the bench and stared at her lap.

Luke bent closer. "Mary and I will take care of you. You can live in the apartment over my harness shop."

Hannah lifted her chin and looked at him. "*Ach,* Luke, you're not thinking. With the bishop set against me like he is, you could get shunned for such a thing. And for sure it'd ruin your good standing with the church." Hannah took a deep breath. "I've been branded, Luke, and that will never go away."

"But what about that...guy?"

"Paul? He fled the moment he discovered I was pregnant. I knew he would."

"You ain't exactly given him time to adjust."

She rose. "I'm not living every day of my life hoping he'll come back. I couldn't stand that. Even if he comes to realize I'm innocent, what's he going to do—still want to marry me? Besides, he's not coming back, and I don't want to live in a lonely world with no hope of a future, barely being tolerated among our community, while Paul finds a new love, gets married, and has children." Her body trembled, but her eyes blazed with determination. She'd obviously thought this through.

A uniformed man strode by. "Train for Pittsburgh will begin boarding in two minutes," he called out. "Please have your tickets ready."

Luke felt panicky. He had to change her mind. "So you have some things to work through. It's the hand you were dealt, Hannah, but Mary and Matthew and I will help you. We'll set things right with the church. It may take some time, but…"

A man wearing a red cap stopped in front of them. "If you wish to ride the elevator to the platform, I'm heading that way in just a minute."

Hannah drew a deep breath and stared at Luke. "Think, Luke, just really think about this. Would you want to stay if you had to face what I'll have to face for the rest of my life?"

Luke searched his sister's face. She'd borne so much grief and condemnation that she was no longer the girl he'd known only six months ago.

God, help me. What do I say?

No one spoke as he waited to get some inkling, some word of wisdom.

Let her go.

His heart sank. He wanted the chance to do things right, but this wasn't about him. "You will write to us or call Mary and let us know when you're settled?"

"I will," she said, her eyes misting. "I promise."

The redcap returned, pulling a long flatbed dolly behind him. Matthew stood and passed the man Hannah's bag and a ten-dollar bill. "Make sure to carry this bag onto the train for her and get her a seat."

"Absolutely, sir." The man grabbed her suitcase and placed it on the dolly. He then turned to collect some of the other passengers' bags.

Matthew gently placed his hands on Hannah's shoulders. "You're sure about this?"

She stroked the two tickets in her hands. "Yes." She hugged him tight. "Good-bye, Matthew."

He squeezed her gently. "Bye, Hannah. You take care and write to us."

She backed away. "I will." She turned to Luke. "I'm going to be fine."

Luke swallowed hard. "Can you at least tell me where you're going?"

She shook her head. "It's best that no one knows."

Luke hugged her, wondering if he would ever see his sister again. "You're probably right."

When he let her go, she looked at him for a long moment. "Thank you." She grabbed one of Luke's hands and one of Matthew's. "Both of you."

The redcap paused in front of Hannah. "You ready, ma'am?"

She let go of their hands. Matthew's returned to his side, but Luke held on to his sister. A shadow of insecurity came over her face.

Luke released her hand and turned to the redcap. "She's ready."

<center>~~~§~~~</center>

Hannah glanced at her boarding passes, one for the first leg of the trip to Pittsburgh and the other for the Amtrak passenger train that would take her to Alliance. Gripping her tickets as well as her ID, she felt her resolve weaken. At the moment, hope only slightly outweighed her anxiety.

Grateful Luke had come and shared his feelings, Hannah fell into step with the small group of people following the redcap as he pushed the dolly filled with luggage. After twenty or so steps a hallway came into view on her left. The beauty of the Harrisburg Train Depot ended abruptly as gray concrete seemed to cover everything except the dingy-looking elevator doors.

She turned and waved at Matthew and Luke. They both waved back, looking torn between supporting her decision to leave and wanting to keep her near. Pulling her attention away from them, she walked to the elevator and squeezed in with the few others who weren't using the stairs.

The redcap pushed a button. As the doors began to close, realization of what she was doing hit Hannah like an ice storm. A voice inside her head screamed at her to grab a piece of luggage off the dolly and shove it between the doors. Was she making the worst mistake of her life? How could she leave everything familiar behind? Could the pain of knowing that her daughter might have lived if she'd handled things right have caused her to imagine God was leading her away from the source of her pain?

She fought to get control of her fears. How could she, a girl with an eighth-grade education who'd just given birth and buried her child, move to some foreign place and start over?

Closing her eyes, she remembered the whispery voice, and her fears calmed a bit.

s the sun went down for the second day, Paul made another round through Owl's Perch. He'd known the Amish community could keep its silence, not even giving an impression of politeness if they thought an outsider was subversive, probing, or inappropriate. Regardless of who knew what, those he approached either turned away from him or closed a door on him without sharing a bit of information.

In spite of knocking on Matthew Esh's and Mary Yoder's doors, he hadn't convinced anyone to share more than a hard countenance and an unwillingness even to hint where Hannah might be. Mr. Esh had informed Paul that Matthew and his mother were gone for the night. When Matthew returned, Paul could ask whatever questions he wanted. Matthew was a grown man, and he could decide for himself what he wanted to say on the subject of Hannah Lapp.

Her name seemed to be poison on the man's lips. "Ya don't need to knock on the door again, asking for him. When he gets home, someone will hang a towel on the front railing." During the curt, brief conversation with Mr. Esh, Paul got the feeling that Matthew's being gone was in some way related to Hannah. Maybe he'd taken her somewhere to hide while the community calmed down.

With nowhere else to turn, Paul had gone to Gram's the night before and had slept a few hours before beginning his search again. He'd straight-lined it for the Esh place, but there was no towel hanging out. As he drove on, going through the community again and again, he had to face that his willingness to accept Hannah's reality might be too late. She'd gone into hiding somewhere, and unless Matthew helped him locate her...

His heartbeat quickened when he spotted what looked like an Amish woman riding in a van, sitting next to a driver, with an Amish man in the backseat. Paul's fatigue fell to the wayside as the car drove into the Eshes' driveway. He pulled up beside the other vehicle and jumped out. The woman barely looked at him as she closed the car door and trudged toward the house. When the man climbed out of the backseat, Paul immediately recognized him.

"Matthew," he called.

Matthew glanced up before turning back to pay the driver. The driver shook his head, refusing the money and drove off.

"I'm Paul Waddell. I'm looking for Hannah."

Matthew looked at him with eyes that were every bit as unfriendly as Mary's and Hannah's father's had been. "She's gone. My mother and I took her to the train station."

Paul's heart seemed to stop beating. "Where did she go? How can I contact her?"

Matthew shook his head. "She didn't say. She doesn't want anyone to know where she's going."

Paul struggled to stay standing.

Matthew stepped forward, his features changing from coldness to puzzlement. "Why did ya take her money?"

As if a second fist had hit Paul in the chest, he gasped. "What?"

"The money in the account that belonged to both of you. Why did ya take her part of it?"

"I never… It's gone?"

Matthew nodded.

Paul's chest constricted as he carried on a conversation that had nothing to do with helping him find Hannah. "I only use that account twice a year, putting money into it after all expenses have been paid out for a six-month period. But…is it possible that Hannah lost the bankbook the day I gave it to her, the day she was raped?" Paul rubbed his forehead, feeling unbearably dizzy. "If her attacker got his hands on the bankbook and emptied the account, then maybe the police will have a lead to find her attacker. Will you go with me and tell them what you know about it?"

Matthew dipped his head and sighed. "I don't know. I disobeyed the bishop on some things concerning Hannah, and I'm in a lot of hot water with him...and my girlfriend."

"I...I didn't realize you had a girlfriend."

"I did..." Matthew shrugged before he reached into his pocket and pulled out a letter. He handed it to Paul. "Hannah said you'd come looking for her at some point."

Paul snatched the letter as if he'd been thrown a lifeline. He tore it open, hoping it would tell him where to find her.

Paul,

If you're reading this note, then you've come in search of answers, perhaps in search of me. I have no way of telling how much time has passed. Maybe you have a family of your own by now.

I'm not sure how much help I can offer you, but I had to go. It seems that no one believes my account of how I conceived a child. The injustice of this is more than I'm willing to bear. I need to get away, to start fresh. I had to put everything behind me and begin anew, like putting new wine into new wineskins, ya?

I hope you find peace, Paul. I don't hold you responsible for your reaction. I hope you don't hold resentment against me for mine. I wish you well.

Hannah

Feeling as if he'd been thrown into a deep pit with no way out, Paul held tight to the letter. "How will she support herself and a baby?"

Matthew didn't answer.

Paul searched Matthew's eyes, looking for hints of things he wasn't saying. "Does she have a plan? Is she going someplace where they'll help her and the child?"

Matthew folded his arms across his chest. "Hannah went into labor a couple of days ago. The baby died."

A loud, unstoppable groan left Paul. Unable to stand on his own, he placed the palms of his hands against the roof of Marcus's car. She'd given birth since he'd seen her a few days ago?

God, how can anyone survive all this alone?

"She'll get a job," Matthew went on.

Paul drew several deep breaths, needing the cold air to keep him from turning into a raving maniac. "But if she has no money…"

"She didn't leave empty-handed. She has enough to take care of herself in any way she needs until she's on her feet. I…I made sure of that."

Paul lowered his head into his hands, too hurt and tired to know what to think.

Matthew placed his hand on Paul's shoulder. "She needed to go. Trust God with that."

God wasn't the issue here. It was Hannah, who'd chosen to run off while Paul had spent nearly two days and most of a night looking for her. Why did she have to keep the pregnancy such a secret? Couldn't she have found a way to tell him months ago so they at least had a chance of working through all this? Who would she go to for help now?

Frustrations and fears melted together until Paul had no idea what he felt—or what he should feel.

"Paul, trust that Hannah figured out what she needed and that she's doing it."

Paul lifted his head and gazed into Matthew's eyes, seeing the same kindness and understanding Hannah must have seen. Matthew lowered his hand as Paul began to reread the letter.

Hannah wanted a fresh start. As he read, the frustration of nearly thirty hours of riding through her community searching for her released its grip on him. The phrase "new wine into new wineskins" was biblical symbolism he'd shared with Hannah on several occasions. Despite his anguish, a gentle peace slowly eased over him. The young woman he'd always thought had the heart of a lion had just broken free of her cage. A smile tugged at his lips.

Maybe Hannah and Matthew were right. Perhaps she did need a clean break from the scandal and grief that the rape had caused. But he wanted to be with her.

"You say she has plenty of money and a plan?"

Matthew nodded. "She's safe, Paul, and probably enjoying the freedom to find her own path in this world."

Paul walked to the edge of the driveway and gazed across the snow-covered pasturelands to the distant hills. The view was almost a perfect image of the dreams that had haunted him night before last. "Two days back I dreamed throughout the night that a voice was calling to Hannah from across the lands to *kumm raus.*"

"Paul." Matthew's voice broke with emotion, and Paul turned to look at him. Matthew's brows knitted tightly, and shock covered his face. "She heard the same words call to her as we stood near her infant's grave site. She even answered it aloud."

Paul couldn't budge as Matthew's words worked their way into his understanding. He studied the horizon, mystified at this assurance of Hannah's departure.

Confusion and heartache lifted somewhat as optimism surrounded him. Confidence that she would return one day took root. He would hold on to that hope and continue to pray that the Lord would heal her and complete the work He had begun in her—in both of them.

Godspeed, Lion-heart. Godspeed.

After stepping off the elevator and onto the train platform, the redcap asked Hannah to wait on a bench while he boarded the others first. He reassured her that he'd reserve a seat for her that had room for her carry-on. As she waited, her thoughts turned up the heat on worry.

Her community and other family members besides Luke had to know by now that she'd left Owl's Perch. The Yoders and even her own parents didn't want her living under their roofs, but that didn't mean they would accept her leaving. The faster she could put more distance between her and her people, the better.

For them and for her.

The minutes seemed to drag by, and her heart palpitated several times before the redcap returned. He led the way as they followed the yellow line, passing several cars in the process.

He came to a stop. "This is your car, ma'am." Without leaving the platform, he passed her bag and ticket to a uniformed man on the train, who seemed to be expecting her.

Before she'd decided whether she should tip the redcap again or not, he'd disappeared.

With the porter leading the way, Hannah strode down the aisle. He motioned to a seat near where baggage was being kept. "I'll put your bag right here in front of you. If you need anything, let me know."

She eased onto the thick blue chair, glad she had the whole row to herself. Through the train window, she could see people on the upper level of the building she'd left minutes earlier. People young and old were gazing through the glass from inside the building, waving their good-byes to loved ones. Neither Matthew nor Luke was anywhere to be seen, and she wondered if they'd already headed home.

Doubts tumbled through her mind while grief and uncertainty assaulted her emotions. Maybe the voice that had called her to *kumm raus* was simply her mind playing tricks on her and she'd been foolish enough to follow it. She closed her eyes and leaned her head back, wondering how she could plan a future based on a nondescript, unspecific voice.

The train shifted forward smoothly, and her misgivings quieted some. As it began swaying and picking up speed, Hannah's hope stirred again. Soon she began to feel as if she were soaring like an eagle rather than gliding and jolting along on train tracks. She was beginning a journey between her and God. It had to be worth taking.

As the hours passed, Hannah watched the ever-changing scenery outside her window. Every time the train stopped and then pulled out from another depot, she sensed she was leaving behind a bit more of her overwhelming sense of powerlessness. It became easier and easier to breathe as the train moved northwestward. She hadn't expected that.

As she stared through the window, a soft whisper crossed her soul. *Nevertheless.*

It was an odd word coming to her at an odd time, but it kept circling through her mind, whispering hope. Life hurt. Nevertheless, it was a gift worthy of honoring.

Nevertheless.

The word came stronger this time, immediately lifting her spirits and causing sprigs of new faith to grow.

Her infant had died. Nevertheless, Rachel was now with God.

Hannah's relationship with Paul was over. Nevertheless, God's strength would pull her through.

If everything ended with God, then those who were in Him had a good ending—eventually.

A deep warmth comforted her.

If she already felt this much healing before she'd even gotten on the second train, what healings lay ahead as she learned about life and God over the next few months or years?

She closed her eyes and basked in the warmth of her renewed faith in the God who loves His children.

She'd find her aunt and make plans from there. For now, that's all she knew. And for now, that was enough.

A desire to write to Paul swept over her. He needed to know about *nevertheless*. Regardless of the way things turned out between them, God had a plan.

Acknowledgments

I'd like to give a very special thanks to three women without whom this book and its sequels would not be possible: Miriam Flaud, my dear Old Order Amish friend, who opened her home, her family life, and her heart to this writing endeavor; Linda Wertz, who knows the Amish community well and opened doors for me, chauffeured me tirelessly whenever I landed in Pennsylvania, and never questioned if it would all be worth it; and Kathy Ide, editor, mentor, and friend. You in no way doubted that I could do this, even though you saw the roughest drafts of them all.

I'd like to thank everyone who had a hand in making sure all fictional patients responded in ways that were medically accurate: Rebecca T. Slagle, BSN, MN, neonatal nurse practitioner; Kim Pace, RN, BSN, manager, NICU/Nursery, Northeast GA Medical Center; Jeffry J. Bizon, MD, OB/GYN; Terri Driesel, physical therapist; Elizabeth Curtis, RN.

Thank you to my critique partner, Marci Burke, whose fast-paced imagination, problem-solving skills, and faithful diligence can get any author out of a writer's block and back to work long before he or she is ready!

To Kathy Port, Kathy Bizon, Lori Petroni, and others who offered prayers and bits of time and creativity to various aspects of this project.

Thank you to Karen Kingsbury, who found time to reach out to me, even with a husband, six children, and a writing career.

Thanks to Deborah Raney, whose critiques, brainstorming, and encouragements are too numerous to list.

Thank you to Shannon Hill, who believed in this work from the moment she read the first chapter. I'm so grateful for the privilege of working with you.

And to all the staff at WaterBrook Press. You're absolutely amazing!

Glossary

ach—oh

alt—old

Ausbund—a hymnal

begreiflich—easy

Bobbeli—baby

Buhnesupp—bean soup

Christenpflicht—a book of prayers

dabber schpring—run quick

Daadi—grandfather

Daadi Haus—grandfather's house. Generally this refers to a house that is attached to or is near the main house and belongs to a grandparent. Many times the main house belonged to the grandparents when they were raising their family. The main house is usually passed down to a son, who takes over the responsibilities his parents once had. The grandparents then move into the smaller place and usually have fewer responsibilities.

Daed—dad or father

dankes—thanks

deerich—foolish

dich—yourself

die—the

do—here

Druwwel—trouble

du—you

du bischt—you are

du kannscht—you can

Dummkopp—blockhead or dunce

duscht—do

ehrlich—honest

Englischer—a non-Amish person. Some conservative Mennonite sects are not considered *Englischers*.

entsetzlich—awful

es—it

Fraa—wife or woman

Gaul—horse

Grossmammi—grandmother

gut—good

hatt—difficult

Haus—house

Herr Jesu Christ, er führt mich—
    Lord Jesus Christ, he leads me

ich—I

im—contraction meaning "in the"

iss—is

Kammer—bedroom

kann—can

Kapp—a prayer covering or cap

kumm—come

langsam—slow

letz—wrong

liewe—dear (adjective)

Liewi—darling; dear (noun)

Mamm—mom or mother

Mammi—shortened term of
    endearment for grandmothers,
    as in *Mammi* Annie

mei—my

muscht—must

net—not

Ordnung—The written and unwrit-
    ten rules of the Amish. The
    regulations are passed down
    from generation to generation.
    Any new rules are agreed upon
    by the church leaders and en-
    dorsed by the members during
    special meetings. Most Amish
    know all the rules by heart.

Pennsylvania Dutch—Pennsylvania
    German. The word *Dutch* in
    this phrase has nothing to do
    with the Netherlands. The origi-
    nal word was *Deutsch,* which
    means "German." The Amish
    speak some High German (used
    in church services) and Pennsyl-
    vania German (Pennsylvania
    Dutch), and after a certain age,
    they are taught English.

raus—out

rei—in

rumschpringe—running around

saage—say

schick—behave

schwetze—speak or talk

Sitzschtupp—living room

uff—on

un—and

verschteh—understand

was—what

was denkscht?—what do you
    think?

wie—how

wunderbaar—wonderful

wunnerlich—strange

ya—yes

zerick—back

New York Times BESTSELLING
AUTHOR OF *When the Soul Mends*

When
the
Morning
Comes

~⧳ A NOVEL ⧖~

Cindy
Woodsmall

SISTERS OF THE QUILT, BOOK TWO

To my dear friend and amazing critique partner
Marci Burke

Hannah gripped the railing as the train squealed and moaned, coming to a halt. Her body ached from the absence of the life she'd carried inside her only days ago. When the conductor opened the door to the outside, a cold blast of night air stole her breath. He stepped off the train with her bag in hand and turned to help her onto the platform.

"It's bad out here tonight." The man glanced across the empty parking lot, then passed her the traveling bag. It weighed little in spite of carrying all she owned—all she'd begin this new life with. "You got somebody meeting you, young lady?"

Wishing she had a decent answer to that question, Hannah studied her surroundings. The old depot was dark and deserted. Not one sign of life anywhere, except on the train that was about to depart. She glanced the length of the train in both directions. There wasn't another soul getting off.

The conductor's face wrinkled with concern. "The building stays locked 24/7. It's no longer an operating depot, but we drop people off here anyway. When somebody lands in Alliance, they better have made plans."

A few hundred feet to her right stood a small blue sign with a white outline of a phone on it. "I've got plans," she whispered, hoping he wouldn't ask any other questions.

He nodded, grabbed the two-way radio off his hip, and said something into it. Of course he wouldn't ask anything else. He had a job to do—a train to catch.

As he stepped back onto the train, it slowly pulled away, its whistle sounding long and loud. For hours as she'd traveled from Owl's Perch, Pennsylvania, heading for Alliance, Ohio, the train whistle had stirred a sense of hope and well-being within her. But as her haven of shelter and food disappeared around a bend, a deep feeling of aloneness shrouded her.

She turned toward the sign with the emblem of the phone on it. Unsure whether she had enough information to get her aunt's phone number by calling 411, she began to realize how foolhardy she'd been not to make calls during the layover at Union Station in Pittsburgh. She'd been so afraid she would miss her next train that she had stayed on a seat, waiting.

Wrapping her woolen shawl even tighter around her, she made her way to the phone. But once she stood in front of the sign, she saw there wasn't a phone after all. She walked around the pole, searching. She spanned out a bit farther, circling the empty lot. The sign was wrong.

God, what have I done?

She'd freeze before morning.

Walking around the building again, Hannah searched for a nook to shelter her from the wind. Finding nothing, she crossed the graveled parking lot to the edge of the paved road. To her left was a hill with a sharp curve and no hint of what lay beyond it. To her right, down about half a mile, groups of lights shone from high atop poles.

Shivering, she set out for the lights, hoping they would lead her to shelter of some sort. Each step made her abdomen contract in pain.

In her great efforts to keep Paul, she'd lost everything.

Everything.

The word went round and round in her head, draining her will. In the distance to her left, she could make out the backsides of a few homes that looked dilapidated even under the cover of night. It appeared that Alliance, or at least this part of it, was every bit as poor as she was.

She approached the lighted area. Sidewalks and old-fashioned stores lined each side of the street. Most of the shops had glass fronts, and each was dark inside except for some sort of night-light. Desperate for warmth and too weary to worry about laws, she wondered if one of the doors might be unlocked. The door to each store sat back a good six to eight feet between two walls of storefront glass, like a deep hallway. The moment she stepped into one of the passageways, the harsh wind couldn't reach her. She knocked on the door before trying the knob. The place was locked.

She walked to the next store and tried again. It, too, was locked. Moving from doorway to doorway, she grew uncomfortably sleepy.

Too tired to try anything else, Hannah leaned back against the cold plate-glass window of the dime store and slid to a sitting position. She pulled out the two dresses she'd packed in her traveling bag and put one dress over her and scooted the other one under her, trying to get some distance between herself and the icy concrete. She removed her prayer *Kapp*, loosened her hair from its bun for added warmth, and tied her Kapp back on tight.

Sleep came in sporadic measures as her body fought to stay warm. Every time she nodded off, thoughts of the life she'd left behind startled her. Her family's gray stone farmhouse, set amid rolling acreage. The Amish heritage that had once meant roots and love. Memories of her mother teaching her how to sew, cook, and tend to infants. Mary, her dearest friend, standing by her even when it meant she'd lose her fiancé, Luke, Hannah's own brother.

Images of Paul filled her mind, making the thoughts of her family vanish. She chided herself for longing for him. But her inner chastisement did nothing to stop the memories of him from pelting her. She could hear his laughter as they played board games, see the strength that radiated from his hands and arms as they worked the garden side by side, and feel his joy on the day she accepted his proposal.

Stop.

Her body shook harder as cold from the concrete seeped through her clothes, and she wondered if she'd wake in the morning or freeze to death during the night.

From somewhere on the sidewalk came the sound of footsteps. Prying her eyes open, she glimpsed through the dark shadows of night and drowsiness to see the silhouette of a man at the end of the long, glass entryway. Her heart pounded, but waking to full consciousness seemed impossible. Maybe he wouldn't see her.

The next time she forced her eyes open, the broad shoulders and lanky body of a man were directly in front of her. Still unable to get fully awake, she couldn't see any more than his profile.

With no energy or place to run, Hannah waited—like an animal caught in a trap.

He removed something from around him and placed it over her. The miserable chills eased, and she could no longer control her eyelids as warmth spread over her.

Perry County, Pennsylvania

rumbling to herself, Sarah grabbed her winter shawl off the peg and headed out the back door to fetch a load of wood. Early morning sun gleamed against the fresh layer of snow. As she made her way to the lean-to, the strange events of yesterday weighed heavy.

She tracked snow onto the dirt floor of the covered shed as she crossed to the stacked woodpile. Placing a split log in the crook of one arm, she mumbled complaints about Samuel not getting his chores done last night. *Daed* would hear about this.

The sound of a horse and buggy approaching made her turn. Matthew Esh was driving, and his mother, Naomi, sat beside him. As Sarah stood under the lean-to, watching them get out of the buggy, Matthew spotted her.

He dipped his head to come under the low roof. "Sarah." He nodded his greeting rather coldly, then without another word proceeded to stack firewood in the crook of his arm.

Of course he has nothing to say to me.

He was Hannah's friend. And once a man saw the perfect beauty and poise of Sarah's older sister, he never glanced her way again.

Daed came out of the barn and spoke to Naomi for a moment before taking the horse by the lead. He motioned for her to go into the house. Through the open double doors to the barn, Sarah could see Levi still mucking it out after milking the cows and wondered where Luke was. Before she thought to ask Matthew what he and his mother were doing here, he strode down the hill toward her home. Sarah followed in silence.

When she entered, her three younger siblings were eating at the kitchen table.

Naomi stood in front of the wood stove, warming her hands. "It's awful bitter out there." Her voice sounded different today.

Matthew unloaded the wood and headed out the back door again.

"*Ya*, it is cold." Sarah dropped a couple of split logs into the woodbin and closed the lid. "The potbellied stove has been eating wood like it's candy, and the house is still a little cool."

A few minutes later Daed stalked into the kitchen from the coatroom, looking no one in the eye. Since he'd pulled off his mucky work boots, only his black woolen socks covered his feet. "Sarah, fix a pot of coffee while I fetch your mother."

Matthew came in the back door with wood piled so high in his arms he could barely see over it. Sarah moved to the woodbin and lifted the lid. Then she removed a few sticks off the top of his load.

"That's all right, Sarah. I got it." Matthew's words were void of his usual warmth.

Normally, from the moment Naomi and Matthew arrived, he and her father engaged in easy banter about horses, cows, and such. But this didn't have the feel of a normal conversation.

Sarah decided her best chance of being allowed to stay and hear a few bits of gossip was to get something into the oven as quickly as possible. After putting the coffee on to brew and filling the cups with hot tap water to warm them, she began kneading the batch of sourdough that Esther had made and set out to rise last night.

When *Mamm* and Daed came into the kitchen, they said nothing to her about leaving. But they told Esther, Rebecca, and Samuel to take their breakfast upstairs and stay there until someone called for them.

By the time Sarah returned from helping Esther get their two youngest siblings up the steps with their plates of food and drinks, the coffee was almost ready. She set the cream and sugar on the table before dumping the water from the cups down the drain and pouring the fresh brew. Placing a mug in front of each person, she was relieved that she seemed invisible to them. While they fixed their coffee, she placed a few leftover cinnamon rolls from breakfast on the table. The long, awkward silence in the room made her wonder if any of them would say what was on their minds before she was banned to the upstairs with the others.

Daed tapped his spoon against the rim of his cup and focused on Naomi. "I suppose this visit is about Hannah."

Watching everyone out of the corner of her eye, Sarah stood quietly at the counter, molding a handful of dough into a dinner roll. Her insides quivered. Just the thought of Hannah's fall from on high made her feel guilty as well as triumphant.

Naomi cleared her throat. "I think the community was kept in the dark about the...about Hannah's secret for far too long."

Hannah's secret? The wad of dough in Sarah's hands plopped onto the floor. She grabbed it up.

"Sarah." Her father's voice vibrated the room.

She wheeled around. "Yes, Daed?"

"You shouldn't be in here."

She wanted to beg for permission to stay, but the look in Daed's eyes kept her from asking.

Matthew pushed his coffee cup to the center of the table. "Zeb, there's no keepin' what's taken place a secret. If ya don't share it, your children will have to rely on the rumors they'll hear to try to figure things out." Matthew closed his eyes and drew a deep breath before opening them again. "But this is your home and your family."

Her father clicked his tongue but gave a slight nod, letting Sarah know she could stay.

Naomi smoothed the front of her apron. "I've never seen our bishop so set in his mind against a body like he was Hannah. It was his and the preachers' stand concerning anything she said that made them force her to stay alone..."

Sarah couldn't catch a breath. She'd gone to the bishop and told him things about Hannah, but surely that wasn't what had caused this trouble.

Daed pushed his coffee mug away. "What new actions by my eldest daughter have caused you to come see me?"

Naomi looked to her son briefly. "Zeb, Ruth." She paused. "I hope you can find it within your hearts to forgive me."

Mamm's eyes opened wide. "Forgive you? You've done nothing wrong."

Daed glanced at Sarah. "We all know the tricks Hannah pulls. Don't take on guilt for her."

Sarah turned her back as if she hadn't heard him and washed the dough off her hands, hoping this conversation wouldn't end up pointing a finger in her direction.

He continued. "If you've come here thinking something is your fault, you're wrong. No one can take blame for the birth except Hannah herself."

Sarah turned to face her mother. "Hannah has a baby?"

Her mother stared blankly at the table. "Don't repeat that, Sarah."

Matthew rose from his seat. "None of what's happened is gonna stay a secret." He pointed Sarah toward the bench seat. "I think ya should tell her."

Sarah sat, unable to accept what she was hearing. How could her unmarried sister have a baby?

Daed buried his head in his hands. "Okay, okay. Ruth, tell her, but make it brief. Clearly, Naomi and Matthew have something they need to talk about."

"I...I don't know what to say." Mamm shook her head. "Do I tell her what Hannah said is true or what you think is true or what the bishop says is true?" Her eyes misted. "Tell me, Zeb. What am I to say about Hannah and about my firstborn grandchild?"

"Ruth." Naomi's calm voice cut through the freshly loosened anger. "I was there after Hannah gave birth. I would stake my life, even my son's life, that the child Hannah gave birth to was indeed conceived the way she told you."

Mamm clamped her hands on the table and buried her face against them, wailing, "Oh, God, what have we done?" She looked up at her husband. "What have we done?"

Resentment carved Daed's face as he shook his head. "Naomi has the heart of a mother. Of course she believes what Hannah told her."

Naomi stood, facing the head of the household in his own home. Almost instantly the sadness etched across her face disappeared, and fury replaced it. Sarah had never seen any woman face a man with such anger.

Matthew wrapped his hand around his mother's arm and motioned for her to sit. When she did, he nodded his approval. "Mamm was in the room and overheard Hannah praying about the attack. Hannah didn't even know she was there."

The room fell silent.

Hannah was attacked? Sarah dismissed that idea immediately. Her sister had made that up to cover her sin.

Zeb shoved the teaspoon into the sugar bowl, dumped a scoop into his coffee, and stirred it briskly. "More likely that you heard her repenting for telling us she was attacked when she wasn't."

Naomi rose, pointing a shaky finger at Daed. "Don't you dare spread lies about your daughter, Zeb Lapp, because you can't face the truth." She snapped her shawl tighter around her shoulders. "No wonder she didn't want you to know where she was going. She knew you'd never believe her; that you'd only condemn her." She turned to Matthew. "Get your coat. This man would rather listen to the sounds roaring inside his own head."

Mamm rose, looking horrified. "My Hannah's gone?"

Suddenly it became clear; this piece of information was the reason the Eshes had come here today.

Naomi placed her hand on Mamm's shoulder. "Matthew and I took her to the train station yesterday. She told no one where she was heading."

Daed looked to his wife. "But the rumors about her being out at night," he mumbled. "And I saw her with my own eyes in the arms of that *Englischer* doctor. The bishop saw her kissing that man she confessed to being engaged to—a young man who isn't even Amish. She was sneaking around behind our backs mailing letters and who knows what else."

Stiff and mute on the outside, Sarah was relieved there was a lot of evidence against Hannah that went way beyond the pot Sarah had stirred.

Mamm plunked into her chair, staring at Daed. "Is your list of wrong-doings against Hannah all you have to say about this?"

Her mother's look of disbelief at Daed rattled Sarah even more than this news.

Mamm reached across the table and grasped Sarah's hands. "The baby was born the night Mary came to stay here—" Mamm broke into sobs, unable to say anything else.

In spite of the years of frustration that had built between her and her sister, Sarah needed someone to admit that they were all pulling a meanspirited prank. But the grief in her parents' eyes told her this was no hoax.

A horrid scream banged against her temples, making her fight to hold on to her good sense. She looked to Matthew, hoping he had some words of comfort for her. But he seemed torn between anger and sympathy.

His eyes bored into her. "The church leaders had insisted Hannah spend a night alone to rethink her account of how she came to be pregnant. I went to check on her anyway and realized she was in labor and needed…"

His mother eased over to him and placed her hands on his shoulders. "Matthew and I tried to get help for her, but the phone lines were down because of a storm, and…the baby died within minutes of being born."

Matthew reached inside his shirt and pulled out a small stack of folded papers. "Hannah wrote these before she left."

He started to lay them on the table, but Daed took them.

Dazed, Sarah didn't budge. She hadn't liked it when the whole community put Hannah on an undeserved pedestal, but she hadn't wished for this either.

"Sarah," Matthew said, "don't you have something you need to say?"

Her skin felt as if it were being peeled off. Heat ran through her arms and chest. "N-no, of course not."

But God knew she did. Did Matthew know it too?

~~∽

Luke waited outside the Yoder home for someone to respond to his knock. The hour was awful early to be making a call, but during the night a desire to apologize to his fiancée for their serious disagreement had nagged at him. He needed to share the conversation he'd had with Hannah yesterday before she left and hoped it would bring Mary some measure of peace.

The door swung open, and Mary's mother, Becky, stared back at him.

She didn't step back or open the door farther. "She doesn't want to see you."

Luke resisted the urge to push past her. "I'm sure of that, but I need to talk to her anyway."

She shook her head. "This thing with Hannah is just too much for us to deal with."

He inwardly winced at the lies people believed about his sister. Sadder still, until Hannah was about to board the train, he'd believed them too. "Mary has to be hurting because Hannah's gone. Don't you think it'd be best for Mary's health if she and I talked things out?"

John Yoder came up behind his wife.

"Go home for today, Luke. Just go on home." He shut the door.

Luke stared at the closed door. He knew it'd be a battle to win Mary back.

He moved to the steps of the porch, brushed snow off them with his boot, and sat down. He propped his elbows on his knees and stared out over the snow-covered land. Acknowledging his prejudice against Hannah hadn't been easy. He was as good at pointing an accusing finger and deciding who was right and wrong as his father was.

The memory of his venom against his sister still haunted him, even in the wake of the forgiveness she'd offered him before she boarded the train. The horrid reality was, she'd been raped. And she had borne the trauma and the pregnancy in absolute isolation while rumors devastated her.

Luke groaned. "Father God, how could I have been so stupid? Please help Mary forgive me."

The prayer crossed his lips, and he rose and walked to the buggy.

Before getting in, he looked toward the first story, where Mary slept these days since climbing steps was still difficult for her. She was standing at the window. He lifted his hand and held it there.

He saw her moving about, but she didn't leave the window. A moment later a popping sound came from the window, and she lowered the top pane. She opened her mouth as if to say something, then stopped.

Luke lowered his hand. "I was wrong about Hannah."

Her pale face didn't change. She did that chin-tilting gesture, telling him that although her body still dealt with some frailties from their buggy accident, her will was not as easily defeated. Mary had a bold spunk he'd only become aware of recently. His sister's influence, he was sure.

As he stood outside her home watching her, part of him wanted to speak up and let her know her place as his future wife. But without Mary's frustration with his behavior, Luke wouldn't have questioned whether he was right about Hannah. He would have pressed onward in his anger, blaming his sister for the horse-and-buggy accident and believing the scandal about her.

"Why, Luke?" Mary wiped a tear from her face. "Why couldn't you believe her, believe me, when it would have made such a difference?"

There was no way to explain things he didn't understand. There had been no proof of Hannah's innocence.

He walked to the window, glad to see Mary up close, even if she was furious with him. He studied her features, looking for signs of strength and health. He wasn't sure he saw any. "Hannah and I made our peace, and she forgave me before she left. Can you please consider forgiving me too?"

Mary shook her head. "Don't fool yourself, Luke. If you hated Hannah when you thought our accident was her fault, you'll hate me now that you see it was my fault." Pain filled her eyes, and Luke despised himself even more. "I'm the one who wrapped the horse's reins around the stob of the buggy. I was supposed to take the leads, but I let the horse meander onto that dirt road. Me, Luke, not Hannah."

"Mary, please. I was so wrong to—"

Mary raised her hand, interrupting him. "Yeah, you and Sarah both. I always knew that girl had problems, but I thought I understood who you were—a loving, forgiving, kind man. But now I see how quick you are to judge. You allowed your thoughts to twist the truth into lies just so you could blame someone." Mary closed the window and then the blinds.

Chapter 3

Alliance, Ohio

unlight danced off the storefront windows as Hannah opened her eyes. Not only had she survived the night, but she felt reasonably warm. As she rose to her feet, two woolen blankets fell from her. No wonder she was so warm. But where had they come from?

The shuffling sound of shoes against the sidewalk made her look down the narrow entryway. A woman, about her mother's age, came toward the store's entrance, searching through her purse. When she was just a few feet from Hannah, she looked up, stopped abruptly, and gawked.

Hannah could imagine how out of place she must look, standing there with her long hair hanging loose under a prayer Kapp, two dresses lying on the ground along with blankets and a traveling bag. She stooped to gather her clothes. "Hello. I got caught out in the weather, and it was warmer back in this cubbyhole. I'll be out of your way in a moment." She glanced up.

The woman's eyes grew large. "You stayed outside all night?"

Shoving the dresses into her bag, Hannah felt her cheeks flush. "I arrived by train, and the phone at the depot was missing."

"Oh my goodness." The woman took a set of keys out of her purse and shimmied past Hannah. "Come inside. I'll get some coffee going and heat up a pastry while you use my phone."

Hannah grabbed her bag, not at all sure what to do with the mystery blankets. She tossed them over her arm and followed the woman into the store. Warmth, blessed warmth, filled the very air she breathed. An aroma of old wood filled her nostrils. The square clock hanging on the wall said the time was a little before eight. She must have slept pretty hard after all.

The woman set her purse on a shelf behind the counter. "So what brings you to Alliance?"

The heated room and the promise of food suddenly lost their appeal. With so much to hide, Hannah couldn't afford to start answering questions.

"How old are you, girl? You can't be much more than sixteen."

Hannah hated deception, but telling the truth—that she was a seventeen-year-old runaway—wasn't an option. She looked out the glass door, considering whether to bolt or lie.

A long shadow in the shape of a man covered the sidewalk leading up to the door. When she looked farther down the street to see who the shadow belonged to, all she saw was a blur moving away from her. A hazy memory of a man covering her with a blanket came back to her.

"I...I think I see someone I need to speak with." Without another word, Hannah left the store. Once on the sidewalk, she spotted a tall, black, teenage boy walking away from her. He turned his head and stole a glance at her, then kept going.

She strode toward him, holding up the blankets. "Are these yours?"

He stopped and turned before shrugging. "You got them now, so they're yours."

The dark-skinned youth was probably only a year or so younger than Hannah, but she felt considerably older. Maybe she'd never feel young again.

"If you put these on me, I really appreciate it."

He shrugged again. "It was nothing. You looked terrified when you saw me, but you fell asleep the minute I put the first blanket on you."

Hannah sighed. "That seems to be the story of my life these days: terrified or asleep."

He held out his hand. "I'm Kendrick."

She shook his hand, realizing she'd never spoken with a black person before. "Hannah."

He released her hand. "So, Hannah, what's with the odd getup? You Amish or a lost pilgrim?"

Fresh realization of how she looked bore down on her.

"Well, don't panic, or I'll have to put those blankets over you so you'll go back to sleep." His voice carried enough sarcasm that she should feel intimidated, but she didn't. Something about him seemed trustworthy.

"Kendrick, I'm in a fix." Trying to think in spite of the grief that clung to her, she decided to aim for a bit of humor. "But if you could assist me without asking any questions, you'd help keep a pilgrim alive through another harsh winter."

He chuckled. "I ain't never met a pilgrim."

"That's okay. Before today I'd never met a black man."

He studied her for a moment. "Well, I guess I better make a good impression then." He smiled. "What can I do to help?"

Hannah told him the name of her aunt she was looking for and the address she'd memorized from the letter she'd discovered back home.

He pulled a pencil and paper out of his pocket and jotted down the info. "I don't have money for car insurance, so I don't drive. I walk to work and stuff. Guess that's a good thing, since that's why I saw you and brought you some blankets from my house."

She held out the blankets again. "Your mother will be looking for these soon enough."

He nodded and took them. "One of my co-workers at the pizza place has a connection to the Amish. I'll give him a call and see if he can get her phone number. If that doesn't work, we'll find you a driver."

He led her to a drugstore that had a pay phone inside. While he made the call, she went into the rest room, determined to shed her Amish look. If her parents had sent word to the Ohio Amish to search for her, she didn't want them or the police to spot her as an Amish girl.

From the backseat of the car, Hannah watched out the side window. The driver scratched his head. "By the way, I don't really care what you call me as long as you call me for dinner, but my name's Gideon."

"Thank you for driving me around today, Gideon."

He smiled and nodded without asking her name. He was a large man who looked old enough to be a grandfather, but Kendrick said he knew his way around this region of Ohio. While on the phone with Kendrick, Gideon had agreed to chauffeur her around for several days if necessary, but he hadn't asked any questions then either. He'd promised Kendrick they'd do their best to find her aunt today, but because Hannah wasn't willing to chance not having a warm place to stay by nightfall, Gideon had helped her locate an inexpensive motel room before they set out. He'd even offered for her to stay with him and his wife tonight, but she declined. She couldn't imagine staying with strangers and fielding the questions they might ask.

The motel was an awful place, a battered one-story brick building with a decaying roof and peeling paint around barred windows, but she wasn't willing to pay for a better place. If she didn't find her aunt, she'd need to conserve what little money she had.

While the car jolted along the rough roads, grief and hope dragged her first one way and then another. The last six months of her life had been horrible, but if she could find her aunt, everything might change.

The snow-covered landscape was sprinkled with homes and farmsteads. In spite of her heartache, inklings of excitement danced within her as she thought of meeting the aunt she hadn't known existed until six months ago.

The driver's voice broke through the long silence. "Hanover Place should be just a few more miles ahead, miss."

"Thank you."

A beautiful brick house came into sight. Electric lights from inside shone warmly against the grayness of the day. Something akin to desire—or was it coveting?—ran through her. Did people who lived like that ever get cold and hungry or stay in a rundown motel?

A mile or so later Gideon turned right and continued a few more miles before slowing the car. Snow crunched under its tires as he pulled onto the shoulder of the road. "This is it—4201 Hanover Place." He pointed to the faded address on a rusty mailbox that sat near a long, curved driveway covered in untracked snow.

He inched the car along the drive, and they passed a small shed that had seen better days. The scene felt right somehow, like a snapshot of a hundred no-longer-used outbuildings she'd grown up around. It wasn't well cared for, but it matched real life: used and still standing.

Gideon stopped the car in front of a house as worn-out as the shed. The peeling paint on the clapboard house was its best feature. Parts of the roof were caved in, as if something had smashed on top of it. Boards crisscrossed the doors and windows, pinned in place with rusty nails. She couldn't imagine why someone would bother to board up such a dilapidated house.

She pulled the door handle and climbed out of the car. Surely there had to be another house somewhere around here. She made a complete turn, looking in all directions for signs of a different homestead along this driveway. All she saw were gently rolling hills, tattered fences, oak trees, and the old shed. Her focus returned to the house.

"You sure this is the right address?" Gideon's question bounced around inside her brain.

Was it possible she'd memorized the address wrong? The wind sliced through her clothing, making her wish she hadn't tried to hide her Amish roots so much that she'd left her homemade woolen shawl along with her apron and Kapp back at the motel.

"Young lady, we ain't beat yet. I promise you that."

She could hear the man, but she couldn't find her way to answer him.

Since burying baby Rachel three days ago, she'd dreamed of arriving at Zabeth's. This was to be her refuge, her direction, her help.

Hannah searched herself to find some sliver of hope to hold on to. But her dream of finding a safe haven in Ohio appeared every bit as ruined as her relationship with Paul.

Soft cries from nondescript voices floated across the fields, becoming more distinct with each second that passed. *Nevertheless,* they cried.

The whisper grew louder. *Nevertheless.*

Nevertheless.

It was the word that had come to her on the train, giving her hope and strength.

She looked at the house. "Nevertheless," she whispered.

⁓ஜ

Darkness overtook the afternoon as Gideon headed them back to the motel.

"I don't mean to pry or nothing…" His gravelly voice filled the vehicle. "But I'm gonna stick by you until we find your aunt. Maybe you're remembering that address wrong."

Too drained to respond, Hannah shrugged. "Maybe."

The man glanced back and forth between the road and the rearview mirror. "Just take a few relaxing breaths, and try to think." The skin around his sagging eyes crinkled in a smile. "If you come up with a different address, we can give it a try tomorrow."

Nodding, she closed her eyes and backtracked through time. She remembered discovering the envelope in her parents' bedroom. The realization that her father had a sister, maybe even a twin sister, had caused curiosity to overpower her, and she'd dared to read the letter.

Hannah shifted against the cloth car seat, trying to recall what had been written in the upper-left corner of the envelope. There hadn't been a first name, only a last name—Bender—and the street address: 4201 Hanover Place, Winding Creek, Ohio. She could see it clearly in her mind's eye.

Against her will, a few tears ran down her cheeks. The place was nothing but an unlivable shambles.

In the rearview mirror she saw Gideon avert his eyes to watch the road. She wiped her face and sat up straight. "Th-that's the address I remember."

He nodded. "Well, I was in a bind like this in my younger days. You got a name for this relative, right?"

"I think so."

"Then that's where we'll begin tomorrow." Gideon drove up to the motel entrance and stopped the car. "You sure about staying here? My wife is a wonderful cook." He patted his rounded belly and laughed. "She's got some Plain roots in her childhood." He smiled, as if he knew Hannah's secret.

She pulled from her purse the wad of money Matthew Esh had given her and handed Gideon the portion they'd agreed upon. The money seemed to be dwindling awfully fast.

He hesitated before taking it from her. "Tomorrow, if ya like, we can search for your aunt using the computers at the local library."

Paul had told her he used his computer to find almost any information he needed. She figured there was no avoiding them or the Internet now that she was living as an Englischer. She stuffed the remaining money deep into her purse. "Yes, I'd like that. But I also think I'd best spend part of tomorrow applying for a job."

A startled look flashed through his eyes. "You're not giving up on finding your aunt already, are you?"

"I...no..." After last night, she wasn't ever going to chance not having a place to stay. Even a crummy roof came with a stiff price in her estimation. "I've got to plan for what can't be foreseen. And even if I find my aunt, I'll be paying my own way."

He smiled, as if he understood. "Got any ideas where to start?"

"Not yet."

From the seat beside him, Gideon passed her a newspaper. "Read the Help Wanted section. If you find something that looks like a possibility, I'll drive you there."

She blew a long, slow stream of air from between her lips. She needed a driver's license so she could go places herself, but then she'd need a car. The list of her needs in this Englischers' world seemed to spring up like weeds in a summer garden.

"Thanks." She swung open the car door. "Gideon?"

"Yeah?"

"Could you not tell anyone that you saw me or that you know where I'm staying?"

The big man turned in his seat, looking at her directly. "How old are you, missy?"

She bristled. "Old enough to know what I'm doing."

I hope. Oh, dear Father, I do hope.

He stared at her before he nodded. "I was on my own at fifteen. I don't reckon you're that young, are you?"

"No, Gideon, I'm years past that. I turn eighteen in eleven days."

"Good enough."

"Thank you. I'll call you in the morning and let you know my plans for tomorrow."

When she'd stepped out of the vehicle and closed the door, Gideon slowly pulled out of the lot. Tucking the newspaper under her arm, Hannah dug in her purse for her room key. The on-site manager came out of his office and stood in the frigid air, watching her.

Maybe he knew.

Maybe he'd already called the police.

As she fought to get the small gold key inserted into the lock of her motel-room door, the number eleven filled her thoughts. In eleven days, when she turned eighteen, freedom would become a reality. Fear of being dragged back to a community that hated her would end on her birthday.

Eleven days. Eleven days.

Since before she departed the train, the number of days until her birthday updated daily and hounded her continually. And encouraged her.

While she jiggled and cajoled the obstinate lock, a lightning zap of pain shot through her lower abdomen. She leaned her shoulder into the door for support and silently counted to ten. The pain would go away as it always had, ever since it began the day after she'd given birth.

As desperate as she was to get out of the cold and off her feet, she refused to ask the manager for his assistance—even though he wasn't doing anything but staring at her.

"Mach's schnell, du Dummkopp—" Her angry whisper, "Make it quick, you dumb—," ended the moment the key turned.

She shoved open the door, entered the dimly lit room, and deadbolted the lock behind her. Her breath came in shallow spurts as she made her way to the shoddy-looking bed. Sitting on top of the frayed bedspread, she closed her eyes and tried to fight off the sense of panic.

Images of Rachel's tiny body lying inside that homemade pine box buried beneath the frozen earth disturbed her. If only she'd handled things differently—

Refusing to be plagued by a past she could do nothing about, she opened her eyes, trying to dispel the image. The room might be drab with worn carpet and faded paint, but it was warm.

She slid out of her clothes and stepped into a hot shower. While the hot water soothed her taut muscles, she tried to think of another way to find Zabeth.

After drying off, she put on her nightgown and sat on the side of the bed, longing to curl into a ball and cry the night away. If Paul could see her now, he'd think her irrational on top of his other negative opinions of her. But whatever he thought, at least she didn't have to face him.

Hannah slid between the cold sheets and placed her hand over her aching stomach, refusing to cry. She had little doubt that she needed medical attention. But she couldn't go to a doctor, not yet, not as a runaway minor. Odd, but it seemed that living under the *Ordnung* and the bishop was easier than finding ways around the Englischers' laws. But all that would change the day she turned eighteen.

She thought about when she'd called Paul the night before she left Owl's Perch. After placing the call, she remained in the motel room near the train station for nearly fifteen hours—waiting, hoping he'd call her back. Hoping he might still want her. He never returned her call, letting her know that he wasn't even willing to say good-bye.

How could she have lost his love so quickly?

A sob ripped through her, and she could no longer hold back her emotions. Rolling onto her side, she buried her face in the pillow and let her tears flow.

*P*aul Waddell paced outside the police station, arguing with himself as to whether he should file a missing person report. Hannah had left of her own accord, and maybe she needed a little more time to choose to return. But he had given her two days.

He'd spent most of yesterday trying to make sense of the missing money from his joint checking account with Hannah. Mr. Harris, an officer at the bank, agreed to begin an investigation—if Paul would sign an affidavit swearing Hannah hadn't taken the money. Paul had no problem doing that. Matthew had told him the account was already empty when she tried to get her portion of the money.

Regardless of who had removed the money, Mr. Harris said the bank would not replace it. Too much time had passed. All Paul's years of working as many hours as possible around his schooling, all his weekends and holidays away from Owl's Perch in order to build for their future and support a child at House of Grace—all of it for nothing. Hannah was gone. And all his time away from her had been spent—on less than zilch.

Brilliant plan, Waddell.

As it stood, the only thing left was to hope the bank's investigation would cause the police to get involved, and maybe it would lead them to Hannah's attacker. In the meantime, Mr. Harris suggested Paul return to his normal life.

Paul scoffed. Normal life?

He'd helped chase into hiding the one person who meant life to him.

And to make matters worse, he seemed to be searching for Hannah by himself. There was no way her family would turn to a government agency and allow it to meddle in their private affairs. So if he didn't file a missing person report, no one would.

Reading the letter Hannah had left with Matthew had given Paul some peace, but it had faded over the last two nights, leaving in its stead a churning anxiety to do something to find her.

But what?

If the police found her and dragged her back to her father's house, that could cause her more complications than trying to live on her own for a while.

Paul shook his head. She was in no position to make it alone. She needed him.

He rubbed the back of his neck as he continued pacing the asphalt lane that ran beside the white masonry building.

Even though he believed she was right to leave her community, he ached to join her and build a life with her. That was only possible if he could find her. He headed toward the police station.

The solid blue door to the station reflected the sun. He backed away, wavering in his decision. He moaned aloud. If only he'd heard her out the night he discovered she was pregnant, she wouldn't be in some distant place trying to survive.

How could he have thought that Hannah, his beautiful girl who didn't even kiss him until after they'd been engaged for months, was guilty of giving herself to a man?

His anger had been a reflex, as if he'd taken a sucker punch and had come up fighting mad.

Now he had to find Hannah. He'd messed up by not being there for her, but from this point on, he would be—if he could find her. If the police became involved, they had the authority to get the train records; they'd know where to start looking. He prayed that the Lord would soften her heart toward him and that she'd trust him enough to give him another chance.

Sure of his decision this time, Paul entered the small police station.

~~✒~~

Hannah stared out the car window at another brick medical building. It was the fifth one today she'd gone into and applied for work. If she needed another assault on the fragment of self-esteem she had left, applying for more jobs was the best way to do it. She and Gideon had spent a few hours early that morning trying to track down her aunt using the Internet, but everything led to a dead end.

Pain sliced across her abdomen, reminding her that instead of applying for work at a medical facility, she needed to be a patient. Waiting on the pain to lessen, she promised herself that if she wasn't better by the time she turned eighteen, then she'd go.

Longing for life to give her a break, Hannah eased her fingers over her mouth and whispered another plea for God to help her. She had no idea whether her prayers would be heard since she was without her prayer Kapp. Maybe God would never listen to her again until she came under the authority of the church.

Her pinned-up hair had a bit of a stylish, puffed-out look to it, with curly wisps escaping here and there. The solid blue caped dress resembled the Plain Mennonites much more than she wanted it to, even though she'd made a belt by cutting the ties off her discarded black apron. When there was money, she wanted a new styled dress, one that didn't set her apart so easily.

"Miss?" Gideon interrupted.

"Oh. Sorry." Hannah opened the car door.

"I got some other errands to run, and since you said you're not hungry, I'm gonna eat while you're puttin' in applications in that building. I'll be back for ya in a couple of hours. Okay?"

She nodded and got out of the car. The large building loomed in front of her, daring her to think she had any qualifications to work there. She stood on the front sidewalk, staring at the place. Maybe her strong emotional pull to and fierce thirst for the medical field were signs of her mental instability. Rather than looking for employment at a place where she couldn't possibly get it, perhaps she needed to seek psychological help.

Drawing a deep breath, she ignored the negative thoughts. She could wallow in the misery of her stubbornness and stupidity later as she spent another long night in the motel.

Half a mile in the distance, down in a small valley, smoke rose from the chimneys of a few homes. Voices of children playing in a patch of woods, climbing trees a couple hundred feet away, danced across the snowy fields. Desire to see her three youngest siblings burned within her. She wanted to help them scale trees and to hear them tease one another about who would reach the highest point.

Feeling like homemade taffy being pulled in two directions at once, she drew a deep breath and headed for the building. She'd chosen a path, and there was no sense in looking back.

She walked through the foyer, past a packed waiting room, and went to the front desk. A sliding glass partition separated her from the office staff. A thirty-something woman with smudged eye makeup and a short crop of fuzzy blond hair glanced up before she turned her attention back to her computer screen. Using a phone headset, she talked while she typed. Behind the woman sat several other women, all busy with phones, computers, or paperwork. A fresh charge of intimidation ran through Hannah. She knew she had few skills to offer a place like this, but she wanted a job at a medical facility of some type, where she could put to use all she'd learned from the nurses who trained her to take care of Mary for all those months. That was her plan, unless she had no other choice.

Without removing the phone headset, the woman behind the counter opened the glass partition. "Can I help you?"

Hannah swallowed, trying to brace herself for another rejection. "Hi, I'm looking for a job."

The woman motioned to the worker behind her. "On a day like today, any one of us would give you ours." She chuckled and pointed to a door at the far end of the room. "Go through that door, pass the first set of counters, and turn right. Human Resources will be the first door to your left."

"Thank you."

A woman named Mrs. Lehman seemed to be the entire department. Mrs. Lehman said they were looking to fill a few entry-level positions as soon as possible, and she asked how quickly Hannah could start work. When Hannah said, "Today," the woman passed her an application, then told her to fill it out and wait for an interview. Hannah wasn't sure what "entry level" meant, but she was hopeful.

Before long she was sitting in a chair outside the Human Resources office doing her best to fill out the application. Her hands shook as thoughts of lying on the application tempted her. She had no desire to be dishonest, but she couldn't list her real name after all she'd been through to get this far. Besides, she might change her last name just as soon as she was eighteen, had the money, and knew how to do it. With her decision made, she filled in her name as Hannah Lawson.

The office door beside her opened. "All set?"

Hannah stood. "Yes."

Mrs. Lehman took the clipboard that held the application. "Come on in." She entered the room behind Hannah, leaving the door open, and read the application as she walked to her desk. "Do you have any computer skills?"

"No."

Mrs. Lehman frowned. "None?"

Hannah shook her head. "I was at the library this morning, working with someone who showed me a few things about connecting to and searching the Internet."

"Oh." Mrs. Lehman took a seat and flipped the application over. "You haven't graduated from high school?"

Hannah shook her head. "No."

The woman took a deep breath. "You didn't fill out the year in which you were born."

Hope began to dwindle. "Is that really important?"

The woman raised her eyebrows. "Yes, I'm afraid it is, along with schooling." Mrs. Lehman tapped the application. "Or lack of it. We need someone with office skills. I'm sorry. We do need help, but you don't meet the qualifications for any of the available positions."

Hannah blinked, trying to dispel the tears that threatened. "I see. I…I learn pretty quick."

"I'm sure you do. Did you take keyboarding in high school?"

"Excuse me." A man's voice from somewhere in the building interrupted them. "Does anyone here speak German?"

Hannah rose. "I do." Without waiting for Mrs. Lehman to respond, she walked in the direction of the voice. A boy about five years old stood in the middle of the waiting room, looking panicked.

A man wearing a white lab coat was squatting in front of the boy, holding on to his shoulders. "Don't you speak any English yet?"

"Dabber schpring! Dabber schpring!" Tears fell from the boy's eyes.

Hannah crossed the room and knelt in front of the boy. *"Shh, liewer. Es iss net hatt."*

The boy jerked air into his lungs, and the panic across his face eased a little.

She took his trembling hands in hers. *"Was iss letz?"*

He let out a sob and opened his mouth to speak, but all that came out were a few broken syllables.

Hannah smiled at him with a calm she didn't feel. She gently rubbed his cold hands between hers, as her mother had done for her when she was little. *"Seller Kall will hilfe."* She nodded at him, assuring him he was able to say what was on his mind. *"Du muscht schwetze."*

Her words of encouragement, mixed with a touch of firmness, seemed to settle him a bit more. Through his sobs he shared broken pieces of what had taken place.

Hannah glanced at the doctor. "His sister has fallen from a tree, and she's not moving." She patted the boy's chest, assuring him they would help his sister. *"Gut."*

The man turned to a woman wearing scrubs. "Get our coats and my medical bag." He pointed to another woman. "Call an ambulance. Watch what direction the boy leads us, and send them that way." He gestured at Hannah. "Where to?" He slid into his coat and clutched his medical bag in one hand.

Hannah asked the boy if he could show them where.

He grabbed her by the hand. *"Kumm! Kumm!"*

They ran out the front door, made a sharp left toward the patch of woods, and crossed over fields that lay covered in untrodden snow—except for the deep, small prints the boy had made on his way to the medical building.

Determined not to fail in this task, Hannah forced her aching body to keep moving.

As they entered the woods, she saw a little girl about six years old on the ground, lying faceup and perfectly still.

The doctor knelt beside the girl and shoved his fingers against her neck. Then he started pushing on her chest. He told a woman to get things out of his black bag. Within ten seconds, she had some kind of apparatus over the girl's mouth and was squeezing a bag. The boy screamed at them to stop.

Glancing at Hannah, the doctor pointed to a different area of the woods. "Get him out of here."

Without hesitation, she reached for his hand. The boy kicked and flailed against her, screaming that they were killing his sister.

Understanding his distrust, she whispered in Pennsylvania Dutch that the doctor was trying to help his sister. When the boy tried to pull away from her, she lifted him onto her hip. Pain ripped through her, causing her knees to almost buckle.

"Du muscht schtobbe!" Hannah spoke firmly.

The boy obeyed and stopped fighting her.

She walked with him on her hip, getting him out of eyeshot of what was taking place. He wrapped his arms around her neck and cried.

All her physical pains seemed to quiet under the tenderness this child stirred within her. Spotting a recently fallen tree, Hannah plodded to it, dusted snow off a small area, and sat down. She rocked the boy and sang to him, ignoring the screeching sounds of the ambulance when it arrived and the distant voices of the medics as they worked with the boy's sister some two hundred feet behind her.

In spite of the mysterious break from the pain in her abdomen, nausea and lightheadedness mounted within her.

Through a series of gentle questions, she learned the boy's name and where he lived. As he relaxed, exhaustion took over. Before long he dozed off.

Blinking, Hannah tried to keep her eyes open as blackness tinged her peripheral vision and closed in. She grabbed a handful of snow from the log and drew it to her lips. The woods spun, and she was no longer sure which way was up.

Had she fallen?

"You okay?" an agitated male voice said.

Pretending she could see clearly, Hannah nodded. "Yes. How's the girl?"

"We don't know yet. She went quite awhile without oxygen, but the cold temperature and lying in snow may have slowed her body's systems enough that she could fully recover."

The man in front of her was shrouded in a thin black veil, and the woods appeared cloaked in dusk, causing Hannah to wonder if night had fallen.

The man lifted the boy from her arms. "I'd like your help to find the girl's parents and explain this to them in the language they are most comfortable with."

"Sure." Hannah forced the word from her lips in spite of the strong urge to lie down and sleep. "But anyone in their family past the first grade will speak English." Hannah stood, using a tree to steady herself against.

"Yes, I know." The doctor nudged the little boy, trying to wake him. "Did he tell you where he lives?"

"Yes." Hannah closed her eyes and reopened them, trying to focus as the trees danced and jiggled like half-set pudding. Feeling an internal darkness pull at her, she grabbed a handful of snow off the log and rubbed it over her face.

When she opened her eyes, the doctor had shifted the boy to one of the uniformed women and was directing his intense stare at her. "I'm Dr. Lehman, and you are…"

Aware of the risk, she didn't answer his question.

"What were your symptoms when you came to the clinic today?"

"I didn't come in as a patient." She tried to stay upright, but her legs folded under her.

She heard Dr. Lehman's frustrated voice. "She's hemorrhaging. Get my bag. Call for another ambulance."

She fought against the dark hole that was trying to consume her. "The boy's name is Marc."

"She's going into shock."

Hannah narrowed her eyes, trying to see something besides darkness. She looked down and saw red snow. "The boy lives at 217 Sycamore. It's half a mile behind…your clinic, past the ridge—"

"Yes. Yes. We can find it. Give me information on how to contact your—"

Something more powerful overtook her, and she had no choice but to go with it.

Chapter 5

A chill ran up Paul's back.

"So." The police chief tapped his pen on the legal pad holding his notes. "What I have so far is that there's an almost-eighteen-year-old girl named Hannah Lapp who's missing. Her parents won't file a missing person report, and if the police show up to talk to them, they are likely not to admit she's gone or even that she exists, for that matter. There are no photos of her, and none of your friends have ever met her."

Paul barely remained in control of his tone. The man's sarcasm was not appreciated. "She does exist. My grandmother can vouch for that."

At the thought of how alone and desperate Hannah must be, a sense of panic stirred within him. But fear would do him no good. He needed a lead, a direction…a miracle. "Hannah's a minor, and she's been traumatized by—"

The man glanced at his notes. "…an attack that took place at the end of last August." He looked up. "The question is, does she want to return?"

"She's a minor, and she needs help. And I need your cooperation in order to find her."

"Look, I agree with you. She got a bum deal, and she deserves a break. But she's less than two weeks from turning eighteen, and she has a friend who says she left of her own accord with money to live on and some sort of a plan. Those details make this a low priority for us. By the time we get the info out on her and anyone has a chance to recognize her, she'll be a legal adult." The man shrugged. "We'll do what we can, but I can't guarantee anything."

Paul clenched his forehead with his fingertips. If the police weren't going to help, he had to get out of here and do something himself.

Grabbing his coat off the chair, Paul headed for the door.

The police chief rose. "You could try hiring a private investigator."

Pausing for a moment, Paul nodded. "Thank you."

He hurried out the door of the police station and hustled down the asphalt alleyway toward his truck. As he reached for the door handle to his old vehicle, he spotted a red brick church with a bell tower two blocks up the street. The place stood resolute, inviting him to come search for peace within its walls. Deciding he needed to pray before trying to figure anything else out, he sprinted toward the aged church.

Dear God, please. I don't know what to pray. Please help.

He whispered his pleadings as he climbed the concrete steps, opened the oversize wooden door, and walked through the sanctuary. Thankfully the place was empty. Paul went to the altar and began quietly praying.

As the panic of the last few days quieted underneath the blanket of prayer, anger at the man who'd attacked Hannah pushed to the forefront of Paul's mind and heart, but he was clueless what to do with it, what he should do with it.

If I could get my hands on him…

Yet, even as the fury caused sickening feelings, he knew he had to let the desire for revenge go. Not only was the desire against everything he believed, but it had no power to help. Only God could help. Only He was stronger than what any enemy could dish out. Paul's and Hannah's families would never agree on much, but all Plain folk had one thing in common: they believed in nonresistance, that forgiving and letting God take vengeance was the only way to live.

"Help me focus on You, God. Not on what's been done, but on what can be done to restore," Paul whispered.

Voices from somewhere inside the church caught Paul's attention, and he glanced at his watch. He needed to go.

Driving toward Penn State, in Harrisburg, he spotted a pay phone and pulled his truck into a parking spot. There was a phone at his apartment, but if he stopped by there, his three roommates would bombard him with questions he didn't want to answer—couldn't answer. He called Gram to see if she'd heard from Hannah or had learned anything about her from Luke or Matthew. She hadn't, but she told him that Mr. Harris from the bank was trying to reach him. He assured Gram he'd make contact with the man and then be home as soon as he could.

Hours later, in the dark, he drove into Gram's driveway. His time with Mr. Harris had been totally discouraging. He got out of his truck and made his way around the side of the house. Stomping the snow off his boots, he climbed the few steps to his grandmother's back porch. The starless night air was bitter cold and the darkness so thick it seemed to smother life itself. He crossed the threshold of the enclosed porch, haunted by its memories. He and Hannah had spent many a long summer day shucking corn or snapping beans right here on this porch.

He plunked onto a padded wicker chair, wondering what his next move should be. Every possible hint of a way to locate Hannah had become a dead end. Aside from Matthew, no one in her community would even talk to him. Maybe a private investigator was the answer.

Through the porch window, he caught a glimpse of his grandmother's silhouette as she entered the kitchen. A dim light flicked on inside the house, and then the door to the back porch opened. Gram tightened her thick terry-cloth housecoat around her as she stepped onto the porch.

She knew why he chose to live here in Owl's Perch with her during the summer and on school breaks rather than spend time in Maryland with his parents. She'd hired an Amish girl to help her around the house three years ago, and after Paul met her, he spent as much time here as he could manage. Gram had reservations about his future with an Old Order Amish girl, but she had come to care about Hannah too.

Gram grabbed a blanket off a nearby rocker and draped it over her shoulders. "Any news concerning the missing money?"

Paul sighed. "The footage of the person who withdrew the money from our account shows a young woman, either Amish or dressed like one."

"What? How did she get hold of the bankbook?"

"We don't think she did. Our best guess is that somehow Hannah's attacker got it, and he either tricked an Amish person into withdrawing the money, using a photoless ID, or he hired someone to act the part."

"Now what?"

Paul shrugged. "It's another dead end, Gram."

Faint streams of light filtered through the kitchen window onto the dark, cold porch. He knew Gram had a meal inside waiting for him; she always did. But Paul didn't want to enter the warm, familiar home. He wanted Hannah.

She needed him, if he just knew how to find her.

"Paul." Gram's voice trembled.

Realizing it was too cold for her to be out here, he nodded toward the door. "Go on inside, Gram. I'll be in later."

She shifted from one foot to another. "I don't want to get your hopes up, but…"—she shoved her hands into her pockets—"a letter arrived in the mail for you today." She pulled out an envelope. "I don't think it's from Hannah. The handwriting doesn't look like hers."

Paul took the envelope and held it in the dull light that streamed from the kitchen window. "That's Hannah's writing. It's more wobbly than usual, but it's hers." He studied the envelope. It had no return address, but it'd been mailed from Pittsburgh two days ago. He ripped the envelope open and removed the letter.

At the sight of his name scrawled across the top of the letter, his eyes clouded. Light flooded the porch. Gram had turned on the overhead lamp and gone inside.

He read the letter.

Dearest Paul,

I wrote a letter to you and left it with Matthew, but then I realized you would not receive it unless you came looking for me.

I'm on the train I boarded in Harrisburg, and I needed to share a word that has caused such hope to grow within me that my strength for life is returning.

Nevertheless.

It's a great word. Ya?

Paul nodded as tears blurred his vision. He wiped his eyes with the palm of his hand.

If all our dreams lie shattered before us—nevertheless, God can sustain us and even build new dreams.

I conceived a child because someone did not place his desires under God's authority—nevertheless, God's power over my life is stronger than that event.

Rachel died—nevertheless, she is now with God.

You and I are no more—nevertheless, God is not without a plan.

Ach, what I feel in my heart is so much stronger than I can manage to put on this paper. But I laugh as I think—nevertheless, God will give you understanding.

He closed his eyes and could hear her soft, gentle laugh. She was growing in ways that were good for her, and he was thankful for it.

I know you had to walk away and start a new life without me. I think I'll always miss who we once were. I'm guilty of Rachel's death. I tried to hide that she existed when I should have sought medical help. Nevertheless, God speaks to me. Let Him speak to you too.

In hope forever,

Hannah

He shot out of the chair, off the porch, and into the yard. He gulped in a lungful of frigid air. Closing his eyes, he felt the burden of confusion ease a bit as it tried to give way to acceptance. A snippet of hope took root, and he sensed that Hannah must have experienced a similar feeling when she discovered the nevertheless idea.

Paul folded the letter, assured that if anyone could make a success out of this mess, she could. He lifted his face to the heavens. "I need to hear from you again, Hannah. I need to know you're safe and have found someone to help you. God, please."

As he stared into the vastness of the jeweled sky, he wanted more from God than just this note.

He sighed.

Nevertheless, he'd heard from her, and it was a good note.

"Thank you, God." He whispered the words and tucked the letter into his shirt pocket. In that moment, all lingering desire for vengeance against her attacker melted. Whatever the destruction, God would not let the story end there.

*S*et on seeing Elle Leggett first thing today, Matthew climbed into the buggy and pulled to a stop in front of his home to wait for his brothers. If he didn't get some time with Elle this morning before she began teaching, his heart might fail him—right there in the schoolyard in front of everyone.

"Peter! David! *Loss uns geh!*" He should've have ridden there by himself rather than let Mamm talk him into giving his younger brothers a ride to school. He pulled a pair of work gloves out of his coat pocket. So it was cold. If they didn't hurry up, he'd let them walk.

"*Kummet mol!*" he bellowed.

David moseyed out the front door, pulling on his winter coat. "We're coming. Hold your horses. I mean horse."

Nothing was the least bit humorous to Matthew right now. He wanted to see his girl.

David knelt on the porch and tied his shoes. Peter ran out the door, panting, carrying two brown-bag lunches. "Sorry. I didn't realize you wanted to leave this early today." He dropped one of the lunches next to David. "Forget this?"

"Oh, ya. I'd miss that about lunchtime, huh?" David climbed into the buggy.

Peter jostled into his spot on the bench seat. "Elle would share her lunch with you. She's a real nice teacher."

Matthew tapped the reins against the horse's back and clicked his tongue. "Geh."

The horse plodded forward.

David shoved his lunch bag between his feet on the floorboard. "Yeah, she'd share it with any student. Can't say she'd do the same for you, Matthew."

David squirmed around to face him. "So, why's our teacher so frosty whenever your name comes up lately? I thought ya were her beau."

"Just ride." Matthew flicked the reins, stepping up the pace of his horse. The chaos that had led to Hannah's departure made him unable to keep up with what was happening in Elle's life, but he'd bet she'd heard plenty of rumors about him and Hannah. He slowed the buggy and turned right, entering the long dirt road that led to the one-room schoolhouse.

His last exchange with Elle played through his thoughts. They'd argued over where his loyalties were, with her or with Hannah. He'd ached to climb into the buggy with her and go for a long ride, talking until everything was aired out. But he had agreed to help Hannah leave Owl's Perch and had to keep that promise first.

Today he had time to talk, if she would listen. Pulling the buggy to a stop beside the schoolhouse, Matthew took note of the smoke coming out of the chimney. Elle's driver had already dropped her off. He pulled the brake and wrapped the reins around the stob before climbing down. "Get wood from the shed, and stack it on the porch, but don't come inside until someone else arrives."

"You and Elle feudin'?" Peter asked.

Without responding, Matthew gathered an armload of wood and strode toward the school. He tapped on the door, giving her warning someone had arrived early, then went inside. Elle was sitting at her desk with a pencil in hand and looked up when he came through the door. She pursed her lips and returned her attention to the papers in front of her.

Matthew made his way to the woodbin. Stalling, he unloaded the split logs one by one, hoping the right words would pop into his head. Brushing the dirt and moss off his hands and into the woodbin, he studied her.

"Elle." He walked to her desk and waited for her to look up again. She didn't.

"You got something honest to say, say it."

"Could you look at me, please?"

She slammed the pencil onto her desk, folded her arms, and looked him

WHEN THE MORNING COMES   377

dead in the eye. "What am I supposed to think of you never having time for me? Could you just tell me that?"

"Han—"

She rose, toppling her chair backward. Her porcelain skin and reddish hair radiated beauty, even in her anger. "Could we manage one conversation without mentioning Hannah? Just one?"

Matthew had no idea what to say if he wasn't supposed to mention Hannah's name along with a list of apologies. He fidgeted with the edge of the student's desk behind him. "I had to help her, but I care for no girl but you."

She moved to the side of her desk, just a foot away from him, and sat on it, leaving the toe of her shoe on the floor. Her eyes of lavender mixed with blue, a combination he'd never seen before he met her, were a regular reminder that she hadn't been born to Amish parents. She played with one of the ties on her prayer Kapp. The way her eyes probed him, looking to understand things she wouldn't ask aloud, left him no doubt that she still cared deeply.

"See, neither me nor Hannah meant to cau—"

Elle rose and placed her fingers over his mouth. "I don't want to hear about her." She whispered the words as her fingertips slid across his lips. Her warm hands moved to his cheeks, and she gently pulled him to her until their lips were a mere inch apart. "I was hoping..."

Matthew clasped his hand around the back of her head, feeling the lump of her hair bun under her prayer Kapp. An image of her without her Kapp, her strawberry blond hair flowing over her shoulders, flashed in his mind's eye. Of course, for him to see her like that they'd have to be behind locked doors and have taken their marriage vows.

He closed the gap between them until her soft lips brushed against his.

The sound of children approaching made Elle dart from his arms and retreat behind her desk before he had time to react. The door to the schoolhouse flung open, and several children scurried in, chatting feverishly.

Elle ran a finger over her lips. "Yep, that's what I was hoping for." She turned to the children and motioned to the pegs on the back wall. "Please put your coats on the pegs and lunches near the stove, and take your seats."

Matthew chuckled. She went from sounding like his future wife to a schoolteacher as fast as the speed of that opening door.

Aching for another kiss, he moved to the opposite side of her desk and behaved like a visiting adult should, but it wasn't easy. "How about if you have the driver bring you by the shop after school? I'll see to it you either get home later or can stay at the Bylers'."

She picked up her teacher's attendance book, avoiding looking at him. "Okay. I'll bring David and Peter with me."

He turned to leave.

"And Matthew?"

He wheeled around, hoping to see a warm smile, but she was still fiddling with things on her desk.

"The girl we're not talking about—she left me a letter. It sounds like there was something you haven't told me." She lifted both eyebrows, waiting on him to answer.

He gave a slight nod. "We'll cover *everything* tonight."

~∿৪০

With the bacon frying, coffee perking on the stove, and a huge batch of sticky buns in the oven, Sarah glanced at the kitchen doorway and whispered, "Mamm?"

"Hmm?"

Although she had responded, Sarah knew her mother hadn't fully come out of that faraway world she lived in lately. Mamm had called Sarah to her bedroom last night, shut the door, and explained things about how a woman conceived and what had taken place that caused Hannah to become pregnant. Her mother's voice had been but a whisper as tears trailed down her face through the explanation. Then she'd dismissed her daughter without answering the one question that tormented Sarah.

"Mamm." She said the word more firmly, hoping her mother would break free long enough to talk to her.

"What?"

"Do you really think Hannah's baby died?"

Moving eggs from the basket to a small container, Mamm answered, "Yes." She opened the refrigerator and set the eggs in it.

Dread so thick it seemed to be suffocating her wrapped around Sarah. As much as she'd hated her sister, it was too horrid to think she'd given birth to a child who hadn't survived. That couldn't be true. It just couldn't.

It was your own words, Sarah Lapp, that turned Daed and the bishop against your sister.

She rubbed her temples, trying to clear her head. "But how do you know? I mean, couldn't she have taken the baby with her?"

Her mother faced her. "I know it's a nightmare, Sarah, but it's all true."

Thoughts tripped one way and then stumbled another, all leading her where she just couldn't accept the story the Eshes had told them yesterday.

Why, Sarah had seen how that oldest sister of hers had everyone jumping through hoops and doing her chores while she lay around pretending to be sick. With Sarah's own eyes she saw Hannah climb into a buggy with some man, going off for a joyride at midnight in her nightgown!

Sarah turned the bacon over in the skillet, trying to keep the hot grease from spattering. If Hannah was so sneaky as to use Mrs. Waddell's place to meet her beau and had sent and received letters for years without anyone in her family knowing, what else was she capable of? Maybe she'd never boarded that train. Was she hiding out right here in Owl's Perch with her baby?

"Just how trusting are we supposed to be?" Sarah mumbled under her breath.

"Did you say something?" her mother asked.

"Are you sure she buried the... I mean, did you see the baby before..."

Mamm shook her head. "We saw the casket that Matthew made being lowered into the ground." Mamm sat in a chair, looking too tired to remain on her feet. "Just as well, I suppose."

"Do you think Naomi saw the baby?"

"I imagine. I know this is hard to accept, Sarah, but—"

"Can I go see Naomi after breakfast?"

"You've got chores. Just because you're done with your schooling days—"

"Please?" Sarah interrupted her. "I just need to see her."

The back door opened, and Sarah heard the menfolk stomping around as they pulled off their work boots.

"Okay, after breakfast you can slip out," Mamm whispered. "But be back before Esther and Samuel are home from school."

~~⚬~~

Sarah knocked on the Eshes' door and waited. A moment later the door popped open.

Naomi's eyes widened at the sight of her. "Why, Sarah Lapp, what are you doing here with everything your Mamm's going through?"

"I brought you some sticky buns."

Naomi accepted the plate from Sarah and walked toward her kitchen. "My guess is you've got more on your mind than sharing food."

Sarah shut the door, peeled out of her cloak, and followed her. If anyone would give her straight answers, it'd be Naomi. Why, she'd been awful outspoken with Daed yesterday. Sarah bet she was aching to spill all she knew.

Naomi set the plate on the counter. "Take a seat, and tell me what's on your mind."

Laying her winter cape beside her, Sarah climbed onto a tall, swivel-backed counter stool. "I was hoping to understand a little more about what happened with Hannah."

"I really don't think we should talk about that. Your sister had a baby out of wedlock. How your parents want to address that with you children is up to them."

Outspoken indeed.

"Did you see the baby that night?"

"Yes. She was a tiny thing."

A pitiful noise, like a baby crying, came from somewhere outside the house. The sound made Sarah's insides jolt, but Naomi didn't respond a bit to the cries.

The awful sound repeated with no reaction from Naomi. Was she just pretending not to hear it? Was she hiding the baby?

Realizing Naomi wasn't going to tell her anything and ready to search for what was making this noise, Sarah rose. "I was hoping you'd say something that could help me understand."

Naomi straightened her pinafore. "I'd like to know some things too, like where she was heading when she boarded that train."

Wrapping her cloak around her, Sarah asked, "Did you see her get on the train?"

"Oh, honey, I sure did. You don't need to worry about that. She got on that train safe and sound with her tickets in hand."

Sarah nodded. So Hannah did leave Owl's Perch. That actually brought Sarah a measure of relief, although she couldn't figure out why. She excused herself and slipped out the door and listened for the sound. It was coming from Matthew's shop.

Hoping Naomi didn't look out her window, Sarah scampered across the yard to the shop. After looking everywhere on the first floor, she climbed the ladder to the storage loft. She looked behind every crate for signs that someone was hiding Hannah's baby. She found none. But it had to be alive somewhere.

When the front door swooshed open, Sarah jumped.

A moment later it closed. She tiptoed in the direction of the ladder, cringing with every moan the wooden floorboards made.

"Hello?" Matthew called.

No way around it, she was caught. With her heartbeat going wild, she hollered down, "Hi, Matthew." Her voice sounded guilty, even to her. Navigating each rung of the ladder carefully, she made her way to the ground floor.

"I saw Old Bess hitched to a buggy out front. I figured it'd be you that came over here, but I guessed you were in the house."

Shaking the dust from her dress, Sarah refused to look at him. "I was. I brought your family some sticky buns, but then I came out here to see you."

"In the attic?" he scoffed. "What are ya really lookin' for, Sarah? Peace?"

"That's ridiculous. I'm not the one who's done anything wrong."

Folding his arms across his chest, Matthew rocked back. "Ah, now I see how you're living with yourself."

She brushed dust off her black cloak. "Well, aren't you just cheeky and rude when you're by yourself?"

"Sticking with Hannah's wishes, I ain't told anyone what I know. But don't let that piece of information make you think it'll stay that way."

"What're you trying to say?"

"Your sister was better to you than anyone. You can mark my words on that. She saw you for what you are and loved you anyway—until you ruined her whole life."

His words stung something horrid, but she wasn't about to let him know that. "And to think I held you in such high esteem. It's clear enough that Hannah has cast her spell over you just like she did my Jacob."

"It ain't like that between me and Hannah. But I'd like to know one thing from you, and then maybe I won't tell your secret."

The shrieking cry filled the room. Sarah jumped, a gray eeriness settling over her. "What was that?"

Matthew rolled his eyes. "A tomcat killed all the mama cat's babes. She ain't quit hollering over it yet."

Sarah swallowed hard. A mama cat?

The baby's not dead. It's not.

An image of a tiny coffin lying in a grave with dark soil being tossed onto it flashed through her mind. She sucked in air and scrunched her eyes closed, trying to free herself of the sickening thought.

"You okay?"

"Of course," she snapped. "I need to go."

"Not before you've answered my question."

"What?"

Matthew leaned against the planked wall, blocking her exit. "I'm not going to ask why you told everyone about Hannah going out for a late night ride. It happened. You told—out of jealousy is my guess. But why did you lie about how long she was gone?"

"I'm not jealous!" she fumed.

"Answer the question."

"I didn't lie." She just wasn't sure, that was all. Most of her life she'd lost track of time easily. Had she lost track that night?

"Wrong answer."

"Well, if you're so smart, how long was she gone?"

"Less than five minutes, and we never left sight of the house, just like she said."

Sarah drew back "We? You were with her? That can't be. I saw her in a tourist buggy with a horse I ain't never seen before."

"Look around you, Sarah. Part of what I do is take old buggies and refinish them, some of them for touristy places. I go to the racetrack and buy horses and train them, sometimes for those same places."

The screaming returned, banging against her temples and shrieking at her. "But—"

"There are no *buts*. I'll put my hand on the Bible and say how long we were gone that night. Will you stick by your story that well?"

Beads of sweat rolled down her back, and suddenly the door loomed in front of her. Pushing it open, she gulped cold air and ran to her buggy. Shaking like a leaf, she flicked the reins and started toward home. As the horse lumbered onward, guilt inched into her thoughts, feuding with the fear of what would happen when the community found out she'd been wrong.

Her thoughts suddenly became dull and confused, as if a tornado had deadened a path through her mind.

Matthew met Elle at the car and took the books from her hands as she got out. Peter and David wasted no time heading inside the house—for food, he was quite sure.

"Come on." Matthew led her into the privacy of his repair shop. Once they were sitting on the couch, he drew a deep breath and told the whole story of his and Hannah's buggy ride, how she came to stay at his repair shop overnight, and why he'd kept secrets for Hannah.

Elle rose. "That buggy ride everyone talked about… It was you she was with?" She gaped at him in disbelief.

"The rumors are lies. We weren't gone no thirty minutes. I bet it wasn't even five."

"Every time I think things are straight between us, something else concerning Hannah comes up." She rolled her eyes. "If it's all so innocent, why keep it a secret from me?"

"Hannah asked me to, and I was afraid you wouldn't believe me."

"And keeping secrets was your way to win my trust?"

Matthew stood. "See, Hannah and—"

She rose on her tiptoes and pushed her finger against his chest. "If you don't quit talking about Hannah, I'm going to scream."

"You are screaming."

She narrowed her eyes and growled at him. "Make the point, Matthew—without Hannah's name being mentioned—before I show you just how loud I can scream."

"Elle, none of the rumors are true. I don't know what else to tell you."

She propped her hands on her hips. "It's just all so infuriating. I want to believe you. You know I do."

Matthew inched closer, fearing she'd step farther away, but she didn't. "Elle, there was a time when I thought maybe I'd enjoy taking Hannah home from singings. It was just a thought, no real emotions or desires attached to it. Then I met you."

"So I have two choices: believe you and maybe play the fool for life, or believe the rumors and go find someone else."

"For life?" Matthew smiled.

"Oh shut up." She stormed off to the far side of the room.

"You know, you're a mite easier to get along with in the morning than in the afternoon."

A short burst of laughter escaped her. Matthew had the sneaking suspicion he'd hit on a truth about her that she already knew. He crossed the room and pulled her into his arms.

"We're not finished arguing." She pushed against him, but he didn't let go.

He ran his finger over her lips. "Could we take a break and return to arguing later?"

Expecting a snippy remark, Matthew was caught off guard when she slowly kissed his finger.

He lifted her chin and kissed her the way he wished he'd had time to do that morning. "Marry me, Elle," Matthew mumbled between kisses.

Someone banged on the door, making them both jump. A moment later the door swung open.

"Dad," Elle whispered.

*D*eep darkness became a reddish black as Hannah tried to open her eyes. Papers were rustling somewhere close by.

"Can you hear me?"

A machine near her head made little bleeps faster and faster.

"It's okay. Stay calm. You're in Alliance Community Hospital."

A wave of nausea ran through her. She couldn't be in the hospital. How would she pay? They would find her, and her father would come. Her eyes refused to open. The dark world tugged at her, and she struggled to stay awake. She tried lifting her arms, but they barely budged.

She forced enough air into her lungs so she could speak. "I won't go back. I won't."

Plastic wrap crinkled right beside her. "Well, I don't know where 'back' is, but if you're angry with somebody at home, you just might change your mind when you realize how close you came to not surviving."

She heard water being poured. Licking her dry lips, she commanded her eyes to open. They didn't obey.

"Good thing for you that your body started responding positively. You gave us a scare for nearly twenty-four hours. Then your vitals improved, letting us know you would survive. That took place around this time yesterday." A straw touched her lips. "Take a drink."

Sipping the cool water, Hannah began to come out of that dark place. She pulled away from the straw, scrunched her eyes, and managed to lift her eyelids for a moment.

Standing over her was the doctor from the last clinic that wouldn't hire her. Fragmented thoughts sprang to her mind, too disconnected to make sense.

The straw pressed against her lips again. She drew cool water into her mouth, feeling more clarity with each swallow. She tried shifting in the bed.

Parts of her body were working now—her arms, shoulders, and legs. But with her torso feeling like dead weight and the soreness across her lower body, she couldn't move. "You may not remember, but I'm Dr. Lehman. How are you feeling?"

Forcing the correct response, Hannah whispered, "Okay. The girl…at the clinic, how is she?"

"She made a complete recovery and went home yesterday. You, on the other hand, are still quite sick. You're in ICU. You had what's called a retained placenta. Our best guess is that when that boy kicked against you, the pool of internal blood broke loose from its clot. It was merciful timing to happen near the clinic, that's for sure. The surgeon did what he could to repair your uterus. Until yesterday you were on a ventilator. You were given a ten-pack of platelets and a unit of fresh frozen plasma. Now that may not mean a whole lot to you, but trust me, you should read up on it and thank your lucky stars you survived."

Embarrassed that an entire surgical team knew her secret, Hannah closed her eyes. She didn't want to know what they'd done. The only question she wanted answered was how she would pay for this.

He cleared his throat. "Okay, I've covered all that a doctor is supposed to tell you. Now there are some things I need you to tell me. We'll start with your name."

"Hannah," she answered, hoping he wouldn't push for more information than necessary.

The man drew a deep breath. "That's a start. On the application, you gave Lawson as your last name. Is that real or made up?"

Hannah shook her head without opening her eyes. "I've got money to cover part of the bill. I'll pay the rest when I get a job."

The doctor didn't respond.

Hannah pried her eyes open. The doctor was perched on the edge of a chair next to her bed.

He ran his hands through his thick gray hair. "An older man named Gideon came looking for you the day you passed out. He says he's been driving you around since Tuesday morning, but he knows nothing about you other than you pay in cash and you're staying in a motel." He shifted in his chair. "I know you're Amish—otherwise, you wouldn't know the language so well. You're underage, or you would have put your date of birth on the application. Since you're staying at a motel, you're probably a runaway."

Hannah winced as fear rose within her. He'd figured out a lot about her.

"I also know you've recently given birth to a baby, and you're lucky to be alive, considering the amount of blood you lost when you began to hemorrhage." He drew a breath.

Wooziness washed over her. She closed her eyes, drowning in the awareness that this wasn't the life she'd expected to find. Loneliness. No safe harbor. A cheap motel. Constant fear of getting caught. And now this.

God, please.

Uncertain what else to say, she ended her prayer at two words.

"The surgeon did what he could to repair your uterus. I think you'll recover nicely, but due to the extensive damage..." He paused. "Hannah, I'm sorry to have to tell you this, but it seems unlikely that you'll ever conceive again."

Panic choked her. "Unlikely?"

"The damage was quite severe. It's highly unlikely, probably impossible, that you'll ever have another child."

The words rolled over her. She covered her face with her hands. Was her dead child truly the only one she'd ever have? As if a hidden part of her had just worked its way free, she realized she'd still been harboring hopes of a life with Paul. Somewhere inside, dreams of one day bearing his children were fading.

Something touched the backs of her hands, causing her to lower them. Through teary eyes she looked at the doctor.

"Here." He shoved tissues into her hands, staring at her. "I'm sorry this happened to you, but you had to know you needed medical help long before you passed out."

Accusation pointed an ugly finger at her. He was right—she'd known.

"Where's the baby you gave birth to?"

She shook her head. Her life was none of this man's business. And if he knew the truth, he'd try to send her home. She couldn't go back. She just couldn't.

He shifted. "I need to know that you haven't abandoned your newborn somewhere. If you don't convince me, I'll call the police right now, and you can finish recuperating wherever they take you."

The sternness reflected in his eyes matched his tone. There was no doubt he wanted answers. His motives for prying into her life were sound enough, but she couldn't make herself answer him.

"Fine." He stood.

Hannah tried to lean forward. "Okay."

He turned to face her. "Where's your baby?"

She wondered what the authorities would do with her after she explained what happened. "She died. We buried her."

"How far along were you?"

Hating not knowing, Hannah closed her eyes and wished he'd just go away.

"When did you conceive?"

Hannah fidgeted with the sheets. "I don't know how to figure that."

"Were you sexually active?"

"No!" She stared at him. "How can you just blurt out such wrongdoing at someone?"

Dr. Lehman returned to the seat beside her bed. He sat in silence, as if waiting for her to volunteer information. "Hannah,"—his voice was barely audible—"when were you raped?"

She pursed her lips as tears worked their way free against her will. That day would linger with her forever. "August thirtieth." A sob escaped her. "Paul asked me to marry him that morning." She closed her eyes. "On my walk home a man in a car came up and…"

The doctor patted her hand. "Take a breath, Hannah. I understand enough. According to the surgeon, you gave birth less than a week ago. That means you had a miscarriage, Hannah. The child was not developed enough to survive—unless born in ideal circumstances—and even then it probably would have had serious complications if it had lived." He passed her a few more tissues. "Where are your parents?"

She wiped her eyes. "When rumors started spreading, they thought I was lying about how I became pregnant. I couldn't take any more."

"So you are a runaway."

"I turn eighteen soon."

Dr. Lehman drummed his fingers against his thighs. "How soon?"

"March ninth."

"You should have waited until then to leave home. You're a minor, which means I have to inform social services. Besides, issues between parents and their children can almost always be worked out. Your folks may not have responded as they should have, but you were wrong to run off."

She wanted to scream at him. He didn't know what it was like to have an entire community set against you or to have your parents trick themselves into thinking you were the problem. If she had stayed, the People would have continued to ostracize her. Then her only choice would have been to work for Gram and live with her or with others close by who weren't Old Order Amish. Then she would have been forced to endure her worst nightmare: having a front-row seat as Paul fell in love with someone else, got married, and had children.

She closed her eyes and covered her head with a pillow.

"I'll contact the authorities, and someone from child services will be here in the next few days. In the meantime you'll be staying here."

She swallowed hard and waited to hear him leave the room.

The glass door made a swooshing sound as it slid open.

"I'm sorry, Hannah," Dr. Lehman whispered.

She flung the pillow off her head, waves of anger replacing her misery. "You're sorry? Then try being right instead of lawful. You can't think it's right to send me back home when I'm just days away from being an adult. My family despises me!" She gasped for air. "I'll have to wear a scarlet letter for the rest of my life because of things that weren't my choice." She paused, realizing she was yelling at the man. She lowered her voice. "I'm begging you. Please don't make that call."

He studied her, and for a moment Hannah thought maybe he'd see this her way. But then he shook his head. "I can't break the law, Hannah." With that, he left the room.

The nurse at the station outside Hannah's room stared at her before returning her attention to her desk. No wonder the Amish avoided contact with policemen and doctors. They followed the law, whether it held any wisdom for the individual or not.

If she had any strength, she'd find her clothes and get out of here. But whatever was wrong with her had left her weak.

Staring at the ceiling, she mourned the loss of something she'd never fully had: freedom.

If she had any chance of winning Paul's heart again, she could endure going back. If she could bear him children, he might forget that she'd once carried a child concealed from him. But the news that she'd never be able to have another child slashed the last threads that might have bound her and Paul together.

Oh God, help me. I can't go back. I just can't.

*S*itting in the enclosed buggy, Luke tapped the reins lightly against the horse's back as he drove down the dirt road toward his harness shop. In spite of how broken his relationship with Mary was and how much he loved her, that's not what he'd try to repair first. If he could go back and do things over, he would treat his sister right. He'd stand against his father and the bishop, even knowing he'd be frowned upon and ostracized, if not shunned.

He spotted a man about his age tossing loose hay into the snowy pastures that bordered the Waddell and Lapp properties. Considering Mary's description, Luke would've bet this was the guy Hannah had been secretly engaged to. The Lapp and Waddell homesteads were a mile apart, but until now Luke had never laid eyes on the guy. Of course the man didn't live in Owl's Perch year round. He only came here during his summer breaks from college—just long enough to make his sister believe she was in love with him.

Torn between indignation and the reminder of his own mistakes with Hannah, Luke had no idea what to think of the man who had tried to steal his sister from her Amish roots. As he rode closer, the stranger glanced his way. Intending to ignore the man and keep going, Luke looked straight ahead. A scene flashed through his mind, causing the hairs on his arms to stand on end.

The night of his and Mary's accident, a car had rammed into their buggy, and he went sailing through the air. When he woke in the grassy field, he couldn't find Mary. He remembered looking toward heaven and praying, "God, please." Shame had swallowed him. He knew he wasn't worthy of God helping him with anything. When he made his way back to the road and saw what was left of their upended carriage, his legs had buckled, and he'd landed on his knees, begging, "Please, Father, if You will, help us."

It had been a feeble prayer from the lips of a man totally unworthy to ask or receive anything from God, but immediately warmth had run through his body, and he had known what he needed to do to find Mary.

Unable to justify coldness to Paul when God had been so merciful to him, Luke tugged on the reins and came to a stop a few feet from where the man stood. Fighting against his prejudice, Luke wrapped the reins around the stob on the dash of the buggy and just sat there, waiting—for what, he didn't know.

The man stepped forward. "Something I can do for you?"

If Luke was going to do penance for how he'd treated Hannah, this was the place to begin. By an act of his will, he climbed down from the buggy and offered his hand. "I'm Luke, Hannah's brother."

"Paul Waddell." He used his teeth to pull off a work glove and then held out his hand to Luke.

Now that he was standing eye to eye with the man, Luke felt like a gamecock ready to attack. Instead, he shook Paul's hand firmly. "I'm right sorry for all that's taken place."

Paul's eyes bored into his. "Have you heard anything from her?"

Luke shook his head. "No, but I'm sure she's doing fine." He shrugged. "Hannah's not like most girls."

Paul seemed relieved to hear something encouraging about Hannah's circumstances. "She's tender-hearted. Courageous. And..." His voice cracked with emotion.

Dislike for the man drained from Luke. "And stubborn. If will has anything to do with making a success out of her new life, she'll stroll back to Owl's Perch someday just to let the bishop know he didn't win."

Paul studied the fields. "Just as long as she returns."

Luke didn't respond. When his sister did return, he wanted to see her grow fresh roots among her own kind, the people God had placed her with.

Paul shoved a glove into his jacket pocket. "If you hear anything..."

"I'll let you know." Luke buttoned his coat against the cold air.

"How's Matthew doing working things out with the church leaders?"

"They seem to have nothing to say to him or anyone else over the events concerning Hannah. But his life is not what he'd hoped. His girl, Elle, was born English and raised by Amish parents after her mother died when she was ten. Her father had been trying to make contact with her for a few weeks. Since he showed up, he's been pushing her to leave the only family she's known for the last ten years and come live with him."

"Is she going to do it?"

Luke shrugged. "I guess so, 'cause—"

Sounds of a horse and buggy made both men look toward the road. The rig turned onto the driveway of the harness shop. Mary's oldest brother, Gerald, was driving, and his wife, Suzy, sat beside him. Luke hurried to the buggy before it came to a full stop. "What brings you two out this way?"

Gerald glanced at Suzy, but neither one answered him.

"Is Mary all right?"

Gerald gave a slow wave of his hand. "Yes and no." He spoke casually, as if they were discussing plowing fields. "Daed insisted Mary go see her specialist yesterday, with all the stress of this business with Hannah and you."

Suzy leaned forward. "I don't know what that doctor said, but whatever he told her has her acting funny—all quiet and withdrawn like." She spilled the words quickly. "Speak with her, Luke. Make her open up to you."

Luke wanted to talk to her so badly he could barely stand it, but she wanted nothing to do with him.

Gerald released the hand brake. "If anybody asks, we didn't say a word." He clicked his tongue and slapped the reins, continuing up the driveway so he could turn around and head back out.

Luke turned to find Paul still standing beside him.

Paul pulled a set of keys out of his pants pocket. "I can drive you in my truck and have you there in no time."

Luke hesitated. It might not go over well with his or Mary's father—or the bishop—to be seen with the likes of Paul Waddell. But Paul could get him all the way to Mary's in less time than it'd take Luke to go a mile by horse and buggy.

Luke grabbed the reins to his horse. "Just give me time to pull the buggy under the shed and put the horse to pasture."

Within three minutes he was climbing into Paul's truck.

Paul jerked the stick shift into gear. The old jalopy rattled even worse than a horse and buggy, and the fumes stank more than Mamm's old gas-powered washing machine, but it moved quickly, and for that Luke was thankful.

They rode in silence, and within ten minutes Paul slowed the truck in front of Mary's home. Luke opened the truck door and paused. "I'm glad we met, but when Hannah comes back...I can't side with you about her leaving the People. I think our ways are the right ones for her. Our community hasn't handled things right, and we've got some repenting to do and some things to learn." Luke swallowed hard. "But she was born Amish, and I believe she's supposed to be with us."

Paul gave a brief nod. Luke figured it wasn't really in agreement as much as a silent acceptance not to argue. "Will you let me know if you hear from her?"

Luke climbed out. "I think that's a reasonable thing to ask." He shut the door to the truck and headed across the yard as Paul drove away.

The front door opened before he even knocked, and Mary's father stepped outside. "What are you doing here?"

Luke took a deep breath. "I came to see Mary."

John Yoder eyed Luke from top to bottom. "She's been in the *Daadi Haus* since last night, but she said she didn't want no company."

"I'd like to go see her. I'm not likely to be able to make things much worse, but I'll do all I can to help her."

John nodded. "Just leave the front door open, and keep the storm door unlocked."

Within thirty seconds, Luke was tapping on the door to *Mammi* Annie's house. When Mary didn't answer, he stepped inside. "Mary?" He walked through the small house, searching for her.

He found her in a chair in the living room. She twitched when she saw him. A spool of thread fell from the quilt in her lap and rolled across the floor.

Luke grabbed it, noticing how pale she looked. "Is that our 'Past and Future' quilt?"

She didn't answer him.

The quilt had been Hannah's idea, a gift for Luke and Mary's marriage bed. She and Mary had worked on it since Mary was released from the hospital in early October. Hannah had gathered patches of cloth from their childhood for the past side of it. He wasn't sure what they'd done for the future side.

He held the spool toward her. "I guess you're hurting awful bad about now, missing Hannah."

She took the thread from his hand without looking at him.

He sat on the ottoman, his knees almost touching hers. "I heard you had a doctor's appointment yesterday."

She repositioned the quilt and ran the needle through an edge of it. "The basting on the future side of the quilt gave way. I don't know why."

He ran his finger along the sleeve of her sweater. "What did the doctor say, Mary?"

She shoved the quilt into his lap, rose, and walked away from him. Luke resisted the desire to stand in front of her and try to bend her will to his. He stayed on the ottoman, watching and listening. The room was silent for several minutes as Mary rummaged through a stack of material. She unfolded a piece of black broadcloth, her hands caressing it gently.

"Who will you sew a pair of pants for?" he asked, hoping her answer might give him some clue as to what was going on in her heart.

She tossed the material on the chair, her eyes focused on the cloth. "It doesn't matter." She turned her attention to him. "Not anymore. It's all ruined. All of it."

Luke rose and went to her. "It doesn't look ruined to me."

Taking a step back, she gestured toward the quilt. "Parts of it are already sewn into our future part of the quilt." She gasped for air. "And now…"

He was clueless as to why she was so upset but fairly sure he had the answer. "I'll buy you a whole bolt of black broadcloth, however many bolts you want."

Grabbing the material, she mumbled, "You can have it." She picked pieces of lint off the cloth. "Someone else can make pants for you."

Ah, so the material is for making my pants. At least he understood a little more, but the pain that crossed her face when she stumbled over that sentence added to his confusion. She folded the material and passed it to him, staying as far away from him as possible.

Luke eased up to her. "Mary, what's all this about?" When she tried to turn away from him, he stepped in front of her. "I need you to talk to me, Mary. I can't stand what's happening to us. I was wrong about Hannah, but I've already done all I can to fix that. And you have the power over *our* future."

"That's just it, Luke. I don't have the power. The doctor has removed it from me. And you'll up and lea—" She stopped, picked up the quilt, and moved back to the chair. The only sound in the room was the ticking of the clock.

Luke returned to the ottoman, waiting for her to finish her sentence. Doctors grated on her nerves easily. They were quick to give her lists of things she had to do, like take physical therapy and nutritional supplements. They also gave lists of things she couldn't do, like stay on her feet for more than six hours each day. He was curious what they'd demanded of her this time that had her so frustrated.

"I think I'll give Paul this quilt." She grabbed the spool and unwound some of the thread. "From the work Hannah put into it, it has more of her in it than anything else she owned."

Though not thrilled with the idea of her so easily giving away their marriage-bed quilt, he gave a slight nod. "If that's what you want."

Mary looked up from her sewing. "You'd not balk at me giving this to Paul?"

"I met him today. He's not such a bad guy. And I think he's hurting awful bad." Luke placed his hands over hers. "But that's not who I'm worried about."

She lowered her head, her fingers tightening around his. "I'm sorry, Luke. But I can't marry you."

Fighting the urges to argue, walk out, or pressure her for an immediate answer, he rubbed her fingers. "Can't or won't?" In spite of his anxiety, his words flowed calmly.

She shook her head. "It's time for you to go."

"Not yet. First I need you to answer that question. You can't marry me, or you won't marry me?"

"You need to find somebody else—" Her face crumpled with sadness.

"Mary, you're scaring me. I feel like I did during those awful days before you woke in the hospital. Does this have something to do with what the doctor said yesterday?"

"It's not like that." She stood. "The doctor says I'm doing great, just as long as I follow his orders."

Relieved, he took a deep breath. "Then what's wrong?"

Her lips curved down, causing a half-dozen little dimples to develop on her chin. "He said I can't plan on getting married this fall."

Shocked, Luke gazed up at her, hoping she meant what it sounded like. "Does that mean you're still interested in marrying me?"

"Of course I am." Her cheeks seemed to flush. "I mean…"

He raised an eyebrow at her. "It sounds like I still stand a chance of being your husband." He reached for her hand and gently tugged on it.

She knelt in front of him.

He caressed her cheek. "I love you, Mary."

"But…" She tilted her chin back as if she wasn't ready to forgive him.

A bolt of laughter escaped him. "Hannah would be proud of that chin-tilting thing. But she was better at it than you."

She smoothed her apron without looking at him. "Oh, Luke, it's not funny. The doctor said I'm not to get pregnant for…fi—for several years. And you know the bishop won't allow…" Pink tinged her cheeks.

Birth control. Not only was she thinking of marrying him, she was imagining the nights they'd share. "Mary, I can wait. You're a bit young to be getting married just yet anyway. I ought to wait for you. You shouldn't try to rush things for me. Right?"

Her lips pouted. "You could at least want to appeal to the bishop."

He encircled her in his arms. "Oh, I'll appeal, all right," he whispered in her ear.

With the head of the hospital bed angled upright and a food tray in front of her, Hannah watched as Bugs Bunny paraded across the television screen. She'd been moved from ICU within hours of waking, and this morning she'd discovered that some of her strength had returned. The rabbit popped his head out of a hole, smacked loudly on a carrot, and looked around. "I knew I shoulda taken a left toin in Albuquerque." He'd made the same mistake an hour ago and landed in a whole different set of troubles.

Glad for the way this cartoon distracted her thoughts, she took a bite of her scrambled eggs. Her face contorted at the plastic feel in her mouth. She poked at the eggs on her plate with her fork, wondering if they were real, then pushed away the tray.

For the first time since she'd awakened yesterday, she wasn't trembling like a newborn calf. Trying to mask the taste of the eggs, she took a long drink of her orange juice. Maybe tomorrow the IV could be removed, and she'd be able to slip out of this place and go into hiding somewhere.

The door to her hospital room opened, and Dr. Lehman strode in. "How are you feeling this morning?"

Hannah set her juice down and wiped her mouth. "A lot better. Plenty well enough to take care of myself."

The doctor pushed the juice toward her, silently expressing his will. "That's doubtful. Nice try though." As she finished the drink, he pulled a chair close to the bed and took a seat. "I did a little reading last night on runaways. Most of those who flee home have a reason for heading in a certain direction."

A nervous tingle ran down her spine. Wondering if he intended to help her or work against her, she set the empty cup on the bedside tray.

He rubbed his chin. "So why did you come to Alliance? Was this your destination or just a stop along the way?"

Smoothing her hands across the bedcovers, she answered, "Alliance is the closest train depot to Winding Creek, which is where my aunt lives."

"Ah, so you did have a specific place in mind because you knew someone here."

She grimaced. *"Know someone* might be a bit of a stretch."

"You don't know your aunt?"

Hating to admit that part, she fidgeted with the hem of the sheet. While stalling, she decided her best way of getting this man on her side was to be honest with him. "I didn't even know she existed until about six months ago. But I'm sure I can find her."

Dr. Lehman took off his glasses and pinched the bridge of his nose. "You didn't know she existed? That's odd, especially among people as family oriented as the Amish."

"I figure she's been shunned, but I won't know anything for sure until I meet her. I discovered a letter from her, and that's where I got her address."

He nodded, seeming satisfied with her answer. "There's one question that came to me last night and has been nagging at me ever since." He slid his glasses back into place. "I'd like you to answer it, okay?"

She stared at him, wondering how she was supposed to agree to something without knowing what that something was.

He slid his hands into the pockets of his lab coat. "Why apply for a job at a medical office? Why not apply at a restaurant or at a day care?"

For the first time in too long, Hannah felt a smile tug at her face. Science was the most fascinating subject on the whole planet. While working with the nurses in charge of Mary's recovery, Hannah had learned some specifics about how cells form into organs and how each system has its unique job and needs. The needs part was where medical knowledge could help people get well, could even save lives.

She searched his face. "The desire to work where I can learn medical things is in here." She patted her chest. "Learning about healing and medicine draws me like..."—she closed her eyes and tried to think of an expression that matched her desires—"like a new mother longs for her child." She pulled a long breath into her lungs, feeling embarrassed that she'd just shared so much of herself. "You know?"

After a long silence, he scratched the back of his head. "Look, I'm not sure what the laws are, but your chances of not being sent back home have to be better if you can find that aunt of yours. Maybe I can help you."

Pinpricks of excitement swept through her, and she knew she was gaping at him.

"Clearly you have trust issues." He clasped his hands and laid them in his lap. "But I really do want to help you. I've already run some interference for you with Admissions; otherwise they'd already have contacted the police."

She studied his face, trying to determine his true motives. "Why?"

"Maybe I've just turned into an old fool."

Some of the heaviness she'd grown so accustomed to lifted. "You won't regret it. I'd promise to repay you if giving oaths to man wasn't against God's Word."

"And you don't think disobeying your parents and running away are sins?" The wrinkles across his brow deepened as he seemed to dissect her responses.

Hannah lowered her head. "I've wondered about that." She tugged at a loose thread on the top sheet, drowning in the thoughts that rose within her, thoughts she couldn't believe were hers. "But I've decided it isn't a sin to protect yourself, whatever it takes."

He sighed and pulled a pen and pad out of his pocket. "I'm going to take a chance on you. What's your aunt's name and address?"

"I got that driver to take me to her address. It was an unlivable old house."

"Why don't you give me the info anyway and let me see what I can find out?"

She wanted to answer, but her throat seemed to have closed up.

He stared out the window for a few seconds. "Listen, if we're going to have any type of relationship, regardless of how temporary, you're going to have to trust me, or at least pretend."

A whispery laugh escaped her. "I can do that. Pretend, that is."

He chuckled.

"Her name's Zabeth Bender. Her address is supposed to be 4201 Hanover Place, Winding Creek, Ohio."

He scribbled on the notepad.

"What happens to me if you can't find her?"

"One bridge at a time, Hannah."

She wasn't asking for a bridge. She wanted an escape plan, some trace of hope that this kind man had a backup plan that would save her from having to return to Owl's Perch even if he couldn't find her aunt.

He shoved the pad into his pocket. "If I discover anything solid, I'll let you know. In the meantime, rest. And you ought to call your parents and let them know you're safe."

"They don't own a phone."

Dr. Lehman scowled at her. "Don't misdirect me, Hannah. I know a little bit about how the Amish live. I'm sure you can call someone who has a phone and get them to take a message to your parents."

Her cheeks burned. "I don't mean to be dishonest. But I didn't go through everything I have just to be found."

Pulling a small phone out of his pocket, Dr. Lehman growled. "Use this. The number's unlisted, so no information will show up on caller ID or a bill."

Hannah stared at the strange gadget. "I don't know how to use that."

He flipped it open. "Punch in the numbers, with the area code, then press the button with the green icon of a telephone receiver."

Area code? Icon?

She took the phone from his hand and looked at it, then at him, and back again.

"You'll figure it out. I have rounds to make. I'll be back for it later." He lifted an eyebrow at her and looked meaningfully at the phone. "And a full report."

She watched him leave before turning her attention back to the tiny phone in her hand. The man just didn't understand what he was asking of her. No one wanted to hear from her. Well, almost no one. She had promised

Mary, Luke, and Matthew that she would write, but aside from her brother and two friends, everyone else fell just short of hating her. Maybe they did hate her. She didn't know. She didn't want to think about it. Her dream was to start fresh, not deal with old things.

Staring at the phone, she huffed. The doctor had put a task before her, one that had to be done or he wouldn't help her. What had Paul told her about making a long-distance call? She closed her eyes, trying to remember.

He had said to dial 411 if she knew the name but not the phone number. Would calling that three-digit number work for locating area codes? She pushed the only green thing she could see. She put the phone to her ear but heard no dial tone.

Paul had taught her a thousand things over their years of friendship, but he hadn't owned a cell phone, so he'd never showed her how to use one. The ache of missing Paul stole her sense of relief. Hope in Dr. Lehman's words couldn't stop the awful hurt of facing her future without Paul.

After trying several ways to make the phone work, she finally reached directory assistance. It wasn't all that hard—press the digits and then the button with the green image of a receiver. Once she had the area code to go with Mary's phone number, Hannah punched the numbers in. The phone rang.

In her imagination she could hear the shrill ring of the phone echoing across the fields of the Yoders' farm. If someone besides Mary answered, would they hang up when they realized who was calling? Would they pass a message to Hannah's parents, assuring them she was safe? If they hung up or refused to take a message to her family, would Dr. Lehman refuse to help her?

A clicking noise let her know someone had just lifted the phone from its cradle.

C losing the door on his way out of Gram's house, Paul wondered how to go about finding a reliable private investigator. He headed for his truck, hoping the police might offer him some direction. Money was a problem, but he'd figure something out. He refused to return to school or work right now. It was way past time for Hannah to be his top priority.

The sound of a horse whinnying caught his attention. Coming across the back pasture was a man dressed in the black trousers, coat, and hat of the Amish. Paul hurried toward the cattle gate, not sure if it was Luke or Matthew coming toward him. He knew no other Amish person who would come see him.

As Paul opened the gate, the man lifted his head.

Luke.

Although his jaw was set as the horse trod through the snow and muck of the back fields, he didn't look as downtrodden as he had yesterday. The horse slowed its pace as they approached. "Whoa." Luke brought the horse to a stop.

"We heard from her." He exhaled, causing billows of vapor to disperse into the cold air.

Paul drew a deep breath, taking in the heavens. *Thank You.*

Luke's laughter caught Paul's attention. "You should see Mary. Just knowing Hannah was somewhere safe brought some color to her face and relief to her eyes."

"Who spoke with her?"

"No one. The phone is in a shanty some sixty feet from the Yoders' house, so nobody heard it ring. But they have an answering machine, and she left a message."

"What did she say?"

Luke rode the horse through the opening. "Not much. I mean, she said she's fine and safe. She has a place to stay and someone helping her. That's about it."

Songs of praise silently ran through Paul's mind as he closed the gate. "Did she leave a number where she can be reached?"

"No." Luke slid off the horse, his smile fading. "She didn't leave any information about where she is. But she sounded good, hopeful, and at the same time really tired."

The inward songs faded, like a radio being turned down, as he realized there was no way to reach Hannah. "Can I go to the phone shanty and see if we can do anything to get the number she called from?"

A look of concern covered Luke's face. He pulled the loose ends of the reins through his hands several times. He slapped the leather against his palms, clearly mulling over what to do.

Paul waited, hoping he didn't have to figure out how to talk Luke into something he was set against.

Luke patted the horse's neck. "I don't like the idea of taking you to the Yoders' phone. If we're seen together, it won't help my position within the community any. I've risked being seen with you once, and I'm gonna need the bishop's approval over some things." He studied Paul. "But I've been right where you are, so concerned about Mary I thought I'd die. I can't imagine not knowing where she was or not being able to hear her voice." Luke shrugged. "Even when she's mad as a wet hen at me."

"I'd settle for Hannah's wrath over this."

"Good. 'Cause I figure when she does come back, she'll have been stripped of her somewhat-restrained self, and you'll definitely catch it."

They both laughed.

Luke nodded toward his harness shop, some hundred feet off of Paul's property, and to the small barn beside it. "Come on. Let's put her away for a spell and then use your truck to get back to Mary's. But when we get there, we gotta make it quick. I just hope news of us being together doesn't make it back to the bishop. Mary and I don't need him mad at us."

"I thought you and Mary were in everyone's good graces."

"We are as good as can be, considering the stench of trouble he had with my sister. But we need his permission about something sort of private-like." Luke shrugged, looking reluctant to say more.

Grateful that Luke was less like his father and more like his sister when it came to hearing and responding to the needs of those around him, Paul fell into step beside him.

~~~

Paul walked back into his gram's house. He'd heard Hannah's voice on the answering machine, and that was wonderful. But after exhausting every possible way he knew to get the number she had called from, he had come home empty-handed.

Added to that letdown, the message from her was in their first language, the only one they spoke among themselves: Pennsylvania Dutch. Paul longed to hear her speak words he could understand. If he were like most of his branch of Mennonites, he'd speak the native tongue too. But both sets of his grandparents had been Mennonite missionaries in other countries and hadn't taught their children Pennsylvania Dutch, so neither of his parents spoke the language.

Even with the communication barrier, he sensed she wasn't faring as well as he'd hoped. Every word seemed to come from a dark place of grief and exhaustion. He couldn't voice his concerns to Luke, because the moment they stepped out of the truck to go to the phone shanty, Mary came outside and joined them.

According to Luke, Hannah had said she had a place to stay, had made a friend who had helped her the night she arrived, and had been to see a doctor. She gave her word that she would write to Mary and Luke in a few weeks.

She made no mention of Paul. None. Was she starting her life over without him, believing he hated her? Surely not. She had written him a warm letter. But when she called, she hadn't left a number, nor did the Yoders have caller ID. When Mary told him they had the star-69 feature, he had hopes—

until he punched in the code and discovered that Hannah had called from an unknown number.

He was grateful to know she was safe, somewhere. Incredibly grateful. But it wasn't enough. He had to find her and set the record straight. Then if she wanted nothing else to do with him, he'd cope.

Who are you kidding, Waddell? You'll never accept losing Hannah.

Fixed on locating her, Paul went to his room, pulled out his laptop, and connected to the Internet. He figured the Net was the best place to start trying to locate private investigators. After finding the names, phone numbers, and even Web sites of several private investigators in Pennsylvania, he decided to make some calls. He called half a dozen places before he found a man named Drew, who seemed worthy of consideration. Balancing the phone between his shoulder and his ear, Paul jotted down notes as the private investigator rattled off a long list of missing-person cases. "Out of all those incidents, how many people have you actually located?"

"Well…," Drew hesitated. "That's harder to answer than it sounds. Finding someone depends greatly on why they're missing. If they don't want to be found and are smart enough to cover their trail—" A phone rang in the background, causing him to stop without finishing his sentence. "Paul, can you hold on one moment? I need to catch my other line."

"Sure."

Again doubts about pursuing Hannah weighed on him. She had left of her own accord, and she'd called using an unlisted number. Maybe she needed more time. Perhaps he should stick to their dream of his graduating and becoming a full-time social worker. That way, when she did return, he'd be settled in the job they'd always dreamed of—helping children in need of an advocate.

His frustration over the empty bank account surfaced again. It wasn't just the money being gone that bothered him. Something else in all this nagged at him. He just wasn't sure what it was.

As he closed his eyes, understanding dawned. House of Grace. He and Hannah had saved for years so they could sponsor a girl at House of Grace.

From the moment he'd shared about the home for girls, her eyes had lit up. For the first time in days, a smile worked its way to Paul's heart.

Remembering that an envelope had arrived from them a few days back, Paul began searching through the mail. Finding the ivory-colored envelope, he noted the words *Global Servants* stamped in purple on the far left side with an image of Thailand beside them. This was the ministry that had caused Hannah and him to unite in determination to reach beyond their lives and help a girl avoid being sold into prostitution. He slid his fingers into the envelope and pulled out the letter.

In the folds of the letter lay a photo of a young girl with a big grin, holding up a name placard. The white sign had the name A-Yom Muilae written in large letters across it. He could help this girl if he stayed focused on fulfilling Hannah's and his dream. He laid the picture on the table and read the note.

Dear Sponsor,

The words typed across the page shared how thankful they were that Paul Waddell and Hannah Lapp had joined forces to feed, shelter, and educate a young girl. It explained how God provided ways for the organization to acquire the girls, without buying them, before they were sold by their families. The letter gave details of how to prepare and send packages for Christmas, birthdays, and even an "I love you" gift throughout the year.

Remember, it is your willingness to give that makes the girls feel loved. Every gift you send, even the smallest gift, says, "I care about you and your future. I love you!"

It wasn't overly expensive to sponsor a girl. It just took some planning and effort, which he and Hannah had been doing since they learned of the plight of these girls. He'd been nineteen and Hannah only fifteen at the time. Even at just sixty dollars a month, plus gifts, he knew it would require planning and sacrifice to continue this journey until the girl was grown. They'd worked for three years toward this goal, and now they had a girl assigned to them.

The phone clicked. "Paul?" Drew asked.

"I'm here." He lifted the photograph again. Her smile seemed genuine, but her eyes appeared to be begging for someone to truly care. Paul knew he had to keep this commitment for the sake of all three of them.

The sound of car wheels crunching against the gravel driveway caught Paul's attention, and he moved to a window. His parents. One glance at their solemn, upright posture, and Paul knew he'd avoided this encounter as long as he could.

"Drew, I need to go. I'll think about all this and get back with you."

"Yeah, sure. Just remember, the trail grows colder with every hour that passes."

Paul disconnected the call and headed for the front door. His mom, bundled in a heavy coat over her caped dress and wearing a black winter scarf over her prayer Kapp, didn't wait for his dad to get the door for her. The two of them stepped out of the car in unison as Paul walked down the steps to greet them. He gave his mother a hug that she barely returned and then gave one to his father, who squeezed him warmly.

His dad placed a hand on Paul's shoulder. "We need to talk."

"Sure. Come on in." Awkwardness joined the array of emotions bearing down on Paul. He was inviting his dad into his own mother's home.

Without another word, his parents moved up the steps and into the living room and took a seat. Too antsy to sit, Paul shoved his hands into the pockets of his pants and waited for one of them to speak. The tension radiating from his mom and dad made him regret he'd kept everything about Hannah so secretive. Last Saturday when he began searching for Hannah, he'd called them and asked them to remain by the phones in case she tried to reach him there. That's when they'd learned their only son was interested in and even engaged to a girl they didn't know.

His mother intertwined her rough-skinned fingers. "So all your years of ignoring us every summer and coming here were because of this Hannah person."

He chafed at the flippant description of the woman he adored. "I didn't ignore you."

Silence lay thick between them.

His mom gave his dad a look he couldn't decipher. "I blame us for part of this. We've allowed you too much freedom. Your sister told us that she and William have gone to a few spectator games. My guess is you've gone too."

He knew professional sports were frowned on by most Plain Mennonites, but he enjoyed them, and he had always intended to take Hannah to see a game as soon as he could. It was a game, for crying out loud, and if his mother wanted repentance, she was looking at the wrong offspring.

She sighed. "I take it you don't care that your sister, William, and Dorcas had to talk to the church leaders about this."

Did his mother really expect him to care about some minor infraction right now?

She rested her head against the back of the couch. "Your sister, who clearly knew about Hannah before we did, said the girl left here with money and a plan and that she is believed to be completely safe, right?"

He'd answered a few of Carol's questions when she called him earlier in the week, but he hadn't realized she was giving a full report to their parents. "That's what we believe. She called—"

"We?" his dad interrupted.

Taking a seat, Paul counted to ten, trying to calm his mounting frustrations. Contrary to what his folks believed, he was an adult, and they were the ones out of line. "I talked to her brother Luke yesterday, and earlier today he came to talk to me."

His mom glanced at his dad before turning back to Paul. "You've been in Owl's Perch all week?"

"Of course." And he'd be here all next week too. "My fiancée is missing. Am I supposed to go about life as if nothing has happened?"

His parents retreated into silence again.

"Paul," his father began gently, "regardless of how we may sound, we're sorry for the pain you're going through. We really are. This is all quite a shock to us, and—"

"And you weren't honest with us," his mother interrupted.

"Hazel," Dad chided.

"He wasn't," she insisted. "Nearly three years ago you sat at my kitchen table and promised me you'd never get involved with any of those Englischer girls on campus. I've asked you about it since then, and each time you gave me your word. And not once did you mention this Amish girl, not once." Her eyes flashed with anger.

"I know, Mom. But you have to understand—I was trying to protect her."

"From who? Me?" she screeched.

Paul wiped the palms of his hands on his pants. "You have relatives in Owl's Perch. It was best to keep it a secret for her sake."

"I won't mention how well that seems to have worked for you, but I will tell you that you must return to school and work. She's gone. I know we don't sound like we're sorry, but we are. If for nothing else, for the pain this is causing you."

She was right about one thing—they didn't sound the least bit remorseful.

"Let her go, Paul," Dad added gently. "If she'd wanted to stay, she would have."

Apparently they expected him to put aside the fact that Hannah was gone and simply move on with his life. "I've been thinking about teaming up with a private investigator and going to find her." He stared at his shoes, wondering how Hannah would feel about being tracked down when she obviously didn't want to be found.

His mother harrumphed. "You have obligations here."

Standing, Paul rubbed the back of his neck. She was right, and he knew it; he just didn't want to give in to it. Hannah had left everything behind. Couldn't he?

Compassion shone in his dad's eyes. "I never doubted you had someone out this way." Dad cocked his head, with a half smile on his face. "But here's the problem, Son. Against what most of our sect of Mennonites believe, you talked us into allowing you to go to college, saying you had to have a specific college degree to carry out your dream of helping families. I know you've worked hard to pay for your truck and insurance, gas, books, food, dorm, clothing." He made a circular motion with his hand as if the list could go on and on. "But if you leave school now, you'll lose the scholarships that were based on your finishing school and working in state for two years. You can't afford to pay for your schooling without those scholarships, and neither can we."

His mother grabbed a pillow off the couch and pulled it against her chest. "If you want to help families, start with your own. You can't leave us drowning in bills from this educational venture of yours while you're chasing someone who left you."

"The scholarships don't work that way, Mom. You and Dad will not be held accountable if I fail to keep the agreement. It's my responsibility and my problem. But you don't understand about Han—"

"Maybe you're the one who doesn't understand," his mother interrupted. "She hasn't called you. She hasn't let you know where she is. She obviously doesn't want you to find her."

"I appreciate your voice of concern, Mom."

"Do not get smart with me, Paul Waddell."

He stifled a groan. Their adult-child relationship needed help, but now wasn't the time to argue that she was guilty of dishing out sarcasm too. "Don't believe the gossip about her. I know it's not true."

"I have no doubt that most of the rumors I've heard are lies." She shrugged, as if Hannah's innocence was unimportant. "However, what I believe or even what you believe doesn't change anything."

Paul shoved his hands into his pockets. "How can you say that? You never met her, so she doesn't seem real to you. This isn't some silly crush. I want to marry her."

"And because of that, I'm glad she's gone!" His mother rose, anger carved in her face. "How could you think of marrying someone I've never met? Someone who was pregnant for months without you even knowing it? Her whole life has been one secret after another, and when her house of cards fell, she ran—without regard for you."

As his mother sliced him with her anger, it seemed he'd never really known her.

"Hazel," his father scolded before he drew a deep breath and offered her a peacemaking smile, "why don't you go upstairs and wake Mom from her nap. I need to talk to Paul alone."

She turned and strode out of the room. Watching her climb the steps, Paul knew she had no respect for him as an adult. Oh, she loved him dearly—as long as he did things her way. But to her, his feelings were as insignificant as a child's tears over a dropped candy bar—temporary and easily appeased.

"She's hurting, Paul. I've tried to tell her for years that you had someone, but she wouldn't believe you'd hide such a thing from us."

"It had to be that way—"

His father held up his hand, stopping Paul in midsentence. "I get it." He offered a weak smile. "If anyone in this family can understand, it's me, along with your Uncle Samuel."

"Uncle Samuel? How can an old bachelor understand this?"

He motioned Paul closer. "Gram doesn't like anyone to talk about this. Consider it a family skeleton."

Paul moved in and took a seat.

"When Samuel was about your age, he fell for a Catholic girl. Both families were ready to disown their children if they didn't stop seeing each other. It broke both their hearts. Samuel was willing to leave his family over her, but she couldn't do it. In his own way, he did leave the family over it, even though he still joins us for holidays and such. I've watched my older brother carry pain unlike anything I had ever imagined, and he did so for years."

"What happened to the girl?"

"She eventually married someone her family approved of and had children. Your Uncle Samuel's ache turned to stone, and he's never been the same. Your mom was in the family throughout most of it. It's part of the reason you've finagled too much freedom out of us; we've tried to handle your wanting more Englischer-type freedoms differently than my parents handled Samuel. Your mom thinks you never should have spent four years in college rooming with Englischers. You've become self-willed, Son. And expected too many family members to cover for you."

Paul realized afresh the position he'd put Gram in. No wonder she kept waffling between respecting his feelings and putting up roadblocks to Hannah's and his relationship. She didn't want to carry the burden of standing between them, and yet she understood how Mr. Lapp felt about his daughter marrying outside their Amish community.

He drew a breath. "Hannah called."

"Here?" Uncertainty flicked through his dad's eyes.

Shaking his head, Paul glanced at the stairway and lowered his voice. "She called her best friend, Mary. They have a phone shanty and an answering machine."

"What did she say?"

"That she's safe and…" Nothing. She'd said nothing else—not really.

"She's not coming home, is she?"

Paul shook his head. "But I've talked to this private investigator, and—"

"Son," his dad interrupted him, "what are you going to bring her home to? An angry community, family, and bishop? To join your family, which will be another set of stresses to work through. Aren't those the very things she needed to get free from?"

"Dad, I can't just—"

"Can't what? Give her time? Respect that she's in the throes of grief and deserves a little space?"

"What if she doesn't return?" Paul moaned.

His dad tapped his fingertips together, thinking before responding. "Making her come back to this mess isn't the answer—at least not yet. Finish school. Keep your scholarship by working in state for two years. We both know the church leaders may have some concerns if you choose to work for the state beyond your internship." His dad smiled. "I think your job choice is fine, always have. But if it's going to pull you away from your faith, find a different line of work. It sounds like Hannah has enough help. And she knows your phone number, right?"

Paul nodded. "But she thinks I abandoned her."

"That's the toughest part to live with. Still, she has to know what caused you to react the way you did. If she really loves you, she'll reach out again, at least once more before giving up." His dad leaned forward. "There's something else on my mind. The preacher and bishop want to talk with you. That has your mother every bit as upset as your intent to marry a girl we've never met. You need to make plans to meet with them. They're going to question you on points of the church disciplines. They know you joined the faith at fourteen. What they want to know is how faithful you've been. For four years your roommates have been watching television, going to movies, and partying. Our church leaders want to know where you stand."

Paul nodded. He had nothing to hide. It was never his intention to use his freedoms for anything but pursuing Hannah—and maybe an occasional Senators game. Pursuing an Amish girl wasn't against any part of the church disciplines, and even going to a game wasn't considered a huge issue—just things he needed to agree not to do again if he wanted to remain in good standing with his church.

The two men sat in silence until Paul finally rose. "I need more time to think through your advice about Hannah. You might be right about giving her some time and returning to school and work. But even if that's what I do, if she lets me know where she is, I'm out of here."

Without waiting for a response, Paul went upstairs. Feeling as if he'd climbed into the very cage his Lion-heart had been freed from, he went to his room and closed the door. With his mind and heart elsewhere, Paul wondered how he was supposed to cope with the pressure of school and work, especially with the added issue of being a week behind on everything.

When the phone in his room rang, he snatched it up. "Hello."

"Paul? It's Dorcas."

"Hey." He tried to keep the fullness of his disappointment from his voice, but he knew it was a vain effort.

"I guess you heard that we confessed to the preachers."

"Yeah." And he wasn't going to apologize for the choices she'd made. He'd never once invited her to a game. His sister did that. Last time they all went to a game, Dorcas had on a dress with lace and had a ticket in hand, all set to go whether he joined them or not.

"I don't mean to bother you. I just thought you might want to talk." She paused.

Suddenly Paul had an idea. Dorcas was only a few years older than Hannah. She hadn't been raised as strictly as Hannah, but the similarities could be useful, and she definitely had the mind-set of a female. His parents knew what they wanted. Paul knew what he wanted. But maybe Dorcas could help him figure out what Hannah might be thinking and feeling. "Now that you've called, I'd like your opinion on something."

ℋannah lay still as the nurse removed the IV needle from the back of her hand. Soon she wouldn't have to wait on Dr. Lehman's plans, all of them relying on various ifs. If he found something solid, if he could locate her aunt—if, if, if. As soon as the nurse left, Hannah would get dressed and sneak out.

The nurse put a Band-Aid in place. "All done."

"Thank you." If Hannah had realized removing the needle was that easy, she'd have done it herself last night and been long gone by now.

"You're welcome." The nurse removed the needle from the IV bag and placed it in the small, red plastic container that hung on the wall behind the head of the bed. She wrapped the tubing loosely over the IV stand before grabbing the thermometer off the table she'd set it on when she entered the room.

While the nurse took her temperature and pulse rate, Hannah thought about what the doctor had said yesterday. His offer to help was nice, but she'd already ridden to her aunt's place. It was abandoned. There was no sense in waiting for the doctor to come back with that news and bring social services with him. No one was going to make her return to the land of persecution— no one. She owed the hospital money, and she'd pay them, but not today. Right now she needed to slip out of this place before—

"Temp's good. Pulse is good." The nurse gathered the pieces of tape, Band-Aid wrappers, and the thermometer's sheath and threw them into the trash. She removed the bed coverings and gently pressed on Hannah's abdomen. "Any pain?"

"No."

"Good." She replaced the sheet and blanket. "You're healing remarkably well. Keep it up, and you'll be out of here in no time. Probably within a few days."

Oh, I'll be out of here in no time, all right. The minute you leave—

The door to her room swung open, and Dr. Lehman strolled in, carrying a short stack of papers. Hannah chafed at the interruption.

Lifting the almost-empty IV bag off its perch, the nurse glanced up. "Your patient is doing much better today than yesterday."

"The benefit of youth…" Dr. Lehman took a seat as the nurse left the room. He raised both eyebrows before closing his eyes and sighing. "I'd bet money on what you're planning, Hannah. Don't do it."

A prickly feeling, as if she'd been caught stealing eggs from the henhouse, ran through her body. This man seemed to know her thoughts and feelings as soon as they came to her.

He rolled his eyes, clearly frustrated at her lack of trust. But if she couldn't trust her own parents or even Paul, she wasn't about to give this stranger a chance to ruin her future. He sat there, skimming his papers. She wished he'd hurry up so she could get dressed and go.

He turned his attention to her. "Hannah, I think it's a great idea for you to pursue this dream of learning about the health field. But getting a degree in any area will be difficult. It's hard enough for honor students who have graduated from high school, but as a seventeen-year-old with an eighth-grade education, you'll have years of learning to make up for."

She bristled. "Every summer for three years Paul brought me his college textbooks and taught me things from them. I can do this. I know I can."

He cocked his head, studying her. "Is this the same Paul who asked you to marry him?"

Hannah nodded.

"If he was in college, then he's not Amish." A troubled look crossed his face. "You weren't planning on remaining among the People, were you?"

She tilted her head up, irritated by his grilling. "No."

Dr. Lehman tapped the papers in his hand. "With all that's happened to you, I can understand why you left the way you did. And I can't see asking you to return—not until you're emotionally, physically, and financially on your feet enough that you can walk away from your parents, if need be."

He's not going to send me back? Suddenly she wanted to jump out of bed and dance around the room.

Dr. Lehman sighed. "And I certainly can't ask you to try to work things out with Paul. What can a seventeen-year-old girl possibly know about choosing a life mate?"

Something defiant in her quaked under his attitude. She'd been so sure about Paul, who he was, who they would be together for a lifetime. But it all changed in the length of time it took him to brush against her rounded stomach, run to his truck, and then take her portion of their money before she could get to it. If that wasn't enough to break her, he'd had some girl in his apartment the one time she'd tried to call him before she boarded the train.

Dr. Lehman showed her the first page of the papers in his hand. In bold letters across the top were the words "Stark State College, Alliance Satellite, State Street." The very idea of attending college raised thoughts of failure, causing a disconnect from all joy.

He glanced at her and then at the papers, a frown creasing his brow. "You can go to classes to study for a GED. It's equivalent to a high-school diploma as far as qualifying you to begin the process of getting into college. Then you'll need to attend college classes in science and math to qualify for whatever medical field you intend to enter. That may take years longer than you're thinking, but your future will be in your hands." He scratched his brow. "You haven't been using your best asset in trying to get a job. You speak Pennsylvania Dutch. Look for work and training at clinics based on that. Why, I might hire you myself to help in my usual line of work if I needed someone and you knew how to log info into the computer."

"What do you usually do?"

He rolled the papers up and tapped them against his leg. "Well, I don't work at that clinic you came to. I was just there filling in as a favor." He stifled a yawn. "Aside from managing a women's clinic for the poor, I'm the doctor at two home-style Amish birthing clinics. I work in conjunction with some nurse-midwives. With a little effort, I could learn the language, but I always have one Amish woman on staff so I'll know what's being said when a patient is talking to a family member. That way I can address some of their fears or concerns they might not ask me directly. And the Plain women are willing to ask them questions in private. The assistant then comes to me, I answer, and she shares that answer in their native tongue. It's the best way I've found to spread medical advice to the Plain communities. You understand the need for that kind of information. You came close to dying because of the lack of it. Well, that mixed with your stubbornness."

"I can't work at an Amish clinic."

"Sure you can. You think you're the first girl not to be baptized into the faith? And give the Amish community a little respect, will you? Even if they learned the truth about you, most wouldn't want to make you go back. Actually very few would dare meddle in such a decision."

"Says who? I'm the one who kept receiving letters upon letters begging me to repent or be ready to pay the price."

"That was different. Members of your own household and your church leaders were probably instigating the letter writing to stop you from sinning. Besides, here no one has to know who you were."

The man was crazy. She wasn't jeopardizing her freedom in order to become some type of public-service announcement over medical advice she knew nothing about.

Dr. Lehman tossed the rolled-up papers onto her lap. "It's my best guess that with enough time and training, you'd be a first-rate midwife, Hannah— regardless of how far you're able to go in school. But that idea is pretty far into the future—" His pager went off, interrupting him. He took it off his hip and focused on it.

Midwife?

Words her mother had spoken as far back as Hannah could remember tugged at her. *Someday you'll make a good midwife, Hannah.* But she herself would never again conceive. How would she stand helping other women bring their babies into the world?

He clipped the pager back onto his belt. "But for now there are family clinics for the Plain, and there are Plain folk who go to Englischer clinics. Those will be good places for you to look for work. Just tell them you speak the language and are willing to go to night school to become trained and that you'll learn how to use a computer."

Not at all sure she liked his plan for success, she laid the scroll of papers on the side table. His leathered wrinkles softened into a smile. "I'm willing to arrange things where you don't have to go back."

Goose bumps ran up her arms. He'd hinted at this a minute ago, but did he really mean it?

He leaned back in his chair. "But I'll expect you to agree to a few terms."

"What kind of terms?"

"You'll need to attend counseling for victims of rape."

A rush of embarrassment swirled through her.

He cocked his head. "There won't be any men at the meetings. And every woman there has been a victim of the same crime—a lot of times even the counselors."

Disbelief at his request surged within her, but somewhere inside she knew she needed the kind of help he was talking about. Just an aroma like one from that day or a sound or a glimpse of blueberries, like the ones she'd been bringing home in a bucket that day, made her chest constrict and her mind cloud with confusion and panic. "Okay."

He patted her arm. "Now that we've got all that settled, there's someone I want you to meet." He opened the door.

A thin woman using a wooden cane came to the doorway. She was about the age of Hannah's parents and looked much too young to need a walking aid. A silky, navy-blue scarf covered her whole head, leaving no strand of hair in sight. Her eyebrows were very thin, and Hannah wondered if she had any hair under her head covering. She wore a matching caped dress, and she looked amazingly familiar, though Hannah couldn't place why.

They soaked each other in before Hannah broke the silence. "Are you Zabeth?"

The woman dipped her chin, looking disappointed. "Your father must not have ever spoken of me, or you'd know how to pronounce it." She lifted her head, looking determined not to care.

Dr. Lehman chuckled. "Well, there's no doubt you're related. Not only do you two favor each other, but you have some of the same gestures. I noticed that when I met your aunt last night."

Indignation nipped at Hannah. "You met her before you had me agree to go to counsel—"

Her aunt stepped forward. "It's pronounced Zuh-beth. It's short for Eliza-beth. So it's said just like the name without the first three letters." She smiled and shifted the cane to her other hand. "Hannah, once I was able to prove to his satisfaction that I am indeed your aunt, he talked with me about you going to counseling and getting an education. We decided that you need to make your own choices about your future. I sew curtains and bedspreads for a living, and you're welcome to join me in that."

Hannah wanted to set her aunt's mind at ease. "I'll pull more than my weight, and I'll—"

Dr. Lehman pointed a finger at her. "Not for a while you won't. You need to stay off your feet and rest for at least three weeks. During that time you can decide what you're going to do—go on to school and train at clinics or go to work for your aunt. While you're recuperating, you'll use the money you arrived here with to cover food and such. When your surgeon gives the go-ahead, you can find a job and start paying off your hospital bill."

She'd always worked as hard as she felt like, without anyone telling her otherwise. Then again, she'd barely survived her last round of stubbornness. She nodded. "Okay."

Dr. Lehman offered a brief smile. "Good. I need to go. Bye, ladies."

When the door closed behind him, Zabeth propped the cane against the bed and gingerly walked to the window. "How's Zeb?"

Her mouth suddenly dry, Hannah licked her lips. "I don't know. He's physically well enough, I suppose. Aside from that, he's angry and unreasonable."

Turning from the view to look at Hannah, Zabeth sighed. "I was hopin' he'd changed." Sadness filled her eyes. "Dr. Lehman said you were determined not to return home. But he didn't say why you're in this hospital or how you came to arrive in Alliance."

"I came hoping to find you."

Zabeth toyed with the blinds. "How did you know about me?"

"I found a letter from you hidden in my parents' bedroom."

"Ah, now things are making more sense." Zabeth eased to the side of the bed and sat down. "What happened to make you leave?"

Hannah liked the woman. Her mannerisms said she was reserved, but her words were laced with honesty and gentleness. Unable to stand the idea of keeping any more secrets from those she lived with, Hannah began sharing the events of her life in almost a whisper. Before long she was speaking in a normal tone, summing up what her life had been like since last August.

When she had finished, tears ran down both their faces. Zabeth passed her a box of tissues before grabbing a handful herself.

"And now Dr. Lehman says I'll never have babies."

Zabeth wrapped her frail arms around Hannah and held her. She didn't try to offer any words of comfort. For that Hannah was grateful.

Zabeth pulled away and smiled at her. "I'm glad you've come to be with me, Hannah-girl."

Hannah nodded. "Why were you banned all these years?"

"I wouldn't repent." Zabeth scrunched the tissues in the palm of her hand. "I can't. I'm not wrong."

A laugh broke from Hannah along with fresh tears. "That's exactly how I feel. But what did you do?"

Tossing the tissues into a trash can, Zabeth took a deep breath. "I fell in love." She bit her bottom lip, smiling. "His name is Music." Zabeth's gray blue eyes locked on Hannah's. "I was a baptized member of the faith when I began baby-sitting for a woman while she taught music lessons." Zabeth covered her heart with her hand, and serenity covered her face. "The first time I heard her play the clarinet, I was swept away by the rich melodies. Oh, Hannah, there's nothing like the pleasure of music. Nothing."

Hannah couldn't imagine anyone leaving the fellowship of the People over something like music.

Zabeth paused, drawing a deep cleansing breath. "My teacher, Lauraine Palmer, understood my need for secrecy. She taught me how to play a few songs on the piano, and I did really well. Later on, I snuck off to play in recitals and such. What a glorious feeling! Then one day news of my playing at a recital got back to the bishop. He confronted me and insisted I repent and follow the oath I'd taken before God. I stood my ground, insisting there was nothing wrong with music. The community shunned me, but I kept taking lessons and playing in recitals. It wasn't until your father started hating me that my life took a hard turn."

There was a lot Hannah could say against her father, but it'd take more strength than she possessed. "Did you marry a Mennonite or an Englischer?"

Zabeth shook her head. "Things happened within the Palmer household, and I never married. I just stayed busy with them."

"Then why is your last name Bender?"

Zabeth wiped her forehead with the back of her hand, reminding Hannah of her father. "It seemed important at the time. Zeb was dogging my every step, determined to make me—"

A tap on the door interrupted her.

"Come in." Hannah tucked the sheet around her upper body.

A skinny woman with short black hair, bold makeup, and tight blue jeans opened the door to the room. "I'm going to the parking lot for a smoke. You can just meet me at the car when you're done."

Zabeth motioned for her to come in. "Hannah, I'd like you to meet my music teacher's daughter. Faye was just a child when I baby-sat her, and her baby brother came along some twenty-six years ago. Now she has two adorable children of her own, a three-year-old girl and a four-year-old boy. Faye Palmer, this is my niece, Hannah Lapp. "

The woman's features looked cold and uncaring, but there was something more than just that about her. She seemed different somehow, and not a good kind of different—if Hannah's gut reaction was right. And why, if she had two children, did she have the same last name as her mother?

Faye pulled a piece of gum out of her purse as she sank into the chair.

"Hi, Hannah." She unwrapped the gum and popped it into her mouth without ever making eye contact. "Care for some?" She held out the package.

"No, thank you."

She offered it to Zabeth, who took a piece.

"Hannah's going to move in with me."

"Really?" Faye chewed hard on the gum and glanced at Hannah. "Hope you're used to roughing it, 'cause Zabeth's idea of living fancy falls a bit short." She blew a quick bubble and popped it. "She came out of the Old Order Amish lifestyle to live semi–Old Order Amish." The sarcasm bothered Hannah, but Zabeth didn't look a bit frustrated.

Zabeth placed both hands on her hips. "Hey, I have electricity, a piano, and a clarinet. What else does a person need?"

Faye smacked on another bubble. "She has two outlets and two of those hang-from-the-ceiling-type light bulbs. No phone, no computer, no radio, no television, no air conditioning, no electric dryer, and she says she's not Old Order."

"I have four outlets—one in each room of my house—and indoor plumbing." Zabeth's eyes danced with humor.

"Sounds good enough to me," Hannah said. The news that Zabeth was planning to take her home sounded like freedom's ring.

Faye sighed. "After all you've sacrificed for our family, Dad ought to have you living in a mansion."

Zabeth removed the gum wrapper. "That's enough, Faye." She folded the gum into fourths before placing it into her mouth.

"Well, good grief, when Mom died, you gave up everything." Faye elongated the word *everything*, and Hannah wondered what all Zabeth had given up. Faye rolled her eyes. "And took over running the whole household and raised Martin before he went off to college, while Dad went right on making money, money, money."

"Faye." Zabeth angled her head, trying to catch Faye's downcast glare. "Hannah has no need to know all this. None."

Faye shrugged. "Somebody ought to know it."

"Look at me, please." Zabeth waited. "I don't want you talking about family history. Not now. Not later."

Faye huffed and then nodded her head. A jingly piece of music shot through the room. Faye opened her purse and grabbed a two-inch-long oval thing that looked like a fat beetle. She opened it and stuck it on her ear, making it light up blue. "Hello." She wrinkled her nose. "Hi, Martin." Faye studied her chipped, burgundy-colored fingernails while listening. "Hang on and I'll find out." She lowered the object. "Zabeth, my little bro has had his fill of watching the kids. He wants to know when we'll be home. Seems his niece and nephew aren't as important as the date he has tonight."

Hannah pointed at the odd thing in her hand. "What is that?"

"It's a phone piece, for talking and hearing."

"You're kidding."

"Nope. Here, say hi." Faye passed it to her.

"You mean somebody's still on the line?"

Faye laid the odd thing on the bed beside Hannah. "Yep."

She shook her head. "I couldn't."

Faye held up both hands, backing away from Hannah. "You have to say hi, or he'll be on hold all day."

Feeling silly and curious, Hannah picked it up and put it to her ear. "Hello? Is someone there?"

"Wow, Sis, your voice sure has changed. Your accent too."

"This isn't Faye. I…I'm just checking out this beetle thing."

"I object to being called a beetle thing—at least before you've seen me."

Hannah laughed. "Not you. This thing I'm talking into."

The deep voice resonated with laughter. She could hear the gentle chatter of a preschooler in the background. "Can I talk to my sister again? I—" Hannah heard a *ka-thump*. "Whoa, young fella, you can't dump the can of peaches on the floor until after Mommy gets home. Listen, uh, phone girl, tell my sister if she doesn't get home within an hour, she can pick her kids up at the local orphanage. Do they have orphanages anymore?"

"I wouldn't know."

The man chuckled. "Tell her I have a date, an important one. Bye, phone girl."

"Bye." Hannah held the device toward Faye. "He said he has an important date, and he said something about an orphanage."

"Brothers. And to think this hot date will be convinced he's cool." She shook her head. "But we do need to go. You ready, Zabeth?"

"I'm ready." She pulled a card out of her purse. "We'll be back when you're released from the hospital. Until then, here's Faye's phone number. Call if you need anything. She'll get me any message from you right away."

Faye pulled a set of keys from her purse. "That's me, a carrier pigeon."

Zabeth gave Hannah a hug. "You take care." She kissed her cheek. "You done right to come here, Hannah. It won't be a picnic, but I'll take as good care of ya as I can."

As Zabeth followed Faye out of the room, Hannah realized she still didn't know where her aunt lived. She had a thousand questions, but the pieces of what she did know bothered her. The illness Zabeth had written about in the letter along with her lack of hair and frailty of body said her aunt was probably fighting some type of cancer. Hopefully one she could win against.

And Faye? She left uneasiness in her wake. Or was that Hannah's imagination?

*S*tudying Mrs. Waddell's house in the distance, Sarah hoped the woman was gone to church. She tugged the reins and made a right turn onto the driveway that led to Luke's harness shop. The midmorning chill sat heavy on her, and she pulled the lap blanket tighter. Sometimes having church only every other Sunday was the most freeing part of living Amish. It reminded Sarah of slipping into a warm pair of lace-up boots that didn't pinch her feet. As a matter of fact, if it weren't for being able to watch Jacob across the way in the men's seating area, church Sundays would hold nothing for her. But the few words she shared with Jacob during the after-services meal made the going bearable.

Pulling under the huge lean-to designed as sheltered parking for Luke's customers, Sarah had other things on her mind besides trying to share a glance or a word with Jacob Yoder.

Hannah's baby.

It wasn't dead. Sarah knew that. Not one thing in her doubted that the infant was alive somewhere. Clearly her sister had given birth and left, but no one had directly confirmed that the infant had died—not even Naomi, who was there that night. So far, Sarah hadn't seen any hint of a new baby in anyone's home, and she'd spent plenty of time this week looking. She'd baked items and used that as a reason to make visits to people's homes. And for her efforts, all she knew for sure was the community was grieving something fierce over what had taken place with Hannah. Sarah clicked her tongue in disgust. Why should she grieve when she knew it wasn't true? She'd never seen the likes of such guilt as she'd encountered this week. But when she proved to them Hannah's baby wasn't dead, their grief would disappear, and rejoicing would return, not to mention a renewed dislike and distrust for Hannah.

She pulled to a stop and removed the blanket from her lap. Feeling confident she'd find signs that Mrs. Waddell was keeping Hannah's baby, Sarah trod across the mushy, snowy fields that separated the Lapp and Waddell properties.

She tiptoed up the steps and across the back porch of Mrs. Waddell's home. Rapping on the glass, Sarah peered through the window. The large farmhouse was quiet inside, with no signs of movement. As she waited, her excitement grew—just as she'd expected, no one was home.

Without wasting any more time, she went to the storage cabinet and searched for the spare key. Mrs. Waddell kept it in here somewhere. After shifting baskets, tools, and some junk around, she finally found it.

Triumphant, she unlocked the door and stepped inside. The warmth of the place surrounded her, filling her with hope. She was close to finding Hannah's baby. She could feel it.

Mrs. Waddell had some really nice things—fancy things—but she couldn't let them distract her. Sarah looked in the refrigerator and pantries for any signs of infant formula or bottles. When she found none, she worked her way through the living room, looking in drawers and closets as she went. Upstairs she searched through each bedroom and its closet.

Nothing.

She sank onto Mrs. Waddell's bed, wondering where else Hannah might have left the baby. Her fingers danced over the lace-patterned coverlet, the softness triggering some recollection. She'd seen this print, these yellows and purples, elsewhere in this house. But where?

Her mind jumped to the guest room. There she'd seen a baby crib and diapers. Maybe…

Paul helped his grandmother up the steps before he unlocked the front door. They entered the warm house and slid out of their coats without speaking. The fact that lately they both seemed to live in their own worlds nagged at him.

He put his hand on her shoulder. "Can I fix you a bite to eat before you lie down?"

"I didn't ask to leave Sunday school so we could eat." She pointed to the steps. "I'm tired."

As Gram made her way up the stairs, Paul went to his place of refuge—the back porch. It faced the dirt roadway, and if Luke or Matthew were to come visit him, he'd spot them. He'd sat out here for hours, even in the cold, and remembered the dozens of times Hannah had walked across the pastures up to Gram's.

He'd just opened the back door when he noticed someone had tracked snow and mud across the porch. Walking to the edge, his eyes followed a fresh set of prints from the porch to Luke's property. From the size of the marks, they appeared to have been made by either a woman or a younger boy. Wondering if someone had come to see him when he wasn't home, Paul headed toward Luke's shop.

He heard a window open. "Paul!" Gram whispered loudly and motioned for him.

He ran back to the house and up the stairs. "Gram?"

He went to the room she'd called from. She wasn't there. Hurrying through the place, he glanced inside each bedroom door as he passed it. When he came to the guest room on the far end of the second story, he stopped short. Gram stood near the foot of the daybed. An Amish girl was on the floor, sitting on her heels, with her back to him. Every piece of baby clothing his Gram had held on to over the years seemed to be scattered around the girl.

Hannah? Elation soared. Fear raced. But his body wouldn't budge. If it was Hannah, sitting in the middle of the room strewn with baby clothes…

Concern shone in Gram's eyes. "It's Sarah."

The girl turned to face him. Unlike the family resemblance that Luke shared with Hannah, the girl's face bore no similarities to her sister's.

"Sarah?" Paul stepped into the room.

With each fist holding one end of a cloth diaper, she yanked it. He figured if she'd had any strength, it would have ripped. "Where is she?"

Paul crouched. "I don't know, Sarah. I wish I did."

She lifted wild eyes to him. "She isn't here?"

Uneasiness crept up Paul's spine. Did her father realize how unbalanced this poor girl was?

"I've been searching for her all week. She's safe. That much I know for sure." Paul stood and held out his hand to help her up. "Does your family know where you are, Sarah?" He repeated her name as he spoke to her, hoping to help center her.

Shaking her head, she took his hand and stood upright. "I came looking for her by myself."

He glanced at his Gram and nodded toward the door. "Come on, Sarah. Let's get you home."

With Paul in the lead and Gram behind, they walked downstairs and through the house. Once on the porch, they paused.

Gram ran her hand over her chest. "I'd better be the one to take her home. If Zeb sees you—"

"Then what, Katie Waddell?" Zeb Lapp came around the side of the house and stomped onto the porch.

Gram jumped and tightened her hand against her chest.

"Easy, Gram," Paul assured her. "Go on inside and rest. I'll talk to Mr. Lapp."

The man opened his mouth to speak, but Paul raised his hand, signaling him to stop. Surprisingly, he hushed and waited.

Paul opened the door and helped Gram inside. "Go lie down, Gram."

She nodded, and he closed the door.

Mr. Lapp pointed a wrinkled finger in Paul's face. "Stealing one of my daughters ain't enough?"

"It's not like that."

The man wrapped his hand around Sarah's biceps. "Stay away from my family."

Sarah trembled, but the faraway, glazed look only seemed to deepen.

"Mr. Lapp, Sarah needs help. I think she's struggling with—"

"Yeah, she's struggling," Mr. Lapp interrupted. He pulled himself to his full stature, which was about four inches shorter than Paul. "Just like the rest of us. We're all living in the wake of you messin' in my daughter's life."

As the man breathed threats on his grandmother's porch, Paul struggled to control his tongue. "I know you blame me for Hannah's troubles. But if you ignore what's going on with Sarah, you're going to lose another daughter."

"Whatever happens, it'd be best to make sure you are not involved in that process. Do I make myself clear?"

Paul stepped back. "Are you saying you don't care if you lose a second daughter as long as I'm not the cause?"

"I'm saying my family is none of your concern! If you'd kept your hands off my Hannah, none of this would be going on. None of it!"

The man's face turned purple, and he shook all over, making Paul wonder if he might have a heart attack. Did he remember enough from his CPR courses to keep Mr. Lapp alive until an ambulance arrived? Paul flinched at the dark thoughts of not performing CPR if the opportunity presented itself.

"Mr. Lapp, set aside your resentment toward me for just a moment, and look at Sarah. Truly see her, please."

Mr. Lapp hesitated, then he studied his daughter. Some of the anger drained from his face. Placing his arm around her shoulders, he bent his head toward her. "Let's go home, child."

*J*t made no sense to Hannah. After all her determination to get here and find Zabeth, her elation had settled, and now she felt oddly uncertain. She eased onto the side of the bed, combing her wet hair. The shower had dispelled the bit of chill that clung to her each time night fell. But all her thinking during the long shower brought her no answers.

Dr. Lehman and Zabeth had put her future into her own hands. Unfortunately, neither one could see into the future to know what she ought to do.

What if she did go to work at an Amish clinic and her Daed and bishop found out? Or what if she wasn't smart enough to pass the GED and go further with her education? What if, after all her hopes for the future, the best thing for her was to work with Zabeth in the solitude of her home?

In some ways, it seemed easier when others made the decisions for her.

This approach of your-life-is-in-your-own-hands was uncomfortable territory, for sure. How could she have been so confident as to arrive in Alliance by herself and now, with life looking more hopeful, be completely unsure of what she wanted?

She went to the bathroom mirror and wiped off the steam. Looking past her features and into her eyes, she wondered who she really was. And she wondered how she could find out before she needed to give Zabeth and Dr. Lehman her decision.

There was a tap on her door before it swooshed open.

Hannah peered around the bathroom door. "Gideon!"

He held up her traveling bag. "The motel called me."

She moved to the bed and sat down. "It's good to see you."

He set the bag on the bed beside her. "I've come a couple of times, but you were asleep."

She pulled the bag into her lap and unfastened its latch. "Yeah, I was unconscious for a few days, and then I slept a lot. I get to leave tomorrow."

"Where to?"

"A man named Dr. Lehman found my aunt."

A broad smile shifted his deep wrinkles and loose skin in different directions. "That's great."

Hannah dug through her bag until she found the anatomy book Dr. Greenfield had given her. She pulled it out, glad to have it in her possession again. "Gideon?" She opened the book and slid her hands across the slick pages. "How do you make decisions? I mean, you said you were on your own really young. How'd you know what to do next?"

He chuckled. "Ain't much to decide when you're tryin' to survive. Each day sort of decides for you."

Hannah nodded. He was right, although she hadn't realized it until he said it.

He tugged at his baggy pants before sitting in the chair across from her. "But when there is a choice, trust what you know about yourself. What do you know about Hannah?"

She shrugged.

Gideon crossed his arms over his large chest. "Well, let me tell you what I know. You know how to take blind steps and trust you'll have what it takes to face whatever is ahead. You're strong enough to pay the price of your decisions—even if it means staying in a run-down motel by yourself." He paused. "What has you so spooked that you're confused about everything after you've gotten this far?"

That was what she wanted to know. His words about taking blind steps and trusting she had what it took to face the next step seeped into her thoughts.

She drew a deep breath and whispered what was really nagging at her. "Every decision has a price."

He gave a hearty nod. "Every lack of decision has a price too." His gravelly voice rumbled through the room.

She traced the image of the respiratory system with her fingertips. "I was raised Amish, Gideon."

"Had that one figured out the first moment I saw you. It's part of the reason I was interested in helping you even if you weren't eighteen yet. The Amish are exacting people, so I understand needing to get free. You came here looking for more than just your aunt. If you hadn't found her, you were determined to find a job and get by. What's so different now?"

She pulled the book to her chest. "Before I left home, I told myself that, if need be, I'd carry my fears with me, but I wouldn't let them stop me. But it's not that easy."

"Oh, so it's *easy* you're after. See, now that you know what you want, you'll know what to aim for."

She studied him, feeling a little less confused. That wasn't what she wanted. She wished for guarantees, and there were none. She tapped the book. "I want knowledge, Gideon, medical knowledge. I think it's what I've always wanted, but…"

Gideon raised his hand, motioning her to stop talking. "No one else may ever understand how scary this is for you, a young girl facing her dreams with little money and even less formal education. But what do you want from life in five, ten, or twenty years from now?"

She knew the answer to that. "I think I need to talk to Dr. Lehman. If I'm gonna go to school while taking a chance on working with the Amish, I want it to be with him at the birthing centers—whether he thinks he needs me or not."

～め～

As Faye drove along the back roads toward Zabeth's place, it was hard for Hannah to believe how things had turned around for her, and she said a silent prayer of thanks. Across from Hannah in the backseat of the beat-up vehicle, Zabeth chatted with Faye. When they passed the same fine brick home Hannah had seen the last time she was out this way, an eerie sensation slid up her spine. It was only last Monday that Gideon had driven her down this street in search of her aunt.

She'd called Dr. Lehman last night. At first he said he didn't have the need or the time to train her, but when she laid out all the coincidences that had brought her across his path, the phone line went completely silent, as if he needed time to absorb it all. Finally he spoke, agreeing to hire her. Of course he had concessions she had to agree to, like using some of her recuperation time to train on his office computers. The decision she'd made about stepping into the medical field to work with the Amish felt good, and she could only hope it was right.

But she knew she'd never really feel free unless... "How hard is it to change a last name?"

Zabeth's eyes grew large for a moment. "I can help you do that."

Faye glanced back at her. "You'll need your birth certificate though."

Her heart skipped a beat as she turned to her aunt. "I didn't bring it."

Her aunt reached across the seat and patted Hannah's hand. "A good lawyer will know how to get a copy of that through a courthouse without your Daed or anyone else knowing a thing. Trust me."

Faye slowed the vehicle and turned right onto the same long driveway Gideon had taken her on. "I wouldn't suggest changing your first name. That's too hard to get used to. But women are pretty comfortable changing their last names. My boyfr—husband, Richard, can put you in contact with people who can help."

Faye passed the dilapidated house Gideon had brought Hannah to last week. A few hundred feet beyond, after a row of thick hedges, she slowed almost to a stop before turning right. Hannah couldn't believe how close she and Gideon had been to her aunt's place when they gave up and left.

Zabeth's forehead wrinkled. "What would you want your last name to be?"

"Well, I wouldn't want it to be the same as yours. My parents might think of that—" She lost her train of thought as the car topped a knoll and a small log cabin came into sight. Smoke swirled out of its chimney, reaching toward the heavens before it dispersed. A porch ran the length of the cabin, and there was a clothesline with dresses shifting under the frigid breeze. Her eyes misted at the sight.

When the car came to a stop, Hannah climbed out, never taking her eyes off the view before her.

Faye slammed her car door shut. "I told you there wasn't much to it."

Around the side of the yard Hannah could see a place where the snow lay in neat rows. A garden was buried there, just waiting on spring.

She cleared her throat and turned to tell Zabeth it was perfect. *"Es iss fehlerfrei."*

Zabeth nodded and wrapped her in a hug. *"So denk ich aa."* She drew back, looking into Hannah's eyes. *"Des iss aa alleweil dei Heemet. Ya?"*

Hannah's emotions were too thick for words as Zabeth told her this was her home now. She fell into her aunt's embrace. "Ya."

"Okay, guys, the least you could do is insult the place in a language I can understand."

Hannah stepped back, too surprised at Faye's words to respond. Her eyes moved to Zabeth, and they broke into laughter. Obviously Faye didn't understand Zabeth's love for this place.

"Come on, child." Zabeth led her up the front steps while talking over her shoulder to Faye. "Perhaps such a fancy Englischer as yourself can get Hannah's bag out of the trunk and join us in our fine abode…if you can stand it."

Faye huffed, but she went to the trunk of the car.

The front door was made from three vertical planks of rough-hewn wood and had a tiny peephole drilled in it. Zabeth opened the door, and they stepped into a small, scantly furnished room. One lone bulb hung from the middle of the ceiling. Nothing hung on the walls but a plain, round clock. A tiny kitchen sat off to the left, too small for even the dining table to fit in it. The table and chairs were in the main room. To her right, two open doors led into what Hannah figured were bedrooms. The place was more plain than Hannah's own home—except for a shiny piano. She stared at the instrument.

Zabeth shrugged. "I guess that does look a bit out of place." She gestured across the room. "I have a stereo and stacks of CDs in my bedroom that fit no part of this landscape either."

Faye closed the door with her foot and dropped Hannah's bag in front of a couch that had clearly seen better days.

Zabeth slid out of her coat. "So, Hannah, you will need to have a last name. What will you choose?"

Hannah's cheeks burned. She'd put the name on the application, but saying it out loud was asking a lot. "I like the name Lawson, although I don't know why. It just came to me when I was filling out an application."

"Well, Miss Lawson, your room is right there." Zabeth pointed to one of three rooms directly off the living room. "The room next to it is mine. The bathroom is the only other door, and it doubles as a coat closet. That's the whole place." She chuckled.

Faye sat and propped her feet up on the coffee table. "You know, Richard works construction and travels a lot for business. So if you want to write letters home now and then without revealing your whereabouts, he could drop them in the mail for you from different cities and states."

"I did promise to write to Mary, Luke, and Matthew, and I'd like to do that without worrying about being traced."

Zabeth set her glass in the sink. "And by this time tomorrow, I hope to know who Mary, Luke, and Matthew are."

Hannah cocked her head. "And I'll know all sorts of things about you too, right?"

Zabeth paused. "Sure." Grasping the scarf at the base of her neck, she tightened the knot.

Hannah swallowed. "What illness were you referring to in your letter to Daed?"

Zabeth shook her head. "It doesn't matter. You turn eighteen soon enough, and I'm here now."

Hannah took a sip of her water. She only had *now*?

*H*eavy-eyed from a long night of wrestling with her fears and her conscience, Mary placed the "Past and Future" quilt onto the brown
paper and folded the sides around it. Having come to some decisions, she was
grateful for the rules of privacy over her medical charts. Unfortunately the
reason for her thankfulness boiled down to one goal: deception.

Just a tad—nothing major like Hannah had done.

But Mary wasn't going to lose Luke—no matter what it took.

The doctor told her that she appeared to be healing quite well, although
he wanted to read the results of her next CT scan before he allowed her to
resume all her previous duties as the only daughter of a large family.

He'd been quite firm about her not marrying unless she was very careful
for several years not to get pregnant.

Easy for him to say. He believed in using birth control.

After explaining a hundred things that sort of made sense and sort of
didn't, he'd looked her in the eye. "The baby would be fine, but a pregnancy
for you, specifically the labor and delivery, could be very dangerous. I don't
know how to make it any plainer, Mary. You either need to use birth-control
pills or not get married for at least five years. Okay?"

She grabbed a piece of scrap material and wrapped it around each side of
the package. No, it wasn't okay. Thoughts of the latest news she'd learned
pressed against her. It was a bad enough indication of her future that Hannah
had up and left two weeks ago. Now Mary had learned from her father that
Zeb Lapp had done the same thing some twenty-two years ago—abruptly
moved away from his Mamm, Daed, and all his siblings. All her father
remembered about Zeb's arrival here was that something had happened in his
old community that didn't sit well, so he left. When he decided to settle in
Owl's Perch, the bishop verified he was in good standing with his old church

and welcomed him into their fellowship. That information, along with knowing how quickly and easily Hannah had decided to leave on her own, had opened Mary's eyes to what could happen. She didn't think Hannah knew what her father had done. She doubted if Luke knew it, but pulling up stakes and leaving everyone behind was in their blood. Had to be.

Luke was so frustrated with his family and the church leaders for how they'd handled Hannah that Mary feared if he had to wait on her to marry him, he might just leave Owl's Perch for a spell. Through the grapevine, she happened to know that Mervin Stoltzfus had already offered Luke a job in Lancaster. And while he was working and living there, he might find someone else. But if she and Luke began to make plans to marry in the next wedding season, then he'd be hers forever.

She tied the material into a bow. It was time to give this to Paul and see if Luke had talked to the bishop yet. Maybe he'd give them permission, and she wouldn't need to fudge on the truth.

She suddenly felt flushed.

When the doctor took follow-up pictures of her injuries from the buggy accident, if it all looked healthy and strong, then why should he tell her to wait?

Doctors. Sometimes they wanted too much say over her life. Regardless of what that doctor wanted, she would begin her instruction period in April and join the faith in September—all in preparation to marry Luke the next wedding season.

She grabbed her shawl and the package. Buggy rides made her miserably nervous since the accident, but what was on her mind was more important than trembling hands and an aching chest. Besides, she'd talk her Daed into dropping her off there and then going on. Luke would see to it she got back home.

Paul wanted a chance to talk to Luke before he returned to school and work on Monday. He'd missed two full weeks of school and was no closer to knowing where Hannah was than before. It was time to try to catch up and graduate as planned. Hannah had made her decisions, and if she changed her mind, he was fairly confident Luke would contact him.

He used the newly worn path between Gram's and the harness shop. When he walked inside, an Amish man was at the counter ordering something from Luke.

"Welcome. Be with you in a minute." Luke didn't even look up as he spoke the words.

Taking a moment to look out the window, Paul noticed that Gram had a visitor pulling into her driveway. Oddly enough, it looked like the Millers from his Mennonite community in Maryland. If it was, that probably meant their eldest daughter, Dorcas, would be with them.

The car stopped and let Dorcas out before pulling on up to Gram's house. Dorcas opened the mailbox and checked inside it, then closed it and started walking toward Gram's. Paul was curious but turned his attention back to Luke as he told the customer bye.

"Hey." Luke grabbed a poker and stoked the wood stove, though the place was already way too warm to suit Paul. "Mary wanted to see you. She should be here any minute."

"She wanted to see me?"

Luke chuckled. "You see somebody else I could be talking to?"

Paul shook his head, not at all sure he cared to hear what Mary might have to say to him. He'd met Mary for the first time two weeks ago when he'd demanded to see Hannah and then sped off without hearing her out.

Luke set the poker next to the stove. "I spoke to Matthew the other day. The church leaders are looking for a midyear replacement for Elle. She teaches at the school. If they don't find one, she'll finish out the school year, but then she's going away with her dad for six months. Matthew and I are thinking about using that time to expand our businesses by joining under one roof—E and L Buggy, Harness, and Horses."

Paul frowned. "Buggy, harness, and horses? All three? I don't think I've ever seen all three combined into one business before."

Luke wiped his hands down his workshop apron. "It's a hunk to try to pull off, but if it works out, we'll add three new rooms onto his place, and this building will become storage."

"But can't you do just as well separately without such a big gamble?"

"See, as it stands, when one of us needs to travel to get supplies or drum up business—like when Matthew needs to deliver things to an out-of-state customer—the shop has to be closed for several days. But if we work together, one of us can mind the shops while the other travels for business. Plus we can combine our energy and creativity and really make a go of this business."

"Sounds like some long days of hard work ahead."

"Yeah, if Mary isn't well enough for us to wed this season, I might rent out our upstairs apartment and even spend a bit of time in Lancaster. Mervin Stoltzfus needs some help and is willing to pay good money and give me a place to live while I'm there."

"But if you're trying to build a new business here, why would you take that on too?"

Luke moved behind his work counter. "A new business needs money. I can make good money working part-time for Mervin and sink that money into E and L. Besides, the new business shouldn't require both of us to be here all the time. Just don't tell Mary about the Lancaster deal. It's something I'm only thinking about."

"Sure. I can keep it a secret..." Paul rubbed his fingers and thumb together. "For a price."

Luke laughed. "Renting out my apartment upstairs will be a good source of income, but the idea of living at home when I'm not in Lancaster is a miserable one."

Through the small window to his left, Paul saw Dorcas walking toward the shop. Gram must have told her where he was. He appreciated Dorcas's opinion on certain things, but she seemed to have taken on the powers of a bounty hunter of late. Though tempted to moan and complain to Luke about her, he resisted.

He turned his attention back to Luke. "Maybe while you're enlarging Matthew's shop, you should build yourself a place to sleep there. You could take your meals and showers at the Esh place or with Mary's folks."

Luke's face lit up. "That's a good idea." He slapped Paul on the shoulder. "I knew you college boys were good for something."

Paul chuckled. "Thanks."

The door popped open, and Dorcas entered with a smile. "Sign says you're open for business. Should I have knocked?"

Luke turned. "Knocking isn't necessary when we're open. Can I help you with something?"

"Luke," Paul said, "this is Dorcas Miller. She's a friend of my mother's, and she's not in need of any leather." *Unless we can use it to strap her to a chair in her house in Maryland.*

Dorcas entered the shop, but before she closed the door, they saw Mary getting out of a buggy.

"Mary,"—Luke went to the front door—"come warm up by the stove."

Mary had a package in her hand as she paused just inside the door. "Did you speak to the bishop?" Her voice was hushed, but Paul heard her clearly.

Luke put his arm around Mary's shoulders. "I tried, but before I got started, he said there's too much going on right now for him to make any more decisions. He'll talk to me in a few months."

Disappointment covered Mary's face before she looked at Paul and held the package toward him. "I brought you something."

He felt nailed to the floor.

"Hannah and I made it, but she did most of the work, and it was her idea."

Paul's mouth went dry. He slid the brown paper off, letting it fall to the floor.

Running his hand over the thick, textured quilt, he couldn't believe Mary was giving him anything.

Mary smiled as a tear trickled down her cheek. "It has more of Hannah in it than anything else we own. Luke and me wanted you to have it."

He stared into Mary's eyes, wondering how she could so easily forgive him. He looked to Luke, who nodded his approval.

"I don't know what to say."

Skimming her delicate hands across the fabric, she whispered, "It'll keep you warm until Hannah returns."

The realization that Mary hadn't given up on Hannah's marrying him sat well with Paul. Suddenly the quilt meant even more. "Thank you."

Dorcas stepped forward. "This is amazing. Did you say Hannah made this?"

Mary stroked the blanket. "Yes. She called it a 'Past and Future' quilt. It has patches of cloth from our childhood and patches of material from fabric we plan to use for our clothing in the future."

A car door slammed, breaking the spell of the moment. The front door opened, and a man strolled in.

"May I help you?" Luke asked.

The man pointed toward his car. "I'm thinking about getting a leather cover for my seats."

"Sure." Luke went behind the counter and pulled out a catalog.

While Luke prepared to assist the newcomer, Paul turned to Mary, touching the edging of the quilt. "I can't believe you're giving this to me. Just saying thank you doesn't seem like enough."

*I*n spite of the whispers inside her head that made her feel crazy, Sarah refused to give up on her quest. Hannah's baby was alive and well, and someone had to know where. She tugged on the reins, guiding the horse to slow down. Since she had baked some goods for others in the community, Mamm had said she could go out visiting for a while as long as she didn't go on foot or by bike. Clearly Daed hadn't told her where he'd found Sarah during her last trip out *visiting*.

She pulled the buggy off the side of the snow-and-muck-covered dirt road just before the knoll. On the other side of this hill, maybe two hundred feet away from her, sat Luke's shop, and not far to the side of that was Mrs. Waddell's place.

John Yoder had come to the Lapp place, saying that he'd dropped Mary off at Luke's and that he thought he saw Paul Waddell inside the shop too. Sarah would bet next year's garden that the whole lot of them were meeting to discuss Hannah's baby. She needed to know where the child was, and they weren't going to tell her, so she'd just have to eavesdrop. Looping the reins around the fence, Sarah shivered. It was awful cold for March, and her wool cloak did nothing to stop the winds from howling up her skirts. Ignoring the constant murmuring in her head, she mapped out the best way to get to Luke's harness shop without being seen. Pulling her cloak more tightly around her shoulders, she followed the side of the ridge that ran parallel to the shop. From the top of the ridge, she saw the roof. She sneaked behind the tree line that went up to the back edge of his place. Hurrying to the side of the shop, she kept a watch on the surrounding yards in case someone was out and about. Then she flattened her body against the side of the building.

If it was any season but winter, the windows would be open, and she'd be able to hear as clearly as if she were standing in the room with them. As it was, she couldn't hear anything. She carefully peered in the window. Mary, Paul, and a young woman she didn't recognize stood around looking at something in Paul's hands. Luke was at the counter, showing a man some leather goods. As she adjusted to get a better angle, the woman beside Mary spotted her. The stranger, wearing a different type of prayer Kapp and cape dress than the Amish, gave Sarah a slight nod.

Sarah jumped back from the window and plastered her backside against the clapboard siding, hoping the girl didn't call attention to her. There would be no way to explain herself, and then everyone would be sure she was crazy.

Sarah heard the door to the shop open.

The girl from inside peered around the side of the shop. "Hi," she whispered, "my name's Dorcas."

A mixture of miserable feelings kept Sarah from finding her voice. If the fields weren't so covered in snow, she'd take off running just so she wouldn't have to answer any questions about her secretive behavior.

"You look awful worrisome over something." The girl smiled and stepped closer. "Anything I can help you with?"

Dorcas's kindness surprised Sarah, and she pointed at the building. "They say anything in there about a baby?"

"Why, no."

Sarah pressed her back against the house, trying to escape her stare. "My sister had one. They told me it's dead."

Dorcas's eyes focused on her, making her feel like the stranger cared what she thought. "Are you Hannah Lapp's sister?"

She nodded. "You know her?"

"I haven't met her, but I've heard plenty about her. Just last week I heard she came up pregnant outside of being married. I also heard her baby died."

Shivers ran up and down Sarah. "It ain't true. I know it's not."

"She wasn't pregnant?"

Sarah trembled. "Yeah, that part's true. But it didn't die. Those who say it did must've made it up."

Dorcas stepped in close and placed her hands on Sarah's shoulders. "Maybe we should talk to someone and tell them what you're thinking."

"You can't tell anybody. Please. If my Daed finds out…"

Lowering her hands from Sarah's shoulders, Dorcas glanced around. "Are you Sarah?"

Sarah nodded. "What are they all looking at in there?"

"Mary gave Paul some kind of quilt. It had a name."

"The 'Past and Future' quilt?" Sarah shrieked before covering her mouth. Lowering her voice, she continued. "She can't give that away to some half Englischer. That quilt's got pieces of Lapp and Yoder family history in it. It even has material from my childhood. It's an Amish quilt for Amish folk."

Dorcas looked distressed before she turned and left without saying anything else. Feeling as if she'd been slapped in the face, Sarah hurried down the snow-trodden path she'd made on her way to the shop. Hoping no one saw her and that Dorcas didn't tell anyone she'd been there, Sarah topped the hill and turned right, then began traipsing back toward the road.

"Sarah." A whispery male voice echoed around her. Eeriness shot through her. The image of a newborn's hand reaching through the snow dominated her mind. She feared she'd pass out from the horror of it.

The voice came again. A hand grabbed her. She screamed.

"Sarah, it's me, Paul."

She wheeled around.

The man was breathing hard, puffs of white clouds filling the air. "I didn't mean to startle you. I've been trying to catch up with you."

"The quilt's not yours. Mary had no right—"

His face reflected no annoyance that she was speaking her mind. "I can see where that'd be upsetting, but the quilt was Mary's to do with as she chose." He shoved his hands into his pants pockets, and she realized he didn't have on a coat. His blue eyes studied her face. "How are you, Sarah?"

Put to silence by his kindness, she folded her arms, feeling like a demanding child. "I'll not accept any part of my sister's past or future being in an Englischer's life. And don't try saying you're not one—your ways speak louder than your sect's name."

He gave a slow nod. "I'm not trying to be Plain or English. My goal is to find the path God wants me to take. If parents or friends or relatives have a problem with that, they need to take it up with Him."

"Where is she?"

A wobbly smile crossed Paul's lips. "I've told you already. I honestly don't know."

The sound of snow crunching underfoot made them both look behind Paul. Dorcas carried something in her arms as she waved a hand and scurried toward them.

Visibly catching her breath, Dorcas held out a coat to Paul. "Mary and Luke think we've gone back to Gram's."

Paul took the jacket and slid his arms into it, then turned to Sarah. "We know Hannah is safe. She left a message on the Yoders' phone the other day."

Sarah kicked a patch of snow. "I wasn't asking about Hannah. I want to know about the baby."

Paul took a step back, looking baffled. "Is that who you were asking about when you were at Gram's?"

Sarah huffed. "Of course."

Concern crinkled his forehead. "I assumed you were asking about your sister. Every answer I gave you was about Hannah. I didn't mean to confuse you."

Paul glanced at Dorcas before looking at the horizon. His eyes lingered there, and then he ducked his head. "I'm sorry, Sarah, but Matthew and Luke buried the baby just a few hours after she was born."

The silence that filled Sarah lasted only a moment before the horrid shrieking started again. All she had wanted was to put Hannah in her place, and now she was guilty of shedding innocent blood.

Sarah tore out toward the horse and buggy.

"Sarah, wait," Paul called after her.

She ran faster, crunching new snow underfoot. After crawling between the slats in the fence, she grabbed the reins and climbed into the buggy. Releasing the brake, she hollered for the horse to get moving. By the time she settled onto her seat, the horse was in motion. "The baby can't be dead. She can't be."

Paul was briefly tempted to try to stop Sarah, but she needed much more help than a few minutes could give, especially from an outsider.

Hannah loved her deeply; he knew that. Still, he doubted if either sister realized how much of a connection they had with each other. A lot of Hannah's letters over the years had centered on Sarah and how to help her cope with her anxiety. But he could only guess at all that had happened between these two young women in the past year.

Dorcas cleared her throat. "We probably better head back before we're missed."

The buggy moved farther down the road and closer to Sarah's home. Poor girl, she lived under Zeb Lapp's roof, with no safe place to share the pain she was carrying.

Dorcas tugged at his coat. "You okay?"

He turned and looked into her green eyes. "You did right to come get me, and I appreciate what you said to Sarah." Paul sighed. "It's such a mess, Dorcas. Everyone needs to see Hannah and set things right. Maybe I'm wrong not to go after her."

"I'll say it again, Paul. If I were Hannah, I'd never forgive you if you made me return to this situation. She knows how to reach you."

Paul nodded. "I've told myself all that over and over."

She gave a nod toward the narrow, snow-trodden path. "Can we go back to the shop to get your quilt and then go on to your gram's now?" She turned and started down the trail.

As he fell into step behind her, resentment welled. Hannah was intentionally covering every trail, and she was good at it.

But maybe by the time he graduated in May, she would relax in her determination to use untraceable phone numbers and to send letters without giving a hint as to where she'd gone.

Or maybe she'd return by then.

The warm May air buzzed with insects. Under the shade of a black oak, Matthew held Elle's soft hands and listened as she tried to convince herself she was doing the right thing.

Her father sat in his idling car, waiting for her. Although Matthew refused to say it aloud, it irked him that the man who had abandoned his daughter and left her in the hands of Amish neighbors more than a decade ago had returned wearing an air of superiority and hoping to keep his daughter from joining the faith. Matthew feared that Sid Leggett dished out more pain and confusion than he knew. Matthew had concerns about what this could mean for Elle and him, but her removal from Abigail and Kiah Zook's home, for even a few months, meant far more than Sid understood.

The back door of the Zook home opened, and Abigail came out carrying a basket of home-baked goodies. The Zooks were childless, and their years of raising Elle had brought them untold peace as they slowly came to accept they'd bear no children of their own. Elle's desire to be baptized into the faith and take an Amish husband had filled them with a hope nothing and no one else could have given them.

Sid stepped out of his car, took the basket from Abigail, and placed it in the trunk.

Matthew released Elle's hand. "I'll be here when you get back." He didn't ask for reassurances from her that she would return. What could she possibly say—besides promises she might not want to keep by the time the agreement with her father was up? Sid had told her that if she'd come away with him for six months, he would honor her desire to join the faith and marry Matthew.

Sid had wanted her to leave with him when he showed up in March, but the school board had been unable to find a replacement until last week, so Elle ended up almost finishing the school year. Sid had been determined to pull her away as soon as possible, probably afraid that, given more time, Elle and Matthew would connect so strongly she might refuse to go. Because Sid had managed to need Elle regularly over the last three months to help with his newly owned bakery, she'd spent most of her weekends with him in Baltimore.

Matthew thought it unfair to Elle to show his displeasure, so he had kept his mouth shut and been as supportive as he could.

Kiah came from the barn and walked to Elle. He wrapped her in his arms. "This is the right thing to do, Elle." He pulled back from her, looking into her eyes. "You were born English. If that is your destiny, then embrace it. If it is not, then you'll be glad for the proof this time away brings you." He kissed her cheek.

Abigail moved forward. "You'll always be welcome here, Elle. If you choose not to be baptized in our faith, you'll be just as welcome then as you are now."

Elle squeezed her tight. "I'm coming back." She looked to Sid, who stood at the back of his car, watching her. "I'm coming back. I'm joining the faith and marrying Matthew."

Her father closed the trunk. "We need to be going, Elle."

She turned to Matthew. "I'll talk him into allowing me to come for a visit, maybe two, between now and then. I agreed to no phone calls, but we can write each other."

"He just wants you to be sure about your decision, Elle. I don't much like it, but I understand it."

Elle kissed his cheek. "I love you, Matthew." She whispered the words against his skin before going to the car.

She waved as Sid pulled out of the driveway.

"Care to come in for a spell?" Kiah asked.

Matthew wasn't in the mood for visiting or eating, but he nodded. "Abigail, did you save any of those goodies for a couple of hungry men?"

She smiled. "You know I did."

It was late afternoon when Matthew climbed into his buggy to head for home. It'd be quite a long drive back to Owl's Perch, but he needed the time alone. The rhythm of the horse's hoofs against the pavement seemed to echo: wait, wait, wait, wait. The phrase beat against his temples, making him even more restless.

Matthew had a sudden urge to chop several cords of wood. He drew a deep breath. But what could he do? Sid was her father, and he'd begged Elle to give him a chance, saying he was sorry he ever left her. If she did this his way, he'd give his blessing on her decision to join the Amish faith. He'd even agreed to return for visits regularly as she raised her children right here, near Abigail and Kiah.

Matthew rode toward home in silence as the horse's hoofs beat out the tempo. Wait. Wait. Wait. Wait. But he wasn't sure whether he was waiting for Elle to marry him or to find out she never would.

Paul sat in the large auditorium, dressed in his blue cap and gown. Navy banners with gold tassels hung behind the department heads, who sat on stage facing the graduates. Rows of seats held what looked to be more than a thousand excited family members. His family was here, but they were far from thrilled. When he tried to hold a conversation with them of late, his voice seemed to echo back to him, unheard by his family.

He studied the rows of people in the stands until he spotted Dorcas. She waved, grinning broadly. He gave a slight dip of his head. She was excited enough to make up for his whole family. The work it had taken to get to this point hadn't bypassed her understanding in the least. Tonight had been long awaited, although he'd just as soon not participate in the ceremony. They could have mailed him his diploma. But he was here because missing it would have caused continual hassles from his college friends.

His meeting with the preacher and bishop had come and gone and would come again in a few months. He was honest, and they found little fault in the way he'd lived his college life. But his secret relationship with Hannah caused them to bristle. It wouldn't have bothered them to bring an Amish girl out of her community and into their fold—except she gave birth to a child before disappearing. Her pregnancy issue aside, the men expressed displeasure in Paul for keeping Hannah a secret from his family. He should have been more open with them.

The meeting ended with both men strongly requesting that Paul never attend another game and that he repent quietly in front of them. Paul said he'd consider their words. His lack of hearty agreement to do as they requested didn't earn him any respect within the church or his family. The men prayed with him before they left, hoping he'd get on the right path to avoid his name going before the church.

But Paul had something else on his mind that his church leaders would be worried about. He wanted to continue his education and get a license in counseling. If families knew how to really talk and listen to each other, they'd bond rather than rip apart. He hadn't had this desire until his life exploded and he saw how easily relationships were damaged and how hard they were to fix. He wanted not only to understand more about family dynamics and counseling, but he wanted to help others learn how to communicate. So while Hannah worked her way back to Owl's Perch, he'd stay busy taking more classes and serving umpteen hours as an intern. Hopefully he'd come to understand more of what had brought such destruction to Hannah's and his relationship and how to help them rebuild.

Life's journey involved so many changes and winding roads that it was often hard to tell which direction was the right one. He'd never have imagined Hannah and he would end up like they had—separated when they were finally capable of being together. He wondered what Hannah was doing and if she realized what today was—or if she cared. It was hard imagining Hannah these days. He'd only seen her as the Amish girl next door, and he couldn't envision who she was now.

She'd been gone two and a half months. How much longer would it take before she ran out of the money Matthew had given her and realized she couldn't make it by herself? No one could. He considered himself reasonably independent, paying for his own education and living expenses, but he had a home in Maryland and at Gram's place in Pennsylvania, not to mention his church as well as Gram's—all filled with people who were there to help him.

Who was there for Hannah?

~~~&

Standing barefoot in the budding garden, Hannah scraped the hoe along the soft dirt, ridging the potatoes as the last rays of sunlight danced on the toiled earth. Pausing, she gazed out over the fields. It was no wonder Zabeth didn't mind living with such sparse niceties; the setting made up for any possible lack.

At the edge of the knoll sat a long wooden bench where she and Zabeth spent the evenings when Hannah was home. Each morning Hannah joined Zabeth at the piano, where she was learning praise songs she'd never heard before. She liked starting out the day hearing music fill the home and then carrying the tune with her wherever she went. They'd also spend a few minutes reading a Bible verse and saying a prayer. Zabeth looked at life differently than anyone Hannah had ever known, and she enjoyed learning from her.

Closing her eyes, she listened to the songbirds' low tones as they began to settle for the night. The two and a half months she'd spent in Ohio had been beyond her wildest hopes—in spite of her heart yearning for things that could never be.

Zabeth's health.

Paul's love.

A memory of Paul surfaced, and she shuddered at the ache it caused. Hoping to find more peaceful thoughts, she jabbed the hoe into the dirt again. The counselors at the rape center said thoughts and emotions that ran in opposite directions were normal. They also said it helped to work through a wide variety of thoughts and feelings until a person could settle on something, like reading through a menu of meal options.

Though she found it hard to believe, she almost liked going to the center for the group-therapy sessions. Sometimes when they talked, a piece to her life's puzzle seemed to float right into her hands. A lawyer Zabeth knew had taken care of getting a record of Hannah's birth certificate and changing her last name.

The pleasure of the warm soil against her bare feet and the rich scent of earth filtering through the air faded as her latest round of frustrations with Faye crossed her mind. It was becoming clear that her first impression of Faye had been too kind. The woman seemed to think Zabeth ought to baby-sit for her at any time. When Faye had brought her two children by a few hours ago, Hannah had to insist she not leave Kevin and Lissa for the night. Thankfully the whole scenario took place out front, before Faye even got her children out of the car and while Zabeth was down for a nap. It was ridiculous for Faye to assume the children could spend the night when Hannah was on call and might have to leave. There was no way to know whether Zabeth would have the strength to tend to Kevin and Lissa or not. It wasn't something Faye should be willing to test—for Zabeth's or her children's sake.

The screen door creaked, and Zabeth held up a glass of ice water. Hannah propped the hoe against a tree and went to her aunt.

Zabeth smiled. "The garden has never looked better, even in my best days."

Hannah took the glass and helped her aunt down the steps. "Did you love gardening or just need the produce?"

Zabeth dipped her head. "Love is for people and music, not for plots of dirt." She whispered the words conspiratorially while chuckling.

Hannah laughed. "Yeah, but without that dirt, it'd be hard to feel anything but hunger."

Zabeth wrapped her arm around Hannah's waist. "You're too practical to be just eighteen." Her laugh joined the rustling of the leaves, and Hannah took in the moment.

They slowly made their way to the bench. Here, with her beloved aunt, Hannah's world was sewn together with the most delicate of threads. But it was a seam that could begin unraveling at any point. A second round of combination treatments for epithelial ovarian cancer had severely weakened Zabeth's heart. How long it would be before the illness grew more powerful than Zabeth was anyone's guess.

But five weeks ago the doctor had given Hannah permission to take on as much as she felt up to. Since then she'd done her best to juggle her time with Dr. Lehman and with Zabeth. She hadn't begun studying for her GED yet. Every spare minute not working with Dr. Lehman was spent at his clinic learning how to operate the computer, how to use the Internet, how to log patient info into the computer, and how to answer patients' health questions.

A peaceful silence settled between them as they watched the last rays of sunlight make shadows that turned and flipped in the breeze that shifted the leaves of the huge oaks. Darkness took over, and the birds slowly grew silent while the crickets and frogs picked up the chorus.

Zabeth drew a deep breath. "Did you get that letter to your parents written and sent off like I asked?"

Hannah gave a slight shrug. "I wrote it. It's basic and not worth much, but I gave it to Faye, who gave it to Richard to mail while he's in Columbus this week."

"That's my girl." Zabeth patted Hannah's leg. "Now, tell me how things went at the clinic last week."

"I've already told you. And each time I repeat it, I feel like I'm bragging."

"But I'm so proud of you, Hannah-girl. And so happy you've come to live with me." Zabeth nudged her shoulder into Hannah's. "You're proving how smart you already are without even taking any formal classes. Tell me again."

If her aunt knew she was procrastinating on getting her GED, she wouldn't be nearly as proud. The idea of schooling was intimidating. A one-room Amish school filled with family and friends was one thing. But attending North Lincoln Educational Center for her GED and later going on a college campus—well, she just dreaded it.

Hannah nodded and talked about how well her time at the Amish clinic was going. Dr. Lehman had set her up in a quiet office, and each patient had to meet with her privately before seeing him. Hannah asked a few basic questions and then shared what she'd been taught in a manner fitting the Amish lifestyle. Sometimes a bit of Pennsylvania Dutch slipped into the conversation. Once in a while someone would ask about her background, and although anxiety tried to steal her courage every time, she briefly explained she'd grown up in an Old Order Amish home. Without fail, the women told her they'd pray for her to return to her People and her parents, as she should, but they always assured her they'd not tell anyone but God about the ex-Amish girl who worked at the clinic.

Hannah paused, taking a sip of her water. "The calls to come in and see me have increased so much that we're trying to think of ways that groups of women could come at the same time."

"I've got an idea." Zabeth pulled several patches of fabric from her pocket. "Quilts. One afternoon a week Amish women can gather in a closed room with you at the clinic and ask and talk while working on a quilt. Their husbands won't think a thing about them doing community service work, and once they are there, the conversation can have a specific health topic or just roam onto whatever's on their minds." She bobbed her head up and down. "That way the shyer women who aren't comfortable seeing you one-on-one to ask questions will come to a gathering and just listen while they're sewing. You could even have a box for them to drop in questions, and you could answer those during the gathering without anyone knowing who asked it."

"Zabeth," Hannah gasped, "that's a wonderful idea. Dr. Lehman will love it." She brushed an ant off her foot. "You know, it's so odd. The thing I feared most about this job, that Old Order Amish women would turn my name over to their bishops and eventually make a trail for Daed to find me, isn't something to fear at all. They seem to accept my choice—even if they're praying for me to choose otherwise."

Zabeth reclined against the bench's wooden back. "I think you've under-estimated how strong and loyal the Plain folk are. You were ostracized because of a misunderstanding and a set of circumstances no one knew how to deal with. But the People have tons of inner character, even your father in all his stubbornness."

Hannah gave a nod, unsure what to think. She took another sip of water. "I love what I do at the clinic, especially answering questions the soon-to-be-married or young married girls have about women's health, the marriage bed, and having babies."

"Are you still being asked questions you can't answer without talking to Dr. Lehman?"

"All the time." Hannah's body flushed hot with embarrassment even now. Talking to Dr. Lehman about intimate subjects wasn't comfortable. "It seems there's no end to good questions. Why, even Dr. Lehman doesn't always know the answers. Sometimes he needs time to research before he can respond."

She breathed in the evening air and tried to settle her emotions. "Dr. Lehman has received permission from the hospital management for me to shadow him when he goes to the newborn nursery and the neonatal intensive care unit."

"I've heard tell that some of those babies don't weigh any more than a pound."

Hannah nodded. "Because of the hospital's policy, I can't handle the babies, but I can observe and learn. My first time to do that is next week—"

The phone in the side pocket of Hannah's dress rang out, jolting both women. Their laughter echoed off the hills as Hannah answered her phone.

"Hannah, Jeff here."

"Hi, Dr. Lehman."

"I know it's nearly bedtime, but we have three women expected to give birth tonight, and I could use an extra set of hands. And you could use the experience. Do you think it's too late for Faye to give you a lift to the clinic? I'll pay her extra this time, and I'll give you a ride home sometime tomorrow."

"Faye can't, but Gideon probably can since I warned him you might need me."

"The term is *on call*, Hannah. You're on call this weekend."

"Hang on." She looked questioningly at Zabeth. She might be on call, but leaving Zabeth didn't always sit well.

Zabeth smiled. "You go, Hannah-girl. Grab every chance you get to learn."

She nodded. "Dr. Lehman, I'll try Gideon. But if he can't bring me, I'll hitch up Ol' Gert."

"No. I don't want you riding by horse and buggy in the dark. Besides, by the time you get here, all three babies could be born—and celebrating their first birthday." He chuckled at his joke.

Hannah stood. "I'll be there within the hour, even if I have to find another driver."

~∾§∾~

The freshly cleaned newborn in Hannah's arms seemed to look straight at her, asking where he was and who it was that held him. Wordlessly, she diapered him, wrapped him tightly in a soft blanket, and put a little knit hat on his head. She'd expected dealing with babies to cause her grief since she'd buried her own three months ago and would never have another one, and in many ways it did. But even then her feelings stayed on an even keel better than she'd expected, and she felt good about responding professionally.

The birthing center was once a small, older home, and the residence made a peaceful place to learn about using computers and the basics of midwifery.

Nancy, one of Dr. Lehman's resident midwives, came up beside her. "I've got the blue room. Jeff has the green. Casey just arrived. She's assigned as my RN for the night. As soon as you're done in here, Dr. Lehman needs assistance."

Hannah nodded as she nestled the newborn in his mother's arms.

"Thank you." The mom looked straight into Hannah's eyes, and she felt it in her soul. She stared into Hannah's eyes as if she'd had something remarkable to do with the new life that had, with great effort, moved from the woman's womb to her arms. Dr. Lehman and Nancy had done the remarkable stuff, although just being in the room made Hannah feel like she was part of something as important as the dawning of time. Oddly, seeing how much joy labor and delivery could bring to a family brought no sense of joy to Hannah, only awe at the observable science of life.

"He's a fine, healthy boy—"

"Hannah," Dr. Lehman gently called from down the hall. "Now, if you can."

"Excuse me." She scurried to the green room, peeling off her latex gloves. She tossed them into the trash and grabbed another pair.

"The cord is being a bit of a problem," Dr. Lehman instructed. "Stand on the X, as I showed you last week, and just follow my directions."

A tremor shot through her, and she couldn't budge. "Can't Casey..."

"Hannah," Dr. Lehman's calm voice was a front for the frustration he was trying to hide. "Casey's assisting Nancy right now. Everything will be fine. I just need some help."

She moved forward.

Time passed in odd increments of panic and delight as each person on duty worked most of the night to deliver the three healthy babies. The sun was peeping over the horizon as Hannah finished bathing the newest arrival.

She laid the babe on the changing table and was wrapping a prewarmed blanket around the little girl when her phone rang.

Hannah turned to Casey. "Can you take over for me?"

"Sure."

Hannah removed her gloves while stepping out of the room. She tossed her gloves into a trash can and pulled the phone from her pocket. "Hannah Lawson speak—"

"Hannah, it's Faye." The slurred words interrupted her. "Listen carefully because time is running out. I took the kids by GymberJump yesterday. It's an all-night stay 'n' play, but they close at six. Someone has to pick them up by seven, or they'll call social services. Can you do it?"

"Faye, what's going on?"

Faye broke into sobs. "Can you do it? I called Martin." She sniffed. "He's not willing to get them."

"Why?"

"Please, Hannah. You can't let social services take my children."

"Do you have a phone number for this place?" Hannah jotted down the number as a male voice barked that Faye's time was up. "I'll get there somehow. Where are you?" The line made an odd noise. "Faye?" When there was no answer, Hannah closed her phone.

Without a clue what was going on, Hannah tucked the piece of paper into her skirt pocket and went to find Dr. Lehman.

Inside his office, Dr. Lehman rested in his chair. "Yes, Hannah. He spoke without opening his eyes.

"How did you—"

He opened his eyes and sat up straight. "When you walk, only an occasional floorboard creaks. When it's one of the midwives or nurses, their uniforms make a scrubbing sound." He rubbed his face. "Your dresses continually become more modern though." He pointed to her yellow dress with small flowers and tiny white buttons running down the front. "Maybe one day you'll be comfortable wearing scrubs."

She doubted that. A modest dress was one thing, but pants? "I need to get to a place called GymberJump by seven. Do you know where it is?"

"Never heard of it. Is it in Alliance?"

"I don't know, but I have a phone number."

He let out a long sigh. "We need to add driving to your list of 'must learn.' " He shifted the mouse to his computer. "I'll get directions to this place and take you, but you owe me."

"Owe you?" Hannah laughed. "You took me on when you didn't need me, and you have your trained staff constantly teaching me stuff. I can't possibly owe you more than I already do."

"I think you owe me another apple pie." He grabbed a pen and jotted down some information from the computer screen.

"You didn't even ask why I need to go there."

"I figure if you need me to know, you'll tell me." Clutching the paper in one hand and his keys in the other, he glanced at the clock. "We have forty minutes to get to a place that's supposed to take fifty. We'd better move."

~~∽~~

Hannah glanced at the directions and then at her watch. "We've only got six minutes."

. Dr. Lehman squinted against the morning sun. "I think it's just up here on our left. Keep an eye out for the sign." He yawned. "When we get there, I've got to doze for a few minutes."

Hannah searched each sign, desperately hoping they'd make it in time.

She spotted one with the right words and pointed to the driveway. "That's it. We found it."

He slowed his vehicle and made a left turn. Pulling to the side lot under a huge oak tree, he pressed a button to lower a window.

Hannah opened the car door before he came to a complete stop. "I don't know how long this might take."

Dr. Lehman drew a sleepy breath and tilted his seat back. "The longer, the better for me."

She got out and closed the door. Trying to gather her confidence, she entered the brick building through a set of glass doors. Anytime she was away from Zabeth's cabin, the strangeness of her new life made her feel awkward and fainthearted. But she did her best to ignore the emotions while she went on about her business.

A thirty-something, brown-haired woman at the counter looked up. Black makeup circled the edges of her eyes. "You here for the Palmer kids?" Her irritation rang out loud and clear.

"Yes."

She got out of her office chair. "This is going to cost extra, five dollars for every minute. The policy clearly states that any child left here for night care is to be picked up by six. It's one minute before seven. I was just about to call social services."

"Five dollars a minute? But Faye didn't—"

"I'll need your ID and a fax from one of the parents stating you have permission to take the children. The signature on the fax will have to match the one we have on file."

Hannah placed her ID on the counter, wondering how Faye would send permission through a fax machine. "Where are Kevin and Lissa?"

"They're in their sleeping bags, snoozing in one of the birthday party rooms." The woman lifted Hannah's ID off the counter and frowned. "This doesn't have a photo on it. I've got to see a photo ID."

"I don't have one. Not yet anyway."

The woman shoved the ID back across the counter. "Is the mother sending a signed fax, giving permission for me to release the kids to you?"

"I don't think so. Does she know she needs to?"

The woman shrugged. "She's supposed to know that if the person picking up the children is not on file, she has to send written permission via a fax."

The glass door swung open, and a dark-haired man stepped inside. The scowl on his face deepened as he pulled his sunglasses off. He stepped forward and slapped his driver's license and a credit card on the counter. "I'm here to get Kevin and Lissa Palmer."

Hannah spoke to the woman. "But Faye sent me."

He turned, as if seeing her for the first time. His green eyes skimmed over her before he turned back to the woman in charge. "My signature's on file. If you could speed this up, I'll add a tip to the late fee."

"Sure. She didn't qualify anyway." The woman took his driver's license to the file cabinet. Hannah swallowed, wondering if this was Richard or Faye's brother. "Um, excuse me, but I just inconvenienced my boss to get me here because Faye said no one else was coming."

The man leveled a look at her. "Of course I was coming. Faye knew that." He spat the words at her like she was stupid.

Heat ran through her, as did a desire to spit back at him. "Who *are* you?"

The woman placed his license on the counter. "Everything checks out. You're cleared to go." She pointed to the credit-card machine. "Credit or debit?"

"Debit." The man swiped his card and punched some numbers. "Since I check out with this place as a viable guardian and you don't, maybe you should tell me who you are."

His arrogance left her speechless.

He slid his ID and debit card back into his billfold.

"But you can't just take her children without her knowing—"

The woman pointed to a door. "I'll go get the kids."

He glanced at his watch. "ASAP, please."

"Faye told me no one else was available to pick up—".

"I heard you the first time." He whispered the words, but his tone clearly indicated that he doubted her intelligence. He studied her. "You look younger than most of Faye's friends, so I'll give you a piece of advice. Find a new group of people to hang out with before she and her entourage drag you down too." With his sunglasses in hand, he gestured from her shoulders down. "And what's with this outfit? Trying to pretend you're well behaved so they'll hand over the kids to you? Or was it retro night at the local bar?"

Suddenly feeling outdated as well as stupid, Hannah fought to keep her composure. "You can't just take her children without telling me who you are."

The man scoffed. "If you were half as intelligent as you are cute, you'd figure out pretty quickly that I wouldn't know the kids were here unless she'd sent me. She sent you for backup." He shooed her away from the counter. "When you talk to her, tell her this is the last time she pulls something like this. I'll call the authorities myself next time."

He leaned toward her. An aroma of musky aftershave offended her senses. "Got it?"

Unable to think of one thing to say, Hannah walked out. He had come to GymberJump, obviously knowing the children were here. He had the ID, a signature on file, and had paid the ridiculous late fee. There was nothing else she could do but leave.

s one hour drifted into two, Martin's irritation with Faye calmed, and he chided himself for his rude behavior toward the young woman at GymberJump. He was sure she was the same girl he'd had a run-in with once before because of Faye, only it'd been dark the first time. At times his sister's behavior seemed to turn him into someone else entirely. And that girl had been in his path when his tolerance for Faye was at an all-time low. Every time Faye and Richard had problems, she took to drinking or drugs. Or maybe every time she took to using, she and Richard had problems. He didn't know. Didn't really even care. But he hated having the responsibility of his niece and nephew dumped on him, and he hated telling them half truths as he tucked them into bed after feeding them breakfast. GymberJump allowed the kids to play on the trampolines until well after midnight. Kevin and Lissa would probably sleep most of the day.

Taking care of Faye's rug rats when she got all strung out had been Zabeth's job before she got sick. If his sister thought he'd start pulling Zabeth's shifts with the children, she was stupider than he'd given her credit for.

He checked his watch. Nina, the daughter of some friends, would be here in a minute so Kevin and Lissa could sleep while he pulled music duty at church. He was running later than he ever had. Tempted to call Pete and just bail on trying to get there before the service started, Martin wondered if Zabeth might make it to church today. A few years ago she was the one who'd drawn him back into going, but her attendance hadn't been too regular of late. At least she'd had her Amish niece helping for the last couple of months.

He stopped cold. Surely Faye wouldn't pull Zabeth's niece, the visiting teen, into…

He spat a curse. Of course she would.

"Somebody tell me I didn't just insult Zabeth's niece." The room echoed his voice, but there was no one there to answer him.

He had been so sure she was the girl he'd argued with on Faye's front lawn one night a few months back, the one he suspected of getting his sister involved with drugs. He pulled his phone out of his pocket and called Pete to say he wouldn't make it to church. As Nina entered the house, Martin left.

Less than twenty minutes later he was driving his Mazda RX-8 up Zabeth's long dirt driveway. He hated taking his car up this rutted mess Zabeth called a lane.

Since she had someone staying with her, he knocked on the screen door rather than just going in.

Zabeth came into view, walking toward him with a cane. "Hi, Martin." She gestured for him to come in. He hadn't seen her since her niece had landed here, because Zabeth had asked him for six to eight weeks of uninterrupted time.

He hugged her carefully. "How are you doing, Zebby?"

"Not bad. It's good to see you, Martin. What brings you out here?"

"Well, I figure if you can't come to church to see me…" He studied her face. She looked happier and more peaceful than ever—and more frail.

"Is that why you're here?" Her voice held a touch of humor, reminding him just how well she knew him.

"Well, no, but it sounded good." He forced a laugh. Sometimes facing Zabeth hurt. She reminded him of everything his family had once been, before the separation, his mother's death, and his sister's guilt.

She gave him a tender smile, like a mom waiting for the real truth. "What's on your mind?"

He hesitated. He couldn't just ask for a description of her niece or inquire where she had been around seven o'clock that morning. If he did, she'd want to know why. He sighed. This was Zebby. She deserved better than the facade he presented to everyone else. He maintained eye contact. "I had a run-in with someone this morning."

She chuckled. "Ah, that explains everything."

He wished he could join her in the laughter. He didn't want her to know

Faye was strung out somewhere, probably too incapacitated to drive, and he had her children. That seemed like too much for her since her diagnosis, although she'd done all she could in the past to help Faye through her bouts. He glanced to the doorway of what had been the extra bedroom. "Is your niece around?"

Zabeth studied him for a moment before shuffling into the kitchen. Martin followed her.

In spite of how little they had seen each other since her niece's arrival, he and Zabeth usually spent time together. Because he had to be at church early for music practice, he paid a driver to bring her to church, and after services he'd take her out to eat, and they'd spend part of Sunday afternoon together. On Friday nights, Zabeth would come to his house, where a gathering of musicians would hang out. But she was less reliable since becoming ill.

She pulled a Mason jar down from a cabinet. "Funny you should ask. A couple of hours ago, not long after she arrived home, she asked me what Richard looked like. That didn't seem to satisfy her, so she asked what you looked like." She flicked the water on and held the jar under it. "Acted like she was just curious, but I didn't buy it. She worked hard around here all day yesterday and then worked all last night at a birthing clinic, yet she's still awake—working the dickens out of that garden on a Sunday." Zabeth plunked some ice into the glass and handed it to him. "Was my niece nearby when you had your run-in with someone?"

He took a sip of water, wishing he had a different answer to her question. "I think the run-in may have been with your niece."

She folded her arms across her waist and stared at him. "I'm gonna say this once. You'll get along with Hannah at all times. Do you hear me?"

"You're not even going to ask how we met or what caused the blowup?"

"Martin, she's all I'll ever have in the way of a blood relative, and she's the most genuine person you'll ever meet. That makes whatever happened your responsibility to fix. And I mean that."

"Thanks, Zebby." He rubbed his hand across his chin. The girl he had the run-in with wasn't all that remarkable, but obviously bias overruled reality. "Where is she?"

She nodded toward the back door. "I saw her move to the bench a few minutes ago. You remember where that is, right?" She cocked an eyebrow at him, humor dancing in her eyes.

They shared a smile, easing the tension. "Yeah. Most of the blisters from building it turned to scars."

She laughed, and he headed for the back door.

"Martin."

He stopped and turned to face her.

"I appreciate that you dropped everything and came here to make this right." She leaned into her cane and drew a ragged breath. "Your sister might benefit from being on the receiving end of that kind of niceness."

Martin shifted the glass of water he held, trying to think of what to say. "Faye only uses anyone who tries to help her." He searched for something honest yet hopeful. "But I'll try to think of a way that might be possible."

Looking pleased with his response, she nodded.

As Martin went out the back door and across the lawn, he thought about Zabeth's words. He knew she desperately needed to see the Palmer family come together again. He just couldn't imagine how that would happen.

Hannah pulled her feet onto the bench and wrapped her arms around her legs. Stifling the rush of negative emotions, she wondered if all Englischer men were so blatantly disrespectful to females. This morning had been hard, although she didn't fully understand why. There'd been something humiliating about staring that man in the face and realizing how much he knew and understood compared to what she knew. Powerless. That's how she'd felt. Only it had nothing to do with him having authority over her.

She missed Paul more than ever right now. Before their relationship fell apart, he never once made her feel anything but appreciated, smart, and fun to be with. Was this new world filled with people like that man at Gymber-Jump—conceited and educated, with the ability to shoot invisible poison darts at will?

But he knew the ins and outs of life, like Dr. Lehman and those mid-wives she worked with.

Whatever else she'd realized this morning, she was now determined to check into North Lincoln's GED program. No more procrastination. The next time she stared some arrogant person in the eyes, she'd be as educated as she could get. Her fears about going to school had shrunk under her new desire to—

"Excuse me."

Hannah jumped before turning in the direction of the voice. Her eyes lingered on him, as if looking into his eyes might explain why the encounter with him had bothered her so much. Finding no answers, she turned away and resumed watching the fields.

"Look, I'm sorry."

If he was waiting on her to talk to him, he'd have a long wait.

He walked in front of her and pointed at the empty place on the bench beside her. "May I?"

She didn't respond.

He took a seat. "I shouldn't have talked to you the way I did. The call from Faye really made me angry. When I arrived, I thought you were some-one else, someone Faye barhops with." He rocked back as if he planned to be there awhile.

A good ten minutes passed without a word being spoken. Surely he'd up and leave eventually.

"Are you going to talk to me?" He looked out over the fields. "I never expected silence. Yelling, yes. Quietness? What's a guy supposed to do with that?"

Propping her chin on her knees, she gave a slight shrug of her shoulders. She wished he'd just go home.

"It's gorgeous here. I helped build this bench. If you knew my skills as a manual laborer, you'd either be impressed or jump off the seat."

She slid her feet off the bench and looked at him. Her mind was zipping with retorts—"If you were half as intelligent as you are good at gabbing…"—but she kept quiet.

Looking away from him, she wondered how much longer he'd stay. The minutes droned on, but he didn't rise to leave.

The man clasped his hands together and propped his elbows on his legs. "You think you could teach other women this trick? I can think of a few who could use some lessons in silence."

His words made her want to tell him what she thought.

"Just say it," he growled in a whispery voice. "I can tell you're tempted to speak. Whatever it is, just say it."

Sensing a little brashness well up, she nodded. "I can think of a certain man who could use that same lesson."

He laughed. "Wow! You looked all sweet and innocent, and then slam." He continued chuckling and held out his hand. "I'm Martin."

She didn't feel any friendlier than when he arrived, but she shook his hand. "Hannah. And you can't just remove Kevin and Lissa so I can't get to them. I told Faye I'd take care of them."

He released her hand. "Nice to meet you, Hannah…"

"Law…Lawson." She stumbled over her new last name, feeling foolish that it didn't just roll off her tongue like it should.

"I don't think Hannah LaLawson is it. Try again."

Zabeth and Faye said it'd be their secret, that only they and Dr. Lehman would ever know the truth.

He looked around as if spies might be lurking nearby, then whispered, "Phone girl?"

She smiled, remembering how much she'd enjoyed the snippet of conversation that day, but now she was disappointed at the man behind the voice and humor. "That was you, wasn't it?"

"Beetle thing. That's me."

A hawk swooped down in the field in front of them and snatched something off the ground. But if he was the man she'd talked to that day at the hospital, then his tolerance of Faye's children in his life was probably very limited.

"You joked about taking her children to an orphanage."

He gave a nod. "Not very funny right now, I know, but at the time it seemed funny."

"You wouldn't really—"

"No, of course not. It was joke. If I was going to dump them somewhere, I'd have let you, a total stranger, pick them up."

"So where's Faye?"

He shrugged. "No way to know for sure, but I'd guess she went to where Richard's been working lately, argued with him, got drunk or stoned, and then crashed somewhere. When she woke, she was either too out of it to drive or too far away to pick up the kids on time." He sighed. "It happens."

Hannah brushed wisps of damp hair off her neck. "It's my fault."

He chuckled. "What— This should be good. Just how is this your fault?"

"She came by here yesterday, wanting to leave Kevin and Lissa, and I refused to let her."

"Really?" He raised his eyebrows. "Zabeth let you tell Faye no?"

Hannah shook her head. "She was taking a nap, and I hurried out the front door when Faye pulled into the driveway. I knew I might get called in to work, so I put my foot down before she got out of the car."

"Good for you. Zabeth can't seem to tell Faye no." He placed his hands on the bench on each side of his legs. "I'm really sorry about this morning. I thought you were someone else, someone I'd seen for just a minute one time."

"Someone you didn't like?"

He nodded. "When it comes to Faye, things get pretty unfriendly before I realize what's happening."

"Oh."

"But you know, I've not been in trouble with Zebby since I was fifteen and took something of hers that'd been packed away in a box." He propped one leg on the other. His mannerisms spoke of relaxed confidence unlike anything she'd ever noticed in someone before.

"What'd you take?"

He cupped his hands, demonstrating. "Some white net-looking hat thing that'd I'd never seen her wear. It was great for catching minnows at the creek."

Hannah knew her eyes were bugging out as she tried to speak. "You used her prayer Kapp to catch live bait?"

"Only once."

Hannah scoffed. "Yeah, I bet."

"So, you fish much, Hannah?"

"Excuse me?"

"You used the phrase 'to catch live bait,' which means you know something about fishing."

Hearing Zabeth rattling dishes, she rose. "I'd better go help. She's probably trying to fix us dinner."

"You know, phone girl, you're not great at answering my questions."

Hannah gave an apologetic shrug as she entered the house with Martin right behind her. As she helped Zabeth get the meal on the table, she was aware of Martin's presence in the room. She silently speculated about the Englischer tendency to be overly friendly when it suited them and rude when it didn't. Were they all this fickle when it came to their beliefs as well?

The mealtime was a bit stilted as the three of them tried to find subjects they could or were willing to talk about. She learned that Martin was twenty-six years old and lived just outside Winding Creek. He was a civil engineer for a company he owned, but he wasn't a registered engineer yet.

"So where does your father live?"

"He and his wife live in Australia. We own some business ventures together, and he's more than fair to me financially, but I don't see him very often—not since I turned eighteen and went off to college."

Hannah knew firsthand the difficulties of trying to stay bonded to someone who was away at college. "I'm sorry he's so far away. Faye's husband is gone a lot too, isn't he?"

Zabeth's movements paused. "Richard is gone a fair amount, but…he's not exactly her husband."

"Oh, I…" Hannah felt like she had said the wrong thing. She was only trying to make conversation, not pry.

Martin took a sip of water. "He's a common-law husband."

Unwilling to ask anything else, Hannah examined his face, hoping for clues in his expression.

He set the glass beside his plate. "That means they've been living together so long even the law's not clear on whether they're live-in lovers or husband and wife. But Kevin and Lissa are too young to realize their parents aren't married."

A wave of nausea caused Hannah to set her fork down. Drugs, drinking, and a live-in boyfriend. "Why would Faye be willing to live like that?"

A look passed between Zabeth and Martin, one that said they knew but didn't talk about it.

Martin grabbed the salt shaker and shook the granules over the roast. "Faye has issues. Big ones."

Hannah smoothed the cloth napkin across her lap. "Why doesn't someone do something?"

He set the shaker on the table. "Like what?"

"I don't know. Isn't there a group of church leaders who could put limits on her?"

Zabeth reached across the table for Hannah's arm. "No, child. The only people who could be informed are the police, and family members don't call the police because someone gets drunk or uses drugs occasionally. It's just not done."

Hannah took a long drink of water, wondering if there wasn't some middle ground between the Amish church authorities, who sought too much control, and Englischer families and friends, who had no control.

"But I don't understand what would make someone willing to live like she is rather than fighting back."

Martin studied her. "I don't know that the kind of clear-cut answer you're wanting exists. Faye has been trouble for as long as I can remember. When I was twelve, our parents separated, and she got even worse. One day Mom and Faye had a huge argument. I don't know what it was about, but Faye stormed out. After a few hours, Mom went to look for her. It was raining, and the roads were bad."

Zabeth shook her head as if Hannah had wandered into forbidden territory. "Their mother died in a car accident."

Hannah took another drink of water, concerned she'd asked too many questions and determined not to make that mistake again. Martin shared the tragedy, telling just enough facts for it to make sense, but something about his tone said there was a lot more to the story.

He lifted the biscuits toward Hannah, offering her one. When she declined, he took one and set the bowl down. Cutting the bread in half, he asked, "So how long are you visiting?"

Zabeth smiled. "She's going to live here."

"Really?" He buttered his biscuit. "There's no car out front, and someone else was driving when you left GymberJump this morning. Are you old enough to drive?"

Zabeth nodded. "She turned eighteen in March."

Martin's green eyes fixed on Hannah, and he smirked. "Then next on the list is a car and driving lessons, right?"

That's what Dr. Lehman had said too, but Hannah shook her head. "I'm not interested, and from what Gideon told me, I can't afford the insurance, let alone lessons or a car."

Martin propped his elbows on the table. "We'll work something out. Every girl needs a way to help me out." He chuckled. "I mean, needs a way to get around."

Zabeth pushed her plate away. "Yeah, having you here with me, buying groceries and getting me to doctors' appointments, has already made Martin's life easier."

He nodded. "The moment she said you were here and would be helping her for a while, I was able to get to some out-of-town jobs that needed my attention months ago."

Zabeth laid her napkin next to her plate. "Did you get caught up on the Malcolm Crest job?"

"Pretty close. Stayed a night there last week trying to get everything straight and back on track."

Hannah enjoyed how comfortable Zabeth was with Martin, how much they seemed to know about each other's lives. "If anyone cares, I'd really rather hire a driver as needed."

Martin pushed back in his chair. "It's settled, Hannah. You're learning to drive."

"But…"

Zabeth grabbed her cane, which was never far from her, and used it to stand. "I'm going to lie down. You two work this out, but I will say, Hannah, that I think it'd be a mistake not to learn to drive with all you have coming up."

Hannah sighed. "I see how it is with you two."

Zabeth stopped behind Hannah, bent down, and gave her a hug. Hannah gently squeezed her arm. Silence between her and Martin prevailed until Zabeth's bedroom door closed.

Martin tossed the homemade cloth napkin onto his plate. "Zebby needs you. And my life is a ton easier since you arrived, but you'll never be all she needs unless you can drive."

"But cars are so expensive."

Martin smiled. "I'll find you a good used one."

"Can I get a loan for it?"

He shook his head. "That won't be needed."

She stood and started clearing the table. "Yes it is. I'll not take a handout."

He rose, grabbed his plate, and followed her into the kitchen. "Keep your backbone intact for Faye, but work with me, okay?"

She set the dishes next to the sink. "You pay for Zabeth's drivers?"

"Or drive her myself, yes."

"Then find me a used car with a small monthly payment. You can apply whatever would be the normal monthly cost of Zabeth's drivers toward the payment, and I'll pay the rest."

He laughed. "Then I'll end up paying the full car payment, plus all insurance and gas, and you'll get money to boot."

"Really?"

He nodded.

"Does she know that?"

He shook his head and held a finger to his lips. "Shh. There's a lot about finances that Zabeth doesn't know. And she shouldn't have to. I cover certain expenses, and my dad takes care of other stuff."

"Faye doesn't know that, does she?"

"She and my dad haven't spoken in thirteen years. And I refuse to tell either of them what's going on in the other one's life."

Hannah studied the man in front of her. If she'd had to deal with Faye for thirteen years, she'd have been out of sorts at GymberJump too. "I forgive you for this morning."

He laughed. "I had to earn it, eh?"

"Saying you're sorry and meaning it are two different things. I wasn't going to ease your conscience if you didn't deserve it."

"Well, phone girl, you'll be a good protector for Zebby where Faye's concerned. I can't tell you how glad I am that the cavalry arrived." He held out his hand.

"The what?"

"Cavalry. Ah, between your being a girl and being raised Amish, I guess that wasn't the best word choice. It's a military term for soldiers who often arrived just in the nick of time and fought mounted on horses."

"Oh, well, thanks. I guess." She shook his hand, but she knew it was Zabeth who had rescued her. Her aunt had caused her to find a life worth living and was urging her toward the freedom to live it.

Rays of late-afternoon sun streamed through the broken clouds as Paul drove into Gram's driveway Friday evening. It had been his ritual since he graduated to come to Gram's every weekend, mostly in hopes of hearing something about Hannah from Luke, Mary, or Matthew.

He parked the truck and got out, then headed for the house. This was the summer he and Hannah had dreamed of. Graduation was finally behind him. He would be living with Gram full-time if Hannah were here. Instead, he was entering graduate school next fall and spending thirty-two hours a week as a caseworker in Harrisburg. He no longer lived in the on-campus apartment but rented a one-bedroom place halfway between Harrisburg and Owl's Perch. It made more sense to keep moving forward in life than to spend every moment in Owl's Perch, hoping to hear something about Hannah. Becoming a counselor was heading in a different direction, but the goal was the same—to help others. Rather than spending his life rescuing children from bad situations, he hoped to reach out through counseling before things in a family got that far off track. With all he and Hannah had been through, this new step would fit well into the next phase of their life.

The snows were long gone, and the fields were lush with greenery. The grass grew faster than he could control. It'd take him from sunup to sundown to cut Gram's ample yards tomorrow. A rectangular patch of odd-looking weeds caught his peripheral vision, and he stopped before walking to the edge of it.

Hannah's garden.

It was hers more than his, even though they'd worked it together. She loved it: smelling the soil, working the land, producing a bumper crop from tiny seeds. He always figured it was symbolic of the hope she carried for life, and he loved that about her.

He reached down and pulled up a clump of weeds by the roots. Then another. And another.

A need to plant seeds and watch the fruit of them grow to a harvest nudged him. Hope, from the size of a seed to full harvest—that's what he needed. Dusting off his hands, he headed for the house. After telling Gram he was home and that he'd be in the garden if she needed him, he went to the barn to get the rototiller.

He filled it with gas and cranked it, and his whole body vibrated with the machine as he directed it toward the garden. While walking slowly down the rectangular patch of earth, tilling the soil, Paul wondered if his gift to A-Yom Muilae had arrived and if the little girl liked what he and Dorcas had picked out for her.

When someone called his name above the roar of the machine, he stopped. An Amish woman about his mother's age stood at the edge of the garden. He turned off the rototiller and wiped the sweat from his forehead.

"Hi." He stepped forward.

She stood in silence. His best guess was that he was looking at Hannah's mother and that she thought he knew nothing of gardens to begin planting the first part of June. She cleared her throat. "I'm Ruth Lapp."

"Paul Waddell." He held out his hand, and she barely shook it. He glanced toward Luke's harness shop and saw a horse and buggy parked there—probably hers.

"I…I was hoping to have a word with you—now, if you will."

"Sure." A smile crept to the corners of his mouth. Her reserved but polite succinctness reminded him of Hannah. He motioned toward the porch. "Care to have a seat?"

She shook her head. "I'm needed at home. I got two things on my mind, and I'll tell ya up front, one is sort of a way to haggle for what I want."

Well, this woman seemed to have little in common with her husband. She was calm and forthright.

"You have my full attention." Paul used his hand to block out the sun's rays that were coming from behind Mrs. Lapp.

Her gaze moved over the garden. "Sarah told me a few weeks back that she talked to you the first week Hannah was gone and that you helped her a lot. I want you to know I appreciate that. She has a tougher time with life than any of my other children. I never knew a body to get so nervous."

"How is she?"

Pain seemed to flicker in her eyes. "She keeps…searching for things, making her behavior every bit as hard to explain as it was the first week Hannah went away."

Paul figured Sarah needed more help than the few minutes he'd had with her. "I'd be glad to talk with her again, do whatever I could to help her. Because I'm taking courses about these areas, I know of some good professionals who could help her—"

Mrs. Lapp held up her hand, causing him to stop in midsentence. "Our community wouldn't take too kindly to that idea. Besides, Sarah's always been flighty. It's just her way." She reached into the bib of her apron. "I wanted to show you something." She pulled out an envelope. "Hannah wrote to us a few weeks back. I've been debating whether to share it with you or not, then Sarah told me about your talk with her."

The two months of sleepless nights spent pacing the floors, praying for Hannah, all seemed worth this one moment. Maybe this letter would lead him to her. Maybe she was coming home. Maybe…

Paul took the envelope and noticed it contained no return address, but the postmark indicated Columbus, Ohio. That was about six hours away.

He turned the envelope over and read the words on the outside.

But the words were disappointing.

I gave this note to the husband of a friend to mail while he was on a business trip.

So Hannah hadn't mailed it from where she was living. He wasn't surprised, not even deeply disappointed. He had come to peace with God on this issue. Hannah needed time. He opened the unsealed envelope and pulled out the letter.

Greetings,

Please tell all who are interested that I'm doing well. I have a job, and my employer is very kind. He has patiently trained me, and I hope I'm learning fast enough that he's pleased with me. Life here is interesting. I seem to be sandwiched between the Plain life and the Englischers' life. Day to day is strange among the English, but in many ways they are much like the Amish, some easygoing, others uptight. I cannot say more, for I haven't been here long enough to know what I think about many, many things. I am truly doing well and hope you are the same.

Hannah

It struck him how formal this was compared to the note he'd received from her with "Dearest Paul" written as a greeting and the epiphany she'd shared with him. Unlike the paper in his hand, she'd revealed parts of her true self to him, and that gave him hope. Still, her words made it clear she needed more time away before she knew what she thought about many things. He refolded the letter, grateful for every word.

"Thank you for sharing this with me, Mrs. Lapp." He slid the note into the envelope.

She pushed a clod of dirt with the toe of her shoe. "I figured it was only right to share it. But to be honest, I'm hoping to use it to get what I want."

A little amused at her boldness, he held the letter out to her. "If it's your leverage, you shouldn't have let me read it first."

She searched his face before they shared a small laugh. "I guess I won't make a good businessperson anytime soon."

"Mrs. Lapp, I haven't heard from Hannah other than a letter she left for me with Matthew and one she mailed within a few hours of leaving Owl's Perch. The second letter was much like this one, no return address. Its postmark said it was mailed from Pittsburgh."

"Do you think that's where she is?"

"No. That's a hub for Amtrak. I think that's probably where she changed trains before heading elsewhere."

She gave a solemn nod, looking pained beyond what her lack of tears showed. "Thank you. If you hear from her, you'll let me know, right? You'll come to the house and…"

He didn't mind going to the house, even if he was not welcomed by Hannah's father. "I'll let you know. But if she doesn't want to say where she is, I won't tell that part."

She clenched her lips and drew a deep breath. "I understand. But if she does contact you, please tell her to write to her Mamm and give me an address where I can write to her. I can keep it a secret if she needs me to…just like you and she did." Her voice broke, and a sob escaped her before she clenched her jaws and gained control.

"Yes, Mrs. Lapp. I give you my word."

She pointed to the rototiller. "I'll let you get back to your work."

Paul held out his hand, needing some way to make physical contact without daring to lay a hand on her shoulder. "I appreciate that you came here and let me read the note. It helps."

She shook his hand, and without another word she strode toward Luke's old harness shop, where her horse and buggy stood waiting. He was glad she'd come to see him, and her note made him more sure than ever that Hannah just needed time away from her family. She had a job and wouldn't return as soon as Matthew's money ran out, but she would return. He felt sure of it.

 ideon got out of the car at the same time Hannah did.

"You're staying?" Hannah's nerves were bad enough without an audience.

Gideon shut the car door. "Last time I dropped you off at some unfamiliar building, you wound up in an intensive care unit, fighting for your life."

That thought did nothing to calm her nerves. She headed for the DMV building. What she wanted to do was stand in the middle of the DMV parking lot and just scream at the sheer frustration of constantly battling to catch up with everyone else her age in this Englischer world.

Well, that was silly. She'd never stand somewhere and scream. That'd be downright useless—not to mention embarrassing, although her boundaries of what was embarrassing kept expanding.

Ignoring the rogue thoughts, she entered the building with Gideon right behind her. She had all her papers in order, including a statement from her doctor that she was in good health. Martin had explained that not everyone needed papers from a physician, just those who'd been hospitalized or unconscious in the past six months. He'd wasted no time bringing a driver's manual by Zabeth's place for Hannah to study. She had to wonder how many rituals she'd go through before the events of each day stopped molding her into someone unrecognizable.

Gideon took a seat. Hannah stepped behind the last person in the shortest line, hoping she would leave here with her learner's permit.

Sometimes she missed the routine of everyday life among her people. Aside from her garden at Zabeth's, nothing in her life was similar to before. Right now a day of doing laundry by a wringer washer and rinsing the items by hand sounded like a pleasant escape. It was what came with those tasks that kept her rooted in this constant storm of newness—that and the fact she'd never leave Zabeth.

When it came to being pushed into the fullness of the Englischers' life, Martin was the one behind her, shoving. She hadn't been there when he'd dropped off the driver's booklet, but that didn't stop him from making it clear he wanted her learning how to drive—yesterday.

That'd been nearly two weeks ago, and she'd been at North Lincoln, talking to Rhonda, the office manager, about what had to be done to earn a GED. North Lincoln was an old elementary school, a three-story, red-brick building snuggled in the midst of an older neighborhood—not nearly as intimidating as she'd expected.

Rhonda was probably twenty years older than Hannah and really nice. By the time Hannah had toured the building and asked way too many questions, she didn't feel so hesitant about trying to get her GED. It was all a matter of taking one step at a time and studying until she was ready for the next step. There was no set timetable for achieving her goal. Rhonda said whether it took her two years or two months was nobody's business but Hannah's— and her instructor's. There was no way Rhonda could know how much her words meant. For a brief spell in her life, Hannah had stopped feeling like an oddball—until Gideon pulled in front of the DMV building. She drew a deep breath, hoping she wouldn't have to face Martin tonight and tell him she'd failed her first test in the Englischers' world.

And, pass or fail, she'd have to see him tonight. Zabeth woke with a bit of energy and wanted to be at tonight's music gathering at Martin's place. There would be fifteen or so people Hannah didn't know, all playing musical instruments and singing songs she'd never heard. She'd hoped to get out of going by being on call, but Dr. Lehman had insisted she take the night off.

The world she now lived in and the one she'd been raised in seemed to battle within her constantly. Each pulled her in an opposite direction, as if she were the rope in a tug of war. She wanted to experience new things, and yet the moment she did, she questioned if it was the right thing to do. Sometimes her only reprieve was during the Bible study time with Zabeth each morning and evening.

When she read the Word, life made sense. When she went out to live it, confusion dogged her. Among the Englischers, everything was subjective: modesty, stewardship, needs, wants, and even honesty. Nothing seemed to be black and white—just a hodgepodge of folks trying to figure things out as they went, depending on the situation.

"Next," a man called without looking up.

The person in front of Hannah stepped forward. A nervous tingle ran through her. She would need to move forward in a few minutes. If she passed, it'd be another step into the stress-filled world of the Englischers, but there always seemed to be a bit of hopeful news along the way. Like the fact that North Lincoln Educational Center also had a School of Practical Nursing right there in the same building as the GED studies and pretests.

In Rhonda's words, that was way cool.

The man behind the counter gestured for her. His face was void of anything resembling friendliness. Martin and Gideon had both warned her about the DMV staff.

She laid her stack of papers on the counter. "I'm here to get my learner's permit."

He took the papers and read through them. "Do you live at this address?"

"Yes."

"Are you registered to vote?"

"No."

"We can do that here."

"No thank you."

He scowled and slid a paper toward her. "Fill in your Social Security number here."

Hannah wiped her sweaty palm down her dress before taking the pen in hand and following his order.

The moment she was done, he took the paper back. "Look through the eyepiece and read the bottom line." His voice was as empty of emotion as his face.

She stepped over to the vision-testing device. Reading the letters aloud one by one, she wondered if the man was paying any attention to her accuracy or was just going through the motions.

"You pass." He pointed to the sidewall. "Fifth computer. Just follow the prompts."

"The prompts?"

"The screen will tell you what to do. Just do it. It'll make sense once you get in front of it."

Hannah reached for her papers.

He put his hand over them. "I'll keep these for now."

She crossed the room and sat in front of computer number five, hoping she knew enough to operate it without asking for assistance. Following the prompts, she was soon reading questions and clicking on answers. The questions had blanks and multiple-choice answers.

"A broken _____ line separates…"

A broken harness *line separates the horse from its buggy, leaving the driver unable to steer the buggy and yet moving onward, horseless.*

She read the question again, chose an answer, and clicked Next.

"If your car stalls on railroad tracks, you should…"

…have been in a horse and buggy. A horse would never stall on a railroad track. It might bolt at the sound of a train whistle and not slow for a good mile. But stall? Never.

Trying to stop the instantaneous visualization of horses and buggies and think instead about cars and highways, Hannah realized her biggest problem wasn't operating this computer but rather controlling her internal wiring.

Staying on the trodden path surrounded by the ever-growing grasses of the hayfields between Esh and Yoder property, Mary hurried to find Luke. The long-awaited meeting with the bishop was supposed to have begun some thirty minutes ago, so it was probably over by now. She wiped a bead of sweat off her neck, fussing at herself for sitting down in her cushioned rocker, feeling as sleepy as she did. She had fallen sound asleep and had awakened with a start. If she hadn't been so uptight about today and unable to rest well for weeks, she wouldn't have fallen asleep unexpectedly.

As she topped the grassy hill, she spotted Luke, facing away from her with his forearms on the split-rail fence. The bishop stood beside him, talking. Luke nodded, but his stance—with his shoulders drooped—was not that of a man receiving a favorable decision.

Tinges of nervousness rippled through her as she took in the scene. Without having heard the conversation, she was sure the bishop's decision was no.

Of course he hadn't made a decision they wanted to hear. The marriage bed was about trusting God, not about man deciding the timing and delivery of a family's future. This she knew deep within her, and the truth of God's sovereignty within the marriage bed sat well with her, except she intended to marry Luke this coming wedding season—doctor's permission or not.

Paul had lost Hannah—at least for now, maybe forever.

Elle might never return to wed Matthew.

Mary wasn't going to wait and see what lay ahead that might cause Luke and her to suffer the same fate—no matter what it took.

But could she lie to him? The whole idea of lying made her queasy. Surely there was another way.

Bishop Eli caught a glimpse of her as she came near. He smiled. "Hi, Mary."

Luke turned around, his eyes carrying a distant look even though he, too, smiled at her.

The bishop nodded as he used his bony hand to point toward Yoder property. "If I'd realized you were planning to walk the fields in this heat, we'd have met at your place."

Mary eyed Luke, wondering what he was thinking. "It didn't make sense for Luke to lose any more work time than necessary, Eli. How are you today?"

"I'm doing right well. It's my fervent prayer that you do well with the news I brought to Luke." The man paused, watching her intently.

He wasn't a bad man, even if his decision over Hannah had been harsh.

The church leaders had no way of knowing that making Hannah spend a night alone would have such consequences. Eli could be strict and sometimes wrong, but Mary never doubted his heart in the matters. Besides, what happened with Hannah… Well, she was quite pregnant and had kept it a secret. Nobody could put that on the bishop's shoulders.

Eli removed his hat, wiped his brow, and put his hat back on. "I was telling Luke that none of us, the church leaders or the community, can allow a marriage, knowing you're too weak to carry a child."

She wondered why it'd taken him so long to say the very thing he'd known from the beginning—the Old Ways did not tolerate birth control. It'd been nearly five full months since Hannah had left. Maybe he'd waited until Luke was calm about the reasons for Hannah's departure and had no desire to blame anyone for the way events had played out.

Eli looped his fingers through the triangle where his suspenders attached to his pants. "Luke's request is a serious matter that goes deep into the heart of trusting God beyond our own understanding."

That was it!

She didn't have to lie. She just needed to trust God.

Luke offered her a lopsided smile before looking at Eli. "I…think you're right. Conceiving a child should be left in God's hands. It's the way things should be, but I appreciate that you considered it."

Eli studied him, as if he'd expected a bit of an argument. She knew better. Luke was asking because she wanted him to. He'd mentioned several times over the last few months that it might be right to wait rather than use some intervention to not conceive…

Eli held out his hand. "You've taken this like a man who's submitted to God. I can't tell you how glad I am to see such maturity."

Luke shook his hand.

Eli focused on Mary. "I'll see you during instruction…"

He left the sentence unfinished, and Mary knew it was more of a question than a statement. He wanted to know if she'd choose to stop going to class. Without the instruction classes, she couldn't be baptized. Without the baptism, she couldn't be wed.

Without Luke, none of it mattered.

"Yes, I'll be there each Sunday until time for the baptism, and…" She stared at the ground, unable to look Luke in the eyes. "And soon after, Luke and I will marry. I…I spoke to the doctor, and…I mean…" She could feel Luke's gaze boring into her. "He said the results of the last CT scan, along with my other progress, shows that I'm all healed." She held on to as much honesty as possible and hoped they didn't hear what she *wasn't* saying. She hadn't talked to the doctor recently, but the last time he'd read the CT scan, he did tell her she was healed and everything looked good.

"Well, how do you like that?" Eli chuckled. "That's why you were late. You were talking to the doctor?"

Her skin felt like it was on fire as she gave a slight nod.

Eli slapped Luke on the back. "I guess this means you won't be partnering with Stoltzfus's Harness in Lancaster after all, eh?"

Mary lifted her eyes, realizing all the rumors about this were true and wondering if Luke would ever straight out tell her of his plans.

Eli smiled. "Well, I'll just leave you two to talk, and I'll see you both on Sunday."

She was still gawking at Luke when she heard the sounds of the buggy pulling onto the paved road.

Suspicion covered Luke's face. "You talked to the doc—"

She gestured toward him, stopping him in midsentence. "What's this about you partnering with somebody in Lancaster?"

Luke's countenance changed. "It was just an idea, a way of making extra money while we waited for your doctor's okay to marry."

Determined to keep him right here in Owl's Perch, Mary whispered, "We h…have permission."

Luke smiled. "So I heard." He stepped forward and took her hand.

The warmth of his touch spread through her. Like the bishop said, this matter went to the heart of trusting God. The CT scan said she was healed. The doctor had given her a clean bill of health, except he'd said…

Never mind what he said.

"Mary?" Luke placed his finger under her chin and lifted her head. She looked into his brown eyes.

There was nothing wrong with trusting God in these matters.

"We can get married this wedding season," she whispered.

Hannah squeezed the steering wheel as she pressed the brake.

Gideon looked out the open window on the passenger's side, acting like he wasn't nervous about Hannah wrecking his older model Buick.

From the backseat Zabeth tapped Hannah on the shoulder. "You think we'll get to Martin's sometime tonight?"

Gideon and Zabeth both broke into laughter. Gideon drew a heavy breath. "I ain't even sure we're gonna get to the end of the lane before morning."

Hannah didn't respond to their playful jests. This machine had real horsepower, about two hundred of them according to Gideon, which made no sense to Hannah. If she had two hundred horses hooked to a buggy, she couldn't imagine it being able to go sixty or seventy miles per hour—although however fast it went, the trip would completely tear a buggy to pieces. She was fairly sure that stopping a vehicle at a red light would be easier than stopping two hundred horses.

Coming to a stop at the end of the driveway, she pushed the lever for the blinker up and waited for a car to pass. Zabeth gave directions as they eased onto the road and sweat inched down Hannah's back. It was quite a drive to Martin's place, and the car seemed much hotter than a buggy.

"We made it...before it's over," Zabeth chirped. "It's that second house on the left. Right there."

The second...

Hannah turned into a paved, circular driveway and stared at the two-story, smooth-stoned home with high arching windows and stacked-rock columns. "Zabeth?"

Zabeth chuckled. "Yeah, we're at the right place. His father taught him how to invest money and gave him a few thousand to invest each year for his birthday since he was twelve. Something about making some savvy choices in the stock market before he even graduated from high school."

She put the car in Park, set the brake, and turned the engine off. She pulled the keys out and passed them to Gideon. "You want to come in for a while?"

"Nah, it's been a long day of driving and…being driven." He smiled. "Since Martin will see to it you guys get back, I'm ready to go on home."

Hannah paid him while Zabeth went to the front door. She made arrangements for Gideon to pick her up the next day and then went up the steps to Martin's home.

Soft, unfamiliar music pulsated through the room as she entered through the opened door. Zabeth was busy talking to people Hannah didn't know. Martin was nowhere in sight as she closed the door behind her. Polished woods and colorful rugs covered the floors. Fancy lights with fans hung from the ceiling, and the walls were covered with photos. Seemed to her the place looked awfully shiny and clean for a single guy.

She meandered into the adjoining living room and stopped in front of a group of pictures on the wall. Her heart palpitated at the sight of photos of family events. Melancholy washed over her as she stared at a picture of Zabeth when she was a few years older than Hannah, holding a one-year-old in her arms and a little girl by the hand—probably Martin and Faye. Another frame had a man and woman standing behind a young boy and older girl. That had to be Martin and Faye with their parents. Several photos had Martin in sports uniforms; one showed Faye wearing a ballerina costume.

"Hey, phone girl." Martin spoke over her shoulder.

She glanced at him before pointing to a photo. "Did Faye take ballet as a child?"

Martin shook his head. "That's a Halloween costume."

"Oh." She touched the silver-framed picture of Zabeth holding a baby. "Is this you?"

His confident nature seemed to melt as he nodded.

Hannah looked around the room. "This isn't how I thought a single man's place would look."

A half smile crossed his lips. "I hired a decorator, who put everything that was worn, torn, or too guylike into the storage room. And I have a cleaning lady who keeps everything shiny and tidy—when I'm not baby-sitting Lissa and Kevin." He rolled his eyes. "So, I heard you inched...I mean, drove here tonight."

She mimicked his roll of the eyes.

He laughed. "Now if you practice that a little, you can tell a person off without ever opening your mouth."

From somewhere she heard Lissa chattering. "Is Faye here?"

Martin shook his head. "The musicians always hire a sitter for our parties. And never underestimate the power of Faye to use any available sitter." He slid his hands into his pockets. "How'd things go at North Lincoln?"

She still chafed under the guilt of pursuing an education, and yet part of her was overjoyed at the opportunity—torn between the ways of her people and the choices offered in the Englischers' world, without a hint of how to pray her way to peace.

She cocked an eyebrow. "You and Zabeth talk too much."

"Nah. Not all that much, but she's a tad interested in you getting on your feet ASAP..." He shook his head. "Sorry. I tend to think about things like they're a business deal and what needs to be handled in what order, and I just saw concern for Zabeth's health flicker through those brown eyes."

Hannah drew a deep breath. "The cancer *is* in remission. Even with the heart condition the treatments caused, she could live for..."

"Yeah, I know." He stepped closer. "And no one wants that more than you and me, but she'd like to see progress made, okay?"

She nodded and opened her purse. "You won't believe this, but the Robert T. White School of Practical Nursing has a program that starts at the first of the year." She pulled a small stack of informational papers out and passed them to him. "Admission testing takes place in time for me to begin the two-year program this January."

He read through the first page, not looking all that impressed. "Are you sure you want to go here?"

"Ya. It's perfect for me. It's close; it's part-time. The classes are at night, so you'd be available for Zabeth while I'm in class. *And* it's even housed in the same building where I'll study for my GED, so I'm pretty comfortable with it." She pointed to the criteria for admissions. "This plan gives me a chance at passing my GED and getting everything in order to begin the two-year course without having to wait until next fall."

He flipped through the papers. "But you won't finish with an associate's degree, just a diploma. There are other schools, nursing schools where you'd have a degree at the end of two years and really good schools where you could earn a bachelor's in four...or a little more."

She took the papers from him. "But I *can* do this one." Clearing her throat, she shoved the stuff back into her purse. "It's only part-time plus a clinical rotation every other weekend. Martin, I've never spent any time in a classroom that wasn't a one-room schoolhouse. Maybe you stepped right into a college campus full-time, but this feels right for me."

His green eyes narrowed. "I didn't mean to..." He held her gaze before offering a smile. "I apologize. This is a huge step, one that makes you happy, and I should've looked at it from your perspective, not mine. So let's try again." Martin pointed to her purse. "That school is perfect, and I think you'll be comfortable there. If you want a better chance of passing the entrance exams, we'll get you a tutor, the GED study book, and whatever else you need to prepare for nursing school. I'll find you a car to drive by the time you get your license. And—"

She held up her hand, interrupting him. "Did you invent the to-do list or something?"

He grimaced. "Sorry. We'll talk about it later." He motioned. "Come on. I'll give you a quick tour and introduce you to everyone."

The kitchen, music room, and open spaces, as he called them, were incredibly lavish. Upstairs he had an entire room devoted to a huge-screen television. He called that the entertainment room. It had leather couches, stained-glass shades on lamps, and bookcases with glass fronts. Lissa and Kevin were sprawled on the couches, along with some other kids, none of whom even looked up from their show.

She followed him back downstairs and into the kitchen. She'd known he had money because he spent it so freely, but she didn't realize this was what having money looked like on the inside: mahogany cabinets, tiled floor, stainless-steel refrigerator, oak table and chairs, and two granite islands.

Martin opened the fridge. "Care for a bottle of water?"

She looked at the shiny faucet, set in green marble, then back to him. "Is there something wrong with the tap water?"

He closed the refrigerator. "Not that I know of. But bottled water tastes better, and then the container can be thrown away."

"I'm fine, thanks."

"How about some food?" He held a platter of fruits out to her: strawberries, bananas, apples, and red grapes.

She picked several grapes off a vine and popped one into her mouth. Their conversation was disrupted by what sounded like a herd of cattle clomping down the stairs.

Martin propped his forearms on the island. "I guess they got to a part in the movie where they were willing to hit Pause."

"Yeah, I guess so." She held up a grape. "These are really good."

"Hannah," Lissa shrieked and wasted no time jumping into Hannah's arms.

She squeezed her. "Hi, sweet girl. Been riding or feeding any horses lately?"

Lissa's silky black hair and dark eyes were almost a mirror image of her mother's. "Nope. Didja bring Ol' Gert with you?"

Hannah laughed. "I tried carrying him, but he complained."

Lissa giggled. "No you didn't. Ol' Gert's too big."

Hannah glanced at Kevin, who stood back, watching. Until this moment she hadn't realized how much the young boy favored his uncle, in spite of having straight, light brown hair and fairer skin. "Hi, Kevin. How's the bug catching going?"

He poked an elbow into his uncle's thigh. "Uncle Martin ain't much good at catching bugs, but he has no problems squooshing them."

Hannah's eyes met Martin's. "You know, I'd think a beetle thing would show a little respect for his kind…and hope I don't start squooshing all bugs."

He laughed. "Watch it, phone girl."

She turned back to Kevin. "Maybe we can catch some tonight and hide them from the bug squoosher."

"Yeah!" Kevin's face lit up. "She's good at catching fireflies, Uncle Martin."

"Well, then that's one more thing she can do that I don't have to, right?" He set the water bottle on the counter. "We'll begin jamming in a few minutes. You'll enjoy seeing just what Zabeth adds to the group. She's really good and not the least bit shy."

A teenage girl walked into the room wearing skin-tight shorts and a tank top.

Martin lifted Kevin onto the counter. "Hannah, this is Nina. She's doing the honors of baby-sitting for us tonight."

Hoping she didn't look as uncomfortable as she felt around a half-clothed girl, Hannah shifted Lissa in her arms and held out her hand. "Hello."

Nina shook it. "Hi." She turned to Martin. "Dad called and said he's running late but you should get started without him."

Lissa reached for Martin. He lifted her from Hannah's arms. "Nina's parents are Dave and Vicki Slagle. They're good friends I'd like you to meet when they get here." He looked to Nina. "That's fine. I knew he had a lot going on today. Why don't you take the kids outside for a while? That's where we've set up all the band equipment."

"Okay." Nina helped Kevin jump down.

Martin tickled Lissa's belly. "You're going to be good for Nina tonight, right?"

Lissa giggled and nodded, and Martin set her feet on the ground. "Go on." He gave a nod for her to follow Nina, then took a swig of water. "According to Zabeth, you're not interested in coming to church. Is there a reason?"

"I…I've never…" She shrugged.

"Been to church?"

"Not an Englischer one."

"I see. Well, Zabeth had already made those transitions long before I was born, so I guess I hadn't really thought about how you might feel." He backed against the island. "You need to—"

She held up her hand, interrupting him. "I know. I need to put that on my list."

He opened the fridge and grabbed another water bottle. He took the lid off and passed it to Hannah. "I hated church as a teen. Zabeth had Dad's full backing, and I went, even though he didn't go. Then after college, I started going again, but only for Zabeth. It sorta grows on you, but it took awhile to fit in. Maybe because I had to work out some stuff with God before I could really tolerate it." He slid onto the counter, looking relaxed and comfortable with his confession.

His words didn't sit well, although it seemed like they should. "That's… that's not… I don't have a problem with God…"

"So what's the problem?"

She shrugged.

"I saw something in those eyes, Hannah. Just say it."

"The only thing I was thinking is that I don't know why, but I just don't want to be in church. Okay?"

Martin smiled. "It's okay with me. I get the idea it's not so okay with you."

She sighed. "There's a phrase that comes to mind whenever you're around."

"Yeah? Are the words *charming* and *intelligent* involved?"

"Nope." The desire to tell Martin to "shut up" had risen within her since they'd met, but she couldn't imagine actually saying it.

He laughed. "Why am I not surprised?"

The sounds of drums and guitars vibrated through the air. "Palmer, front and center." The male voice echoed through the amps.

"Come on. Zabeth said you have a great singing voice." He grabbed her wrist and pulled her toward the back door.

This was an item he'd put on her list that she wasn't at war with herself over—well, not completely anyway. She'd been looking forward to learning new songs and how to sing with instruments. She'd always loved singing a cappella at the church meetings, but most of the songs were about religious martyrs. Surely that wasn't the only kind of music God enjoyed.

With everyone settled into bed for the night, Sarah slipped out of the house. Earlier in the day she had seen Daed in the tack room putting a folded piece of paper into a tin box before he shoved the container behind some loose slats on the wall.

She hoped that's where Daed was hiding the letters Matthew had passed to him, the ones Hannah had written and left for them before she boarded that train six months ago.

Six months!

It was ridiculous that Daed hadn't shared the letters with them in all this time. It wasn't his place to be the keeper of what wasn't his. Of course, her sister might not have written to her.

Sarah had been caught on many occasions trying to find these letters, but no one had figured out what she was looking for. Maybe because she wasn't always looking for the same thing. When caught, she'd make up some missing item and say she was hunting for that. They'd look at her funny, but then they'd walk off and leave her alone.

But now she knew right where to go. Walking into the musky-smelling barn, she headed straight for the tack room. Through the darkness she ran her hands along the shelf, gently searching for the kerosene lamp. When her fingers touched the smooth glass, she grasped the lamp and set it on the workbench. After finding the matches on the same shelf, she lit the lantern and slid the matches into the bib of her apron. She held up the light in front of the area where she'd seen her Daed move the boards.

Placing the lamp on the bench next to her, she giggled. Hannah just might have told where she was going and what she did with her baby... Why, the little thing would be sitting up by now.

Instantly she could imagine a sweet little babe growing and happy. That thought seemed to be all that kept her sane these days. The board had a nail at the top, but with some pressure it swiveled onto the boards next to it and out of Sarah's way. The tin box reflected the firelight, and she pulled it from its hiding spot. Her hands trembled as she removed the lid and grasped the papers in her hands. She laid the stack on the workbench and opened the top one.

Day four:
I keep looking for her return. Wake at every sound…

Sarah flipped past that page and several others before reading the last line on the final page.

Six months:
Each night I lie awake, wondering…

Sarah groaned. That wasn't written by Hannah. She tossed the letters to the ground and grabbed one from the bottom of the stack.

Dear Sister,
What has hap—

"Sarah?"
She jumped at the sound of her father's voice. When she turned, he was in the doorway of the tack room.

"I thought we had a thief or something. What are you…" His eyes landed on the papers and then on the gap in the wall as he walked toward her. Concern drained from his face, and anger replaced it. He bent and snatched the papers off the ground and pulled the letter from her hand and the others off the bench. He shook them at her. "Is this what you've been searching for, worrying your poor mother over? Wanting this?" He pulled a handkerchief from his pocket and removed the globe from the lamp.

"Daed, no, please!"
Ignoring her, he held the bundled letters over the flame until they caught

fire. He turned them sideways, letting the orange and yellow flames leap. Before the fire reached his fingers, he tossed what was left into a bucket. She watched as the last scripted words blazed and then turned to thin, black ash.

"Go to bed, Sarah." He pointed to the door.

Staring into the bucket, she wondered what had been written before fire destroyed the words.

"Go!"

A thin trail of smoke danced in a circular motion, rising into the air before it disappeared.

Never before had she dared to really look... She lifted her gaze to meet his. It was odd seeing him eye to eye. "Did you see how fire removed what had been written?" She stared into the bucket. "Did it erase the truth with it?"

"There was no truth there, Sarah."

She stooped next to the bucket and smelled the aroma of fresh fire. "Or if there was, it's better to burn it than face it. Ya?"

"Go to bed, Sarah."

Sarah pulled her attention from the ashes, rose, and headed for the house.

Matthew whistled softly as the horse trod toward the Zook place. The heat of the August day was over, but it'd be daylight for hours yet. Elle had been gone four of the six months she'd promised to her dad, and she was back for a visit, probably arrived at the Zooks' less than an hour ago. She was leaving again first thing tomorrow morning, but he'd been looking forward to this visit since she wrote him a few weeks ago, sharing her plans. He missed her something fierce—from the moment he woke each day until sleep took over. The need to see and talk to her never seemed to lessen.

The upside was the number of hours he could pour into expanding his business. He was working sixteen-hour days, six days a week.

All those hours were paying off too. Really paying off.

But he'd gladly give that up for more time with Elle.

Bits. His mind jumped subjects on him. He had to remember to go by the storage shop and get a package of bits before tomorrow.

Well, he and Elle could swing by there tonight while they were out riding and talking.

Luke was a really good partner, and surprisingly enough, his own brother David was a lot of help. Between him and Luke, they were gaining customers from other states.

He slapped the reins against the horse's back. He could have hired a driver to take him as far as the Zooks', but he was hoping to bring Elle to see his updated and expanded shop. And he wanted to do so in as slow and private a manner as possible. A hired driver provided neither slowness nor privacy.

He hummed for a while and then prayed for a while as the horse clopped along. As he pulled in front of Kiah and Abigail's home, he could smell the feast.

"Hello," he called as he hopped down from the carriage.

The doors and windows were open as they always were when it wasn't winter, but no one responded to his call.

He strode to the screen door and knocked.

"Come on in," Abigail said. A moment later she came around a corner, smiling. "Matthew Esh. Come in, come in."

She sounded surprised that he was here.

He entered the house, looking for Elle. "It sure smells like ya been busy today."

"Busy canning."

Just canning?

"So"—Abigail wiped her hands on the corner of her apron—"what brings you out this way?"

He scratched his head. "Where's Elle?"

"Elle?" Abigail's face was serious. Her eyes narrowed before she winked at him. "Why, I have no idea." She pointed to a door, a closet door from the looks of it.

Matthew walked to it. "Oh, well, I guess I got the days mixed up, and she won't be comin' tonight." He opened the door, expecting to see his fiancée, but what he saw left him speechless.

A huge camera lens stared him in the face as a bright light flashed. He covered his eyes. "What are you doing?"

Elle stepped out of the closet. "An Amish man caught by surprise," she laughed. "Now that should sell." She took the strap of the camera from around her neck, held the bulky contraption away from her in one hand, and gave Matthew a one-armed hug. "Hey."

He laughed. "Leave it to you." He returned the hug, thankful she was in his arms.

She pulled away and took another photo.

"Elle," Matthew protested, "you do remember you're in an Amish home, right?"

Elle made a face at him as if he was making a fuss over nothing.

Her hair was pinned back in a ponytail with reddish blond wisps dangling about her face and neck. Her straight blue-jean skirt and sleeveless knit top gave her a very modern look—a modest one by Englischer standards—but Matthew wasn't comfortable with it.

He looked to Abigail, who pulled a kitchen towel from the bib of her apron and snapped it in the air. "This is my defense."

"You pop her with it?" Matthew looked around the kitchen. "Where's mine?"

"Matthew!" Elle scolded.

"No, it's not for smacking anyone." Abigail frowned at him before shaking the towel. "You've seen the captions that say 'Amish woman avoids camera.' Well…" She draped the towel over her head and face.

They shared a laugh, but Matthew wagged his finger at Elle, not sure how amused he really was. She lifted one shoulder, angling it toward him while raising her eyebrows. But rather than looking like a shrug, her move looked like a dare. Abigail removed her towel just as Kiah came in covered in a sheet with two holes cut out for his eyes. Everyone broke into laughter. Kiah looked like an Englischer kid, a really tall one, dressed as a ghost on Halloween.

Matthew held out his hand. "Elle." He said it firmly.

She harrumphed but placed the camera in his hands. "I told my teacher I'd do a complete photo shoot inside an Amish home. Don't know how a girl is supposed to do that if she can't include some photos of real people."

Her voice and mannerisms said she was joking—sort of.

Kiah pulled the sheet off his head and wrapped the camera in it. "I am real, and so is Abigail."

"Uh, yeah, real covered," Elle retorted.

She took a stack of plates out of the cabinet and began setting the table. It wasn't long before they all sat down to eat, talking about the lack of rain and the price of horse feed.

"Matthew's business is doing so well you might've heard of it all the way in Baltimore. He's got customers from at least seven states—Amish, Mennonite, and Englischers." Kiah stabbed another fried pork chop and plunked it onto his plate. "All wanting buggies, horses, and leather goods from E and L Buggy, Harness, and Horses."

All hint of a smile left Elle's features. "Is it really doing that well, Matthew? You've said nearly nothing in your letters."

Matthew wiped his mouth with a napkin. "It's doing good. Just about better than we can keep up with. Rather than writing about it, I thought I'd show you the additions to the old shop after dinner."

She gave a sullen nod. "Seems like you would've told me…"

He pointed to the counter where the camera sat hidden inside the sheet, letting her know she hadn't shared everything going on in her life either.

She smiled. "I was waiting till I saw you in person."

"Yep. Me too." He returned her smile. "So how about a buggy ride after dinner?"

"All the way to your place? No way. I'll drive."

"Drive?" He glanced out the window. "I didn't see a car."

"That's because I hid it behind the barn." She giggled. "Worked too, ya?"

He nodded. "So you have your license now?"

"Oh, good grief, yes. Do you know how difficult it'd be to get to DC's School of Photography regularly without being able to drive myself?"

Each person froze, staring at Elle.

She blinked. "What?" Somewhere between staring at them and thinking about what she'd said, it dawned on her. "Oh." She lowered her head. "I was going to talk to you about that, Matthew, when we had time alone." She shrugged. "Had planned for us to go for a drive."

The meal wrapped up in silence, and Abigail shooed them out the door, saying she'd clean up without their help.

Elle grabbed her camera, its case, and a large black bag of some sort. She pulled a set of keys out. "Why don't you put the horse to pasture, and I'll drive."

That wasn't the way he'd pictured tonight at all, but he led the mare into the barn, unhitched her from the buggy, and put her in the field. Elle slid behind the wheel, and he got in on the passenger's side, feeling a complete lack of dignity.

Over the next hour, as they drove everywhere and nowhere at the same time, she told him all about living with Sid, helping to run his bakery, and taking photography classes. "See, the school teaches classes two ways, through sessions—which is what I've been taking. Or through an actual professional program—which is what I'd like to take." She paused.

Matthew nodded, feeling rather foggy about what she'd rattled off.

She adjusted the rearview mirror. "Well? What do you think?"

"I think it's an odd hobby for someone who's planning on being baptized into the faith."

She nodded. "Yeah, I know. But if I take photos of people who aren't Amish and photos of scenery, the bishop will make an exception."

Matthew propped his elbow on the car door next to the window. "I'm not so sure he will."

"Of course he will."

"Do you ever lack confidence in what all you can talk people into?"

She turned, frowning at him. "What's that supposed to mean?"

He shook his head. "Let's talk about something else."

"Okay, what?" Her tone was clipped.

"How about if I show you the expansion on our shop?"

She nodded, used a stranger's driveway to turn around in, and headed for Owl's Perch. It was dark now, making it even harder for Matthew to gauge her thoughts.

They crossed into Owl's Perch. "Could we go by Luke's old harness shop and let me pick up some supplies first?"

"Sure. I'm glad the business is going so well for you."

"Thanks. It's a handful, that's for sure."

They drove on for miles in silence. He'd never once thought they might have trouble finding things to talk about. They never had before.

She drew a deep breath. "Matthew, I…I've applied for the professional program."

"What's that?" He took notice of the Lapp house as they passed it.

"I told you…didn't I?" She slowed as the road went from pavement to gravel. "It's a course where I can get a diploma in photography."

"In photography?"

"Well, don't sound so skeptical. It's a viable course."

Wondering what she meant by *viable,* he nodded. "I guess."

Dust churned under the wheels until she slowed to enter the driveway. Putting the car in Park, she drew a deep breath. "The program starts next month and takes eleven months to finish."

He just sat there, staring at her silhouette through the darkness. "Eleven months?"

She fidgeted with the steering wheel. "I know that sounds like a long time, but I really want to do this. I'm good at it, and I've never really been good at anything before."

"Yeah, but…" Firelight from inside the shop caught his eye. He studied the place, seeing a flicker inside as if someone had lit a match. Even though the apartment above the shop-turned-storage-room was rented out to a young Amish couple, no one but Luke or Matthew was supposed to go into the storage area—not that they ever locked it.

Matthew opened the car door. "Wait here."

She turned the car off. "But we're in the middle—"

"I know," Matthew interrupted her before getting out of the car and tiptoeing onto the porch. As he peered through the front window, disbelief ran through him.

Sarah?

She had a thin stick held up to the flame.

He tapped on the door, giving her a warning before he opened it. "Sarah?"

She jumped back, dropping the burning twig onto the floor. Matthew hurried over and stomped the tiny flames out. "What are you doing here?"

"I…I was looking…"

He grabbed her by the elbows. "Do you have any idea how easily these boxes and crates would catch on fire?"

She looked around and shook her head. "I…I didn't think… I'm sorry." Tears filled her eyes. "I…I'm sorry."

He released her and put the globe on the kerosene lamp. "Sarah, are ya not any better in all these months since Hannah left?"

She stomped her foot. "I'm fine! Everybody thinks everything is all about Hannah, even after all these months." She mimicked the last part of the sentence, mocking his words. "You got no proof, you know?"

"Proof?"

"That you and Hannah were only gone five minutes." She stretched her neck, like she was looking down on him.

He sighed. "I'm not going to try to set that event straight, Sarah."

"Why not?"

"Because if I do, it'll only cause trouble—too much of it—for you."

"So you think Hannah's the only one with enough gumption to handle trouble?"

"Do you want me to tell, Sarah?"

Sarah stared at him, looking both petrified and defiant—if that was possible. She grabbed the matches off the counter. "Did you know that I heard fire can erase things? As if they'd never happened." She struck a match. "Don't remember where I heard it though. Do you think that's true?"

"No. But what I do think is that it's time for you to give me the matches and go home."

He was part of Sarah's community, and that meant looking after each other, like being members of the same household, but tonight was for Elle, not Sarah. She blew on the match, making the flame disappear.

The front door opened. "Matthew?" Elle called.

He turned. "Come in, Elle. I found Sarah in here, and she was just leaving. Right, Sarah?" Holding out his hand for the matches, he waited until Sarah put them in his hand. "Don't play with matches, Sarah."

She ran out the door.

Elle frowned. "What was that all about?"

"I didn't take the time to find out." He moved to the back part of the shop and grabbed a box of hardware for the leads and harnesses.

Elle looked around the overcrowded shop. "You must be staying awfully busy to afford this many supplies."

"Beyond anything I thought possible." Matthew pushed against the door with his back and held it open for Elle.

"Will you miss me at all while I'm gone for the next year?"

Matthew let the door close behind her, and they walked to the car. "I didn't realize that issue was settled."

Elle gave a slight shrug and opened the trunk to her car.

Matthew set the box inside, feeling frustration mount. "Elle, is it a settled issue?"

With butterflies in her stomach, Hannah slid out of the driver's seat and locked her car, then crossed the parking lot of Alliance High School. It was the official test-taking site for her GED. Eight in the morning on a Saturday and a beautiful fall day at that. Not a cloud in the sky. She paused, looking at the life-size jet mounted on school property. It seemed sort of... What was that word she learned last week?

Chapter 21

Apropos.

That was it. It meant "befitting," and it was definitely apropos to view this aircraft as she entered the building. The day Paul had proposed she'd felt like she was soaring. She remembered thinking that wherever jets took people couldn't be as exciting as where her dreams were taking her.

Now she knew—dreams weren't what took people places. Circumstances were, followed by decisions and determination. Right now her circumstances required her to pass this GED test, or she'd not be able to get into the nursing program anytime soon.

She had to push through her days with the same determination as in her other, Plain life, just with more right to speak up and make her own decisions. She liked the part about making her own choices, mostly. At least, she thought she would eventually like it. If she could figure out what God really thought about education, television, movies, clothing styles, hair, makeup, and all the other fancy things that were part of the Englischer lifestyle.

She walked into the empty building, thinking it would have been easier to concentrate today if the test site was the same as the studying site. She went up the stairs to the second floor and located room 256. One glance said she was the first student to arrive because she was sure the man in the room was the examiner.

He looked up from the papers in his hand. "Ah, the first test taker has arrived. Just show me your ID, and then find a desk that suits you." He glanced at his watch. "We have four more, who should arrive within the next fifteen minutes, and then I'll give instructions and pass out the tests."

She showed him her driver's license and then took a seat, wondering if she'd pass the test. Around four this afternoon she'd be finished, and within two weeks she'd have the results. But tonight Martin would come by the cabin and want to know what she thought about the test; tonight Zabeth would have a cake to celebrate her taking the test, whether she made the grade or not.

The two of them were quite a pair, prodding and supporting. It was an odd family she'd landed in, but they'd taken her in as one of their own—even Faye had, in her semifunctional ways. Zabeth now had a short crop of coarse black hair, and although the damage to her heart was slowly taking its toll, she was still the core of this unit. Martin seemed to be the leader and organizer, Faye was clearly the rogue, and her children made this strange group of people feel like a real team.

Why was it that every family had a Faye? Or at least a perceived one. Hannah filled that role within the Lapp household, so she felt a kinship with Faye on some level.

Zabeth never wavered in her belief that Faye would find God and would change. Hannah was less certain, but her aunt's belief in people was totally refreshing. It wouldn't bother Zabeth if Hannah came home saying she had a new dream, as long as she was willing to pursue it, whatever *it* was. After growing up in a community where members were forbidden to do anything differently from the forefathers, she found that this life was as confusing as it was exhilarating. Zabeth said she'd get used to it and come to a place where freedom meant boldness to follow God, not fear of displeasing Him.

And Faye was always around to challenge Hannah at every turn, offering makeup, new styles of clothing, and nights out with other girls. None of which she had taken her up on. Not yet anyway.

"Hannah." A male voice spoke her name as he laid the test packet on her desk.

A nervous tingle ran through her. The others had arrived while she'd been daydreaming. Now it was time to see if she was as smart as Martin and Zabeth said she was.

~~∽~~

Mary tried to remain calm as the preaching part of the church service ended and each youth who intended to be baptized today rose from the benches. Six young people followed the bishop and deacon out of the Bylers' barn, while everyone else remained seated.

It was time.

In a few minutes the bishop and deacon would speak to her privately and ask if she was sure she was ready to take the vow. It was a serious matter, and they would look each person in the eye and ask if they were sure they were ready to take on the full responsibility of laying all worldliness aside and living in submission to the *Ordnung* and the church leaders.

Mary had no doubts—plenty of guilt, but absolutely no doubts. She'd take her vows. And she intended to keep everything in the *Ordnung* down to the least jot and tittle. But she'd keep her secret.

Her faith was in God, not in doctors who said she was healed. If she was healed, then why tell her she wasn't to conceive a child for several years? *Verhuddelt.* That's what those doctors were. Confused.

Within a few weeks she and Luke, along with every other engaged Amish couple across the States, would be published and could begin preparations for the wedding. She quietly waited her turn, hoping neither the bishop nor the deacon saw anything reflected in her eyes but a desire to be the best Amish woman and wife they'd ever known.

"Mary." The bishop motioned for her. She walked the hundred or so feet to the side yard and stood in front of the two men.

"You may raise your head and look at us, child."

Time seemed to trudge ever so slowly as she fought to lift her head.

The bishop's small eyes were targeted firmly on her. "Is something troubling you, Mary?"

She shook her head. "I have no doubts about joining the faith. I want to keep the ways of our people and trust God with all things."

He glanced to the deacon, who nodded his approval. "Very well then. You may return to the others who wait while we talk to a few more."

It wasn't long before the six youths were following the bishop and deacon back into the service. They kept their heads bowed, but she knew Grace, the bishop's wife, and Elizabeth, the deacon's wife, had moved to the front of the church to help their husbands with the ceremony. When Mary and the others sat on the bench, they bent over and kept their faces covered. Soon enough her back ached as they remained in that position while the service continued. She heard words being spoken over the people being baptized ahead of her and water spattering on the ground.

Was she wrong? Was she taking a solemn vow as she concealed a lie from everyone around her, or was she truly trusting God?

She felt Grace remove the pins from her prayer Kapp and slowly lift it from her head. The bishop's hands were now cupped over her head as the deacon poured water into them.

Oh, dear God, I pray this is a step of faith and not deceit.

Water poured down her face and neck, but it didn't carry the cleansing she'd expected. The bishop's wife replaced Mary's prayer Kapp before kissing her and welcoming her into the fold.

She never should have taken such a vow while hiding her lie from Luke.

With Dorcas moving way too slowly, Paul held the door as they entered the mall. He needed a wedding gift for Luke and Mary, so he'd requested Dorcas's help in finding a suitable present.

Surprisingly, he'd received an invitation, although if he went, it would cause turmoil among Mary's and Luke's families and even throughout their extended families who would come from other states for the wedding. Paul seemed to be really good at causing friction these days—even among his church leaders, among the families in his place of worship, and within his own family.

Maybe it was time he branched out and shared his "golden" touch.

Paul sighed, weary of how the conservative beliefs of his people worked to mold his life. The church leaders were still waiting for him to repent over the ball games.

"Any ideas?" Dorcas asked.

Paul shoved his hands in his pockets. "That's what you're here for. I could draw a blank on what to get Luke and Mary all by myself."

Dorcas grabbed his arm. "Slow down. I can't walk that fast."

He slowed. "We're walking at the pace of an old lady as it is. I've got to find something, get it wrapped, and…" For the first time he wondered, if he didn't go to the wedding, where would he take the gift? He only saw Luke on rare occasions. Since it was fall, and he'd begun school again, he wasn't in Owl's Perch very often.

Nonetheless, he'd received an invitation.

"Think I should go?"

"Go where?"

"To the wedding."

"Oh." Dorcas shrugged. "I don't know. Do you want to go?"

"That's a good question. Because Luke and Mary invited me, yes. For the reaction Luke and Mary might experience from relatives and friends because of me, no."

"Hmm. I would go."

"Why?"

"Because it'd give you some insight into what life would be like if you married into that family."

"If? Thanks, Dorcas." There was a store in front of him with all types of timepieces. "A clock would make a nice gift, wouldn't it?"

"I guess. You go look while I sit on that bench."

He frowned. "You that tired because of walking from the truck to here?"

"I just sort of ache all over." She reached for him.

"You weren't moving this slowly when we bought presents for A-Yom and shipped them off."

She shrugged. "I'm just not feeling good today. That's all."

He placed his hand under her forearm. "You want us to get a drink at the food court and rest there awhile?"

She sat on the bench and looked up at him, seemingly surprised by his offer. "I thought you were in a hurry."

"Sounds like it's time to slow down a bit." Paul took a seat beside her, deciding his tendency to use her to help him was self-centered. He hadn't been a friend. As long as she was helpful, he tolerated her.

That's just wrong, Waddell.

As if catching a glimpse of his life from the church leaders' perspective, he began to wonder if they were more right than he'd given them credit for. There were agreed-upon goals for the Plain society, and either you agreed with those goals, or you separated from the church.

He'd done neither.

"Dorcas." Paul rubbed the back of his neck. "I've been really headstrong and difficult, haven't I?"

Her green eyes fastened on him. "I figured it was your more-buried self coming out."

"What's that supposed to mean?"

She shrugged. "You never considered not being Plain, because the step from Old Order Amish to Plain Mennonite was as much as you'd dare ask of Hannah."

Paul leaned back, wondering if she was right.

A group of teenagers passed them, and he took note of how they dressed and behaved. It took about two seconds to see they were rebelling. Tattoos everywhere, multiple piercing with chains connected to half a dozen parts of their body, and ugly, two-word sayings hand painted on their filthy clothing.

Well, he hadn't taken rebellion that far. But the desire to map out his own set of beliefs and follow them had become a good-sized part of who he was. No wonder his church and parents were so displeased with him. He knew the aim of his people but constantly fought it. Sort of.

When he talked them into letting him get a degree in social work, he knew he was pushing the limits—studying subjects that gave his people cause for concern. The word *forbidden* was usually left to the Amish. His people would say the subjects were to be *avoided* or *approached with great caution*, but he'd pursued his dream anyway. Then there was his going to Senators' games—neither stepping away from his church nor yielding to their wishes. It was as if he wanted to remain Plain, but he wanted to mold it into something it wasn't, wanted to do it his own way.

Dorcas rubbed her wrist as if it hurt. "No one at the church thinks you'll come back under the preachers' and bishop's authority. They figure you'll leave."

He nodded. "I guess I'd think that too if I was watching my life from their perspective." He looked about the fancy mall. "Do you think Hannah is living Plain?"

She shrugged. "What I think is that you'll be a good counselor, Paul, no matter where you land—Plain or English. But I just can't believe you wouldn't use your education to help your own people. There are places that offer counseling for the Plain community. With your foundation and education, you could cast a good net for catching and helping our people."

Paul shifted, removing his arm from the back of the bench. "I guess it's time either to follow the church leadership and lay down the parts of my life that don't fit or to decide I'm not Plain after all."

"I can't imagine not being Plain. Not only because it's who I am—who we are—but because leaving would cause a permanent rift with my family and community."

"Hannah was going to leave her family."

"Yeah, but clearly she finds leaving those who love her pretty easy."

Paul wanted to argue, but the evidence was stacked against him.

avid stood on one end of the wagon and Matthew on the other as they placed another long wooden table in the bed of the cart. With Luke and Mary getting married tomorrow, he and a lot of others were working all day to set up for it. The Yoder place was buzzing, with thirty couples working together to cook a celebration meal for tomorrow. He wasn't part of the teams of couples who would provide the wedding meal. He couldn't help with that part without Elle being around.

The upside was that she was coming tomorrow. She couldn't get away on a Tuesday morning, so she'd miss the actual ceremony, but she'd be here in time for the meal, songs, and games that would last until midnight. Matthew would carry Luke and Mary from the Bylers' place, where the wedding ceremony would occur, to Mary's home, where the meal and the rest of the festivities would take place. After Elle's last visit, nearly four months ago, they could use an afternoon and evening of songs and games. It'd do them good. And all the fellowship and laughter would remind her of the best parts of being Amish.

Then maybe her letter writing would pick back up. She still wrote, but just short notes and not very often.

David brushed his hands together. "Have you heard that Sarah's been found wandering about at night by different folks in the community? I don't mean being with anybody, just by herself, out roaming around. Jacob's done washed his hands of her, says she's weird."

Matthew shifted the benches, trying to secure them. "I've heard. Don't make nothing of it. She's having a hard time, and the quiet evening air clears her mind. And if you ask me, Jacob's washed his hands of her because he's got eyes for Lizzy Miller."

"Yeah, well I heard that her Mamm's trying to cover for her, not lettin' anybody know just how bad she is, and trying to keep her close, so she don't get in any real trouble." David jumped down from the wagon. "Wanna place a bet what month Mary gives birth? I suspect she'll have a baby within a month of their anniversary."

Matthew stepped off the back end of the wagon. "We'll need more chairs. So go find some and a sense of respectability while you're at it." Betting on how long it'd take Luke to father a child. Good grief. Thinking it was one thing, but speaking it out loud? Where did his brother come up with such brazenness?

But David stayed put, watching the house. Matthew studied their home to see if his brother had his eye on something specific. They both had grown up in the farmhouse, as had their father and their grandfather before them.

Seeing nothing in particular, Matthew tightened the rope across the benches. "Is there somethin' on your mind, aside from foolishness?"

"Yeah."

"Well?"

David grabbed a piece of old straw from a corner of the wagon. "You won't get mad?"

"Depends. What'd you do?"

David stuck one end of the straw in his mouth. "Nothing, not yet."

Matthew moved to the last rope and checked it. "Meaning?"

"I haven't done nothing, but I got things stuck in my mind, and they won't leave me alone."

"You and everybody else. So what's weighing on you?"

"Didn't you think Hannah would've come home crying long before now?"

Matthew shrugged. He figured Hannah was finished crying and had no desire to ever return. She'd been treated poorly and given no options. It was a huge part of the reason Matthew stayed so patient with Elle. Demands were not the answer. Some freedom to make choices was.

David gestured toward the paved road. "Maybe it's not as hard to live *draus in da Welt* as we think."

Wondering if his brother had some romantic idea of life "out in the world," Matthew sat on the back end of the wagon. "You do plenty of living in the world right here. Besides, there's nothing out there worth chasing."

"Then why's Elle living there and not here? Something more than her dad is drawing her. And if Hannah can make it on her own, maybe it's worth a try."

"You're only thinking about this from a money standpoint. How about what you believe?"

"I believe there's other ways to live besides this. I don't want to give up riding a four-wheeler and playing my guitar in order to join the church."

Matthew wondered who'd helped David purchase these mysterious items and where they kept them hidden. "Those are temporal things. They aren't significant."

"Well, they must be pretty important, or they wouldn't cause such a stink."

Matthew didn't care to admit that a misshapen shirt collar could cause trouble under the right circumstances. "Our lines are drawn to keep us from going deeper and deeper into the ways of the world. The desire for more never stops if you don't stand against it."

David took off his hat and gestured toward the skies. "Doesn't it drive you crazy to think about living like this forever? No music, television, or cars is bad enough, but I'm sick of being too hot in the summer to sleep and busy year round hauling pews from one place to another. I'm tired of dressing in a way that makes me stick out whenever I go into town. Most days I feel like I'm gonna bust."

"It gets easier. You'll find someone special, and living by the faith will take on new meaning."

"That's what Kathryn said. She even showed me Bible verses about some stuff, but how can ways as old as ours take on new anything? I want to make my own decisions, and if I thought I could make it out there, I'd be gone already." David turned to face him. "Do you think Elle might help me get a job and find a place?"

Matthew's head ached, and he was sorry to find himself in the middle of this conversation. "If Mamm and Daed hear you talking like that, it'll make them despise Elle for sure. She's coming back to be baptized into the faith. She's not interested in helping anyone, including my family members, separate from the Old Ways."

Matthew went to the barn to fetch the horse, hoping David didn't end up breaking Mamm's heart over this.

As Hannah pulled out of Zabeth's driveway, she pushed the knob to the radio and turned the volume up. The stick shift was fun to drive and made her feel free and modern. The car was used and six years old, but it had everything: speed, locks, heat, air, a digital clock, music, and a plug so she could recharge her cell phone if she forgot to do it at home. Amazingly, she could travel home at midnight from the clinic and feel completely safe—although Zabeth said she was a bit compulsive about repeatedly hitting the lock button.

Thirty minutes ago she'd come home from North Lincoln on her way to the clinic to make sure Zabeth ate a few bites of the stew Hannah had put in the Crock-Pot before daylight. Zabeth was well enough to feed and care for herself, but she often skipped meals if Hannah didn't intervene. Faye tried to come by and stay with Zabeth a few hours on Hannah's busiest day, Tuesdays, but as often as not she didn't make it. When Faye couldn't check on her during the middle of the day, Hannah had to push the speed limit to be on time for the quilting group. After that she had her meeting at the rape crisis cen—

"Oh, peaches and bunnies." Hannah held the steering wheel with one hand and grabbed her purse with the other. Rustling through it, she located her cell phone. While glancing from road to phone, she scrolled to the clinic's number, punched the button, and waited. Removing the phone from her ear, she shifted gears. Maybe she needed one of those beetle earpieces like Faye's. She put the phone to her ear, waiting for someone to pick up or the answering machine to get it.

The machine picked up. When it beeped, she began. "Hey, guys, Hannah here. This message is for Dr. Lehman. I was working on Lydia Ebersole's file when you asked for it. I noticed you hadn't returned it last night, so if you could please put it on my desk, I'll finish up the reports before tomorrow. Thanks." She started to close the phone. "Oh, and Emily Fisher's file needs to be on my desk too. Also, remember that it's an afternoon of quilting, so although you'll see my car on the premises, don't forget I'm not available, and my phone will be turned off. Thanks. See you later."

By the time she pulled her car into the driveway of the clinic, there were four sets of horses and buggies already lined up in front of the quilting shop. Since it was a Tuesday during the Amish wedding season, she hadn't been sure anyone would be here this afternoon. But so far, at least three Amish women had made it for each quilting. Some Tuesdays she had up to twenty women and fourteen buggies.

She pushed the button to turn off her radio as she went past the clinic and up to the quilting house—seemed the respectful thing to do. The quilting house was an outbuilding to the clinic. It'd probably been a carriage barn in its day, which seemed befitting to Hannah. She and the Amish and Mennonite women met in this building rather than in a room inside the clinic. Each week when their sewing hours were over, they could leave everything set up. More important than that, the carriage house was very private. Anyone could say anything, and laughter could peal out as loudly as they wished and not be overheard by lurking husbands waiting on their wives to deliver. The room held secrets and tears and vibrated with laughter every session. It was the one place where Hannah's striving to fit into the Englischers' world stopped.

She got out of her car to see Nancy, one of the nurse midwives, motioning for her. So much for seeing the clinic workers later. Hannah shut the car door and walked toward the clinic. Taking care of Zabeth, working for Dr. Lehman, and studying for next month's entrance exam into nursing school all pulled on her constantly. But whatever was going on in her life, this November sparkled like diamonds compared to last November. With the exception of Zabeth's health, everything happening to her was good and freeing.

"I'm not here, Nancy. Remember?"

"Yeah, I know, but this will only take a minute. There's a woman from the courthouse on the phone, and she says she needs to speak with you, something about the Coblentz twins' birth certificates."

"She couldn't just leave a message?"

Nancy shrugged. "She balked, and I gave in when I saw your car pulling up the driveway. She's on line four."

"Okay, thanks." Hannah walked into the clinic and down the hallway.

Of course this new life had a ton of responsibilities and a controlled panic to it that she'd not yet grown accustomed to. Computers tended to crash at the worst possible moment. Babies were born while the office phones rang and e-mails piled into the in-box. There were always stacks of paperwork to fill out at the end of each day. And even more piles of textbooks, waiting for her to make time to open them throughout the day. Oddly, she wasn't very worried about the entrance exam. Confidence said she'd pass it; she'd passed everything so far.

Punching the fourth red button, she tucked the phone between her shoulder and ear, noticing the stack of written messages on her desk. "Hannah Lawson speaking."

After answering the clerk's question about the birth certificates, Hannah disconnected the call and read through the list of voice-mail phone numbers on her computer. She clicked on the number from Martin's office.

Phone girl, I bet you haven't checked your messages on your cell phone, and I wanted to be sure you knew what was up. It's a crazy week at work, so I can't be there for our tutoring session until late on Friday. If you need help before then, call me.

He was right; she hadn't checked her messages today and probably wouldn't until late tonight. She headed out the back door to the quilting shop. Since the building had no phones or electricity and was completely unadorned, it was a comfortable place for the Plain women to meet.

Leaving all her Englischer stuff in her car and office, Hannah went straight toward her haven, where, for just a few hours each week, juggling to keep up with the fancy life was not a part of her world. The soft light of the sun filtering through the windows, the muted voices of the women, and the lack of hurry put Tuesday afternoons high on her list of enjoyable times.

She walked inside and took her place at the table.

Sadie King, a soon-to-be-grandmother, slid the question box along with a quilt patch toward Hannah. "Glad you could make it."

The touch of sarcasm struck a chord with the other women, and they giggled softly.

"*Denke,*" Hannah replied before she opened the box, pulled out the first note, and read it:

Mary and Joseph never had sex while Mary was pregnant. Does that mean it's wrong while pregnant? And if not, is it safe for the baby?

Wondering if the woman who'd written the question was in the room or if the question had been put into the box earlier in the week by someone who wasn't here today, Hannah set the paper to the side and grabbed a needle and thread.

That was one of the nice things about being here: they didn't expect an immediate answer, just an accurate one. Although she was more comfortable answering the medical question than the moral ones, the mixture of the two was the norm, and she was glad the women trusted her enough to ask. Whether they agreed with her answers or not, she didn't know.

She drew a deep breath, enjoying the aroma of the fairly new rough-hewn planking some of the husbands had installed over the dirt floor. The potbellied stove gave off the perfect amount of heat, making the place feel more like a kitchen than a slightly remodeled outbuilding. After the men installed the floor and wood stove, the women helped her clean the place from top to bottom and add some shelving. It was a perfect place to counsel young brides-to-be, women entering menopause, and those who needed medical advice but didn't want to ask Dr. Lehman. And odd as it seemed, it was here that Hannah fit in best.

"Mary was to conceive and give birth as a virgin, so…"

~~♒~~

The midnight November air was nippy as Matthew walked from the Yoders' barn toward the road. Voices and laughter echoed from the barn as the games continued. The antics of his friends were amusing, but Elle had never shown up. He knew Elle was safe somewhere inside her Englischer life. She wasn't here because something came up or she forgot or…

He had a catalog of emotions banked. Fear was the first one—fear of what was happening to them. He did not want to lose her. Sure they had things to work through. Every couple did.

The barn doors swung open wide as friends of Luke and Mary cheered. They strolled out, Luke laughing and Mary blushing visibly even in the dark night. Mary's hand was clasped in Luke's as they headed for Mammi Annie's house. It would be their honeymoon place. That way they'd be right here when it came time to finish cleaning everything tomorrow. They were going to live with Mammi Annie and keep renting the apartment to the Millers. It made the most sense. Mammi Annie's was close enough for Luke to walk to work and go home for lunch, much like he'd been doing for the past nine months.

"Matthew?" Luke called.

Matthew jogged over to him. "Hey."

"What are you doing wandering around out here?"

Matthew ignored the question and chose to tease. "I'll expect to see you bright and early tomorrow for work, right?"

Luke pushed against his shoulder. "You can expect it all you want. I ain't coming in until Friday."

Matthew laughed. "Since you'll not be shaving that huge, ugly face of yours anymore after tonight, you should have plenty of extra time for work. Keep him straight, Mary. Don't let him get all lazy on us now that he's king of something besides a shop attic with a bed."

Luke put his arm around her shoulders and pulled her close. "Mary has enough integrity to keep us both straight."

Mary's smile disappeared.

Luke squeezed her shoulders. "Tell him, Mary."

A look of discomfort crossed her face before she smiled at him. Matthew figured she was having a bit of prehoneymoon jitters.

"Ya," she whispered.

"Well, good night." Luke waved and directed Mary toward Mammi Annie's place. "You are going to keep watch on the place and make sure no one pulls any pranks, ya?"

"Absolutely." Matthew nodded before he shook his head. "Not." The three of them laughed. "If you want no pranks pulled, be vigilant yourself."

Luke opened the door for Mary, muttering about the difficulties of having Matthew Esh as a partner.

The camaraderie between Luke and Mary made him miss his girl even more, and he wondered when his and Elle's friends would get to prank their wedding night.

annah tapped her pen on the form in front of her. It was an application for a loan for nursing school. The entrance exam wasn't until next week, but she needed to make sure she had funding before she took the exam. If she borrowed money, she'd probably be the first in her family for hundreds of years back. In this case the idea of being the first at something wasn't consoling.

But that was only part of what was bothering her—a large portion, to be sure. The real snag, however, seemed to be that if she took this step, she was locking her life into a definite path for the next two years.

Two years?

Zabeth crossed the room one slow thump at a time. Her frame had a little more weight on it than when Hannah had arrived nine months ago, but the heart condition caused a lot of swelling as her body fought for oxygen. She eased into the kitchen chair across from Hannah and set her cane to the side. "You've been in that chair for nearly two hours, Hannah-girl, and you're not one little dot further than you were before you sat down, are you?"

Rolling the pen between her hands, Hannah sighed. "I…I'm not sure about taking out a loan."

Zabeth folded her arms on the table. "We have other sources. I still have some money put back. You're more than welcome to all I got. Vince, Faye and Martin's dad, would give or loan money gladly, and he'd not miss it any more than dropping a penny on the ground. Martin doesn't have money like his dad, but he could pass you the ten thousand you need without it making much difference to him."

Hannah thought about Zabeth's offer, but it just affirmed that the loan wasn't what was bothering her. So what was the problem?

"Hannah-girl?"

Hannah stared at the forms. "Hmm?"

"What ails you?"

"Luke and Mary's wedding was today. I read about it in *The Budget* a few weeks back."

"I didn't realize you were reading the Amish-Mennonite newspaper."

Hannah shrugged. "Dr. Lehman subscribes to it, and I..."

Zabeth reached across the table and placed her hands over Hannah's. "It hurts to miss the events of loved ones. I know." Zabeth's swollen and slightly blue fingertips rubbed Hannah's hand. "Is that all that's bothering you?"

She brushed Zabeth's hands before pulling away. "Remember me telling you about Paul?"

"Yes."

She pushed the papers away from her. "While I was at a hotel the night before my trip here, I called his apartment. Some girl answered and promised she'd give him the message and phone number. I was in that hotel all night and half the next day, waiting for him to call me back." She tapped the end of the pen on the table, slid her fingers down it, and flipped it over.

"And now you're not sure he got the message."

"I shouldn't care. I know that. He deserted me, no questions asked. He took all the money from the bank. He..." Hannah sighed. "Oh, I don't know."

"I do." Zabeth slid the cell phone from its spot on the kitchen table toward Hannah. "You should call him. Be sure he got the message. See if he had a reason you weren't aware of for moving your money from that account. Find out if what you had was real or if you'd do better to build a life here."

"But you need me."

"Oh, Hannah-girl. I love you, but Vince Palmer would hire round-the-clock nurses if I asked. I want you here. But I don't need you. And now that we know each other, you could come back to visit anytime."

Although her words sounded nice, Hannah doubted if Zabeth had ever directly asked for anything from Vince, Faye, or Martin. Still, she couldn't see arranging her life to be fastened to payments and schooling for the next two years without making sure how Paul felt.

"He's always at his grandmother's the day before Thanksgiving, helping her get packed to go to his parents' place in Maryland."

Zabeth brushed her unruly, curly locks of black hair away from her face. "That's just next week."

"What if he really doesn't want anything to do with me?"

"Then you're no worse off. You can't wonder the rest of your life if you left too soon. I knew I hadn't. Remember, I told you I stayed for a long time even after being shunned. I knew for sure when I left everyone behind, Hannah. Do you?"

"I'm pretty sure."

"But not positive."

"I don't know if I can stand being rejected by Paul a third time."

"Third?"

"The night he left, when he never returned my call, and now this."

"I thought you were ready to move on without ever looking back, and I quote, 'to the likes of Paul Waddell again.'"

"I was... I mean, I am..." Hannah paused, unable to understand the multitude of emotions assaulting her. Paul had betrayed her, yet here she sat, longing for life to be different. Still longing for him.

Zabeth gave an understanding nod. "You'll find he doesn't have the power to hurt you as badly this time. It's the way things work with loved ones. The question is, who are you, Hannah Lapp Lawson? A young woman too afraid to find out the truth? Or a young woman who'd rather suffer the hurt and be sure of her path?"

Hannah laid the pen on the forms and set them to the side. "There's a lyric in one of the songs you sing with the band. It says when we wind up lost and alone, that's when we find ourselves...or something like that."

"Close enough for now. And I think that's true. Bumps and hard places make us both find and face ourselves."

She knew she'd rather suffer humiliation and hurt than hide from her destiny. And she had eight days to find the courage and the right words.

The sun was rising as Matthew rinsed the razor under hot water and stared at himself in the mirror while shaving. Luke would be shaving only part of his face today—his mustache area and his high cheeks, that's all. He'd grow the beard that told all the world he was married. Aching to be in that position, Matthew wondered about his own future.

Through the closed window, he heard a car horn toot. He lifted the green shade and peered out.

Elle.

He wiped the shaving cream off his face, pulled his suspenders on, and finished buttoning his shirt. When he came out of the bathroom, his Daed was putting on his housecoat as he came out of the bedroom.

"It's Elle, Daed."

His Mamm eased around his father, dressed and weaving a straight pin into her hair and Kapp. Concern showed in her eyes in spite of the motherly smile on her face. "I'll have breakfast ready in twenty minutes if you want to invite her to stay."

Grabbing his coat off the rack, he answered, "We'll see." He slid it on and buttoned it as he went down the steps and out the front door.

His first glimpse of Elle was not reassuring. She had on blue jeans and a red coat.

She came toward him. "I'm sorry, Matthew. You gotta believe me. I intended to be here."

"What happened?"

She placed her palms over the breast of his coat. "Don't be mad, please?" She tilted her head, half flirting and half pleading.

"I'll ask again, what happened?"

She played with the button on his jacket. "See, this fantastic opportunity to assist at a photo shoot came in. And I thought I'd be done in time to get here by midafternoon."

"You said you'd be here by noon."

"I know, but…" She pulled her coat tighter around her. "Can we talk in your shop?"

"Sure." He signaled toward the shop, and she turned to walk with him.

They took several steps before she stopped in midstep. "Wow, Matthew. We never made it by here the last time I was home. Look at the additions to your shop. They're amazing."

"We created each shop like a separate building, but they all have either a doorway or covered walkway into the old shop. More like a minicomplex."

She laughed. "A minicomplex? That's a bit too fancy for the Plain life, isn't it?" She grabbed his hand and ran toward the closest building. "Come tell me all about them."

Matthew allowed her the change of topic and showed her each shop and the stacks of orders that kept coming in.

She ran her hand along a row of shelves filled with handmade buggy parts for all the fancy carriages the Englischers were ordering. "Sometimes when you're talking, it's like you're not the same guy who fell off the roof of the schoolhouse the day we met."

Matthew propped against the workbench. "Nor do you look like the Amish teacher I met."

She glanced at her clothing. "I know." She moved in closer. "I hate that I missed yesterday. I'd looked forward to it for weeks. It's my fault. I thought I could squeeze everything in. I drove to Pleasantville, New York, for a photo shoot."

"You drove to New York? How long did that take?"

"About four hours. I assisted at a formal wedding and didn't finish until too late to get here."

Matthew wished he knew what to think, wished he could see into their future and know if he was waiting for her to return or if he was playing the fool. He hoped for the first one, but he was beginning to think the second one was laying a trap for him.

Elle walked to him and stood just inches away. "I know you're not pleased with much of anything about us right now." She looked into his eyes. "But try to see this from my point of view. You get to do this business for the rest of your life, but once I become a wife and mother, stretching my wings is over, Matthew. I look forward to that time—I do. But I need you to understand that you're learning new things and using all your passion to pursue what you want without limits. It's not like that for women, Amish or Eng-lischer. I've found something I can hold in my heart and know for the rest of my life I was really good at it. And I'm hoping you're the kind of man who can understand my needs."

"It makes little sense that your father asked for six months, and ya offer to give him a year and a half."

"He's changing, Matthew. His heart is becoming more tender toward you and me as I stay longer."

"Sid is gettin' just what he wanted to begin with, so of course he's becoming more pleasant. Ignoring that, what's happening with us is because of your choices. You're the one who picked going to photography school. You're the one staying so busy that your letters are just plain-out sparse."

"Yeah, okay, but look at it this way. I missed this year's instruction be-cause my dad wanted time with me. There isn't one next year, so our plans have to follow the schedule laid out by the community. All that's different is I'm not living here while the time passes. That's all." Her warm hands sur-rounded his face. "Wait for me, Matthew. Give me my time now, and I'll give you the rest of my life." She placed her lips over his.

Every frustration melted, and Matthew wrapped his arms around her, making up for every kiss he'd missed while she'd been gone. Slowly he pulled away. "I'll wait." He sighed. "But you knew that before you arrived, didn't you?"

Her eyes clouded with tears. "I hoped. You won't regret it. I'll make it up to you…if we have to have eight children."

Matthew laughed. "Girls or boys?"

"Yes." She gave him a quick kiss. "How was the wedding?"

"Luke and Mary both glowed. I bet their Christmas present to each other next year is their firstborn child."

"Well, we can't match that, not by next Christmas anyway."

Matthew reached behind her and tugged her ponytail. "I guess I can understand your need to do a few things before the childbearing begins. Just visit more often."

"That's not a good idea, and you know it. Your family is almost as tolerant as the Zooks, but I'll not traipse in and out and tax your parents' tolerance before I join the family."

Matthew didn't like it, but he knew she was right. Because of her heritage, they'd accept her as an Englischer friend or as an Amish prospective wife, but she couldn't maintain regular visits while living in both worlds at the same time.

"Ya, I guess you better save that taxing my parents' thing until after we're a couple. Just don't take too long out there among the Englischers, okay?"

"I won't. I'll be living here by next fall. Promise."

That seemed so far away. "Mamm invited you to breakfast."

"I picked up drive-through on the way here." She glanced at her watch. "I'm going to be late opening Dad's store if I don't skedaddle." She grabbed his hand. "Walk me to my car."

Drive-through? Matthew walked with her, trying to shake off his discomfort at the gaping differences that separated them. All he could do was hope the canyon didn't grow so wide a bridge couldn't be built.

~~∽~~

Pacing the length of her now-desolate garden, Hannah pressed the numbers on her cell to call Gram, stared at the digits written across the screen, and closed the phone without hitting the green icon. Her palms were sweaty, even with the November air so chilly she had on her woolen shawl. She drew a deep breath and redialed it. Again she closed the phone.

Tired of the game, she punched the numbers one last time…she hoped. A nervous tingle ran through her as she hit the connect button. Gram's phone rang.

Once.

Twice.

Three times.

"Hello," a young female voice answered.

Was it the same one who had picked up at Paul's apartment? She didn't know, but she wasn't going to identify herself this time.

"Hi. I'd like to speak to Paul, please."

The girl paused before asking, "Hannah?"

"Yes."

"Have…you reached him…before now?" The stranger's voice quivered.

Hannah didn't think it was any of this woman's business, but she answered, "No."

"Please don't do this. He's just now out of the straits with our church leaders. His mother has finally stopped crying herself to sleep over him caring for…" She inhaled. "He's repented for being stubborn in his own ways and has agreed to stick to the ways of his people. Please, just let *us* alone."

The way she said *us,* Hannah knew there was more to her being at Gram's the day before Thanksgiving than just coincidence. It had been her and Paul's day, one of fun and laughter after being separated from late August until Thanksgiving every year.

"Are you and he…"

"It's what I want, what I've always wanted, and his family is completely behind this union, as is our whole community."

Union?

"Please." The girl sobbed. "He didn't return your call the first time. He's made his choice. It has taken time, but he's happy and content. To hear from you now will only cause more turmoil, but his decision will be the same. He's had to make some changes to line up with our beliefs, but he's glad for the changes—all of them."

Hannah gazed at the cabin, smoke coming out of the chimney, pre-Thanksgiving foods in the oven, and a life that was begging to be chosen. It held love and freedom, but why was it so hard to let go of what was clearly dead and fully embrace what lay before her? It was foolishness. That's what it was. She'd been idealistic beyond reason where Paul was concerned, hoping for a life that was not hers. Even if he'd once shared that dream, it obviously had died an easy death for him.

The girl lowered her voice. "Can't you see? You've left your family. You've got nothing else to lose, but he'll have to break every relationship to be with you."

Hannah felt warm tears slide down her cold cheeks. "Yeah, okay." She disconnected the call.

"Hey, phone girl," Martin called to her.

She was in no shape to turn around. The back screen door slammed shut, and each footfall caused leaves to crunch. The barren trees swayed in the wind. Zabeth had told her he was closing his office today at lunch, but she hadn't realized that meant he was coming by here.

"If a man is alone in the garden and speaks, and there is no woman to hear him," Martin asked, "is he still wrong?" He touched her shoulder. "Hello?"

She turned to face him, and his smile disappeared. "Not now, okay?" She looked at the phone in her hand before sliding it under her shawl and into her dress pocket.

"Yeah, sure. But since Zabeth hasn't felt like getting out much the last few weeks, I've invited the gang to set up the band here tonight. I thought I'd forewarn you."

"For when?"

Martin pushed the sleeve of his leather jacket off his wrist and glanced at his watch. "Um…ten minutes ago not enough notice?"

She laughed and wiped her cheeks.

Martin gave a half smile, watching her intently. "With those hedges, a whole fleet could arrive out front and you'd never know from back here. I brought plenty of snacks, and I knew the place would be spotless, but I guess I didn't figure on everything."

She cleared her throat, demanding the tears to stay at bay. "Me either."

"Anything I can do?"

She looked out over the barren fields, dreading another winter. It felt like just yesterday that she'd survived her first winter's night here in Ohio. "I hate cold weather. I didn't used to."

"The propane tank is full, and there's nearly a cord of wood in the shed. You can burn both at the same time, and if you need more before winter's out, I know who to call."

His sincere concern eased her anxiety. Whenever he tutored her, they always skimmed general topics and shared a dozen laughs, but the need to share her hidden side nudged her. She knew the relationship wasn't one-sided. They tag teamed certain areas of life, like covering Zabeth's health needs, handling Faye, and even managing Kevin and Lissa. On more than one occasion, his *Civil Engineering Reference Manual* in hand, Hannah quizzed him for the professional exam he'd take in two years. She knew she could share her insecurities with Zabeth, and she had begun to feel she could share them with Martin too.

"A few days ago, while filling out forms at the clinic, I signed my name wrong."

Martin's brows knit. "Huh? I can't say I've ever had that problem."

Hannah pulled her Amish cloak tighter. It was all she had in the way of a winter coat. "That's because you've always had the same name."

"And you haven't?"

She shook her head.

Martin motioned to the bench, and they began walking toward it. "Why did you change your name?"

She took a seat. "I thought I was doing it so my family couldn't find me, so my community couldn't write to me and…say things I didn't want to hear."

Martin sat beside her. "What was the real reason?"

"Paul Waddell," she whispered.

"Oh. I didn't realize you… So who's Paul?"

She closed her eyes and took several deep breaths. "He was my fiancé, and I loved him so much that I was willing to separate myself from my family."

"Because?"

"He wasn't Old Order Amish. By the time things ended between us, I'd made enemies of my whole community, and when I landed here, I knew if I kept my last name, I'd keep hoping Paul would come looking for me." She sighed.

Martin laid his arm along the back of the bench. "Really, you changed your last name so you could begin a new life. Is that it?"

She nodded. "I tried to call him today…for reasons that make no sense."

"And it didn't go well."

"Times a hundred." She watched a flock of starlings circle. "There's more to the story, a lot more, but I don't want to talk about it."

He put his arm around her shoulders. "Whenever you do, call me. See, I'm no expert at love, but I bet, with a little time and a few dates here and there, in a few years you'll forget what's-his-name."

"You really think so?"

"Absolutely. The saying is that there are lots of fish in the sea. And I can tell you that's very true. Just find a new fish. And then one day you'll see him for what he was and be grateful you didn't marry the idiot."

She laughed. "I look forward to being glad he's not in my life."

"Yep. And in the meantime, I brought an extra bag of red seedless grapes for the youngest member of the band."

"The youngest member…" She dropped the sentence, realizing she'd been adopted or hoodwinked or something. "I'd like a few minutes, okay?"

"Absolutely." He stood. "The afternoon will be fun. Guaranteed to lessen the disappointment of"—he pointed at her dress pocket that held her phone—"that."

He went inside to join his friends and her aunt, leaving her alone with the barren trees and cold winds. But it didn't take her long to realize where she'd gone wrong. She'd set her mind on a new life and then looked back. That's not where her future was. It was time she took out the loan and prepared to go to nursing school. And just as God had brought her to a better place this Thanksgiving than last, she was sure next year would be even better.

"This life, God. I choose this one."

A blast of off-key music sounded, followed by boisterous laughter. She was sure they'd hit those sour notes on purpose.

She crossed the yard and went inside. Zabeth and about half the band turned in her direction. Some clapped that she'd finally arrived. Others made weird noises with their instruments.

Behind the keyboard, Martin smiled. Her cheeks warmed. He often reminded her of those men she'd seen on advertisement posters in the mall:

thick, dark hair; beautiful green eyes; and a grin that could melt the winter snow.

She returned the smile before peeling off her cape and taking a seat next to Zabeth. "Hey, I'd love to hear that song 'Inside Your Love.'"

"Sure thing." Martin thumbed through his songbook and grabbed the sheet music. He held it out to Hannah. "You have to help us sing it."

Perched behind the electronic drums, Greg held the microphone toward her.

Zabeth nudged her. "Take it."

"Adopted or hoodwinked," Hannah mumbled as she rose to her feet.

Martin pulled his mike close and spoke in a raspy, dramatic voice. "Hannah's life lay before her like a desert, nothing but school, work, and pushy musicians controlling her for years to come." He played the death march on the keyboard.

Greg followed it with the drum roll they always played at the end of a joke. Zabeth broke into laughter. Hannah interrupted the clashing music, laughter, and sarcastic remarks by starting to sing a praise song Martin wrote after he'd started going to church again: "You and You alone are my Alpha and my Omega…"

Martin immediately started playing the tune and joined her in singing. "My life is hidden in You. All I hope to be is kept safe inside Your love…"

Within a few lines, each member had found his spot and joined in playing and singing.

"Inside You we find our path."

With one hand on the steering wheel while waiting at a red light, Hannah fumbled through her purse, trying to find her sunglasses. She felt the frames just as the light turned green and quickly put them on. Her eyes were light sensitive when driving. Martin said it was because she was getting old. She teased back that, if she was old, what did that make him? Charming and intelligent, was his answer, but for her birthday he bought her a pair of sunglasses.

She merged onto the main road with ease as Kevin and Lissa prattled excitedly about what games they'd play with their Amish friends while the women quilted.

Kevin kicked the back of her seat. "Hannah, will Noah be here today?"

"I don't know. I hope so."

Lissa clapped her hands. "And Mandy too?"

"If Noah is there, his sister will be there too." She glanced at the rearview mirror before changing lanes. At seven years old, Noah spoke some English. Unfortunately for Lissa, Mandy didn't. But Noah enjoyed interpreting for the two of them. Hannah found the warm acceptance of her—and now the Palmer children—by the Amish women quite surprising. Maybe this relationship worked because she came to them as an extension of an Englischer doctor who operated an Amish birthing clinic. She didn't know, but whatever the reason, she found it refreshing.

Martin's iPod lay on the seat next to her. He'd dropped it off at Zabeth's last night while she was at school and had left a message that there was a list of songs he wanted her to hear, but she hadn't had time. Back in November, after her last attempt to reach Paul, she'd begun opening up to Martin, and she wasn't disappointed. Even though he had a tendency to be blunt and sarcastic sometimes, he'd turned out to be a good friend. And for a guy, he seemed pretty much in tune with life. He was definitely right about her getting over Paul. Of late, more days than not, Hannah didn't even think about him. And when she did, it no longer shot pain through her but only caused a dull ache.

She'd turned nineteen two months ago, and before going out to eat with Zabeth and Martin for her birthday, she had walked into the field by herself and told Paul good-bye. He'd told her that through his actions, but this time she told him. At first she'd felt silly talking out loud as if he could actually hear her. But later, when she sat at a candlelit table in a fine restaurant with Zabeth and Martin, discussing her schooling and career possibilities, the euphoric feeling of taking flight once again stirred within her. She knew she was free of what might have been with Paul and had chosen to look straight into the future at what could be. Not only was she hopeful about all of life, but prayer, along with the Tuesday-night meetings at the counseling center, had brought her acceptance without shame concerning the rape.

Acceptance without shame. That seemed to be the greatest sense of peace she'd received this past year. God had cultivated it; she enjoyed it. The beauty she felt each time she prayed told her He wasn't finished yet.

As she pulled into the driveway of the clinic, Kevin unfastened his seat belt. "There's no one at clinic."

Hannah got out of the car and opened the door beside Lissa. "It happens sometimes." She heard a cat meow as she unbuckled Lissa and lifted her from her seat. It had to be Snickers, a stray cat the midwives had adopted. If Snickers knew what was good for her, she'd hide before the children found her. "The clinic is open for appointments every Monday. After that the doctor and midwives come in when they're called."

Kevin shut his door. "Now how's an Amish person who has no phone gonna call if no one's here?"

Hannah chuckled. He was bright for a five-and-a-half-year-old. She thought he should be in kindergarten, but school attendance wasn't mandatory before age six, and, along with a great many other inconsistencies in her children's lives, Faye said she wasn't sending him. "Some Amish have phones, just not inside their homes. But the midwife keeps a cell phone with her, and she gives the patient a cell phone to use. Make sense?"

"Yeah." He pointed to the end of the lane.

Three Amish buggies were pulling in, one behind the other.

"I see Noah!" Kevin reached into his pocket and pulled out two identical plastic horses. "One for me and one for my friend."

Hannah rubbed the top of his head. "He'll like that."

Lissa brushed her hair back from her face. "You gonna pin my hair up like Mandy's?"

"Sure. I have the stuff for it right here in my dress pocket." Hannah ran her fingers through Lissa's hair and twisted it.

Another round of pitiful meows came from somewhere, and Kevin started searching under the car for the animal.

"It's not there, Kevin, but I appreciate your confidence in my driving skills."

Without noticing her humor, he looked around the yard. "Where do you think it is?"

Before the buggies came to a complete halt, Noah jumped down. "Kevin, you're here."

Hannah opened the screen door and held it, greeting each of the seven women as she entered the building. The children set out to find the cat.

Sadie, looking every bit the grandmother, stopped in front of Hannah with a plate of cookies in hand. "I think eating while working on a quilt is just asking for stains, but my daughter said to bring these to you. Said you helped deliver her baby."

"I only helped because it meant you'd bring me cookies." Hannah took one off the plate.

Several children ran into the shop, knocking into Sadie while yelling something about the cat. Hannah steadied Sadie with one hand and grabbed the plate of cookies with the other.

Sadie's hands instantly clasped Hannah's shoulders. "Forget the cookies, girl. They almost plowed me under."

"Yeah, but I saved the important part."

The women enjoyed a hearty laugh. Hannah gave each child a cookie and shooed them outside.

"Clearly, Hannah thinks my cookies are the answer to everything. Does anyone even know what the children were carrying on about?"

"They are happy and outside. Does anybody care?" Lois mumbled around a bite of cookie.

Chatter went in a dozen directions as they settled down to work on their latest quilt, a log cabin star quilt.

Sadie placed her hand over Hannah's. "My Katy was scared when she was in hard labor but not dilating. She said you stayed, assuring her she was fine, for eighteen hours straight. Thank you."

Hannah nodded and squeezed Sadie's hand.

Kevin and Noah ran inside, one prattling in English and one in Pennsylvania Dutch. Neither was understandable.

Noah's mother, Lois, jabbed a needle into the quilt. "Boys, what is going on with you today?"

"The cat's stuck way up in a tree."

Lois's eyes grew wide. "Still?"

"Yes." The boys nodded.

"What do you mean 'still'?" Verna asked.

"I came by here yesterday to leave a box of material, and it was way up in a tree. I figured it'd climb down before now."

Kevin grabbed Hannah's hand. "Come on."

The women hurried out the door and soon were gathered around the trunk of the medium-sized tree. "It must be twenty-five feet up that tree," Verna said.

Lois squinted. "The poor thing has climbed even higher since yesterday."

"Think just looking at it will make it come down?" Sadie nudged Nora with her elbow.

"We could try bribing it with a cookie," Fannie suggested. "It would work for Hannah."

The women giggled, but the poor cat clung to the tree, meowing itself hoarse.

"Think the fire department would come rescue it?" Nora asked.

Hannah shook her head. "There was a write-up in the paper recently, explaining that they stopped rescuing cats long ago."

"So what are we going to do?" Fannie asked.

Hannah rolled her eyes. "Climb a stupid tree. But I can't climb back down while holding on to that cat. It'll scratch me to pieces, and we'll both fall."

Sadie wiped her hands on her apron. "You can drop the cat, and we'll stretch something out to catch it."

"Oh, that's a good idea. Let's get a sheet from the clinic. And I have a set of scrubs in my car that I can put on."

"Scrubs?" Katy asked. "You gonna clean the cat while you're there?"

"It's my nurse's uniform, and it has pants. No one can climb a tree in a dress."

Sadie propped her hands on her hips. "Yes, we know. It's the reason Amish women agreed to wear only dresses hundreds of years ago. Our foremothers banded together and decided if we never wanted to climb up after a cat, we'd better make a dress code."

Lois motioned toward Hannah. "But this is the first time their reasoning has ever come in handy."

The women all nodded in agreement before bursting into laughter. The cat startled at the noise and climbed even higher into the tree.

"You're all a lot of help."

"Denke," the group chorused.

"I'll change. You get the sheet." She gave Sadie a key to the clinic.

Within minutes, the women were showing the children how to hold the sheet for the cat to land in. Hannah climbed higher and higher.

"Hey, Hannah?" Sadie called. "If the fire department doesn't rescue cats, does it rescue girls who go after cats?"

The women's personalities often reminded Hannah of those she'd known in Owl's Perch. Even when Hannah felt overwhelmed in this Englischer world, these ladies—and Zabeth—were steady reminders of her heritage.

She was finally high enough to grab the cat by the scruff of the neck. It writhed and whined, trying to get its nails into her arm. She held it over the sheet. "You ready?"

"Ya."

She let go of the cat. The children looked up at the screeching fur ball as it hurtled toward them. They dropped their portion of the sheet and took off running. The women laughed so hard they could barely stay standing as the cat hit the sheet and darted toward the woods. The children chased after it, screaming for Snickers to come back.

Hannah held on to the tree, her arms scraped, her scrubs dirty, and her body shaking all over as she tried to control her laughter so she wouldn't fall the twenty feet to the ground—all for a stupid cat.

The upside was that the next time she saw Martin, she'd have an amusing story to share. She could hear him laughing already.

Kneeling beside her marriage bed, Mary ran her hand over her flat stomach, whispering words of repentance for the thousandth time. The delay in conceiving should have been a relief to her, but it only reminded her that she'd sinned. Last year she'd bowed before God, receiving the baptism of faith, while hiding a secret. Her first-year anniversary would soon be upon her, and her shame weighed heavy.

A sob escaped her. She alone knew why she wasn't yet with child. No one asked any questions, but every other couple in her community who had married during last year's wedding season either had a babe or would deliver one before the winter's end. This year's wedding season had begun, and she wondered if she'd have to endure seeing these new brides hold a baby in their arms before she did. Right now she wished the wedding season only happened every other year, just like the Amish instruction period did. Then at least there wouldn't be a whole group of new brides coming up pregnant when she wasn't.

Would she not conceive until she told her husband the truth?

In deciding to put matters in God's hands, not once had she considered that she might not get pregnant. Her thoughts had fully centered on trusting Him to help her survive childbirth; that's where the doctor said the problems could come, wasn't it?

Then she should be grateful she didn't have to face that concern. But she wasn't.

Luke cleared his throat, startling her. She opened her eyes to see him in the doorway of the bedroom. He was so handsome in his best Sunday clothes, dressed for the wedding they'd attend today.

Mary rose to her feet, feeling her cheeks burn.

He fidgeted with the black winter hat in his hand. "The buggy's hitched. You about ready?"

She fought tears. "Ya."

With Luke's eyes glued to her, she slid her Sunday apron over her dress and began pinning it into place.

Luke stepped toward her. "We'll have a baby when it's time, Mary." He ran his hands through his dark hair. "If you could just accept that this is God's hand of protection."

Unable to look him in the eye, Mary nodded.

His protection?

What would her husband think if he knew her empty womb was God's hand of judgment—one she might not ever get free of even if she told Luke, her Daed, and the church leaders the truth? How would Luke feel when he learned she hadn't trusted him to keep his vow to marry her, that she'd withheld information so he would marry her? She'd taken her instruction and baptism with a cloud of deceit hovering around her—a fog of self-deception mostly. Tricking herself into thinking she was trusting God for her life when all she was doing was using that *trusting God* phrase to hide her selfish motives. But somewhere inside her she'd known what she really thought...or else she would have told Luke everything and let him have a say as her future head. She'd removed that right from him, not because she trusted God, but because she was spoiled.

Luke stood directly in front of her. "Mary."

The gentleness of his voice washed over her. This was the voice he used when the doors were shut at night and the pleasure of being married lingered. Her resolve broke, and tears welled in her eyes. He drew her close and held her before he kissed her long and deep. Warmth and hope rose in her as his lips moved across her face and he nibbled down her neck.

"I'm sorry." She whispered the words, wishing she could tell him what all she was sorry for.

Luke kissed the top of her head and wrapped his arms around her. "Next week it will only be a year, Mary. Just one year. Try not to take this so hard."

She nodded and pulled away from him. Grabbing the wedding gift off the dresser, she decided it'd be best if she changed the subject. She hadn't meant for Luke to see her kneeling by the bed, brooding under her load of guilt and fear.

Passing the gift to Luke, she straightened her dress. "Will Elle be there today?"

Luke put his hat on. "Last Matthew heard she was still out west, assisting in a photo shoot for some calendar company."

Mary slid into her winter cloak. "I fear she will end up hurting him."

"She broke her word about moving back home this fall, saying she'd be here before instruction time arrived. I can hardly believe it, but Matthew didn't end things with her over it. He doesn't like it, but it seems she's gallivanting all over the U.S. working with some photographer." Luke's words were gruff and had no give to them. "She's already broke his heart, if you ask me. The only thing missing is that she's not told Matthew yet." He took a step back. "She's strung him along so she could have her way, an Englischer life and an Amish man on the hook."

Mary's heart skipped a beat as guilt pressed in on her. She placed her hand on Luke's chest. "Maybe she hasn't broken her word. Maybe she's planning on returning, just like she said, just eight or so months later than the time she and Matthew agreed on."

"I can't believe she stayed a year past the six months her dad asked for. And now she's staying until spring." Luke sighed. "You mark my words, Mary. She won't be here for this spring's instruction period either. Then will she want Matthew to wait through two more summers until the next instruction period?" He grabbed the brim of his hat and pulled it down firmer on his head. "I hate what's happening to Matthew, but our community has a lot more important things to think about than Elle Leggett."

Sarah.

Mary took even breaths, trying to quiet the nervous shiver that went through her every time Sarah was mentioned. Rumors of Sarah not being right in the head weighed on him and the whole Lapp family. Hannah had been gone for more than a year and a half, and Sarah seemed no better. She had weeks, sometimes months, of normal behavior, and then the oddities would begin again. Maybe time didn't heal all wounds. Maybe it just gave the injuries time to fester and turn malignant. A few days ago Edna Smucker had found Sarah asleep in her barn in the middle of the day. No explanation. No excuses. Just there, asleep…with torn quilt patches in her hands.

Sorry she'd let her husband see her despair, Mary took the present from him and set it on the bed. He needed her to help him carry the weight of life, not add to it. She slid her hands under his coat. "Let's forget all the bad stuff and just have fun today, ya?"

Looking down at her, he smiled. "I'd like that."

She pressed her hands against his back and pulled him close. After a long kiss that stole her breath, she backed away. "Maybe we should go and pick this topic up later, ya?"

Luke chuckled. "I'd like that too."

Mary smiled, hoping that maybe this time God would forgive her secret and she'd conceive.

*H*is arms full of presents, Martin knocked on the cabin door and then opened it. "Man in the house." Christmas music played softly, and the delicious aroma of baked sweets filled the air.

"Martin." Zabeth's raspy voice welcomed him.

He'd spent every Christmas Eve with her since he was born. He would be here tonight regardless of anything else going on in his life, but his friendship with Hannah was a definite attraction these days. It more than made up for the distress his sister would cause when she showed up later in the evening.

"Merry Christmas, Zebby."

From the recliner, Zabeth motioned him closer. "Merry Christmas." The puffiness and paleness of her face and body made her almost unrecognizable as the person who'd sat here last year. He and Hannah had spent a few long nights at the hospital with her since last Christmas. Her heart was failing. The doctors had adjusted her medicines and put her on full-time oxygen, but beyond that there was little they could do.

Her spirit and love remained intact. She still had good days, sometimes a good week, and as often as not she made it to church.

Wondering where Hannah was, Martin set the presents under what he called the neither-Amish-nor-Englischer tree. It was an evergreen inside their home, so that counted for something. The string of popcorn and a few home-made ornaments kept it from looking too barren.

He gave Zabeth a kiss on the cheek before sitting on the coffee table in front of her. "How are you feeling?"

"Fine, just fine." Her breathing was labored even with the constant flow of oxygen through the nasal cannula.

"You warm enough?" He slid out of his coat, glad he'd worn short sleeves. It was always too warm in this place for him.

"Yeah." She barely said the word before she closed her eyes and dozed off.

He tucked the lap blanket around her and moved to the couch. A sound of movement from the bathroom let him know where Hannah was. A moment later the door opened. Her hair was wet and cascading down her left shoulder as she came out wrapped in a thick housecoat and carrying a towel.

Martin leaned forward. "Merry Christmas."

She sandwiched her hair in a fold of the towel and rubbed it while walking to the wood stove. "There's no hot water."

Martin laughed. "That's what happens when you don't wish people a Merry Christmas."

She giggled before putting her hands on her hips. "Uh, yeah, but it happened before then. I knew it was only lukewarm a few hours ago, but it didn't dawn on me there was a problem until I was in the shower. Brrrrr." She shivered. "Can you fix it?" She slanted her head, dangling her hair near the wood stove.

"Not likely. And there aren't any plumbers available tonight or tomorrow."

"Merry Christmas," she said sarcastically before their eyes met, and they both laughed.

This relaxed, genuine relationship added more meaning to his life than any other, although he had no idea how to define it. She stood there with wet hair, her usual look of no makeup, and men's socks—probably his.

"I heard you were called into the clinic today. I wasn't sure if you'd be here until I saw your car."

"It was a doozie of a day. I needed a long, hot shower to wash it off. So much for salvaging a bad day."

"How so?"

"We had two Amish dads who'd been, uh…" She tilted her thumb toward her lips and her pinky in the air, the sign for drinking. "They were in the waiting room being just as loud as they pleased. I asked nicely for them to tone it down. Next go-round I explained the rules. A few minutes later I had to stand eye to eye and try to reason with them while they looked at me like I was some stupid girl, which is exactly how they saw me. Beneath them. Someone to not just ignore, but to prove they didn't have to listen to."

"Where was Dr. Lehman?"

"Delivering a baby. But it wouldn't have mattered if he'd been standing around drinking coffee; he told me to handle it. What those men didn't realize is that I knew their Achilles heel."

Martin had to smile. Sometimes he hardly recognized her as the girl he'd met eighteen months ago. "Yeah, what was that?"

She glanced at Zabeth before putting her finger to her lips, letting him know the story was not to be repeated to her aunt. It was another part of their relationship that he valued. They shared all sorts of aspects of life with each other, just the two of them, things that were too much for Zabeth to know about. "Nancy was afraid I'd come across unwelcoming to the very people the clinic was established for. I don't think so. If they chose to feel unwelcome, it's because they were in the wrong and not my fault. So I told them I'd call the police."

"Hannah Lawson," he chided, teasing her.

"No one hates the police more than Plain men who are breaking the law. They shouldn't have crossed the line of propriety and then pushed my buttons."

"So did you call the police?"

"I picked up the phone and dialed two numbers before they left. When they came back an hour later, they came in quiet and well behaved, although they wouldn't speak or look at me." Her eyes lit up. "Oh, I want to show you a gift I received." She disappeared into her bedroom.

Last year for Christmas he'd bought her an electric blanket to help her feel better about long winter nights. He couldn't spend much on her because she'd made him agree to a limit—a really puny limit. But she seemed to have absolutely loved his gift. When he'd dropped by unexpectedly on a few winter evenings, he'd found her on the couch, wrapped in the blanket while studying.

He just hoped he'd done as well on her gift this year. A couple of years ago, before Zabeth was diagnosed with cancer, he was enjoying a Sunday afternoon with her right here at the cabin. While they talked, he pulled out his digital camera, set a timer, and took a photo of them on the bench—the same bench where he and Hannah had met and talked for the first time, where they still spent time talking every Friday night at the end of her tutoring lesson. Since she really liked the photos of Zabeth on his walls, he figured she'd treasure this gift forever.

For his Christmas last year, she'd given him a gift booklet with several "I owe you" cards for her to make his favorite dinners. He'd taken her up on them too, eating most of the dinners right here with her and Zabeth. But one of his best memories was the time she'd come to his place and prepared a meal. He'd invited his friends Dave and Vicki to join them. They weren't a young couple, yet the four of them could not have had more fun together. It was his favorite memory of the year. After the meal, they went out and played Putt-Putt golf and bowled until two in the morning. Teaching Hannah how to bowl had been an absolute riot, one where they laughed and quipped at each other until it became clear to him just how much this friendship meant.

Zabeth shifted slightly without waking up. The fact that he cared deeply for her niece might have bypassed Hannah's perception, but it hadn't escaped Zabeth's notice. Thankfully she had no objections, as long as he agreed to keep Hannah's best interests above his own. He fully agreed. Aside from an insane desire to kiss her, the relationship was close to perfect.

Zabeth woke, blinking hard and breathing even harder. "How long did I sleep?"

"Just a few minutes."

"Where's Hannah?"

He pointed as she bounded out of the bedroom carrying a leather tote bag. She stopped by Zabeth and gave her a kiss on the head.

"An oversize purse?" Martin asked.

"No, you goof." She sat Indian style on the couch and faced him. "Look." She opened the bag and passed him a small cylinder and something that looked like tongs.

"What am I looking at, Hannah?" He held it up to Zabeth and made a face. The swelling in her features could not block the smile as she watched them interact.

Hannah shifted it. "It's an infant-sized laryngoscope. These are the blades for opening the air passages, and this is the handle." She wiggled her finger through the blades. "The endotracheal tube goes through here." She pulled out another item. "This is a resuscitator." She laid that on his lap and grabbed something else. "And?" She dangled two items in front of him.

He touched each one. "Blood-pressure cuff and stethoscope. Those I know."

"And?" She held what appeared to be a huge set of tweezers.

"Eyebrow pluckers for an orangutan?"

She laughed. "Yeah, that's it, Martin."

He deflected her as she tried to pluck his eyebrows. "So what is it?"

"Forceps. But Dr. Lehman doesn't believe in using them unless absolutely necessary. There's other stuff too. It's a medical bag. Dr. Lehman gave it to me for having a year of nursing school under my belt."

"Belt? What belt? I've never seen you wear a belt."

She sat up straighter, tightening the belt to her housecoat, and even Zabeth laughed. "And..." Hannah pulled a small, wrapped item out of the bag. "This is for you from Dr. Lehman."

Martin hesitated. "For me? Is this a gag gift?"

She shrugged. "I wouldn't think so, not from Dr. Lehman. Open it and let's see."

Her almost-dry hair had become a thick mass of curls, making her one of the sexiest women he'd ever seen—even in a thick bathrobe and men's socks. He removed the red tissue paper. It was a plaque with an inscription that said "Ohio's Best Tutor," plus restaurant gift certificates with "Dinner for Two" printed on them.

Hannah peered over. "Ohio's best? Yep, it's a gag gift."

Martin slapped the top of her head with the gift certificates. "Hey, that's no way to talk to the man who helped you pass math."

"So what's this?" She took the gift certificates from him and glanced at them. "Oh."

"Well you don't have to sound so disappointed. It's a nice gift."

"I have a right to my opinion."

He thumped the certificates. "What's wrong with the gift?"

She shrugged.

When Zabeth was up to it, Hannah drove her to church and stayed throughout the service but rarely went out to eat with them afterward. She usually headed straight for the birthing clinic to either work or study in her office. When he'd asked her why, she said she wanted him and Zabeth to keep their Sundays as they always had been before she arrived. But today he got the feeling there was another reason. In spite of how much they'd come to know about each other, there were still things she didn't tell him, like what those Tuesday-night meetings were about.

He took the certificates back. "I think I'll just hang on to these."

Zabeth raised her hand, and all attention focused on her. "Maybe you should keep them for ten weeks…" She drew a slow, heavy breath. "It'll be Hannah's twentieth birthday. You two could have a great evening out together."

"Yeah, what she said." Martin pointed to Zabeth and winked at her.

Hannah stuck her tongue out at him. "I'm not interested in being one of umpteen dates you take out to eat, but thank you anyway."

He laid his hand across the back of the couch, wondering how long they'd dance around the truth of how he felt about her. It was scary to be twenty-seven and fall for a nineteen-year-old.

Deciding he really didn't want to go any further with the conversation, he dropped the subject. Hannah began putting each piece of the medical equipment back in its exact spot in the bag. He'd been wrong about that nursing school. It fit very well around the other needs in her life. She went to school on Monday, Wednesday, and Thursday nights and had clinical rotation every other weekend. She had to study a good fifteen to twenty hours a week, but that could be done right here at the cabin. Then she worked for Dr. Lehman each Friday and every other weekend. The only other thing in her schedule was whatever meetings she still attended on Tuesdays. Her life was busy but very grounded and focused for a nineteen-year-old. She stayed with Zabeth all day throughout the workweek, sewing curtains for the orders Zabeth wasn't able to keep up with and tracking her intake of nutrition and medicine like a hound dog. Martin kept a check on Zabeth by phone or sat with her when Hannah was gone.

Faye came and went at will, leaving Kevin and Lissa with Hannah regularly. If she didn't seem to enjoy them so much, he'd try to put a stop to it. But she said the house was more like a home since the two rug rats spent three to four days a week here. And then there were times when Faye helped with the in-home care of Zabeth.

His best guess was that his sister was a functional addict, but he had no proof. If not, she was borderline, using whenever it suited her. Using what, he wasn't sure. He only knew she acted very odd at times. There were days and weeks when she had energy to burn and played supermom, so he guessed maybe she used methamphetamine some of the time. Other days she slept round the clock. And still other times she smelled of alcohol. What worried him was that nobody who used part-time to get through the day stayed that way for long. They became hardcore addicts.

Zabeth took hold of her cane, and in a flash Hannah was at her side, helping her up. "Did one of you feed Ol' Gert?"

"We always take care of the horse, Zebby. But I think it's way past time to sell her."

"No way," Hannah retorted. "I take Kevin and Lissa for buggy rides and bareback rides."

Zabeth nodded in agreement. "We're not getting rid of Ol' Gert. I'm going to putter around in the kitchen." She thumped her way slowly, wheeling her oxygen tank behind her.

Hannah sat back on the couch beside him. "Never tell her no when she chooses to go *putter* in that kitchen."

Martin chuckled. "What is puttering anyway?"

Hannah wrapped the blood-pressure cuff around his arm. "Doing little odds and ends in a slow manner."

Martin frowned. "What are you doing?"

"What does it look like I'm doing?"

"Checking my blood pressure."

She put the stethoscope on. "Yep. And your pulse." She squeezed the bulb. "The chest piece goes on the antecubital, and you're to remain still until I'm finished." She took the reading. "Ohhhh, you're one cool cucumber, huh?" She released the pressure in the cuff. "Why am I not surprised?" She patted his arm, letting him know he could shift it so she could get the cuff off. "Okay, I'm done."

He didn't pull his arm away. "Do you have to be?" he teased. "I mean, you could keep checking my blood pressure just for the fun of it."

Her brown eyes locked on his in a way they hadn't before, dancing with mischief. She laid the stethoscope around her neck. "Well, it won't be any fun unless we do something to make your pulse increase." She whispered the words and held her index finger over her lips.

He was sure his heart rate had just increased—substantially. "Mmm, and how do you propose we do that?"

She bit her bottom lip and gazed up at him, making him long to kiss her. "I don't think you're old enough for us to cross that bridge *yet*." She whispered the words and laughed.

Wondering if she was flirting with him or just being spirited tonight, Martin put one hand on each side of the stethoscope that hung around her neck. "I'm not old enough?" He pulled her closer, within five inches of his lips, and then a horn tooted, ending the moment abruptly.

The noise let them know Richard, Faye, Kevin, and Lissa were pulling into the driveway. Zabeth came out of the kitchen.

Hannah rose, untying the belt to her housecoat. She slid the housecoat off, revealing a typical Hannah dress—stylish and modest. She pulled off his socks and passed them to him. "Slightly used but all yours."

"You're pretty entertaining tonight, you know that?"

She ran her hands through her hair and began twisting it. "Yeah, well, you know how it is. I'm here to please."

"What kind of mood is this?" he asked. "Did those men at the clinic share their booze with you?"

She clicked her tongue at him. "Can't a woman have a little Christmas cheer without being accused of being tipsy?"

Zabeth chuckled. "Obviously not."

Martin grabbed Hannah's clip off the coffee table and held it up to her while she wound her hair into a loose bun. As far as he knew, he and Zebby were the only ones who ever saw her with her hair down. He just sat there, watching and wondering if they'd ever become all that he wanted from their relationship.

Hannah took the clip from his hand. "Maybe if Faye is, uh, void of too much Christmas cheer, we can play some board games like we did last year."

"Board games?" Martin frowned at her, sounding as serious as he could. "That's spelled B-O-R-E-D, right?"

She pouted while pinning up her hair. "I thought I was entertaining."

When her eyes met his, reflecting some of the same feelings he had for her, he knew that Paul Waddell no longer owned her heart.

The door opened. Kevin and Lissa ran inside with their parents behind them.

Kevin held a Matchbox car out toward Hannah. "Look!"

Hannah scooped up Lissa. "I see that. It looks like your uncle's car."

Kevin climbed on the couch next to Martin. "It's not the same, is it?"

"Well, let's take a look at this." He put the toy in the palm of his hand and talked to Kevin while still thinking of Hannah. She'd taken up residence in his soul, whether he fully approved of it or not.

Hannah eased Lissa onto Zabeth's lap, turned and gave Faye a hug, and welcomed Richard before grabbing her medical bag and taking it to her bedroom.

Satisfied with Martin's answers, Kevin moved to an empty area of the hardwood floor and sat down to play. Martin choked out a few niceties to his sister and Richard, recognizing the hollowness in his voice as he tried to find something pleasant to say. When Zabeth struck up a conversation with them, he went to see what kept Hannah.

Hannah's back was to him when he tapped on the open door. Pulling a fleece jacket from the closet, she glanced his way. "Hi." She put the pink jersey on. "You can come in."

He stepped inside the room for the first time in years.

She pointed to the living room. "What do you think?"

He knew what weighed on her mind. "She doesn't look high or drunk tonight."

Relief filled her eyes. "I thought the same thing."

"I know what I want for Christmas."

"Yeah? Did you know Christmas Eve is not the time to have spontaneous wants?" she teased him.

"It is when it's doable."

She sat on the chair, looking up at him—half flirting, half just being friendly. "Okay, as long as this is equitable, I'm game."

"Do you even know when you're flirting?" He hadn't intended to sound so flat and accusing but knew it came out that way.

"Well, that's a mean thing to say. I don't flirt."

"Then I got my answer, didn't I?"

She rolled her eyes. "So for Christmas you'd like us to argue?"

When they were studying together, Hannah knew how to hold her own if they argued. She'd make him apologize for his rude behavior if he threw out some overly snide or sarcastic remark, but she'd never cried or said her feelings were truly hurt. He liked that. Actually, it was a quality he'd always hoped to find in someone special.

"I surrender." He held up both hands. "Whatever you say."

She raised one eyebrow. "Anything I say? Hmm, let me ponder this awhile."

"And yet she doesn't see it," he mumbled, deciding they could discuss the fact that she *didn't flirt* another time. "Tuesday nights. Where do you go?"

All trace of cheer drained from her face. "What?"

"It's what I want for Christmas, please." He teased her, but the smile didn't return to her face.

She lowered her eyes. "The Rape Crisis Center. At first it was mandatory because Dr. Lehman said I needed it. Now I counsel others."

Martin heard the words *rape center*, but he couldn't make himself respond.

Hannah gestured toward her bed. "Need to sit?"

He tried to regain his composure. "I never once thought…" He sat down across from her. "I'm really sorry."

"Me too. I wanted to tell you, but I didn't want you to know. Rape is so embarrassing."

"And you thought I'd think less of you?"

"There's always that chance, but more than that, I wanted you to learn to like me for who I am, not out of pity."

He enfolded one of her hands between his. "Fair enough. But I think you should have trusted me to figure out and separate my own thoughts and feelings, don't you?"

"Is that how you treat me—able to hear the whole story and figure out my own thoughts?"

"That's different, Miss Not-Yet-Twenty-Years-Old."

She pulled her hand away and folded her arms. "Yeah, but I'll always be nearly eight years younger than you."

"I know. You're just going to have to trust me. Okay?"

She shrugged "So are you ever going to ask me out?"

His doubts about the type of relationship they were in vanished. "Give me a break, Hannah. I don't date teenagers."

She whispered, "But you almost kissed one."

"I was sort of hoping you hadn't noticed that."

She caught his eye, and they both broke into laughter. "So now what?"

"We wait…just like I've been doing."

"You call what you do waiting?"

The first thing he'd called it was trying not to care for someone so much younger than himself. Then he labeled it as giving her time to get over Paul, but he couldn't see ruining their moment by sharing too much honesty. He pulled the gift certificates out of his pocket and laid them in her hands. "You hold on to these."

The dreary skies outside Paul's office window seemed to go on forever, only broken up by skeletal trees. It was barely winter, with Christmas just behind him, yet he was tired of the grayness, and he wasn't looking forward to the New Year—although he knew he should be. He lived in a free country and had a loving family, plenty of food, and a good internship at the Better Path. But the holidays had felt empty, just like Thanksgiving and Christmas had last year and this year. It was the year before that where his thoughts always lingered—his last real time with Hannah.

She'd been gone twenty-two months, and he'd survived every day of that time in hope of her returning. He could understand that she hadn't returned yet, but that she hadn't even called? *That* he just didn't get. He'd blown it with her. No doubt. And sometimes in life when you blew it, you didn't get a second chance, but if she'd make contact, just once, they could start to work through things.

While gazing out the window, thinking, Paul saw movement a few hundred feet away. A closer look indicated it was an Amish or Mennonite woman walking here and there in the patch of woods near the mission. He studied the movement, trying to figure out what the woman was doing. She appeared to be gathering brushwood. A bicycle leaned against a tree near her. He eased back in his chair, watching.

The graduate program and internships suited him well and helped keep his mind focused on something other than Hannah's eventual return. Since he really liked working at the Better Path, the facility he was in right now, he volunteered here regularly. It was run by an independent, nondenominational Christian organization that fed, clothed, and counseled people of all ages, races, and religious backgrounds. The place had thirty beds and a dozen different programs to help people, including one of his preferred programs—

after-school care for teens. And best of all, at the end of the day he drove ten miles down the road to Owl's Perch.

The woman carried a huge armload of sticks to the ditch and dumped it. That seemed odd. Deciding to take a closer look, Paul stood. He peered through the window just as the woman turned and seemed to look straight at him.

"Sarah?"

It couldn't be. Surely she didn't bike this far. It was near freezing outside. He grabbed his coat, went down the stairs and out the side door. Jogging across the road and into the woods, he couldn't spot anyone.

Looking about, he called, "Sarah?"

A few moments later she stepped out from behind a tree. Not a trace of emotion showed on her face—no smile, no fear, not even recognition.

"Sarah, what are you doing here?"

She took a step toward the road, not even looking at him. "Have you seen her?"

Paul stood mute.

"She'll come back here, you know. Right here." She pointed at the mission home.

"How did you get here?"

"I saw this house in a dream. And Hannah was inside, looking out that window." Sarah smiled and pointed to the only empty room in the place. "So I set out to find the place, and here it is. She was staring out the window, looking for me. And she still loved you, but you didn't know it. It'll happen, just wait and see."

Paul knew she hadn't needed to dream about this place to be aware of it. She'd passed it dozens of times, and Luke or Mary must have mentioned he was working here. Her imagining Hannah was here was the next natural step. Sarah wasn't delusional; she just got things confused in her mind.

"Sarah, listen to me. You're eighteen years old now. If you want to leave home and seek a doctor's help, you don't have to explain it to your dad or even go back there. There are counselors in the mission." He knew she needed someone different than him, someone who wasn't emotionally invested and who wouldn't stir her community to anger merely by existing. "There's a Dr. Stone, who comes in once a week. She can work out a plan to help you."

Sarah looked him dead in the eye. "Daed burned Hannah's letters, the ones she wrote before she left Owl's Perch. She wrote me one, and he burned it. But he's not the only one with power." She reached inside her hidden apron pocket and pulled out a box of kitchen matches.

Those weren't just sticks she'd gathered; they were kindling. "Come on, let's go inside, and I'll see if I can get Dr. Stone on the phone."

"Everyone's whispering that I'm crazy. I thought so too for a while, but I see things. Just wait. You'll see that I'm right. Hannah will be right there." Sarah pointed to the same empty room of the mission. "And you'll see her, but you won't." She cocked her head, gazing at him. "That's the real problem, isn't it? We see people, but we don't." She waved at him and took off running, then paused and turned to face him. "You got a chance to hear her and didn't. You'll get a second chance, Paul."

~~◦~~

Hannah stared in the mirror, wondering if she could actually make herself leave the cabin looking like this. Faye had helped do her hair, scrunching it while using a hair dryer on it. It was awful wild looking to Hannah, but Zabeth said it was classy. Faye said it looked sexy.

Classy? Sexy? In public? Do I really want to do this?

Faye adjusted the inset tie on the side of Hannah's rose-colored wrap dress while Zabeth looked on from her wheelchair. The flutter sleeves and V-shaped neckline were different than anything she'd ever worn, but it was the way the fabric gently molded to her body that gave her reason to pause. She'd picked out the pattern herself, but was she falling for the ways of the world?

Faye stepped back. "Okay, Hannah, let's take a look at you."

Faye had promised to stay with Zabeth tonight, making arrangements with Richard to watch the kids, so Hannah and Martin didn't need to stay in Winding Creek for this occasion.

Hannah looked at her aunt's reflection in the mirror. Her complexion was ashen, and her lips and fingertips were slightly blue. The swelling in her legs and her physical weakness caused her to use a wheelchair these days. "How much did you pay for the material to make this?"

"None of that. It's your birthday, and you look beautiful, Hannah-girl, not much like the scrawny, pale girl of two years ago."

Hannah swallowed. "I feel just as out of place tonight as I did then."

"Well, of course. That'll fade with time and some experience, but you look like you could own the world. Enjoy it." She adjusted the tubing to her nasal cannula that fed her a constant stream of oxygen.

Faye winked. "I bet you'll be on Martin's top-ten list of best-looking dates ever. Now that's saying something."

"Thanks for the constant reminder of Martin's past dates, Faye. It's very helpful. Really."

Faye rolled her eyes. "It's the way it is—or was before you came. Deal with it. But maybe you'll be the last. Who knows. One thing's for sure, he's not likely to ever hook up with anyone younger."

Zabeth held up her hand, letting them know she intended to say something. She drew several deep breaths of pure oxygen before trying to speak. "You just got a bad case of nerves. You'll have a wonderful time."

"Sit." Faye pointed to the bed and opened a small makeup kit. "We'll just use a touch of color on your lips, cheeks, and eyes."

Not sure she liked this idea either, Hannah sat and let Faye fill in as a makeup artist. Hannah wondered if Martin was the least bit nervous about tonight. She hoped he was.

As she'd learned over the last two years, Martin's heart was pure gold. He drew her, despite his occasional raised voice and sarcasm. He'd drop anything at any time when she called him. Even if he was in the middle of some important meeting when she called, he would make time for her. He had helped her with tutoring, with Zabeth's illness, and in hundreds of other ways, showing her how much he cared.

She knew the things she really liked about him were practical, but practical counted for an awful lot in her opinion. Paul had always needed her to wait. Wait. Wait. Whatever her needs were, they had to be put on hold to fit with his schedule.

And there was another side to Martin, one that caused her cheeks to warm when she found him staring at her from across the room. He wasn't as tall or broad shouldered as Paul, but she discovered she really liked that. With her being in heels tonight, he'd only be an inch taller than she was. There was something wonderful about being able to stare a man in the eye when walking or talking or…almost kissing.

His confidence mesmerized her. It seemed contagious, and she needed that, like a garden waiting for the spring rains.

Faye dusted Hannah's cheeks and eyes with a light rose-colored powder while Hannah wondered what it would be like to be kissed by Martin. Maybe even tonight.

"Man in the house." His voice startled her, and she gasped.

Zabeth chuckled. "You're going to need my oxygen tank if you keep that up."

"We're coming," Faye yelled, then reached for a tube and stroked the pink gloss across Hannah's lips. Faye grinned and backed away. "All done. I'll wait in the living room with Zabeth."

"Thanks." Hannah grabbed the matching pouch Zabeth had made as her purse and tucked the lip gloss inside it.

She drew air into her lungs, counted to three, and stepped out of her bedroom.

Martin whistled. "Man alive." He held a bouquet of roses and orchids toward her.

"Thank you. They're beautiful." She drew them to her face and breathed deeply.

Suddenly feeling more awkward than nervous, she hoped to get past this and find their typical comfort zone.

He held a vase out to her. "I figured you'd need one of these."

She shook her head. "I'll keep them with me for now."

Setting the vase on the table, Martin eyed her and smiled. He looked like he wanted to say something, but Hannah knew he would wait until they were alone.

Faye moved in front of her and rearranged a stray hair. "Well, this is one night you won't be sleeping with your date, right, little bro?"

Feeling as if she'd been slapped, Hannah staggered under the realization of what Faye had just said.

"Shut up, Faye." The words came from both Martin and Zabeth, but it was too late.

Hannah dropped the flowers and reached for her keys that stayed in a bowl in the center of the table.

In one fluid move, Martin snatched them before she had a good grip. "Hannah, wait. I can't change the past."

Faye scoffed, "But *she* can change your future."

He glared at her. "Stay out of this, Faye."

Zabeth's face furrowed, and Hannah knew she had no choice but to smooth things over and leave with him if she was going to keep her aunt calm.

Hannah forced a smile. "Forget the past and look straight ahead, ya?" She bent to kiss her aunt on the cheek. "I'll be in to see you when I get home, okay?"

Zabeth nodded and placed her hands on Hannah's cheeks. "Happy birthday, Hannah-girl."

"Thank you." Hannah allowed Martin to help her slide into her coat. With his hand on her back, she walked out the door, leaving the flowers. When he closed the door, she pulled away.

"Hannah." His smooth voice offended her. "I wanted to talk to you about this, at the right time. It's just absurd to talk about it before a first date."

She stared at the barn, refusing to make eye contact. "You sleep with your dates?"

"No." He paused. "Well, I did. In another lifetime, before church and half a decade before I met you."

Her heels tapped against the steps as she descended them.

When she was on the bottom step, Martin's warm hand took hold of hers. "Talk to me, Hannah."

She pulled her hand away. "I don't like it."

"Me either, times a hundred." He rubbed his forehead. "But there's nothing that can change what's been done. Nothing."

Hearing both desperation and resolve in his voice, she remembered the night Paul had discovered her secret. If he could have seen her heart in spite of the circumstance, he might have realized that the only thing that mattered was their future, not the past. If he'd chosen to deal with the events and decisions that made him uncomfortable, they could have moved into a deeper relationship. But instead he took a stand on one issue and ruined everything.

"The very idea of you…" She took a ragged breath. "It makes me feel insecure and…and jealous."

He moved in close, and she could smell his cologne. "That's because you think every relationship means something special. It has for you. But our friendship is the only one that's ever meant anything to me. I don't know where we'll land, but we don't have a chance if you cut me off because of my past mistakes. It's only between me and God at this point."

"No it's not. It will never just be between you and God, not for me. Can't you see that?"

Odd as it was, Martin didn't defend himself; he seemed to be waiting for her to judge him and make a ruling. A dozen emotions rolled through her before stopping on a single thought. If they could find peace and unity over this issue, they'd be able to overcome their sexual history—his through poor choices, hers by force. But both had to be reckoned with.

Suddenly his past seemed less of a threat and more like equal footing—like a trade-off of baggage to be dealt with. Beyond that comforting realization, Hannah wondered, if God had forgiven her for all she'd handled wrong in life, could she withhold forgiveness from Martin?

She slid her hand back into his. "I overreacted, and I shouldn't have."

He gently squeezed her hand. "You were sucker-punched, and I'm really sorry."

She drew a deep breath, ready to start the evening over. "I've never been on a date."

A soft grin eased the tension on his face. "How does a girl get engaged without dating?"

She shrugged. "Let's not talk about that." She felt a hair clip in her coat pocket. "I don't want to wear my hair down."

He laughed. "I didn't think you would."

She pulled out the clip and pinned up her hair. "Am I date umpteen hundred for the month?"

"No. We made a deal at Christmas, remember? Besides, I'll tell you a secret." He looked around the yard conspiratorially. "I haven't been on a date in more than nine months."

She felt calmer, knowing their time together had caused him to stop dating early last summer. Standing directly in front of him, she waited for him to look into her eyes, say something witty or sweet or even sarcastic, and make her forget everything but the moment.

But he didn't say anything at all. He just stood there, smiling at her.

"I'm no longer a teenager."

"Mmm, I know."

"If you almost kissed a teen, maybe you could come closer this time."

"Well, last couple of years my rule has been that I don't kiss until the fourth date. That way I don't freak out later when I realize I didn't like the girl. If someone lasts through four dates, she's worthy of a kiss." He caressed her face. "But I could make an exception."

He slowly brought his lips to hers, and every speck of loneliness that had remained with her for two years was swept away.

*M*artin stared at the casket perched on the hydraulic lift designed to lower it into the ground. The green indoor-outdoor carpet under his feet covered the loose dirt that had been removed to make room for a woman he loved like a mother. The trees around them were in full end-of-May bloom.

People had gathered in droves. Most of them he went to church with. But none had brought any sense of comfort. It wasn't for Zabeth that he grieved; it was for Hannah most of all, and for Faye and her children, and then for himself. Zebby had died in her sleep at the cabin with Hannah right beside her. But Zabeth was free now. He knew that. Even so, it'd be a long year of grieving, with years of lesser grief. That was just the way it worked.

In spite of how taxing the last few days had been, Hannah had responded with a quiet reserve, doing whatever needed to be done. She'd put up a stoic wall, and for now he was allowing her to cope in whatever manner she chose. She'd provided Dr. Lehman addresses for all of Zabeth's family and asked him to send letters, informing them of her death. For reasons Martin would have thought she was past now, she'd asked Dr. Lehman to use his own name, address, and phone number as the contact person or to refer people to the funeral home. The burial had been delayed as long as possible to give Zabeth's family time to reply to the letters they'd received by overnight delivery. But no one had responded.

His sister's cries broke through the heavy silence, her uncontrolled grief a stark contrast to his own silence. For days she'd behaved as if nothing existed but her own pain, not even her children or Hannah. Faye had acted this way when their mom died, and it had been Zabeth who had comforted her then. Had that really been sixteen years ago?

Across from where he stood, Hannah sat quietly on a white folding chair.

He wanted to go to her, but he kept his distance. His sister was beside her, sobbing without control. As if losing Zabeth wasn't enough to sink Faye, Richard had walked out on her last week. He'd been coming home less and less until he finally told her he was seeing someone else. Kevin and Lissa didn't yet know their father had left them. They had enough to deal with this week, losing the only grandmother they'd ever known and bearing the pain of their mother pulling even further away from them. Leeriness at what life held for Faye, Kevin, and Lissa made Zabeth's passing even harder.

Delicate fingers shifted inside Martin's hands. He glanced down.

Lissa looked up at him, her dark brown eyes swimming in tears. "I want my daddy."

Martin knelt beside his five-year-old niece. While he tried to think of something to say, a small hand patted his shoulder. When he turned, he found six-year-old Kevin staring at him, desperate for comfort. Reflected in their eyes was an ache deeper than they could convey in words, and he didn't know how to fix it. They needed promises for their future, and he had none.

Hannah unlocked the cabin door but couldn't make herself go inside. The eerie silence would swallow her. It'd been this way since Zabeth died, and today, the day of her burial, it was even worse. She took a deep breath and pushed open the door. Stepping out of her shoes, she flicked on a light before sinking onto the sofa.

She wished Faye hadn't gone to the gathering after the funeral. Her speech was slurred and her movements clumsy. Hannah could only conclude she'd been drinking. Faye had made a spectacle of herself as she wailed about Richard leaving her. When the commotion started, Martin's eyes met Hannah's from across the room, and he hurried the children out of the house. Too weary to deal with one more thing, she had slipped out to her car and come home. She looked about the cabin.

Home. Even today, it still held some of the appeal it had the first day she'd seen the place.

She flipped through the mail. Still, not even one of Zabeth's family members had responded to the letters Dr. Lehman had sent. Laying the junk mail and bills to the side, Hannah rose from the couch and walked into Zabeth's room. She ran her hand over the old dresser and the bed and along the wall until she came to the closet. She went into the small room and pulled an armful of Zabeth's dresses to her face, breathing in the lingering aroma of her aunt—a wonderful scent of fresh air and the expensive soaps Martin gave her.

She wiped away a tear and whispered a prayer of thankfulness. She had found her aunt and had treasured twenty-six months with her. In spite of the hurt, she'd always be grateful for that. But she'd just buried the only person who'd ever known all there was to know about her and yet had loved her unconditionally.

A car horn tooted three times in quick succession. That was Faye's signal when she was coming up the drive—although it seemed odd that she'd drive here since her one saving grace was that she didn't drive while under the influence.

Too drained to deal with anyone, Hannah muttered, "Not tonight, Faye."

Car lights flickered against the bedroom window as the vehicle slowly approached. Hannah closed the door to Zabeth's bedroom and went to the front porch. It was hard to tell in the dark, but the vehicle that came to a stop didn't look like Faye's.

Martin climbed out. With his body between the open door and the car, he faced Hannah. "I just wanted to come by and check on you. You disappeared pretty quickly."

Hugging her arms tightly around herself, she didn't move closer to him as she wanted to do. "I'm sorry I left early."

"There's no need to apologize. Faye's enough to run anyone off."

Hannah ached to feel the warmth of his arms around her, but she kept her distance. Death and funerals were a part of life, and she refused to get all needy because of them. But it'd been a week of sidestepping Martin's comfort, and her resolve was growing weaker.

He closed the car door and walked toward the porch, reaching into his shirt pocket. He pulled out an envelope. "I wrote down the names of every-one for my own use, but I thought you'd want to keep all the cards that were on the flowers."

"Thanks."

He sat down on the top step of the porch.

"Who's watching over Faye?"

"She's asleep. I didn't think Nina should be responsible for her, so I asked her mom, Vicki, to keep an eye on her as well as Kevin and Lissa for a bit."

Hannah sat down too, feeling the oddity of being here alone with him. No one spoke, reminding her of the day he came here and apologized to her—two years ago.

Across the field, mist rose from the creek banks, looking purplish under the night sky. Crickets sang loudly, and an occasional bullfrog croaked. Peace seemed to slip right into the place where anxiety had been only moments ago. But it wasn't just the scenery. She could have that by herself. It was having Martin near.

He drew a deep breath. "It's nice here. Quiet and peaceful, and it suited Zabeth, but…I think it's a bit too lonely out here for you by yourself. Don't you?"

"You're going to bring this up now?"

"It's on my mind." He faced her. "Remember when you called me a bee-tle thing?"

She laughed. "I didn't mean to." She dared to finish her thought. "But had I known it was so befitting…"

His deep laughter filled the night air, and she wished he could stay and sleep on the couch as he'd done on occasions when Zabeth returned home after a hospitalization. Desperate for a reprieve from the loneliness, she rose from her spot on the porch and pointed to the step below where Martin sat. A gentle smile formed on his lips, and he shifted his legs. She sat down.

He wrapped his arms around her. "How are you, phone girl?"

She swallowed hard and shrugged, but the warmth of being in his arms made her grief more bearable.

Martin rubbed her shoulders. "So how about we find you a better place to live? You can sell the place in a few weeks and find somewhere not so isolated or quite so plain or—"

She stopped him. "It's home, and I'm staying."

"If you change your mind…"

"Yeah, thanks."

She turned her head, looking Martin in the face. He placed his hand against her cheek and neck and rubbed his thumb back and forth.

Slowly he lowered his lips to hers. "Mmm. I could have used that a week ago."

Enjoying his closeness, she nodded and kissed him again before turning back around.

Martin propped his chin on her shoulder, as if he needed the warmth of her touch as much as she needed his. "I always felt guilty about Zabeth."

"Guilty? Why?"

"It was my mother's influence in Zabeth's life that ended up causing a division between her and her people. Mom swooned over Zabeth's ability to learn music, lined her up in recitals and gigs. When her community learned what was going on, Mom offered her a place to live."

She pondered his words before answering. "Your mother was not what led Zabeth away from the Amish life. That came from years of living under rules that demanded one thing while her heart wanted something else. Your mother just lit a path that Zabeth's heart was already searching for."

"I needed to know that."

The tenderness of being held eased through her, giving her strength to face the night alone. For the thousandth time Hannah wondered how Faye had gotten so lost when she had two women of such high caliber trying to show her the way, but Zabeth never wanted the subject mentioned. "Zabeth loved your mother, especially for bringing music into her life. I don't think she ever regretted the sacrifice it took to have that joy. And I know she never regretted raising you, loving you like her son."

"Thank you." His voice wavered, and he cleared his throat.

"Martin," Hannah paused, wondering if maybe there was a better time to ask her questions.

"Just say it, sweetheart."

He'd never used that term before, and it stirred her like when he played her favorite songs, making her feel they were meant to be. "You shared a sketchy version when we met, but what really happened to get Faye on this substance-abuse path?"

He brushed wisps of hair off her neck. "And we were having such a nice conversation." He pulled back from her and pushed a button on his watch, making it glow. "I don't think now's the time. I'd better go, but if anything comes up, Hannah, anything at all, you call me."

Frustrated that he'd cut her off so quickly and that he'd rather leave than talk to her, she rose, making it easier for him to stand.

He pulled the keys from his pocket and headed for his car.

Hannah followed him. "I don't like that you're suddenly treating me like a kid sister who's too frail to live alone in her own home or too weak to get a straight answer. If something is too much for me, I'll let *you* know. And you're the one who uses the phrase *just say it*."

He stopped and studied her. "I've never treated you like a sister. That's just disgusting, Hannah. I do my best never to push you in this relationship. That's all."

"And I admire that. I really do. But there's a difference between respecting who we can be, given time, and refusing to talk about things with me."

He ran his hand through his hair and walked to the split-rail fence near where Ol' Gert was standing. Hannah followed him.

Ol' Gert put her head across the fence, and he patted her. "I was twelve when Mom accused Dad of using her like a maid, never having time to raise us, never being a part of our lives. She wanted him to stop working and traveling so much. I think she just missed him, but I'd never seen my dad so angry, accusing her of using him. He said she wanted his money and the house, the cars, clothes, whatever. He said she wasn't his maid because she'd suckered Zabeth into being one." Martin shook his head. "That wasn't true.

My mom loved and treated Zabeth like a sister, not hired help. But the fight unleashed years of garbage. It went on for weeks before my dad finally packed his bags and moved out."

Hannah rubbed his back. "I...I shouldn't have asked this question, not today of all days."

Martin faced her. "For being so close, there are still things we hold back, aren't there?"

Dread of telling him that she'd once carried a child and was unable to ever carry another one washed over her. "Yes."

"It's time to move past those things, okay?" When she gave a slight nod, he continued. "The separation went on for months before things got totally out of control. Faye and Mom were arguing one day—I'm not sure about what—but it ended with Faye telling Mom she didn't blame Dad for moving out and she didn't know how he'd stood it for as long as he had. Then Faye stormed out, got in her car, and left. You know the rest. Mom followed her and never made it back."

She took in several deep breaths. "I'm so sorry." She gazed at him, searching for some sense of how to piece together what she knew of the Palmers. "Did your father ever comfort Faye, ever talk to her and tell her it wasn't her fault?"

Martin shook his head. "They barely spoke. Then less than two weeks after Mom's death, Faye disappeared. She'd pop back up every couple of months, always more needy and less stable than before. I was just a kid, so I didn't realize how heavily she drank and used. Zabeth stayed, making things as stable as possible. Dad stopped traveling as much. He became all that Mom had wanted to begin with. He came to my baseball games, taught me all he knew about business and the stock market, and gave me birthday money each year to invest."

"And Faye, did she get any of these benefits?"

"She wasn't there."

"You said she was there some of the time. What did he do to—"

He put his hands on her shoulders. "It's really time for me to be going."

"But..."

He lifted his hand. "No more, please."

She nodded. "Sure, I understand."

Placing his hand on the small of her back, he slowly kissed her. "That's what I came here for." He smiled before pulling his keys from his pocket again. "Will I see you in church on Sunday?"

"I'm on call, so there's no way of knowing right now."

He opened his car door and paused. "I'm glad Zabeth had you with her for the last two years."

Without waiting for a response, he got into his car, leaving Hannah to wonder how Vince Palmer could abandon his daughter to her guilt—even if she were to blame. And she wasn't. It was an accident, an awful one that seemed too heavy for both Martin and Faye. Faye needed her father to look her in the eye and tell her it wasn't her fault.

She ran her fingers over her lips, the sweetness of Martin's kiss clinging to her. If he could so easily see his sister drowning and not reach out to her, would he do the same to her if she made a mistake?

*T*he sound of the phone shrilled through the open windows as Mary wrapped the freshly baked muffins with a towel. She hesitated, unsure whether to try to make it to the phone shanty or not. It was quite a jaunt from Mammi Annie's kitchen to the shanty, and she wasn't sure she wanted to run—not in her newly pregnant condition.

Deciding not to dash to the phone, she placed the muffins on the table and turned to rinse her hands. The call would be from one of her mother's sisters. When the phone did ring, which wasn't often, it was always one of her aunts.

Mary had long ago given up on Hannah calling again, but that wasn't all she'd given up on. If Hannah didn't call or write, she wasn't going to return. And life moved on. Although Mary wasn't sure it had moved on for Paul. He'd be finished with his graduate degree by summer's end, but that wasn't a sign he was making progress emotionally. She and Luke would go to his grandmother's and see him later in the day. She hoped for his sake that he'd stopped waiting. Hannah had been her good friend while growing up and while Mary was recovering from her injuries, but Hannah had made a poor decision when she tried to hide her pregnancy from everyone. That's where most of the troubles came in.

Mary brushed a damp cloth down her apron, cleaning off the flour. Mammi Annie entered the kitchen, wiping sweat from her top lip. "Is there a reason why you're baking instead of planting your garden?"

"Ya, but not one you want to hear."

Mammi Annie smiled and shook her head. "I'll tell you what, Mary. You're too excited about that upcoming baby to settle down and take care of this year's crop, but you'll regret that if Luke has to buy food come winter because his wife didn't do as she should."

"I'll get to it next week. Tonight we're going out visiting."

"Well, is that really what should come first?"

She knew Mammi was trying to gently prod her to settle her whirlwind emotions, but the garden held no interest whatsoever. It was already the middle of May, and she hadn't put a seed in the ground yet. As usual Luke was patient with her and listened each night as she prattled endlessly about being pregnant.

"Where are you two heading this time?"

"To Mrs. Waddell's."

"To visit with that Paul fella?"

"Yes. He came by E and L a few weeks back and made plans with Luke for us to visit him. Until he came by the shop, neither of us had seen him in ages."

"You're not going to tell him or his grandmother of your news, surely."

"No, of course not."

Keeping herself from shouting to the world that she was expecting come November was really hard. She knew it wasn't something proper families told, but Mary wanted everyone in Owl's Perch to know her good news. Fact was, she wanted to put the information in *The Budget* and let the whole Amish world read that she was entering her second trimester, according to the midwife. But so far, only the adults in her and Luke's immediate families knew. Thankfully, her days of nausea were behind her. Because Hannah had explained certain things to her and because she'd longed to conceive, she'd known early on that she was pregnant. She'd used one of those at-home pregnancy tests to confirm her suspicions. Well, actually she'd used a dozen of them over as many months, but finally one had given the positive sign.

After taking longer to conceive than any other girl who'd married during her same wedding season, she couldn't contain her excitement.

Nor her health concerns.

She pressed her hand down the front of her dress, unable to feel even the slightest bulge through her clothing yet. At night, when she undressed, she slid her hand over the slight bump. It was such a miracle. One day a toddler would play near her as she worked her garden or hung laundry on the lines. One day she'd have a child who had once lived inside her.

"Mary?" Luke was in the driveway sitting in the buggy when he hollered through the screen door. "You ready?"

"Ya." She grabbed the muffins. "Don't wait up, Mammi. Paul said something about staying and playing a board game or two."

Mammi Annie harrumphed. "If that don't beat all, you and Luke hobnobbing with the likes of that man. You know the gossip spreads like wildfire whenever he is involved."

"If you don't say anything about where we're going, then nobody will know. Ya?" Mary didn't wait for her to answer before walking to the buggy. "Seems Mammi Annie disapproves of us visiting Paul."

Luke slapped the reins against the horse's back. "I can give you a short list of things she does approve of: you and our baby."

Tingles of excitement ran through Mary. From the day she'd learned she was pregnant, she'd felt like she was soaring with the hawks. Once in a while her conscience still nagged at her, but she'd made it this far without telling Luke the things he didn't want to know about his wife. She would not share her secret now.

It was a long ride to Paul's place, giving them lots of uninterrupted time to talk.

"Did you invite Matthew to come tonight?"

"Ya. He's not in a sociable mood of late." Luke guided the horse off to the side, letting several cars pass. "All I know is Elle ain't kept her word that she'd be living here by now, but she hasn't asked Matthew to release her from her promise to marry him. And he just keeps hoping things will work out."

"Just like Paul. Waiting and hoping. I hate this for both of them."

"Yeah, I know you do, but it's not yours to take on, Mary. Matthew's building a good business, and if it don't work out with Elle, then it don't. I think Paul's moved on too. I think that Dorcas girl will be there tonight, so don't be upset if she is."

"I won't be upset. I can't blame the man, and Dorcas seems nice enough. I just never thought Hannah'd stay gone like this. Did you?"

Luke shook his head. "Not once."

She slid closer to him. "I never knew what to think of Elle returning or not, but I always thought Hannah would come back to Paul when her pain and grief eased." She wrapped her arm around his. "I'll always be grateful we made it though."

Luke pulled into the driveway of his old shop. "I wish Matthew would forget about Elle and find somebody worthy of him."

"Yeah, I do too."

He helped Mary down, and they crossed the weedy path between the Lapp and Waddell properties.

Paul strode onto the porch and opened the door for them before they had a chance to knock. "Hi."

"I brought you these." Mary held out the muffins, noticing how full of life Paul appeared. When Hannah first left, he looked pale, and he lost a lot of weight in the weeks that followed. But tonight he looked robust and self-assured.

"Thanks. These'll go perfect with the coffee I have brewing. Come on in." He gestured toward the back door of the house.

As Mary crossed the porch, she saw several people in the kitchen she didn't know and one she did: Dorcas. For Hannah's sake, Mary hurt for what her friend could have had if tragedy hadn't struck.

She covered her stomach with her hand, grateful for what her future held.

Hannah pulled into Faye's gravel driveway. Her place wasn't nearly as nice as her brother's, but then again Martin worked hard and invested wisely. Faye didn't work, had no investments, and now that she didn't have Richard to support her or the children, Hannah wasn't sure what Faye would do. Her need to find work while buried under the grief of losing Zabeth and Richard weighed on Hannah. More important, it weighed on Martin even though he didn't talk about it.

She got out of the car, crossed the concrete porch, and knocked on the door. Even though Faye was close to no one now that Zabeth had died,

Hannah hoped to reach her. She was sure it'd mean a lot to Martin if his sister could find her way free of substance abuse. Plus, Hannah wanted both children enrolled in school this fall. It was absurd for Faye to pawn them off on any available sitter and then refuse to send them to school until it was mandatory. Kevin's age demanded he go this year, but Hannah knew it'd be good for Lissa to enter kindergarten—mandatory or not.

It wasn't easy trying to befriend Faye. She used people rather than bonded with them. She never considered returning favors or chatting over a cup of coffee. Her attitude wore on Hannah, and if it wasn't for Martin, Kevin, and Lissa, she'd bail out of this relationship.

Lissa opened the door. "Hannah!" She squealed and jumped into her arms.

Hannah gave her a long hug.

Kevin came running into the room. "Did you bring us lunch?"

Hannah put Lissa on her hip. "Are you hungry?" She looked around the messy room. "Where's your mom?"

Lissa covered her mouth with her finger. "Shh. She's asleep."

Kevin licked what looked like peanut butter from his fingers. "I was tryin' to make peanut-butter sandwiches, but we just got one slice of bread."

Wondering why Faye hadn't brought the kids by the house, she held out her hand for Kevin. "I'll fix you something."

She took him by the hand and went into the kitchen. A quick peek into the cabinets and fridge said Faye needed a trip to the grocery store. She heated a can of soup and found some crackers to spread the peanut butter on. While they ate, she made a list of items to get at the store, making sure she bought plenty of foods Kevin could fix for them. When they were finished, she sent them outside to play and went to Faye's bedroom.

She knocked on the door. "Faye?" Calling to her again, she entered the room. "Faye."

The shades were pulled tight and were taped around the edges to keep out the light. "Faye." Hannah shook her.

Faye moaned. "What?"

"Get up!" Hannah shook her again. "You cannot leave Kevin and Lissa alone while you sleep. There's almost no food in the house. The door wasn't even locked when I arrived. You're a social services nightmare. Do you realize that?"

Faye took a deep breath and sat up. "Are the kids already up for the morning?"

"It's afternoon, Faye. I know it's hard losing Richard and Zabeth, but if you don't pull your act together, you're going to lose your kids too."

Faye pulled at Hannah's dress. "Don't turn me in. I'm a good mother. You know that."

"I know you want to be. There's a difference." Hannah jerked the tape off the sides of the black-out shades, peeling paint and fraying the shades at the same time. "Get up, take a shower, and let's go to the store."

"Yeah, okay." Faye staggered to her feet.

"If you ever pull this again, I'll take the children from you myself. Got that?"

She nodded. "I'm trying, Hannah. I swear I'm trying."

"Why didn't you bring them to me like you usually do?"

"I...I took a few drinks and..."

"Didn't drive."

"See, that's a good thing. You should be glad for that part."

"You don't drive because you don't want to get a DUI. What lame excuse would you like to give for not calling me? What you've done this morning is dangerous, Faye. Your children were hungry, and Lissa opened the door for me without even knowing who it was. Kevin was trying to figure out how to turn on the stove. He's six years old! Do you get that?"

Faye sank onto the bed holding her head.

"You're depressed too. You need help, Faye, professional help."

"Oh good grief, Hannah. That makes Zabeth a whole lot smarter than you. Open your eyes. I'm beyond help."

Hannah remembered well the feeling of being trapped, and she regretted sounding so harsh. "No one is beyond help, Faye—not unless they're dead. And you're not dead." She eased onto the bed beside her. "This is really hard to explain, but I'm convinced it takes two things to survive on this fallen planet. One is forgiveness, because when we forgive, we're saying what was done to us is not more powerful than God's ability to redeem us from it."

Faye stared at her as if her words might be sinking in.

Hannah put her arm around Faye's shoulders. "You need to forgive yourself. You need to believe what you did is not more powerful than what God can do from this point forward. I can't see that as I look around your life, and I know you can't either, but that's where the faith part comes in. Now you think on those things while you get your shower, and we'll talk some more."

~~∽~~

Luke pulled the mail from the box and read the return address on each envelope. He looked around the property for his wife and spotted her in the garden.

Walking toward the garden, he opened the letter from her doctor's office. "Mary Yoder, please be advised that you have missed your last two appointments. We have concerns about your rehabilitation and wellness program and would appreciate it if you would contact our office at your earliest convenience." Luke mumbled the words and closed the letter.

When he came to the edge of the garden, Mary saw him and stood straight, holding her back. "I've been at this all day. But here's the deal, I'm doing the planting, and you'll do the weeding, right?"

Luke held the letter out to her. "What's this?"

She took it and glanced over it. "It...it must be a mistake."

"It still has you listed as Mary Yoder."

She nodded. "I saw that."

"You're keeping up with those visits and everything, right?"

"Oh, Luke, I'm seeing the midwife now that I'm expecting, and there's no reason to keep going to those expensive doctors for them just to tell me I'm healthy. Ya?"

"Well, it's different with you, and I don't know..."

"Luke, I'm fine. You know I am. The doctor has given me a clean bill of health over and over again. It's time to forget the days of the accident and live like they never happened."

"Mary Yoder?" He lifted the letter from her hand and read it again.

"Mary Lapp, thank you very much." She washed her dirty hands off in the pail she'd been using to water her newly planted crop. Wiping them on her apron, she gazed up at Luke. "Unless you care to change your last name instead."

Luke scratched his forehead. "It just seems they'd get the name right."

She grabbed the pail and stood. "It also seems you wouldn't walk around in wet clothes."

"What?" He looked up from the paper just in time to see his wife throw water on him. "Mary Yoder!"

She burst into laughter and ran from him. "Who?" She grabbed the hose and held it toward him. "Even my husband calls me by my maiden name?"

"It was a mistake."

"Ya, and so was this."

Water smacked Luke in the face, and he charged her and wrestled the hose from her, all the while enjoying her laughter. She'd shed too many tears afraid she might never get pregnant. This new joy was a welcome thing.

When he had control of the hose, he drenched her good before she slid down on the grass. He dropped the hose and ran to her. "I'm sorry. Are you okay?"

Laughing, she grabbed a handful of loose dirt and tried to rub it in his face. He pinned her hands to the ground, chortling before they both grew serious as he lowered his lips to hers. "It's definitely Mary Lapp," Luke mumbled. "I remember that clearly now."

With Kevin and Lissa in tow, Hannah entered the church doors, returning a dozen greetings. She made her way to their children's church classrooms and signed them in before giving them hugs and heading for the sanctuary. The place wasn't very churchlike from the outside. It had once been a shopping complex, but that was impossible to tell once you were inside the renovated building. The praise music filled the air. A hint of unease clung to her as she maneuvered through the place without Zabeth.

She'd already arranged for Vicki and Nina to get the children after church and take them home. Either she or Martin would pick them up later. She took her seat in what had been Zabeth's and her spot. Martin was behind the keyboard, totally absorbed with the band. Although she missed a lot of Sundays due to her work at the clinic, she loved most parts of going to church here: the teaching, the music, the prayer time, communion, watching the altar calls, and the friendliness of the members. Other parts she could do without. Actually there was only one other part: the clothing worn by a lot of the women, especially the ones around her age. Jeans, short skirts, and tight tops seemed not to bother anyone but Hannah. But if men came here to worship God, why would a woman dress in such a way as to totally distract them? Wasn't God allowed one day, in His own house? She just didn't get it.

Then again, she figured it was her problem. She couldn't even manage to wear her hair loose, so what did she know? It'd taken her far too long to become comfortable wearing the mandatory scrubs when doing clinical rotations for nursing school.

Martin looked her way and raised his brows, showing his surprise. If he thought her making it to church when she was on call was unusual, she might need to get the ammonium carbonate out of her medical bag for the next shocker.

When the musicians moved to their seats for the preaching, Martin headed her way as he'd done every Sunday since last Christmas. As he took a seat, she could smell his cologne.

He placed his arm on the back of the bench. "I'm glad you made it. You doing okay?"

"Sure. You?"

"Yeah, I am. Listen, I'm having a memorial type gathering at my place this Friday. I can count on you being there, right?"

"For Zabeth?"

"Yeah, just a time with the band, singing her favorite songs."

"That should only take about three days."

He coughed into his hand to hide his laughter.

Howard, the man in front of them, turned around, smiling. "We know how to separate the *youth* when they get rowdy during service."

Martin pointed his thumb at Hannah, like it was all her fault. The man chuckled and turned back around. She folded her arms across her waist and frowned at Martin.

Pastor Steve opened the service, the PowerPoint slide behind him declaring the subject in bold, black letters. "Today's topic is intimacy and sexuality."

Hannah's breath caught. Martin leaned in, rubbing her shoulder sympathetically. "Breathe, phone girl. It's a five-part series," he whispered through his laughter.

She swallowed, wondering what all would be covered from a pulpit.

The pastor unbuttoned his bright red sports jacket. "Intimacy can be thought of as *in to me see*. And we let very few people really see who we are, but when we're a couple under God's direction, we long for that. But how do we get it?"

Hannah's cheeks burned mild to flaming as the service went on, but the teaching was insightful and filled with humor. As the pastor brought the service to a close, Martin got up to head for the keyboard. Before leaving the pew, he pointed at her. "You stay."

She gave a nod. When the service ended, she hung around in the sanctuary, chatting with people while waiting for Martin to finish playing the last songs. She was totally engrossed in answering some questions from a grandmother-to-be when she felt the warmth of Martin's hand on the small of her back.

"You about ready?" he asked.

The woman took her cue, thanked Hannah, and left.

He studied her, not looking his normal, confident self. "I'm starving, and you're not going to make me eat Sunday lunch alone, right?"

"Actually, no."

"Wow, can't say I saw that one coming."

Hannah straightened his shirt collar. "We need to talk." She patted his chest. "I brought us a picnic lunch."

He looked suspicious. "Where to?"

"Somewhere no one will hear you screaming at me."

"Hmm, I don't like the sound of this." They headed toward the exit. "There are picnic tables beside my office. No one will be anywhere near there on a Sunday." He pulled his keys from his pocket. "I'll drive and then bring you back here to pick up your car."

She dangled her keys. "I'm the one with the food. I'll drive and bring you back here."

He got in the car and made himself comfortable, punching the radio stations and making smart remarks about her driving. His sarcasm kept things lively from the time she got into the car until she pulled into his office parking lot. The manicured lawns and walls of windows gave the one-story, red-brick building a very classy look.

She put the stick shift in reverse and set the brake. "Nice place."

"Not bad." They opened their car doors in unison and got out. "I'm looking at leasing a new building next year since we're outgrowing this place, provided I pass my engineering exams in October."

"Have you turned in your board application forms?"

"Yep."

They chatted over little things while covering the table with a cloth, setting out the food, and eating lunch, only pausing to say a prayer before eating. The conversation meandered throughout the meal, but when he tossed his napkin onto his paper plate, an obvious transition took place.

"Okay, I'm full and completely satisfied, so what's on your mind, Esther?"

"Esther?" Hannah repeated before she realized he was referring to Queen Esther and her appeal for her people. "You're no king, and I'm not afraid anyone will lop off my head." She gathered the dirty plates and put them back in the basket.

He chuckled. "So what gives?"

After putting the rest of the items into the basket, she took a seat. "You do, I hope."

"What do you want?"

"You to get Faye into rehab and go to counseling sessions with her. Talk your dad into doing phone sessions on a regular basis. He's got the money. Get him to fly here for a few weeks. We need to help Faye get free of this unfair burden of guilt she carries. Shift the focus from her being the black sheep to the reality that she's a victim in this too."

He sighed. "Hannah, sweetheart, your motives are good, but Faye is a lost cause."

"I don't think so, but this isn't just about her. I mean, I've seen her at least three times a week since I met her. Under that veneer and deeper than her drug use, she's really sweet and hurting. I think you have enough influence on her that if you pushed in the right ways, she'd go into rehab, but—"

"No, she won't. Underneath it, she's an addict, Hannah. I'm sorry. That's just the way it is. She's not willing to go to rehab or counseling. And even if she would, I'm not going with her, and I'm certainly not asking my dad to get involved."

"Your dad wouldn't even call during a session to help his daughter?"

Martin stood, picked up the basket, and walked toward the car. "You'd have to know him."

She followed him. "What's he like?"

"Distinguished, filled with charisma, and bitter at Faye. Your plan isn't going to work. Faye has to want this, and she doesn't."

Hannah opened the trunk of her car. "But if you presented it…"

He placed the basket in the trunk. "No human can control another one's will. She doesn't want help."

"Sure she does. She just might not realize it yet, but if you—"

He slammed the trunk shut. "You're the one who…" His words came out mocking and condescending before he stopped. He walked away from her before turning. "I'm not willing to spend time and energy to land in the same freaking place with her I've been in for the past sixteen years—only to fail again. Do you know what it takes to be my age and run a business like this?" He waved his hand toward the building. "I have forty employees who all have personal issues, but at least they fight for success. Faye has no fight in her, and that's not our fault. The answer is no."

She stepped in closer. "And if you can do that for your employees, think what you could do for your sister. And you."

"Me? Are you saying I need help?"

"I…I'm saying if Faye gets help, it'll help you too."

He raked his hands through his hair. "There's nothing to help. I resent you implying that I need *Faye's* help."

He was yelling at her, and she knew he'd rather fight with her than for his sister.

"I'll keep Kevin and Lissa during every session. It won't be easy, but it's doable. You and your father haven't really tried. She's been left alone. You were a kid. It wasn't your fault, but it's time to—"

"You haven't been here but two years, and you have it all figured out—who's right, who's wrong, how you can fix it. Just butt out, Hannah."

"Fine." She opened her car door.

"Zabeth would never ask this of me."

"She was a mother to you. I want more. I want what you can't give me unless you can reach past your apathy and anger and help your sister." She angled her head, catching his eye. "Is that what you want from this relationship, for me not to ask more of you than Zabeth?"

An expression she couldn't read crossed his face. "No, of course not. Although a little of Zabeth's nondemanding ways would be appreciated about now."

"She wanted you and Faye and your dad—her family—to find a resolution to the nightmare that stole everything. All I'm asking is that you go with Faye and try to find some answers."

He shoved his hands into his pockets and walked off. "Why?" he shouted at the sky before facing her. "Why is jumping through hoops for Faye so important?"

In spite of his sarcastic tone, it was a fair question, but she could feel embarrassment burn her skin at the thought of answering.

She swallowed hard. "It's not just for Faye that I want this, or for you. *I* need this."

"You?"

Hating that she'd backed into a corner where the only way out was to share things she didn't want to, she made herself speak. "Look, I know this is unfair, but I need to know that when I make stupid decisions and you get caught in them, you'll reach out to me. Your sister made a mistake, and it feels like you just washed your hands of her."

He closed the distance between them. "That's ridiculous, and you're not making sense. You'd never do anything as—"

She placed her hand over his mouth, unable to hear his declaration of faith in her. "Everybody does hurtful stuff, Martin. I need this from you." Lowering her hand, she forced the next words out. "I never told you, but I became pregnant from the attack, and I tried to hide the whole thing from Paul." She crossed her arms, hating that her eyes were misting. "I knew if he ever found out about the rape, he'd end our relationship. He did, within two minutes of learning the truth. The baby died, and I came here." She shuddered. "Your sister made a mistake and has paid too high a price."

He took her hand into his. "I'm sorry Paul was a jerk. And I'm sorry for what you went through." He paused before giving a nod. "I see your point that it's easier to walk away than anything else." He sighed. "I'll see what I can do to get Faye into counseling, but you can't get upset when this plan does nothing to help her."

"It'll work. I know it will."

He rolled his eyes, took a step back, and opened the driver's door for her. "From now on, I'll know to beware of beautiful girls carrying loaded picnic baskets."

"Yeah?" She laughed.

He bent, giving her a kiss.

She caressed his face. "Thank you for doing this."

"Yeah, yeah, yeah, that's what you say now. Just wait until it all blows up in our face."

"It won't."

*M*atthew read the letter one last time before scrawling his name at the bottom. He folded it and shoved it into the envelope addressed to Elle. Against everything he'd spent years hoping for, he went to the mailbox, placed it inside, and lifted the red flag. An early-morning summer breeze carried the burnt smell from the Bylers' barn. The memory of flames leaping toward the sky last night left a sick feeling in Matthew's gut. But that didn't compare to the twisting ache that breaking off with Elle was causing.

Trudging into his workshop, he couldn't help but rehash how little he'd seen Elle since she went to live with her father more than two years ago. Each trip back she was different, more of an Englischer and less of the Elle he'd fallen in love with. He'd seen the look in her eyes, the one that said she no longer admired who he was or what talents he possessed. He wasn't in the same class of people as she was, and her visits seemed only to confirm that for her.

She'd spent the last year driving all over the U.S. while snapping pictures, but somehow her car just couldn't make it down these familiar roads very often. She'd signed some sort of contract without realizing exactly what it meant, and Matthew had been patient as she tried to get in her hours so the contract would be fulfilled. When it was time for instruction to begin, she had to get special permission to finish out her contracts among the Englischers and yet still be allowed to take instruction classes. As a testimony to Elle's ability to talk people into things, her bishop agreed. At first her efforts to be here for instruction had given him hope, but she hadn't made it for the last two lessons, nor had she called or written him.

Her agreement with her father not to call Matthew had ended quite a while ago, but her letters and phone calls had dwindled to nothing, and it was time he accepted reality. Her father had won. Elle would never be baptized into their faith.

Pulling on his tool belt, Matthew ran down a mental list of what he needed to get done today.

Luke was traveling, taking a week to handpick supplies and stock up for this next year. This was the fourth buying trip in as many months. Matthew went on the last three. Luke had avoided going for a while because of Mary, but now he wanted to get his time in so he wouldn't need to travel as Mary grew closer to her November due date.

Sarah drove the half-loaded produce wagon toward Miller's Roadside Stand.

She was sick of her parents always whispering about her odd behavior. Her hand had a burn on it, and she didn't know why. So what? If the constant gray cloud that clung to her thoughts would go away, maybe she could explain how she felt. But it never did.

Weariness made her movements hard during the day, but the nights were even worse. Fires blazed everywhere, creeping across Amish land until they burned right through her home. She shuddered.

After pulling the wagon under a shade tree at the roadside stand, she climbed out and looped the horse's reins around the hitching post. The stand had a blue and white tentlike covering, lawn chairs for the vendors, and plenty of parking for customers. The Millers' home was at the high point of the property, just a couple of hundred feet from the street. They rented a portion of their stand to anyone who needed a good place to sell things. Since the Lapps' house was so far off the main roads, this was one place they had always come to sell the extra yield from the family garden.

Leaning over the side of the wagon, she grasped the handles of the bushel basket.

"Sarah," Lizzy Miller called from her front porch.

Setting the heavy container on the ground, Sarah figured the girl was helping her mother collect this month's rent for the roadside stand. Sarah waved, letting her know she'd heard her. Then she reached into the wagon and unloaded the rest of the baskets while Lizzy hurried down the hill toward her.

"Did you hear?" Lizzy panted. The girl had graduated the eighth grade with Sarah years ago.

"Hear what?"

"The Bylers' barn burned down last night, all the way to the ground!"

The words shot through Sarah, making her feel woozy. Was her nightmare coming true? She set the small baskets of raspberries on the ground and straightened. "You sure?"

"Go see for yourself."

Without answering Lizzy, Sarah climbed into the wagon and took off.

It was quite a jaunt to the Bylers', but within thirty minutes she was pulling up at their place. Smoke was still rising from a few spots. Lizzy was right; there wasn't a salvageable piece of timber anywhere.

Unable to remove her eyes from the damage, she got out of the wagon and edged up to the smoldering embers. The barn had been a full, strong structure. She'd been to singings and church meetings here throughout her life. Hannah had taught her how to jump from the loft into a pile of hay in this barn. Stepping around the smoldering parts, Sarah walked through some of the ashes. How could such a strong building, with thick timber running in all directions for support, be reduced to this?

The tongue is a fire, a world of evil…and sets on fire the course of life.

A shudder ran through her, and those words looped through her mind again and again.

Aiming to find where the loft had crashed from its high position to the ground, Sarah continued walking around the edge of the building. Sadness deeper than any laughter or joy she'd shared in this building twisted inside her.

Wondering if the tiny corncob dolls she and Hannah had made and buried under the ground in the tack room more than a decade ago were still there, Sarah went to the spot where she thought they should be buried. The area had been along the outer wall. No smoke rose from that area. She held her hands over the cinders. They gave off no heat. Soot covered her hands and dress as she moved a few burnt two-by-fours. When a portion was cleared, she grabbed a piece of burnt tin from the roof, knelt where she thought they should be, and began digging.

~~♊~~

Matthew heard the door to the paint shop open. David had finished his other chores and had arrived to add another coat of shellac to the fifteen buggies that were close to being fitted to their undercarriages. Matthew worked another spoke into place on its wooden-hoop frame, hoping to get a dozen wheels done before nightfall.

As the morning wore on, sounds of the outdoors echoed through the open windows, allowing him to hear when the mail carrier approached. A desire to run to the mailbox and snatch back the letter gripped him. His palms became sweaty as he imagined the postal vehicle slowly heading, mailbox by mailbox, toward the Esh place. Ignoring his anxiety, he wrestled to line up the spokes that sprawled from the wooden hub with the hand-drilled holes in the circular frame.

He reminded himself that long before Elle's father showed up, her bishop had asked her to wait until she was at least twenty-one to join the faith. At the time he hadn't understood the reason, but the bishop had turned out to be right. Some Englischers had tried living Amish. It never lasted for more than a few years before they pulled out of the faith, sold their places, and returned to the easier ways of the fancy folk.

He'd thought it would be different for Elle since she'd been raised Amish half her life. As the mail carrier closed the metal lid on the Esh mailbox and drove off, Matthew went to the barn and bridled his fastest horse. He needed a few minutes away from the shop.

Holding on tight, he spurred the horse across his property, jumping every fallen log, trampling through the creek, and riding at breakneck speeds across the flatlands. The warm breeze whipped through his shirt, cooling the sweat against his body. His straw hat flew off, but he didn't slow. He should have known Elle wasn't likely to return to the Plain life. He tightened his grip on the reins and dug his heels into the horse, wishing he could outrun reality.

When Matthew spotted the profile of a female across the meadow, he slowed the horse to an amble. She seemed to be kneeling in the grass. He tugged at the rein and clicked his tongue, heading the horse in that direction.

As he came closer, he could make out a white prayer Kapp on her head. He thought it odd that the woman didn't seem to hear the approaching hoofbeats against the dry ground.

A childlike voice drifted through the air. "The tongue is a fire, a world of evil...and sets on fire the course of life."

"Excuse me." Matthew brought the horse to a full stop. The girl jumped up. "Sarah?" She was covered in soot, and the hems of her skirts were torn. "What are you doing out here?" He scanned the edges of the fields. "Is someone with you?"

She shook her head, looking terrified. Dark soil covered the green and brown grass beside her, and he realized she'd been digging in it. "What are you doing?"

"I...I was burying something for Hannah."

"Hannah?" He steadied his horse. "When did you talk to her?"

She turned her back to him, knelt, and put whatever was in her hand into the hole in the ground and covered it. When she stood, she stepped on the fresh dirt, packing it down. "I haven't spoken to her." After wiping her dirt-covered hands down her apron, she turned her palms upright, as if she were offering him a gift. But her hands were empty.

"How did you get this far from home without a horse?"

"I came to bur—" She didn't finish her sentence.

Matthew tried again. "Did you drive a horse and buggy to the Yoders and then walk to this spot?"

"I went to Miller's Roadside earlier, then drove the horse and buggy to the Bylers'. From there I drove to the back part of your property and walked."

Matthew was even more confused now. Sarah had always been skittish and odd, to his way of thinking, but this behavior left him more uneasy than ever. Her hands trembled as she tried dusting them off. He decided not to try to figure this out. He'd just talk to Luke about it when he got home. "Can I give ya a ride back to your buggy?"

She nodded, and he reached a hand down to help lift her onto the horse's back. She wrapped her hands around his waist. Not liking this one bit, he dug his heels into the horse. "Geh."

artin stared into his sister's almost-black eyes, weary of this conversation. He'd been at this session for more than an hour. Hannah was baby-sitting Kevin and Lissa at his house, and he'd told her he'd be home by five. It was Friday, so she didn't need him to relieve her for classes or the clinic, but she did have plans of some sort.

Faye needed to live at the rehab center for a few more weeks, but all the intervention had accomplished so far was schedule chaos for Hannah and him. Hannah arrived at his home by six in the morning, and she needed to leave his house by five in the evening, Monday through Thursday—except on Tuesday. Tuesdays were the worst. She had that quilting thing at the clinic and often ended up taking Kevin and Lissa with her and dropping them at the house before going to the crisis center. He had to leave work at four in the afternoon, cutting off at least three valuable hours of work time to care instead for his sister's children.

With Dr. Smith listening silently, Faye had gone through a whole box of tissues, but they'd landed in the same place they always did. She claimed that everyone in the family hated her because they blamed her for her mom's death. Martin denied it. He didn't blame her for that, but the drugs and alcohol abuse were her choices. She had to be accountable for that.

But not for the accident.

Still, what led to the shattering of their childhood made more sense each time he came here. Occasionally when she shared a recollection, it caused other memories to flood his mind, and in some ways he understood both Faye and himself more now.

When Martin talked to his dad about doing phone sessions, he refused. Flat out. Martin didn't intend to tell Faye he'd contacted their dad. It was hard enough to get her into rehab and counseling without reminding her how little their dad wanted to do with her.

She grabbed another tissue. "Can't you see how Dad manipulated me to fight with Mom and then, after the accident, he just abandoned me?"

"Dad's never manipulated anybody. You ran off, Faye. But even then, he kept giving you money, supporting you."

She sniffled. "Don't you ever wonder why he did that?"

"He's done nothing but try to help you."

The counselor shifted in her chair. "Okay, we've covered a lot today. I think this session has been extremely helpful."

The doctor continued talking, drawing things to a close, but Martin wasn't listening. He'd heard plenty, and none of it was new. Faye just didn't get it. No one blamed her but herself. She had destroyed her own life, not Mom or Dad or him. Surprisingly, on this trip he'd heard one encouraging thing: she was attending chapel services.

After the counselor closed the session with prayer, Martin left without another word.

Thanks to his sister, he had a mess of a life to keep up with, including juggling her two children—with Hannah's help.

Hannah.

Despite having built a good friendship beforehand, he and Hannah were being taxed by this stuff with Faye. Hannah had cut her hours at Dr. Lehman's clinic, but she couldn't cut her school, study time, or clinical rotation hours.

She worked harder than anyone he knew and continued to amaze him. For quite a while after first meeting her, Martin kept dating, looking for other possibilities—because of her age and background. But a part of him kept hoping that when she was older, she'd be the one he'd been waiting for. The one he'd been looking for since he'd realized the importance of God in his life.

When he was a kid, his mother had told him, "When you get old enough, date, date, date, but never settle for less than the one you know in your heart is right for you." He'd like to hear what advice she'd give him now.

But she was gone, thanks to his sis—

Oh God, please…

His stomach clenched in a knot, making him feel sick. He had to pull to the side of the road. Like a spray of cold water in winter, chills crashed over him.

Faye was right.

Dear God, I do blame her.

Memories of how he'd coped after Mom died seeped into his mind from somewhere he didn't know existed. He'd always believed he and his dad were good people caught in an awful situation, but where did that leave Faye? And why hadn't he seen any of this before now?

He turned the car around to go see his sister.

With Lissa and Kevin playing in the yard, Hannah sorted through another box in Martin's storage room inside the cottage behind his home, looking for items to donate to the women's shelter. Martin cared nothing about this stuff from his childhood and Lissa's and Kevin's infancy. It was time to put it to good use. Since Martin was late again, she continued digging through it. She'd already brought out a bassinet from the storage room, cleaned it, and set it up. The washer and dryer had worked all day on old blankets, sheets, and baby clothes.

Through the screen door, she could hear the children's voices as they made pies from outdated flour, eggs, and milk she'd found when cleaning out Martin's fridge and cabinets. Kevin and Lissa were mixing the items with sand and had a table set for a bake sale. Their childish excitement over old foods had made her smile.

Even though she was still living at the cabin, she spent more time on Martin's property than at home, and it was unexpectedly stressful. She'd discovered that the cottage behind his place was more her style than his house. His fully air-conditioned, electronically endowed, television-crazy home made her long for the cabin. Most of all she missed having time to enjoy her garden. Martin's manicured lawns, maintained by paid help, were picture perfect, but they didn't compare to the beauty of the landscape at Zabeth's place. As soon as Martin came home today, she'd head for the cabin and weed the garden.

In a few weeks both Kevin and Lissa would begin school. She'd updated their immunizations and taken care of the paperwork. Martin had enrolled them.

Remembering she'd seen one more box of items she hadn't gone through yet, Hannah went back to the storage room. She opened the box and pulled out folded sheets and blankets one by one. As she came to the bottom of the box, she noticed frayed edges of fabric under a store-bought blanket. She removed the top item, revealing a patchwork quilt that showed clear markings of being designed by Zabeth. Pulling it out and laying it in her lap, she noted the tiny black squares of material added to the defined pattern. Hannah smoothed her hand over the well-worn quilt. It was Zabeth's work all right, and it looked like someone had abused it before packing it away. The fabric patches—leopard skin, white silk, pink tulle, crimson satin, brown suede—were not Zabeth's usual choices, which meant she'd made it for someone special with fabrics from his or her personal life. It had to belong to a Palmer—Faye, Martin, or their parents. Whoever received it hadn't understood; a quilt was like a person, possessing strength and honor as well as frailties and needs. Right then, she decided to work on the quilt at the next quilting.

Hannah took it to her car. As she was closing the door, Martin pulled into the driveway.

She waved as he got out of his car. "Hey, you're even later than usual."

"Yeah, I know."

"The kids have eaten, and there's a plate for you in the oven if you want it."

"You're leaving now? Are you on call or something?"

"There are only so many hours of daylight, Martin, and it's hard to weed a garden in the dark. I have rotation this weekend. That makes this my only time to do something outside of school, work, and baby-sitting."

He scoffed and pulled his checkbook out of his back pants pocket. "Just let me write a check to cover what you'll make on that garden."

Hannah blinked. "What?"

"Oh, come on, Hannah. This is ridiculous." He filled in a check and held it out to her. "Forget the garden. We're both pulling double duty as it is, and this will more than compensate."

"Do you think money is the answer to everything?" She pulled her keys from her dress pocket and got into her car.

"Get out of the car, Hannah. Now."

She rolled the window down. "Excuse me?" She released the brake and pressed the clutch. "I resent being treated like a child. Moreover, I refuse."

Before she pressed the accelerator, Martin stepped behind the car. She slammed on the brakes, turned off the motor, and jumped out. "Are you crazy?"

"Don't get angry with me and just leave. Stay and scream until all the neighbors hear you, but don't ever do that."

In that moment she realized that a similar situation was how he'd lost his mother. She shut the car door. "You want me to stay and scream? Fine! Your all-air-conditioned, highly technical, very modern house is driving me crazy!"

"Yeah?" He screamed back. "Well, when you go off by yourself, you drive me nuts, and I have no cabin of refuge!"

They stared at each other.

Hannah propped herself against the car. "I drive you nuts?"

He shrugged. "Maybe."

Standing in front of her was her closest friend, a man who'd made himself vulnerable by reaching out to his sister because she'd asked him to. "I'm sorry."

"Yeah, me too. And I won't ever try to put a price on that stupid garden of yours again."

She laughed. "Deal."

Kevin ran from the backyard, carrying a pan of *pies* with him. Stress was etched on his young face, and Hannah realized the raised voices had him in a panic. Lissa was right behind him, looking as if she was about to cry.

Before she could say something, Lissa pulled on Martin's leg, her dirty hands leaving imprints. "Who's leaving?"

Martin put Lissa on his hip.

Hannah picked up Kevin. "Nobody. Not right now. I might go to the cabin later."

But the concern in their eyes said they'd heard the anger between the adults and didn't believe her. "Your Uncle Martin and I were playing. That's what you heard, but you know what I think? I think your uncle is hungry and needs a nap."

Martin nodded. "May I please have food and a nap?"

Kevin giggled. "Naps are for babies."

"Are not!" Lissa yelled.

"Whoa." Martin held up his hand. "Answer my question first."

Hannah pointed at him. "You may have food, but it's too late for a nap. So…after you eat, you, Kevin, and Lissa may come with me to the cabin."

"I'd rather have a nap."

Lissa shook her finger at him. "You better watch it, Uncle Martin. Hannah won't let you have a snack with your dinner."

Martin gaped mockingly at one and then the other. "What?"

Lissa giggled. "And even if you're good, she doesn't allow television."

He touched the end of her nose with his index finger. "Yeah, I've heard that before. But that means you're just happier when I'm home, right?"

"Thanks, Martin."

He chuckled as he set Lissa's feet on the ground. "No. I thank you, Hannah."

Hannah put Kevin down and took the *pie* from him. She bit her bottom lip and bounced the pan filled with gunk up and down.

Martin pointed at her. "If you start this, I'll finish it."

She stepped in close. "Promise?" she taunted right before smacking him in the chest with the pie. She took Lissa into her arms and took off running to get another pie.

Martin whispered something to Kevin, who ran into the house. Instantly they were divided, the girls against the boys. From the pie-making area, Hannah grabbed a handful of gunk. Kevin came back outside with a bottle of ketchup and mustard. He passed the ketchup bottle to his uncle. The two guys moved in close, and she flung the goop at Martin, missing completely. He mocked an evil laugh and stepped in closer.

"Don't you dare, Mart—"

He squirted the red sauce over her bare feet and across her dress. He then aimed the bottle at her face. He roared with laughter before aiming the bottle at Kevin.

"Yeah, get me, Uncle Martin. Get me!"

The next ten minutes were spent with Kevin and Lissa playing dodge ketchup. When the bottle was empty, the four of them were a mess.

Martin and Kevin went to one bathroom to get cleaned up, and Hannah and Lissa went to another. Twenty minutes later the kids were clean and dressed in warm clothes and sent back outside to play, with all yucky stuff off-limits for the night.

Martin and Hannah went into the kitchen. She pulled his plate of food from the oven and set it on the table. He grabbed a bottle of water from the refrigerator.

Hannah sat at the table, waiting for him to say something.

Martin stabbed a forkful of potatoes. "I got a little too angry."

"And too demanding. But I might have been a little testy myself and a bit desperate for the solitude of the cabin."

He took a bite of the grilled pork chop. "That's so good," he mumbled.

"Was it bad at work today?"

He shook his head. "The average hassles. But I had to put everything aside again to meet with Faye. The session with her was really long and difficult."

"Why didn't I know you were seeing her today?"

"I guess because I don't like to think about the sessions, let alone admit when I'm going to them."

"Do you want to talk about it?"

"Well, 'want to' might be pushing it, but I will." He winked at her. "Can I have a promise first?"

"I promise."

"Do you know what you just promised me?"

She nodded. "To not get angry and leave but to stay and work things out."

"Nope. You just promised to marry me."

She burst out laughing.

He set the fork down and covered her hand with his. "I need you to keep your word on that, Hannah. Since we first met at GymberJump, you've shown your tendency to turn your back and just leave. On our first date, I had to take the keys."

"I just get angry way beyond what's happening right then, and I don't know what to do with it other than get away."

He sat up straight and picked up the fork. "I really don't understand it from someone as levelheaded as you are, but you've got to give me your word—no more leaving during the heat of an argument."

"I promise."

He nodded. "It was a good session with Faye, the best we've had yet. Only it was draining and just made me feel nauseated. I faced some things I didn't know about myself."

He ate and talked. Later they moved to the chairs in the backyard. Lissa and Kevin climbed into the hammock and went to sleep to the sounds of adults discussing events in their week. When the children dozed off, Martin and Hannah began talking about deep things again. As Martin told about the progress Faye was making and the self-realizations they were both having, hope for the Palmers' future warmed her. Faye was coming home next week. They would still need to help juggle Lissa and Kevin so she didn't get over-whelmed, but she was coming home.

"Hannah?"

Her head was against the back of the chair as she watched the leaves of the sycamore sway softly under the glow of moonlight. "Hmm?"

"Do you feel like you know what you want in life?"

The sounds of crickets rode gently across the night air while she thought about his question. Voices from the past demanding she live by the *Ordnung* rose, then faded. An image lingered of who she once thought she'd become— in a caped dress and prayer Kapp, trying to live an obedient Plain life but determined to find enough freedom within to discover her real self.

Looking across the lush lawn to the electric lights shining through the windows of the stately home, she was again struck by the contrast of her life now. Then Hannah's eyes focused on Lissa and Kevin, snuggled under a blanket. They were so precious. She smiled at Martin, who watched her intently. "Most days."

"Think you'd care to take our dating more seriously? You know, make a verbal commitment?"

She laughed. "And ruin whatever this game is that we play?"

"It's called the game of growing up, and you've played it quite well."

"It's a shame I can't return the compliment."

"Cute."

"So, after accepting the challenge of committing to date just one girl, you want to step up that pledge?"

He took her hands in his. "Truth is, even though I went out with all those girls, I've always been looking for you, and then you landed here— entirely too young to do anything about it and from a different world."

Somewhere inside her, his words snuggled against her soul and the magnetic pull of being this close to him made her head swim. But she was in too deep already since she hadn't told him the one thing that might cause him to change his mind. "I don't really see a need to step up what we have. We're dating. We've agreed you won't see anyone else."

"Just me?" he mocked.

She gave him a kiss. "Yep, just you. I better head home. Good night, Martin."

$\mathcal{M}$atthew lifted off the back of the truck the last box of supplies from Luke's most recent trip to the wholesale stores.

Nate McDaniel, their truck driver and Englischer neighbor, who lived some fifteen miles down the road, clapped his hand against Matthew's back. "You got quite a stack of papers mounded in your old workshop."

Perching the edge of the box on the tailgate, Matthew chuckled. "Yeah, I know. We hired a cousin of Esther Byler to come in and help out. She starts later today, but a person might go in there and never come out."

Nate laughed. "Buried alive by paperwork." He pulled keys from his pocket. "Hope whoever you find is up to the task." He glanced at his watch. "I gotta run. It took me and Luke two days more than we figured on to get all that stuff. I imagine the missus has a honey-do list a mile long."

"Thanks, Nate." Matthew hoisted the box. "We should be all set for quite a while." As Nate pulled his truck out of the driveway, Matthew carried the load into the storage room.

With a clipboard in his hand, Luke stepped in front of Matthew and jotted down the inventory numbers off the side of the box. He then pointed to a section of boxes. "Let's put it over there."

Matthew slid the carton into place. "Where's David and Jacob?"

"Tending horses and lallygagging, in that order." Luke lowered the clipboard to his side and bounced it against his leg. "I know Jacob is Mary's brother and all, but we gotta do something about him."

Matthew nodded. "I know. But right now we need to talk about somethin' a lot more serious." Wasting no time, Matthew told Luke about finding Sarah covered in soot and burying things in an unused field.

Luke wiped his brow. "What do you think she was doing?"

"I have no idea. I took her to her buggy that she'd left near Mary's house, but I didn't go back to the field and dig up whatever it was she buried. That just seemed wrong." Matthew propped his foot on top of one of the boxes. "You know how bad she got right after Hannah left. Well, I hate to say this, but she seems really bad again. Maybe the Bylers' barn going up in flames made her slip right off that ledge again. It's the only reason I can figure why she'd be going through the ashes."

A car door slammed, causing Luke to go to the window. He turned to Matthew. "I think I'll go to the Yoders' and let Mary know I'm back. Then I'd best go to the folks' place and see what's up with Sarah. And, uh, good luck, Matthew. Looks like you're going to need it."

"Huh? What are you talk—"

"Matthew Esh!" Elle's voice vibrated the walls as she entered the front door of the shop.

Luke passed the clipboard to Matthew and slipped out the side door of the storage room. Matthew walked through the connecting hallway and into his old shop.

Elle waved papers in the air. "This is how you wait for somebody?"

He recognized the pages in her fist. He was surprised she hadn't been relieved by his letter and figured she was more insulted than disappointed. "Hi, Elle." He went to the file cabinet, which had more papers stacked on top of it and beside it than in it. "You mad 'cause I dared to do what you wanted to but wouldn't, or 'cause you actually care?" He removed the inventory sheets from the clipboard and opened a cabinet drawer.

She shook the letter at him. "This stinks, Matthew, and I'm disappointed in you."

"In me?" Unable to find the right file, he shut the drawer and added the papers to the large stack beside the cabinet. "I'm not the one running around like it's my *rumschpringe*."

"That's ridiculous! I'm not using any freedoms to…" She didn't finish her sentence, and he figured her conscience had stopped her cold. He felt like a parent with Elle, the rebellious teen, sneaking around behind his back.

He pointed at her hair, which she was now wearing shoulder length with wild curls going every direction. He'd wanted to see her like this, no question, but he never thought she'd walk around for everybody, hair flying. "Nice, uh, outfit."

Pushing the sides of her slinky, printed green and sky blue skirt against her legs, she pointed to its length, which came just below her knees. "This is perfectly modest," she growled at him. "And it's a reasonable compromise while I finish up my contracts with that photography studio."

"Yeah, I know. Life is all about everyone making compromises while you half fulfill your part of the agreement."

"I signed a contract, Matthew. It was based on hours logged, not a set number of months. I told you all this." She shook the letter in the air. "So I found some interests out there and asked you to give me a bit of time. How is that not fulfilling my part of the agreement?"

"You know how to write, but I seldom receive a letter anymore. You own a phone, but I don't even remember the last time you called me. You own a car, but you rarely come to visit. You've missed the last two articles of instruction. You can lie to yourself if you want, but I'm tired of it. Your dad wanted you away from us, away from me, in order to break us up, and he's accomplished that goal. You wanted to go to that photography school, and I agreed to give you all the freedom you needed, but I never signed up to play the fool."

"I've been busy trying to get my hours done!"

"And I've given you lots of room and time. But this isn't about how busy you are. Your heart is no longer invested in us. You're supposed to be living here and dressing Amish to take your instructions, but you've sidestepped everything to fulfill this contract you shouldn't have signed in the first place."

Her gorgeous eyes fastened on him, and he was caught off guard by her moment of calmness. "The way I've been dressing is really just camouflage, if you'll think about it. I mean, in the real world no one thinks anything about dressing like this."

The real world?

Irritation ran hot as she avoided his points and then insulted him, but he chose not to take up an argument over her meaning of that phrase. He clasped his suspenders. "Look me in the eyes and tell me you're every bit as sure about us as you try to make yourself sound."

She hesitated, and Matthew thought his heart would sink into his shoes. "You been going out with someone while I've been waiting?"

"Of course not—"

"I'm tired of the games, Elle. Do you understand?"

The screen door swung open, and Esther Byler's cousin, the new hired help, walked in.

"Kathryn, we're in the middle of something here. Can you give me a minute to finish up before we begin on the paperwork?"

As Kathryn's dress swished out the door, Elle slapped him in the chest with the letter he'd written to her. "I can make up for missing the two article lessons. The bishop said so."

Matthew took the letter from her and shrugged. "No doubt you did a fine job of talking him into it."

"This isn't about how I'm acting or dressing or how busy I've been. This is about you. You've become this successful, wealthy man since I moved away. I bet girls are just flocking your way from all over the state. Maybe you don't want the embarrassment among your Amish peers of marrying some ex-Englischer, even if I were ready to take my vows."

Matthew folded the letter. "I didn't back away, Elle. You did."

She jerked the papers from his hand and ripped them in two. "Fine." She threw the torn papers at him and ran out the door.

He hurt all over as he watched her drive away, but his resolve hadn't been shaken one bit. She was no longer the Elle he'd fallen in love with, and she had no real desire to leave the ways of the Englischers and live Amish. She couldn't even be honest enough with herself to acknowledge the clear truth of her choices.

It hadn't been easy, but he'd ended things for both their sakes.

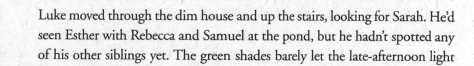

Luke moved through the dim house and up the stairs, looking for Sarah. He'd seen Esther with Rebecca and Samuel at the pond, but he hadn't spotted any of his other siblings yet. The green shades barely let the late-afternoon light in. As he topped the stairway, he saw the shadowy outline of his mom sitting in her rocker.

"Mamm, where is everybody?" When she didn't move, Luke eased into the room and removed his straw hat. "Mamm?"

Like cold molasses being poured from its container, she turned her face toward him. "Any word from Hannah?"

Since the community phone Hannah would call was at the Yoders', Mamm asked that question every time she saw him.

"Not for a long time." He squeezed the brim of his hat. "You okay?"

"Yeah." Mamm pulled her shawl tighter. "But Hannah would know what to do…if we could just contact her."

"Know what to do about what, Mamm?"

She rose from the chair and went to the chest at the foot of her bed. After kneeling and opening it, she pulled out something wrapped in newspapers. Closing the lid, she rose, removed the paper, and held the bundle in front of him. "Sarah came home in these a few days ago." Mamm took a corner of each side of the fabric and let it unfold in front of Luke.

It was the soot-covered dress and apron Matthew had told him about.

His mother took a step back and sat on the bed, looking worn-out. "She tried to hide them in the trash," she whispered. "You don't think she had anything to do with the Bylers' barn burning down, do you?"

"No." Luke took the dress from her and rolled it up. "No, Matthew saw her in a field behind his house the day after the fire. You must have seen her in these clothes the morning after the fire, and they weren't damaged then. Right?" He grabbed the newspaper off the floor and wrapped it around the clothes.

The lines across her face eased, and a half smile tugged at her lips. "Yes, that's right."

He put the wrapped clothing back in the chest and closed it.

Mamm drew a deep breath. "I should've thought about the timing of it all. She took some bushels of produce to the Miller's Roadside Stand that morning. She came home at the end of the day without any empty baskets or any money. According to Deborah Miller, Sarah just up and left every-thing there first thing that morning, but she didn't come home until nearly dark." Mamm fought tears. "I'm getting scared. I don't want to lose another daughter."

Luke eased onto the bed beside his mother, wishing he knew the answer, any answer that would bring comfort.

Mamm rubbed her head firmly. "Why didn't I stand up for Hannah when I had the chance?" A sob burst from her before she gained control.

Luke gave her a pat on the shoulder and tried changing the subject. "Where's Daed, Levi, and Sarah?"

"Daed and Levi are hauling pews to the Millers' for Sunday's service. I have no idea where Sarah is." Mamm wiped her tears. "Something's wrong with her. She's always been jittery and has spoken before she thought, but I was sure she'd outgrow her oddities. Now they grow like weeds in the garden. You've got to help me talk to your Daed about her."

Luke was fairly sure Paul could help Sarah or would know who could, but his Daed wasn't going to allow that. Luke and Mary saw Paul here and there. They'd had dinner with him at his grandmother's place a few times. He was nearly finished with his schooling and worked a fair amount of hours at a mental-health clinic not far from here.

Mamm searched his face before she rose to her feet and paced the length of the room. "Why didn't I speak up? I knew in my heart Hannah wasn't any of those things they accused her of." She stopped all movement. "I can't stand it any longer. My anger burns against—" She covered her mouth, as if sud-denly aware of what she was saying.

"Against the church leaders?" Luke finished for her.

She shook her head. "They responded based on what they knew, but we betrayed her." Mamm stared into his eyes. "If I'd done Hannah right, Sarah wouldn't be having these problems."

"That's not true, Mamm."

"Yes, it is. And I've got to look my eldest daughter in the eye and tell her I'm sorry I failed her. I'm sorry her father and I turned against her."

"Ruth!" Daed's voice boomed from the foot of the steps, followed by his clomping up the stairway. "I'll not be talked about behind my back in my own home."

Expecting his Mamm to lower her head and apologize, Luke witnessed a shadowy image of Hannah in his own mother as she lifted her head and squared her shoulders. "Fine, then I'll say it to your face. I've not spoken of this with anyone before today, so don't think I've been sowing bad seed. I've held my tongue until my heart holds nothing but venom and anger. I followed you, Zeb Lapp, when I felt it was wrong to do so. And I'll swallow poison before I bow to your great and mighty wisdom again."

His mother wasn't just angry with Daed; she was bitter. And as Luke stood there, he vowed to always give Mary a voice. They were a team, and he might be the leader, but he'd not ever think Mary should hold her opinions while doing things his way. They'd talk and pray and decide together. Even if they made the wrong choice because he gave her too much say, they'd go through whatever happened in unity. Any bad decision made and worked through together had to be better than what his father had done to his mother.

Mamm pointed a finger at his father. "You despise Naomi Esh for speaking to you the way she did, but at least she was honest. Heaven forbid a female see something a man doesn't and tell him he's wrong."

"Ruth! You will get control of your tongue immediately."

"I won't. God gave me a mind and a heart, and you've trampled all over them. Rather than stand before the church leaders and tell them they were mistaken, you sided with them."

"Is it my fault Hannah snuck letters to that Mennonite boy and lied about why she was going to Mrs. Waddell's? How do you know that child she carried wasn't his?"

In spite of his fear, Luke knew it was time to speak up. "Daed, I know Paul. I met him the first week Hannah was gone. The baby wasn't his. They were secretly engaged, but he's as good a man as I've ever known. Even though he's got that education in psychology, he planned to work for you and win your approval. I don't doubt that he kissed Hannah, but it went no further. I believe that, and if he had any reason to think that was his child, he would have married her. Fact is, he came back for her and intended to marry her anyway, regardless of how she came to be pregnant."

His father stared at him as the clock ticked the seconds into minutes. Finally Daed's shoulders slumped, and he sat on the bed, looking up at his wife. "Do you hate me for this, Ruth?"

Mamm stared at him, and Luke thought she just might.

She knotted her hands into fists. "I want my daughter back—if only so we can stand before her and confess our sin. I think she'd know how to help Sarah. She's in a bad way, and she's only gotten worse since the day she learned of Hannah's troubles. Hannah would know what to do. I believe that."

Mamm went downstairs, leaving Daed without an answer to his question.

Luke's father ran a rough hand over his face, swiping his misting eyes. "I...I'd like to be alone for a while."

Luke closed the bedroom door as he left. He went downstairs, gave his mother a long, wordless hug, and walked out of his house. As he climbed into his buggy, a windstorm of emotions pounded against him. But he didn't know anything he could do to change the situation. Not one thing.

$\mathscr{H}$ annah stacked the books into the crook of her arm and whispered a prayer as she locked the cabin door. Days of poring over pages of nursing care for each stage of a person's life would do her no good if she was late. Schooling didn't get easier as time went on, but in months she'd have her nursing certificate.

And probably run down the aisle to receive her diploma, at least on the inside. She opened the passenger door and laid her books on the seat. A car horn blasted long and loud three times. Even though she wasn't able to see over the knoll, she was sure it wasn't Martin. He arrived at work early and stayed until nearly bedtime—except on Fridays, when they went out.

But that wasn't the way Faye blew the horn either.

Faye's vehicle topped the knoll, spewing dirt in every direction before it fishtailed. The driver regained control and flew toward Hannah before slamming on the brakes. Faye climbed out of her vehicle. Her unkempt hair and dirty clothes turned Hannah's stomach.

"Faye, is something wrong?"

Faye didn't even look at her as she opened the backseat to her car and unbuckled Lissa. Kevin climbed out behind his sister.

"I…I have class tonight, but you know we planned for Kevin and Lissa to come here on Saturday after my rotation and to stay until Monday evening."

"No!" She slammed the car door.

Hannah started toward her. "Faye?"

Faye set Lissa's feet on the ground and nudged her away. "Go," she snapped at both children. Kevin and Lissa joined hands, staring at their mother.

Hannah stepped between Faye and her children. Hannah reached for her, but she jumped back and glared. Icy fingers of anxiety wrapped around

Hannah's throat, making it difficult to breathe. This was no tantrum or bad mood. Faye's pupils were dilated. She was using again.

"What have you done?" Hannah whispered through clenched teeth.

Faye pushed her backward. "I can't do this anymore. I just can't."

Hannah easily regained her footing and ignored the physical shove. "You *have* to be able to do it. We'll call Martin. He'll go with you, talk to the counselor with you."

"I'm done, Hannah."

"Done? You can't mean that!" She silently counted to three, trying to control her anger. "I know your life has been unfair and filled with a ton of grief. Our lives are a lot alike in that. But you've gotta keep fighting. I'll help you more. My schooling will be over soon." Hannah managed a smile, wondering how much of what she had said was getting through the drug-induced fog.

Faye backed away from her. "You know nothing about my life! You waltz in here and become Zabeth's hero. I'm the one who stole her dearest friend!"

"I…I…" Stunned at this viewpoint, Hannah struggled to find some words. "Faye, this isn't about me or Zabeth or Martin or even your mom. You've got to fight for your life, the one God gave you, regardless of anyone else—including your own past. I landed here and—"

Faye covered her eyes. "And you lived happily ever after." The hopelessness in Faye's voice sounded painfully familiar.

Hannah took Faye's trembling hand and looked into her eyes. "Oh, come on, Faye. You know where we met and how I changed my last name. Half the time I just manage to cope."

Faye's steely eyes looked a little softer for a moment. "That's all?"

Hannah sighed. "It's enough." She rubbed her throbbing head. "My drug of choice is absolute determination."

Faye shook her head, hostility returning to her expression as she opened the trunk of the car. She took out two large boxes filled with crumpled clothes and toys, tossed them on the ground, and shut the trunk. "Take care of my babies." Faye climbed back into the car.

"What?" Hannah glanced around, looking for something that made sense. "Wait. When are you coming back?"

She slammed the door and slung pebbles and debris as she sped off.

Hannah wanted to scream and run after her, but instead she smiled at Kevin and Lissa. "Hi, guys." She knelt in front of them. "Why don't you go get some eggs out of the refrigerator and some mixing bowls to make mud pies with?"

Kevin wrapped his arm around his sister's shoulders, as if to ease the weight of their mother's departure. "Sure." He turned his back on Hannah. "Come on, Lissa. You can cook those pies using some muffins tins, just like Aunt Zabeth showed us."

Hannah pulled her phone from her pocket and called Martin.

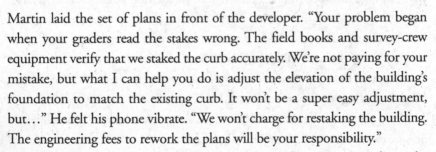

Martin laid the set of plans in front of the developer. "Your problem began when your graders read the stakes wrong. The field books and survey-crew equipment verify that we staked the curb accurately. We're not paying for your mistake, but what I can help you do is adjust the elevation of the building's foundation to match the existing curb. It won't be a super easy adjustment, but…" He felt his phone vibrate. "We won't charge for restaking the building. The engineering fees to rework the plans will be your responsibility."

The man stared at the plans, clearly needing a few minutes to digest the bad news.

Martin ignored the buzz of the phone hooked to his belt. The last four calls had been from Faye. He'd read the screen and continued with his business meeting. He'd call her later. Maybe in a day or two. He'd spent the last three days dealing with issues on this job site, and he wanted to stay on track so he could get out of Columbus by midnight.

"You say the construction crew read the survey stakes wrong?"

"Yes, that's what the surveyor and I showed you earlier on the job site. The elevations on the stakes do not match the curb that was poured, but—"

Without removing it from his belt, he shifted the phone to hit the Reject button and caught a glimpse of the screen.

Hannah.

She'd called him a total of four times since arriving in Ohio—the first three were when Zabeth needed to be hospitalized, the fourth was the night Zabeth stopped breathing. He grabbed the phone and pulled it to his ear. "Hey, what's up?"

The developer smacked the papers. "How much money are we talking about?"

Martin held up his hand, signaling for the man to give him a minute.

"She dropped off the kids with large boxes of their stuff and told me to be good to her babies. Martin, I…I don't think she's coming back."

"What?"

The developer rattled the paper. "Can we get back to this, please?"

Martin didn't miss the man's ill-tempered tone, but he walked out of the room and closed the door behind him. He glanced at his watch. "Call Nina and take the kids there. I know it's a school night and all, but this is sort of an emergency deal. Her parents will understand. Then you go to class. Tell her to put them down in sleeping bags in the living room and someone will pick them up in the morning."

"No." She elongated the word. "I can't. They know what's going on. They watched Faye leave them, and I'm not going to hurt them worse by dropping them elsewhere."

"Hannah, just do it. Attendance is ninety percent mandatory at all times. You can't afford to—"

"I didn't call for you to give me a list of orders, Martin."

The dull headache he'd had all day increased, sending a twisting pain down his neck. "I'm trying to keep you on track. That's all, Hannah. I can't just drop everything, and neither should you. Let me try to reach Faye, and I'll call you back later."

She didn't answer him.

"Hannah?"

"Yeah, I heard you. Bye."

Disconnecting the phone, he realized that whatever she'd hoped for when she called him, he'd let her down. He didn't understand certain aspects of Hannah yet, but this much he got: she hadn't wanted him giving directions like he was her boss or her parent.

He walked back into the room. "Dale, I have to go."

"You can't leave now."

He began rolling up the plans. "There's a family emergency, and I need to go."

The man pulled a leather billfold thick with cash from inside his suit coat, visually sending a reminder of his strength. "I believe in the Golden Rule. The man with the gold rules. Stay, and we work this out. Go, and I'll find someone else."

"A very smart woman once asked me, 'Do you think money is the answer to everything?' I have a family issue, and I'm going home." He slid the prints into the cylinder container. "I'm sure I'll be available next week. If that's not good enough, we'll send all the information we have to whoever you hire."

Martin walked across the parking lot wondering what Faye would have done with Kevin and Lissa if Hannah hadn't been home. He piled the plans and his laptop into his car. He wouldn't arrive in Winding Creek for nearly three hours, but it was the best he could do. He tried to reach Faye, and he tried calling Hannah back. Neither woman answered her cell. He called Dr. Smith to see if she'd heard from Faye or knew where she was headed. The doctor talked to him for over an hour, sharing pieces of encouragement. It all sounded nice, but the reality was bleak and heavy.

It had long been night by the time he pulled into Zabeth's drive. His frustration had grown with each passing hour. As the car lights hit the front porch, he saw Hannah sitting on the steps. He parked the car, wishing he'd come across as less of a jerk and more of a friend when she'd called him. Hannah stood, and he walked to her.

He smiled. "You okay?"

She shook her head. "I was so sure we could make a difference." She closed the distance between them. "I'm sorry."

He wrapped his arms around her. "You don't need to apologize."

She laid her head against his chest.

"We did our part, Hannah. That's all anybody can do." He laid his cheek on the top of her head. "How about we get you moved into the cottage so it'll make life easier while we get this mess sorted out?"

Without answering, she pulled away and turned toward the cabin. He saw a rustic cabin, a relic, and not something to regret leaving, but he doubted that Hannah viewed it the same way.

Martin stepped next to her. "I can help you pack. It's not like you own much, mostly clothes and books, right? After we get the cars loaded, we'll move Kevin and Lissa, hopefully without waking them. Then—"

She placed her hand on the center of his chest. "But it's my home."

He sighed and nodded. "I know, sweetheart. I do. But I don't know how we can juggle everything with you way out here. It's the school year, and their district doesn't bus this road. And even when I leave early, I can barely get home from work in time for you to leave for your classes. I certainly can't make it here."

Without a word she walked to the fence and patted Ol' Gert. He followed her. She had a passion for certain things, and he loved that about her—even if it meant working through their different, equally headstrong opinions.

He took her hand. "Talk to me, okay? Say what you're thinking."

She tilted her chin, looking resolved. "There's nothing else to talk about. Kevin and Lissa need a stable environment—for now that means living in a way that keeps them from being shuffled around like they're a burden."

"I agree, but that's just your decision, Hannah. I asked for your *thoughts*."

She shrugged. "Even without the *Ordnung* instructing me, I think desire comes second to doing what is right."

"You're pretty amazing, you know it?"

"I know you think so. Far be it from me to disagree."

Martin chuckled, running his fingers over her soft cheek. "I'm sorry for barking orders at you when you called."

"I know." She kissed him. "What are we going to do about Faye?"

"I've got meetings all day tomorrow, but then I'll start looking for her while you keep Lissa and Kevin, okay?"

She nodded. "Let's start packing."

~~∽~~

With Lissa in her lap and Kevin sitting beside her, Hannah finished the last page of a picture storybook of *Heidi*. She hadn't sent them to school today. They were nervous about Hannah and Martin disappearing on them. She figured it was just one day, and they'd return on Monday.

Hannah closed the book and patted Lissa's pajama-covered legs. "Okay, bedtime."

Kevin jumped up. "I'm not going to sleep. I'm gonna turn out the lights and watch the stars glow that we put on the wall today. When Uncle Martin gets home, I'll show him all the constellations we designed."

Hannah set the book on the coffee table. She figured if he stayed in bed watching the stars long enough, he'd go to sleep. "Okay by me."

He hurried toward his room. Lissa stood on the couch, wrapped her arms around Hannah's neck, and held on tightly as Hannah walked upstairs. Lissa giggled the whole way.

Hannah set her on the bed and waited while she scurried to her sleeping spot. She tucked the blankets around her, sat on the side of the bed, and kissed her tiny hands. How could Faye just walk out on her little girl?

"Hannah."

"Hmm?"

Lissa gazed up, her big dark eyes absorbing everything. "What's *buoyant* mean?"

Hannah stroked Lissa's hair. "You want to run that by me again?"

"But I'm in my p.j.'s. Where do you want me to run?"

Hannah repositioned herself on the bed. "Nowhere, sweetie. That means I need you to repeat what you said."

Her face blossomed with wonder. "So you don't know what *buoyant* is either?"

A deep chuckle made Hannah turn toward the doorway. Martin leaned against the doorframe, looking as confident as ever.

Lissa giggled. "Uncle Martin!"

She started to get up, but Martin held out both hands in a stop-sign fashion. "Stay, Rover, stay."

She snuggled back under the covers. Hannah moved to the foot of the bed. Martin sat down beside Lissa and patted her head. "Good girl."

She broke into giggles. "He pretends I'm a puppy sometimes."

Hannah nodded. "I see."

She sat up, encircling him with her arms. "I love you, Uncle Martin."

Martin gave her a gentle hug. "Back at ya. Now snuggle down, and let's say good night to God." He lowered his head and said prayers with her.

Suddenly Hannah was swept back to her own childhood. Her Daed used to tuck her in each night, lay his hand on her head, and say a silent prayer. In the silence she used to imagine he was begging God to make her be a good girl. She never quite managed goodness, but she missed the warmth of hearing his last words of the day as he tucked her in.

Martin whispered her name, drawing her out of her thoughts. The prayer was over, and he was standing next to her. He nodded toward the door.

He turned out the light and pulled the door almost shut as they left.

Hannah began descending the stairs. "Any signs of Faye?"

"None." He sounded tired. "I talked to every friend and acquaintance I could find. I visited homeless shelters, talked to Dr. Smith. I came up completely empty-handed." Martin touched her shoulder, and she stopped in midstep. "She might not come back."

There was no sense in asking him what they were going to do if that happened. He didn't know. And yet they both knew.

They heard a door open, and Kevin appeared on the landing.

Martin drew a deep breath. "Hey, sport, what's up?"

"Come look at what me and Hannah did to my room today."

Martin glanced at Hannah, not looking all that pleased that the guest bedroom was being transformed into a kid's room. "I'm in the middle of—"

Hannah tugged at his shirt sleeve and gave a slight nod toward Kevin.

Martin's body tensed with frustration. "I'll be right there."

Kevin went back into his room, and Martin sighed. "Listen, we need help this go-round. I know you think it's pawning the children off on someone who doesn't love them, but I intend to find someone who can come into the home. You've taken on more hours at the clinic, and you have school most nights. I already have a good list of candidates to fill either a full- or part-time position as nanny. I want to begin interviewing."

"I could take a leave of absence. Kevin and Lissa need stability and lots of it. I just don't think hired help is the answer."

"That's because you think if you work at something hard enough, you can fix it. You can't heal the damage Faye and Richard have done, and dropping everything in our lives to baby the kids isn't the answer. I want you to go on with your life as much as possible. Hiring part-time or full-time help is the ans—"

Hannah held up her hand, stopping him. "Maybe you're right."

Martin moved in closer. "I know I am."

"Of course. So do you have someone on that list you're already considering seriously?"

"Depends."

"On what?"

He took her hand in his and caressed it. "On whether you're going to get angry if the answer is yes."

"Are all men like this?"

"No. Very few climb to this level of honesty."

She laughed. "How do you have a list already? She left yesterday."

He looked at the ceiling and whistled innocently until she smacked his shoulder. "I started looking for someone when Faye was in rehab, but a certain young woman I know wouldn't even consider it."

"All right. You know my schedule. Just set up a time and date. Have whoever it is come here right after lunch one day. I'd like to see her in this environment, and she can have dinner with us."

"Uncle Martin." Kevin sounded exasperated.

Martin looked to the landing. "I'm coming. Go on back to your room." They waited for the door to close. He turned back to her. "This is a good decision, Hannah. It'll be just what we need so that Kevin and Lissa are taken care of but we get more time to date without kids in tow."

"Ah, so that's the goal, huh?" She went to kiss his cheek, but he pulled her into a lip kiss. She inhaled sharply. "Your plan sounds promising." She finished descending the steps. "See you sometime tomorrow."

"Hannah?"

She stopped and turned. "Yeah?"

"Is the cottage comfortable enough? Anything I can do or buy that would keep me from having to hear you complain about it later on?"

"Yeah, earplugs. Good night, Martin."

"Good night."

With the aroma of new leather permeating the small shop, Luke sat behind the commercial-grade sewing machine, stitching a well-oiled piece of rawhide around the padding of a horse's collar. The gas-powered motor that provided the strength for the heavy needle to do its job sat outside, right behind the wall where he was sitting. His thoughts seemed to move in rhythm with the steady *flub-dub, flub-dub, flub-dub* of the machine's engine.

Joining Matthew in business and renting his old harness shop out to an Amish couple was the best thing he could have done. It seemed if Matthew put his hand to something, it became a huge success. Why, with the rent money he was making and the income he was earning as Matthew's partner, he and Mary would be able to build a home of their own soon.

Luke cut the heavy-duty strings, loosened the rawhide from the machine, and rose to assemble another collar.

A shadow fell across his workbench, causing him to look up. "Daed, I didn't hear you come in."

The man stood in the middle of the room, reminding Luke of a statue. "The fact that divorce is unheard of among the Amish does nothing for a man if his wife hates him."

Luke had no words of comfort, and now wasn't the time to try to get his Daed to see his fault in all this, so he remained silent.

His father walked to him and held out a piece of paper in his trembling hands. "I never meant to…" He shut his eyes. "I got a letter from a Dr. J. Lehman in Alliance, Ohio." His eyes watered. "My sister died, and a doctor sent me a note about it. The doctor mentioned that a relative had delayed the funeral to give any of Zabeth's other relatives time to come. If I had my guess, I'd say the relative he speaks of is Hannah. I don't know how she

learned of my sister or her whereabouts, but none of my relatives had anything to do with my sister."

Luke took the envelope. The doctor's name was the only readable part.
The return address looked as if drops of water had hit the ink and smudged
it. He opened it, but there was no letter inside. "Daed?"

He gave a fatigued nod before pointing to the paper. "I know that's not
much information to go on. I had shoved the letter in my pocket, and it went
through the washer, but it seems the envelope fell out and wedged itself under
the washer. Maybe you know someone who can help you figure out how to
find her."

Luke shook his head. "Not unless I ask Paul. He'd know—or know how
to find out."

His father pointed to the envelope. "If that's the only person, then that's
who you should take the information to." His eyes reflected hurt so deep that
a physical pain shot through Luke. A sob broke from his Daed's throat. "I've
tried standing true to Sarah, like I shoulda done with Hannah. But her nervousness just gets worse, and she's mumbling to herself and turns up in the
oddest places. Yet she doesn't seem to know why she's at those places. She's
locked inside herself, and no one has been able to reach her."

Dismayed, Luke couldn't respond, and he watched his father turn and
leave the shop.

Luke stared at the envelope, wondering what to do. Was it fair for his
Daed to use Paul to find Hannah when he hadn't spoken a nice word to or
about the man in the two and a half years Hannah had been missing? Besides,
Paul seemed to have moved on, with Dorcas. And clearly Hannah still didn't
want to be found. She hadn't written in a long while, but last he heard from
her, she was going to school and felt good about where she was.

And although Mamm longed to see Hannah, she'd had her chances too,
hadn't she? Instead she chose to let Hannah grieve in solitude after her baby
died. She never went to her.

But Sarah—she hadn't been the same since the day she'd learned of her
sister's plight. If there was a reason for Paul to help find Hannah, Sarah was it.

Unsure what was the right thing to do, Luke tucked the paper into his leather apron and returned to the work at hand. Figuring this out would take awhile.

~~§~~

Martin walked to the cottage. He thought Hannah might want to know how well the interview had gone with the potential nanny, Laura Scofield, a sixty-two-year-old woman with excellent credentials. More than that, he wanted a few minutes with Hannah. He tapped on the door. It was almost eleven o'clock, but she'd just pulled into the driveway a few minutes ago. The hour was the downside of taking night classes. The truth was he couldn't wait for her to get her diploma and end this continual rivalry he felt with her schedule.

She opened the door, looking gorgeous and tired. "Hey." Stepping back, she invited him in.

"I took all the laundry by the dry cleaners." He held out the basket of washed and folded clothes.

"Thanks. Care for a drink?" She set the basket on the table.

He grabbed two bottles of water. "I interviewed Laura Scofield, the nanny I mentioned to you. I'd like you to meet her as soon as you can, and perhaps you should set up that appointment. I think Laura is a perfect choice, but I feel pretty strongly that because of your age, you need to establish yourself as her authority concerning the children so no issues ever crop up in that area."

"Ah, leave it to you to think about such things. I'll call her tomorrow and schedule her visit."

He held up a bottle of water. "Want one?"

"Yeah." She stifled a yawn. "Kevin give you trouble going down for the night?"

He opened her bottle of water and passed it to her. "Has a cat got a climbing gear?"

"Taking care of two children is probably not how you'd like to spend your evenings."

Martin sneered. "Not hardly, but it's growing on me. It's not nearly as bad as I thought it'd be."

Hannah took a sip of water. "The Amish consider a baby the most precious gift on this planet. The People cherish them—just because they exist."

"Yet they don't seem all that warm and inviting once people are adults. My mom told me Zabeth's troubles were plenty. And you left at seventeen and changed your name. So what happens between infanthood and adulthood?"

She motioned to the porch.

"Sure."

They moved to the porch and sat on the steps. It seemed their best conversations took place outside, especially at the end of the day.

She pulled her legs in and propped her chin on her knees. When nothing but the gentle hum of crickets filled the air, Martin wondered if she'd answer him or not. It was never a given that she'd answer his questions.

She stretched her legs out and ran her hands down the row of buttons on the front of her dress. "I left because I refused to repent. I think the reasons for leaving are as varied as people themselves."

Wondering what she had needed to repent of, Martin asked, "Is Paul still the reason you've never gone back home?"

"For a while I didn't think I could stand seeing him with someone else." She paused and seemed to shudder. "My father saw me the night I'd been attacked, witnessed the trauma, and yet later on he chose to believe I'd had a fight with Paul or something that night. I don't really know how he twisted it in his mind, but he didn't believe how I came up pregnant."

"What happened between you and the rest of your family?"

She slowly explained each piece of the story until he understood things she and Zabeth had been silent about since he and Hannah met.

He moved in closer and put his arm around her shoulders. "Do you still miss Paul?"

She gazed at Martin, a smile crossing her lips. "I've found an unusual fish in the sea, a bit self-centered, but a remarkable man nonetheless."

He pulled her closer and kissed her cheek. "Well, this fish is pretty happy to be caught. But sometimes I get the feeling you're still unsure about us."

"It's not just a feeling. I am unsure, because I haven't been ready to tell you everything."

"This is everything, right?"

She shook her head. "I wish." She paused. "Because of complications after I gave birth, I...I can't have children."

In her voice he heard the depth of loss she felt for the children she'd never bear. "I'm sorry."

"I wasn't sure when to tell you. It seems presumptuous to bring it up too soon and wrong to have waited this long."

He removed his arm from her shoulders and slid his hand over hers. "No guilt over the timing."

She watched as he kissed and caressed her fingers. "Don't just rush in to make me feel better, Martin. You have dreams for your future, and maybe I don't fit as well as you'd thought."

"And maybe you fit better. I should have told you this, but I didn't want to scare you away. I don't want children. Even after getting serious about life and God, I stopped seeing some women because I didn't want children, and I realized they did."

"You'd put your hand on the Bible and confess that's true?"

"I've never told a girl something in order to sound nice or to soften the blow. Not that sweet a guy."

She pushed him back. "Yeah, but this is me. We're different together, more bonded for reasons I don't need to explain."

"True enough, although I didn't realize you knew that." He rose. "I know what I want, but I'll give the younger member of this band time to think and process. Good night, Hannah." He headed toward his house before stopping in midstride. "If we'd both known that being honest about who we really are would have helped rather than caused problems, we might have actually told the whole truth earlier on."

She shook her finger at him. "You're making that phrase circle inside my head again."

"The one missing the accurate adjectives *charming* and *intelligent*?"

"That'd be the one."

"So what is it?"

"Shut up, Palmer."

He kept a straight face, knowing she'd just answered him. "You're not going to tell me what it is?"

"I did."

He laughed. "Yeah, I know, but something with *charming* and *intelligent* would be much more accurate."

"I'm fully aware of that."

He chuckled and went inside his house.

nside protective services' small office, Paul clutched the phone against his ear as Luke shared that Zeb Lapp had information about Hannah's whereabouts and was hopeful Paul could help locate her. The day had started like any other, with a miserable longing for Hannah. And now…

"J. Lehman, Alliance, Ohio." Paul repeated Luke's words as he wrote them down. "Did your father say when he received the last letter from Hannah?"

"The letter didn't come from Hannah. It came from someone notifying him of his sister's death."

"He has a sister?"

"Did. And that was news to me too. She died in May." Luke paused. "Daed gave me this info in August, over a month ago, but I wasn't sure it was right to get you involved. Asking you to find Hannah isn't about what Daed wants or even Mamm. I'd not have called you if this was for them. But Sarah…"

"I've had a few encounters with her since Hannah left. She doesn't seem to be coping very well. Is she doing better?"

"Worse. From what Matthew and Mamm have told me, whatever you saw is nothing compared to what she's like of late. I think if Sarah could just talk to Hannah one time, she might get better. If you can find a way for us to reach Hannah, a phone number or address where we could send a letter, it'd mean an awful lot to me."

Paul wasn't going to tell Luke about his last encounter with Sarah, but there was no doubt she needed help. "Luke, I appreciate that you contacted me with this info. I'll do what I can and let you know."

They said their good-byes, and Paul hung up. He was done with waiting for Hannah to return on her own. If he'd ever thought she'd be gone for more than two years, he would have hired that private investigator before the trail became impossible to pick up.

But this way, she'd been gone long enough to find peace and healing on her own terms. Now she needed a reminder of the worthy things she'd left behind and of the gaps her absence had caused. Her sister needed her. Paul loved her. It was time for her to come home. And now he had enough information to find her and nudge her to do just that—come home. He began an Internet search for any Lehman's phone number in Alliance. It didn't take long to learn there wasn't a single Lehman listed. Paul widened his search to a twenty-mile, then fifty-mile radius of the place and jotted down all the possibilities.

Starting at the top of the list, Paul began dialing.

As the hours passed, he scratched through possibility after possibility. He'd skipped lunch, and his co-workers had left for the day. But all he could think about was hearing Hannah's voice again. He was unsure what his hopes were beyond that. For her to come home immediately? For him to go to her first and them talk for a month solid until they knew each other again? Too many thoughts and emotions hounded him to discern any of them with clarity. Only one thing he knew for sure: he longed for Hannah to be in his arms. Things were different from when she'd left. The gossip and anger had dissipated. She'd lived on her own long enough that no one would expect or demand she line up with their desires or repent of things that weren't her fault. It was all different, and he had information in hand to finally contact her and let her know.

He dialed yet another Lehman number.

"Lehman's Birthing Clinic. Midwife Nancy Cantrell speaking."

"Hello, this is Paul Waddell, and I'm looking for a Hannah Lapp."

"Is she one of Dr. Lehman's patients?"

"I…I don't think so. She's a friend, and I'm trying to locate her."

"This is an Amish birthing center, sir. You must have the wrong number."

Amish? On the contrary, he must have the right number. "Is Dr. Lehman's first initial J?"

"Yes, Dr. Jeff Lehman."

This was too much of a coincidence. Hannah had to be connected to this doctor.

"But there's not a Hannah Lapp who works for him?" Paul suspected the woman was leery, more interested in getting off the phone with as little said as possible than in helping him. "Does he have any other offices?"

She hesitated. "Yes. He has another clinic and a main office. But there are privacy laws concerning patients and workers."

Confidentiality laws. As a counselor, he dealt with them all the time. "I'd still like to have those numbers if you don't mind."

With the note in hand, Paul connected to the Internet. In less than two minutes, he had the man's main office address. This Dr. Lehman or someone on his staff might not be willing or able to tell him anything over the phone, so Paul's best bet was face to face. He grabbed his suit jacket and headed out. There was no reason to leave tonight since he wouldn't arrive until nearly midnight. But by lunchtime tomorrow, he intended to be in Ohio.

Leaning over the drafting table in his office, Martin tried focusing on his work. His thoughts were everywhere but on the set of engineering plans in front of him. Mostly they were on the brown-eyed girl living on his property.

But even with all their progress toward a lasting relationship, in Martin's ears echoed the sounds of prison doors clanking shut. Even if Faye returned and succeeded at living clean and being a good mom, as if that were possible, he'd still never be fully free of the responsibility to keep things stable for Kevin and Lissa. At least Hannah had agreed with him about hiring Laura. She'd only work part-time, but it would free them from some of the schedule juggling and give them an occasional evening off. Even if Laura became a live-in nanny, he and Hannah would never have the kind of freedom and bonding time he'd always dreamed of having. He loved Kevin and Lissa, but he chafed at the nonstop patience and effort it took to raise them.

He wondered what he'd be like in this situation without Hannah's influence.

His thoughts jumped to when he'd lost his mother. Zabeth had stepped forward and never once made him feel unwanted. On the contrary, she'd made him think he was the greatest thing to ever happen to her life. But was he? He'd been a bit hardheaded and rebellious at times.

As he allowed his mind to drift, a memory surfaced that he hadn't thought of in more than a decade. A few weeks after his mother's death, he got off the school bus to see Zabeth in the driveway, talking to a man. Whatever was going on was intense, because they never even noticed him. Looking back now, he realized how young Zabeth had been—single and in her early thirties, only a few years older than he was now. Funny, she'd always seemed like someone's mother.

The man had put his arms around her. "Take a few months and get the boy past the worst, but you have a life of your own, Zabeth. A future with me."

"Can't we find a way to blend our lives? Must it be a choice?"

"My ranch is in Wyoming, Zabeth. You've known that all along, said you'd move there come summer."

"I know, but—"

Martin had dropped his book bag, causing Zabeth to notice him. He couldn't really remember much more, other than being introduced and feeling that the man hated him. He never saw the man after that day. Obviously, Zabeth had made her choice, and she chose Martin. Fresh grief for Zebby rolled over him, and before he even realized it, he was praying that he'd become the type of guardian she had been. One who sacrificed without grumbling, loved without resentment, and gave freely, making the kids in his home feel like treasures. When he opened his eyes, he ached to hug Kevin and Lissa. It wouldn't hurt anything if he checked them out of school a little early.

If Hannah wasn't too busy today, maybe he could pick up all three of them, and they could go for ice cream or something where they could talk and laugh, and he could let them know he truly did care. Whether he had planned it or not, these children were a part of his life, and he intended to make sure they knew they were a part of his heart.

He picked up the phone and hit the speed dial. A rap on the doorframe interrupted him. Amy Clarke held up a blueprint tube containing a set of plans.

He pushed the disconnect button. "What's up?"

She stepped inside and moved to the leather chair in front of his desk. He placed the receiver in its cradle. Amy was a couple of years older than Martin and rented space in the adjoining office for her landscape-architect business. This kept Martin from needing to hire and run a whole different department under his engineering firm. Even though she thrived on spontaneity, she maneuvered through the orderly business world with a cool savoir-faire.

"A land plan was sent to McGaffy that I didn't approve." She thumped the tube against the palm of her hand. "And it shows more lots than the county will allow on that parcel."

"Send a corrected land plan back to McGaffy that the county will approve, and the developer can take it or leave it. I'm not willing to work the extra hours to get a variance with the county to make the developer happy." He placed his hand on the receiver, ready for this conversation to be over. "I'm heading out for the weekend. If anything else comes up, it'll need to wait until Monday."

Her blue eyes opened wide, and she tucked one side of her blond hair behind her ear as she rose. "Okay, if you say so."

"We can talk about this more next week if we need to." He picked up the receiver and punched the speed dial for Hannah's cell phone. "Amy, please close the door on your way out."

⁓⫯∽

Paul parked his car in front of a clapboard house with white columns, black shutters and trim, and a gray porch and steps. It sat on a tiny plot of ground, flanked by dilapidated homes on both sides of the street. The large wooden sign with fancy black painted letters said this was a women's clinic, with doctors on site Mondays and Wednesdays only. Even though today was Tuesday, an Open sign hung on the glass door.

Paul glanced at the cellophane-covered bouquet he'd bought at the local florist shop, lying on the passenger seat beside him. He knew he shouldn't have bought these. Such a move was premature and undoubtedly out of place, but he couldn't resist.

Climbing out of his car, he prayed that this place could lead him to Hannah.

As he opened the door, a bell jangled, making him cringe at the noise. A grandmotherly woman behind a desk to his right glanced up and smiled. "Can I help you?"

He eased up to her and held out his hand. "Paul Waddell."

"I'm Sharon. Nice to meet you, Paul. What can we do for you?"

"I'm looking for a friend of mine."

"Is she a patient?"

"I...I don't think so. I believe she's a friend of Dr. Lehman's. Is he here?"

The woman chuckled. "Dr. Lehman is almost never here. He has a couple of doctors on staff and a slew of community-service volunteers. Maybe the friend you're looking for is one of his volunteers. What's her name?"

"Hannah Lapp."

The woman slowly shook her head. "No. There's no Hannah Lapp. He has a Hannah Lawson, who works really closely with him."

Paul's heart leaped. Would she use a different last name? Of course she would. Changing her last name was probably one of the first things she did.

"Is she here?" he asked, his voice trembling.

"She doesn't work out of this office. She helps Dr. Lehman at the Amish birthing clinics and counsels at the rape crisis center."

"That's got to be her!"

The woman's eyebrows shot up.

He took a breath, choosing to sound calmer. "Can you tell me where his clinics are?"

"Sure. But she's on leave right now, taking care of her new family." She shrugged. "I don't know her, but I heard Dr. Lehman saying that the man has two children and that Hannah took some time off to help them get settled."

Feeling a bit unsteady, Paul dropped into a chair.

Maybe the woman was mistaken. Or perhaps this wasn't really his Hannah after all. "Do you have an address for her?"

Sharon hesitated. "I'm not sure I should…"

Paul pulled a business card out of his billfold. It wasn't an ethical thing to do. If this got back to the board of the Better Path, he could be in serious trouble since the card could be misleading, but he gave it to her anyway. "Her father is trying to get in touch with her. He asked me to—"

She took the card and read it carefully. "I do remember overhearing Dr. Lehman tell his wife that Hannah had moved away from home rather abruptly and something about they'd tried to reach her family…" The woman spun her Rolodex to the Ls, then pulled out a card. "Let me jot this down for you." As she wrote Hannah's address, she asked, "Until she moved, she lived in Winding Creek. Her new place is just south of there. Do you need directions?"

"That would be very helpful. Thank you."

Following the directions the woman had printed out for him, Paul drove toward the south side of Winding Creek. Within twenty minutes he pulled up on the street across from the home bearing the address Sharon had given him.

It was a nice two-story, slip-form stone house with stacked-stone columns. He even caught a glimpse of a cottage behind the house. Everything about the place spoke of a comfortable lifestyle. If this was where Hannah lived, it was no wonder she hadn't given up on surviving in the Englischers' world and come home.

Leaving the flowers in his vehicle, he strode up the sidewalk. He rang the doorbell and waited. His mouth was so dry he wasn't sure he'd be able to speak if someone did come to the door. When no one answered, he returned to his car.

Laughter and silliness rang out from the three of them as Martin pulled into the driveway. Lissa was sound asleep. He and Hannah got out of the car. Kevin unbuckled himself and jumped out. Hannah unfastened Lissa's restraints and lifted the sleeping girl from her seat. When she stood, her eyes met Martin's. In the silence, her eyes told him everything he wanted to hear. She was happy. While the kids had played in the sandbox at the park, he told Hannah what he'd realized about himself and why he'd come home during the middle of the day.

Lissa mumbled. "Where are we now?"

Martin smiled. "You're home." The words were simple enough, but they stirred him.

Hannah eased Lissa's head onto her shoulder. "But you can stay sleeping." Walking toward the house, Hannah whispered, "I'm going to lay her down. Keep the house quiet, okay?"

Martin nodded and opened the trunk of the car. He grabbed the Nerf football he'd bought earlier today. "Okay, go out for a long one."

Kevin took off running.

Martin chortled. "Not that far. Come back." They tossed the ball back and forth, and Martin tackled him a few times before Hannah bounded back out the door and into the yard.

He tossed her the football. Surprisingly she caught it.

"Tackle!" Martin yelled.

Kevin came running at full speed. Hannah put her hand in front of her. "Whoa, guys. Girl on the field."

Martin took the ball from her, tossed it to Kevin, and wrapped his arms around her, facing her. "Yeah, I know. Cute one too."

She pushed against him, but he didn't let go. He glanced at Kevin, who was throwing the ball into the air and catching it.

Martin touched her soft face and gently guided it to his. He lowered his lips almost to hers, but she backed away.

"Hannah." He gazed in her eyes and stroked her cheeks with his thumbs, waiting.

When she relaxed, he eased his lips to meet hers and was again struck by the powerful physical and emotional reaction he had to her.

After an intense kiss, she put a bit of space between them. Her lips curved downward, and she shrugged. "Not bad."

He laughed.

She snickered. "I love your sense of humor."

"Good. Because I haven't found anything about you I'm not in love with."

"You lie."

"Do not." As he brushed loose curls away from her face, he resisted her push against him. "So how do I move past not bad?"

She pressed her palms against his chest, clearly ready for him to let her go. "I…I think you should throw the football with Kevin."

"Uh-huh, and I think you should kiss me."

Frowning, she stood on her tiptoes and barely touched her lips to his, as if that would be sufficient and he should go play with Kevin now. But in the instant after touching her mouth to his, something in her seemed to shift, and she ever so lightly kissed him again. Once, twice. Her hands no longer pushed against him but balled into fists that held his shirt as she barely skimmed her lips over his—four times, six times—before he received the tenderest, most powerful kiss of his life.

Martin took a step back and drew a deep breath, trying to pull his stare away from her. "Uh, you know, it's really not necessary for us to wait any longer before we get married."

"What kind of a proposal is that?"

He clasped his hand around her neck and looked into her eyes. "A desperate one."

She laughed. "Good grief, Palmer. I feel like you're trying to close a business deal."

"It'll be the best deal I ever made." He took a few steps toward Kevin before turning back to Hannah. "I love you, phone girl."

Knowing she needed time to process every new curve in life, he jogged to the middle of the yard and clapped his hands. "All right, buddy, put one here."

Watching Hannah from inside his car, Paul sat speechless, his hopes shattered. The optimism that had kept him hopeful for the past two and a half years was destroyed. There was no reason to get out of his car and see her face to face. She had a new life: a gorgeous home, a husband, even a family. She worked closely with that Dr. Lehman.

Englischers. All of them.

Well, he hoped Mr. Lapp was pleased with the outcome of his strictness. If his goal was to keep Paul out of her life, he'd certainly accomplished that. Unable to stomach blaming someone else, he closed his eyes and tried to center himself. He was the one who'd walked away while she was begging him to listen. He was the one who didn't return for her until days later. There was no one else to blame.

But somewhere beyond the growing ache he felt, he was grateful she seemed happy.

After all the years of praying for the best to happen for her, God had honored his requests.

And yet he felt betrayed.

He'd been so sure she would find wholeness and then return. Well, she had found it—without him. Pouring more salt in his wounds, no one in the happy family even noticed him sitting in a parked car across the street from their house. Suddenly unable to imagine what it would be like to look in her eyes knowing she was married, he started the engine. He had the information the Lapps needed to contact her, and he'd take it to Mr. Lapp himself, but it'd be best if Paul left here unannounced.

He put the vehicle in gear and drove away.

*M*atthew dipped up a bowl of his mother's hot-fudge cake and slid a spoon in it. His brother had been having lunch with him when the shop's phone rang out across the yards. David had taken off running since it was his day to field calls. Sometimes keeping up with the growing business was a hassle, but they managed. Now Matthew figured he at least owed David a bowl of dessert. He pulled a clean dishtowel out of a drawer and placed it over the bowl. He'd trained Kathryn to take orders and handle most of the office stuff, and she was good at it, but her sister had given birth, and she'd gone to help out for a few weeks.

His mother sank the lunch dishes into the sudsy water. "Keeping some of that separate so I can't eat it all while you're gone? Or you got someone else in mind?"

"The horses," Matthew answered with a grin. "We're low on hay, and I didn't figure they could tell the difference."

"Uh-huh. That's why you ate a bowlful of it yourself." She looked up at him with those tender mom eyes.

He poked her with his elbow. "You're a really good Mamm, you know that?"

She gave him his routine hug before he returned to work some hundred feet away. "You're not such a bad son either."

"Not bad? Me? I'm terrific. Yep, nothing like the rest of my family." He tried to keep a straight face, but he grinned anyway.

She pointed to the bowl. "Take it and go, or you can stay and wear it."

Chuckling, Matthew went out the front door and across the yard. He'd take this to David and then go back to working in the carriage shop, where he was attaching the underpinning of a buggy to its body. His Daed, along with six other men and two wives from the community, would soon be back from the carpentry they'd been doing in Maine. The women helped do the cooking and kept an eye on the men, so the wives back home never felt unsure of what their husbands were up to.

Although it was September, the summer's heat had yet to break. He wondered if David had dared to run the three-inch, battery-operated fan he'd bought for him or if his whole face would be glowing with color and sweat. As an employee, he was nothing like he was as a brother. He was diligent and willing—even to leave the rest of his lunch to catch a phone. As much as it surprised him, he liked having David work with him. If his obstinate brother was this good, he wondered what Peter would be like when he graduated this year. If things continued as they were going, there'd be enough work to go around.

Gasoline fumes rode the humid breeze, stinging his nostrils. He lifted his head, sniffing the air. The dimness of his shop made David's job of reading and filing all the paperwork harder. It had been built to hold in heat in winter and keep out the sun in summer. Unfortunately, that made a kerosene lamp necessary to read and file the receipts and orders.

But the odor he smelled now wasn't kerosene. And the closer he drew to his old shop, the stronger the smell became.

A car pulled into the shop's driveway, and its horn tooted.

Matthew paused, waiting for the car to come to a stop. The driver came into view.

Elle.

She got out, looking a lot different from the last time he'd seen her, a month ago. Her hair was pulled back, and her dress was every bit as modest as the caped ones the Amish women wore.

She had a rather guarded smile on her face. "Matthew." She closed the car door. "Could we talk a minute?"

His first impulse was to say yes, but reservations mounted by the second. It had taken him too long to end things between them. He wasn't interested in opening his heart to her again. The jagged scent of gas cut through his thoughts, and he decided to get this over with and check on the source.

Her eyes found his, and she smiled again. "You don't have anything to say about the new attire?"

"It's your life, Elle. However you choose to dress and act no longer matters to me." He turned away from her, looking toward the motorized engine at the back of the shop as the possible cause of the fumes.

"You know, after the way you stood by Hannah through everything, I thought you'd stand by me."

His body flushed with heat at the shadowy accusation, and he stepped closer. "I helped Hannah carry a load that should not be put on anybody, and I helped her follow through on her choice to leave. Seems to me I've done the same for you, Elle Leggett. If Hannah had been my girl and asked me to wait indefinitely while she whooped it up among the Englischers, I woulda refused. I'm tolerant, not stupid."

"Matthew, we need to talk. I mean really talk. You're too distracted around here. Let's go for a ride and—"

"I…I need to check on something." He strode toward the shop and had nearly reached the door when Elle caught his arm.

"I've come here in humility and honesty, and you walk off? Has everything about this business of yours changed the man I fell in love with?"

Her words about loving him cut through his resolve. The very thing he wanted to avoid had happened. Traces of who they'd once been stood before him; memories of kisses tempted him. Through the screen door he could see David sitting at the desk. He glanced up, his face frowning at Elle's presence.

A breeze ran through the open windows of the shop and whisked through the screen door, filling the air with fumes. "David?" Matthew slung the door open. "Any idea where that—"

A flash of orange light exploded from the attic overhead. Something fell from the ceiling, knocking David out of the chair and to the floor. Burning fumes and smoke pushed Matthew down and scalded his lungs.

"David!" Struggling to keep his eyes open, he worked his way back to the door and into the smoke-filled room.

His eyes felt seared, as if they, too, were on fire. Staggering, he held his hands out in front of him to feel his way to the file cabinet. "David!" Heat surged around him. Through the murkiness of his vision, he could make out flashes of orange light.

"David!" Remembering what he'd always been told about smoke, he dropped to his knees. It was impossible to keep his eyes open. They burned too badly, and the stinging smoke made it worse. Grit from the floor buried itself in his palms as he crawled toward David. At least he hoped he was going in the right direction.

He felt papers and a piece of wood. "David!" he yelled over the sound of creaking timbers and lapping flames before the smoke choked him.

Outside the shop he heard Elle and his mother screaming. Luke was barking orders. "Stay back. The ceiling's about to collapse."

"Do something!" His mother's voice pierced the crackle of fire. "Do something!"

"Matthew!" Elle called.

"Someone ride bareback to the Yoders and dial 911. Hurry! Jacob, find every hose you can and conn—"

"I've got a cell phone in my car," Elle cried.

Matthew's hand landed on a thick piece of coarse material. He grasped it and tugged. When it didn't budge, he followed it, patting the floor in front of him as he went. His fingers landed on something soft, like flesh. Running his hands over the lump, he realized what it was. His lungs felt tighter than even a moment before.

David.

He tried to lift him, but he didn't have the strength. Unsure which way the door was, he wished he could still hear the noises from outside. Grabbing David by the arms, Matthew shuddered. There seemed to be no life in his brother. Tugging on him, pulling him across the floor inch by inch, he felt his own strength draining. Blackness threatened him as he tried to backtrack out of the building.

A faint popping sound came from above. Specks of smoldering embers fell from the ceiling. A crack sounded. He moved to cover David's face and torso. Something crashed to the floor a few feet from him. Pain seared his back as burning splinters landed on him. Matthew forced himself to hover over David, protecting him.

When the noise from the ceiling stopped, Matthew struggled to his knees, unable to catch more than a shallow breath.

Noises from outside became clear again. His mother continued to scream for David and him. He dragged his brother in the direction of her voice. Water from somewhere drenched his back and legs, making it even harder to tug on David.

"You're out of the building, Matthew." His mother sounded as if she was right beside him, but he still couldn't focus his eyes. "You're out. You can stop now." Mamm whispered the words, but she didn't touch him, and he couldn't see her.

"Matthew? Can you hear us?" Elle called.

"David! No!" His mother's sobs filled the air.

Matthew reached for David's shoulder, wanting reassurance he'd gotten them both out of the building okay, but all sense of his surroundings slipped away, and there was only darkness.

"Shh. Stay here," Sarah told Esther and the rest of her younger siblings, who were already seated at the kitchen table. In her bare feet, Sarah tiptoed through the living room and to the front door. Their home had been like a bus stop lately. Day before yesterday Hannah's Paul had arrived during mealtime. Just moments ago it was Jacob Yoder who'd knocked on their front door, right in the middle of dinner, and Mamm and Daed had gone to the porch to talk to him.

Sarah stood beside the open window. She'd managed to hear the conversation with Paul this way. He'd given Daed a piece of paper. Paul said it had Hannah's address and phone number on it. He said he'd come to pass the information on to them, but he wasn't going to contact Hannah, and he didn't say why.

Now Jacob was here, and Sarah didn't intend to miss one word of what was said.

"I-I," Jacob stuttered and then paused. "I came to tell you…there was an explosion and fire at Luke and Matthew's place."

Sarah thudded against the wall as Jacob's words swirled inside her, tearing at her. "Oh, God, please, this can't be happening." She whispered the half prayer, half accusation.

The tongue is a fire, a world of evil…and sets on fire the course of life.

First the Bylers' barn, now Matthew's shop. The flames were getting closer and closer. Her house would be next, and it'd be all her fault. She'd said things about her sister she shouldn't have said. She'd started the gossip on purpose.

God is not mocked: for whatsoever a man soweth, that shall he also reap.

She moaned. Matthew's shop had caught fire. She couldn't believe it. According to Jacob, David and Matthew had been injured and were on their way to a hospital, the extent of their injuries unknown.

Silently she screamed for God, but if she didn't confess her sins before the bishop, God wouldn't help her. If she did confess her sins, God Himself couldn't save her—not from her father.

But Hannah could. She'd faced their father whenever he discovered one of Sarah's wrongdoings, and she had not let him lay a hand on her until he calmed down. Daed had grown to appreciate that about Hannah, although when they were younger, she'd taken a switch in Sarah's stead on many occasions.

Jacob's quaking voice interrupted her thoughts. "The bishop is calling for a community meeting at his place. There's talk that someone in the community is starting these fires."

Her tongue had set the fire. Unable to breathe, Sarah closed her eyes and silently begged for God or someone or something to help her.

An idea struck her, and her legs wobbled at the excitement of it. For the moment confusion melted away.

Hannah's phone number. She hadn't dared look for it after Paul brought it by and Daed took it to his room. Fear that he'd burn it, too, had kept her from even trying to find it. But now she had nothing to lose.

She rushed through the living room, darting to avoid being seen through the windows, and up the stairs. Sweat dripping down the back of her neck, she went into her parents' room and closed the door behind her. She went to her Daed's dresser and began opening drawers.

"It's in here somewhere," she mumbled to herself as she pushed T-shirts and socks to one side and then the other. After searching through each drawer, she was empty-handed. Scanning the room, her eyes stopped when she came to the chest at the foot of the bed. As she knelt in front of it and opened it, a stomach-turning smell of scorched material made her gag. She dug through the stuff until she found a piece of burnt material. Unfolding it, she realized it was the dress she'd worn the day she went to the Bylers and poked through the ashes. Her parents must've found the dress she'd thrown away.

They were collecting evidence against her. Did they know?

Tossing the dress back into the chest, she figured they probably didn't *know* anything or she'd have been confronted by now. Beaten. Thrown out of the house. Disowned forever.

Her chest hurt, and she could hear Hannah telling her to slow her breathing and picture herself sitting on the pier, dangling her feet in the pond. There wasn't time for that. Sarah pulled quilts and old baby clothes out of the wooden box until a piece of paper floated to the floor. It'd been tucked in a quilt, safe from prying eyes during the warm month of September.

"Sarah?" Her father was in the room.

She froze, too frightened to look up. She clutched the coveted piece of paper in her fist.

Her father wrapped his hand around her arm and lifted her to her feet. He took the paper from her and unfolded it. "You will tell me what you're doing going through things that do not belong to you."

She couldn't even catch a breath. How was she supposed to talk?

"Right now, Sarah." His words came out purposeful and hard.

She fought for air. "I...I've got to call Hannah."

"Why?" He barked the word at her.

She shook her head, unable to think with him in the room.

Daed clenched his jaw before he wrapped his hand around her wrist. He slowly turned her hand over, palm side up, and stared at it. He looked into her eyes and pressed the paper into her hand. "The decision is yours."

*P*aul walked the rows of yellow squash in his mother's garden, twisting ripe ones from the vine and tossing them into the bushel basket. His attempt to break free of his disappointment and pain wasn't working. Over two years of believing Hannah would return and they would reunite was hard to let go of. He'd convinced himself she was somewhere mending while gaining maturity, that by the time she came home, she'd no longer be too young to marry. He swallowed hard. Clearly she wasn't too young to marry.

He'd held on to the dream of her return for so long that he felt ridiculous. And yet he still loved her. His life would never be what he believed it could have been with Hannah.

Nevertheless, it went on.

He'd known from the time she was fifteen that she'd tug on many a man's heart. There was no way around it. He twisted another squash off its vine. Five years of his life had been devoted to waiting on Hannah to love him the way he loved her.

But she'd grown to love someone else.

An Englischer. An upper-middle-class one at that. He could hardly believe his Lion-heart would fit into that lifestyle. It was his fault, really. He'd led Hannah to desire a lifestyle beyond her community. He'd always talked about the freedoms of electricity, computers, education, and cars. He'd put idealistic views into her head, thinking he was helping her see the value of stepping out of the Old Order ways. In many respects he'd acted more like a fancy Englischer than a Plain man, and he'd done so in front of an impressionable young woman.

Paul's family and community weren't like Hannah's Old Order Amish life, with no electricity or high-school diploma, but his roots were in the simple ways. When she left, he'd had one foot in each world. If he hadn't, she might not have found it so easy to leave the Plain life.

His regrets wouldn't solve anything. He'd lost his temper when he learned she was pregnant, and he'd always pay the price for that, but it was time he let go of his guilt and turned toward home and the roots he believed in. He refused to handle his loss the way his Uncle Samuel had. He wouldn't grow a heart of stone and live out his days single, pining for what might have been. He'd taken the paper with Hannah's phone number and address to the Lapp home yesterday. Her family could contact her or not as they saw fit, but he was finished longing for Hannah Lapp.

Completely finished.

The dinner bell rang. He grabbed the bushel basket and headed for the house. His sister and her husband, William, were here with their two boys and new baby girl. The Miller family was visiting too. Dorcas had brought the ingredients for homemade ice cream. It was a celebration in honor of his securing a full-time position at the Better Path and finishing his graduate program—although he planned to skip the commencement ceremony this time. Working at the Better Path wasn't much of a job as far as pay or benefits, but he could do more preventive work as a counselor for families than as a case-worker.

Placing the basket on the back porch, he peered through the window. Dorcas was laughing with his mom about something while arranging candles on an oversize cake. She'd been feeling really ill lately, even having days where she could barely get out of bed, but she seemed fine today.

She glanced up, spotting him. Her eyes grew wide, as if he were spying on what she was doing. She wagged her finger at him before joining him on the back porch.

"Hey." She nodded toward the house. "You gonna be able to stand all the family ruckus over you?"

"I always do," he teased back, focusing on her. She wore the clothes of her People. He'd never seen her without a prayer Kapp. Her heart was as respectful of the Mennonite ways as any he'd ever seen. She'd remained his friend throughout all his pining for Hannah. They didn't have the same level of camaraderie as he and Hannah had shared, and they rarely laughed together, but that could change with some effort.

He went to the edge of the porch and studied the horizon. "She isn't coming back."

Dorcas came up beside him. "I'm sorry."

He turned to face her. "No, Dorcas, I should apologize to you. You've been patient and hopeful for me that she'd return. But you didn't really want her to come back, did you?"

She closed her eyes, and her face twisted with emotion. "No. You're not angry at me, are you?"

He watched the fields, trying to let go of his desire for Hannah's return. "No, not at you." He willed himself to give attention to the present, but like a hurricane gaining strength, bitter emotions churned inside him. "After dinner, would you care to go for a walk?"

She looked surprised. "You know I would love to. But I thought you were going to Gram's to take care of the garden after dinner."

Hannah's garden.

The one he'd tended for three summers, waiting on her to return. "It can grow weeds." He motioned toward the house. "Let's go celebrate."

While the band held the last note of a song, Hannah laid the microphone down. Ready for a break, she walked into the kitchen. Placing a coffee filter into its basket, she heard Laura upstairs playing games with all the kids. Laura was just working part-time for now, giving Kevin and Lissa time to bond with her while Hannah and Martin were close by. Nina was glad for the reprieve and hadn't even come over with Dave and Vicki tonight. Hannah filled the basket with fresh grounds and poured water into the coffee maker, then watched fresh brewed coffee immediately begin to fill the decanter. The band sang a song by Rascal Flatts about forgetting the past and moving on.

Memories of life with Zabeth circled through Hannah's mind. How grateful she was for the chance to have been a part of Zabeth's life, but she missed her.

The musicians began another song. Laughter and loud voices echoed through the house. She grabbed a grape from one of the prepared trays and popped it into her mouth. Life in Martin's house was amazingly easy, and most day-to-day problems were solved in the time it took him to write a check.

"Hey." Martin strode into the room, all smiles. Whiffs of his cologne followed him as he placed his hand on the small of her back.

She couldn't help but smile. "Hi."

"Any chance I can talk you into us going away for the weekend with Vicki and Dave?"

"Ah, chaperones, huh? And you think that'll cause me to at least consider this rather brazen request?"

"Exactly." He grabbed a mug and poured himself a cup of coffee. "Come on, Hannah." He filled her cup and set the decanter back in place. "We have Laura now, and we need some time without Kevin and Lissa." He drew the cup to his lips.

She added sugar and powdered cream to her coffee. "Okay. It's probably time I learn to trust your judgment more."

He choked on a sip of his coffee. "You're going to kill me being so agreeable about things without warning. But since you're in such a generous mood, maybe we could catch a movie during this weekend outing?"

"A movie?" The bottom of her mug scraped against the countertop when she wrapped her hand around it. "I've never been to a movie theater or watched the DVD thingy here at the house."

"Good. Makes it easier to work out what movies you haven't seen yet." He smiled.

She giggled. "True enough. If I agree to this, do I get the infamous expensive popcorn and candy to go with it that I hear people talk about?"

"You can have anything you want, Hannah. Date night or not."

Hannah believed that. She just hoped she never took advantage of it.

Lissa ran into the room, laughing. "Me and Kevin's being good tonight, huh?"

"Yes, you are," Martin answered. Hannah nodded in agreement.

"Can I have some soda?"

"How about either juice or water?" Hannah asked.

Lissa brushed strands of hair off her face. "Apple juice."

Martin took a cup and lid from the cabinet and opened the fridge.

Looking from Martin to Lissa, Hannah couldn't imagine ever living a solitary life at the cabin again. The adjustment to living on Martin's property had taken some time, but now this is where her life took place—where schedules were juggled, where any and every thought or emotion was welcome to be freely expressed. She smiled to herself. Where music reigned supreme and lights flicked on in one room and off in another without a care given to it, where friendships were built and opposing opinions were listened to with respect.

Martin poured the drink and snapped the sippy lid on it.

Warmth and gratitude radiated from deep within her as if it were Christmastime and she were sitting in front of a roaring fire.

Wrapping her hands around the mug of coffee, Hannah watched him interact with Lissa. He'd changed a lot in the time she'd known him.

Kevin and Lissa still had times of crying for their parents, especially for their mom. Hannah had little doubt they would continue to miss their parents, but they knew they were loved, and surely that would cause abundant life to grow.

Lissa took the drink. "Thanks."

"You're welcome." Martin patted her head. She leaned against him, hugging his legs, and he rubbed her back before she ran out of the room. He returned his attention to Hannah. "Care to tell me what's on your mind?"

She shrugged. "Nothing."

His green eyes fastened on her, making her feel like everything about her mattered to him. "I think there is."

She smiled. "You're right. There is."

"Come on, phone girl, talk to me."

"I've just been thinking…" She shrugged. "That I'm very glad. That's all."

He moved in close and slid his arms around her. "Ah, are the words *charming* and *intelligent* coming to mind much these days?"

She put her palms against his chest. "You just can't not tease, can you?"

"Nope."

"Well, just for your information, those words are included. And more."

He kissed her forehead. "I like the sound of this. Those brainwashing tapes rigged to play in the cottage while you're asleep must be working." He brushed her lips with a kiss.

She felt safe and warm, loved and respected. In his arms, life never seemed as heavy.

"Any other words you want to share? There are children and friends in the house, so, you know, keep it decent."

She laughed. "That's enough for now. I wouldn't want you to be tempted to sin by thinking too highly of yourself."

"Oh, come on. Just one more thing?"

Her cheeks were burning, and he was fully amused. "Shut up, Palmer."

Laughing, he hugged her tighter. "I'm pretty thankful for you, Hannah. You probably have no idea."

"That's exactly what I wanted to tell you."

"That you're thankful for you too?"

She smacked his arm. "You're difficult. You know that?"

"And you have trouble telling a person what you're thinking and feeling. You know that?"

"Well, duh." She pulled him close, and he responded by brushing her lips with kisses, slowly and gently. "I...love you."

He stopped kissing her and stared.

"Well, breathe, Martin. If you pass out,"—she took a step back—"you're on your own." She tapped the floor with her foot. "Thump."

They shared a laugh before the phone interrupted them. She glanced at the caller ID, then looked at Martin. "It says it's John Yoder. You think that could be the Yoders from Owl's Perch?"

Martin reached for the phone.

She stopped him. "I'll get it."

With her pulse racing, Hannah grabbed the phone. "Hello?" She pushed her finger against her free ear, trying to block out the music and voices in the background. She walked out the back door.

"Hannah?" A young female voice wobbled and screeched.

"Yes?"

"You gotta come back, Hannah. You gotta." Her sister sounded rattled.

"Sarah, what's wrong?"

"Matthew's shop burned down, and the bishop's looking for who did it. It's my fault, Hannah. Me and my tongue, we did it."

"Matthew's shop?" She looked at the back door, hoping Martin had followed her. He was right behind her, watching. "Did anyone get hurt?"

"Matthew and David are in the hospital."

"How badly are they injured?" She felt Martin's hand on her back, comforting her already.

"I don't know." Sarah cried harder. "I'm sorry for the stuff I spread, Hannah. I...I'm sorry."

"Hush now, Sarah, hush." Hannah almost choked on the words. Of all the people she'd missed since moving here, Sarah was not one of them. She had betrayed Hannah too many times.

Sarah drew a ragged breath. "It's my fault. Because of what I did to you. The fire's coming for our house. Don't you see? First the Bylers' place, now Matthew's. It's moving closer. It's coming for me."

"Oh, sweetie." Hannah reverted to the tone she'd used in their childhood when Sarah would get so nervous she couldn't catch her breath. "I'll head for home by midmorning. Everything will be okay."

"Really?"

Hannah's breath caught. The idea of going home didn't hold near as much terror as it once had, but it was far from appealing. "Yes, I'll be home by tomorrow night."

Through broken sobs, Sarah whispered, "Thank you."

A dial tone buzzed in her ear. After a moment, she pushed the disconnect button.

Martin grabbed a lawn chair and pulled it up behind her. "What's going on?"

She sat. "That was my…my sister Sarah. There was a fire. I…I need to go home."

Concern flickered across his brow. "How long?"

"Just a few days."

"How did she get my phone number?"

"I don't know."

Martin knelt in front of her. "Will you be back before school on Monday? If you miss, with their policy of mandatory—"

"I don't know, but I'll be home by Wednesday for sure."

"I'll take time off from work and go with you. Laura can keep Lissa and Kevin here."

Hannah shook her head. "You don't understand, Martin. My family may not even allow me in the house. The community will be cold, to say the least. If I take you, I'll be treated worse than an outsider. If I have any hope of doing what needs to be done or of helping Sarah, I've got to do this alone."

"But I can make this easier on you."

"Not this time. You're more likely to lose your temper and make things worse. I'm not treasured in Owl's Perch like I've been since I landed here. You'll have to trust me about this."

He gave a reluctant nod. "What's wrong with Sarah?"

"She's a lot like Faye, only she doesn't need the addiction to be an emotional wreck. She said her tongue set the fire."

"Her tongue?" Disbelief etched across his face. "Is this the same Matthew you told me about?"

Nodding, she caressed Martin's cheek. "Yes. He stood by me, helped me leave, and gave me money. I've got to go to him."

Martin placed his hand over hers and rubbed it. "Hannah." He stood and guided her to her feet. "Once you're there, you'll be faced with figuring out all sorts of things."

"I think I'll be figuring out how to get back to you, Kevin, and Lissa quickly. I'm coming back just as soon as I can." She snuggled against him. "This isn't going to be enjoyable, Martin."

He kissed her forehead. "You'll question what you really want, where you really fit in—that kind of stuff. I love you, Hannah Lawson. Don't forget that."

"I won't, not for a minute. And I'll return as quickly as I can." She took a step back. "We need to explain this to Kevin and Lissa. And I need to pack."

"We need to go over directions of how to get on the Ohio Turnpike."

She took him by the hand and led him toward the cottage. "Before all that and before we talk to the kids, I have something I want to give you. It was supposed to be for your birthday in two weeks, but now's a better time."

Martin tugged at her hand. "I need to get something too and let the others know where we've gone."

"Sure." Hannah went into the storage room and lifted the repaired quilt from a box. She unfolded new wrapping paper across the kitchen table and laid the quilt inside. She still wasn't sure who it had originally belonged to. The only thing she knew for sure was Zabeth had designed and sewn it. And since Hannah and her Plain friends at the quilting gatherings had repaired it, she was going to give it to Martin.

When she heard the knock on her door, she hurriedly put the last piece of tape in place and turned the package over. "Come in."

Martin popped open the door and walked inside.

"I've been working on repairing something for you, so it's not new."

He took the gift from her. "May I open it now?"

"That's the idea."

He unwrapped it, tearing the paper at will. His face drained of emotion for a few seconds before he looked at her. "Where...did you find this...and how did you find the time?" He ran his finger over a corduroy square in the blanket.

"It was at the bottom of a box in the storage room. The Tuesday afternoon women's group at the clinic always sews quilts for charity." She grinned. "You'll be glad to know you qualified."

Martin chuckled. "Thanks." His green eyes lingered on her before admiring the quilt again. He spread it out over the kitchen table. "I've missed this thing for years. Zabeth and Mom made this when Faye and I were children. Zabeth placed it over me at night every winter for years after my mom died, so it became mine."

"Don't put it in the washer, or it'll fall apart again."

"I didn't know that." He gazed at the multicolored patches. "This was from my mother's wedding gown," he said, pointing to a square of white satin. "And this," he said, his finger moving to a patch of faded-blue denim, "is from my grandfather's overalls. Did you know he was a dairy farmer?" His fingers skimmed each section tenderly. "This is from my first pair of cowboy pants, when I was four. This quilt is a patchwork of Palmer life—before it became a train wreck."

"You're doing the best anyone can to make things right."

He laid the quilt on the chair and took her hands. "Hannah, I have something for you, but maybe it's not appropriate as you head back to your Amish community." He reached inside his jeans pocket and pulled out a small box. "It's a birthstone ring."

She opened the box to see a gold ring with two stones nestled in an S-shaped loop.

Martin removed it from the box. "It's sort of a strange gift. One is Kevin's birthstone, and the other is Lissa's." He chuckled. "Lissa's stone is a diamond, and Kevin's is a ruby—well, actually his is a garnet, but I think the ruby is the same basic color, right? And it's a higher quality stone." He lifted her left hand. "I know you haven't said yes to anything, but if you'd wear this on your left hand, it'd mean a lot to me."

Hannah watched as he slid it onto her finger. "Ah, so it's an honorary mother's gift, yet somehow it tells everyone I'm spoken for even though I've not accepted your rather brazen, albeit romance-free proposal. Have I missed anything?"

Martin kissed the finger that now wore the ring. "You know me entirely too well. But you skipped the fact that I am in love with you."

"Oh, I never skip that part. I think about it all the time." She slid her arms around his shoulders and hugged him. "Thank you for everything. I wouldn't want to face Owl's Perch without knowing I have you here waiting for me."

"There's one more thing." He pulled some papers from his pocket and passed them to her.

She opened them. "A trip to Hawaii." She glanced up. "Over Christmas?"

"Before you say no, consider this: Dave, Vicki, and Nina are going too. As are several top employees from the company. Kevin and Lissa aren't near as likely to miss their parents as badly over Christmas if they are in a whole new setting. You'll be finished with school, and we should celebrate. And my idea is perfect."

She couldn't deny the idea was exciting—to get on a plane and fly, to see a beach for the first time in her life, and in Hawaii. "That's you, isn't it? Thinking through every angle of something and then going for it." She folded the papers and passed them back to him. "I'll look forward to it every day between now and then."

Martin kissed her, sealing her determination to get back to him as soon as possible.

~~∾~~

Luke paced the floor of the hospital while the Esh family talked with the doctor at Matthew's bedside. The orangy smell of cleaning products was all too familiar, and it brought back awful memories from Mary's time at a medical facility.

Elle waited at the end of the hall, looking like an outcast.

Mary came to his side and took his hand before laying her head on his shoulder. Luke turned and wrapped her in his arms. They'd survived their accident three years ago and recovered. But this time was different. There'd been a working cell phone and a car. Luke had the power and the means to make decisions.

Yet David hadn't survived.

Matthew's parents, Naomi and Raymond, came out of the room. Luke and Mary went to them, but Elle hung back, listening. Naomi stared straight into Luke's face and spoke flatly. "He was awake and asking for you, but the pain medicine must've taken over, and he's asleep for now. When he wakes, just know his eyes are covered with bandages, so he won't be able to see you. None of the burns will require a skin graft." She brushed her hands down the front of her apron.

"Does he know about David?"

Naomi nodded. "Yes."

"And that the business is gone?"

She nodded again. "We told him everything."

"Will he get his eyesight back?"

"Ash and soot from the ceiling fell into his eyes, but the doctor thinks that when the bandages are removed in a couple of days, he'll be able to see."

Grief was etched on Naomi's and Raymond's faces. They'd lost one son. Hopefully just one. Luke feared the weight of what had happened might break Matthew, even if he regained his eyesight. Raymond led Naomi to a chair and sat beside her.

Elle went into Matthew's room.

Ignoring the ways of his people, Luke placed his hand on Mary's protruding stomach, so thankful she hadn't been near the shop when the explosion occurred. Everything dear to him was right here in his arms, but Matthew had lost his business and his brother. And if anyone asked Luke, the man had never had Elle to begin with, certainly not since her father returned.

He dreaded the realities that would beat Matthew without mercy for a long time to come. He walked to the doorway of Matthew's room. An IV was attached to one arm, and he was lying on his stomach. Aside from the temporary problem with his eyes, nothing but the skin on his back had received burns. Elle stood beside the bed.

Matthew stirred. "Luke?"

Elle placed her hand over his. "It's me—Elle."

Matthew pulled away from her. "Go home, Elle. Just go."

"Matthew, please. I'm so sorry—"

"Get out."

Elle glanced up, spotting Luke. He nodded toward the door, confirming Matthew's words.

~~~

Anxiety over Matthew and facing her father wore on Hannah as she drove across the Pennsylvania state line. She'd been foolish and desperate when she'd left home two and a half years ago, thinking freedom could be found in running away.

She'd arrived in Alliance broken; nevertheless God had given her Dr. Lehman, and he, in turn, had found Zabeth. And Zabeth had brought Martin, Lissa, and Kevin into her life, and Hannah loved them.

Her freedom had been found in the love they offered her.

But was anyone ever completely free?

She didn't think so. Never free of troubles or of human need. But she was free to make mistakes or get caught in a trauma and still be loved. That was something Owl's Perch couldn't give her.

In spite of her reluctance to return, she looked forward to seeing the friends she'd left behind. And Paul? Well, it should be easy to avoid him. If she had to face him, she wouldn't share how badly he'd hurt her. It wasn't any of his business. He might be married to that Dorcas by now, or at least engaged, but Hannah had moved on.

Thoughts of Martin filled her mind. She'd done more than just move on, and even though her nerves said otherwise, Paul Waddell was simply someone she'd once thought she loved.

Nevertheless. For the first time in years, the word spoke softly in her spirit. She'd face her father before leaving again.

Nevertheless.

She'd take these few days and find peace with her past. Then she'd return to Martin, Lissa, and Kevin.

Content with those thoughts, she drew a deep breath.

She didn't know what would happen in Owl's Perch, but she trusted the One who held her heart. The One who'd taught her that He was more powerful in her life than any injustice—past or future.

Acknowledgments

With deep gratitude I thank those who've faithfully helped me with this project.

My dear husband, your love and support make this possible.

Miriam Flaud, my dear Old Order Amish friend, who opens her home, reads each manuscript, and answers questions via her phone shanty because she has a heart of gold.

Eldo and Dorcas Miller, whose expertise about the Plain Mennonite community mixed with their willingness to teach me have been a tremendous blessing.

Joan Kunaniec, a wonderful Plain Mennonite who willingly shares her love and respect of the Plain ways.

Rick and Linda Wertz, whose readiness to help with research, photos, and accurate navigation of the Pennsylvania roadways is a gift in my life.

Jeffry J. Bizon, MD, OB/GYN, and his wife, Kathy, who make time to keep the medical information correct; I couldn't have done this without your help.

To all the awe-inspiring people my husband and I met while spending a week in Alliance, Ohio. Your warmth and openness lingers with us still.

Mrs. Rhonda Shonk, Office Manager, Alliance City Schools Career Centre and the Robert T. White School of Practical Nursing, whom I relied upon to keep Hannah's schooling experiences accurate.

Don and Jean Aebi and Sue Feller, residents of Alliance who shared information via e-mail after I returned home to Georgia. You made the nuances of being an Alliance resident come to life.

Steve Laube, my agent. I'm forever blessed to be one of your authors. You're everything I'd hoped for in an agent. You have calmed my nerves and answered my newbie questions with the patience of Job. Thank you.

And a special thank-you to my editor extraordinaire, Shannon Hill, who is clearly skilled at molding lumps of clay. And to Carol Bartley, whose keen sense of story balance never ceases to amaze me. And to everyone at Water-Brook Press, I'm very grateful for all you do.

Glossary

aa—also or too

ach—oh

alleweil—now, at this time

da—the

Daadi Haus—grandfather's house. Generally this refers to a house that is attached to or is near the main house and belongs to a grandparent. Many times the main house belonged to the grandparents when they were raising their family. The main house is usually passed down to a son, who takes over the responsibilities his parents once had. The grandparents then move into the smaller place and usually have fewer responsibilities.

dabber—quickly or at once

Daed—dad or father

dei—your

denk—think

denke—thank you

des—this

draus—out

du—you [singular]

Dummkopp—blockhead or dunce

Englischer—a non-Amish person. Mennonite sects whose women wear the prayer Kapps are not considered Englischers and are often referred to as Plain Mennonites.

es—it

fehlerfrei—perfect

geh—go

gut—good

hatt—difficult or hard

Heemet—home

hilfe—help

ich—I

in—in

iss—is

Kall—fellow

Kapp—a prayer covering or cap

kumm—come

kummet—come

letz—wrong

liewer—dear

loss—let

loss uns geh—let's go

mach's—make it

Mamm—mom or mother

Mammi—shortened term of endearment for grandmother

mol—on

muscht—must

net—not

Ordnung—The written and unwritten rules of the Amish. The regulations are passed down from generation to generation. Any new rules are agreed upon by the church leaders and endorsed by the members during special meetings. Most Amish know all the rules by heart.

Pennsylvania Dutch—Pennsylvania German. The word *Dutch* in this phrase has nothing to do with the Netherlands. The original word was *Deutsch,* which means "German." The Amish speak some High German (used in church services) and Pennsylvania German (Pennsylvania Dutch), and after a certain age, they are taught English.

rumschpringe—running around

schnell—quick(ly)

schpring—run

schtobbe—stop

schwetze—talk

seller—that one

so—so

uns—us

verhuddelt—confused

was—what

Welt—world

will—will or wants to

ya—yes

---

* Glossary taken from Eugene S. Stine, *Pennsylvania German Dictionary* (Birdsboro, PA: Pennysylvania German Society, 1996), and the usage confirmed by an instructor of the Pennsylvania Dutch language.

NEW YORK TIMES BESTSELLER

When the Soul Mends

~❧ A NOVEL ❧~

Cindy Woodsmall

AUTHOR OF *When the Heart Cries* AND *When the Morning Comes*

~ SISTERS OF THE QUILT, BOOK THREE ~

To my husband

*I could fill a thousand books with words of love
and still not have shared but a small portion
of who you are to me.*

*H*annah's car faded into the distance of the paved horizon. The cold concrete chilling Martin's bare feet and the lukewarm cup of coffee in his hand confirmed that this was no way to begin a Saturday morning. Watching the place where Hannah's vehicle had disappeared, Kevin and Lissa slowly stopped waving. For the first time since Hannah had landed in Ohio—two and a half years ago and not yet eighteen—she was on her way back to her Pennsylvania home and the Old Order Amish family she'd left behind. Maybe he should have insisted on going with her.

Lissa tugged at the hem of his T-shirt. "She packed a lot of stuff."

His niece's big brown eyes reflected fears she didn't know how to voice at five years old. Martin tried to catch Kevin's eye to see how he was doing, but he stared at the ground. Hannah really hadn't packed very much, but this had to feel like a replay of when their mother ran off months ago. When Faye had packed a lot of things into her car, she dropped Kevin and Lissa off with Hannah while Martin was at work, and never returned.

Martin suppressed a sigh, tossed the brown liquid from his cup onto the green grass, and held out his hand to Lissa. "She'll be back, guys."

Lissa slid her hand into his. "Promise?"

"Yes. Absolutely." Martin gave her hand a gentle squeeze. "Her sister called to say that a good friend of Hannah's had an accident and is in the hospital. She'll probably be back in time for her classes on Monday. Wednesday at the latest."

Kevin shoved his hands deep into his pockets. "I didn't know she had a sister."

Martin shrugged, unwilling to say too much about Hannah's past. "She hasn't been to see her family or friends in Pennsylvania for years." With the coffee cup dangling from his fingers, he put his hand on Kevin's shoulder. "Now they need her for a bit." He headed for the house, leading the children.

Earlier this morning, while Hannah called possible hospitals her friend might have been taken to, Martin found an Ohio-Pennsylvania map. Once she knew the name and address of the hospital, they studied the map together while he highlighted the route she'd need to take. He didn't know which caused her the most nervousness: her injured friend, having to see her family again, or driving in unfamiliar territory, but right now he wished he'd pushed a little harder to go with her.

He thought about the gifts he and Hannah had exchanged last night. He'd given her an honorary mother's ring and had slid it onto the ring finger of her left hand. She hadn't agreed yet to marry him, saying his proposal a few weeks back had been brazen and romance-free, which it had. But when he took her to Hawaii over Christmas, he'd find the most romantic way possible to propose.

A smile he couldn't stop seemed to spread across the morning.

Martin opened the front door. "How about some Cracklin' Pops cereal and cartoons?"

The muscles across Hannah's shoulders ached. With the toll roads and service plazas of the Ohio and Pennsylvania Turnpikes behind her, she pulled into the parking lot of the hospital and found a space for her car.

Her frazzled nerves complained, but she was here now—whatever *here* held in store. Trying desperately to remember who she'd become over the last couple of years, not who she'd once been, she stopped at the information desk and waited for the woman to end her phone conversation.

Her sister Sarah had managed to get hold of her phone number and had called last night to tell her about Matthew being hurt in a fire. Hannah promised to come—a pledge she now regretted. In some ways it'd been a lifetime since she'd last faced her Amish community, yet the quaking of her insides said it'd been only yesterday.

The gray-haired woman hung up the phone. "Can I help you?"

"Yes, I need the room numbers for Matthew and David Esh."

The woman typed on the keyboard and studied the screen. She frowned and typed in more info. "We have a Matthew Esh, but there's not a David Esh listed." She jotted down the room number on a small piece of paper. "It's possible he's already been released or perhaps was taken to a different hospital."

"Maybe so. I'll ask Matthew." Hannah took the paper from her. "Thank you."

She went to the elevator, trying to mentally prepare to face Matthew's visitors—people she knew, people she was related to, those who'd accused her of wrongdoing before they washed their hands of her. Nonetheless, she'd come home.

Here. Not home. She corrected herself and felt a morsel of comfort in the thought. These people didn't own her and had no power to control her, not anymore. She stepped off the elevator and headed toward Matthew's room. Odd, but the place appeared empty of any Amish. She gave a sideways glance into the waiting room as she passed it. There were no Plain folk in there either.

Stopping outside the room, Hannah said a silent prayer.

Ready or not, she pressed the palms of her hands against the door and eased it open.

A man lay in the bed, but she couldn't see his face for the bandages across his eyes. He turned his head toward the door.

"Hello?" His voice echoed through the room.

"Matthew?"

His forehead wrinkled above the bandages, and he clenched his jaw. "Just go home…or wherever it is you're livin' these days. I got no more use for you."

She froze. If this is what awaited her from Matthew, one of her few friends, what would the community be like? But maybe the man wasn't Matthew. His body was larger, shoulders thicker and rounded with muscle. His voice was raspy and deeper than she remembered. And Matthew would have visitors, wouldn't he?

"Matthew?"

He shifted in the bed, angling his head.

"It…it's Hannah."

Only the soft buzzing sound of electronics could be heard as she waited for his response. Wondering a thousand things—whether the eye damage was permanent, why he didn't have a marriage beard, and where everyone was—she moved closer to the bed.

Finally he reached his hand toward her. "Hannah Lapp, at last back from the unknown world."

Ignoring his unsettling tone, she put her fingers around his outstretched hand and squeezed. "How are you?"

The stiltedness of their words said that a lot more than two and a half years had passed between them.

He shrugged and then winced, reminding her of the pain he must be in. "I've lost David…and every part of my business. How do ya expect me to be?"

David is dead?

The news twisted her insides, making her fight to respond. "I'm so sorry, Matthew."

He eased his hand away from hers. "I'm grateful you came all this way, but I'm too tired to talk right now."

"Sure. I understand. Where is everyone?"

The door swooshed open, and a nurse walked in. "I'm sorry, miss.

He's not to have visitors." She held up a laminated, printed sign that said No Visitors Allowed. "It'd slipped off his door."

That explained why he didn't have friends or relatives here, but he didn't appear to be in bad enough shape for a doctor to give that order. Hannah studied the nurse, but she just shook her head without saying more. The only reason he wouldn't be *allowed* to have visitors was because he'd requested that of the staff. And clearly he didn't want to make an exception for her.

"Okay." She slid her hand into his once more, wishing she could at least know more about the condition of his eyes. But he seemed in no mood for questions. "I'll come back when you're feeling better."

"There's no sense in that. I'm goin' home tomorrow. But…David's funeral is Monday." His voice cracked, and he took a ragged breath. "If you're still here, we could meet up afterward while *Mamm* and everyone is distracted with the gatherin' at the house."

The words Matthew didn't say weighed heavily. He didn't want her going into the community to see anyone. He wanted to meet her alone, in secret.

Unable to respond, she grappled with the space separating them. She'd expected distance from her *Daed* and Mamm, the church leaders, and even Gram, but she hadn't for one second thought Matthew would sidestep her. He'd understood, even disobeyed the bishop to help her. Built the coffin for her baby, dug the grave, and said the prayer. Taken her to the train station, bought her a ticket, and stayed with her until time for the train to depart the next day. Did he now regret that he'd stuck by her?

Unwilling to push for a specific plan, Hannah gave his hand a final squeeze before pulling away. "Sure. I…I'll catch up with you then."

Desperate to clear her mind, Hannah hurried out of the hospital and into her car. She pulled out of the hospital parking lot and drove—to where, she didn't know. Old feelings of loneliness washed over her, but she kept driving, as if she could outrun the sting.

By the time her emotions began to settle, she had no idea where she was. Glancing in the rearview mirror, she pulled her car onto the shoulder of the road. Fields of yet-uncut hay seemed to go on forever as cars whizzed past. Unsure of the county or town she was in, she grabbed the map off the seat beside her and searched for her location. Nothing looked familiar. Realizing the stupid thing was upside down, she flipped it around.

At this moment all she wanted was to be at home with Martin, but the next few days had to be walked through first. She'd given Sarah her word. Even as that thought crossed her mind, she wondered if there was more to it. If maybe some deeply hidden part of her wanted to be here. Desperate to hear Martin's voice, to feel like she did when with him, she took her cell phone out of her purse.

"Hey, sweetheart, where are you?"

A sense of belonging washed over her the moment she heard his voice. "I was hoping you could tell me."

He laughed. "Are you serious?"

"Yeah, sort of."

"Do you know the name of the road you're on?"

"No. All I know is I want to be there, not here." In spite of her effort to sound upbeat, she came across as pathetic and didn't want to imagine what Martin must be thinking about now.

"Look at the directions I printed out, and tell me what point you got to before you became lost."

"I turned left out of your driveway."

His low chuckle was reassuring. "Very cute."

Determined to show Martin she could handle this, she studied the map. "Yeah, you've told me that before, only then you could see me." She angled the map sideways. "Wait. I got it. I know where I am." She pressed her fingertip against the map and followed the line before realizing she was wrong. "Lost without you."

"Metaphorically, I love the sound of that, but you should have let me take you there. You've never driven anywhere outside a twenty-five mile radius of Winding Creek."

·"You're not helping."

"It's a little hard to help from here with no"—he mockingly cleared his throat—"POB to work from."

She heard the familiar beeps of his laptop starting up. "POB…ah, engineering lingo."

"Yep. Point of beginning. I'm logging onto Google maps right now and will try the satellite visual. Tell me about your surroundings."

"Oh yeah, that's a great plan. I'm surrounded by cow pastures and no houses. Found the right spot yet? There's a Holstein watching me."

"On Google maps, no. The right spot for you? Yes, it's right here in Ohio with us."

She heard the rustle of fabric. "Did you go back to bed after I left?"

"I ate breakfast and watched cartoons with Lissa and Kevin. But then Laura arrived, so I let the nanny do her job while I took a nice long nap, until you became a damsel in distress. The Mary Jane to my Peter Parker."

"What? Damsel in distress," she muttered. "So what does that make you when you don't know the difference between a skillet and a pot?"

"A typical male who just happens to be…" He paused. "Come on, work with me here, phone girl. Who just happens to be…"

"Charming and intelligent." She mimicked his clearing of the throat. "According to him."

He laughed. A loud crash echoed through her cell. Lissa screamed, and Hannah's breath caught.

A bang, as if his door had been shoved open and hit the wall, filtered through the receiver. "Uncle Martin, Laura said you better come see this. Lissa might need stitches."

"Phone girl, I'll need to call you back in a few. Okay?"

The next sound she heard was the complete silence of a cell-phone disconnection. Wondering what she was doing here rather than being there to help Martin, she closed her phone. At sixty-two, Laura was a skilled nanny, but Hannah wanted to be the one with him going through whatever the day brought.

Looking at the map one last time, she thought about calling Dr. Lehman. He was more than just her boss, and he regularly visited relatives in Lancaster, some forty miles southeast of here, so he might be able to help her. But rather than chance disturbing him, she decided to continue driving until she found a landmark she recognized. She pulled back onto the road. After a solid hour and many times of turning around, she found the road that led to Owl's Perch. Martin hadn't called her back, and she hadn't been able to reach him. His voice mail picked up immediately, which meant his phone was turned off. Whatever was going on, she bet his Saturday was tough, nanny's help or not.

The oddest sensation slid up her back as she drove alongside the Susquehanna River. She'd been in this very spot three years ago, heading for Hershey Medical Center because Luke and Mary had been taken there by helicopter after their accident. She remembered the days that followed, months of hiding her rape from everyone but her parents and hoping against hope that she wouldn't lose Paul.

"Brilliant, Hannah, you were afraid of losing a jerk." She mumbled the words, then turned the radio up louder, trying to drown out the whispers of resentment against him. The familiar territory had to be the reason for the fresh edge of offense that cut against her insides. In all the time she'd known Paul, he'd lived on a college campus not far from here, except for the summers, when he stayed with his Gram. She'd only seen this area twice before, once on the way to the hospital to see Luke and Mary and again about two weeks later on the way back home, but in each instance she'd been keenly aware that she was in Paul's stomping grounds. At the time she felt connected to him, hopeful they could overcome the obstacles that stood between them and getting married.

Silly, childish dreams.

Needing a stronger diversion than worship songs, she pushed the radio button, jumping through the stations until she found a familiar song by Rascal Flatts, "I'm Moving On." She cranked up the sound full blast and sang along, assuring her anxieties that she would survive the oddity of being here as well as the misery of not being with Lissa throughout whatever ordeal she faced.

The waters of the Susquehanna weren't brown and frothy this time. The river looked crystal clear as the afternoon sun rode across the ripples. In less than an hour she'd be in Owl's Perch, and as badly as she wanted to arrive, she didn't want to face her father. What was she going to say to him?

A dozen songs later, that question was still on her mind as she drove into her parents' driveway. Her mouth dry and palms sweaty, she got out of her car. The cool September breeze played with her dress and loose strands of her pinned-up hair, but there wasn't anyone in sight, and the wood doors on the house were shut. Without any sounds of voices or movement coming through the screened windows, she was pretty confident no one was home. She knocked loudly anyway. It was rare for everyone to be gone if it wasn't a church day.

When no one answered, she made a complete circle, taking in the old place, its chicken coop, barns, lean-to, and smokehouse. A sense of nostalgia reverberated through her as she absorbed the homestead where she'd been born and her mother before her. The tops of the huge oaks rustled. She walked to the hand pump, pushed and pulled the handle until water poured forth, and filled a tin cup. Taking a sip of the cool water, Hannah sensed an odd connectedness to her ancestors. A great-grandfather on her mother's side had dug this well, and springs that fed it had been sustaining her family for generations.

The quiet peacefulness moved through her, making her realize how much she'd once cherished parts of the Plain life. She hadn't expected this, and for the first time in a long time, she wished she understood herself better. Spotting the garden, she walked up the small hill to the edge of it. The last of the corn had been harvested weeks ago, and now all that remained were the cut-off brown stalks. The pea plants had been pulled up for the season. The cold-weather plants—broccoli, cauliflower, and cabbage—were thriving. She'd loved gardening from the first time her Daed had placed seeds in the palms of her hands and helped her plant them. Daed and she had come to the garden every day, watching, weeding, and watering. In the end those seeds produced enough food for her family to eat well all year long. Suddenly missing who her Daed and she had once been, her eyes misted. How much easier it would be to sort through her feelings if she understood the magnitude of emotions that came out of nowhere and took her to places she didn't know existed. Perhaps in that one thing, she and Sarah weren't so very different. Her sister seemed to respond immediately to the emotions that marched through her, and Hannah stood against them, but either way they left a mark.

Her mind returned to the strange conversation she'd had with Sarah—the jumbled words and thoughts that circled with no destination. She needed to find out what was going on with her. Deciding to go see Luke and Mary for answers, she went to her car. She backed out of the driveway and headed down the familiar dirt road she used to walk regularly when going to Gram's. The hairs on her arms stood on end as the paved road turned into a gravel one, the one where the attack had taken place. She locked her car doors and turned the music up to blaring, trying not to think about it. A few minutes later she pulled into Luke's driveway.

Getting out of the car, she noticed that his shop didn't appear to be open. The windows, blinds, and doors were closed. It seemed like he'd have the place open on a Saturday. She knocked loudly before trying the door.

When it opened, she stepped inside. The shadowy place didn't look anything like a usable shop. It looked like a storage room for buggy parts, not leather goods. Waiting at the foot of the stairs that led to the second-floor apartment, Hannah called, "Luke? Mary?"

The door at the top of the steps creaked open, and a half-dressed young man stepped out. "They don't live here. Never have. We rent the place."

He might be Amish, but she couldn't tell for sure since he only had on a sleeveless T-shirt and pants.

He descended a few steps.

Hannah backed up. "I'm sorry for interrupting you."

"No interruption at all."

Luke and Mary never lived in the home above the harness shop, both of which were built by the community just for them? Unwilling to ask any questions, Hannah went to her car.

Opening the door to the vehicle, she spotted Katie Waddell's white clapboard home amid fenced pasturelands. The once-worn footpath from here to Gram's was thick with grass. Hannah closed the door to her car. Maybe it was time to push beyond her fears. She headed for the old farmhouse. Except for a few fences that needed mending, the place looked good. Her heart pounded something fierce as she crossed Gram's screened porch to the back door.

"Look at me, Hannah." As if catapulted back in time, she could hear Paul's voice and feel the soft rumble of his words against her soul. *"I've been aching to talk to you before I return to college. There are some things I just can't write in a letter."*

She shuddered, trying to dismiss the memory and ignore the feelings that washed over her as she knocked on the door. No one answered. She peered through the gape in the curtains that hung over the glass part of the door and knocked louder. After several minutes she gave up, left the porch, and moved to the side yard, thinking Gram might be in the garden. But one look at the garden said no one had been in it for quite a while. Paul's old rattletrap of a truck sat under a pavilion near the garden, the hood up and the engine dangling above by a thick chain.

Eeriness crawled over her skin as if she were trapped in one of those *Twilight Zone* episodes Martin had told her about. Whatever was going on, life seemed to have changed for everyone else as much as it had for her. She headed for her car. It was time to find the hotel near Harrisburg where Martin had made reservations for her and settle in for the night. She could have stayed at a hotel closer to her community, but according to Martin, the one he'd chosen was nicer: very safe, with breakfast included, and a business center in case she needed Internet access. Unfortunately she'd be stuck there all day tomorrow since it was a church day. Visits by estranged Amish may not be tolerated any day, but especially on a Sunday. And Matthew had made it clear she needed to wait until after the funeral to be seen by the community as a whole and by his family in particular. If that's how strongly Matthew felt, her father would magnify that sentiment a thousandfold.

Regardless of what it took, she'd get through the next few days with her dignity intact. They'd trampled her spirit once. She'd not give them another chance.

Chapter 2

Hannah.

Paul woke with a start.

The nighttime breeze rustled through the sheers of the half-open window. He turned the alarm clock toward him. Three a.m. Regardless of the time, it wasn't likely he'd go back to sleep.

He pushed her "Past and Future" quilt off him.

"Past and Future." Paul stood and began folding the quilt. Even in the dim glow of street lamps, he could see the handiwork of the Amish girl who'd promised to marry him. Last Tuesday he'd found her—seen her, rather—in front of an upscale Ohio home in the embrace of her husband.

It was time to get this thing off his bed and out of his apartment. Mary had given it to him after Hannah left, saying it had more of Hannah in it than anything else. It was supposed to keep him warm until she returned and they wed. He wasn't sure what to do with it just yet, but it wasn't staying here.

Dark gave way to light as he sat with a coffee cup and a stack of his clients' files on the table in front of him. Reading and taking notes on Andrew Brown's family, he continued to map out the issues each family member dealt with to see if he could find a common thread, a connected problem he was missing. He'd head for work, then go to Gram's and mend a few fences before nightfall, but right now these moments without interruption belonged to him.

The shrill ring of his phone ended his private study time, and he knew Monday had begun.

He rose from the table and lifted the receiver. "Paul Waddell."

"Paul, it's me, Luke. I hate to call you so early in the morning. Should have thought to contact you sooner, but it's been crazy around here."

"What's going on?"

"I'm sure you've heard by now, but I thought I'd call anyway."

"I've been in the mountains all weekend, camped out with friends."

"E and L shops burned to the ground Friday."

Paul's thoughts jumped to each person in the Lapp and Esh families. "I'm really sorry. Is everyone okay?"

"No." Luke paused. "David died." His voice wavered. "And Matthew was injured. Aside from needing therapy and some scarring on his back and shoulders, Matthew will be fine." Luke's words came out quiet and slow. "David's funeral is this afternoon, one o'clock, at our Old Order cemetery."

Funeral. Hating what this meant for Matthew and his family, Paul couldn't manage to respond.

"Things haven't work out between Elle and Matthew, and… well…I think it'd do him good for as many friends as can to be there."

"Absolutely, I'll be there."

"Good. I knew I could depend on you. But, uh, look, I should warn you." Luke took a heavy breath and talked even slower. "Sarah found the paper you brought to the house with Hannah's phone number and address. She called her and asked her to come home. We haven't seen anything of her yet, but Sarah swears she promised to come for a few days and was supposed to be here two days ago. Sarah came up missing early Saturday morning, and when we figured out she'd hired a driver to take her into Harrisburg, we all went there looking for her. We found her at the train station, determined to wait for Hannah."

Paul appreciated the sentiments behind Luke's explanation, knowing his friend was trying to prepare him for bumping into Hannah. "Well, if she does come, it'll be a good time for your community and family to make peace with her before any more time passes. I'll see you this afternoon, and if you need anything, just call."

Paul drove to work, second-guessing himself as to whether he should take the day off or not. He pulled into his parking space and headed for his office. Throughout the morning he tried to hear every word his clients spoke, but he found the clock jumping in time and he'd taken no notes during the sessions. It wasn't so much knowing Hannah was supposed to come back as feeling concern for how her family would react to her. She bore few traits of having been raised Plain. That was obvious the moment he saw her last week—wearing a short-sleeved, thin cotton dress with no pleats while laughing and kissing a man.

Feeling like a second-rate counselor, he checked the clock. "Andrew, our time is up for today, but if you can allow extra time next week, I'd like to go back over some of this."

"My wife likes what she's seeing in me. I do too. Even m-my son seems better."

Andrew's stumbling over the word *my* reminded Paul they had quite a bit of road to cover before healing included the father-and-son relationship.

Paul rose. "I'd like to see your wife and children again as soon as it fits their schedule."

Andrew followed his cue and stood. "You're a lot of help, Paul. I haven't lost it with the kids for over a month."

He walked Andrew out of his office and down the carpeted stairway. They stopped at the receptionist's desk, which sat in the large open area of the old foyer, dining room, and living room combo—all of which were furnished in home-style comfort for clients of the Better Path. The office space and mission was an old homestead, and everything in it was designed to retain the homey feel.

"Halley, would you put Andrew on the books for the same time next week, and he won't be charged for this week."

"Really?" Andrew looked surprised.

Although guilt shadowed Paul, he couldn't tell Andrew why he wasn't charging him. It'd taken too long to build a rapport with the man to undermine his confidence with a confession of not hearing all he had said today. "Take care, Andrew, and I'll see you next week." He turned back to Halley. "Did you reach my appointments for this afternoon and reschedule?"

"Yes. And Dorcas called."

Paul nodded. "Did she say what she needed?"

"No, but she asked you to call her before you leave today."

"Okay, thanks." Paul went back up the stairs and into his office. It'd feel good to talk with Dorcas, to try to connect with reality over any lingering dreams of Hannah's returning to him.

He lifted the phone and dialed the Miller home.

"Hello." Dorcas sounded tired.

"Good morning. What's up?"

"Paul." The excitement in her tone was undeniable, and he smiled.

"Did you doubt I'd call back?"

"I wasn't sure how long it'd take you to get the message and then find the time. I wanted to remind you of Evelyn's birthday today. Everyone's meeting here for dinner. Your parents are arriving around five. I'd hoped you could be here by seven."

He'd totally forgotten about her sister's birthday celebration tonight. "Did you hear about the fire in Owl's Perch?"

"Yeah, I heard. My mother's cousin Jeanie called. That's so awful."

"I'm going to the funeral, and I want to stay around here today in case there's anything I can do for Matthew. Sorry."

"Oh." She sounded disappointed. "I should have thought of that. Of course you're going."

On a whim Paul came up with a plan she would like. "Since I'm pulling weekend duty at the clinic, I'm off tomorrow. I need to get some fences mended at Gram's. Care to spend the day there with me?"

"You're serious?"

"Sure, why not?"

"Well…no reason. You've just barely shown any interest in…well, you know, and your invitation is just surprising, that's all."

He paused, willing himself to open up to her. "I've been thinking about things this morning, and maybe I'd held on to the idea of Hannah's coming back because I didn't want to admit defeat more than I actually wanted her back."

"That makes sense."

"I guess I should've figured this out way before now."

"Do you think she'll return for the funeral?"

"Maybe, but I'm sure you'll feel better when you hear that she's married."

"She's married?"

"Yes, I found out when I went to Ohio last week."

"I'm really sorry."

Confident she wasn't all that sorry, he imagined she was probably relieved and quickly becoming hopeful. Paul placed his latest notes on Andrew into the appropriate file. "That's nice of you, but it's water under the bridge and long gone. Do you want to come to Gram's tomorrow?"

"Absolutely."

He slid the file into the cabinet and locked it. "I'll come get you in the morning, and we'll go out for breakfast first."

"Oh, Paul, that sounds wonderful."

"Good. I need to run. The funeral starts in an hour."

"I'll see you tomorrow. Okay?"

"Sure thing. Bye." Paul hung up the phone, feeling more on track with his life than he had in years. Why had it taken seeing Hannah married and happy before he could connect with his own life?

He grabbed his suit jacket and headed for his car. Driving toward the cemetery, Paul was thinking about the Esh and Lapp families, wondering what, if anything, he could do to make this time easier. He'd sure like to help get the shop back in working condition—if they would accept his help. The community itself felt nothing but distrust for Paul, as if maybe it was his fault Hannah had been pregnant and had run away. Thankfully, Luke and Matthew didn't feel that way, but whether Paul would be allowed to pitch in and help rebuild was another matter.

Speculating whether Hannah would actually come home for this or not, he trailed behind the long line of horses and buggies as they slowly wound their way to the cemetery. Thoughts of the last two years with Dorcas floated through his mind. Maybe he hadn't been waiting for Hannah to return. She'd been seventeen years old and six months pregnant when he left her standing there crying after him. Maybe guilt had more to do with his waiting all this time.

The stark black buggies set against a nearby field with large rolls of golden, baled hay looked picturesque, but the reality of life, anyone's life, never seemed to match the peaceful image of a quick glimpse. He parked his car near a group of horses and carriages in a dirt and gravel area across the street from the burial spot. Those who'd come to pay their respects quietly made their way to the site.

Unlike most Amish funerals, all parts of the ritual would be conducted with a closed casket because of the fire. Their heritage kept them from having a photo to set up on a table near the casket like *Englischers* might.

Hanging back with the other non-Amish neighbors, Paul spotted Matthew near the grave as men prepared to lower the casket into the ground using ropes. Matthew was the only Amish man here without a jacket on. It had to be due to the burns on his back. Since Paul had come to assure Matthew he had people who cared, he stepped around the crowd, including Hannah's parents and younger siblings, and went to Matthew and offered his hand. "I'm really sorry."

Matthew didn't even look up as he shook Paul's hand. "*Ya*. It's a miserable thing."

Luke caught Paul's eye and gave a nod, and Paul returned it. Mary stood beside him, leaning heavily into her husband.

He reached to clasp Matthew's shoulder, but Matthew pulled away. "Second-degree burns leave the nerves exposed. It's more pain than I can tolerate most days."

Wishing for the right words, Paul nodded. "I should have thought… Matthew, when you're well enough and begin clearing the debris and rebuilding, I want to help."

Staring at the freshly dug hole, Matthew sighed. "Hannah came to see me Saturday." He gave a stiff shrug. "I wasn't sure what I thought of her returning—still not. But I'm sure I came across unwelcoming and—"

An Amish man spoke loudly. "Dear ones, let's bow in silence."

The weight of today settled over Paul as he closed his eyes. The gentle winds across his face and the warmth of the sun made the day one that should be enjoyed. Instead the focus was on loss.

Death seemed like such an odd thing. One did not have to die or know anyone who'd died to experience it. Death came without pallbearers or grave sites. The death of a dream, hope, and even love. He hadn't realized love could die. One day breathing. One day in poor health. One day dead. Never to be resurrected.

But it didn't have to be that way, not for every family that became ill. What had happened to Hannah and him had been horrible, but the death of a family—one that had taken a vow before God—that's where he wanted to stop death. Like with Andrew's family and…

Another image of Dorcas filled his mind, making him long to connect with life. It was too precious and too short not to spend it on love and family. Life beckoned to be lived. Love called to be embraced. And he intended to do both.

When the preacher said *amen,* another Amish man stepped forward and began reading a hymn while the pallbearers slowly placed dirt on the coffin. Paul looked through the crowd, praying for the families that were represented. Movement off to the left caught his eye. He glanced in that direction, just beyond the trees and near the shoulder of the road where a few cars had parked.

Hannah.

She was wearing a dark green dress and leaning against a gold Honda a hundred feet away. She removed the sunglasses from her face. An air of control and poise surrounded her like an aura. He thought she was right not to come too close, to handle this quietly and with no fanfare. Yet she was present for Matthew's sake…and maybe her own. Even if her people could recognize her, they wouldn't see her where she stood, not unless—

"Hannah!" Sarah's scream pierced the formality.

Her father grabbed her arm. "Hush."

Every eye turned to where Sarah was looking and saw Hannah. Mary gasped and started to head for her, but Luke put his arm around her and whispered something.

Sarah broke free of her father's grip and took off running. "Hannah!"

Zeb Lapp followed her, unable to keep up with her all-out sprint.

Hannah dipped her chin and rubbed her forehead. Paul hated this. He wanted to step out and go to her, to give her at least one person as a shield against the murmurs and stares. Someone to be a friend. But he'd only make things worse for her if he did.

He understood anew why she'd given up and left once she lost hope in their relationship. The reason she hadn't returned—until her sister made contact, needing her—stared hard at him, and he got it. There simply was no winning inside Owl's Perch for Hannah Lapp.

Chapter 3

*E*very person Hannah had known growing up turned to stare at her.

Her Daed was still a good thirty feet away when he finally caught Sarah's arm. "Stop this. Now."

But she flailed her free hand and kept heading for Hannah. "You came! I knew you'd keep your promise!"

Her Daed lost his grip, and she took off again. He took long strides toward Hannah, and when his gaze met hers, she felt like an unruly child. "Well, do something."

Hannah read his lips and his expression more than heard his words. She nodded and closed the gap between them. Sarah grabbed her, almost knocking her over. Unexpected warmth flooded Hannah. No one could have made her believe the feelings she had for her sister right now. Sarah had caused such harm to Hannah's life in the past. And yet the tie to her younger sister was undeniable.

The hug lasted a good minute before Hannah removed her sister's arms. "You have to go back now, Sarah. We'll have all the time you need later."

She glanced at the funeral and back to Hannah. An expression crossed her face as if she'd forgotten where she was and why. She looked at her palms and began scrubbing a thumb against the palm of her other hand.

Hannah slid her hands into Sarah's, stopping her sister's odd gesture. She squeezed her sister's hands and nodded toward the cemetery. "Go on."

Sarah looked a bit calmer.

Daed arrived, out of breath and definitely out of patience, if he'd had any to begin with. He paused, his face red. His eyes narrowed, and he skimmed her from head to toe.

"What were you thinking?" Her father whispered the words. "Gone for more than two years and arrive just in time to interrupt a community funeral. And look at you." He pointed at her hair and then her dress. "You didn't remain Plain."

Wondering if she looked that different or if she simply wasn't what he'd expected, she shook her head. She wasn't Plain, but she was his daughter.

He pointed to her car. "Go on to the house, and Sarah will meet you there later."

Hannah looked across the crowd that stared at her with heads grouped in pairs, whispering. Refusing to allow powerlessness to engulf her, she lifted her chin, squared her shoulders, and slid her sunglasses on. Before closing her car door, she heard the preacher speaking loudly, beginning the service again. Hannah drove away.

Of all the possible times to cause a scene, a funeral had to be the worst. She never should have come.

Doing as her father told her, she pulled into the driveway of the Lapp homestead. When she'd talked to Martin yesterday, he'd told her that Lissa had climbed his five-tier glass shelves, and it broke with her on it. She received four stitches in her left leg on Saturday. Lissa couldn't be in better hands than Martin's, but that didn't keep Hannah from wishing she'd stayed with them.

She got out of the car and headed toward the bench that sat on a knoll behind the Lapp home. It favored the one at her aunt Zabeth's cabin, the one where she and Zabeth used to sit at the beginning and ending of each day as oft as the weather permitted.

Drawing a deep breath, she took in every familiar aroma she'd grown up with. The smells changed with the seasons, but September's fragrance brought a flood of memories—summer's heat breaking, the last of the garden's produce, and the aroma of freshly cut hay. Her childhood had been as idyllic as allowed any human on this planet. It wasn't until she hit her teen years and began wanting things that weren't Old Order Amish that life under her father's roof became bumpy.

She let her mind wander, and it filled with a dozen hayrides, take-a-pet-to-school days, and summertime produce and lemonade stands. Memories of laughter ringing across the fields as she played with her siblings eased in and out of her thoughts. In the midst of them all, a vision of Paul crept in, and before she could stop it, she heard his voice as clearly as the day he asked her to marry him.

"Hannah, you are all my thoughts and hopes... There's no one for me but you..."

A shudder ran through her, and she slid her fingers over the diamond and ruby ring Martin had placed on her finger before she left.

The sounds of a horse and buggy approaching interrupted her thoughts, and she stood. There wasn't a male in the buggy, just Mamm and Sarah. Before Mamm pulled the buggy to a stop, Sarah jumped off, ran to Hannah, grabbed her hand, and pulled her toward the barn. "We gotta talk."

Hannah tugged back, stopping Sarah from leading her anywhere. "Yes, I know. That's what I'm here for, but I need to see Mamm first."

Her mother pulled the buggy to a stop beside Hannah and sat there, staring. Feeling as if she'd just stepped out of a Victoria's Secret ad, she reminded herself how modest her below-the-knee, dark green cotton dress was. Her favorite dresses were made of mostly polyester with enough spandex to make them fit and flow in a way that wasn't appreciated among the Amish. She'd chosen her dress today carefully, knowing how ingrained the views toward clothing were.

Her mother's brown eyes locked on hers. "Hannah?"

The doubt in her voice said she had changed in more ways than just her clothing.

She swallowed hard, unsure how to break the ice between them. "Hi, Mamm."

Mamm set the brake, gathered her skirts, and climbed out of the buggy. She stood in front of Hannah, saying nothing. Her mouth opened a few times as tears welled in her eyes.

Hannah slid her arms around her and hugged her. "I'm fine, Mamm. I told you that in the letters."

Her mother engulfed her, her body shaking as she sobbed. "Oh, child, how could you stay gone so very, very long?" She took a step back and stared into Hannah's eyes. "I've missed you."

Hannah knew nothing to say. If her parents had tossed any understanding or affection her way before she boarded that train, she might have stayed. But now she couldn't receive an unspoken apology without question.

"How did you see me that night, put balm on the gashes in my hands, and dry my tears, yet decide later that I hadn't been attacked after all?" Her insides quaked as she dared to speak her mind. In Zabeth's home, openness had been cherished more than restraint, and Hannah longed for that with her Mamm.

Her mother's eyes grew wide with disbelief, and Hannah knew she'd just burned the bridge Mamm had wanted to cross.

Hannah slid one hand into the side pocket of her dress, wishing she could talk to Zabeth about all that was going on. "How did you get my number?"

Sarah clutched Hannah's arm firmer. "Paul brought it to the house last week."

Paul knew how to reach me? The slap in the face stung a bit even now, and she wouldn't mind being able to return the favor. A wallop of one. He knew how to reach her, which really wasn't the point—not any longer. What did she care? Years ago he could've returned her call the night she stayed at the hotel, waiting until time to go to the train station, and yet he didn't.

Hannah focused on her sister, thinking maybe she was mistaken. "He brought my address and phone number to the house?" She searched Mamm's eyes for understanding. "Here?"

Mamm nodded. "He's made a bit of peace with your Daed. I think he and Luke are friends. Matthew too."

Disbelief rang in her ears, making her lightheaded.

For the first time ever she realized the man played games. He had to. It was the only thing that explained his behavior. He didn't return her calls or try in any way to make peace with her, and yet he'd become friends with Matthew and Luke, and he'd brought information about Hannah's life to her Daed.

Of all the nerve…

Mamm shooed a fly away. "I talked to him once myself. He…he doesn't seem to be such a bad guy after all."

"Oh good grief!" Hannah took a step back. Paul had them totally bamboozled. "You know what? Let's not talk about Paul."

Sarah started clearing her throat in long, weird sounds while rubbing her right thumb across the palm of her left hand again. Hannah remembered the odd sounds as an old habit of her sister's when she was tense. The palm-rubbing thing was newer.

Mamm looked bewildered. "But, Hann—" Her mother shook her head. "You're impossible to understand. What's wrong with me thinking he's okay? Isn't that what you wanted?"

She thrust her hands, palms up, toward her mother. "I wanted that when it might have mattered, and there's no way you would have ever given him a chance if I'd stayed, but now you do?" She sighed. "And I'm the one who's impossible to understand?"

Sarah began rocking back and forth on her heels. "The male cats eat the mama cats' babies." The words pushed out through labored breathing. "And fires destroy truth that's not even there." She put her thumb on her middle finger and turned them, as if doing the motion for the itsy, bitsy spider song. She sang the words. "The tongue sets on fire the course of life."

Chills climbed up Hannah's back and through her scalp. What was wrong with her sister?

Mamm clapped her hands. "Stop it, Sarah."

Her sister stopped moving her hands. Her eyes darted back and forth. "You can't hate each other." She moaned.

Hannah reeled under the shock of her sister's words. She didn't hate Mamm, not even close, but her mother had stood silent as the men decided Hannah was a liar and guilty of sexual sin.

Sarah's lips were turning blue as she continued breathing fast and heavy.

Hannah put her arm around her. "Mamm, get a lunch bag and bring it here." She forced a smile. "Sarah, look at me."

This breathing issue was new, wasn't it? Sarah turned her head, avoiding her gaze.

Mamm stepped forward. "What's going on?"

Hannah placed her fingers on Sarah's jugular, taking a quick assessment of her heart rate. "She's hyperventilating, best I can tell. Get a lunch bag, please." Hannah took Sarah's cheeks into her hands. "Sarah, look at me. I want you to imagine being in a field of flowers. Remember that game?" Hannah did. When they were kids, she spent as much time trying to calm Sarah down as she spent doing chores.

Mamm came out the door with the lunch sack. Hannah took it, shook it open, scrunched the top part, and put it over Sarah's mouth.

She tried to claw it away.

Hannah resisted. "None of that. You called me to help, and you're going to let me help, right?" She covered Sarah's mouth with the edge of the bag. "Imagine that we're lying in the field, counting all the different types of wildflowers: black-eyed Susans, morning glories, daisies, forget-me-nots..." She prattled on like when they were younger.

But this was different. Sarah was different. Worse. Whatever was going on, it wasn't a bad case of nerves or a meanspirited sister or even jealousy, as she'd thought for years.

Sarah's breathing eased.

"That's my little sister." She lowered the bag, but she intended to keep it with her.

Sarah's fists were clinging to the sleeves of Hannah's dress. "Where's the baby?"

Hannah blinked. "What?"

"You…you gave birth. Where is the baby?"

Hannah looked to Mamm.

Mamm's face paled. "After you left, Sarah began looking for things. We didn't know what she was searching for." Tears streaked down her face. "I…I guess the baby's been it all along." Mamm wiped her face with her apron, closed her eyes for a moment, and then began again. "Sometimes she has burns on her hands that no one can explain. The day after the Bylers' barn burned, I found charred clothing in the trash."

The oddness of being in some alternate world pushed against Hannah, making her feel like she was stuck inside a dream. Was it possible her sister was guilty of setting fires? Hannah moved to the steps of the porch. Nausea came in waves.

Did her mother understand that if Sarah was guilty of setting fire to Matthew's business, she was guilty of manslaughter in the eyes of the law? And belonging to an Amish community that was willing to protect its own from the courts would not stop the legal system.

Hannah studied her sister. Sarah clearly had times of acting normal, like now as she stood there looking ordinary and…and perfectly sane. But was she? The questions about where Hannah's baby was and the odd little sayings and songs had ended abruptly, leaving her to appear like any other Amish girl.

Hannah swallowed. "Sarah, you wanted us to talk. We can go for a ride in my car or use the horse and buggy."

Sarah shook her head, her fingers trembling. "Daed might not like it if we go off together."

Their Daed might not like it? Sarah was an adult! Irritation swelled again, forcing her to stockpile it. Under Zabeth's tenderness and support, she had forgotten how infuriating life with Zeb Lapp could be.

Mamm looked to the door, and Hannah waited to be invited inside, but the invitation didn't come—probably a verdict passed down from her father. Hannah gestured for Sarah to sit next to her on the porch steps, unsure what to think, let alone what to do next.

Doubts as to whether her mother and she could ever recover the closeness they'd once shared pressed in on her. Hannah rubbed Sarah's back, reassuring her through physical touch of things that couldn't be promised in words. In the Englischer world, words flowed quick and cheap, saying things that shouldn't be said, telling things that shouldn't be shared. But here, words were too rare and perceived fate accepted without a fight. How many Englischers ran for help and medicines, spewing the ills of their life to anyone who'd listen? And here, how many Amish stood stalwart in silence, reaching out to no doctor and telling no professional of the pain they bore?

Wasn't there any balance in the world?

Determined to weigh each word, Hannah began. "Mamm, Sarah's changed a good bit since I left, don't you think?"

Her mother gave a nod.

"I think she needs to see someone professional."

"No." Her mother studied Sarah, who sat quietly as if she'd withdrawn into a world they couldn't enter. "All she needed was to see you."

"Mamm, what just happened was not someone who only needed time with her big sister."

"But she's such a clear thinker some of the time, as if…" She paused.

Grief for Mamm settled over Hannah. Having a willful, difficult husband was one thing, but watching helplessly as her children's lives slipped from her arms into chaos was too much for any woman.

Needing to talk with Sarah without adding to the heartache Mamm was dealing with, Hannah took Sarah by the hand. "We'll be back in a bit, okay?"

"I'll fix us… Do you drink coffee?"

"I do." ,

A faint smile crossed her mother's face. "I'll set a pot on the stove."

Hannah and Sarah walked across the road to the dock. Sarah removed her shoes and stockings and sat on the edge of the pier, dangling her toes in the water.

Having given up the traditional black stockings long ago, Hannah slid out of her shoes and sat next to her sister. Bream swam near their feet, looking for morsels of bread. "Samuel could catch five or six fish with one scoop of the net today, ya?"

Sarah swooshed her foot through the water quickly, scattering the fish. "Ya."

"And we could spend hours cleaning his fine catch of the day to produce half an ounce of meat per fish."

Sarah giggled. "Our aim was noble though, to prove he could provide a meal for the family."

"Is that what we proved? All this time I thought our aim was to keep him out of our hair that morning while you and I worked the blackberry patch without his"—Hannah cleared her throat—"help."

They shared a laugh, and Sarah wrapped her arm through Hannah's. "I'm not crazy."

"Me either," she offered.

Sarah laid her head against Hannah's shoulder. "I feel crazy sometimes."

Hannah kissed the top of her head through her prayer *Kapp*. "Me too."

She squeezed tight. "You won't leave me again, will you?"

Hannah leaned her cheek against the top of Sarah's head. "What's going on? I mean really and truly, all the dirt, no secrets."

"Like we used to do...before going to Gram's became more important to you than being with me?"

Taken aback that her sister knew when she began pulling away from the family, Hannah lifted Sarah's chin and gazed into her eyes. "Yeah, like we used to."

"If I tell you everything, will you take me to see your baby?"

"Talk to me, Sarah."

"Jacob's seeing Lizzy Miller these days," Sarah began, and Hannah let the conversation meander wherever Sarah wished.

If Hannah was hoping for some encouraging news, she didn't get it as her sister made perfect sense some of the time but then talked in circles about Hannah's baby, the fire, and how things were different with everyone since she left. As her sister talked, it became clear she had issues that went way beyond Hannah's scope of understanding of the human psyche. She'd veer off into nonsense, and Hannah couldn't figure out how to bring her back around to reality. She wasn't even able to give a straight answer to what she meant about starting the fires.

"Sarah, everyone needs help at times. I received a lot of mine from counselors at the Rape Crisis Center. I think you might find help by going to a different kind of counselor. Maybe he or she will know about medications that can clear your thoughts a bit."

"I'd like that."

"Good. Come on." Hannah walked back to the house with her. As they crossed the road that separated the house from the pasture with the pond, Mamm came onto the porch, holding a tray with a coffeepot, cups, and cream and sugar.

They came to a stop at the foot of the concrete steps. The awkwardness between Hannah and her mother seemed to stand sentry, keeping them from each other. "I need to take a rain check on the coffee. I really have to go, but I'd like you to consider letting Sarah see someone."

The dishes clanked and rattled as Mamm set the tray down on the top of a wooden keg they used as an end table. "It's not up to me. You know that."

"I know, but you have an influence, Mamm. Use it with all the power you can muster."

Her mother pursed her lips, looking displeased that Hannah would be so bold. Hannah gave Sarah a hug. "You stay close to home, and we'll talk again soon. Okay?"

Sarah held on, making Hannah forcibly remove her arms from around her. Mamm grasped Sarah's hands and pulled her into a hug. The two stood side by side as Hannah went to her car.

"Hannah," her mother called.

She turned. Her mother walked to her and stared into her eyes. "I…I'm sorry for not standing by you, for not coming to you after your Daed refused to let you come home."

And in that moment, Hannah saw traces of the long journey of regret written on Mamm's face.

Mamm shuddered. "Even when your Daed and me got word of what had happened and came to the funeral, I stood mute, so lost inside my own grief and so shaken by the rumors that I didn't even embrace you."

There were things Mamm wasn't saying, like the fact that she'd started to come to Hannah that day by the grave site, and Daed had stopped her. But Mamm wouldn't lay blame. She'd only confess her part and leave the rest alone. Hannah longed for forgiveness toward her mother to sweep through her, but it didn't. The Amish way was to forgive, or at least confess forgiveness, but she couldn't.

Wondering if her years of hiding out in Ohio had more to do with her own inability to forgive than anything else, Hannah hugged her mother. "Let's handle Sarah with as few regrets as possible. Okay?" She stepped back, looking at her mother.

Mamm nodded. "Ya."

Hannah got into her car and pulled out of the driveway. Her mind ran in a thousand directions without finding solutions to any of the issues at hand. It'd take more than a name of a therapist to convince her family it was absolutely necessary that Sarah see a counselor and get on medication.

Her Daed seemed to barely tolerate Hannah's being here, even at a distance. What would he or the church leaders be like when she asked them to handle things more like the Englischers did?

Matthew weaved through the crowd of church folks and relatives in his Mamm's kitchen and walked outside. People stood in small groups on the front porch, talking in muted tones and eating. All eyes moved to him, and he nodded and spoke briefly before going into the barn. He bridled his horse and mounted it without a saddle. If he stayed at the house one more minute, he might lose his will to live.

The sadness in his mother's eyes was too much, and he'd already grown weary of trying to comfort her. He aimed the horse west and let it amble along. The brokenness and guilt made him unsure if he'd ever get out from under it. He'd worked so hard and had nothing to show for it. Nothing but debt from money received and promises made for a product he could no longer make. But that didn't compare to the Grand Canyon–size ache inside him for David. If he'd spent more time with his brother, he might have some sense of peace. Instead, he'd stayed too busy to really listen when David tried talking to him.

And Elle.

Whatever patience David needed, Matthew had probably used it on Elle.

Elle. Born an Englischer. Raised half her life in an Amish home. Left two years ago, promising to return, join the church, and marry him.

He'd loved her. Believed in her. Worse, he still longed for her. He had to be the biggest fool ever born.

Her father's request for her to come away from the Amish community that had raised her and to live with him in Baltimore for six months had ended long, long ago, and yet she continued living there. Her reasons were numerous—helping her dad in his bakery, attending photography school, keeping her part of the contracts she'd signed with a studio—and her promises of returning and joining the faith continuous. When he'd written to her, releasing her from the promise to marry him, she'd returned, complaining about his lack of faithfulness to give her time.

What bothered him the most was that he didn't really know how he felt about Elle. He wanted to be free of her while he longed to hold her.

From the crossroad he saw a woman kneeling beside David's grave. He pulled the horse to a stop, taking in the scenery. Feeling some odd connection to life for the first time since this had happened, he wanted a closer look. He guided the horse along the edge of the paved road until he came to the grass and dirt entryway. Dismounting, he winced in pain. He led the horse to a hitching post and wrapped the reins around it before heading to the grave site.

Kathryn.

She ran her hands over the fresh dirt as tears splashed onto the ground. Matthew's eyes clouded for a moment. He'd seen her a dozen times at his house since the fire, helping Mamm dress and serving meals to his Daed and Peter, but never once did he think how she must be feeling. Until this moment all of David's comments about talking with Kathryn and admiring her hadn't clicked. But whatever the two had going, it probably hadn't been romance, especially since David had been only sixteen. She was older and seeing someone from her own community, a man he'd met for the first time earlier today. Yet that seemed to do nothing to dull the pain he was witnessing.

"Kathryn."

She gasped and stood to her feet. "Matthew." Her lips quivered as she wiped at tears that didn't slow. "I'm sorry."

He shook his head. "No need to be sorry. I envy the tears."

She scoffed. "And I the lack of them." Without any sign of the tears stopping, she looked at the grave, and a soft moan escaped her. "He had so many dreams and desires. It's so unfair."

Surprised that she didn't say what everyone else was saying—that God knew best—Matthew found comfort in her words. "A fallen planet is no easy place to live."

"Ya, but heaven is." She drew a deep breath. "We talked a few weeks back. I know he told you he was unsure about remaining Amish, but I showed him scriptures of what it takes to be saved, and he prayed with me. He accepted the forgiveness Christ paid for and chose to believe God's Word above all circumstances; he just wasn't so sure he'd join the Amish church."

Although her words would be considered heresy by many, they poured salve on his aching soul. Most of his fellow Amish who'd joined the faith spent their lives trying to live as pure as possible, hoping salvation would be theirs at the end of the journey but always unsure. He understood their belief, agreed with it for the most part. It seemed some sects of Englischers wanted to believe one prayer did it all; after that they could do things their own way until death took over. Kathryn's confession of confident salvation through a simple prayer would stir quite a hornet's nest if news of it reached certain church leaders, but it brought waves of peace to him.

Tears worked their way down his face, the first ones since he'd lost his brother. Odd as it seemed, they brought a sense of relief. "I didn't know…thank you."

"I shouldn't be thanked. I can't do spit." Kathryn mimicked a country accent. "How many times have you had to retrain me on how to file your work orders? But God—He can make donkeys talk."

Matthew chuckled, and more tears fell.

Kathryn took another useless swipe at her cheeks. "I reminded you of my work skills and made you cry." She giggled through her tears. "No?"

He wiped his face, thankful for the release only crying could bring. "Ya, that's it."

The laughter and talk stopped, and they just stood there, staring at the grave.

"You can rebuild, Matthew." She whispered the words. "I over-heard you telling your Daed that you can't or won't, but you can."

A car engine turned off, and they looked to the road several hun-dred feet away. Elle got out of the car. She waved, clearly wanting to talk. Matthew motioned that he'd be there in a minute.

Kathryn turned from Elle and swiped her apron over her face. "I'll go on back now and leave you two to talk."

Matthew looked around the edges of the field for Kathryn's buggy. "How'd you get here?"

She smoothed her apron back into place. "Walked."

"That's quite a walk. You must've been pretty desperate for time alone."

Kathryn cleared her throat and offered a wobbly grin. "Just me?"

He smiled. "At least I rode a horse. Here, take her. I'll either walk or catch a ride with Elle."

"Ride bareback? In this? Clearly, being raised without the benefit of sisters did nothing for your understanding of the restraints of the female Amish garb."

"You can straddle it or ride sidesaddle. It's a gentle horse, so you won't have a problem."

Looking a bit skeptical, she nodded. "If you say so."

"It was good of your Daed and Joseph to come today. It was quite a ways for them."

"Only a little over two hours by driver."

"Have they already gone home?"

"Daed has. Joseph is staying with the Bylers, hoping I'll be more in a mood for visiting before a driver takes him home tomorrow."

"Go on back and spend some time with him, Kathryn. Mamm has plenty of other help for tonight and tomorrow."

Elle waited by her car as he walked with Kathryn to the hitching post. He laced his fingers together and offered his hands as a step onto the bareback horse. As he stooped to help her, the pain across his back and shoulders was almost unbearable. She slid her foot into his hands and positioned herself on the back of the horse as if she were sitting on a sidesaddle.

Matthew passed her the reins. "Thank you, Kathryn. I needed this."

"Ya, me too." She took the leads. "I'll continue to pray God's best for you and Elle."

"Thanks." He slapped the horse's rump and ambled to Elle's car, hoping his movements looked natural rather than stiff and painful.

Elle angled her head. "How are you?"

"Better." He leaned against the car. "What's on your mind, Elle?"

"I wanted to offer my deepest sympathy. I just don't have any words to share…"

"I understand what you mean, and I'll pass that along to the family. But you didn't ignore my demand for space in order to share your condolences. So I'll ask again, what's on your mind?"

"The same thing that's been on my mind since before the fire: us. I don't want to lose you. Tell me I'm not alone in that."

He stared at the ground and shook his head. "I'm not sure what I feel, Elle, but I can't do this, not anymore."

"I know. Me either. But…"

Matthew lifted his gaze. "But what?"

"Maybe you should give us another chance, consider this as a good time for you and me to start over. It might help if you got out of Owl's Perch. There are so many things you could make a living at with your talent."

"Outside of Owl's Perch or outside of the Amish faith?"

"Please don't get angry again. I can't take it. Just hear me out."

The strength that had entered him a few minutes ago faded. "I'm listening."

"I've thought for a long time that it'd do you some real good to get away from here, just for a while. The business had you so consumed…

changed who you were, but now you can take a break. I think you'd like Baltimore, and it might open up new ideas that'd help you find a different career."

Matthew folded his arms across his chest, wondering if she actually believed the load of manure she'd just dumped at his feet. "I should just give up here and go to Baltimore. Is that what you came here, today of all days, to say?"

She moved in closer. "Matthew, I've not handled us right. I know that, and I couldn't be any sorrier." Dipping her head, she whispered, "You can't imagine the remorse I carry. But I love you, Matthew. I can't get free of that."

He gazed at his brother's simple tombstone, totally unsure of what he wanted to do from here. The idea of getting away held stronger temptation than he'd felt in a lot of years. "This is not the time."

She nodded. "You're right. I know you are. It's just that this is what I came to talk to you about before the fire. I had to come back again and let you know that just because the business is gone doesn't mean your life is too. It's a huge, fascinating world in Baltimore—just entering the city is exciting and will bring encouragement into your life. I needed to share that hope with you."

Hope? Confusion is more like it.

She reached out and cradled his cheek in the palm of her hand. "I'll go now, but you'll call me in a few days, please?" She tilted her head, appealing for a favorable decision.

The warmth of her hand brought up emotions he wished didn't exist, not for Elle. He remained silent, willing himself not to respond to her. Part of him wanted to grab her and kiss her until the awful pain of what life had done to him eased, but that wasn't the answer either.

He nodded.

Finally she pulled her hand away and went to her car. The notion of going to Baltimore echoed through him like the lustful desires of his youth, and he wished she hadn't come by. Not today.

With her cell phone to her ear, Hannah paced the floor of her hotel room. "I know, Martin, and I'm sorry. Your yelling at me isn't going to change anything."

She'd tried to explain her need to stay in Owl's Perch for at least three more days, maybe a week, but he wasn't in much of a reasoning mood.

"I'm not yelling," he snapped. Then silence. Then he sighed. "Hannah, sweetheart." His voice was calmer, and she knew he was trying. "It's ridiculous that these people get another chance to damage your life. After investing nearly two full years in nursing school, will you even be allowed to graduate if you're not here for class by Wednesday night?"

"I don't know. The mandatory attendance rules have a little give, but I'm afraid to ask. Whatever the answer, it changes nothing concerning my plans, and I don't need the anxiety of knowing I'm ruining my chance at graduation by staying here. Sarah needs my help, and I'm going to do what I can."

"It's not that I care about the degree or your being a nursing school graduate. You know I don't. But you've worked so hard for it. Why can't someone else do this?"

"Because it's not a course anyone in the Amish community will pursue for her if I don't. And whether she's innocent of setting the fires or not, you can't think I'm going to leave her in the community's hands. Although I'm not sure what Daed will agree to even if I get a counselor lined up."

"You can't save the world. Doesn't any of this seem uncomfortably familiar to you? You went out on a limb for Faye, and we ended up with two children to raise, a stack of bills for therapists, and she is nowhere to be found. Come on, this isn't your battle."

Hannah wanted to protest his laying the blame solely at her feet for their becoming guardians over Kevin and Lissa, but she'd taxed him over a need-help issue with his own sister, and he'd done it her way. At her insistence they'd gone through a lot to try to get his sister off drugs, only to have her run off and abandon her kids. Until today he hadn't voiced any blame.

"I can't leave. Not yet. I won't drag this out one minute longer than necessary."

"Great. Just great."

She closed her eyes, feeling that awful sense of powerlessness take a seat on her chest. Since meeting Zabeth, it hadn't been a part of her life. "Martin, please don't do this. You can't imagine how hard this is."

"Then come home."

She took slow, deep breaths, trying to free herself of that claustrophobic feeling. "I will, but I need to find help for Sarah and try to figure out if she started the fires or not."

"Just how the…" He stopped short. "How do you expect to do that?"

"I have no idea. I was hoping you'd help me figure it out."

"Sorry, I'm not caught up on my *CSI* episodes."

"It's not like you to act like this. I basically have no support here."

When he didn't respond, she let the silence hang.

"Yeah, okay," he whispered. "I hear you. Kevin's whining nonstop about when you're going to return. I really think he's scared you're not coming back."

"Assure him I'm only gone because of family issues and I'm coming home as quickly as I can."

"And Lissa misses you way more than I expected. The stitches in her leg really bother her, especially at night, and she won't let the nanny get near her once it's bedtime. I guess because she doesn't know Laura well enough yet. I've paced the floors with Lissa on my hip for two nights."

"That's because you're a good man, albeit spoiled and testy from time to time."

He didn't laugh, which was even more unusual than his present disposition. "Was spoiled." He sighed. "Before children took over my bachelor pad. Right now I'd pay anything to buy myself a little sleep and an evening out with just the two of us."

"Mmm. You can buy almost anything, that's true, but are you aware you can't buy my love but it's yours anyway?"

Martin chuckled. "Yeah?"

"Yep."

"I guess I am being a bit whiny and demanding."

"Just a bit?"

"Well, I can't be charming all the time."

"You're telling me."

He laughed. "Man, I miss you."

She refused to remind him it'd only been since Saturday. It'd clearly been a rough couple of days. "I know. I'll get some help for Sarah squared away and be back as quickly as I can manage. Okay?"

"Yeah, I understand, but I don't like it."

"I got that part, loud and clear. Let me talk to Lissa and Kevin."

"Sure, hang on."

Lissa's and Kevin's precious voices did more to ease the tightness across her chest than anything else, and by the time she finished talking to them, she felt more like herself. After disconnecting the call, she went to the business center of the hotel, got on a computer, and started searching for psychiatrists and psychologists who catered to the Plain community. Although it soon became clear this was not an easy task, investigating whether Sarah was guilty of starting the fires would be worse. The community would have no desire to let anyone ask questions or snoop around, and they'd stonewalled her years ago. If she could just figure a way around their avoidance of her, then maybe she could find some answers.

~~∽~~

After another miserable night without sleep, Martin sat behind his desk at work, suppressing a yawn as he shifted the set of blueprints in front of him. Thankfully he'd talked Hannah into letting him hire a nanny a few weeks before the family emergency whisked her out of state. Still, he hadn't realized how much Kevin and Lissa depended on Hannah like a mother. At only twenty years old, she tended to be more nurturing than most of the women his own age.

Remorse settled over him as he spot-checked the curb grades. He'd been really hard on her yesterday and had wanted to call her back several times throughout the night, but it would have been even more selfish to wake her. In all the time he'd known her, he'd never been that difficult. Felt like being that way, yes. Given in to it, no. Dating an Amish girl wasn't easy. She just had this take-the-high-road way about her, a way he didn't get but found equally frustrating and intriguing. When she looked at him with those gentle brown eyes that always held a trace of absolute stubbornness, he did his best to keep a respectful tone. Hannah Lapp Lawson—daughter of the Old Order Amish, niece to his surrogate mom, Zabeth, and a fledgling crusader of women's health—needed his support, not his griping.

The fledgling-crusader part concerned him.

A tap on his door made him look up. Amy stood in the hallway, leaning against the doorframe with her head inside his office. "Hey, lunch plans. Noon. Three engineers, two landscape arcs. We're going to Sperati's. You joining us?"

"Depends. You're not planning on dumping that fried onion thing and its sauce in my lap again, are you?"

She snapped her fingers. "Now you've foiled my plan."

Martin tapped the set of plans in front of him. "Have you come up with a landscaping plan for River Mill yet?"

"I'll have the landscape plan done for River Mill before you have the engineering plan done for Headwaters."

Martin yawned. "No doubt. Give an old man a break, will you?"

She pointed a pencil at him. "Don't start that nonsense. I'm older than you."

"Yeah, by what, a year, maybe two? It's the eight-and-a-half-year difference between Hannah and me, with the add-on of children, that's taxing my ever-thin patience."

She shifted, straightening the gray tailored jacket of her pantsuit. "Patience is a decision, one I'd love to see you make." She pulled her lips in, trying to hide her smile over the teasing jab.

He leaned back in his chair. As professionals who'd worked together since he was a college co-op—earning money and experience while still in school—and she a second-year landscape architect for the same engineering firm, they knew each other decently well. Years later, when the opportunity to buy the business fell into his lap, he was already familiar with the business's clients and procedures. "Hannah wishes that too."

Amy pointed to the stack of books on his desk. "You ready for your engineering exams next month?"

"I hope so, but I hadn't planned on becoming a parent to two kids a few months before the state exams."

"Yeah, I bet. If finding a sitter is a prob, I'll make myself available the day of the exam. Other than that, you're on your own." She stood upright. "Noon. Sperati's. Doug's driving if you want to ride with us. Otherwise, we'll see you there."

Amy's heels clicked against the tiled floors, leaving him to wrestle with his guilt again.

Zabeth wouldn't be pleased with him right now, and if she were still alive, she'd tell him so. But Martin never thought that the needs of

Hannah's family might come into the picture. When Zabeth left her family, all ties were permanently severed. She'd been shunned, and that ended it, unless she had chosen to give up her love of music—playing or listening—which she hadn't.

Clearly, after two and a half years of silence, the voices of Hannah's past had begun to speak. It wasn't what he'd expected, but he would have to adjust.

Uneasy about the day ahead, Hannah rolled the grocery cart toward her car. Her best use of the day would be to return to Owl's Perch and see Luke. Figuring her Daed wouldn't help her, she knew the next best option was her brother. But she'd not spoken to him or Mary, leaving her unsure of her welcome. Nonetheless, he was the oldest Lapp son, and if he were on her side, it'd help…maybe.

She lifted the hatch to the trunk of her car and set two bags of groceries and a bag of ice into the large cooler she'd brought from Ohio. Then she placed the bag containing nonrefrigerated items on the floor of the trunk. Since she didn't want to eat out and she couldn't cook at the hotel, this was the best plan. Yogurt, cereal, milk, fruit, vegetables, and some sandwich items would hold her until she returned to Martin.

She didn't share his love of dining out, even if money wasn't an issue, which it was for her. If she would allow him to put money into her account, she could have plenty of cash at her disposal, but she liked herself better when she lived inside her own budget, meager as it was. Closing the trunk, she retrieved the car keys from her dress pocket. As she pulled out of the parking lot, she heard a loud pop as the car ran over something. A quick glance in the rearview mirror let her know she'd just shattered some type of glass bottle. She thought about stopping and checking the tire, but it seemed fine.

It struck her again how different the landscape looked as she drove in from the east side. Driving this particular route hadn't been part of her experiences while growing up here, but she was getting a feel for the layout of the area. She turned onto the paved street that ran in front of Gram's house and tried to visualize how it connected to the road her parents lived on. The roads ran parallel, with Gram's ample farm as well as Lapp and other properties, between the two, but where was the road that connected the two?

A shudder ran through her. The dirt road behind Gram's place was where the attack had taken place. She flipped the radio up loudly and hit the Lock button on her car. When she spotted Gram checking her mailbox, Hannah thought about stopping. Of all the people who'd rather not see her, Gram had to be way up on the list. Still, the desire to see her, to explain her side of the ugly rumors took over Hannah's insecurity, and she looked at the carport, which sat more than a thousand feet from the road. A quick glance said no one was home but Gram, and Hannah found herself slowing down and turning into the driveway.

With her cane steadying her, Gram turned to catch a glimpse of whoever had pulled in behind her. She tipped her head to the side, her brows knit.

The sight melted Hannah's heart. She turned off the engine and got out of the car. Suddenly caught off guard by not knowing what to call her, Hannah removed her sunglasses. "Hi."

"Hannah?"

She nodded. "Can I visit with you a minute?"

"Oh, Hannah, come here." She motioned for her, and Hannah closed the distance. Gram wrapped her free arm around her and held her. "You never should have stayed gone this long. Never." The raspy voice made her grateful she'd stopped.

It was a good minute before Gram released her. "How are you?" She took a step back. "Let me look at you."

Hannah posed, gesturing with her arms out. They both laughed.

"You look well. A little fancy for my taste, but well." She motioned toward the house. "Ride me on up the lane, and let's have a cup of hot tea and talk."

Since it was still early morning midweek, Hannah felt safe to enjoy a visit without being concerned that Paul might show up.

Gram eased into the car, pulling the cane in after her. "This is very nice."

"I bartered for it, sort of."

"That sounds like you. How'd you manage to barter for a vehicle?"

Hannah explained about landing in Ohio and Martin needing someone to drive Zabeth, leaving out as much personal information as possible. They moved into the house and talked while sipping on tea. Gram didn't mention Paul; for that Hannah was grateful. She kept the topics neutral, things like Hannah's schooling and work. In spite of her reason for stopping by, Hannah couldn't make herself talk about the rape or pregnancy.

Gram set her teacup in a saucer. "So, are you home because of the trouble at the Esh place, or is that just a coincidence?"

"I'm here because of that, yes."

"And how's Sarah these days?"

"I…I'm not sure I should…"

"As tight-lipped as ever, Hannah?" Gram lifted the flowered teapot, offering to refill her cup.

The words stung. She'd kept so many secrets in the past. "I have plenty, thank you."

She set the pot on the table. "Your sister just fell apart after you left. Came here looking for the baby. Paul and I arrived home from Sunday school one time and found her sitting in the middle of the guest room with baby clothes strewn all around her. Paul talked to her as best he could, tried a couple of times to help, but your Daed wouldn't have it."

"As outlandish as it may be, I hope to change his mind on that topic." Hannah rose. "It was really good to see you, but I need to go."

Gram stood, leaning heavily on her cane as she grabbed a piece of paper off the counter. She held it out toward Hannah. "You pass me your address and start writing to me, at least twice a year. And you call me Gram. None of this avoiding using my name or wavering on what to call me."

Surprised Gram had picked up on her evasion, she smiled. "Gram, it was really good to see you."

Hannah wrote down her address and cell number before leaving. She went out the back door and across the screened porch. Grateful to have spent some time with Gram, she realized she had a friend in the elderly woman, which surprised Hannah a lot. She cranked the car and put it in reverse.

Thud-ump. Thud-ump.

She paused and then continued backing the car down the long asphalt driveway. The thumping noise grew louder and faster as she picked up speed. Stopping the car a couple of hundred feet from the house, she glanced around inside the vehicle and saw nothing that might cause a bumping sound. She pulled the lever to the trunk, set the emergency brake, and got out. Everything in the trunk looked secure. She closed the hatch and walked around the outside of the car. When she spotted the flat tire, it took restraint not to kick it.

She knew absolutely nothing about changing a tire.

Paul listened as Dorcas told him the latest goings-on at their home church. He went to church with Gram more Sundays than he made it to Maryland to attend with his family and Dorcas. But that needed to change.

"So, old man Mast was standing near the back door of the church when Norene came running inside, terrified of a yellow jacket, and plowed right into him, knocking him off his feet."

"Hopefully he didn't get on to her too badly." Paul slowed the car and turned into Gram's driveway. "Norene has allergic reactions…"

Hannah.

She was stooped by the right front tire, removing lug nuts. A plastic bag of what appeared to be groceries as well as a cooler were sitting on the ground near the open trunk of her vehicle. He glanced at Dorcas, whose eyes were fixed on him. He nodded up ahead. "That's Hannah."

She looked, her lips turning white within seconds. "Talk about getting plowed under."

Paul shook his head. "Don't let this rattle you. I'll pull you up to the house, and I'll go see her."

"Paul, no."

"It has to be done. You know it does." Paul drove onto the grass to pass Hannah's car, which sat in the middle of the narrow driveway. She glanced up, but he could see little expression around her large sunglasses.

After pulling up to the house, he got out of the car, went around, and opened Dorcas's door. He escorted her into the house, came back out, and walked down the driveway.

Hannah glanced up. "I'm fine, but thanks." She pushed down hard on the lug-nut wrench. It didn't appear to budge.

He stepped up to her, expecting her to back away so he could remove the lug nut for her, but she didn't move.

"I said I was fine. You've done plenty. Trust me." The words came out through gritted teeth as she exerted effort against the lug nut. It loosened, and she lost her balance. Sprawling her hands against the pavement, she righted herself and put the wrench on another bolt.

"Hannah, I'm so sorry."

"I know." She nodded. "You have no idea how completely I know that you're sorry." She loosened the last lug nut and dusted off her hands.

In spite of her unjust assessment, Paul refused to defend any part of his reaction that day. "I…I realized you were telling the truth, and I came back…but you had just boarded the train, and no one knew where to."

She removed the lug wrench and tossed it on the ground. "Don't. Okay? Just don't." Straining, she tried to remove the tire. "You want to lie to everyone else, yourself included, go ahead. What do I care?" She fell onto her backside when the wheel came off, got her feet under her, and leaned the tire against the car. "You don't want to have this conversation with me." Shifting the spare tire onto the hub, she tried to get the holes to line up so it'd go on.

"Maybe not, but I'm here anyway."

"Oh yeah, you're here. I happen to be *in* Gram's driveway. Excuse me if I don't faint at the effort you put forth to see me."

"There's not much point in my trying to tell you anything if you're not going to believe a word I say."

Giving up on aligning the spare with the hub, she set the tire on the ground. "Exactly."

"Can you at least let me help you get the spare on your car?"

"You can trust that I'll leave the car and walk for the rest of my life first."

"Well, forsaking things and walking off seem to come naturally, so that's not a real shocker."

She knelt in front of the hub and took the spare tire in hand again. "I learned it from the best." After finally getting it in place, she pulled a lug nut out of her dress pocket.

"Paul." Dorcas's friendly voice called from the front door of Gram's.

"Yeah, Dorcas?"

"I need your help, please."

"Sure thing. Be right there."

Hannah's face glistened with sweat, and her dress was covered in smudges of road soot. Paul couldn't imagine Dorcas ever being so stubborn about anything. "See, some people know how to ask for help when they need it."

Hannah slowly rose to her feet. "Well, if she's putting her life in your hands, she needs to be able to easily ask people for help."

"It must be nice deciding I'm the only one at fault here, Hannah.

Reminds me a lot of your dad, which is sad if you think about it." He turned and headed for the house.

"Yeah, that's it, Paul. I get like this because I'm like my Daed. This has nothing to do with the fact I'm justified!"

Without responding, he went inside.

Dorcas stood near the door, looking pale and stressed.

"What do you need?"

She handed him a jar of mayonnaise.

He opened the lid. "I need some time alone." He went upstairs to his room. How had the conversation with Hannah ended with his being mean? Disbelief settled over him, making him sorry he'd succumbed to her anger. She had a right to hate him. In spite of her mammoth secret, she'd been a traumatized seventeen-year-old girl, and he held no blame against her.

Besides, she had plenty of reason not to believe anything he said. If he'd been thinking straight, he'd have explained about the missing money from their joint savings account. He moved to the window and stared at the dirt road behind Gram's, the road Hannah had walked to come see him every chance she got during the summers. Even her reason for being on that road was his fault. Hating what'd just taken place between them, he leaned against the window frame. "God, forgive me."

Seeing her today and knowing all that had caused her to leave more than two years ago, he realized why he had waited for her to return.

He owed her.

And he had been willing to pay any price she needed because of his hand in creating the devastation of her life. But the love he had for her had grown thin and useless over the years as she had changed from the girl he fell in love with to someone he barely recognized. She'd hidden too much, and he'd left her when he should have stayed, but here they were, years later, needing to find forgiveness for themselves and with each other.

Hannah tossed the flat tire and jack into the trunk, followed by the cooler and bag of groceries. Unable to stop trembling, she climbed behind the steering wheel, hoping the stupid spare wouldn't fly off its hub as she backed out of the driveway.

Just let me get out of here.

Her "sunny" temperament probably had Paul turning somersaults that he had moved on. She choked back tears. She'd never dreamed of acting like a maniac, of raking cutting words across him like a hay mower.

Reaching the main road, she jerked the car into first gear, tears blinding her vision. After years of hoping to never have to face him again, it'd been worse than she'd ever imagined. Much worse.

What was he doing off work at this time anyway? Except for summertime or Thanksgiving, he'd never managed to come to Gram's midweek before, but today, well, he just had to show up.

"Arrrrrrrrgh." She slammed her head against the headrest, feeling like a complete idiot.

Worse, she'd really let him have it, and she was more angry now than before. Tons more. A whole lifetime more.

"Jerk." She pressed the accelerator to the floor. Needing time to calm herself, she wound her way through a few back roads. Soon enough she was passing the Lapp house, but she kept going. The dirt road. She eased off the gas as the fence-lined road with mostly trees on one side and pastures on the other seemed to draw her. Walking this road had been her connection to Paul, her hope for a future with him. When hidden by the lay of the land on the deserted dirt road behind Gram's property, she stopped the car and turned it off.

Her heart burned from racing, not just from her encounter with Paul, but from where she was. Hannah drew a deep breath and got out of her car.

This was where her nightmare began. Closing her eyes, she felt tears sting. There seemed to be no getting free of it. Until she returned to Owl's Perch, she'd been sure all her work at the rape center, facing the past and helping others, falling in love again, and going to nursing school meant that the aftermath of the attack was behind her, not *in* her, stagnant and toxic.

"What just happened at Gram's, Father? I thought I trusted You... had put all the disappointment and anger into Your hands." Even as she said the prayer, anger tumbled around inside her. If the anger unleashed at Paul wasn't bad enough, she reeled, feeling trapped.

But she couldn't just drive away. Sarah needed help, and Hannah intended to see that she got it, because it was clear that Sarah was as trapped inside her mental imbalance as Hannah had been inside her circumstances. No one deserved to be abandoned to either of those. No one.

The man's voice echoed inside her head... *"Can you tell me how to get to Duncannon?"*

Hannah doubled her fists. "God will turn for good what was meant for evil, and I will come out better in life because of the attack. Better! Do you hear me?" She made a complete circle, yelling at her surroundings.

She gazed up at the crystal blue sky, feeling traces of hope that only God could give.

With Mary beside him, Luke guided the horse and buggy down the dirt road he'd seen Hannah driving on just a few minutes ago. When he saw her pass the Lapp house, he figured she might be headed to the apartment where he and Mary were supposed to be living, the place the community had built for them while they were mending from their accident.

When he spotted her car, it was parked on the dirt road itself, not in the driveway of his building. Hannah was leaning against the front of it with her back to him. Why was she here, on this road of all places?

He brought the buggy to a stop, and she turned, catching a glimpse of him before standing and heading his way. The closer she came, the more he realized that she barely resembled her former self. It wasn't just that she'd become a woman and wore the clothes and hairstyle of the Englischers, but he couldn't put his finger on what else made her so different.

"Hi." She stared up at him while playing with the sunglasses in her hand.

"Look at you. All grown up. When I saw you at the train station, a white sheet had more color and shook less in the wind than you."

She smiled. "Yeah, but I survived…" She slid her glasses into a side pocket and pressed her hands down the front of a very dirty dress. "And then life got better."

Feeling as ill at ease as he did when he was a teen trying to hide his emotions, Luke couldn't take his eyes off her.

"Luke." Mary elongated his name.

"Oh ya, sorry." He jumped down and helped his very expectant wife down too.

Mary stumbled as her feet hit the ground, and Luke steadied her. She watched Hannah, staring at her much like Luke was. Hannah's eyes went to Mary's stomach, and a slow smile crossed her face. Mary closed the distance between them, and the two women fell into an embrace.

As he watched his wife tremble, he realized she'd never truly shared with him just how badly or how often she'd missed her closest friend.

When they took a step back, Mary looked unsure and awkward again. Luke pointed at Hannah's hair and clothing. "I saw a glimpse of you at the funeral, but…you're not living Plain?"

She shook her head. "No."

"At the train station you had on Plain clothing."

"Of course. All I had in the way of identification was a photoless ID. The only way that's accepted is if the Amish clothing accompanies it. Did you think I'd been living Plain all this time?"

"I'd hoped."

It seemed the volume of unwelcome discomfort between them could've filled every silo in Owl's Perch. Clearly his sister was now an outsider.

Mary smiled. "I hope ya own nicer and cleaner dresses than this one, or being fancy needs a new name."

Hannah swiped her hands over her stained dress. "I had a flat tire."

She'd done what? Luke studied the car. "You know how to change a flat tire?"

"No, but I figured it out…hopefully. If I didn't, I'll know it when the tire comes off."

Mary nudged him. "Leave her alone already and give her a hug. I know you want to."

He stared at his sister, wondering if she was as different on the inside as she looked on the outside. He moved like he'd been thrown from a horse a few days ago, all stiff and uncomfortable, but he embraced her. "I suppose there are worse things than living as an Englischer, although I'm not sure what they are." He squeezed her tighter. "I've missed you so much. Don't you ever leave here again without telling us how to reach you." He released her. "Ya?"

She nodded. "Wait here."

Hannah came back with a business card. "This has my cell number on it and my work number. You call, I'll answer."

Mary held out her hand for the card. "It'll be less likely to get lost if I keep it."

"Hey." Luke laughed and grumbled.

Hannah passed him a card too. "Take this, and we'll see if you can keep up with it."

"Thanks." He read the card. "So you work for this Dr. Lehman?"

Hannah nodded. "You would be hard pressed to find a better man anywhere than Dr. Lehman."

"Paul said your last name is now Lawson." Luke glanced up from the card. "Seems nothing about you is the same."

"Zabeth helped me change—"

"Zabeth?" Mary interrupted, flipping the card over as if looking for answers.

Hannah's eyes reflected sadness, but she offered a smile. "Daed's twin sister, one he never spoke of. She lived shunned for close to three decades, and…I stayed with her until she died in May. She helped me change my last name when I arrived."

"Changed it?" Feeling offended, Luke fought to suppress it. Neither man nor woman should change their God-given name because it suited them. "Were you that ashamed of being Amish?"

"Luke," Mary scolded him, shock filling her eyes.

Hannah tilted her chin, staring him in the eye. "That had nothing to do with my decision, but I had several reasons. Mostly I had to let go and start over. Will you hold that against me?"

Luke held his tongue in check, wrestling to see this from her perspective.

"Look, I don't want to argue or defend myself. What's done is done, and Sarah called me home."

Especially because she was here for the first time in years, Luke didn't want to quarrel either. "I'm pretty sure Daed thinks you're married."

"It doesn't much matter what he thinks or how he feels on this topic. I'm not married now, but I will be soon enough."

Luke removed his hat and scratched his head, wondering where all the lines of right and wrong were in this. "Except if he learns you're not married, he'll try to persuade you to come under his roof and join the faith. When that doesn't happen, he'll blame himself, making Mamm's life harder."

Mary slid her hand around his arm. "Then maybe it'd be best if we don't say anything."

He fidgeted with his hat, watching his sister. Finally he nodded. "Probably so. For now."

It was a few moments before the awkwardness faded a bit and Hannah gestured at Mary's abdomen. "I see your childhood dreams continue to come true."

Mary's cheeks flushed with pink. "It must be for all the world to see these days, no matter how large and pleated the dress."

Hannah nodded. "When is the baby due?"

"November, right before Thanksgiving." Mary rubbed her stomach. "I've been so excited that I wanted to put an ad in *The Budget*."

The horse nudged Mary, knocking her forward. Hannah steadied her before the animal whinnied loudly, making Mary jump and Hannah and Luke laugh. Hannah pulled a set of keys from her dress pocket and pressed a button on the keyless remote. The trunk opened. She grabbed a bag of baby carrots and opened them.

Luke rubbed the horse's neck. "Do you always carry horse snacks with you?"

Hannah placed a carrot on the palm of her hand. "I bought some groceries so I wouldn't need to eat out so much while here."

"You're staying all week?" Luke asked.

She shook her head. "No, I need to find answers for Sarah and get back to Ohio. Not only do I have a family that needs me, but every day I'm here I lessen my chances of graduating from nursing school come December, and someone else has to take my clinical rotations. If I miss class on Wednesday and Thursday, I'm likely to give up all chance."

"Clinical rotation?" Mary asked.

"It's a lot like doing apprentice work, only in a hospital."

Mary's brows crinkled. "You do that separate from working for Dr. Lehman?"

"Yeah, each requires time every other weekend, and then I work for Dr. Lehman during the week, around my school schedule."

Mary glanced at Luke, her greenish blue eyes mirroring a bit of hurt. "And you have a family? No wonder you ain't been back. You left yourself no room for missing us."

Luke shifted. "What exactly do you want for Sarah?"

"I...I think she needs professional help, Luke."

He didn't respond.

Hannah gazed into his eyes. "You have to see the problems too. Not wanting them to exist doesn't keep them from being real, and it doesn't help Sarah."

"I'm not sure what you think you can get done while you're here, but Daed is not going to agree to Sarah seeing someone. Paul mentioned that to Daed not long after you left, and I wouldn't recommend repeating the idea."

Mary touched his arm, gazing up at him. "If Sarah's setting the fires, we don't have a choice but to try to get her some help." She looked to Hannah. "The family is trying to keep her from running off, but your parents are exhausted from the effort."

Luke put on his hat. "I really don't think Sarah's setting the fires. I got no proof. Just hunches. Sarah's got problems, but it's not like her to hurt someone."

Hannah's forehead creased. "Well, she did plenty of damage to my life, and she meant it too. But whether that was just a sister thing, I don't know." She gazed down the road toward the Lapp home. "I guess it's time for me to talk to Daed. I have to see him anyway before I leave. I might as well stick my neck out all the way while it's on the chopping block."

"I'll stand beside you, if you think it's the right thing to do," Luke offered.

"It'd be great if you and Mary could be at the house, but let me talk to him alone first. If I know Daed, my chances of winning this debate are best if he doesn't think I'm trying to get people on my side and turn them against him."

Luke notched his hat tighter on his head. "Sound thinking."

He was sure Mary would like a few minutes to talk with Hannah alone, but he couldn't suggest she ride with Hannah to the house. If Daed saw his daughter-in-law riding with his wayward daughter, the bishop would be on Luke's doorstep soon enough, with frowns and words of correction for both Mary and him.

"You know, I need to mosey on up to my old harness shop and try to collect rent." Luke climbed into the buggy. "Mary, why don't you stay here, and I'll be back in a bit."

His wife smiled at him. "Sure."

Hannah held out her hand for Mary. With their heads almost touching, the two began talking as if time had stolen too little to really matter.

The sound of a car in the driveway made Sarah drop what she was doing and head for the back door. The plate clanging against the floor meant little to her.

"Sarah," Mamm scolded above the noise of the wringer washer, "you can't let go of everything because you had a new thought."

She paused, turning to look at the twirling metal plate and scattered scrambled eggs. "Sorry."

That was the right word. She was sure of it. It seemed to her that words carried enough weight to change anything, if she could just find the right ones. Without returning to help clean up the mess, she barreled out the back door.

Hannah opened the driver's side door while fidgeting with a cord of some type. She placed a small silver thing in her dress pocket and then got out. "Hey, Sarah, how's your morning going?"

Sarah got right in front of her sister. "You gotta take me to see your baby, then maybe we can all go to Ohio together. I know the babe's a toddler now, but…"

"Sarah, I explained all of that yesterday when we were on the dock. Remember? The baby died. Didn't others tell you this already?"

"It's not true. The baby is alive. We just haven't found where they took…"

"Her," Hannah finished the sentence. "I had a girl who was born too premature to live. It's fairly common with teen pregnancies."

"No!" Sarah screamed the word. "No. No. No. No!"

"What's going on?" Daed came out of the barn yelling. His eyes moved from Sarah to Hannah. "Hannah." He gave a nod.

"Hi, Daed."

Sarah wanted to scratch their eyes out. They behaved so orderly, so stoic, when there was no way that's how they felt. Why couldn't someone in this family say what they were feeling? Why did they hide so much, even Hannah's own child? Well, clearly it was up to her to show the truth.

Hannah wiped the palms of her hands down her dress. "I came to talk…"

Daed nodded. "It's much past time. We have a lot to talk about."

"I spoke with Sarah yesterday, and she'd like some help."

"So that's what you want to talk about?" Daed paused, staring at his eldest daughter. "You lied to me coming and going. Then you're gone for years only to come back to meddle in things that are none of yours. I think your visit has lasted long enough, don't you?"

"Daed, I…I was seventeen, and by our own traditions it was my free time to find a mate."

"The *rumschpringe* is to be used to find an Amish mate, and you know it!"

"I understand that's every Amish parent's hope, but those years are for young people to step outside of parental authority and find their own path. Did you not do much the same during your teen years?"

"You're too much like Zabeth."

"I found her and lived with her until she died. Did you know that?"

"I figured as much. And seeing you now, I can't say it did anything positive to help guide you. From the time you were a little bitty thing, you were too much like her. I was blindsided by trusting you to be who you appeared to be, a dutiful girl who wouldn't lie to me. I got no use for a liar."

Ready to yank her own hair out, Sarah watched as Luke and Mary pulled into the driveway and drove the horse and buggy up to the far side of the carriage house. He barely glanced at Daed, and she bet he had no power to improve things between Hannah and Daed.

She couldn't let Hannah leave.

Flames danced in her head.

Fire.

The thought soothed her rumpled nerves, and Sarah took several steps backward without either Hannah or Daed noticing. She slipped off to the shed, found her stash of matches, and grabbed her push scooter.

With the matches in her pocket, Sarah rode the scooter, propelling it with her foot, as fast as she could to Katie Waddell's.

The fires brought Hannah, and fire will keep her.

Burned wood and ash crunched under Matthew's feet, making him cringe at the memory of what'd taken place right here. Maybe Elle was right; maybe getting away from Owl's Perch was a good idea, a better one than he wanted to admit. What had living Amish gained him so far?

Loneliness and ashes.

She'd said she loved him. He longed to believe that, needed it now more than ever. The half-burned beams were good for nothing but being knocked down. Over two years of hard work gone. It made him sick. The only thing that seemed to bring a trace of hope to life was Elle's invitation to come to Baltimore. Everything else felt as empty and lifeless as this building.

"Matthew." Kathryn's voice called to him from the direction of his house.

How could he rebuild the place that killed his brother?

"Matthew?" Kathryn clapped her hands, drawing him from his thoughts. She stood at the edge of the burned-out place. "You okay?"

"I'm fine. Did ya need somethin'?"

"Your mother asked me to have you come in. She'd like to apply the salve to your back while she's up for a bit."

Matthew lifted a charred buggy wheel. "Elle's asked me to go to Baltimore and stay for a while."

"A few days there while you're healing isn't such a bad idea, I guess. You can't do much here until you heal more, and the newness of Baltimore might lift your spirits and give you a different perspective."

Her voice had the first bit of edge to it he'd ever heard, and he looked up.

She held his gaze. "What?"

"You don't like the idea."

"I have concerns. You'll answer to the bishop about this for sure."

Matthew nodded. "He won't learn of it until I'm gone."

"I don't know what you'll tell your Mamm or Daed—or even your brother, for that matter—that will keep from adding fear and stress to them."

He tossed the ruined wheel onto the ash-covered ground. "It's my life, not theirs."

"Your pain is talking, not Matthew."

He kicked a half-burned leg of a workbench, causing it to fall. "The pain has been burned into me until we're one."

"For now. But it's your choice whether the pain grows stronger than you or whether you grow stronger than it. And I happen to think making choices that hurt those we love will cause the ache inside a person to grow stronger and the true soul to grow weaker."

She just didn't get it. It wasn't her brother that had died, or her back that burned and hurt constantly, or her business that had burned down, or her love that beckoned her away. "That sounds an awful lot like flowery words from someone who doesn't know and can't possibly understand."

"I didn't lose a business. That part's true, but I did lose a brother." Pain flickered across her face, and she paused. "Abram drowned, and"— she closed her eyes for a moment—"I go on."

For the first time Matthew realized who Kathryn was—Elmer

Glick's daughter. When Matthew was about twelve years old, Elmer Glick had lost a son in a drowning. That son was Kathryn's brother, which meant, according to rumors that had flooded in from Snow Shoe some eighty-five miles away, Kathryn had come close to drowning too.

Sick of pain and death, Matthew motioned toward the house. "I better go in and see Mamm."

Chapter 9

The fires brought her, and fire will keep her.

The words tapped a rhythm inside Sarah's brain. She left her scooter near the side of the road and climbed over the cattle gate at the back of Mrs. Waddell's property. A Holstein bull grazed in the adjoining pasture, so she ran full speed across the field. If he saw her and had a mind to, he might come right through that fence that needed mending.

The fires brought her, and fire will keep her.

She opened the gate that led to Mrs. Waddell's yard and went straight to the barn. Looking around the place, she spotted a can of gasoline. Isn't gas what people said caused the fire in the attic of Matthew's shop?

She spread the liquid over some bales of hay, realizing how beautiful the powerful stuff was. Fascinated, she poured it across the dirt floor as she walked out of the barn. Covering her shoes and the ground with the golden fluid, she found beauty in the swirling little pools as rainbows of colors floated and shifted around. She set the nearly empty can beside her.

"Mrs. Waddell," she called. "Mrs. Waddell." When she didn't come to the back door, Sarah called again.

Paul came out the back door.

"Fire brought her, and fire will keep her. Ya?" She pulled the box of kitchen matches out of her pocket.

He ran toward her. "Sarah, what are you doing?"

She put the head of a match to the side of the box. "I told you she'd come back, but she's going to leave again if I don't do something. We can't let that happen."

"Sarah, no." Paul stopped. "Your shoes and the hem of your dress are soaked in gasoline. Don't strike that match."

"I want Hannah to stay and help me find her baby."

"Sarah, give me the matches." He stepped closer.

She ran the match down the side of the box, and a few sparks zipped around, but it didn't light. "Don't come any closer."

"Okay, okay. Tell me what you want."

"Hannah to stay."

A girl came out the back door. "What's going on?"

"Dorcas, you remember Sarah. She's going to give me the matches and come inside so we can talk."

Dorcas came closer. "Hi, Sarah. Wh-why don't you come on inside? We'll visit."

Sarah lifted the box and match at her threateningly. "I want Hannah!"

Paul stepped forward, but Sarah knew what he was thinking. She held the match against the side of the box, ready to light it.

"Okay." Paul stopped cold. "Dorcas, bring me the cordless and the phone number Hannah left for Gram."

"A phone number?"

"I saw it lying on Gram's table. I'm hoping it's to her cell and that she has it with her."

Dorcas ran inside.

"Sarah, move the match away from the box, and I'll call."

Sarah did as he asked, cradling the match in the palm of her hand while pulling out more matches. Dorcas brought him the phone and paper.

Paul took the items from her. "Dorcas, I want you to go inside. If she so much as causes a spark, the fumes will explode, and the gas can will ignite too." He punched numbers on the phone, how many Sarah wasn't sure. "I want you safe. Please."

Dorcas nodded and went inside.

"Hannah, this is Paul. Sarah's at Gram's barn, and she'd like you to come here. It'd be best if you wasted no time, please." Paul paused and then disconnected the call.

"What'd she say?"

"She said okay."

"Nothing else?"

"No, but I'm sure she'll be here shortly. May I have the matches now?"

Sarah shook her head. "Not yet."

Hannah closed the phone, wondering how to handle this. All her hopes of what she might accomplish by staying calm and respectful with her Daed mocked her. Clearly, getting him to agree with her on anything would take more than politeness.

He gestured toward her phone. "Can't go anywhere without being attached to that thing? The whole churchgoing world spends more money on fancy gadgets in a month than they offer to God in a year."

"That can be true of some, I'm sure." She slid her phone into her pocket, chafing at the constant negativity that flowed from her father. "Daed, that was Paul. Sarah's at Mrs. Waddell's."

He startled, looking about the place. "Ruth!" He headed for the house. Luke and Mary came out of the carriage house.

Hannah heard the gas-powered wringer washer turn off.

"Ruth!" Her father yelled again.

Her mother ran outside and paused when she saw Hannah. A look of pleasure graced her face. "Good morning."

"Hi, Mamm."

Daed waved his hand through the air. "Isn't Sarah inside? You're keeping a watch on her, right?"

Terror filled Mamm's eyes. "The last I saw her, she was with you. Has she gone missing?"

Daed opened his mouth, but Hannah interrupted him. "No, she's at Gram's with Paul. I need to go."

"I'm going with you," Daed said.

Mamm wiped her hands on her apron. "Should I come too?"

Daed headed for the car. "You stay here and watch the children."

Her father climbed into the passenger's seat and closed the door.

Hannah turned the key, starting the engine. "You didn't want her to see whatever it is we'll see, did you?"

He shook his head. "It's too hard on her."

She backed out of the driveway and headed for the paved road that led to Gram's. "Harder on her than waiting at home?"

He stared out the window. "Your ways of questioning every decision a man makes is wrong."

Resolved that she'd never really connect with her father, Hannah shifted gears. "And you're right just because you have title of being head?"

"You're talking women's feminism stuff. It's an abomination, and you know it!"

"More than you seeing me minutes after the rape and later deciding I'd lied?"

Her father crossed his arms over his chest and sulked. That worked just fine for her. She carried plenty of wrongs in what'd happened, but she wouldn't bear his share simply because he held the position of head of the household.

She stepped on the accelerator, allowing her father to ride in silence. She pulled into Gram's driveway and up to the house and stopped the car. Running across the yard and to the barn, Hannah wondered what her sister was up to.

Paul came into view but not Sarah.

Hannah slowed. "Where is she?"

He nodded in the direction of the barn.

With a gas can at Sarah's feet and her skirt hem wet, it didn't take

Hannah long to put it all together. Having no idea what to say to her sister at this moment, she looked at Paul. Daed came up behind her, breathing hard from hurrying across the yard.

"Those are matches in her hands." Paul spoke softly. "If I can get close enough, I'll tackle her and take them, but at this distance she could cause a spark while I'm running toward her. It's the fumes of gasoline that are explosive. If she lights a match—"

"No soft voices!" Sarah yelled. "I hate all the murmuring that goes on behind my back! It's everywhere I go—even in the house."

Paul turned his attention to Sarah. "Okay, we won't whisper. Can we move in closer so we can talk without yelling?"

"A little."

The three of them eased forward.

"Stop right there."

Hannah took a few more steps. "Sarah, what's all this about?"

"I want to know what you did with the baby."

"I explained all that. Can't you believe me?" Hannah inched forward. "The night after being accused of wrongdoing in front of Daed and the church leaders, I gave birth too early, and the baby died. I'm not lying."

Daed removed his hat. "Are you saying it's my fault you went into labor that night?"

Sarah's pale face made her dark eyes stand out even more. "No! The baby isn't dead! It isn't!"

Paul took a few steps forward. "Sarah, everyone here knows what happened. What will it take for you to believe us?"

"You only know what she said, and so does Daed."

Hannah stepped closer. "The baby died in my arms. She lived long enough for me to name her, fighting for a breath her lungs weren't mature enough to take. I cried until I thought I'd go crazy. But then the tears had to stop, and I had to find what was left of me and move forward."

Paul inched toward Sarah again. "What do you need from us, Sarah?"

Sarah pressed four matches against the striking surface. "Then it's my fault!"

He stepped in front of Hannah. "Why is it your fault?"

She stepped to the side of Paul, removing him as her shield. "I'm not sure you want to go down that volatile path. Not now."

"We need to diffuse this so we can get the matches."

"I realize that, but..."

"Maybe she knows things we don't. I think she should tell us why it's her fault."

"You're opening Pandora's box." Hannah ground out the words.

Ignoring her comment, he moved forward again. Sarah raised the matches and box. "No closer."

"Did you set E and L on fire?" Daed asked.

Sarah squared her shoulders. "I did."

Her father moaned as he slumped.

Paul pointed to the gas can. "Did you use matches or gasoline?"

"'The tongue is a fire, a world of evil...and sets on fire the course of life.' It doesn't need matches or gasoline."

Somewhat taken aback that Paul had managed to target the issue, Hannah thought maybe his other question had more merit than she'd given him credit for. "Why is the death of...my baby your fault?"

"What's her name?" Sarah asked.

"What?"

"The baby. You said you named her."

Except for the letter she'd written to Paul while on the train to Ohio, Hannah had told no one her infant's name, and she wasn't sharing it now with Daed standing here. She shook her head. "It doesn't matter."

Sarah screamed, like a child throwing a tantrum, as she joggled the matches against the strike plate.

Paul held out his hand, calming her. "Rachel."

Sarah sank to the ground and began to rock back and forth. Paul knelt in front of her, and she held the box of matches out to him. Staring into his eyes without blinking, Sarah whispered, "Help me."

Paul took the matches and put them on the ground behind him, and then he clasped Sarah's hands in his and whispered something that made tears roll down her cheeks.

Hannah glanced to her Daed, who was walking off toward home.

Paul stood and helped Sarah up. He then walked her to the back door, where Dorcas stood watching Paul's every move.

When Dorcas eyed Hannah, a thousand negative emotions roiled through Hannah, but she couldn't voice her thoughts. Paul had once told her that Dorcas attended every family function and that she practically lived at his parents' place half the time. She had positioned herself to be Paul's girl before Hannah ever left Owl's Perch. Hannah had no proof and yet no doubt that was what had happened. Still, she needed to keep this visit to its point and talk to Paul about Sarah, so she stepped forward and held out her hand. "Hannah Lawson."

Dorcas looked to Paul before shaking her hand. "Dorcas Miller."

Paul turned to Sarah, staring into her eyes. "I need to talk to Hannah, just while you get a shower and change clothes. Can you do that?"

Sarah nodded. "Okay."

Paul motioned into the house. "Dorcas, Sarah needs a change of clothing. Can you find her something and stay with her while she showers? I'll be right out here, well within earshot if you need me."

"Sure." Dorcas flashed a condescending look Hannah's way before the two disappeared into the house.

Indignation at Dorcas growled, but Hannah ignored it. Suddenly the great outdoors didn't seem large enough to hold the awkwardness between Paul and her.

He slid his hands into his pockets. "What happened today with Sarah has been brewing for a long, long time. I'm sorry it happened, but

I think it's good you were here, and I think we just witnessed the worst of it."

The only comforting thought Hannah could find at the moment was gratefulness that Martin wasn't here to see just how dysfunctional her family was. "Sarah needs to be checked into the mental health ward of a hospital. How do I go about doing that?"

"That would be a huge mistake, Hannah."

"Could you do me a favor and not use my name like we're friends?"

Paul nodded. "Look, regardless of how you feel about me, the clinic I work at is a wonderful facility and can help her, but a hospital is a mistake for a lot of reasons. The coldness of an institution will push her closer to the edge, and they'll start pumping meds in her left and right."

"Push her closer? Were you out here today?"

Paul studied her. "Are sarcasm and anger your only ways of communicating nowadays?"

To you? Yes.

He stood calm and reserved, obviously waiting for her to give an answer he was willing to work with.

After his help with Sarah just now, she should probably apologize for her tone. Bitterly opposed to that idea, she gave a nod. "Noted." She drew a breath and willed herself to find her nice voice.

Paul shifted. "Look, I shouldn't have said that about your dad and you earlier. And you have every right to be angry with me."

"Contrary to how I sound, I'm really not interested in venting my anger. All I want to do is help Sarah and get out of here, but you had no right to pass my number to anyone without asking me first."

"Your dad sent word through Luke that they wanted to locate you and had received a letter when your aunt died that gave him an idea where you were. Since I knew how to take that bit of piecemeal info and find you for them, I did."

She blinked. "My Daed?"

Paul nodded. "I was surprised too. Look, I was wrong to leave that night without hearing you out. I'm asking you to forgive me."

She shrugged. "Until arriving back here, I thought I had. But now it seems none of the prayers covered actually having to see you."

"I did come back for you."

"Don't." She held up her hand. "*If* you came back, you came back too late."

They stood in Gram's yard looking at each other as if they were strangers—no, it was worse. She saw a man she'd once thought was worthy of her giving up everything just to be with him. There was no telling what he was thinking, but if love was blind, what was happening between them now was more like a piece-by-piece dissection under a high-powered magnifying glass.

He pulled out his billfold and passed her a business card. "I have a counseling license and work at the Better Path. It offers an array of helps for people."

"You're a counselor?" She narrowed her eyes, trying not to gape at him. "This is the more suitable career that your church agrees with? You delved further into psychology, and they agreed with it more than social work?" The last time she'd tried to make contact with Paul, some young woman, maybe even Dorcas, told her that he had to make a career change to please the church leaders. The disbelief in her voice mocked his choice of a profession, and she didn't even try to cover it.

Paul shook his head—a slow, resigned type of shake—as if she were too much of a pain to deal with. "You know, I really am trying—" He stopped short when her phone rang.

She pulled it out of her dress pocket. The caller ID said it was Martin. Ignoring Paul, she pushed the green icon. "Hello."

"Hey, sweetheart, I thought of the solution to all our problems. Have you figured it out yet?"

Warmth and comfort slid up Hannah's spine, and she held the phone tighter. "Not a clue."

"We shouldn't have ever had sisters."

A burst of laughter broke through her current misery, and a tear trickled down her face. The tenderness in his voice made her ache to tell him the horrors of her day, of her own misbehavior of lashing out at Paul...of wanting to lash out even more.

She saw a half smile break through Paul's reserve before he grabbed the gas can and moved it into the barn, giving her privacy.

She walked to the knoll, gazing out over the peaceful fields. "I've been so wrong today. You wouldn't even recognize me. I've ripped people apart, and the thing is...I had no idea that kind of anger and bitterness lurked inside me."

"Phone girl, give yourself some room here. It's okay to lose it a few times with people who said they loved you and then didn't even throw you a life preserver when you were drowning."

Another tear slid down her cheek. She drew a deep breath. "Thank you."

"I'm really sorry for the other night."

"I know, but this isn't a good time to talk, so I'll call you later, okay?"

"Sure. No beating up on yourself, and we'll talk soon."

"Bye." She closed the phone. Walking to the barn area, seeing Paul, being here—it seemed impossible to process it with any sense of reality. "I...I'm off the phone."

With a pitchfork in hand, he tossed the gasoline-soaked hay into a huge metal bin. He glanced up. The lack of condemnation, disappointment, or anger on his face was disconcerting. Was he the jerk who'd abandoned her, taken her portion of their money, and refused to return her call—or not?

He gathered more hay on the tines and pitched it into the bin. "I didn't mean to break a confidence by sharing the baby's name."

Wishing she knew what to believe about this man in front of her, she did her best to temper her answer. "I guess I should have just told her when she asked. I tend to be a little stubborn about things at times."

Paul didn't nod or sneer or even crack some smart remark.

"That's your cue to say, 'You think?' "

He rested the tines of the pitchfork in the ground. "The phone call seems to have helped you find a little perspective on today."

"Yeah." She squeezed the phone in the palm of her hand. "Martin." She slid her phone into her pocket and ran her fingers over the ring he'd given her. "The first time I met him," she laughed, "it was *after* a rather ugly argument."

"So you argued with him and then met him?"

"Yeah. But the argument wasn't my fault."

Suppressing a smile, he answered, "Uh, yes, I...I'm sure it wasn't."

She blinked, staring at him before a whispery laugh escaped her, and he joined her. Silence followed, a welcome kind of truce of some sort. "So now what?"

"You listen to more reasons why the Better Path is the best place for Sarah?"

"Let's skip that for now and assume my opinion is outnumbered by you and Sarah, then what?"

"You take her there and get her forms filled out. I'll follow in my car and do what needs to be done to get a psychiatrist on site. Maybe not today, but some psychological testing will need to be done by tomorrow afternoon and a step-by-step plan developed. The place has full-time, short-term care. She'll be sedated at bedtime, her room locked, and she'll be monitored so she can't do any more slipping out during the night."

"What if she's guilty of starting the fires, of killing David?" Hannah's words barely came out in a whisper as she forced herself to ask about her worst fears.

"Normally that's not something I, or any other psychologist, would tackle, but since it's important to the safety of everyone in the community as well as to her being at peace, I'll work on finding some answers while she's under supervision."

Wondering what the cost would be, Hannah nodded. Regardless of all else, she'd stumbled on a beginning place for Sarah.

*H*annah stood at the window inside Dr. Stone's office, waiting for her to return from taking Sarah to her room for the night. Before leaving the Better Path over two hours ago, Paul had managed to reach the doctor and get her to come in to see Sarah today rather than tomorrow. For that, Hannah was grateful.

Her father's stubbornness seemed no better now than two and a half years ago. Still, she'd need his approval regardless of what Dr. Stone recommended. Sarah required her family and community, a place to live, and someone to provide for her when she was released from this place—all of which meant doing what it took to keep Sarah in the good graces of their Daed.

The receptionist had left about thirty minutes ago, and except for Hannah, the main-house segment of the Better Path was completely empty. A nurse, Dr. Stone, and Sarah were in the patient facility out back, which looked like it'd once been a *Daadi Haus* for an Amish home. The place was probably older than Dr. Lehman's birthing center, but it was nicer with its hardwood floors, refurbished interior, and homey décor. Dr. Lehman's clinics were sparse, functional, and had ancient linoleum floors. She hadn't really thought about it before now, but the windows at her clinic were covered with unopened, aluminum miniblinds to give a constant sense of privacy to the women inside. But here the windows were adorned with opened plantation blinds and lacy valances.

The Tuscarora Mountain stood in the distance with huge oaks spread across the land before it, reminding her of how much she'd once loved the beauty of Owl's Perch. But it no longer felt like home, in spite of the bittersweet longing that had crept up on her once in a while during this trip. Mostly what had flooded her was deep anger. Hoping to temper her reactions from here on, she watched as Paul pulled into the driveway behind the clinic and headed for the *guest* housing, as they referred to it.

Dr. Stone came out of the small house and met Paul, as if they'd timed his arrival back at the clinic with her leaving Sarah in the nurse's care. Meticulously dressed with matching nails and perfectly sculpted short brown hair, the forty-something doctor passed a file to Paul while talking. Trying not to chafe at the absurdity of this situation, Hannah kept a vigil. Paul glanced up to the window where she stood before returning his focus to Dr. Stone and walking with her toward the clinic. Their muffled voices filled the air as they entered the building and came up the stairs to where Hannah waited.

Dr. Stone motioned for Hannah to take a seat as she walked to the front of her desk and leaned against it. "Sarah has decided to stay with us over the next few weeks. It took awhile to help her see the need, but after eighteen it's best if the patient chooses to stay. Otherwise we could need the courts to intervene. If you'll bring her some clothes and any personal items she wants, you can spend a little time with her tonight, but after that we prefer no visitors for at least a week." She tapped the desk with her long, fake nails. "I still have a lot of patients to see at my full-time clinic, so I need to leave now, but Paul is prepared to fill you in on anything you'd like to know."

Not comfortable with the doctor asking Paul to explain what was going on with her sister, Hannah decided to be more direct. "What's wrong with her?"

"She seems to have four overlapping issues. None alone is too serious, and even the four are certainly manageable with help, but she's gone a long time with no intervention."

"We just didn't realize her issues were this serious."

The doctor nodded. "Family members tend to accept the odd behaviors of their own as part of who the person is, and the peculiarities can often increase slowly over years." She glanced briefly to Paul. "I understand you've been gone the last two and a half years."

"I have."

"With no contact?"

Suddenly feeling like her life was on trial, Hannah answered, "I didn't leave a way to be contacted, and I wrote very few notes, which were generic in content. Has that added to Sarah's issues?"

"She does have symptoms of adjustment separation anxiety disorder among other things."

"Was that a yes or a no to my question?"

"It was neither. It's possible your absence contributed to her condition. It's possible it didn't." Dr. Stone pulled a sheet of paper out from a stack on her desk. "She's requested to have Paul as her regular therapist."

"No." Hannah stared straight at him. "Absolutely not."

The doctor frowned. "Is there a reason why you feel he's not a good fit to work with Sarah? He is a Plain Mennonite, which gives him an advantage in understanding her."

Hannah had plenty of reasons for her opinion. In spite of his good showing at Gram's, she simply didn't trust him. Maybe he was who he said and acted like he was, but she had a solid basis for thinking otherwise. "But he's known her for a while. He's friends with our brother and has dealt with our Daed. Doesn't that disqualify him or something?"

Dr. Stone leaned forward. "So you think he's too emotionally involved to hear her without bias?"

Hannah swallowed, trying to maintain some semblance of professionalism. "Look, you're basing this request on what Sarah wants. Earlier today she *wanted* to set fire to herself. Maybe you're mistaken to put so much stock in her opinion."

The doctor gave an indifferent nod and passed the paper to her. "This is a list of our counselors. It's a short list, but each name has a bio. Only Paul works here full-time. The others come in a few times a week or less, so if you decide not to use Paul, you will need to understand the limitations you're placing on Sarah's counseling sessions. You can discuss this with your family and let Paul know. Whether he's her counselor or not, it's very important to her that she feels she can return home when her time here is over." She pointed to Paul. "Which means you will need to talk with her family while you're getting her personal items from home." She glanced at her watch. "I prefer that Paul be present for that conversation for many reasons I don't have time to explain. When you return with her things, I hope you have good news for her. If not, let Paul coach you on the best phrases to use so we can avoid wording things in a way that will upset her."

Hannah glanced at Paul. Daed had to approve this plan for Sarah's sake, but Hannah couldn't even manage to agree with Paul on anything. So how were they going to pull this off?

"Do you have a list of ways we can reach you if need be?"

Hannah pulled the last two business cards she had with her out of her pocket and passed one to Dr. Stone and one to Paul.

She nodded. "Good." She tapped her watch. "Well, I need to go. Paul, we'll have a conference call tomorrow at ten. I think we discussed all other aspects while on the phone earlier. Anything I've forgotten?"

Paul shook his head. "We covered it. I know how to reach you if a need comes up."

Dr. Stone looked at Hannah. "Regardless of who is chosen as the therapist, Paul will be the coordinator for all issues concerning Sarah for the intensity of the next month. After that he can step down and pass the responsibility to someone else." Dr. Stone held out her hand to Hannah. "I'm sure we'll talk again in a few weeks."

The doctor left.

Paul tilted the file in her direction. "We need to discuss a few things on our way to see your Daed."

Despite wanting to object and to drive herself, she simply nodded. This was unbelievable. Aggravating. Annoying. And...maybe the only way she'd get out of here and back to Martin before she ruined her chance of graduating from nursing school on time.

"You ready?"

She'd never be ready for this next venture, but it had to be done anyway. "Yeah."

Paul headed for his vehicle, and she went for hers.

"Han...um, Ms. Lawson, we need to ride together. The fewer vehicles in your Daed's driveway, the less frustrated he'll be, and we need to talk on the way to prep for the visit there."

She'd told him not to refer to her as if they were friends, but calling her Ms. Lawson wasn't the answer either.

"Then I'll drive."

He frowned.

"Problem?"

"No, I guess not...except I saw your effort to bolt that tire on this morning and..."

Caught off guard by his remark, she laughed. Her eyes met his, and for the second time something besides stress glimmered between them— and she was grateful. "Oh, shut up and get in the car, Waddell."

He shrugged. "I'm really hungry and tired. I don't want to get stuck without a spare."

She opened her car door. "I have groceries in the trunk of my car." They both got in, and Hannah turned the key. "So you won't die of starvation if we get stranded."

"So if we get stranded together, what would I die from?"

Hannah chuckled, remembering how well they used to quip their way through things. "I won't incriminate myself."

Paul laughed and opened the file. "Here's the deal..."

~~∿§~~

After pulling into her parents' driveway, Hannah turned off the car.

Paul slid the file between the seat and the console. "It'd probably be best if we left our cell phones in the car."

She'd disagree, except if their goal was to appease her father, Paul happened to be right. She plunked her phone into the console before getting out. Knowing she'd need to remain outside the house, she didn't go to the door closest to them but headed for the front porch. Without questioning her, Paul followed. She knocked and waited.

Her father opened the door.

"Hi, Daed. Sarah's doing much better this evening, and we came to talk with you about where she is and what can be done for her."

Her Daed nodded before he turned back toward the living room. "Luke, get a few kitchen chairs and bring them to the front porch. You need to join us. Ruth, ask Mary to take Esther, Rebecca, and Samuel to see the kittens in the barn until we call them." He then stepped out and motioned Hannah to the porch swing.

From things Mamm and Luke had said, it sounded like her Daed and Paul had met, but clarifying that could cause ill will from her father. And they'd clearly seen each other earlier today; still a proper introduction seemed necessary. "Daed, this is Paul Waddell. Paul, this is my Daed, Zeb Lapp."

Paul held out his hand, and Daed shook it. "Mr. Lapp."

Without speaking or offering any friendliness, her father took a seat next to Hannah, which took her by surprise. Luke came outside carrying two chairs, and Mamm was behind him.

As Mamm walked to her, Hannah stood. Her mother hugged her right there in front of her Daed. "Are you hungry?"

She should be. It was almost dinnertime, and she hadn't eaten since early morning, but she wasn't. *"Denki, Ich bin ganz gut."*

Saying "Thanks, I am fine" in her native tongue felt a little strange. Outside of working with Amish women in labor, she never used the language anymore. Zabeth rarely spoke it, and Hannah followed suit. Dressing like an Englischer seemed to cause everyone to avoid using Pennsylvania Dutch with her, even Mary.

Mamm gently cupped Hannah's face in her hands. *"Liewi..."* Her eyes misted, but she was unable to say more than *dear.*

"I love you too, Mamm."

Her mother sobbed and pulled her close. Daed sat in silence, watching them. Shaking, Mamm pulled away and took a seat in a nearby chair. Hannah sat next to her father. He reached over and patted her hand. Was he offering some type of apology? Or was he simply saying thank you for bringing some peace to Mamm?

Paul leaned forward. "Mr. Lapp, have you had time to share today's events with your wife and Luke, or should I begin our conversation by recapping?"

"I told them enough. Move on with what needs to be said."

Paul remained unruffled in spite of her father's sharp tone. "Sure, no problem. What happened today with Sarah may seem extreme and was probably very upsetting, but I believe her behavior was a cry for help more than a true indication of instability."

Luke placed his forearms on his knees and stared at Paul. "You can help her?"

"Sarah is a good candidate for receiving help. We don't have the lab results back, so we can't be sure yet if some hormone imbalance or physical ailment is adding to her issues, but regardless of that, the physicians and counselors at the Better Path can help her. She's checked herself into the clinic and wants to stay for a few weeks, but she needs to know that she can come home to live and that no one will be angry with her for getting help."

Fully aware that Paul was avoiding saying *he* could help her, Hannah looked at her father. "Daed, Sarah needs more help than we can give her."

He stared at the porch floor, arms folded across his chest. "We? There is no 'we.' You left and intend to leave again."

All hints of the restoration that'd taken place between her and her Daed only moments earlier disappeared. Ten things popped into her mind at once, all sarcastic, albeit true, pictures of why she wasn't a part of the "we," but she held her tongue.

Daed pushed his straw hat back a bit on his head. "I thought when she had time with you, she'd snap out of this stupor of hers. I've been wondering if she's just trying to gain attention, and Paul just confirmed it. I won't have my daughter mixing with the Englischers while those doctors dive into psychology trash and try to get an upper hand over God in her thoughts."

Hannah wanted to stand up and scream, but she determined to speak softly. "That's not what he meant when he said a cry for help. Her reaction today was similar to a reflex. If something is coming at you, you flinch. It's an automatic reflex. That's what this cry for help is like." She looked to Paul. "Is that accurate enough?"

He nodded. "Yes, but if we let Sarah continue down this path, her reflexes, so to speak, will take over more and more of her life, and her chances of regaining control will lessen."

Daed waved his hand as if shooing them away. "This is ridiculous. God knows what He's doing."

Hannah nodded. "Yes, but *He's* letting you see Sarah's need. He has put people near you with answers and help for her. I know you're leery and rightly so. Far too many people follow the trends rather than think things through, but if you ignore what you saw today, it'll only get worse. That can cost Sarah her future."

"She has no more of a future than you did after the unmentionable."

His final words hung in the air. Indignation pulsed through Hannah, burning her skin. She choked back the words that begged to be released.

Paul's eyes stayed on her before he cleared his throat. "Mr. Lapp, Sarah's prognosis—"

"Ah." Hannah interrupted Paul and faced her father. "So, Daed, you're the one who gets to decide who does and doesn't have a future. See, now I get it. If I'd just known that, why, I could have given up years ago." She smacked the palm of her hand against her forehead. "Silly me." She stood, tossing a half-apologetic glance to Mamm for speaking out against Daed. "I bitterly object to you, in your finite mind, deciding I was used up and washed up, and I won't let you decide it for Sarah either." She walked to the edge of the porch steps and paused before looking at her father again. "Your sister understood that love reaches out against all the odds and against all reasonable hope. I learned so much about freedom and hope and faith. Why can't you understand that people and circumstances aren't bound to what you can see in them today? If they were, there would be no need for faith." Hannah descended the steps.

The sounds of hoofbeats interrupted the conversation. Matthew Esh brought the horse and buggy to a stop.

He dipped his head in a nod to the group in general. "Hello."

Everyone except Hannah spoke to him. Unsure whether he wanted her to speak, she waited. His eyes moved to Paul, and she figured he'd like to comment on the oddity of his being at the Lapp place.

Matthew then looked at her. "I came by, hoping we could go for a ride and talk a bit."

Without a moment's hesitation, Hannah hurried closer and stopped when she was near the horse. Matthew studied her. "Well, I haveta say, like the last time we were right here like this, your getup again leaves a bit to be desired."

She didn't need to look at her dress. It was a mess of stains. She smiled. "Are ya saying I'm not dressed well enough to be standing beside your horse?" She lowered her head, hoping to make her voice sound deep. "If the brand-new horseshoe fits, Hannah Lapp…"

They both laughed, which meant he remembered them sharing that bit of conversation. Matthew looked the part of a man now. His eyes carried wisdom, and his frame was that of a man who did a lot of physical work for a living.

"Hannah," Luke called.

She turned.

"Sarah can live with us when she gets out. I'll work with Paul and do what I can to help her."

She glanced at Paul. Luke's words were most welcome, except the part about Paul. "There are other counselors at the clinic."

"Ya, but no one is going to understand being Old Order Amish as much as a Plain Mennonite. It'll help Sarah to have a less worldly viewpoint, won't it?" Luke looked from Hannah to Paul.

Paul remained silent on the subject, but she sensed defeat.

She tried to invoke a professional tone as she shared her feelings. "I'd much rather she worked with someone else."

Her father stood and leaned against the porch railing. "I agree with Luke. If Sarah's to get this so-called help, then at the very least, let her work with someone less in the world than the rest of them."

Mamm nodded.

"We need to talk." Matthew's words were muted and clearly meant just for her.

Hannah turned and studied him for a moment.

He set the brake and leaned toward her. "I know things you don't. Let's ride, and we'll talk."

Hannah pulled her car keys out of her pocket and walked back to the porch. "Mamm, will you get all the items Sarah needs to stay at the Better Path for a few weeks?"

Her mother nodded. Since they trusted Paul so much, he could finish explaining the procedure concerning Sarah and then take her clothes back to her.

She pushed the keyless remote, unlocking her car door. After hurrying to the car and grabbing her phone, she tossed the keys to Paul. Well, they almost made it to him. "In case you need to go."

He grabbed them off the concrete floor of the porch. "I'll head back to the Better Path soon."

Matthew released the brake. "I'll drop her off there when we're finished talking."

That was a long way by horse and buggy, so she figured Matthew must have a good bit he wanted to talk about. She went to the passenger's side of the buggy and climbed in.

Paul got behind the wheel of Hannah's car, unable to fit his legs inside the vehicle until he figured out how to move the seat. With the seat positioned right, he backed onto the main road. Sarah was finally getting the help she needed. It wouldn't be happening if Hannah hadn't come home. She and her Daed didn't get along, but she wielded more power over him than she knew. If Paul had his guesses, that alone caused Zeb to fight her tooth and nail.

Lion-heart.

He'd dubbed her that several years ago because she'd carried the nobility, strength, and fearlessness of a lion. The name had fit more than calling her a sweetheart. It wasn't as if she was void of sweetness, although he'd not witnessed much of it today. To his way of thinking, any sweetness she'd held on to was less her guiding force than the determination that ruled her heart. But he wasn't sure the name Lion-heart fit anymore.

She was more like a sentinel, with cutting words in place of a sword. Under all her anger there seemed to be pure determination. She had some issues to work through, but he hoped she wouldn't let the need to forgive defeat her. Surely after overcoming all she had, she'd find her way to forgiving everyone who needed it.

His cell phone rang. He grabbed it, opened it, and pushed the green icon, barely glancing from the road. "Paul Waddell."

No one spoke, and he tried again. "Paul Waddell."

"Uh, yeah, I heard you the first time," a man snapped. "And you have Hannah's phone because…"

Paul removed the phone from his ear and gazed at it as if it had an answer to the man's question. "While working with Hannah's family to make some arrangements for Sarah, we must have gotten our phones mixed up."

"Where's Hannah?" The edge of anger in the man's voice gave way to a bit of concern.

"She's…" Wondering whether to tell him she was with Matthew or not, Paul hedged. "Not here."

Silence hung, but the man's frustrations were plenty loud.

Needing to shift gears, Paul moved the phone to his other ear. "Martin, right?"

"Yes."

"I'll tell her you called when I exchange phones with her."

"Yeah, thanks."

To the man's credit, he didn't inundate Paul with questions. For that he was grateful, because the last thing he wanted was to cause trouble for Hannah, although she seemed well capable of standing up for herself.

Matthew brought the horse and buggy to a stop outside the Better Path. The sun had slid below the horizon long ago, and they'd talked for hours as the horse ambled along. She'd always thought Matthew had an inner compass that most people lacked, and she saw it now, even as grief tormented him and confusion summoned him to leave Owl's Perch for a spell.

But his firm stance about Paul's innocence in the situation, including the missing money, had been shocking…and very hard to believe. Still, it was Matthew doing the talking, and she loved him as much as she did Luke and had always trusted his judgment without question. Unfortunately that worked against her as he defended Paul's overreaction the night he realized she was pregnant.

The electric lights inside the Better Path contrasted starkly with the Amish homes they'd passed along the way, with the dim glow of the kerosene lamps shining through the windows. The clinic sat nestled in the center of an Old Order Amish fortress, more populated than Owl's Perch. Before returning from Winding Creek, she'd not seen or at least not noticed this clinic that stood outside of Owl's Perch.

Matthew set the brake and leaned in. "I'm glad we got to talk."

Hannah nodded, although he'd said many things she was less than glad to hear. "You should make those appointments like that hospital doctor told you to. Your back needs to be debrided several more times and…"

He shook his head. "I'm fine. I got the salve Mamm can put on my back, and if any signs of infection begin, I'll see a doctor."

"That's a very stubborn way to deal with this. You'll have more scars, and it won't heal as quickly."

"You're awful pushy, aren't ya?" He grasped the leads tighter. "I'm fine. Trust me."

Resigned, she nodded. "You have my address and phone number, so you call or write anytime you have a mind to."

"I'll do that. And you go easy on Paul. In the tragedy that happened to you, he's a victim too."

Not at all sure she believed that, Hannah kissed his cheek. "Take care, and don't be afraid to get away and see life from a different perspective. I think it'll only be good for you."

"Ya really think so?"

"I think it'd be a mistake not to go, Matthew. Challenge your faith. Challenge your thoughts about Elle. Don't let fear stop you."

He straightened his hat. "Then I'll take your advice and get out for a spell."

Hannah climbed down. "Good night."

He pulled away and left her staring at the Better Path with his words of faith in Paul still ringing in her ears. Not wanting to face him and admit she might have been too harsh, she slowly climbed the steps. Through the screen door, she could see him in the kitchen, standing in front of the stove. The aroma of sautéed mushrooms, bell peppers, and bacon wafted through the night air. She eased the squeaky door open, and he glanced her way.

Neither spoke as she made her way into the kitchen and leaned against a counter.

"You hungry?" Paul cracked an egg against a bowl and dumped its contents in with half a dozen others and then wiped his hands on the kitchen towel that was draped across one shoulder.

Her stomach had stopped growling hours ago, but the dull hunger remained. "I'm okay."

His blue eyes glanced at her, reflecting a look that said he was doubtful, but he said nothing.

Nervous at being the slightest bit vulnerable with him, she had to admit to herself that she'd rather die in her wrongness than have any part of her real self exposed to him ever again. That sentiment probably caused her to be unjust beyond reason to him…or at least beyond what Matthew said was reasonable.

With a bit of a hop, she took a seat on the counter. "Matthew said you really did come looking for me, and he explained a lot of things, and…maybe I've been a little unfair in my prejudices against your working with Sarah."

Paul beat the eggs briskly with a fork. "The fact that I came back for you afterward hardly exonerates me. I should have heard you out that night. I should have believed in you." He stopped and held her gaze. "I wish there were words beyond *I'm sorry.*"

She knew that feeling intimately, had felt it to her soul concerning Rachel and trying to keep secrets. For the second time she wondered if it was possible that part of the reason she'd left had nothing to do with the injustice heaped on her. Had she left because she couldn't face how poorly she'd handled things?

Still pondering that question, she was beginning to think he hadn't received her phone message before she boarded that train because he'd been out that night searching for her. And then she left him no way to contact her. Why she'd handled things as she had would take some figuring out, but her personal inner workings weren't Paul's fault. They'd both mishandled things, to say the very least.

"Nevertheless," she whispered.

All of Paul's movements stopped.

Hannah's heart seemed to hiccup under the weight of his subdued shock. "You know, I think I'm hungry after all."

"Good." A slight grin tugged at the corner of his lips. He gestured toward the bowls of various ingredients. "What do you like in your omelet?"

"A little of everything you have there, but go light on the bell peppers."

"You got it."

"Matthew said you didn't take the money. Any idea what happened to it?"

Paul dumped the eggs into the hot skillet. "Not fully."

She heard it in his voice; she'd hit a wall. "And not anything you want to talk about."

Adding ingredients to the eggs, he shook his head. "The money wasn't important, okay? I'd planned on replacing your portion when the opportunity—"

"No," Hannah interrupted, sounding flat-out mean. She drew a breath and measured her words. "I was just...curious. Am I so weak in your eyes that I can't cope with knowing what you know?"

His movements stopped. "No, of course not. I...I just..."

Whatever the rest of his sentence was, Hannah was sure he wasn't going to say it. "Who took our money?"

Paul folded one side of the omelet onto the other. "Not long after you were attacked, a young Amish woman, or someone wearing Amish clothing, went into the bank. She had the bankbook and pretended to be you. I didn't know the money was missing until after you left."

"I thought I'd lost the bankbook, but you think the guy who attacked me got hold of it and put someone up to emptying that account?"

"That scenario matches up with the evidence." He slid an omelet onto a plate and passed it and a fork to her. Without asking, he poured her a glass of orange juice and set it next to her. She remained on the countertop, and when his omelet was done, he leaned against the counter near the stove.

"The doctor gave Sarah a mild sedative when she arrived, and the nurse says she's been dozing off and on the last few hours. I took her the clothes your mom packed, and she asked if you'd come see her when you arrived. She seemed upset that you were out with Matthew, thought you'd be angry with her again. Care to share why?"

Hannah drew a long, ragged breath. "This isn't going to be easy, is it?"

"You mean my being Sarah's counselor?"

Hannah stabbed another bite of eggs. "Yeah."

"It could be worse." Paul shrugged. "You could be my therapist."

His jesting tugged at her, making her want to smile. She pushed a piece of the omelet around on her plate, stalling. "The rumor about the midnight ride in my nightgown, remember the one?"

He nodded.

"Sarah exaggerated it without realizing the person I'd gone for a ride with was Matthew. When he found out those few minutes had turned into a vicious rumor, he only held his tongue because I asked him to. No one doubts anything Matthew says, so if he'd told the community the truth, she would be in really big trouble." She took another bite of food.

"It's not human nature to ask someone to keep a secret rather than set the record straight. Why didn't you let Matthew say his piece?"

"The damage for me was done, and it was only one of several rumors, so clearing that one thing up only held the power to ruin Matthew and Elle, a relationship that began budding shortly after we went for that ride." Hannah took a sip of her juice. "I can't explain it, but Matthew is like a brother. Neither one of us realized how that ride might look." She slid off the counter, wondering how Paul could so easily have believed all those lies about her and left her. She wouldn't ask, whether from fear or some other reason, she didn't know—didn't care to try to figure it out.

Hannah took another drink and set the cup on the counter. "So you think Sarah's afraid of the truth being revealed?"

"Absolutely. I think she should get this off her conscience by telling the truth, not this week and maybe not next, but soon."

"You can't be serious."

"Facing our fears, skeletons, and mistakes is paramount in finding ourselves—in living with ourselves. Once it's done, that fear will be laid to rest, and she'll be stronger for having dealt with it and have more peace because she's not carrying the weight of that fear every day and night."

Hannah put her plate in the sink, thinking how well this new vocation suited him. His career as a counselor should make her uncomfortable, as if he were analyzing her, but he truly seemed to use his schooling only to assess things, like she did with her nursing skills. He wasn't supershrink analyzing, and he certainly wasn't judging.

Assessing. That's what he was carefully doing. It was a skill Dr. Lehman had taught her, even in the emotional realm as she counseled Amish women about their health concerns. She'd expected Paul to peer down at those he counseled, as if he held some secret powers over them, but that's not what he was about, and she found that disturbing for reasons she refused to think on.

"I'd like to see Sarah now."

He set his plate in the sink. "I have to tell you something first."

"About Sarah?"

"No, not at all. Martin called." He reached into his pocket and pulled out a cell phone. "You and the clinic have matching cells."

"What?" Hannah jerked the phone from her dress pocket. "You didn't answer my phone, did you?"

"I thought it was the one I signed out from the clinic."

She'd intended to tell Martin all about today, but there hadn't been time. Hannah sighed. "It's not your fault." She exchanged phones with Paul. "Sarah?"

"Right this way." He motioned to a back door and then stopped, allowing her to go first. They walked in silence across the yard and up the narrow concrete sidewalk.

She took a deep breath of the cool air. It carried the aroma of her childhood—freshly mowed hayfields, livestock, and a hint of honeysuckle.

Paul reached for the doorknob and then paused. "She's been very calm since arriving, but I suspect she'll get upset and try to convince you she can't survive if you return to Ohio. Stay calm and firm in your resolve that you have to go home. It won't help her at all if you give in to her self-image of being weak. She needs help, not babying."

"And for that stance on your part, I'm very grateful. Martin will be too."

"Glad I can help." Paul opened the door.

From a door to the right, Sarah ran out into the hallway and flung herself against Hannah and clung to her. "You're here! You'll stay, right? You'll stay in Owl's Perch and come visit me every day. We can see each other all the time without Daed around."

Hannah hugged her sister. "No, Sarah, I can't stay, but we can write to each other. You can call me when the staff here says you can." She pulled away, looking her sister in the eye. "I have a very busy life in Ohio, and I have to go back."

"But you'll come visit regularly, right?"

Hannah glanced at Paul. She hadn't thought ahead enough to consider what she'd do about visits. "My schedule won't allow much room until after the first of the year."

"But…" Sarah's eyes held panic. "You're leaving me?"

"We can talk by phone regularly." Hannah looked to Paul, silently pleading for some support.

"Sarah, she's separate from you. Remember?" He put one hand on Sarah's wrist and motioned for Hannah to step back. "You have the strength to stand on your own without her and without your thoughts tormenting you. We're going to spend time proving that, and you'll find peace and continue to get stronger while she's gone."

Sarah sobbed. "Don't go."

"Rita," Paul called, "would you help Sarah back to her room, please?" A woman in scrubs came into the hallway almost immediately. "Sarah, I need to talk to Hannah for just a minute, and then she'll come tell you good night before leaving."

Reaching for Hannah, Sarah was guided out of the hallway by Rita.

Paul turned his back to the door Sarah had just gone through. "I have an idea that might help her, but I'm not sure how you'll feel about it."

"And one Lapp daughter's hysteria is all you can handle at a time." As soon as the words left her mouth, she realized her sarcastic side was showing again. When had it become a natural part of her?

"I've never seen you hysterical. Justifiable anger is not the same."

She preferred sarcasm over being patronized. "Your idea?"

"When you left, Mary gave me the 'Past and Future' quilt. Sarah didn't like that it came to me, but I kept it anyway." He shrugged. "Since you designed it and sewed a lot of it with cloth from Sarah's and your childhoods, she might find that comforting for a while. I have it in my car."

"How many years did it take you to learn to make a conversation so generic? And why did Mary pass the quilt to you?"

"Generic?"

"You use odd wording, which causes a lack of clarity in what you mean—which is your point, I'm sure. 'Comforting for a while…' Does that mean you're returning it to me? If you're going to say something, make it clear."

"Noted."

She stared at him. Giving him that one-word response earlier hadn't bothered her at all; receiving it annoyed her. "And you didn't answer about the quilt."

"Mary gave it to me when I was dealing with the shock of your being gone."

"Gave it?"

"Yes."

"And it's in your car?"

"Yes."

"That's it? That's all the explanation I get?"

"I'm hopeful you'll take what I've said and not keep probing for answers." Paul's shoulders were square and his stance unmovable, in spite of the mildness in his words. It was a part of him that she remembered well—respectful noncooperation—and no one ever seemed as good at it as Paul Waddell.

She laughed softly. "I guess you've earned a break. The quilt can be a visual reminder that I'll always be a part of her future just as I was a part of her past."

"Perfectly worded. You tell Sarah while I go after it."

$\mathcal{M}$ artin lay on his bed with the remote control in his hand, flipping television stations at an annoying rate, even to himself. The large red numerals on the digital clock glared the fact that it was past midnight. And he hadn't heard from Hannah yet.

Chapter 12

Paul Waddell.

Disgust rolled through him. Surely this brief encounter—whatever it was—wouldn't resurrect any old feelings she'd once had for him. It'd taken way too long for Hannah to find peace and for her heart to be free of Paul. When she had begun showing an interest in Martin, he'd made her wait until her twentieth birthday before they went on their first date—mostly because the idea of being past his midtwenties and dating a teenager crossed a moral line that U.S. laws didn't cover.

Now he was at home with his niece and nephew and their part-time nanny while Hannah was somewhere in Owl's Perch with Paul Waddell's cell phone in her pocket. He should have gone with her.

Tempted to call again, he jolted when the phone beside him rang. The caller ID indicated it was Hannah. "Hey."

"Hi. Did I wake you?"

"No, I've been waiting to hear from you."

"Yeah, I'm sure. I'd be upset if the tables were turned, but dealing with him was unavoidable."

The fact that she gave credence to his feelings and didn't try to brush off the incident as nothing diluted his concerns. "You okay?"

"I will be when I'm back with you and the children...tomorrow."

"Tomorrow?"

"Yeah. That's sort of why what's-his-name had my phone by accident. It was my fault, but the good news is Sarah's at a mental health facility and I'm leaving for Ohio in the morning. I'd be tempted to leave even at this hour, but I had a flat today, and I'm not traveling at night on a spare."

"A flat?"

"By itself, it may have been the easiest part of my day after I arrived in Owl's Perch. I just want out of here."

Grateful for the sincerity of her tone, he felt more like himself again. "I want you to take the car in tomorrow morning and have a new set of tires put on before you head home."

"It only needs one."

"If it got one flat, they must all need replacing. Just use the credit card, and I'll take care of the bill."

"I'll get one new tire and pay for it myself, but I appreciate your generosity."

He resisted the desire to challenge her reasoning, figuring she didn't need him to debate with her at the end of a rough day. Besides, she'd still do it her way, and he'd end up feeling like the bad guy for trying to take care of her. He'd come up with an excuse to use her car one day next week and have the tires replaced; she'd never know.

Martin changed the subject. "You'll be glad to know it's a teachers' workday tomorrow, so Kevin and Lissa will be off all day."

She cleared her throat, and he wondered if she was crying. "That sounds like heaven."

"You *have* had a rough go of it if you think those two are paradise," he teased.

"But you always manage to be a good uncle anyway." He heard her yawn. "I'm at the hotel and bushed. I'll see you tomorrow. Okay?"

"Sleep well, phone girl."

"Good night."

Golden rays of the new day's sun streaked through the cloud-covered morning as Hannah pulled into Mary's driveway. She hadn't planned on coming by this morning, but she couldn't leave Owl's Perch without more time with her friend. She had even dreamed about her last night. However she had managed to squelch her feelings for Mary in order to begin life anew in Ohio, they'd resurfaced with a tenacious desire.

As Hannah got out of her car, she spotted Mary on her knees in the garden.

Hannah chuckled. *Potato-harvesting time.*

Wishing she'd worn something more appropriate for working a garden, she shielded her eyes from the sunlight and walked toward her. "Are you praying for some help while you're down there?"

Mary jumped and then laughed. "Well, look at you...all cleaned up."

Her words were kind, as they'd been yesterday, but something in her eyes said Hannah was a stranger. On the road yesterday she'd seemed very open, and they'd talked with ease, but the topic had stayed on Sarah and all that had taken place concerning her since Hannah had left. But standing here now, Hannah felt a wall, a thick one—one she wanted removed if it was possible.

"Kann Ich helfe?" Hoping that reverting to Pennsylvania Dutch would make a difference, Hannah offered to help.

"Bischt du zu draus in da Welt?"

Hannah should have known she looked "too out in the world," too worldly, for Mary to be comfortable with her—driving a car, wearing jewelry, attending college, having buttons run the length of her pale yellow skirt.

Hannah covered her heart. *"Ich bin net zu draus in da Welt."* She tapped her fingers over her heart, trying to reassure Mary that she wasn't too out in the world. "Not here, Mary."

Still on her knees, Mary studied her, clearly torn between this different-looking Hannah and the friend she'd once loved dearly.

Mary patted the soil beside her. *"Kumm. Loss uns blaudere bis unsrer Hatzer verbinne."* Come. Let's talk until our hearts unite.

Hannah knelt. She lifted Mary's hand and pressed it against her cheek. "Denki."

Mary's brows knit, and she hugged Hannah tight. *"Mei liewi, liewi Hannah."* My dear, dear Hannah.

Those words seemed to cause the wall between them to completely fall. If it hadn't, Hannah knew it could, if they put a little effort into it. Why had she let her fears and maybe even her ego cause her to hide her whereabouts so completely? Before she left today, she'd make sure Mary knew how very sorry she was for doing such a selfish thing.

At the head of the rectangular table, Martin went down the workload list in great minutia with his project managers. The weekly event often threatened to cause death by boredom, but the process was necessary.

"Doug, how long until the foundation on SWG is ready to be poured?"

"Depends on when the surveyors get the staking done."

Martin turned to Alex.

Alex shrugged. "We can have that done Thursday, but Kirk's requested a walkabout with you and Amy before he signs off on the plans."

Martin nodded. "What's a good time for us to do that, Amy?"

"Christmas."

The men chuckled. Amy's presence always added a bit of flavor to the dull workload process. Everyone in the room and their significant others were headed to Hawaii over Christmas. His employees and Amy worked really hard throughout the year, arriving early, leaving late, and helping this company be a leader in its field. "Anything just a tad sooner, like this afternoon or tomorrow?"

"Sure, either one really, but, uh..." She flopped the pen around on the stack of papers in front of her. "How rough is the terrain on this site?"

Doug tapped his middle finger on the table over and over again. "Jeans and a flannel shirt, definitely. And boots, without heels."

"That rules Amy out," Alex said. "Now if she could wear those black leather pants and those spike heel boots..."

"The thorns would rip my leather pants. But thanks, Alex."

Martin had no idea if she really owned leather pants, but he doubted it. As the only female at these weekly meetings, she took a good bit of teasing.

"Amy?" Martin asked, trying to veer the conversation back to its point.

She folded her hands. "I'll wear old jeans tomorrow, but if I break a nail, I want an extra day in Hawaii."

Alex whistled and pointed out the plate-glass window.

Hannah.

Martin's heart rate increased, and he suppressed the goofy grin that threatened to cover his face. She stood just outside her vehicle, a blue green dress following her hourglass figure as she repinned her mounds of curly hair back into a clasp. It was a vain effort some days, but she didn't wear it down in public.

"Easy, Alex. She's taken."

Alex looked from Hannah to Martin. "Are we looking at 'phone girl'?"

Martin had forgotten that Alex hadn't met Hannah. Amy hadn't either, but the others in the room had come to a few of the band gatherings throughout the year. Martin nodded. "Hannah Lawson is her real name, and if she comes in, try to act refined."

Alex shook his head. "Is she legal? I mean she looks young...for someone your age."

Doug scrunched a piece of paper and tossed it across the table. "Cut the nonsense. You're looking at the mother of his future children."

Ignoring the stabs at humor, Martin rose. "Doug, take over for me."

Martin left the room and hurried down the corridor, heading for the closest exit. He went out the side door and started talking as he walked toward her. "Wow, you drove to Ohio and my office in the same week."

She met him halfway on the sidewalk, a smile highlighting her rosy cheeks and flawless complexion. "A woman of endless talents."

She slid her arms around his shoulders, and he wrapped her in his arms. Her body trembled. "Hey, you okay?"

"Sure."

But he wasn't convinced, and with Hannah he might not ever know.

He held her tighter, grateful she was home. "Have you been to see Kevin and Lissa already?"

She put a bit of space between them and gazed up at him. "No, I came here first."

"Really? I'm impressed." He cradled her face in his hands, wanting to kiss her. "If we weren't being watched..." He nodded toward the window.

She tilted her head. "You care what they think about kissing me?"

"No, but I figured you did."

"Ah, always the perfect gentleman."

Man, how he tried—not just because of who she was in all her Old Order Amish innocence, but also because of how much younger she was. Her age was the only reason he hadn't pushed her harder to agree to marry him. But he was sure she'd say yes when he asked again as they shared a romantic alfresco meal at sunset on the beach in Hawaii.

Her smile wobbled, and something he'd seen before, but never could define, reflected in her eyes as she took a ragged breath. "How about if I pick up a few groceries—maybe fresh fruit, a loaf of deli bread, and a rotisserie chicken—and you take off early? All four of us can go to the cabin before I have to leave for class tonight."

"The cabin?" He laughed and shook his head. His million-dollar home with her own private cottage out back did nothing for the girl, but the scant cabin she'd lived in until the needs of Kevin and Lissa made it convenient for him to get her out of there held her heart ransom. "Wouldn't having a picnic here at the office be easier?"

She poked out her bottom lip, mocking a pout. Since she hadn't requested this in a long time, surely he could stand one night of it. "Whatever makes you happy, phone girl."

She tilted her chin in that way that said her will was set, her resolve complete. But why was this appearing now?

"You." She placed her hands over his. "You and Kevin and Lissa make me happy."

Her uncharacteristic declaration meant more to him than she could possibly understand as a twenty-year-old. He'd navigated living single for too long. Dates were easy to come by, but finding someone who made life more than it was without that person wasn't as effortless. By the time Hannah entered his life, he'd begun to fear it would never happen for him.

Unable to resist, he slowly kissed her cheek several times, breathing in the aroma of everything that made him connect to life in a way that work and financial success couldn't match. He eased his lips across her warm, soft skin until he found her lips. "I love you, Hannah."

$\mathcal{M}$atthew lit a kerosene lantern and carried it with him as he descended the stairway to the ground floor of his home. The rooster crowed loudly, even though the first rays of light weren't yet visible. Thunder rumbled in the distance as the sound of a gentle rain against the windows kept rhythm with the grandfather clock in the hallway. He set the lantern on the coffee table and laced his black boots.

Muted sound and movement in the dark kitchen caught his attention. Once he finished the last knot, he grabbed the lamp and headed toward the sound.

When the lantern cast its glow across the room, Kathryn's attention turned from the stove. "Hey, I didn't wake you, did I?"

He shook his head and set the lantern on the table. "What are you doin' up?"

"Same as you, I suppose. Can't sleep." She wiped her hands on a dishtowel and laid it across her shoulder. "What is it about death that disrupts everything to do with life—hunger, sleep, clear thought?"

Matthew eased into a chair. Kathryn wrapped a potholder around the handle of the coffeepot that sat on the eye of the gas stove. She lifted the pot, silently asking if he wanted a cup. He shook his head, uninterested in food or drink.

She poured herself a cup, dumped some sugar and milk into it, and took a seat across from him. "It'll get easier, Matthew. You have to trust in that, even as these days carry enough pain and guilt to make you believe otherwise."

It was nice to sit in a quiet room with someone who understood. She'd been the only person to acknowledge his sense of guilt. If she hadn't, he might not have understood the thing that seemed to cover him with blame so thick he thought he'd suffocate.

Unable to tolerate the back of the chair touching him, Matthew propped his forearms on the table. "I saw Hannah night before last. She said to tell ya hello."

Kathryn smiled. "I remember seeing her at the annual school sales when we were kids, but I bet I haven't seen her in six or so years. How is she?"

"Different."

"Aren't we all." It wasn't a question, and Kathryn was right. She wrapped her hands around the coffee mug. "We dress and live the same basic way as our ancestors, and yet the changes and temptations that war inside us must rival that of the Englischers."

The softness of her voice, her hope laced inside truth caused Matthew to feel something beyond his confusion for a moment. "But I always thought our sense of community and devotion to the simple life gave us the strength to resist the temptation to doubt or give up."

"And now you're not sure it does?"

Matthew ran his hands across the well-worn oak table his great-grandfather had built. "Can I ask you a question?"

She gazed into his eyes, and he noticed for the first time the golden radiance to her brown eyes. "Always."

Feeling welcome to be himself and to share the tormenting thoughts that ripped at him, he was grateful she'd agreed to stay on for a while. "What happened that day on the pond, and how did ya cope?"

Slowly her hands crossed the table, and she slid them over his, assuring him she'd answer in a few moments. After a bit she withdrew her hands and rose from her chair. In spite of his declining coffee a few minutes ago, she poured him a cup.

After setting it in front of him, she took a seat and placed the pot on a folded dishtowel on the table. "Abram and me and Daed had been at the pond since before sunrise, catching fish and singing loudly because the harvest was over and we were in the mood to play. Daed was sitting on the dock, and me and Abram were in a dinghy in the middle of our acre pond." She paused, turning the mug around and around as if lost in the memory. "Abram was being silly, rocking the boat while I screamed like a girl."

Matthew laughed softly. "Females tend to do that...sound like a girl."

"They both thought it was funny." A smile edged her lips. "The water sparkled, and their laughter echoed. And then everything changed. Green, murky water surrounded me. The boat had tipped, dumping out both of us. I didn't even know which way was up until I saw Abram's feet kicking near the surface of the water. I swam that way, feeling like my lungs would burst before I reached the top. I came to the surface coughing and struggling to get air. He was screaming for me to help him. Daed was on the dock, peeling out of his shoes and screaming for me to swim for the dock." She paused. "I headed for Abram, and Daed screamed my name, pointing his finger at me. He said, 'You obey me this instant!' And I did. He dove into the water, but by the time he got to Abram, he'd gone under, and Daed couldn't find him until it was too late." She lifted her gaze and stared into Matthew's eyes. "While I was making my way to the dock and Daed was swimming out to him, Abram called to me over and over again. There I was, a twelve-year-old girl, flailing in the water, trying desperately to get to the dock so my Daed wouldn't be mad at me." She rubbed the temples of her head as if it hurt. "I hated myself for a long time, wishing..." She took a sip of her coffee, looking lost in pain.

"You know why your Daed wouldn't let you go after him, don't ya?"

She wiped a tear and nodded. "I do now, but I didn't for a long time. I just remember crawling in my Daed's lap every day for months, crying until I couldn't cry any longer. He just held me, assuring me Abram was in heaven, happy and safe, but it was years before I under-stood that my parents would have buried both of us had I disobeyed."

She drew a deep breath. "I think they thought I was traumatized enough without telling me I would have died too. But it seems that in the end all that matters is finding a way to survive the grief and trusting in the goodness of life beyond the pain." She clasped her hands together, staring at them. "You did your best to save David. You were a good and kind brother. What else could be done?"

Matthew nodded, but he still hadn't found the answer to the question that haunted him—how to find *his* way out of the dark hole that surrounded him.

Maybe no one could answer that, but it seemed it was time to go to Baltimore and see if it held any peace or distractions for him. "I'd appreciate if you could stay here helping Mamm while I'm in Baltimore for a few days, a week at most."

"I…I can…"

"But?"

"My Daed's been asking me to come back home since before the fire. I could stay for a week, but he's right; my family is there. When the Bylers' barn burned, I came here to help them because they're our cousins. And…Joseph's patience with me being here is growing thin."

He barely gave a nod.

Her fingers touched the back of his hands. He looked up. "Go. Find some peace and strength. I'll stay until you get back."

"I figure I just need a few days."

Hannah laid the quilt to the side and wriggled her hands into a pair of medical gloves. In spite of the clinic having electricity, only kerosene lamps were used until time for delivery. It gave the place a homey feel the women appreciated. *"Es wunderbaar Bobbeli iss glei do."* Making small talk in soothing tones was important to moms in labor, so Hannah encouraged Lois that her wonderful baby was almost here.

Sweat trickled down Lois's thirty-something face as she moaned through another round of labor pains. *"Net glei genunk!"*

"Ya." Hannah moved to the foot of the birthing bed. Lois was right—not soon enough. It was her fifth child, and labor had begun nearly sixteen hours ago. According to her chart, Lois always had slow, methodical labors. She'd been in labor for several days with her first child.

While Hannah waited for the contraction to ease so she could perform a pelvic exam, Snickers meowed from somewhere outside.

The lines across Lois's face relaxed as the last of the pain subsided. "If that cat's up a tree again, it'd be awfully entertaining to see you go after it...like you did before."

The memory made her laugh. "Lois, that has to be the most legendary Tuesday quilting to date—Amish women poking fun at me while I climbed a tree to rescue a cat. But it's too cold and too dark out there this time."

Lois went almost limp against the pillow, relaxing. "I remember you climbing that tree, hanging that cat over the outstretched sheet us women were holding out. Then when you released it, it plunged through the air, screeching, claws out." She started laughing. "Mercy, Hannah, in one way or another you've been a blessing since you started working here."

"Denki." Hannah raised one eyebrow, dishing back some of the teasing Lois was giving. "Take a deep breath and hold it. I just want to see if it's time to call Dr. Lehman."

"Surely it is."

Hannah checked Lois's cervix and nodded. "I think so." She removed the gloves, washed her hands, and went to the phone.

Although labor had been a long ordeal, interrupting Hannah's Sunday with Martin, she and Lois had made good use of their time, even working on Lois's half-done log cabin star quilt. The pattern was Lois's favorite, and so far she'd made one for each of her children—only this time she was months behind in finishing it. If Lois wasn't so set against getting an epidural for pain, she'd probably have the baby in her arms by now. An epidural often relaxed a woman, and the contractions were able to do their job faster.

Hannah had been here part of yesterday and all night, which meant after Lois gave birth in the next hour or two, she'd have to sleep, then study, and then attend Monday night classes before getting home close to midnight.

The hayfields disappeared from sight as the view turned into asphalt, glass, and steel.

Baltimore.

As they drove toward the city at sixty miles per hour, Matthew watched the scenery, hoping the gloominess that'd taken over his mind and heart would lift. Haze covered the sprawling skyline of buildings, warehouses, and factories with their large stacks filling the sky. Billboards lined the side of the freeway, advertising phones, trucks, gyms—call now, buy now, things and more things. They crossed a huge concrete-and-steel bridge into an area of high-rise buildings butting against stretches of multilane roads. Not particularly feeling the excitement Elle said he would, he turned to face his driver.

"Been here before, have ya, Nate?"

"A few times. My wife loves the National Aquarium, though we haven't been in a while. If you get a chance to go, they might have the sea otters—well, I think they're otters, or maybe they're sea lions—that are outside for everyone to see. Though that may only happen in the summer. Either way, I think you'll enjoy visiting there if you have a chance."

The massive structures did look a little interesting. Nate maneuvered the vehicle this way and that as the minutes rolled on and the view changed again. Long brick buildings with doors and windows that were similar to a home's lined the street. Surely he wasn't looking at some type of house.

"Row houses," Nate said, as if he'd read Matthew's mind.

On second look some had a hint of homeyness to them with curtains in the windows and flowers in window boxes. Others had paint peeling around the trim. As they continued down the street, they passed a section of brick buildings where the lower windows and doorways were sealed with cinder blocks while the upper windows looked like a fire had consumed the insides of the buildings. Across the street three middle-aged women sat on the steps of one house, talking. Parked cars lined the street, leaving two lanes for traffic between them. A young woman in a tight, short dress and a snug leather jacket paraded down the street in high-heeled, shiny boots while pushing a stroller.

Nate pulled up to a curb. "This is it." He put the truck in Park and set the brake.

Matthew stepped out of the vehicle, seeing a few well-placed trees amid concrete and brick everything. The three-story brick place with fancy molding along the cornice looked more like a sardine inside a can—packed in tightly—than a home.

Nate opened the lockbox in the bed of his truck. "You're gonna stick out a bit here unless you get rid of the hat and suspenders."

"More than that girl we passed awhile back?"

Nate pulled out the sacks with Matthew's clothes. "You'll see women dressed in a lot more and a lot less before your week's up."

Elle bounded out the door and down the steps. "You're here and right on time too."

Matthew nodded. "We're here. That's true enough."

She tilted her head. "Can I have a hug?"

"An easy one." He put his arms around her and hugged her, glad his skin wasn't near as sore to touch as it had been. As he took a step back, a tall man wearing a black suit and a fitted hat covering only the crown of his head passed by.

"Nate thought I'd stick out."

Elle glanced at the man. "Nah, if it exists in the world, there will be traces of it here."

Her comments seemed odd, considering things she'd said about needing to wear certain Englischer clothes during her time here, but he didn't want to question or challenge her on it right now.

The half-dressed woman pushing the stroller came toward them.

Elle tugged on Matthew's shirt. "After the shock wears off, you'll find it easy to enjoy."

Nate passed Matthew the two large paper bags carrying his clothes. "I need to go. Told Kathryn I'd be back to pick her up by two."

Matthew shifted the full bags, wondering if he'd brought too many clothes. "Where's she needing ya to take her?"

"My place. With your phone not in working order, the missis invited her to use ours. Kathryn said she needed to use a phone and desk for business of some type. She said the Bylers' phone shanty is too limiting."

Matthew gave a nod. The phone lines in his shop were destroyed. Without the status of operating a business, the bishop wasn't going to approve having a phone shanty put in. But he didn't know what possible business Kathryn could be up to.

Matthew put the sacks on the sidewalk and paid Nate. "Monday morning at eleven. I'll meet ya right here—"

"Actually…," Elle interrupted, "why don't you just call him when you're ready to leave? I have a phone. He has one. It's easier, and I was hoping you might stay longer than just four or five days."

"Longer?" Matthew studied her, wondering just what she was hoping for. "But I told Kath—"

"Okay." She snapped the word, and her violet-colored eyes spit anger, reminding him how little patience she had with any other female being in his life. "You can leave Monday, but why don't you call Nate to confirm rather than put it as a definite?"

"That works too." Matthew slid the rest of his cash into his pant pocket, hoping it'd last him. But as he stood there, he began to unravel a few things about who he and Elle were together—a couple who'd never really had a chance to form an easygoing, enjoyable friendship. His time in Baltimore would help with that.

Nate closed the lockbox. "That's fine. I'll wait until I hear from you to make plans. Enjoy your time here." He waved as he climbed into his vehicle.

Elle grabbed one of the sacks. "Come on. I have your room all ready."

Looking at the tall, narrow, brick building, Matthew had to admit that the trip had already lessened the intensity of his grief. Maybe Elle was right—getting away might help.

They entered through the front door and walked up two flights of stairs before Elle stepped into a bedroom.

She set his bag of clothes on the bed. "This is yours for as long as you want it. When you're ready, I have lunch made. I need to return to the bakery in an hour, but I was hoping you'd come with me, maybe help out since I have to work anyway. You could give our commercial ovens a try or run the counter. Dad said I could have off early tomorrow, so I'll take you to the Inner Harbor and show you a view of the Chesapeake Bay and a hint of Baltimore's nightlife. It'll be fun."

Lace curtains covered the window, a whirling fan with multiple lights hung from the ceiling, and a huge radio with even larger speakers sat on a white dresser. Feeling curiosity stir, Matthew placed the other sack of clothes on the bed. "Sounds like an interesting few days, Elle. I'm looking forward to it."

She smiled in a way he hadn't seen in more than two years and kissed his cheek. "Thanks."

*D*arkness covered the neighborhood as Hannah pulled into Martin's driveway at seven thirty. The question-and-answer time during today's Tuesday quilting ran late, and then paperwork concerning recent births had to be filed before she left. On her way across the lawn, she smelled smoke. She sniffed the air—no, she smelled burned food.

The back door flung open, and a blur of Martin holding a smoldering cookie sheet flashed before her just as he hurled the smoking things in her direction. She screamed and jumped back. Shock registered on his face as their eyes met.

He broke into uproarious laughter. "Hannah, sweetheart, I'm so sorry." With the pan in hand, he stepped outside and walked to her, still laughing. "But it's what you get for not being here to prevent this."

Kevin and Lissa stood in the doorway, watching. Hannah tried to keep a straight face, but it was hopeless. "I don't know what's funnier, burned cookies sailing through the air at me or you in pink oven mitts with a fringed towel tucked in your jeans."

He dropped the pan, jerked the pink things off, and threw them on the ground. "What pink mitts?"

"Too late. I know what I saw, Martin."

"And whose fault is it that my home, a.k.a. the bachelor pad, has pink oven mittens?"

"Yours. You bought them. I thought you'd done it for me, but obviously I stand corrected." She picked up a burned round thing from the grass. "What was this before you got hold of it?"

"Chocolate-chip cookie dough," Lissa yelled out the back door.

Kevin folded his arms over his chest, obviously not happy about the burned cookies.

Hannah bit her bottom lip, thoroughly soaking in the man in front of her. His eyes reflected amusement, and there was a bit of white flour in his thick, dark hair.

He came within inches of her. "Hi."

"Hi." She pulled the towel loose from his jeans. "Need some help?"

"Always." He kissed her cheek while his face reflected desire for a real kiss.

"What's going on?"

He rolled his eyes. "Kevin needs six dozen homemade cookies for tomorrow."

"Six dozen? Tomorrow?"

He nodded.

She put the towel around his neck and pulled him closer. "Why didn't we know this before tonight?"

"I plead the Fifth."

"Why am I not surprised?" She brushed her lips against his.

Lissa banged on the glass of the open storm door. "Hannah, come see what Uncle Martin did."

She narrowed her eyes at him before entering the house. The counters were covered in dirty dishes, and the sink had remnants of burned cookies. "My kitchen!" She clamped her hands over her mouth.

Martin laughed. "You can have it."

Kevin huffed loudly. "I'll never have those cookies, and everyone will…"

Martin held out his hand in stop-sign fashion. "Relax, Kevin. I'll get this done." Martin looked to Hannah. "I will."

Lissa frowned at Kevin. "I believe you, Uncle Martin."

Kevin turned and walked out of the room, mumbling, "I'll believe it when I see it."

Lissa followed him, wagging her finger and complaining at him.

Martin shoved one hand into his jean pocket. "He's a bit sensitive right now. If this doesn't get done, in his eyes it'll be like screaming to the whole school that he doesn't have a mother."

"Ah, would you like some help?"

He gestured at the counters and sink. "Think I need it?" His face became serious. "Some days what Faye's done to those kids makes me so…"

Hannah placed her fingers over his lips. "They have you, and we both know that's saying more than Kevin and Lissa can possibly understand right now."

Martin kissed her fingers. "And you."

"And me." She glanced at the stove. "Hey, 450 degrees?"

"I was hoping to get the cookies done faster that way."

"And how's that working for you?"

"Sarcasm. You know, I wouldn't have coached you to hone that skill had I known you'd use it on me. We need to make a fresh pot of coffee and get the kids in bed…please." He elongated the last word, letting her know he was more than ready for a break from his niece and nephew.

"While you read to them, I'll clean the kitchen. After we tuck them in for the night, we'll get a fresh start. Okay?"

"That seems like a lot of work for a man who only wants some time with his girl."

She grabbed the coffee decanter. "Regular or decaf?"

"Regular and lots of it."

With a long wooden peel in hand, Matthew removed two loaves of bread from the commercial oven. He set them to the side and pulled out a few more. After ten days in Baltimore, grappling through the fog of grief had left him more apathetic than renewed. Still, that was more welcome than the intense pain of loss.

Twinges of guilt pricked him each time he remembered that he'd not kept his word to Kathryn about returning within a few days. He'd called and left a message with Nate, asking him to tell her he was staying longer.

Her voice circled inside his head. *You can rebuild...*

But rebuilding seemed wrong. Why should he get to restore his life when David's was over? Matthew swallowed hard, unable to answer that question.

The bell on the front door of the bakery rang, letting him know the first customers of the day had arrived. What irked him was when he did feel something other than apathy, it tended to be loneliness, and yet he was right here with Elle. It wouldn't be fair to think she could remove any of his grief and confusion, but he'd expected to feel a closeness of some sort.

Elle seemed content enough here. They'd attended a huge Englischer church on Sunday. It'd been...interesting and overwhelming, and he was glad that while on that extended buggy ride, Hannah had told him about the many differences in the Englischer world.

Elle's father, Sid, came into the kitchen through the swinging door. "Hey, Matthew, why don't you slip out of that apron and handle the customers while I take over back here?"

Removing the apron, Matthew went to the customer counter with the glass displays filled with baked goods. Sid had made a dozen statements about how much customers were responding to his presence in the bakery. Although he thought it possible Elle wasn't aware, he wasn't fooled. Sid wanted him at the bakery, not because he needed his help, but because his Amish clothing and accent appealed to customers.

Matthew waited on customers and ran the register. Sid kept the baked goods coming until it was time to shut off the ovens and clean up the kitchen. The place was quiet during the afternoon lull when the bell on the front door rang.

Elle breezed in, all smiles as she slid out of her jacket. "Sorry, the photo shoot took longer than we expected."

Sid came out of the kitchen and looked at Matthew. "You won."

Matthew nodded. "Yep."

Elle huffed. "Won what?"

Sid wiped a wet cloth across the counter. "He said you'd be here around two. I said closer to four. You're always late. We just bet as to how late. You're not nearly as late as usual since Matthew's around."

Elle slid the apron strap over her head. "Are you betting, Matthew?"

"Won a loaf of stale bread to feed to the ducks and the right to leave thirty minutes early."

"Well done." Elle kissed his cheek.

"Think so? It seems a bit stiff for a man who's not actually employed by your father."

She giggled. "I guess I didn't think about it like that."

Sid passed the wet cloth to Elle, a teasing gleam in his eye. "But you have to stay late to make up for the time you've missed."

She stuck her tongue out at him. "Be nice, Dad. We have company."

He moved to a table and sat down. "Matthew, I know you didn't like it when Elle left Owl's Perch, and I probably should've handled that better, but I think you should consider moving in with us. We got plenty of room and plenty of work."

Matthew pulled out a chair from a nearby table, turned it around, and straddled it. "Why me?"

Sid frowned. "What?"

"Why me? There are plenty of people needing jobs."

"Because it'd make Elle happy."

Nodding her head, she smiled broadly, making Matthew wonder if she was in on this with her dad or just an innocent bystander.

Either way, they both knew he was a baptized member of the faith, so this request meant they were asking him to leave the faith, didn't it? He laid his arms across the chair's back. "What made ya want me to come here rather than Elle comin' to Owl's Perch and joinin' the faith as she agreed?"

"Well, I've thought your joining us here was a good idea for over a year, and when your shop burned down, I thought maybe you'd be open to the idea of coming here."

The man made it sound like he'd offered this while considering Matthew's feelings or best interests, but he doubted if Sid was anyone's friend. The man was nice enough outwardly, but from Matthew's perspective every bit of niceness was wrapped around a selfish motive. He seemed to only know the fine art of using people. He'd bailed on his daughter, leaving her to be raised by an Amish family that had befriended her mother before she passed. Never once did he make contact or pay the Zooks anything for childcare. Then he showed up when he needed Elle's help with the bakery, and now—

"You want me to move in?"

Sid nodded. "Sure. I'd love it."

"And if I remove all signs of being Amish, would ya love it then?"

Elle wheeled to face him, shock written across her features. "Matthew."

Matthew shrugged. "It's a fair question."

Sid strummed his fingers on the table, looking as if he'd expected this conversation. "This is a good business, and I'm willing to bring you into it because Elle loves you. You can live rent free and have all the time you want with my daughter. But for this arrangement, wearing your Amish garb is little to ask of you."

"Dad, you're assuming I'll stay here. I invited Matthew so we could have some time together, but I might move back and become Amish."

Sid rose. "You've been saying that for over two years, Elle. Face it, you like it here more than you like the Plain life, but the decision is yours."

She scowled at her dad before she held her hand out for Matthew's. "We're leaving for the afternoon, okay?"

"You guys have fun."

Matthew rose and helped Elle on with her jacket before sliding into his own. As they stepped onto the sidewalk, the afternoon sun against their backs helped take the edge off the cool nip in the air.

She slid her hand into his. "I'm sorry about that. He learned a few months back how much better the Amish bakeries do. I guess he thinks we should try to use that pull if we can. He'd have me wearing the Amish clothing if I would, but I won't. If I wore the dress now after being established as not Amish, it'd come across as fake and offensive to our customers."

Matthew wasn't impressed with her stance. She had known how her father felt, his reasoning and motives, when she invited him here. He freed his hand and slid it into his jacket pocket.

She grabbed his arm, stopping him from walking, and stared into his eyes. "I…I wanted to give you as much time here as I could before we talked, but if you don't like it here and want us to return to Owl's Perch, I'm ready to join the faith and make that commitment."

It seemed he should feel excited, but he did at least sense a break in the fog of confusion.

"Matthew?"

He gazed into the eyes that used to mean hope and a future. Pulling away, he started walking again. She quietly strolled beside him. He'd come here wanting something he thought might still exist, love for Elle. But the longer he stayed, the more he knew that whether she was here or in Owl's Perch, whether Englischer or Old Order Amish, he had no desire to marry her anymore.

Tired of looking for distractions and a way to ease his pain, Matthew felt something click into place. Odd as it seemed, he almost sensed that he *heard* something click into place. Maybe he hadn't really been waiting for Elle to return but only thought he was. Maybe that was the distraction God had used or allowed, but in reality he was waiting for something else.

Someone else.

Elle tugged on his arm. "Hey, let's go to the Inner Harbor tonight."

He gazed down at the most flawless beauty he'd ever seen, fully aware that he wanted more than what she could give him. "Elle, we need to talk."

$\mathcal{M}$ary shoved a clothespin over the edges of the last wet towel before bending to grab the empty laundry basket. A pain caught in her side, stealing much more than just her breath. Cold fear ran through her as she released the basket and waited for the pain to subside. Comparing her due date to today's date, Mary tried to think clearly. According to the midwife, she was due the week before Thanksgiving. It was only the eighth of October.

Chapter 16

What have I done?

The doctor's warning not to conceive a child this soon after her injuries from the horse-and-buggy accident rang inside her head. Although she was at risk, he'd said the baby would be fine, hadn't he?

Mary leaned against the clothesline pole. How could she be this stubborn?

Thoughts of sharing this burden with Hannah released a bit of her anxiety. She'd cut ties with the doctor because he'd wanted to control her life. The midwife...well, no one wanted to say it aloud, but the woman was a gossip. Mary couldn't confide anything in her. But she trusted Hannah completely. Besides, if anyone could understand what she'd done and why, Hannah could. Easing herself upright, she searched the place for her husband. Not seeing any sign of him, she made her way to the phone shanty. With Hannah's business card in hand, Mary dialed her cell.

"Hannah Lawson. Please leave a message."

"Th-this is Mary. I...I need to talk to you as soon as you can." Mary started to hang up but changed her mind. She stole another glance across the yard to make sure she was alone. "I'm scared, Hannah."

Feeling an awful pain down her right side, she hung up the phone. Maybe she should call the midwife. She thought about visiting her surgeon, the one who'd seen her through the physical traumas of the horse-and-buggy accident, but he'd be furious when he realized she'd ignored his instructions. Besides, he always seemed to hold back more information than he actually shared, as if her life was his to understand and make decisions for.

Suddenly all her desire to get Luke to the altar paled as the reality of what she'd done closed in around her. Surely Hannah would have answers for her and could get them through this with both her and the baby safe and Luke none the wiser. Surely. How could she have been so brazen in her decision while hiding secrets and convincing herself she was choosing to trust God over doctors?

This wasn't the first time she'd doubted her actions, but now it was impossible to convince herself the baby and she would be fine. Knowing nothing else to do, she headed for the house. After opening the window nearest the phone shanty, she lay on the couch, waiting for Hannah to call.

Closing her eyes, she counted the beats of the clock, the only noise inside her Mammi Annie's home.

The phone rang, and she pushed herself upright, trying to hurry and be cautious at the same time. Just as she rounded the outside corner of the house, she saw Luke grab the phone.

He motioned for Mary and shifted over, offering her the small bench seat inside the phone shanty. "Last I talked to Paul, Sarah was doing much better, but I talked to Mamm this morning, and she said that Daed was planning to take the church leaders to the Better Path to try to meet with Sarah today. I'll find out from Paul how it went when he comes by here later." Luke talked on, making anxiety ripple through Mary.

There was a time when Hannah knew Mary's hopes and dreams without words needing to be spoken, but were they still that bonded?

Surely Hannah wouldn't ask Luke any questions about why Mary had called earlier. She rubbed her stomach, trying to assure herself all was well. About the time she feared she might just scream and jerk the phone from him, he finally passed it to her.

Hoping her voice didn't give anything away to her husband, Mary lifted the phone to her ear. "Hi, Hannah."

"Mary, are you okay?"

"Sure, I'm fine. How are you?" Figuring Hannah thought she was nuts, Mary ached for her husband to go on about his day and let her have a few minutes alone. Of course, that wouldn't be near enough to explain what was going on, but it'd give her a moment to get advice concerning the pain in her right side.

God, please don't let my sin hurt our baby.

"Mary, what's going on? You're scaring me."

"I…I bet it's been busy since you returned to Ohio, ya?"

Hannah hesitated. "It's been busy, yes." Her voice was a mixture of softness and worry. "Is Luke still there?"

"Yes, he is. Did you want to talk to him again?"

"No, just give him a hug for me. Mary," Hannah spoke softly, "if you're having any sort of trouble, you need to call the midwife. Do you hear me?"

"Yes. It was good to hear from you. Bye." Mary hung up the phone, feeling like a ball of anxiety, but at least Hannah had understood her unspoken words.

Inside his office at the Better Path, Paul read over two weeks of notes on Sarah. He'd worked with her intensely, and even though they had quite a journey ahead of them, her future held promise. That was the good news. The bad news was that the lines in Sarah's mind that separated reality from thoughts, dreams, or feelings did more than just blur. They controlled her actions and motivations. When Sarah had learned of her sister's trauma and the death of her baby, she emotionally experienced the trauma as if it'd happened to her. And she carried a lot of guilt for the trouble she'd caused Hannah. The medications Dr. Stone prescribed for her helped, but she had quite a ways to go.

Using Hannah's business card as a reference, he'd e-mailed a status report to her at the end of each week, not sharing anything confidential, but letting her know Sarah was doing well and continuing to improve. Hannah sent back three words: "Received it, thanks." He'd covered similar info with Luke and Mary in person, and he looked forward to seeing them again this evening. With Sarah moving in with them soon, a discussion at their place would help Sarah adjust back to her world more easily.

"Paul." Halley's voice came through the intercom.

"Yes."

"Zeb Lapp is here to see you."

He could have bet money this day was coming. "Send him up." He put Sarah's file away and went to the landing just outside his door to greet Zeb.

"Mr. Lapp." Paul motioned to his office, followed the man inside, and closed the door. "What can I do for you today?"

"I want to see Sarah."

Paul took a seat at his desk. "I'd like to put that on hold for a little longer. She's feeling less confused right now and is making progress. Unfortunately, how we feel about our relatives, even ones we love dearly, can cause a lot of confusing emotions."

"We aren't interested in confusing her. Just the opposite. We want to ask her to shed some light on a few things. It should help her."

"Is Ruth with you?"

"No."

"Who are the 'we' you referred to?"

"She's my daughter, and this really isn't any of your business."

Paul rose and went to the far window. In a buggy sat three stiff Amish men dressed in black. He returned to his seat. "As I said, in the two weeks Sarah has been here, she's shown a lot of improvement, but she's not ready for any visitors. My professional opinion is that it is not a good idea for you and the church leaders to meet with her anytime soon unless you allow an outside moderator to be present."

"We will meet with her today, without anyone else in the room. They've put everything aside to come here, and you will let me see her."

So the men in the buggy were the church leaders. "Mr. Lapp, I apologize for the inconvenience, but this is about what's best for Sarah. I'll not budge on the issue as long as she's staying here." The meeting with her Daed and the church leaders seemed inevitable, but he needed time to talk with Sarah and prepare her. "If there's nothing else…"

"And she's set to be released when?"

"Well, originally we thought maybe by tomorrow, but that currently doesn't appear to be in her best interests." Not since Zeb and the church leaders were planning on questioning her.

"As her father, can't I have her released early?"

Paul shook his head. "No. She's an adult, and the decision is hers."

"Then let me talk to her."

"I'm sorry. That isn't a good idea for today. I don't think she's ready just yet."

Zeb stood. "I came here in good faith, wanting to meet with my daughter before she was released to start any more fires, and this is the stand you take?"

"We all want what's best for Sarah, but I'm concerned that being asked questions like this will undermine her new sense of having control over her life. Perhaps you could mull over my concerns and we could talk again."

Zeb stood. "We'll be back." He turned and walked out without saying anything else.

Not yet sure how to handle this, Paul checked his watch, gathered his schedules and time sheets, and headed for the board meeting that had begun five minutes ago. If he wanted Sarah's time extended, it'd take some amazing powers of persuasion. Since the Better Path rarely had people who required the kind of watchfulness Sarah did, the staff wanted her released. Although occasionally Rita needed to stay over-night when dealing with patients, this longer-term stint with Sarah had been hard on Rita's family. Ethics and rules didn't allow men to stay with female patients, so Paul couldn't take over for her, and there was no one else trained or available.

Without knocking, Paul walked into the meeting and took a seat.

Bob pushed a paper across the table. "Paul, here's the agenda for today. We didn't start without you, in hopes you had some ideas concerning the—"

A beep came from the intercom. "Paul, there's a call for you from Hannah Lawson on line three. I told her you were in a meeting, but she's insistent that you take the call anyway."

Paul gathered the papers into a pile and left them on the table. "Not a problem, Halley. I'll take it in my office. Thanks." He stood. "I'm sure it won't be a long call, but I need to take it."

Bob leaned back in his chair. "Okay."

Paul went to his office and closed the door. "Paul speaking."

"Listen, I just got off the phone with Luke. Daed is on his way with the church leaders to meet with Sarah. Do not let that meeting take place."

"I didn't. He's already come and gone. When you called, I was in a meeting with the board to see if Sarah's stay can be lengthened so I can keep her environment controlled while I figure out how best to deal with this."

The line remained quiet.

"Ms. Lawson?"

"I really appreciate...and you...should call me Hannah."

"Sarah's safe, Hannah."

There was another pause before she cleared her throat. "I hate to ask, and you're doing plenty already, but I...I need a favor. If I knew someone else to ask, I would."

"Go ahead."

"Mary called my cell and left a message. She sounded really upset, but when I called her back, she acted nonchalant. Luke was there, and I get the feeling that whatever she called about, she didn't want him to know." She clicked her tongue. "I know how this sounds, and it's not a trait of my entire community to hide things from their spouse or... fiancé."

"I'm not anyone's judge, and I wasn't thinking that."

"It's just that if something isn't going well with the pregnancy, she wouldn't want to alarm Luke, and she's not one to trust Englischer doctors any more than most of the community, and..."

"Yeah, I've come to realize over the last few weeks that's quite an issue around here." Paul checked his watch. "I'm supposed to see them tonight about Sarah. I'll go on by their house when I get off the phone and check on Mary."

"Then you won't be able to get an extension for Sarah."

"I'll handle it."

"I'm coming in tomorrow. I intend to face Daed *and* the church leaders and put an end to this meeting they want with Sarah. I should be there by lunchtime, but if Mary is having any tightening across her stomach or any other odd symptoms, she needs to call the midwife immediately."

"I'll make sure to get a few minutes with just her and relay your message. If I think she's trying to ignore any symptoms, I'll call the midwife myself."

She was silent again, and he waited.

"If you talk to her and she needs me sooner..."

"I'll call and let you know. Anything else?"

"Any news about the investigation concerning the fires?"

"Not yet. I really don't think we'll hear anything for a few more weeks." Paul opened the drawer and grabbed Sarah's file. "While you're here… I mean, since you're coming in anyway, there are a few things we—you and Luke and me—need to cover about Sarah."

"Oh…yeah, sure, that'll be fine. Bye."

"Bye." Paul lowered the receiver from his ear.

"Paul, wait."

She'd finally said his first name. And without choking on it too. He put the phone to his ear again. "Yes."

"Thank you."

"Anytime, Hannah."

$\mathcal{H}$ annah ended the conversation with Paul, feeling nauseated at the surly to-do list staring at her. She didn't want to walk down the hall to tell Dr. Lehman that she needed more time off to deal with another family issue. Worse, she'd need to leave Kevin and Lissa again and tell Martin she was returning to Owl's Perch. They were supposed to celebrate Martin's birthday tomorrow night. But the thing she had most hoped to avoid—facing Daed and the church leaders again— loomed before her.

The quiet peacefulness of her surroundings inside the Amish birth- ing center had become a part of who she was. It was one of the beloved places in her new life. The respect she'd gained through her work and school caused her to no longer feel like the shaky, incompetent girl who'd landed in Winding Creek two and a half years ago. But this return to Owl's Perch to deal with her Daed and the church leaders had her nerves taut. Needing a bit of fatherly support, Hannah headed down the hallway to find Dr. Lehman. Over the years she'd grown close to her benefactor. She talked to him about everything, and he'd become like the dad she wished she'd had.

Grabbing the lab reports from her in-box as she passed by the mail center, she noted the empty waiting room before tapping on his door.

"Come on in, Hannah."

She opened the door. "How do you do that?"

He laughed. "If you don't know by now, I shouldn't tell you." His gray hair glistened under the electric lights, and his abundant wrinkles creased with each word spoken. "You have a style all your own, even how you tap on a door." He leaned back in his chair. "Did you get the birthing reports logged already?"

"Almost, but…I need time off again to go back to Pennsylvania."

He laid down his pen. "Issues in Owl's Perch?"

"Yes, I'll be back in time for my classes Monday night and will work here long hours next week to make up for everything."

He gestured toward the overstuffed chair in front of his desk. "We haven't really talked since you returned. How'd things go when you went home?"

She took a seat, glad for the friendship they shared. "Not great. I lost my temper too often, but Sarah's in a safe place to begin getting well."

"In your shoes I'm sure I'd have lost it with them too."

"I…I gave the most grief to Paul."

"Ah, well, we won't analyze why you targeted the somewhat innocent bystander." Dr. Lehman clasped his hands together on the desk in front of him. "Where is Sarah?"

"A place a bit similar to this, only it's set up for counseling instead of birthing babies. It's called the Better Path."

He rocked back in the office chair, looking both relaxed and deep in thought. "I think you're absolutely right to reconnect with your family. That was my hope back when I helped you find your aunt and made a way for you to stay in Ohio. Take whatever time you need, but you should let the Tuesday quilters know what's going on."

"I'm sure this will be the last time I'll need to leave unexpectedly."

"Maybe. It'll be best if you tell them your unpredictability with being here is rooted in the needs of your Amish family. So during Tuesday's quilting you'll cover this, okay?"

She stood. "Okay."

Hannah sat in the carpool line, waiting to drop Kevin off at school. Martin wasn't overly pleased with her returning to Owl's Perch, but after a small explosion, he had helped her pack. To make things easier this go-around, she asked to take Lissa with her. Martin didn't hesitate, saying Kevin was effortless enough for the nanny and him to deal with while Hannah was gone, but Lissa wasn't. Since she was only in kindergarten, she could get away with missing a day or two of school, and Hannah would be home by Monday night for her nursing classes.

While a teacher's aide helped Kevin get out, Hannah went around the car. The aide moved on to open the car door for the next vehicle in line. Hannah knelt in front of him, straightening his shirt. "I'll be back in a few days, so you keep Uncle Martin from staying up too late at night and eating too much junk food." She ruffled his hair. "Okay?"

"Aw, Hannah, it's Friday. Staying up too late, potato chips, and SpongeBob make the weekend fun."

Clearly his uncle had discussed this with him. She kissed Kevin's cheek. "A man weekend, huh?"

"Yeah." He put his little arms around her neck and hugged her. "Lissa ruined it last time, but I didn't say nothing to her about it."

"You're a good big brother." She winked at him and hurried back around to the driver's side. He waited on the sidewalk until she was behind the wheel, and then he waved and went into the school.

With Lissa prattling endlessly for hours about cartoons, friends at school, and the differences between the Amish and Englischer homes, Hannah drove to Owl's Perch. Her mind ran in a dozen directions, but she'd at least decided to see Mary first and deal with Sarah second. Hannah slowed the car as she came to the four-way stop near the Better Path. Why was her Daed's horse and buggy parked under a shade tree behind the building?

She cut into the driveway and put the car in Park. "Come on, sweetie." She unbuckled Lissa and carried her inside the home-turned-clinic. The receptionist glanced up from her computer. "Ms. Lawson, right?"

"Yes." Hannah set Lissa's feet on the floor, and the little girl headed straight for a group of toys in the corner near the desk. "I saw a horse and buggy out back. Do you know who's here?"

"Sarah's father and a couple of other men. They're in a meeting…" She pointed to a closed door.

Hannah took off.

"Wait, Ms. Lawson."

Hannah pointed at Lissa. "You make sure she stays near you." Without waiting for the woman to respond, she opened the door. Sarah sat at the table with Paul, a stranger, her Daed, the bishop, one preacher, and the deacon. Hannah's chest constricted. Why on earth had she trusted Paul?

"What's going on?"

Her father frowned. "Has it become your place to question every man?"

"Has it become your place to interrogate every daughter?"

Paul rose from his seat and walked to her. "Let's step outside, please."

She barely glanced his way. "Daed, surely you're not blind enough to allow this type of meeting again."

Paul tapped her shoulder. "Come on, let's step outside and talk."

Ignoring him, she stared straight into the eyes of the bishop. He wasn't nearly as intimidating as she'd remembered. "And I see no reason why Sarah's health is the church's business."

Paul wrapped his hand around her bicep. "Roger, put all conversations on hold until I return, please." He pulled her out of the room, closing the door behind them.

She jerked against his grip. "Let go of me."

He released her and held his hands up as if proving he'd done so.

She pointed her finger at him. "You gave me your word you wouldn't let this happen."

"Hannah, I'm there with her, ready to defend or end the meeting or whatever else is needed. Roger, an arson investigator, is in there with the results of what started the fires. Sarah was doing great. Let us finish."

"You're an idiot if you think you'll understand the undercurrent of what's being said or implied. I...I went through something similar, and it took me a year to get over those few hours."

"I'm really sorry that happened, but what's taking place today isn't about you."

A small, warm hand slid into Hannah's, and she looked down to see a large set of dark brown eyes staring up at her. Fear creased Lissa's features, and Hannah forced a smile.

She knelt in front of her, brushing wisps of hair from her face. "It's okay, Lissa. Just a little spat between adults."

Lissa frowned up at Paul. "You're not supposed to be mean when somebody comes to visit you."

At least she had her loyalties in place. In this little girl's eyes, regardless of Hannah's outburst, she couldn't possibly be wrong. Still, Hannah was being a horrible role model.

"I apologize." Paul tipped his head as if bowing to her wishes. "I'll be more careful. Halley, why don't you show Lissa the new colt in the neighbor's pasture?"

Halley rose and walked around her desk, held out her hand for Lissa's, and waited. Lissa watched Hannah intently.

She winked. "It's okay. I'll be right here when you get back. Go ahead."

Lissa released Hannah's hand and took Halley's.

They were barely out the front door when Hannah turned back to Paul. "This is just another time of Daed not doing his daughters right. And you said you wouldn't allow that meeting."

"The meeting was inevitable. When Roger had the arson report ready this morning and Sarah appeared able to cope with all of this after I talked to her about it, plans changed. This meeting is better taking place in a controlled environment."

"I expected you to hold your ground and not allow this, though I'm not sure why."

"Hannah,"—he rubbed his forehead—"I've done nothing wrong. Over the last two weeks, between counseling sessions and medication, Sarah has begun to realize the difference between what she actually did and what she dreamed of doing. Your Daed has been calm and careful with his words, surprisingly remaining on Sarah's side the whole time. But when Sarah is released, she will still move in with Luke and Mary for a while. I can help Sarah and maybe, on some level, even your Daed, but I can't make you trust me, and I can't have you undermining Sarah's progress."

Part of her saw the truth in his eyes, despite all her doubt and anger, and told her she was unjustly accusing Paul. Again. She plunked onto the couch and buried her head in her hands, trying to gather some composure. She heard Paul walk off, but her embarrassment for acting like a maniac didn't ease. At least the meeting could continue with him in there and be over all the quicker so she could see Mary and get out of Owl's Perch, the land of perpetual emotional overload.

The sound of ice against glass caught her attention, and she looked up.

"Here, this might help." Paul held a glass of water out to her.

She took it from him, sipped on the cool liquid, and set the glass on the end table.

Paul shifted. "The arson investigation confirmed that Sarah's innocent."

She looked up. "What? Are...are you absolutely positive?"

The lines across Paul's face eased into a familiar smile. "Yes. Roger is the father of a good friend of mine and has been an arson investigator for well over two decades. Since an insurance company isn't involved, he did the investigation as a favor. Even though the Bylers' barn burned quite awhile ago, Roger discovered the possible source to be cigarette butts. Then he poked around, asking questions until a few guilt-ridden teens confessed they'd been smoking in the loft just hours before the barn burned to the ground. He said that investigating the source of the fire for Matthew's shop was pretty quick and easy. Someone had stored gasoline in a leaky can in the attic and then left a lit kerosene lamp nearby. His conversations with David's family verified that David had put the gasoline up there earlier that day to keep it away from some children who'd come in with customers placing orders. Then he lit a kerosene lamp in the attic to search for something and must have forgotten to blow it out. A few hours later the explosion occurred."

"Paul…" He'd done a great job, but she couldn't make herself voice that. "I shouldn't have come in so angry and accusing. It's just when it comes to…well, it's easy to assume the worst."

"I understand."

"Don't you ever lose your temper?"

Paul sat on the oak coffee table in front of her. "Once." He interlaced his fingers and propped his elbows on his knees. "It cost me everything."

Unable to look him in the eye, she wanted to speak, to say something gracious and understanding, but nothing came to her.

He passed her the glass of water. "Look, about the meeting, with the tension between you and your Daed, I think it'd be best for Sarah if you let me handle this."

"Okay." She took a sip of water. "Every time I see you, I act like an uncontrolled idiot."

"Not long after you left, Luke and I agreed you'd return successful…and have quite an attitude for those of us who'd been wrong." He shrugged, a smile tugging at his lips. "We just didn't think you'd take years to return or have a husband when you did."

Hannah set the glass on the table, staring at him.

A husband?

A door jerked open, and her father stepped out. "Roger won't let anyone even speak to Sarah until you return."

Paul glanced that way. "I'll be there in just a minute." He angled his back to the door where her father stood. "I was able to talk with Mary for a minute last night. Privacy with you seemed paramount to her, and she asked if you'd come get her today as early as possible. If you need a place to talk, you're welcome to bring her here. No one in her community will think it odd for you two to be here since Sarah will be moving in with them when she leaves." He motioned to the landing. "Upstairs, first door to your left is an unused office. It has a couple of extra couches and stuff. Just put the Do Not Disturb sign on the doorknob, and no one will even knock. I'd better get back to the meeting."

Mute, she sank back onto the couch.

He thought she was married? She moaned, knowing she should have thought about this before now.

$\mathcal{M}$atthew paid Nate and climbed out of the truck. The white clapboard home with green shutters was a welcome sight. The aroma of burned wood drifted through the air, making him cringe. At least this time he knew why it'd been stealing his desire to rebuild.

The familiar sound of wet fabric being snapped in the air caused him to walk around the corner of the house. The morning sun glistened against Kathryn's white prayer Kapp, her light brown hair evident under it. Her tanned arms stretched to hang out the day's laundry, and awe at the woman in front of him caught him by surprise. She didn't even notice him, and yet her presence inside him was undeniable.

From the get-go, his relationship with Kathryn had been different from what he had with Elle. It was built on things they had in common, on workdays, and the kindness in her heart to offer him true friendship. He wondered just how much Joseph meant to her and if he had any chance of winning her over. Paying her to stay and help his family while he went off with a girl he'd once asked to marry him had probably been the stupidest thing he'd done since he'd met Elle Leggett.

Kathryn grabbed the wooden basket and fiddled with clothespins inside it while walking.

"Hi," Matthew said, causing her to stop right before she ran into him.

The seriousness across her face wasn't the welcome he'd hoped for, but what could he expect from her?

She gave a nod and redirected her route.

He stepped in front of her. "I don't even get a hello?"

"Did you enjoy your extra time in Baltimore? I hope so, because it caused me to break my word."

"I…I'm sorry. Whatever problems it caused, I'll straighten them out."

Kathryn passed him the laundry basket before reaching under her apron and pulling out a letter. "It's my resignation."

He shook his head. "I'll not take that."

She placed it in the basket and walked off. "It's done whether you read it or not."

"Kathryn, wait." He jogged that way and stood in front of her while she plowed on. "Just hear me out. I spent days in a fog, so confused I didn't care about keeping my word to return."

"You had no right to simply call and leave a message that you weren't returning on time."

"Kathryn,"—Matthew grabbed the letter and dropped the basket onto the ground—"give me another chance. I'm here to stay, to rebuild. I made decisions while there, good ones."

She shielded her eyes from the sunlight and stared at him. "Elle is behind you in this plan of rebuilding?"

Matthew shrugged. "I finished endin' things with her. We don't even make good friends. How could we make a good marriage?" He shifted, using his body to shield her from the sun. "She may or may not ever join the faith. I wish her well, but whatever she chooses, I'm glad it's over—in spite of the promise I once gave her."

Kathryn propped her hands on her hips, staring at him. "If you ever tell me one thing and then do another, I'll…"

Curious, Matthew taunted, "You'll what?"

The smile across her face said she'd moved from frustration to teasing. "I'll tell your Mamm."

Matthew chuckled and flexed his muscle. "And what's she going to do about it?"

She laughed. "Daed wants me home and…and Joseph."

At twenty-two she was certainly old enough not to do as her father wanted, but she wouldn't. "Don't you think your Daed will give ya more time if I talk to him?"

She crossed her arms, looking like she might be giving weight to his question.

Still holding the letter, Matthew grabbed the laundry basket. "I guess the first question I should have asked is, are you willing to stay?"

Even if it causes problems with you and Joseph?

But he wouldn't voice that last part. Why invite trouble?

She looked to where the shops had stood. Burned framing and caved-in roofs. "Getting a chance to see E and L come back to life? Ya, I'm willing to let *you* talk to my Daed about that."

Matthew chuckled. "He is a reasonable man, right?"

"No doubt."

"So what is his push to get ya back home lately?"

"I'm not sure, except maybe Joseph is putting pressure on him. My Daed has said from the beginning that he didn't want me staying here so long that I might be tempted to put down roots in a community this far from home."

"I guess I can understand that."

"I'd rather find a way to juggle both, being here to help with E and L when needed and going home for a few days or so whenever I'm not needed. It's expensive hiring a driver to take me the two hours to home and then drive back. But there's no kind of job at home for me that comes close to the kind of satisfaction I get out of running your office."

"I'll talk with your Daed."

"I went through the files while you were gone. Lots of the papers were partially burned, but I was able to figure out who'd done the ordering. I placed a bunch of calls and have a large stack of orders for you."

"Ya figured out who made the orders from what was left of the forms?"

"That, and I remembered some of the orders, and the caller ID on the phone still worked, even after the fire. I was able to retrieve over thirty numbers and call people back to take their orders again."

"And what if I'd not chosen to rebuild?"

"Then I'd have passed the orders on to a place in Indiana. We can't leave people stranded. It's just not right. And speaking of not right, you owe me no promises, ever, but if you give your word, you'd better keep it."

"Or you'll tell Mamm."

Amusement danced across her face. "You got a better threat?"

"Yeah, but I'm not tellin' what it is."

She laughed and took the letter from him and ripped it in two before shoving it into her hidden pocket. Seriousness replaced her smile. "I'm sorry for the added grief you must feel, but I've had concerns about your happiness with Elle."

"But you said you were praying for us."

"Praying the best for you two. Before vows, it's not a given that what's best is marriage."

Her words circled through his mind, and Matthew was hopeful that maybe Joseph wasn't the right man for Kathryn either.

Matthew grabbed the basket, and they walked toward the house. "We have work to do and loss to cope with, but any sadness over things not working out with Elle took place long ago."

From across the kitchen table, Hannah gazed into Mary's eyes, wishing they were alone. With no way to know what was on her mind and no way of finding out until they went somewhere private, Hannah only knew the same thing she came here knowing—Mary had a secret, and she was scared. Mammi Annie sat in the living room, keeping a vigilant ear for every word spoken.

Hannah sipped her coffee. She'd finally been allowed inside someone's home, and this was how the welcome played out? The rocking chair in the corner of the room creaked as Lissa swayed it back and forth while munching on a sandwich. The clock ticked on. It amazed Hannah how the sounds stood out in an Amish home. With no electric buzz from automatic washers, dryers, or dishwashers and certainly no televisions, radios, or entertainment centers, each home carried a peacefulness that Hannah loved—in spite of the stoic restraints that had to be navigated. But at nearly three in the afternoon, they needed to do something.

"We could go for a ride, but I get the feeling whatever is going on, we can't talk with a little one in the car." Her muted tones were quieter than the old timepiece ticking in the living room. Hannah wasn't going to chance Lissa hearing something she could repeat to Sarah. Between Sarah's emotional issues about babies and her ability to share things she shouldn't, it could stir up a lot of trouble for Mary.

Mary's half smile quivered, making dozens of tiny dimples in her chin. "We have to do something."

The only thing Hannah knew to do was return to the Better Path. Although a bit unsure what they could do with Lissa while they talked openly, it appeared to be their best chance of communicating. Since Mammi Annie was listening, they couldn't even whisper without the possibility of being heard.

If Mammi Annie were a little friendlier, Hannah might consider leaving Lissa with her while Mary and she went for a walk. But she had concerns about what Mammie Annie might ask and how Lissa might answer. Whatever tattered reputation Hannah had within Owl's Perch, she needed to guard it for Sarah's and Mary's sake.

"Come on. It's time we went to the Better Path. You need to talk to Paul about Sarah's release, right?"

Mary glanced into the living room and rose. Hannah lifted Lissa into her arms, and the three left the Yoder place. As they drove down the narrow, paved roads, Mary kept rubbing her stomach.

"Does it hurt?" Hannah asked.

"No. I had a few sharp pains hit yesterday. That's when I called you. Then they went away."

"What type of pain?"

"The kind that hurts. What type of question is that?"

Hannah laughed. "A vague one, I guess. Where was the pain?"

"Right here." Mary rubbed her right side near the upper part of her hip bone.

"How deep inside your body did it feel—just topical, like the skin being stretched, or deeper, like a muscle being pulled, or really deep, like an ache in the bone?"

Hannah listened carefully as Mary answered each question, knowing Dr. Lehman would want a complete report when she called him for his opinion. As the Better Path came into view, there were no signs of Daed and the church leaders. Hannah and Mary went inside with Lissa right beside them.

Maybe the argument with Paul had upset Lissa more than Hannah realized, because she clung to Hannah's dress as they entered the building. Not one to be clingy very often, Lissa would be comfortable with her surroundings in a few minutes, but Hannah lifted the little girl into her arms. The conversation with Mary would just have to remain light until Lissa felt like playing at the tire swing or something.

They stepped inside the open space that included a large foyer, living room, and kitchen, with a lot of office doors off to the sides and a stairway that led to more offices. Five people, including Paul, were sitting in the kitchen. A freshly cut cake sat on the table, and they each had a plate with a slice. The soft chatter and laughs ended as everyone's eyes moved to Mary and Hannah. Obviously they were sharing a special celebration break of some kind, but this wasn't the quiet entrance into the place Hannah had banked on.

Paul excused himself and stood. "Hannah, Mary, right this way." He left his half-eaten piece of cake and walked up the steps, leading them. Once on the landing, he opened a door. "If you use my office, everyone will think Mary's here to read over things for Sarah's release. Since her name's been cleared concerning the fires and everything between her and the community is in good order, she'll be released tomorrow, even though it's a Saturday."

Hannah, Mary, and Lissa stepped inside.

He glanced at his watch. "I won't need my office for at least another hour." He looked to Lissa. "You hungry?"

Lissa shrugged, but Hannah knew she was, even though she'd had a sandwich at Mary's place. The tiny girl could outeat the rest of the family and looked like she never ate anything.

Paul slid one hand into his pant pocket. "I bet you could make us both a peanut butter and jelly sandwich."

Her eyes lit up. "Are you hungry too?"

Paul nodded. "And Halley brought a homemade cake."

Lissa stared up at Hannah, silently begging for Paul's plan to be okay with her. Paul had nailed a way to get Lissa to leave Hannah's side. "Go ahead."

He glanced to Hannah as he was closing the door. She mouthed a "thank you," and he nodded.

Mary checked the door to make sure it was secure and then leaned against it. Tears welled and began running down her face.

"What's going on?"

Wiping her tears, she gazed into Hannah's eyes. "I've made a huge mistake. If you can't help me…"

"I'm here to do anything I can." She took Mary by the shoulders, giving a gentle squeeze before lowering her hands to her side. "Tell me what's going on."

"While I was engaged to Luke, the doctor told me not to marry, not to do anything that might cause me to get pregnant. I didn't tell Luke, and…" She slid her hand over her protruding stomach. "I didn't want to lose him…"

Hannah knew this story all too well, not wanting to lose someone and not telling them the truth. "What did the doctor say was the specific reason for not getting pregnant?"

"He said the baby would be fine but labor and delivery could be really dangerous."

"Mary, how could you do this?"

"At first I thought I was choosing to trust God with the marriage bed." Her shoulders slumped, and she shook her head. "But you have no room to be mad at me. You hid your pregnancy from Paul."

"Good grief, have you looked at my life?"

"But this is different, and I thought everything would work out. Please, we've got to find answers. I'm so scared for the baby, and Luke, and me."

Unwilling to share the fullness of her displeasure, Hannah nodded. "Are you having any other symptoms—spotting or anything?"

"No."

"Any tightening of your stomach muscles?"

"No."

"Okay, we'll start with a quick exam of your vitals. I need my medical bag out of the car. We've got to find you a local obstetrician, which probably won't be easy at this point in your pregnancy."

"I...I won't see just any doctor. That's how I got into this fix in the first place. They're pushy and bossy and look down on the Amish. You know they do."

"Not all of them, only a few." Hannah shook her head. "I don't even have a two-year-degree nursing license. If you think I'm the answer, you're wrong."

"Those doctors can't be trusted now any more than when my mother refused to see them. Why, they just walk in, give orders, and you'll do it their way, or you can take the highway." She shook her head. "I'm really scared, Hannah, but for years I've heard about a slew of bad doctors working with Amish because we don't sue, and it sounds safer to choose the highway every time."

The absolute stubbornness was way too familiar to Hannah. No wonder they had bonded so well as children. They were like two mules in full agreement against all reason. And the fruit of it grieved her for both of them. "Mary, you're tying my hands here, and the safety of you and the baby are at risk."

"I thought..." She moved to a chair and took a seat. "Don't you personally know a doctor around here that we could trust?"

"No, but maybe..." Hannah knelt in front of her. "Would you trust Dr. Lehman to examine you and then help us find a physician in the area? I think he'd know someone."

"Would he do that?"

"He literally saved my life a few days after I landed in Ohio. He's trustworthy, but it's asking a lot for him to come here."

Mary stood, grabbed the phone on Paul's desk from its cradle, and held it toward Hannah. "Please?"

She took the phone and set it back in place. How long would Mary have hidden this secret if Hannah hadn't come back to Owl's Perch? "After we get some medical facts about what's going on, you have to tell Luke everything."

Mary backed up. "I can't."

"I won't come back here and have a part in dishonesty again."

" 'Dishonesty' is an awful harsh word."

"What you've done is harsh. I'm not sure you get that."

Mary pursed her lips, and Hannah feared if she wasn't careful, Mary would stonewall her too. Wishing she could see the truth of what she'd done, Hannah put her hand against Mary's cheek. "Are you more concerned about falling off that pedestal Luke has you on than doing what's right?"

"He's going to be so mad at me."

"Uh, yeah." Hannah immediately regretted the sarcastic tone. "But you'd be mad at him too if he'd kept such a thing from you. And the longer he kept the secret, the angrier you'd be when you found out."

Her friend stared off to the side before nodding. "Okay, I'll tell him everything after we have word from the doctor."

n the quiet of her hotel room, with Lissa asleep in the bed next to hers, Hannah ended the phone call with Dr. Lehman. Sleep had been impossible, but his opinion was in line with Hannah's thoughts—Mary's pains were due to pressure and stress on the round ligaments. He was off Monday and said it was time for another visit to Lancaster to see his mom anyway, so he didn't mind going the forty miles out of the way to see Mary. He said he was actually glad for the invitation since he'd been wanting to see Hannah's Owl's Perch and meet some of the people from her past.

His willingness to always support her still managed to catch her by surprise. She sat back against the pillows, the Bible in her lap still open. Her damp hair continued to air dry from the shower she'd taken a couple of hours ago. In all the time she'd known him, Dr. Lehman had never let her down. He constantly trained her to take on more responsibilities at his clinic as a nurse, and sometimes he seemed to expect more from her than from his nurses with four-year degrees, but in many ways he was more like a dad to her than her own father.

Lissa sat up, rubbing her eyes. Without a word spoken, she crawled into the bed with Hannah and snuggled. So grateful for the love Kevin and Lissa brought into her life, Hannah stroked the little girl's hair and kissed her head. "How are you this morning?"

"Hungry."

Hannah rubbed her small back, enjoying the few minutes of having a child in her arms. "Well, then we'll need to take care of that first thing, won't we?" Hannah closed the Bible.

Lissa put her hand on it. "What it'd say this morning?"

"That if someone sins against me and asks for forgiveness, I'm to give it to them."

"Did someone sinned against you?"

Hannah placed her hand on Lissa's head. "I thought they did, and I've not been nice to them, but now I'm not so sure they did what I thought."

"You were mad at somebody who didn't do nothing wrong?"

Hannah slid out of bed, wishing she'd controlled herself rather than screamed at Paul. "Seems so."

"You gotta ask for forgiveness now?"

That uncomfortable idea made Hannah's insides shiver. "Right now I'm going to help you get dressed, and then we'll get you some breakfast."

After Lissa ate fruit, yogurt, half a bagel, and even some cereal at the continental breakfast the hotel provided, they went to the car and headed for Mary's. Sarah should have been released from the Better Path about an hour ago and should be at Luke and Mary's by now. Hannah needed to tell Mary what Dr. Lehman had said, and then she wanted to spend as much time with Sarah this weekend as possible, because when Hannah left this time, she hoped not to return for several months.

The scenery changed from city life to Amish country as Hannah drove out of the Harrisburg area and into Owl's Perch. As she traveled on, Gram's home came into view. She'd once loved this place above all others. Taking note of how beautifully the house and acreage were kept, she spotted Paul mending a fence.

Instead of stopping, she pressed the accelerator.

She didn't owe him an apology. He owed her one.

Her conscience pricked, making her skin tingle like dull pins were poking her. He'd given an apology, several actually, and his words couldn't have seemed more sincere. She'd hidden things from him and then blamed him when he reacted. She clicked her tongue and huffed.

Lissa mimicked her and giggled. Hannah looked in the child-view mirror. Lissa's innocent smile brought a landslide of conviction. What advice would she give to Lissa if she acted as Hannah had—regardless of how justified the reaction may have felt?

Notching the blinker into place, Hannah slowed the vehicle, turned around in a stranger's driveway, and headed back to Gram's. "Lissa, I need to speak to Paul for a minute, okay?"

"Think he needs another sandwich?"

"No, but there's a bridge over a small creek near where he's fixing a fence. You can play on that and toss pebbles into the water while I speak to him for a minute, okay?"

Her little face lit up. "A covered bridge?"

"Well, it's surrounded by trees."

Her head bobbed up and down as if she'd just been given an extravagant new toy. Hannah pulled into Gram's driveway, hoping Dorcas wasn't here today. In the side yard, not far from the house, Paul wrestled with a fence post.

She got out of the car and helped Lissa unbuckle, and they walked across the yard. With each step, Hannah questioned herself. Memories of their past caught her. Of course they did. What had she been thinking to come here? Except for a few extremely short visits, she'd never seen him anywhere but here. This was where they first met. Where they worked together. Where they became friends. Where she'd fallen in—

Stop it, Hannah.

But the memories didn't stop. A weird feeling crept over her when she caught a glimpse of the bridge through the turning shadows of its surrounding trees. As if in those woods she could again see Paul standing in front of her—broad shoulders, hair the color of ripe hay, blue eyes that used to haunt her dreams.

Unable to dismiss the recollections, she couldn't take another step. Deciding this was a really bad idea and she needed to leave before she was noticed, she reached for Lissa's hand. "Come on, Lis—"

Lissa dodged Hannah's grasp. "Hey," she hollered in Paul's direction.

Paul looked up.

He stood straight and pulled the rawhide work gloves off his hands before wiping his brow. The early October air had a nip, and Hannah and Lissa had on thick cardigan sweaters, but Paul appeared to have beads of sweat on his face.

Lissa came to a halt right in front of him. "You need some help?"

"Well, good morning, Lissa." Paul lifted his eyes to Hannah, looking quizzical.

She drew a shallow breath, unable to get a deep one. "I...we...need to talk."

"Sure. We never had a chance to discuss Sarah's progress or some of the suggestions I have that might help her."

Hannah knew professional distancing when she heard it. "This isn't about Sarah. I was hoping to cover some things that...," She lowered her eyes to Lissa. "Look right through those trees." Kneeling, Hannah pointed at the bridge. "Do you see it?"

Lissa nodded.

"You can gather some pebbles and drop them into the water, but you can't go down to the water's edge, okay?"

Lissa turned and squeezed her neck, almost knocking her over with her enthusiasm, and took off running into the wooded area.

Hannah's splayed hand against the ground kept her from losing her balance altogether. Paul offered his hand, and she took it.

After helping her stand, he motioned toward the house. "Give me just a minute, and I'll get us a couple of chairs from the backyard."

Hannah stood where she could see Lissa, who was singing joyously to the creek and trees. A minute later Paul put two resin chairs near her. A sense of dishonor covered her, and she was too antsy to sit.

It was time to say her piece and leave. That sounded matter-of-fact enough, but her head spun, and her insides trembled. Worse, she could feel the edge of tears sting her eyes, which really angered her, but she had to get this over with. "It was never my intention to deceive you,

Paul. Never. But it did turn out that way. Much of what I'm going to say you've pieced together already, but I need to say it anyway, okay?"

Standing just a few feet from her, he stared across the huge pasture behind Gram's place to the dirt road. "I understand. I'm sure it will help both of us."

Lissa's voice rang through the air, singing. Feeling the weight of the two worlds in which she lived, the one that had reason to sing and the one that continued to cause sadness, Hannah sat.

She tried to swallow but couldn't. "The day you asked me to marry you, while walking home on the dirt road, a man about your age pulled up beside me, stopped his car, and asked for directions. It didn't take long to realize I needed to get out of there, but when I tried to run…" She closed her eyes, trying desperately not to relive those few minutes. "That's when I got the scars on the palms of my hands, the ones you noticed the next time we saw each other a couple of months later. Remember?"

"Yes." His gentle voice was barely audible.

"Afterward…he tried to run over me with his car, but somehow I avoided it and ran home." Hannah stared at the ground, remembering how arriving home had only added to her trouble. "I wanted to call you, wanted you to make sense of it and say we still had a future…" Tears eased down her cheeks. "Even though they didn't know about you, Mamm and Daed said that no one would ever want to marry me if word of the attack got out and that I shouldn't tell anyone—not even my own siblings." She raised her eyes, seeing the grief etched on Paul's face. "And that's when I made the choice to hide the rape. I couldn't even say the word until…" She let the sentence drop. "The weeks that followed were all but unbearable. You didn't write. I wasn't allowed to return to Gram's. And I wondered if you'd really asked me to marry you. Now I know I was dealing with shock, then posttraumatic shock, and depression."

As he moved his gaze to hers, she saw his eyes were rimmed with tears as well.

He set the empty chair directly across from her and took a seat. "I know we talked of this before, but I did write. I promise. The letter never arrived at Gram's, and then she began feeling that it was wrong to allow us to communicate through her mailbox when your Daed didn't know about me. There I was at school, longing to be in Owl's Perch with you…as if some part of me knew you needed me, but I made myself stay focused on our future."

Understanding that she wasn't the only one with a list of what should have been done, she began to see the person she'd once believed him to be. One who hadn't lied or stolen or even abandoned her, one who'd made a mistake and paid dearly for it. "I held on to one hope. It was the only thing that got me through everything else—that you wouldn't find out and I wouldn't lose you. But then, in late November, I learned I was pregnant."

"Hannah," Lissa called from the edge of the wood, "can I get a leaf and drop it into the water?"

A faint laugh escaped Hannah. "Yes, Lissa, you can."

He intertwined his fingers, propped his forearms on his knees, leaned in, and whispered, "November?"

She nodded. "Between a lack of knowledge, denial, the depression, and then Mary nearly dying in that buggy accident, I just didn't really put it all together. It wasn't until after our last day to catch a visit that I learned I was pregnant."

Paul straightened his interlocked fingers, staring at them. "The day before Thanksgiving."

"Yes. We hadn't seen each other in so long. My parents didn't know why I wanted to go to Gram's, but they knew I wanted it bad enough to do whatever it took to get here. They insisted I take a home pregnancy test. I took it and immediately left to come here. I spent that day with you, so sure I wouldn't be pregnant, so convinced God wouldn't let that happen because it'd ruin everything. You were right. I was naive.

I caused a lot of the rumors you heard, but I never meant to flirt with anyone."

Paul's fingertips came within inches of hers before he pulled them back. "I know you were innocent, Hannah. My jealousy and confusion didn't last but a few days. How could my fiancée, who wouldn't even kiss me until months after we'd been engaged, be anything but innocent?"

"I wasn't guiltless. I was selfish, wanting to hide the truth of being pregnant, and it may have cost Rachel her life. The night you came to Mary's to talk to me? I didn't know it then, but later I realized I was already in labor."

Paul's intense gaze tightened. "I thought my running out on you might have caused you to go into premature labor."

Hannah's breath caught. What had she done to him? "No, I'd taken something for pain and was in bed when you arrived at Mammi Annie's. Remember?"

He nodded.

She ran her fingers through the side of her hair, pushing some fallen wisps back into place. For the first time she wondered what he thought of her Englischer look. He was the only one who hadn't shown any disapproval. "I met with the church leaders the next morning. I needed them to believe me about the rape, or I wouldn't be allowed to live with anyone within the community. They doubted me, and the bishop insisted I stay a night alone so I could rethink my story. I gave birth that night." Hannah paused and willed herself to finish. "Matthew built a coffin, and we buried her. Daed wouldn't let me come home. Mary's parents said I couldn't stay with them any longer. I...I didn't think anyone would take me." She closed her eyes, taking a moment to gather fresh strength. "When I called the bank, I learned that all the money had been removed from our account. I...I thought you'd taken it."

"If we just could have talked..."

She shifted. "At that time everything was beyond talking about for me. I couldn't voice to anyone what had happened. Besides, when I did manage to call your apartment, a girl answered, so with all those events combined, I convinced myself all hopes of us were gone, and I boarded the train."

The anguish expressed on his face said more than words. "I roomed with three other guys, who always had girls around, but I never received any message that you'd called. And I never had anything to do with those girls. The night you stayed in Harrisburg with Naomi and Matthew, I came looking for you, even borrowed a friend's cell and had people stationed to receive a call from you here, at my parents', and at my apartment."

Her gaze fixed on Paul, and she was unable to break it. The night before boarding the train she'd called his apartment. A girl answered, promising to give him the message. He never called her back. Nine months after leaving, she'd tried again to reach him by calling here to Gram's home. The same young woman had answered the phone, probably someone from his family or friends. Possibly Dorcas.

Hannah wouldn't point fingers or lay blame. Still, she was getting an uneasy feeling that Paul had never received either message. She forced a smile. Whoever she spoke to may have lied, but Hannah was the one who went into hiding. She was the one who didn't push harder to reach him, only calling twice in nine months and then never calling again.

She inhaled deeply, sensing her burden becoming lighter in spite of the truth she was learning. "The thing is, even if we'd talked before I left, I needed to go. Luke questioned me about leaving, saying I hadn't given you much of a chance to adjust to the shocking news. But, Paul,"—she tilted her head, making sure he was looking right at her— "I needed out of Owl's Perch, and even if we'd connected before I boarded that train and you still thought you wanted me, I'd have felt like a charity case, not a cherished fiancée or wife. Can you understand that?"

He nodded. "I knew you needed time. I never wanted to take that from you, but I wanted you to know I believed you and I hadn't taken the money and I was there if you needed me."

But Hannah knew if she'd stayed or even returned soon, she'd have made a mess of his life. His parents and community would not have accepted her, not with the reputation she carried—the scarlet letter she still wore in the eyes of most. And she would never have been able to make herself believe he actually loved her. At that time her self-esteem was gone, her spirit grievously wounded.

She rose. "The good news is that because I left, I met my aunt, a woman I'll always be better for having known. She helped me find myself and a career. She placed seeds in me, assuring me that even a woman has the right to chase her own dream. She modeled forgiveness and hope. I don't regret that time."

Paul straightened his back, clearly relaxing a bit. "I...I always thought you'd return healed and successful."

She scoffed. "Instead, I returned outspoken and difficult."

A whispery laugh eased the rest of the concern lines across his forehead. "Well, I'd braced myself for that too."

They shared a laugh, which brought an odd sense of wholeness to her. As if she hadn't fully moved on until she found peace with others whose lives were ripped apart too.

"Hannah." Lissa sang her name.

"Yes?"

"Can I throw a stick in the water?"

"Yes, and you have about five minutes, okay?"

"Okay."

Being at Gram's with Paul and Lissa caused a sense of wonder at life to dance around her, asking to be let inside.

Hannah drew a deep breath, able to finish with more strength than she'd begun with. "At the end I thought I was losing my mind, but with each little town the train stopped at and then left behind, hope began to stir. I seemed to leave behind more of that overwhelming powerlessness, and I could finally breathe again."

"You wrote me the 'nevertheless' letter."

She nodded. "I wanted to lift some of your burden the way leaving freed me, but then…" She resented that he seemed to have moved on and found someone else within no time of walking out on her. She swallowed hard. "But later on, I began to harbor resentment, blaming you for things that weren't your fault. I'm sorry."

He put one hand on her shoulder, waiting for her to look at him. "You're forgiven."

She shifted her body weight, wishing she'd covered everything and could just go. "In spite of how I've acted, I'm content and not given to bouts of anger. But one of the reasons I came by today is because I refuse to hide things again."

Paul shook his head. "I…I don't understand."

"Within weeks of landing in Ohio, I changed my last name to Lawson."

Lines creased his brow. "That's not your married name?"

She shook her head. "I…I'm not married."

He pointed at her left hand. "But you're engaged?"

With her right hand, Hannah wrapped her fingers around the ring on her left hand, feeling the stones—a diamond and ruby—in her honorary mother's gift. "He's asked, but…"

He stood, turning his back to her.

Hannah blinked, feeling a bit startled. "I haven't said yes, but I love him. We have Kevin and Lissa, and we make a good family."

Paul turned, his eyes mirroring things she'd never be privy to. "She's a sweet girl."

"Yeah, she and Kevin seem to be unusually great children." Hannah drew a cleansing breath. It was over. She'd done what she came to do, and now it was time to leave and pick back up with her life. "Lissa, it's time to go."

On the bridge, through the wooded area, Lissa crossed her arms. "Aw, not now."

"Lissa Ann Palmer."

The little girl hurried off the bridge. "I'm coming." She left the edge of the wood, wiping her dirty hands down her sweater. "Don't nobody start talking about taking my desserts away."

Paul glanced at Hannah. "Hannah," he chided teasingly.

She shrugged. "I need leverage. And you know how she responds to food."

Paul agreed and slid his hands into his pockets. "I'm glad Sarah called you home. Wouldn't prevent one outburst you've had to finally get to this point."

Lissa sang while she ran right past them and toward the car.

Paul walked beside Hannah. "How are things with Mary?"

"I talked to her last night. I think she'll be fine, but there are some steps that need to be taken to be certain."

"I'm sure she's better off just having you to talk to."

Hannah leaned against her car, somewhat taken aback at the corner they'd turned. Paul was much the same as he'd been since she'd arrived, but the resentment she'd let simmer for so long was gone, leaving calmness in its place. "I'm thankful to have her in my life again too, but friendship won't be enough for what's going on with her." She paused, trying to gauge how much to share. "Paul, I may need your help."

"Sure. Anytime. What do you need from me?"

Suddenly feeling vulnerable again, Hannah opened her car door. "I...I'll let you know later...by phone...or I may get Dr. Lehman to contact you."

he Saturday afternoon sun extended across Paul's stove as he stared at the boiling water in the pot. The bubbles, big and small, worked their way to the top and burst, releasing steam. He'd forgotten why he put the water on to heat. Macaroni and cheese, maybe? He wasn't hungry anyway. Confusion covered his thoughts like a pounding headache as his heart thumped like mad.

Hannah wasn't married. Or engaged.

By the time she'd returned three weeks ago, he was relieved to realize he was no longer absolutely in love with her. But since then...well, he'd come to know her again. She was different, quicker to share her feelings, even her most negative ones. She was harder. Yet, everything that had attracted him to her in the first place—her strength, determination, intelligence—and even her newfound and unshakable confidence drew him.

Until this morning when she said she wasn't married, he'd refused to acknowledge the slightest attraction he still had for her, let alone admit to the growing magnetic pull that seemed powerful enough to drag him to her door. But he'd kept even his most private thoughts in check, honoring the vows he'd thought she'd taken.

Of course, she did say she loved Martin. And Paul was supposed to be committed to seeing only Dorcas, although they hadn't talked about that—exactly.

Hannah knew the truth now about his coming back for her and not taking the money and not having any other girls.

He turned off the stove. No wonder she'd stocked up so many negative emotions against him. They could work through those things now, couldn't they? A vision of Lissa popped into his head. Hannah's new family meant life and joy to her. Any attempt to win her back would be treason to the life she'd built.

Still, his desire packed a hurricane force. She'd finally returned, and she wasn't married. If she loved the guy so much, why hadn't she said yes to his proposal?

Was she here to simply give them both closure? Maybe that's all they needed and his other emotions were a reaction to the full realization that she was home, unmarried, and now knew things he'd waited years to tell her. Emotions were a tricky thing. Dead on target some of the time and bold-faced liars at other times.

The way she dressed, who she'd become was no longer Plain, not that he had a clue what that did or didn't mean to him. She was here and not married; that's really all he knew. And that desire burned through him like lava, seemingly destroying all other hopes for his future in its path.

The quiet jingle of his phone interrupted his thoughts, and he picked up the receiver. "Paul Waddell."

"Paul, this is Dr. Jeff Lehman. Do you have a few minutes?"

"Sure. What can I do for you?"

"It seems I need a place to see Mary Lapp. Hannah Lawson recommended that I give you a call since the Better Path may have the facilities I need to give an examination."

"I'd need to take the request to the board, but I have to tell you, as a mental health facility, we don't have an exam room. We do have a lab, but the tech only works part-time, and even then a lot of the blood work has to be sent out. We usually get the results within a few days."

"I travel between clinics. Most of what I need I take with me. The real problem is I'm not licensed in Pennsylvania, which doesn't matter as far as dealing with the Amish community, but it might matter for the licensing and rules of your clinic."

"I'll be sure to bring that up at the meeting. The clinic doesn't have a board-certified medical doctor on staff, but we do have one we can use as an umbrella in certain circumstances, so we may be able to avoid any standards issues through that venue. Bob Marvin is the owner and CEO of the place. He'll have the answers you need, but he's out of town this weekend and left word that he's unavailable."

"I'm off Monday and was planning to go to Lancaster to visit relatives. I'd hoped to swing by Owl's Perch on my way. Any chance you can have an answer for me sometime Monday morning?"

"That shouldn't be a problem."

"Unless we don't get the go-ahead, I'll be there that afternoon, because the sooner this is handled, the quicker Hannah can return to her school schedule."

Paul grabbed a pen and paper off the refrigerator. "I'm sure Hannah's very relieved you're able to help."

"She means a lot to me, and I'm glad to do what I can. I'll give you my number, and you let me know as soon as you have an answer."

"I'm ready." He jotted down the info and ended the call, wondering exactly how Hannah came to know the doctor.

He slid the paper into his pocket. Wishing he hadn't canceled hiking plans with Marcus, Ryan, and Taylor, he moved to his aquarium and fed the fish. Diversion with his friends would be nice about now, especially since focusing long enough to read anything seemed impossible.

Couldn't concentrate. Couldn't eat. Couldn't sleep. Yep, the confusion of Hannah was back in his life, sort of. He moved to the couch and stared at the fish tank. The sun went down, and darkness filled the room, except for the light in the aquarium.

A thunderous knock jolted him.

He opened his front door to find his dad and Dorcas on the stoop. She looked frail and upset.

"What's wrong?" He took a step back, inviting them in.

His dad put his hand on Dorcas's back and escorted her in. "I knocked several times. Did you not hear me?"

Paul shook his head. "I wasn't expecting anyone."

His dad studied him quizzically. "I was on my way to visit Mom. Dorcas asked if I'd drop her by your place."

Dorcas's face was pale.

"You okay?"

She shrugged.

His father placed his large hand on Paul's arm and gave it a friendly squeeze. "I need to go. Your Gram's expecting me. You want to take Dorcas home later, or you want me to come back by here?"

"I'll see that she gets home. Thanks, Dad."

He closed the door behind his dad and turned to Dorcas. He figured she'd gotten wind of how much contact he was having with Hannah. Maybe even Gram told her Hannah came by her place to see him yesterday, but he wasn't sure what to tell Dorcas. "What's wrong?"

She held up a white envelope. "I…I got this in the mail today." She burst into tears and fell against his chest. "What's wrong with me?"

Paul put his arms around her. After bouts of muscle weakness and severe skin sensitivity for nearly two years, she had gone through a battery of tests a few weeks ago. "You received the results?"

She nodded as the sobs came harder.

He patted her back, hating what she was going through. "It's okay, Dorcas. Whatever is going on, your family and mine will help you find answers."

She cried and talked for hours before sleep took over. He eased from the couch beside her, shifted her legs onto the cushions, and placed a blanket over her. She had spent two and half years waiting for him to get over Hannah. She'd been by him through every step of the ordeal as he pined for Hannah.

Now she needed him—desperately.

From his easy chair Paul stared at the woman asleep on his couch, willing his heart to connect with her. He couldn't stand the idea of leaving someone in overwhelming circumstances again. Hannah had someone. Dorcas had him.

He picked up the crisp, typewritten letter from the coffee table. Unfolding it, he leaned back in the chair. A soft stream of light from the hallway crossed the page. Every result had come back negative, which would be good news except the symptoms she dealt with gave her no relief—the joint pain, the skin sensitivity, the inability to think clearly or remember from one minute to the next.

Needing to be there for her, he tried to put lingering thoughts for Hannah into perspective.

Dorcas opened her eyes.

Paul slid the letter between the cushion and the arm of the chair. "Hi. How are you feeling?"

She sat up. "A bit foolish for coming here and crying in your arms until I fell asleep."

"It's not a problem. You were upset, and you should have come here."

Dorcas's eyes held fast to him. "What time is it?"

"About two a.m."

She winced as she tried to sit up.

Paul went to her and extended his hand. "I called your parents so they wouldn't worry. They wish you'd told them what was going on." He helped her stand. "You steady?" The pain across her face twisted knots inside him.

She nodded and wrapped her hands around his arm.

He patted her hand. "How about if I fix you some food or some hot tea before I take you home?"

She put her arms around him. "I need you, Paul."

He rested his head on hers. "And I'll be right here for you like you've been for me, okay?"

*M*atthew turned off the shower, feeling sore, but with more energy than he'd had in a really long time. The ache for David was nonstop, but he was able to grieve and keep moving. That was a welcome improvement. He and Luke had two weeks of hard work ahead of them getting the old buildings torn down. He dreaded facing that, seeing in his mind's eye the day of the fire, the day David died, over and over again as they worked, but it had to be done. They'd begin tomorrow. Today was a church Sunday, and he hoped it'd bring him strength to face the next two weeks.

An aroma of coffee hung in the air as he finished shaving. By the time he slid into his Sunday suit, the smell of scrapple and cinnamon rolls filtered through the upstairs. He stepped into the hallway, almost bumping into his mother as she staggered out of her bedroom.

"Mamm, aren't ya goin' to church today?"

Tears rolled down her cheeks. *"Ich kann net."*

"Mamm, you can." He kissed her forehead. "We need you. Daed's lonely for you. Right now it's like he's lost a son and a wife. Peter still needs his Mamm. He's just a kid, but growing up so fast. And Kathryn shouldn't be tryin' to run the house while helping me rebuild the business."

"I wish I'd been a better Mamm for my sweet David." She brushed tears off her face. "I want another chance."

Guilt. That hopeless, life-choking guilt.

He hated it.

"Kumm." He put his arm around her shoulders. "Please."

She barely nodded, and he escorted her downstairs.

Closing the oven, Kathryn turned. Her gentle eyes surrounded his mother with understanding, but when she looked at Matthew, something else sparked in them. Or maybe he was just hoping he saw something more for him. His Daed thudded through the back door, and Peter slammed the front door as he entered.

"The horses have come inside, ya?" Kathryn looked at his Daed.

He gave a sheepish look, half smiling. "Sorry, I tripped over the feed bucket."

"In the house?" Kathryn looked at Peter.

"So that's what I did with that thing. Sorry."

"You know, I don't get paid enough for this nonsense." She winked at Mamm and poured her a cup of coffee.

When Kathryn returned to the stove and set the coffeepot on the eye, Matthew sidled up to her. "Mamm's guilt is getting worse, not better." He grabbed the plate of scrapple.

Kathryn looked up at him.

He shrugged. "I was hoping you knew something to say."

Kathryn lifted the pan of cooling cinnamon buns off the back of the stove. "I...I have no idea what to say, or I'd have said it already."

"We gotta try something."

She nodded, and they both moved to the table and set the items in place.

Kathryn passed out the cloth napkins and took a seat.

"Mamm, you know Kathryn's dealt with a rough patch of grief too."

Mamm stirred her coffee. "Yes, I know."

Kathryn took a sip of coffee and eased the cup back to the table. "When my brother died, it seemed there was nowhere to put the affection I had just for him. It's like it banked inside me, and I ached to do something for him again. Then I began to constantly relive all the times I fought with him."

Mamm nodded. "Ya, I can see feeling that way."

Daed took a seat and poured himself some coffee. "I'm not short on feeling like I failed him. Over the last few years, I've spent weeks at a time away from home, traveling with the Amish carpenters." His eyes rimmed with tears. "I miss the days when most Amish could make a living farming."

The room was silent, much as it had been since David died, but this time a vapor of hope seemed to swirl, like the unseen aromas of coffee and cinnamon buns.

Peter squirmed in his chair, making it screech against the floor. "I promised him I'd help that day in the shop. If I'd been there, I'd have smelled that gasoline before it could catch fire."

Mamm gasped and grabbed Peter, knocking her coffee over. "No. If you'd been there, I could have lost you too. You have no sense of smell, child. What are you thinking?"

Peter burst into tears mixed with laughter. Kathryn mopped up the spilled coffee. Matthew didn't miss the nod Daed gave Kathryn—a slight movement that carried the weight of his full approval.

When Kathryn took a seat, Matthew slipped his arm around the back of her chair, and she whispered, "Real love—it's the best, most painful thing God ever did for us."

"So really a person should say, 'I'm in pain with you.'" He kept his voice low and tried to hide his laughter.

"Only when they're dealing with you, Matthew Esh."

He laughed out loud, and his Mamm looked at him. He pointed at Kathryn. "It's her fault."

His Mamm's eyes narrowed as she looked from Kathryn to him. He leaned the chair back on two legs so Kathryn couldn't see him as he placed his index finger over his lips and nodded at his mother, answering all the questions she'd never dare to ask. Then he winked at his Mamm.

Inside the Daadi Haus that Luke and Mary shared with Mammi Annie, Hannah rinsed the soapsuds off the last breakfast skillet and stacked it in the dish drainer.

The glow of light from the fall morning danced across the room, turning shadows as fresh air whipped through the barely open window. Luke was like her when it came to open windows. Even in cool weather he wanted a bit of fresh air stirring through a room.

She dried her hands on a dishtowel and grabbed a freshly scrubbed pan to dry it. The kitchen still carried the aroma of a robust breakfast, but the counters were now clean, waiting for the next round of meals. These were the things she remembered most: the steady but calm pace of day-to-day chores, the way daylight filtered through a home void of electric lights, the distinct segments of time—morning, noon, and evening—defined by meals cooked and chores done.

Sarah came into the kitchen, carrying a few glasses. She looked distracted, so Hannah stepped back from the sink. "Did you need to put those in the sink?"

She blinked a few times and then nodded. "I found these upstairs while making beds."

"Okay, thanks." Setting the pan on the counter and grabbing another wet dish, Hannah caught a glimpse of Lissa through the window. The little girl shadowed Mary's every move as they dug up the last of the potatoes for the season. Luke had been ready to go to Matthew's early this morning in hopes that a full day of work would get a portion of the burned-out building torn down today. As he was heading out the door, Mary's Daed and a couple of her brothers had shown up and gone with him.

Sarah's hands shook as she began helping put dishes away. Hannah's time with her over the weekend was something she would carry in her heart for years to come. They'd made cookies, walked the fields, and lazed around while watching Lissa play at the edge of the creek.

Sarah plunked a dish onto the countertop. "I don't want you to go."

"I know. It's been a wonderful visit. I'll be back after the first of the year." Hannah moved to Sarah's seven-day pillbox, making sure she'd remembered her meds yesterday and this morning. She had, and thankfully, she didn't seem to notice what Hannah was doing. In spite of the telltale signs of nervousness, losing small tracts of time, and being a little scattered, her sister's progress seemed remarkable.

Sarah should thank Paul. He seemed really good at his job, able to work with people from all walks of life. Maybe that's how he'd managed to embrace attending an Englischer college while spending each summer with a Plain Mennonite grandmother and falling for an Old Order Amish girl.

Paul.

She drew a slow breath, trying to control the rogue emotions that hit her concerning him. Aiming to refocus her thoughts, she looked out the window and watched Lissa.

"If you're not married, can't you stay?" Sarah asked.

Hannah had clarified she wasn't married, but that news seemed to make Sarah more determined to hold on to her. "No, I can't." She clutched a handful of flatware from the draining basket and dried each piece before sliding it into place in the drawer. Last night Luke, Mary, Sarah, Lissa, and Hannah had sat on the floor near the low-burning potbellied stove, playing a game of marbles. Mammi Annie watched from her rocker, saying she was too old to get on the floor to play a game. It was almost as if nothing had ever ripped them apart, but the weekend had carried a heaviness that Hannah bore in silence.

Mary's secret.

If Mary truly understood the seriousness of what was going on, she hid it well. But whatever lay ahead, it had to be dealt with openly. Luke had to be told…no matter what the prognosis.

If this Amish district had a medical facility the Plain people trusted going to, like the communities in Alliance had with Dr. Lehman, Mary wouldn't be in this position. Years ago if Hannah would've had somewhere safe to go, her life would be completely different.

Lissa ran inside, chortling. Her cheeks were rosy from the cool morning air. Mary came in the back door, smiling.

"Look!" Lissa held up a funny-shaped rock.

Wondering what Lissa thought she'd found, Hannah glanced to Mary. "What am I looking at?"

Lissa laughed. "It's a rock. Don't you know a rock when you see one?"

Hannah, Mary, and Sarah laughed. It was the kind of thing Hannah and Mary would have pulled on adults when they were kids.

Mary placed her hand on Lissa's head. "Sarah, would you help Lissa wash the rock and then her hands?"

Still laughing at Lissa's joke, Sarah did as asked.

Mary waited for the bathroom door to close. "Any word yet?"

Hannah removed the towel from her shoulder and placed it on a peg. "No. You doing okay?"

Mary shook her hands, as if trying to wake them. "As nervous as a body waiting to be told whether they're gonna live or die."

"How did you manage to push this fear off you for so long?"

"It took us awhile to get pregnant, and I thought God wasn't going to let me have a baby until I told Luke the truth. When I conceived, I soared on the clouds for months, confident nothing could go wrong.

When concern tried to creep in, I did a good job of telling it to shut up—until the pains began."

Hannah stifled a sigh. "The part about telling it to shut up—we're just too alike, you know?"

Mary gave a nod. "I'm beginning to see that."

The phone inside Hannah's dress pocket vibrated. She opened it and read an unfamiliar number across the screen. It showed a local Pennsylvania area code, so she pushed the green icon. "Hannah Lawson."

"Hey, it's Paul."

Even if he hadn't identified himself, with one word spoken she'd recognize his temperate, deep voice anywhere, at any time, even after not hearing him speak for more than two years.

Motioning to Mary that she was going outside, Hannah answered, "Any news?"

"The board approved Dr. Lehman coming in. I called to let him know, and he asked me to tell you he's doing all he can to be here by lunchtime."

She had no doubts that Paul had pulled every favor imaginable to get the board to approve this unorthodox visit so quickly, but the news only made Hannah more anxious. What if the prognosis wasn't good? Hannah closed her eyes, praying for Mary.

"Hannah?"

"I…I'm here. Just really nervous, but I appreciate this a lot." Why was she telling him how she felt? Was she no longer capable of holding her tongue when talking to Paul?

"I'm uneasy too, but the favor was no problem. I heard from Kathryn Glick last night. She spent most of the weekend planning a community workday. Has lots of people going to the Esh place today to help clear the rubbish off the foundation. She called me last night. Said she'd been trying to keep it a surprise. "

"Well, that explains why Luke was so flabbergasted when Mary's

Daed and brothers showed up to go with him to Matthew's this morning. I guess Kathryn kept this a secret from Luke and Mary too."

"Are you at the Yoder place?"

Hannah took in the scenery, the hills, pastures, and barns. "Yes."

"I have a client to see first, but then I'm going to Matthew's to lend a hand as soon as I can get there. You know, Sarah should go too and help with lunch."

"You think she's up to seeing something as emotional as tearing down the shops where David died?"

"If it hits her hard, I'll help her deal with it."

"Ah, so you'll be on hand if she wigs out?"

"Wigs out?" Paul laughed. "Is that anything like YoMama from yoTV?"

Laughter escaped her as he quoted bits of an exchange they'd shared years ago when playing Scrabble. Suddenly uncomfortable for sharing a laugh with Paul, she cleared her throat. "I…I better go."

"Just make sure to get only good news about Mary, okay?"

"I'll do my best. Thanks." She closed the phone. Paul loved board games like she did. Maybe one had to grow up Plain to appreciate those types of games, because Martin hated them. He loved computer war games, though, and television and movies, all of which he indulged in regularly while she was at school or work. But when she was home, their lives were so busy she rarely had time to notice something as unimportant as a board game. She slid the phone into her pocket and went to find Sarah.

After telling her about the events at the Esh place, Hannah walked with her across Yoder property to where Esh land began.

Sarah gazed into Hannah's eyes. "When will I see you again?"

"I…I'm not sure, but you can use the Yoders' phone shanty and call me anytime."

Could her sister possibly understand how hard it was coming back to Owl's Perch, even for just a visit?

This time had been a bit easier as a few more of her people seemed to be moderately accepting of her. But she figured each one who'd been more open this time knew the same thing Hannah knew; she'd never really fit in anywhere. Not as an Englischer or as an Amish. She was too much like Zabeth, unable to truly become a part of either world. But like her aunt, she'd made her choice. She'd fallen in love with a master of Englischers, Martin Palmer, and she'd live out her days with him. But she couldn't keep going back and forth from one world to another. And that's how it felt, like traveling to different planets with each reentry bumpy and heated.

Thoughts of building a life with Martin pulled on her. They'd make a good couple, and it'd give Lissa and Kevin a steady, loving home.

Sarah slid her arm around Hannah's. "Can you come home over the Christmas holidays for just a day or two?"

She shook her head. "I'll be in Hawaii with Martin and the children. He's flying his top employees and a few friends there for a two-week stay."

"Hawaii?" She stopped walking.

Hannah tugged on her arm, and they began again. "I'll be back after the first of the year."

The frown on Sarah's face was deep, and Hannah wondered if this news was going to cause a problem for her.

She stopped near where the fields became the Eshes' backyard. "It's best if I go on back now. I don't want to make Matthew's parents uncomfortable by staying, and they aren't the kind to ask me to leave."

"Naomi and Raymond won't mind."

"Maybe not, but I'm not taking that chance."

Sarah hugged her. "I'm sorry you and Paul argued, but I was glad you came barging into that meeting for me." She released Hannah and took a step back. "You really have forgiven me…haven't you?"

Hannah knew she had so much to learn about forgiveness that it might help her to go somewhere quiet and stay there until she understood the true nature of it. But clearly, learning didn't come from time alone in prayer. It began there, and then it seemed it became perfected by messing up, digging deeper, and trying again.

Unable to answer her sister, Hannah gave her one last hug. "Go on. You have work to do."

On the front porch of the Better Path, Hannah waited for Dr. Lehman to arrive. He'd called a few minutes ago to let her know he was close. Mary sat inside the waiting room with Lissa, but Hannah was hoping for a minute alone with Dr. Lehman. The rolling hills were ablaze in fall color, and the air carried the aroma of smoke from a fireplace. The peacefulness reminded her clearly that she was among the Amish.

Why had Paul decided to stay this close to Owl's Perch in such a small, out-of-the-way clinic when his grades and abilities could allow for so much more? Martin would rather die than not use every ounce of his ability to increase his influence and standing in life.

Dr. Lehman pulled up to the clinic, and Hannah hurried down the steps to his car.

He turned off the vehicle and opened the door. "Hello."

"Thank you for doing this."

"This is easy, Hannah, especially with my seeing Mom this week anyway." His voice carried more than just an I-don't-mind-doing-this tone. He sounded pleased to do this for her. Passing her his briefcase with one hand, he grabbed his large medical bag off the passenger's seat with the other. He got out of his car, pushed his glasses higher on his nose, and studied her. "How are you?"

The standard three-word greeting meant more than the simple question.

Hannah rubbed her fingertips across her forehead, wishing she had a more appealing answer to give. "It's been pretty good. Better than the first trip."

Dr. Lehman's brows furrowed. "And?"

She dipped her head, sighing. "I still managed to blow up at Paul."

"Mmm-hmm." They began climbing the steps. "Was he innocent again?"

She rolled her eyes and gave a nod.

The gleam in his eye said more than the crooked smile across his lips. "I saw that side of you when we first met in the hospital and you gave me the dickens for wanting to turn you over to social services."

"Was I that bad?" They stopped on the porch, outside the closed front entryway.

"You were pretty bold for a seventeen-year-old Amish girl who'd awakened to find herself in ICU. You thought I was wrong, and you weren't afraid to say so…as respectfully as possible, of course."

"So far in this with Paul, I've been far from respectful and the only one wrong."

Dr. Lehman chuckled. "You'll survive. And so will he. The way I see it, you were probably born for something that needs spit and fire once in a while. That's bound to shake things up a bit here and there—nothing wrong with that as long as you're either trying to do what's right or willing to go back and make it right."

She squeezed the handle of his briefcase. "My Daed would totally disagree with you…and can quote verses as to why and how your acceptance of my misbehavior is wrong."

"Ah, well, that's a debate I'll never have with him. But we both know you're God's servant, Hannah, not your parents'." He gestured toward the briefcase he'd passed to her. "I spoke with Mary's doctors, but rather than tell you what they said, I'd like you to read the faxes they sent and sum up the diagnoses after her examination. Do you have a vial of blood, a urine sample, and a written report of her emotional state and vitals?"

"Yes. The blood and urine are in the lab, waiting either to be sent out or for you to run the tests yourself."

He moved his medical bag to his other hand. "We won't do anything so elaborate that we'll need it sent out. If she doesn't require immediate hospitalization, which I doubt, we'll see to it that she gets a regular ob-gyn before the week is out."

They went inside. Leaving Lissa in the waiting room playing with toys under Halley's watchful eye, Mary, Hannah, and Dr. Lehman made their way up the steps and into the room provided. The exam didn't take long, and then Hannah and Dr. Lehman went into the adjoining room—Paul's office.

Dr. Lehman sat on the couch, waiting for her to read the chart. "In two sentences or less, summarize what it says, Hannah."

In the overstuffed chair adjacent to him, she shifted. The odd feeling of sitting in the same chair Paul used while with clients made it difficult to concentrate. How had she landed in such a weird place in life? "The concerns are that what was done to stop the hemorrhaging inside Mary's skull when she had a subdural hematoma could blow out upon the increased intracranial pressure during Valsalva."

"Which means?"

"The concerns don't involve any health issues until time for labor and delivery." Tears stung her eyes. "She's in no danger."

"Your medical advice?"

"She has to agree to go to a hospital and have a scheduled C-section a week or so before she could go into labor."

"Exactly. I'll find her an obstetrician who will take her on, but it'll be your responsibility to make sure she follows through." Dr. Lehman removed his glasses, looking at her firmly.

"Yes, absolutely."

He replaced his glasses. "Define Valsalva."

"It's holding the breath and bearing down during labor and delivery."

"Good. Now, in your opinion, why didn't Dr. Hill or one of Mary's other doctors explain this better to her?"

"According to the records, the doctor told her to come in for another CT scan, which she didn't do. He explained that a pregnancy would put the baby in no danger, but labor and delivery would be very dangerous for her. The doctor could've been in a huge hurry and intended to explain more later on, but Mary never went back. Or maybe he didn't think an Amish girl her age would understand anyway. But I think maybe her doctor didn't approve of a teen wanting to get married, so he stayed vague on purpose. Which really irks—"

Mary tapped on the door and then entered. She looked from Dr. Lehman to Hannah, obviously hoping for good news.

Hannah clenched her lips and lowered her eyes to the open chart, trying to restrain herself. It wasn't her place even to hint at the diagnosis. Professionalism at all times meant too much to Dr. Lehman, even today.

Dr. Lehman stood. "I'll go to the lab and run the blood and urine tests myself while you and Hannah talk."

He gave Hannah a nod before leaving the room.

Mary's eyes bored into her. "Well?"

Hannah stood, closed the chart, and laid it in the chair. She took Mary by the hands, smiling so big her face ached. "You and the baby are fine."

Mary engulfed her, clinging to her and crying.

"And you'll be perfectly safe as long as you go to a hospital and have a C-section done." After a long hug, Hannah removed Mary's grasp and stared into her eyes. "You have to tell Luke. You have to be in a hospital a week or more before labor can begin and have a C-section. Do you understand?"

She grabbed Hannah and hugged her again. "I understand…the baby and I will be fine. I'll do whatever it takes to stay that way."

And right then Hannah knew every bit of what she'd been through to work under Dr. Lehman, go to school, and reenter Owl's Perch was worth this one thing.

Hannah shifted gears as she entered the Yoders' driveway. "If I leave for Ohio as soon as I drop you off, I can be there in time for class tonight or at least enough of it to get credit for being there."

Mary rubbed her protruding stomach. "I was hoping you'd stay and answer Luke's questions."

"How badly is he going to take this?"

Mary leaned back on the headrest, closing her eyes. "How bad does any man take learning that his wife lied in order to marry him?"

"You lied?" Lissa piped up. "You're not supposed to lie."

Hannah tapped Mary's shoulder. Mary opened her eyes, and Hannah pointed toward the fields behind the outbuildings. Naomi Esh and Luke walked toward them, coming from the Esh place. Luke's clothes were covered in soot, and he looked almost too tired to walk. Naomi appeared rather worn-out herself.

Mary unfastened her seat belt. "Why is Luke coming back from work in the middle of the day with Naomi?"

"I didn't want to ruin Luke getting to tell you first, but Kathryn organized a surprise workday." Hannah set the emergency brake and turned off the car. "When are you going to tell him?"

"Soon, but not now. Naomi doesn't need the stress of knowing what's going on."

Luke opened Mary's car door. "Where have you guys been?"

"We've been at the Better Path," Lissa offered.

Mary got out of the car. "I heard the good news. How's the workday going?"

"Really good. But Naomi needs to borrow pitchers and sugar and...what else?"

Naomi held up a list. "If it's in your pantry, I may need it." She lowered the list and gazed at Hannah. A slow, gentle smile graced her lips, but she appeared speechless. Deep wrinkles now tracked her face.

Hannah forced herself to speak. "I'm so sorry for your loss."

Naomi embraced her. "Denki." She took Hannah by the shoulders and backed her up. "Let's take a look at you, child. I'd heard you'd been here, but they said you were gone already."

Luke shrugged. "I thought you had to leave in time for classes tonight."

"Hannah," Lissa called from the backseat.

"Oh, excuse me for a minute." She opened the back door of the car and unfastened Lissa from the restraint, glad for the interruption. She placed Lissa on her hip.

Naomi stepped closer. "How've you been, Hannah?"

"I...I'm good." What could she possibly say to sum up all that'd taken place since the day she'd left Owl's Perch and Naomi had helped take her to the train station?

"I've prayed for you every day since you left."

Hannah scooted Lissa to her other hip. "Thank you. I've needed every one of those prayers."

Naomi tugged on Lissa's shoe. "And who's this?"

"Naomi Esh, this is Lissa Palmer. She's...the niece of a dear friend of mine."

With her entire hand, Lissa brushed strands of silky black hair from her face. "She and my uncle kiss."

Hannah's cheeks burned, and she bet her face was now quite pink. "Well, that does make him a good friend, doesn't it?"

"I certainly hope so," Luke added.

Naomi held up the list. "Do you remember Kathryn Glick?"

Wondering what Naomi must think, she managed to hold on to a sense of dignity. "Yes, I think so. I saw her at the annual school sales, right?"

"That's right, along with hundreds of other unfamiliar faces. I think she's a real treasure. On Friday she decided she wanted to surprise Matthew by pulling off a work frolic. She got the word out, but she didn't realize how many supplies it'd take to keep everyone in drinks and food."

Mary took the list and skimmed it. "Luke, maybe it'd be easiest if you hooked a horse to the small cart and used that to tote the items back."

"Good idea." Luke headed for the barn.

Naomi turned to Hannah. "You'll come over too, won't you?"

"I…I…"

Naomi slid her arm around Hannah's shoulders. "Of course it'll be hard, and some—only some, mind you—will whisper and wag their tongues, but it's my house, and I'm inviting you."

Hundreds of insecurities burned inside her head: her Englischer dress, her Kapp-less head, the ring on her finger, her hairstyle, Lissa in jeans and a sweater, explaining who Lissa was, finding the right words for each person, totally giving up on going to class this evening.

But how could she say no to Naomi? She'd lost so much, and if a visit from Hannah was what she wanted, Hannah wouldn't deny her. Besides, Mary needed her too.

"Sure I'll come."

She turned to Mary. "By midnight."

Mary nodded. "By midnight."

Luke came up behind her. "What happens then?"

She jolted. "I thought you were getting the cart."

Luke pointed to where the horse and cart waited to be loaded. "Are you two up to something?"

"These two?" Naomi smiled. "Never."

Luke looked doubtful and glanced from Mary to Hannah.

Mary motioned toward the house. "Let's get the stuff on the list."

They loaded the items into the cart, and while Luke walked beside the horse, Lissa held the reins and drove the wooden rig across the bumpy fields. Hannah's mouth was dry, and her insides felt far colder than the nippy October air, but this seemed to be the right thing to do.

She sat on the bench between Lissa and Mary, not at all sure riding in this jarring rig was a bit easier than walking. It was easy to understand why Naomi had insisted on walking. They crossed the knoll and soon were entering the Eshes' backyard.

Dozens of men in straw hats, broadcloth pants, suspenders, and work gloves knocked down beams with sledgehammers and hauled burned timbers to the back of a large wagon. There were a few Englischers among the mix: Russ Braden and Nate McDaniel, drivers for the Amish, and Hank Carlisle, the milk pickup man. All of them knew her and her past.

Long tables covered in sheets were set up end to end across the flattest part of the yard, and there the large gathering ate their lunch and supper. The women served the men first and waited on them. After the men left the tables, the women would serve the children and then themselves. Staring straight ahead, she tried to brace herself for the afternoon. It wasn't that anyone would physically lay a hand on her, certainly not. They probably wouldn't even question her directly or share their opinions. But she'd get looks and whispers, and when the work was through, they'd get into their buggies or cars and not hold back sharing their thoughts. She'd like to know why something that toothless took so much strength to face.

Hannah viewed the burned shops again. Matthew had added several new ones during the time she'd been gone. Through a rickety, half-standing wall of an almost dismantled shop, she caught a glimpse of a broad-shouldered man helping carry a load-bearing beam.

Paul.

A dreamlike feeling engulfed her again. Luke led the rig around to the front yard, and Sarah came into view, dumping trays of ice into a cooler. Hannah stepped out of the cart and helped Lissa down while Luke did the same for Mary.

Mary beamed up at her husband, placing her palm on his cheek. "I love you." She whispered the words, but Hannah heard the joy in her voice that Mary couldn't yet explain to her husband.

Luke squared his shoulders, clearly teasing. "Of course you do."

Mary lowered her hand. "You'd better get back at it with the men. We're fine from here."

Luke walked toward the shops, but he kept turning back, catching a glimpse of Mary. Hannah believed him to be more in love today than when he married her dear friend, and it warmed her. Mary lifted a casserole from the seat of the cart and headed for the steps to the Esh home.

Naomi passed Hannah an armful of items: pitchers, ladles, and sugar. She then passed a few wooden spoons and cloth napkins to Lissa before grabbing as much as she could carry. "Come on." Naomi nodded toward her home.

Hannah followed, and they entered Naomi's kitchen. Food lined several worktables that were covered with fabric. More than two dozen women were scurrying about to have the next meal ready by suppertime. Hannah remembered well that when dealing with this many mouths to feed, there wasn't enough time, supplies, or energy between dinner and supper.

Naomi cleared a space on the table. "We need however many loaves of bread you can bake, Hannah."

There would be no introduction, no fanfare concerning her return. If some of the women chose to talk to her, they would. If they didn't, they'd pretend she wasn't there. When she looked across the room, a few halfhearted smiles greeted her. The blank stares of others were far from warm or accepting, but no one spoke.

Kathryn Glick, someone she barely remembered, passed her a sack of bread flour. "Hi, Hannah. I'm really glad you're here."

From somewhere across the room, Hannah's mother emerged. Mamm's eyes told Hannah she loved her. Her mother moved forward and hugged her. "I'm glad you came. You do know that, right?"

"I do now." Hannah squeezed her, letting years of ache melt away. When she opened her eyes, she saw several women crowded around. Edna reached for Hannah, and soon tears blurred her eyes as she received hugs from more than half the women in the room.

Her mother wiped tears from her face. "If you'll do the bread, we'll handle everything else, including setting the tables and serving the men."

Lissa gazed up at her, nodding her head. "I'll help."

Hannah placed her hand on Lissa's head. The girl seemed to live in perpetual excitement for life, although her attention span for anything in the kitchen wouldn't last like her love of creeks and water. She'd be by Hannah's side for maybe ten minutes, probably less.

Thankful for a set job, Hannah nodded.

Now, was she still capable of making bread like she used to? It'd been a long time since she'd made a batch of dough in a kitchen without electricity. Determined to give it her all, she walked to the pantry.

fternoon shadows began to creep across the yard as the sun
moved westward. Luke stood still for a moment, trying to catch
a glimpse of Mary. She was setting pitchers of water on the table. He
hoped she wasn't doing too much. In spite of the workday and all the
hope and socializing it brought, the weight of losing David Esh was
heavy on everyone, especially the womenfolk. He'd seen Mary's fears
over their unborn child increase since the funeral. Hannah's return gave
Mary someone she could talk to. That was good. He was glad. Really.
But he got the feeling they were hiding secrets again.

Chapter 24

By midnight.

What did that mean, anyway? He hadn't had any reservations about
the day Hannah helped Mary dig potatoes. But then today they'd gone
out by themselves, ignoring any reservations the bishop might have if
he found out. His wife and sister sure did a lot of private talking, didn't
they? Then again, it was only Hannah's second visit to Owl's Perch in
over two years. Mary spotted him and waved. He trotted to her.

"Hey." The word came out breathless. "Maybe you should get off
your feet for a spell."

"I'm doing great. Why, Hannah was telling me that women who
stay busy and even those who have some extra stress in their lives are
more likely to give birth to healthy babies than the women who live too
soft and easy. She said the baby comes out ready to fight for life."

"You want us to have a fighter?" Luke laughed.

Mary ran her hand over her stomach. "Not if you put it that way."

A deep male voice called Luke's name.

"I need to get back. You take it easy, okay?"

She nodded, but there was something in her eyes, something he'd asked her about a dozen times over the last few months.

"Mary?"

She gazed up at him.

"Something wrong?"

She shook her head. "Everything's great, but I…got some things I want to tell you. Good things, really."

"Can't you just say them right now?"

"No, and not at home either, not with Sarah and Mammi Annie listening."

Luke tried to read his wife. Their bedroom was private enough, but Mary wouldn't let any disagreements be aired out there. That had to be done elsewhere, usually outside when they went for a walk, sometimes at the supper table, in front of Mammi Annie, but never in the bedroom. "I…I thought you said it was good news?"

"It is, but—"

Several more men called Luke's name. He looked up, and four or five of them were watching him, waiting. As an owner of E and L, he was supposed to be supervising. "You hold those thoughts, and as soon as things settle down for the day, I'll come find you."

Hannah turned the last loaf of cooling bread out of its pan and then wiped her hands on the towel that lay across her shoulder. The report Naomi had given about thirty minutes ago was that most of the men had eaten and some had gone on home. Only the younger men were still at it, with sledgehammers and wheelbarrows.

Shouts from several men filled the air, and the few remaining women in the room ran outside. Hannah took a peek through the kitchen window, wanting to spot Lissa. The girl stood near the tire swing with several other children, waiting her turn. Hannah looked out farther, trying to see what'd caused the ruckus. She couldn't see the shop area for the sprawling leaf-covered branches of oak trees, but Luke was walking toward the house. When he spotted her in the window, he motioned for her. She ran outside.

He pointed at the shops…or where the shops used to be. The men had removed almost all the charred debris from the concrete foundation in one day. Impressive.

Luke shook his head. "We were too tired and shoulda quit earlier. Paul's hurt, but he says it's not bad enough to be seen. Will you do me a favor and take a look?"

"If he says he's not hurt…"

"Hannah." Luke lowered his voice, giving an entire lecture in her name.

"Fine. Where is he?"

"There." Luke pointed across the yard to a group of men near a wagon. A pile of charred wood lay on the ground around the men's feet.

They picked up their pace. "What happened?"

"A couple of men were trying to get a load of heavy beams on top of what was already in the wagon. When the load began to slide, Paul caught it with his shoulder, slowing the landslide long enough to give Jacob time to get mostly out of the way before the load came crashing down."

Luke and Hannah closed the gap. Paul's shirt was covered in soot and tattered from the day's work. In spite of the black stains, Hannah saw blood soaking his shirt, starting above his elbow and dripping off the end of his finger.

"Paul,"—Luke motioned to her—"let Hannah take a look."

Paul glanced at her. "I'm fine. Really."

Was he afraid her scarlet letter would once again be shared with him? That any contact with her would break whatever threads of good-will he'd sewn between himself and the Amish community in her absence?

"Then let me look." She stepped closer and pulled at the edges of the ripped sleeve, trying to see the source of the blood.

Ignoring his stiff reaction to her presence, she tore the sleeve of his shirt where it was already tattered and took a look at the injury. "We need to irrigate it, disinfecting it. And you might need stitches." Like changing gears while driving, she let her nursing skills take over. Someone needed to get her medical bag for her. "Where's Matthew?"

Luke tugged at his straw hat, tightening it onto his head. "He went to the Bylers' to use their phone. Since we're getting so much done, he's gone to check prices and delivery for timber."

"Oh, okay. This isn't an emergency, but, Peter, could you bridle a rested horse for Luke so he can go to the Yoders and get my medical bag quicker and easier than walking?"

"Sure thing." Peter hurried toward the stables.

Paul angled his body away from the others, clearly wishing to convey something only to her. "I'd be more concerned about Jacob if I were you."

Hannah looked at the young man, Mary's brother and Sarah's onetime beau. He'd grown half a foot since the last time she saw him, but more important, he was pale and shaking, his breathing shallow.

She removed the kitchen towel from her shoulder and placed it over Paul's wound. "Hold this tight and try to hold the sides of the gash together to slow the bleeding." Stepping over to the young man, she asked, "Jacob, how are you feeling?"

"I...I..."

Hannah took his chin and directed his face so she could look in his eyes. His pupils were dilated. She took his wrist. His pulse was racing, his breathing irregular, and his skin cold.

Was this a reaction to seeing blood flow freely from Paul? Or maybe it was a combination of being startled by the incident and seeing the blood. It seemed an extreme reaction to those things, so maybe he was hurt more than it appeared.

The crowd around them grew larger. Hannah turned and saw Kathryn. "I need several blankets, please."

She nodded and headed quickly for the house.

Hannah placed her hand under his arm. "Jacob, I want you to lie down."

He started easing to the ground, and then his legs apparently lost their power, because he landed on his backside with a thud.

Hannah glanced at the women. "Could someone keep an eye on Lissa for me?"

Mary spoke up, saying she would.

Hannah placed her hand on Jacob's neck and head, easing him to a lying position. "All the way on your back, please."

He complied.

"That's it." She stood and moved to his feet and lifted them. "Just relax." Glancing at the group, she saw Jacob's mom, Becky, at the back of the crowd, trying to see. "Becky?"

She threaded her way through quickly, looking worried, but the more involved Hannah could keep her, the calmer she'd remain.

"If you'll hold his feet about a foot off the ground, that'd be very helpful."

Becky knelt, doing as instructed.

Hannah reached into her pocket and grabbed her car keys. "Luke, my medical bag is in the trunk of my car. It's a brown leather tote bag." Showing him the keyless remote, she pointed to the unlock icon.

Luke stared at her, much like during her first visit to Owl's Perch. "You have a medical bag?"

"It was a Christmas gift from Dr. Lehman, and I always keep it with me."

She showed him the right icon on the keyless remote again. "When you're beside the car, push that twice. Then push the trunk icon, and it'll open."

Luke took the keys and studied the keyless remote. "You sure?"

"Yeah, if it doesn't, you can use this key." She pointed to the right one. "But it doesn't work well on the trunk and has been known to set off the alarm. If it does, ignore it and bring me the bag. Okay?"

Peter arrived with a bareback horse, and Luke pulled himself onto it and galloped off.

Hannah checked Jacob's pulse. It was already a little more even. "We'll have some blankets for you in just a minute." She ran her hands over his chest. "Did you get hit when the accident happened?"

"J-just a bit."

"Where?"

He pointed to the top of his shoulder.

Knowing that couldn't cause any bruising to an organ, she pressed on his sides, kneading his flesh under her hands. "Did any other part of you get hit with the boards?"

He shook his head. Kathryn came back with the blankets, and Hannah spread them over him.

Matthew's Daed walked up with a drink and held it out. "Here, this will help."

She shook her head. "A drink right now isn't a good idea, but thank you. He needs to stay lying down. But I could use a knife to cut his shirt. I need to see the injury."

Someone passed her a knife. The sun hung low in the sky, making it a little harder to see, but he had no cuts or gashes, only a good-sized bruise on his shoulder. She ran her fingers over his shoulder, feeling for any signs of a dislocation or break.

Becky held on to Jacob's feet, stroking his pant-covered legs. "What's wrong with him?"

"I think his sympathetic nervous system is reacting to the situation, which is similar to experiencing mild shock. He seems fine except for the bruise on his shoulder. But I can't tell if anything is torn or broken. He may need an x-ray."

Becky studied her son. "Do you think he needs one?"

"I can't be sure."

"But you know what you think," Jacob's Daed added firmly.

Hannah glanced to Paul. They didn't want the Englischer nurse's version—go let an expert see you, even if you think you're fine. They wanted a trust-your-gut Amish answer—if he's likely to be fine without seeing a doctor, then give that a chance first.

She shrugged. "It's too early to tell. I'd like to give his body a few minutes and see how he reacts. I'll check his vitals as soon as Luke returns. Right now we're going to make a thick pallet beside him and get him off the cold ground, and someone's going to get a chair for Paul."

Several women helped Jacob shift onto the pallet and covered him with a blanket. Both his pulse and color were returning to normal. When Luke returned, Hannah checked Jacob's blood pressure and the reaction of his pupils to the light of her ophthalmoscope. All of his autonomic systems were coming back into normal range.

Jacob tugged at the blood pressure cuff. "Can you remove this thing and let me up now? I feel fine."

Hannah shook her head. "You can sit up, but that's all. If that works, we'll go from there."

His mother released his feet, letting him sit upright. She shooed everyone back. "Go on and eat or clean up or rest or whatever. We're fine. If Hannah needs anything, we'll holler."

The group slowly dispersed, walking back to the Esh home. Paul sat in a chair about five feet away. Someone had brought two extra lawn chairs, and a washbowl filled with clean water sat in one of them.

Hannah paused, insisting her legs keep moving. The oddity of Paul patiently waiting mocked her. She took a deep breath, trying to repel feelings that were a betrayal to Martin. Sitting next to Paul, she pointed at his shoulder. "Let's take a look."

As he eased his hand away, she placed hers over the towel.

Ignoring the strangeness of being so close to him, she focused on her duties. "Are you on any type of medication?" She spoke softly, trying to honor his right to privacy even though Jacob and Becky were just a few feet away.

"No."

"When is the last time you had a tetanus shot?"

"About two years ago."

"Good. You won't need to get another. Do you take baby aspirin or ibuprofen regularly?"

"Baby aspirin?" He laughed. "If you have something to say, Hannah, don't beat around the bush."

She suppressed a smile. "I take it the answer is no?"

"Yes…I mean, correct. The answer is no."

Closing her eyes, she shook her head quickly, as if he were driving her nuts. He laughed.

She slowly peeled the towel off his gash. "Your blood clots fast. For cuts like this, that's generally good, except I have to open the wound back up to clean it out, and it'll start bleeding again. I'm really sorry."

"You sure you're sorry?" he teased.

Willing herself to be painfully honest, she realized humility didn't come easily for her. "Sometimes the words just don't cover it," she whispered, refusing to look him in the eye.

"It's behind us, Hannah. Forgiveness has happened. And now we move forward."

Feeling her mouth go dry and her heart palpitate, she looked up. In that brief moment a piece of her soul seemed to become his. Shifting her focus, she pulled prepackaged items out of her medical bag. "I've been horrid and mean. Is forgiving that effortless for you?" She laid the items in her lap.

Paul held out his arm to her. "Forgiving you is easy. You weren't culpable. Forgiving myself takes a good bit more faith, daily."

She pulled a pair of scissors out of her bag and slid the opened shears up the sleeve of his shirt and then around his bicep, removing the fabric completely. Desperate to turn the subject elsewhere, she thought of a topic. "I...I can't believe how much better Sarah is." Hannah reached into her bag and grabbed a bottle of cleanser. She poured the povidone-iodine solution into the bowl of water and stirred it with her finger.

"Hey," Jacob complained, "can't I get up now?"

"Yes, but stand slowly." She watched to see if he wavered any. He appeared steady. "Are you feeling the least bit sick to your stomach?"

"No, just hungry."

Hannah dried her wet finger on a piece of gauze. "Becky, why don't you see that he eats and drinks a small portion...slowly, of course. And just as a precaution, he should take it easy for twenty-four hours. I'll check the range of motion in his shoulder later, and then we'll discuss getting x-rays."

Becky squeezed Hannah's shoulder. "Thank you."

"Glad to do what I can." Hannah ripped open a package holding a sterilized bulb syringe, filled it with the disinfectant solution, and began cleaning Paul's gash.

He tilted his head, looking at the cleaned-out, slightly bleeding gash. "Can I ask how things went with Mary?"

Hannah filled the syringe again and squeezed its contents onto the gash. "Beautifully. If ever a bad decision turned out well, it's happened for Mary. I just wish Owl's Perch had a better situation for the medical issues that come up."

"The Plain community is in need around here. I agree."

"Every specific group requires targeted medical help they trust—moms of newborns and preschoolers, teens, elderly, athletes, cancer patients. The list is endless and includes the Amish, which is a subgroup all its own, in my opinion."

"And where your heart lands in spite of not wanting it to?"

She cleared her throat, uncomfortable with just how easily he saw some things. "Yes." She paused, trying to find some piece of emotional ground between betraying Martin and being near Paul. "This situation with Luke and Mary will be expensive, but fixing the actual issue is so simple. Time and time again issues that can take someone's life have a relatively simple answer, as long as the patient is informed and willing."

"That's probably why you were drawn to becoming a nurse."

She refused to look at him, but she couldn't stop the smile crossing her lips. "I used to drive you crazy wanting to study your science books each summer."

"It was fun for both of us. Do you still have that anatomy book Luke's doctor gave you?"

She glanced up from his shoulder. "I'm never without it." She pointed to her medical bag. "It's in there."

"The desire to be a nurse was always deep inside you, wasn't it?"

"It sure looks that way."

"Tell me about the expenses you mentioned."

After laying the syringe to the side of the bowl, she dipped a wad of gauze into the solution and cleaned the area surrounding the wound. "She'll have to check into the hospital before she goes into labor and have a C-section, but she's in no danger." She pulled a fresh piece of gauze out of its package and dried his skin. Showing him the container of butterfly bandages, she pulled out several. "These will probably do the trick, but stitches would do a better job of preventing scarring." After laying the strips in her lap, she opened the tube of antibiotic cream and applied it.

"A scar makes no difference to me." He stretched out his fingers several times. "Without insurance, the hospital and surgery will be really expensive for Luke to cover."

She nodded as she wiped the cream off her fingers. "Still, after what they could have been facing, it's a small price to pay. Mary gave her word she'd tell him everything before midnight tonight." Hannah removed the backing from one side of the Band-Aid. "Is your hand asleep?"

"Barely." He flexed his hand, opening and closing it.

She squeezed together the skin at the top of the gash and placed one thin-stripped bandage over it. "If there's any redness or swelling, you need to be seen. If the tingling in your hand or arm continues for even a few hours, you need to be seen. If—"

Paul held up his hand. "I got it, Hannah."

A quick glimpse into his eyes revealed a straightforward openness that startled her. Undemanding. Honest. And steady as the ticking of time. In spite of years of convincing herself otherwise, those things did define him.

How she wished they didn't.

She looked away, gathering items into her medical bag. Being next to the man she'd once loved and intended to marry had every nerve in her body on edge. In his ways she saw why she'd carried feelings for him so long. The force of guilt over Martin ran through her, screaming warnings.

"You're cold," Paul said.

The evening air didn't match the warmth of the kitchen she'd been in most of the day. She shrugged, and while she removed the backing to another butterfly bandage, Paul went to where Jacob had been lying and grabbed a fleece throw blanket. He folded it in a triangle, like a shawl, and placed it over Hannah's shoulders, his warm hands resting there longer than necessary.

"Hannah," Lissa called from across the yard. Sarah was beside her, holding her hand, standing rigid and staring at the ground.

Paul took a seat.

Hannah swallowed, reeling her emotions back in. "Yes?" She ignored the bit of trembling in her fingers and placed another butterfly bandage next to the first one, squeezing the skin together as a stitch would.

"Can I comed over there?"

Hannah glanced up. Her sister stood firm, as if an invisible line lay in front of her and she didn't dare step over it without permission, but her eyes were on the palm of one hand as if she was confused by it. The young woman either still had a long way to go to find freedom, or she'd always have odd ways about her—or both. "Sure."

Sarah released Lissa's hand, and the little girl sprinted to Paul. "Did you cut yourself?"

"A little," Paul answered.

"On what?"

"A nail sticking out of a board."

"Maybe you need some cookies. I cut my leg a few weeks ago." She sat on the ground and rolled up her pant leg. "See?"

Hannah continued putting on the bandages, eager to be done.

"Wow, that's quite a battle scar."

Sarah joined them, and Paul smiled a silent welcome.

Lissa beamed. "I broke my uncle's glass shelves, and he didn't even care. He said I was tougher than nails about the stitches too. On the way back from the hospital, he bought me some cookies 'cause Hannah weren't home to bake them. She was here. He tooked really good care of me."

A wrinkle creased Paul's brows as he looked up at Hannah, but whatever was on his mind, he didn't voice it.

Hannah smoothed Lissa's hair back from her face. "I think someone is missing her uncle about now."

Lissa nodded, the truth of Hannah's words reflected in her eyes. "We goin' home soon?"

"Tomorrow. First thing."

Lissa stood and pulled a broken, lint-covered cookie out of her pocket. "You need a cookie?"

Paul chuckled. "Thank you."

She dusted off her hands. "You're welcome. Can I play on the tire swing, Hannah?"

Spotting Mary near the same area, Hannah nodded. "Yes." She

dumped the bowl of solution onto the grass and placed all the old gauze and wrappers in it.

Paul leaned back in his chair. "Martin is her uncle?"

"Yes, but he's raising...we're raising both her and Kevin."

Silently Paul stared at the disfigured cookie.

Sarah took the bowl, her eyes darting from Hannah to Paul. She looked addled.

"I...I..." She ducked her head. "Never mind."

Paul rose and slid the cookie into his pocket. "She's leaving tomorrow, Sarah. If this is important to you, ask."

The tautness across Sarah's face made her appear unbalanced. "I...know...but it'd help me..." Sarah stopped talking midsentence and stared off into the distance.

"Sarah." Paul spoke firmly.

She slowly pulled her eyes from the distance and looked at him.

He focused on her as if willing her to hear him. "Find your thought and express it. Don't let fear steal your ability to live in the here and now."

Sarah's blank face slowly seemed to gain a more normal look, and she nodded. "If we could walk to where Rachel is buried..."

Hannah froze. She had a right to several things, all of which her sister was intruding upon. Privacy. An undisturbed burial place for Rachel. And her past left alone. Sarah hadn't even known Hannah was pregnant until after the baby had been buried. Why did she need to see the grave?

Hannah rubbed her forehead. "It's not marked at all. It'll look like any other ground under a beech tree in the field."

Sarah stared at one palm while rubbing invisible smudges off. "Paul wouldn't even try going without your permission, and he didn't think I should ask one of the few who know."

His loyalty was disconcerting. She pulled the blanket tighter around her shoulders. "Okay, I'll take you."

Sarah's eyes grew large. "I...I want Paul to go."

Of course she did. Pulling Paul into Hannah's life seemed to be Sarah's gift. Glad to be going back to Ohio first thing in the morning, Hannah gave a nod.

Wearing the small blanket draped like a shawl, Hannah walked in silence as Paul and Sarah talked about putting the past to rest. Paul's words to Sarah wrapped around Hannah's heart, and she recalled the various conversations she'd had with Paul since her first trip back to Owl's Perch three weeks ago. In spite of her resolve to ignore his rock-steady and gentle ways, they fought for attention.

Dusk settled over the fields, and the birds had grown quiet. As they topped the ridge, golden-bronze leaves of the beech that hovered over Rachel's grave came into sight. Hannah swallowed, no longer hearing the words that passed between Paul and Sarah.

But she could hear Paul's voice, see him in yesteryear as clearly as she could turn and see him now.

He'd stood in front of her during one of their rare times together, turned her hand palm up, and kissed it. *"Conversations make a relationship strong. Unfortunately, they won't be a part of our relationship for a while. But we can clear away whatever weeds grow during this time if we hang tough and faithful"*—he'd winked—*"until May."* He'd squeezed her hand lovingly. *"Eight months, Hannah. No problem for us, right?"*

No problem.

Had they been given one small break in any area, it wouldn't have been a problem, not for them. Unwilling for Paul to catch a glimpse of what was happening inside her, she kept her gaze steady on the ground as the three of them continued walking. Her heart suddenly felt too large for her chest as an epiphany hit. Paul had believed in them.

In her.

And he'd waited.

No longer able to resist, she lifted her eyes—tattered shirt, injured arm, blond hair, broad shoulders, and none too weary for the day's work he'd just performed. His energetic steps defied the gentleness with which he spoke to Sarah.

How long had he waited?

It didn't matter. He had Dorcas. And Hannah loved Martin. When she thought of how rare it was to find a quality man, it seemed pretty incredible that she'd managed to find two. Maybe good men weren't as scarce as she'd thought.

Paul's eyes moved to hers and lingered. A hint of a smile crossed his lips. She knew that smile, the one that wasn't born so much from the joy of easy living as from the small pleasures life brought his way.

Edged with a fresh sense of betrayal of Martin, she turned her head without smiling. Scanning the fields, she remembered the whispers she'd heard the day Rachel was buried, calling Hannah's name and whispering, *"Kumm raus"*—to come out.

In the midst of heartbreak, the voice had beckoned and hopelessness gave way. The next day she set out to find a woman she wasn't sure existed. Even today she remained unsure if the vaguely familiar voice had been her inner self begging for freedom, or her imagination, or God's own whispers, or something else. But at the time, it'd kept her from being swallowed in brokenness and had helped her find the courage to leave.

Sarah grabbed her arm, shaking all over. "Look."

Less than fifteen feet ahead of them there appeared to be a grave marker, a headstone.

Sarah tightened her grip and dug her heels into the ground, stopping both of them. "I...I changed my mind. I want to go home."

Paul placed his hand on Sarah's shoulder. "We can't believe our emotions over sound reason. Your emotions are terrified. Reason says there is nothing to fear."

Sarah tugged on Hannah's arm. "Let's go home. I don't like it. Maybe some ghost from the past—"

Paul cupped Sarah's hand, making her ease up on her grip. "You're hurting your sister."

Sarah stopped squeezing but held on. "But who...who would have done such a thing?"

Hannah stared at the grave, goose flesh crawling over her whole body. The perimeter of the tiny grave was edged in white marble the size of bricks and the area surrounding the spot was meticulous, almost like a lawn.

"Someone who cares," Paul offered.

Hannah wrapped her blanket-shawl tighter and moved forward. Sarah balked, and Hannah freed herself of her sister's grip and took a step forward, a thousand memories and emotions ripping at her.

"I...I'm not ready. I can't!" Sarah's scream echoed over the field.

Ignoring her sister, Hannah went to the grave, stunned at what she saw. Thoughts of the many seasons—snowy winters, rainy springs, sweltering summers, and glorious falls—ran through her mind. Yet someone had been faithful. Behind her she could hear Paul talking in muted tones to Sarah.

The sense of loss seemed to be without end, but even so she could feel the trust she had in God to find a way to make up for it. That was part of who He was, wasn't it? Thieves came in and stole, and God redeemed. But standing here right now, she didn't feel redeemed, not when it came to certain things. She was redeemed by Him in a thousand ways—Martin, Lissa, Kevin, school, Dr. Lehman, the Tuesday quiltings, and her Amish friends. Still, the loss of a thousand hopes she'd had before the attack stood firm.

Paul eased up beside her, hands folded and reverent. He stared at the ground. "I'm sorry you dealt with this alone."

If the idea that someone had been taking care of the grave wasn't enough, his reaction made her heart stir. She'd thought all these years that he was...incapable of understanding. Yet as surely as she knew he'd once loved her as she had him, she understood the violence she'd experienced hadn't happened just to her. It had happened to them.

Seems like I should have recognized this long before now.

With her heart beating wildly and her eyes misting, she held her hand out for his. "Nevertheless," she whispered.

He placed his warm, rough hand inside hers, and there in the quiet fields ablaze in fall colors, an unexpected healing soothed her heart. The quiet between them left only the sounds of leaves rustling.

She knelt, releasing Paul's hand. It seemed this odd journey back to Owl's Perch had made her more ready to let go of the past than she'd ever been. She wasn't running from it anymore. She had it in her to rise and move on. And the difference brought a sense of well-being she'd never known existed for anyone, and certainly not for someone who'd been assaulted.

Sarah approached the grave and knelt. "All this time I wanted the baby to be alive..."

Hannah put her arm around her sister's shoulders. "Choose reality, Sarah. It's the only place where strength and faith can begin to work."

Sarah placed the palm of her hand over the grave.

Hannah squeezed her sister's shoulder. "It's time to let go and live."

"You ever gonna do anything to hunt that guy down?" Sarah's voice trembled.

Hannah closed her eyes, asking herself the same question. Cool air whipped through the trees, making the leaves sound like rain as they swirled across the ground. "No," she whispered. "What was done happened over three years ago. I can't identify him. I have no idea what type of car, nothing. The only way the police could start to track him down would be to take Rachel from her resting place so DNA testing could be done, but that would only help if he's already been caught for another crime. I won't do that to Rachel...or to me." She rubbed her sister's back. "Right or wrong, I choose to let go and move on. It's the way we were taught, ya?"

Sarah nodded. "Ya."

Hannah removed her arm. When she and Sarah began to shift in order to stand, Paul held one hand out for each of them. Sarah took his hand, and he helped her get to her feet. Hannah stood up on her own.

"I bet Daed's been doing this, keeping the grave tended to."

"Sarah..."

"No," she interrupted, "you don't know what he's like when nobody's looking. He wrote in a diary about watching for you to return. Pages of stuff, but when I found his secret stash, he burned everything, as if he could think it and feel it but he couldn't stand anyone knowing."

Unwilling to argue, Hannah began walking. The trip back toward the Esh home was done in silence. An odd sense of peace surrounded her more than the darkness of the night. She pulled the blanket tighter around her shoulders. Sarah seemed to have found some resolution about life too.

But somebody had put time and money into edging the perimeter of the tiny grave in white marble.

Someone cared. It couldn't be Daed, could it?

he sounds of hoofbeats made all three of them look up.

Jacob stopped the cart beside them, looking directly at Hannah. "Mamm said I needed to see you first and then give you and Sarah a ride back to Luke and Mary's. Mammi Annie said to tell you that Lissa wanted to go on home with her."

Hannah removed the blanket and passed it to Paul. "I'm not heading back right now, but hop down, and let's check out that shoulder." She had Jacob do several slow range-of-motion moves. "On a scale of one to ten, with ten being the worst, how does it feel?"

"About a three, maybe less."

"I think you're fine without an x-ray for now, but if the pain increases or your range of motion decreases, go in to be checked out. And all those things I just had you do with your arm, do them four times a day, slowly. Okay?"

"Sure. Thanks, Hannah. I guess being a nurse comes in handy, especially out here in the sticks, huh?"

Unsure if he'd understand that she wasn't even a registered LPN yet, she opted not to try to explain it. "It did today."

Sarah gave Hannah a hug. "I'm really tired." She said nothing to Jacob, her old beau, as she climbed into the work cart. "You'll wake me in the morning before you pull out?"

Hannah nodded. "Sure. Good night, Sarah."

In the Esh yard, Matthew's parents, along with a few other men and women, stood chatting in small groups. Kathryn was next to a driver's car, saying good-bye to several men from her community, including a man Hannah recognized as Kathryn's Daed. And the way one of the young men hovered near her, he was either Kathryn's boyfriend or wanted to be.

Closer to the house, Hannah's father glanced up from the men he was chatting with but then acted like he didn't see her. She and Paul walked toward the side yard, where a kerosene heater shed light on a circle of chairs. The tables looked barren and well-worn without the fabric or food covering them. Mary, Luke, and Matthew sat around the heater, talking. Three empty chairs sat in the circle, probably an invitation for her and Paul. If Hannah had her intuition going right, the other chair was for Kathryn.

Of all the day-to-day events that'd taken place while she'd been gone, Matthew and Elle's breakup was probably the most surprising. But Matthew seemed at peace with it, maybe even relieved about it.

More than ready for a few quiet moments alone, Hannah turned to Paul. "I'm going inside. I'm sure there's more I can help with in the kitchen."

"Thank you for doing that for Sarah."

The distant whispers of just how in step she and Paul could be circled inside her. She didn't respond to him, as guilt concerning Martin nibbled at her.

The house appeared empty as she entered it. Void of earlier voices, the kitchen felt secure in ways it couldn't before. The lowing of cows waiting to be fed drifted through the slightly open window and across the room. A kerosene lamp on the windowsill above the sink added a glow not much brighter than two electric night-lights. She moved to the faucet and turned it on, letting the water get warm before she filled the sink and squirted dishwashing liquid into it. As she continued washing the pans, women occasionally came in and gathered their clean dishes. Most of them spoke a reserved farewell on their way out, and she returned it. If they didn't speak, she respected their silence and held her tongue.

The lantern sputtered as it began to run out of fuel. Through the window, she saw several families climb into their buggies and head out, leaving only one more buggy waiting for its owner—her Daed's. But her mother was sitting inside it.

"Hannah."

Her muscles tightened at the sound of her father's voice. Turning her head to face him, she held her sudsy hands over the edge of the sink. "Yes?"

Shadows angled this way and that as the flames of the lamp wavered. Her father stood there, looking as if he had something to say but couldn't. She grabbed a towel off the peg beside the sink and dried her hands.

He eased into the room, crunching the brim of his hat in his hands. "You're leaving tomorrow?"

"Yes." She stepped away from the sink.

"You…you'll write to your mother more this time, ya?"

How could so much lie between two people that they couldn't manage to say anything worthwhile? "Yes."

"Good." He started to leave, but with his head ducked and his shoulders stooped, he didn't appear to have said what he came to say.

"Daed?"

He turned, staring at her as if he still wasn't sure who she was.

"I was innocent."

He wiped his forehead with the back of his thumb. "None of us are ever innocent. I thought you'd understand that much by now."

She fought to keep her shoulders back and chin up. His words were both true and a lie. But he'd never see his part, only hers. Is that what he came in to tell her, that regardless of all he'd accused her of that she hadn't done, she still bore the mark of a sinner?

And with his words spoken, her father turned to leave the house.

"Daed?"

He faced her again.

"The grave site…it…it's been taken care of…"

He clenched his jaw. "I'm not as disloyal as you seem to think."

"We're all disloyal. I thought you'd understand that by now."

He stood firm, staring at her. "You win, Hannah. I haven't been able to stay a step ahead of you since you turned fifteen. I haven't done anything right. But as God is my witness, I tried."

"I wasn't up-front about Paul, and maybe I was wrong about that, but you knew the truth of what'd happened the night of the attack, yet somehow later on you completely justified abandoning me. No, worse, you turned on me and brought the church leaders with you."

He opened his mouth to speak, but then, without another word, he walked out, pulling the door closed behind him.

The door eased open again, and Paul stepped inside. "You okay?"

Her eyes filled with tears. "Always." She cleared her throat, gaining control of her emotions.

"Everyone's gone but Luke, Mary, Matthew, Kathryn, and us. Matthew's parents walked to the Yoder place to look at some lumber John has stored that could be used for rebuilding. I guess Mary will talk to Luke soon, and we'll call it a night." He walked to the table and grabbed a slice of homemade bread from the cutting board. "Since you're leaving tomorrow and we may never meet up again under relaxed and friendly circumstances, I was hoping you'd join us outside." He breathed in the aroma from the slice of bread and gazed up at her. He'd always said he could tell whether homemade bread was made by her hands or not, because he could smell the heat, like the fires from her soul.

Turning her back to him, she reached for a clean pan and then began drying it. They'd walked to the grave and shared something she could never share with another human; he understood things about her no one else ever would. And he forgave her in ways she hadn't known she needed until it was given to her, freely. But now she needed distance.

"I think it would do Sarah a lot of good if you could return and help her find a passion of some sort. She's too old not to have a job that brings her a sense of self-esteem and satisfaction—something she can look at and feel good about."

Hannah faced him. "Like I told Sarah, I can't."

He sat on the edge of the table and propped one foot on a chair. "Yeah, I know, you're too busy until after the first of the year. But maybe after the snows are gone? I think it's important. It'd be better if it could be done before winter sets in, but if you can't, you can't."

"What exactly did you have in mind?"

"I wish I had a clue, but I'm confident you can think of something."

She leaned against the sink. "Sarah should have met Zabeth and lived in that cabin with her."

"Ah, she smiles at the thought of it." Paul's lopsided grin made her remember a hundred others. "What was she like?"

A male voice startled her. Thinking the voice came from the front of the house, she went to the dark foyer and peered out the open front door. Paul followed her.

Luke stood at the foot of the steps. "What were you thinking?"

Mary smoothed her hands over her protruding tummy, her eyes locked on the ground. "I was afraid you'd leave if we couldn't marry right away. Your father left his roots, and Hannah too, and you were angry with your Daed and the church leaders for how they treated your sister, and antsy and talking about going into Lancaster to work and—"

"Those are your excuses for lying to me?" Luke interrupted her. "Telling me the doctor gave you a clean bill of health? You told me—"

She held up her hand, stopping him from saying more. "I know, but I lied to myself. I thought I was trusting God when I was using that as an excuse to get what I wanted. I...I didn't want to lose you."

Hannah eased the door shut, stopping it just short of clicking. From inside the house, she could still hear their voices, but she tried not to listen. "Those words are a red flag, too often spoken right before lies and cover-ups."

"Look at me, Hannah."

"What?"

"If you're talking about yourself, it's time to let it go," Paul whispered. "Just let it go."

The weight of everything seemed to close in—the dark, the empty house, the closeness, the whispers between them. Unable to find her voice and void of knowing what to say if she could, she just stood there, staring at him. Did he feel it too?

He motioned toward the kitchen. "I...I think I'll go out the side door and meet up with Matthew."

He turned, leaving her alone.

Guilt hounding her, Hannah moved back to the kitchen, now completely dark since the lamp was out of fuel, and sat in a ladder-back chair. She couldn't return to the Yoders just yet. She'd told Mary she'd stay close to answer questions Luke might have. Otherwise she'd have returned to Ohio earlier. She hoped he'd have questions and not just anger.

Hannah rested her forehead against her fingertips. That's where she should be, in Ohio with Martin, not here building bridges with Paul.

Matthew came in the side door and motioned for her. "Luke's asking for ya."

She willed the confusion to slide into its hidden place, assured it'd find its way free to be wrestled with later. "Okay." She rose and silently walked out the back door, thoughts of both Martin and Paul lingering.

Kathryn, Paul, Luke, and Mary were sitting around the kerosene heater, stark silence reigning. No one else remained on Esh property. Hannah took a seat in one of the empty chairs, and Matthew followed suit.

"So this is why you stayed?" Luke's sharp tone interrupted her thoughts.

She sat up, clearing her throat. "Yes."

Her brother's face was rigid, jaw set as he stared at the ground. The concern in Mary's eyes was deep, fear of losing his love and respect, of bearing his anger in various measures and ways for years to come.

Kathryn stood. "I...I thought we were going to talk business. I think I'll call it a day. Good night." She walked toward the house, and Matthew jumped to his feet and went with her.

Hannah leaned in, catching Luke's eyes. "You have a right to be angry, but please don't hold on to this."

"Mary should have trusted me to make the right decision based on truth and trusted God with her future." Luke slumped, brooding.

Hannah warmed her hands near the red-faced heater, unable to sit still and unwilling to look at Paul.

Luke gestured in the air, exasperation evident. "So now what?"

Without her permission, Hannah's eyes moved to Paul and stayed. His blue eyes focused on hers as if Luke's question hung between them rather than between Mary and him.

Shifting, Hannah turned her attention to Luke. "Dr. Lehman will find a good obstetrician willing to take her in spite of her impending due date and lack of insurance."

"Explain to me everything, starting with why her doctor didn't want her to get married."

Hannah explained all of it, careful to interject assurances as often as possible.

Luke studied his wife, seemingly torn between anger and complete terror for her safety. "How can he be so sure this plan will work?"

"Because Dr. Lehman is incredibly intelligent and spent hours tracking down every test and every doctor's report concerning Mary's health after the accident."

Luke narrowed his eyes at Mary. He gestured toward Hannah. "Swear to me you two are hiding nothing else."

Hannah held out her hands, palms up. "Nothing. I promise."

"And she and the baby are completely safe?"

She lowered her hands. "As safe as any healthy woman giving birth using modern technology and a skilled surgeon."

Luke slid back in his chair, anger radiating off of him. "I can't just let this go. We should have waited to marry."

Mary broke into tears. "You can't regret marrying me. You just can't. It will taint..." She stood and hurried across the yard toward the back fields where her parents' property met Esh land. And Luke let her go.

Paul shifted in his chair. "Luke."

He looked at Paul, and the two men seemed to hold a silent conversation. Her brother finally nodded, stood, and took off after his wife. "Mary, wait."

Hannah fidgeted with a button on her skirt. "Your silence seems more powerful than most people's words. I'd like to know that trick."

"No trick. We just share enough history from my own mistakes."

Hannah looked up. "And you couldn't have said *nothing* earlier and spared Mary some of this?"

"Luke wasn't ready to hear it earlier."

"Hear what? You didn't say anything."

"Hannah?"

"Yes?"

"You're giving me a headache."

They shared a laugh before Hannah leaned back on the chair, noticing for the first time how clear the evening sky was. Thousands of stars sparkled as if the Susquehanna's surface that gleamed under the sun's rays had been broken up and spewed into the sky. The harvest moon, in all its golden orange glory, was a clear sign that fall was far more than just a chill in the air. In spite of the heater, she shivered.

Paul tossed her one of the blankets from earlier. "This would be our first real time to be together after dusk."

Without sitting up or taking her eyes off the sky, she spread the blanket over her. "Maybe it's not so amazing that we didn't make it…as it is that we forged a relationship around all the constraints."

Paul didn't respond, and she wasn't about to look at him. They'd shared something special earlier today, and clearly they'd been ripped apart years ago against both their wishes, but she loved Martin. She could list his qualities endlessly and felt privileged that he wanted to share his life with her—an ex–Old Order Amish girl who didn't dress or act anything like the hundreds of women he'd dated before her.

Hundreds? Had there been that many? Well, he was eight years older than she was and considered dating a sport he was good at, even up to a year and a half after meeting her.

She shuddered, suddenly wishing she hadn't thought about this. Martin wasn't an outdoor guy for the most part, but when the weather was nice and time permitted, he'd leave his television, computer, game systems, and phones and sit with her. "Some of my favorite times are when Martin and I sit together outside and talk."

Paul reached across the chair that separated them and tugged at her blanket. "I'm guessing that's mostly a summertime event."

She waved her hand at him, shooing his teasing away. Besides, she really shouldn't be here talking with him, and it'd suit her overloaded guilt wagon just as well if they waited out the rest of this Mary and Luke saga in complete silence.

To their left, a hundred feet away, stood Luke and Mary. She had Luke's hand pressed against her stomach. Hannah cleared her throat, trying to dismiss the lump. Love wasn't all that touched their lives on this planet, but it made everything else endurable.

The movement under Luke's hand made his heart thud like a wild man inside his chest trying to get out. His child was inside her, responding to his voice. He held his tongue, and the infant stayed still. He spoke, and the baby shifted. Feeling like a true head of the household, a man with the responsibility to take great care with his words and even his tone, he looked at Mary. "You were wrong," he said softly.

She nodded, fresh tears splashing down her cheeks. "I know, but if you regret marrying me, you'll taint what we've shared…our marriage bed. Remember our first night?"

Luke nodded, recalling many treasured nights.

His eyes stung with tears. He'd trusted her completely. Always had. And now he felt shaken and used. "All those months of crying when you didn't conceive, you should have been rejoicing. I…I don't understand."

"I took my vows before the church, knowing I was hiding the truth from you. I feared God might not ever let me conceive, especially if I didn't tell you the truth. But more than that, I feared you'd never love me the same if you knew the real me."

Luke studied his wife. She wasn't who he'd thought, no doubt. She had flaws and weaknesses he'd not known about until tonight. Now he knew her failing—she feared losing him more than she feared answering to God for a lie. If he wanted power over his wife, something he could use at will for the rest of his life, it'd been given to him tonight.

Mary caressed his cheeks. "I've repented a million times, but it doesn't undo what I've done."

He'd had his own repenting to do since they'd known each other. The reality of their weaknesses ran a long list through his mind. When the doctor had told her to wait about getting married, she was devastated, afraid he'd find someone else. But there was no one else to find, not for him. And the truth was, he would have waited for her, but he'd jumped at the chance to marry her at the very next wedding season. He didn't ask to speak to the doctor; he just married her as quickly as he could.

The list had silly things on it too: the time he'd left the gas-powered refrigerator open all night, the times she made them late for church because she couldn't find her hairpins, and the times he ignored her when she called him to supper, because he wanted to read the newspaper. He guessed this was what being married meant: having someone who knew both the best and worst about you.

With her hands still on his face, he gently took hold of her wrists. "I guess I can only hope you feel as strongly about marrying me today as you did two years ago."

Mary smiled. "You know I do, Luke." She shifted, moving his hand to her stomach again. "We both do. But I shouldn't have loved you or myself more than God, and when I covered truth to get my way, I did just that."

Luke wrapped his arms around her, hoping his wife was as safe as Hannah thought.

M atthew filled the kerosene lamp with fuel and set it on the kitchen table. He struck a match and lit it. Kathryn pulled a calculator from the desk drawer, along with the cost of building supplies. He studied her face. Did she believe their relationship was only business?

She folded her arms in a relaxed manner and stared at the papers. "Do you really think you can start making money on orders before the shop is completed?" Her soft voice soothed his nervousness.

He adjusted his hat. "Completely sure. The storage at Luke's has most of what we need already. After getting a few more supplies, all we need is a place to work that has a roof."

"E and L can't work out of Luke's shop?"

"We could, but it's a distance to get back and forth. That'd cut way down on my time to work on rebuilding for the most part of the day and filling orders during only a few hours."

"I see what you mean."

"You're the only one who understands the orders since the fire. Ya did the work, made hours of calls to make sense of them, even reorganized the storage shop while I was gone. You can line everythin' up— the customer orders, the supplies, the restocking of parts we don't have in the storage at Luke's old shop—while me and Luke use that time to construct the new buildings. If you're willin' to stay and keep everything lined up, we can stop construction for a few hours each day and begin pecking away at filling orders. If we don't have you doin' that part of the job for us, we can't fill any orders until the buildings are completed."

Kathryn folded her arms and leaned back in the chair. "I set up this workday to help you get ahead, and now you come up with this plan?"

"Today was great, Kathryn." And it was, even if Joseph did show up and cause Matthew to turn green a few times. "We got a lot done. My whole family needed this—the distraction, the fellowship, the hope. But…what was your goal?"

"I wanted to make the tearing-down process easier and quicker. Are you disappointed in my plan?"

"No, no, not at all." Matthew rubbed the back of his neck. "Well, a little."

"What's going on?" Her voice was as peaceful as when she was bidding him good morning or good night. This type of calm, reasonable reaction was one of the many things that drew him to her.

He took a seat beside her. "Tonight, as ya told your Joseph goodbye, it dawned on me what all our hard work today meant. That you'd go home for several weeks, maybe all winter, while we got the sides and roof up. I…I don't want that to happen." He brushed the back of her hand with the tip of his index finger. "Surely you know that."

"Matthew, you're barely broken up with Elle. You can't possibly think you're remotely interested in me."

"That's not an exact account. I'd sent her a letter endin' things before you ever came to work for me. Your first day here she showed up to object to me breaking up with her. Then a month later, the day of the fire, she returned again, asking me to reconsider. After the devastation of losing David, I thought I felt a spark of interest."

"So you run off to Baltimore with anyone you think you have a spark of interest for?"

"I went because I was willing to consider and reconsider anything that might help me find my way. What I learned while there is"—Matthew moved in closer and took Kathryn's hand—"it's your friendship, your ways that speak to me."

"Well, okay, friends, yes, but I…I'm seeing Joseph."

"If he means all that much to ya, then tell me so. All I'm askin' is for some time for me to court you."

She wound one string of her prayer Kapp around her index finger. "That's not all you're asking. Us seeing each other is a gamble, one that, if we lose, will end this friendship, and please don't try to tell me it won't."

"And you'll take that gamble with Joseph but not with me?"

"That's different."

"Different how?"

"For one thing it isn't a working relationship with him. You and I work well together. I don't want to mess that up."

"And…"

She pursed her lips, looking really aggravated. "That's plenty for you to know."

Maybe he wasn't being fair to her. The grief over David was still thick, and maybe he was mistaken to think Kathryn cared more for him than for Joseph, but he'd seen her around Joseph today. She was a little cool and distant, wasn't she?

Matthew played with the corners of the papers spread out in front of them. "If ya really care for Joseph, that's one thing. But you don't owe stickin' with him because your Daed wants you to live close to home and Joseph is available."

"Matthew Esh, you're out of line." She pushed the papers and calculator away from her. "And what about the bishop? He's overlooked a lot where you've been concerned, but going off with someone who's not even a church member…"

Matthew sighed. It sounded so much worse when she put it that way. "I've made my share of mistakes, and I'll deal with them with the bishop."

Kathryn played with the strings of her prayer Kapp again, something she did when thinking and deciding. "I…I don't know what to think, Matthew. Fact is, I'm not likely to sort through it until I go home."

"Will you at least come spend some time with everyone tonight?"

"Luke and Mary are arguing. I'd rather not."

"Whatever they're arguin' about, they'll get over it soon. I'm sure of it." He stood. "Okay?"

She rose and put the papers and calculator away. "Okay."

~~§~~

Hannah remained in her seat, watching as Luke and Mary entered the tiny circle of chairs. They walked side by side, glowing.

Wondering if she and Martin ever glowed, Hannah pulled the blanket off her body. "Does this mean I can get some sleep now? And return to Ohio tomorrow?"

Before she finished her sentence, Matthew and Kathryn came out the side door. Luke gestured for Paul to move over one chair. Paul then took the empty spot next to Hannah.

Luke took a seat. "Ohio." He looked about the group. "Does anyone else here think it's odd that she never calls it home?"

Matthew propped his foot on the rough-sawed coffee table. "I noticed that. Paul?"

Paul shrugged. "I'd rather talk about the price of tea in China."

"Knock it off, Luke. You too, Matthew. Zabeth's cabin has been home since I first saw it, but I had to move out of there, and…and Martin's place isn't quite comfortable yet."

Luke's brows knit. "You're living with him?"

"No, of course not. I didn't mean it to sound like that. I live in the cottage behind his home. It makes taking care of Lissa and Kevin easier."

Luke studied her. "Yeah, for him."

Her ire grew, and she leaned forward. "I know how this must look, and I appreciate that you're concerned for me, but Martin and I have needed and helped each other from the first day we met. When Lissa and Kevin's mother abandoned them on my doorstep, Martin and I formed an even tighter team. If anyone has a problem with that, they need to keep it to themselves."

Matthew pulled a well-used deck of Dutch Blitz cards out of his pant pocket.

He ruffled the cards while looking at Hannah. "Ya go to church?"

"Yes, when I'm not on call and helping deliver babies."

Luke shifted. "Martin goes too?"

Hannah reminded herself that they were asking because they cared, but she wasn't used to people prying. In her world no one asked. "He's more faithful about it than I am."

Matthew continued shuffling the cards. "That's because he can tolerate it better. I attended one of those Englischer churches. Give me a hard, backless pew and a three-hour service in someone's living room or a barn any day over the loud music, squealing microphones, and messages on the walls."

A light chortle went through the group.

Kathryn rose and tugged on Matthew's collar. "Before you deal, let's fix some hot chocolate and popcorn for everyone."

Matthew shoved the cards into his pocket. "We'll be back."

Hannah placed her folded forearms on her legs, leaning closer to the heater. "A few unexpected things happened today, so Paul and I made some good progress with Sarah."

"I can't tell you how glad I am to hear it." Luke folded his hands. "She became such a mess after you left, but if we could have gotten her some help then…"

Hannah shivered. "I knew she was dishing out grief to me—spreading rumors and lies about me everywhere—but I never recognized her behavior as a red flag that she needed help. You probably can't imagine how muddled that time was for me. Some parts of it were too vivid, and other parts were so vague it's like I wasn't even there for the events."

Paul turned up the heater. "Yeah, I guess that's a pretty accurate description, isn't it?"

Luke grabbed a blanket off a nearby chair and passed it to Mary. "I know it took Paul days, maybe weeks, to decide whether to hire a private investigator to help find you."

Hannah turned to Paul, not at all sure she could calmly handle hearing about this.

"I wavered in what to do, and I'll never know if I was right or not, but it seemed inherently wrong to track you down when you had good reasons for leaving and equal reasons for not wanting to return. And you knew how to reach me…if you'd wanted to."

Without any lingering doubts, she knew Paul had never received the messages when she'd called. She had to let Paul know about that, didn't she?

She finally understood all, or nearly all, of what had taken place. "You weren't wrong to let me decide for myself. Besides, finding me would have been impossible. With or without a name change, I almost couldn't find myself."

Paul laid his hand over hers. "I'm proud of you, always have been."

Her eyes misted. "I needed that freedom so I could make totally new stupid mistakes all over again."

Paul laughed softly with her. "You and me both."

Hannah was confident that throughout the years to come they'd remain friends rather than merely tolerate the presence of each other. With him so firmly rooted in Sarah's life, respecting each other was a real perk. Still, shouldn't she tell him the truth about his not receiving her calls? What if it was Dorcas who hadn't passed him the messages? Didn't he need to know that? Or had she handled things in the only way she knew to protect Paul?

Knowing she needed time to think this through, Hannah leaned back. "I'm curious, Paul. My shortcomings are easily seen by those around me, but yours?"

He laughed softly. "Are you asking me to spill all my weaknesses?"

"Come on, no one gets off scot-free."

His grin faded. "You've had to survive a few of them, you know."

Hannah tried to piece things together in her mind. "I'm drawing a blank here."

He slumped in mock resignation. "And you just have to talk about this now?"

She nodded. "Yep."

"Women," he muttered, a half smile making him look mischievous. "I have...hopefully it's I *had* a strong tendency to jump to conclusions and then act on them as if they were facts—like when I left without hearing you out or when I assumed you were married because your last name was different."

Luke scoffed. "Well, horse neck, Waddell, weren't you justified?"

"To follow the clues and be mistaken in my conclusions, yes. To act on my assumption without asking questions, digging deeper, and listening, no."

Hannah kept her focus on the gas heater, but she wanted to offer some encouragement to Paul. "Zabeth once said when you figure out where you're messing up and you hate that behavior bad enough, that's where all the good parts of you begin."

"Guys," Kathryn called from the door of the house, "can I have a head count of who does and does not like whipped cream in their cocoa?"

Mary stood. "I should probably just give her a hand."

Luke rose and caught her by the hand. "I'll go with you, just to make sure you don't lift anything too heavy."

"Whipped cream?" Mary paused midstep. Paul and Hannah nodded.

She snuggled under the blanket. "So, what do you do for fun?"

"Ah, a much easier question to deal with." Paul stretched out his legs in front of him. "I hang out with some of my college buddies. We hike, fish, camp out, play some tag football, shoot some pool. You?"

"I work, go to school, and study. Around those things I try to find time for Martin, Lissa, and Kevin."

"It sounds like you're doing your college years a lot like I did mine—all work, no play. I don't recommend it."

"Martin does the event planning for us—band gatherings and stuff—but if he didn't, I wouldn't miss it."

"Don't you have something you do that's just fun, something you'd really miss if you didn't do it?"

"Sure, Kevin and Lissa."

He chuckled. "I meant something indulgent. For me it's ball games, major or minor league. Baseball is my favorite, but football ranks up there too."

"But that's..." She dropped the sentence, not wanting to make him defend himself.

"Not allowed in the Plain life? Uh, if it was, I probably never would have struggled with whether to remain Plain or not."

"But how do you keep up with it—radio, television, newspaper?"

"Yes."

She laughed. "Paul Waddell, you're not allowed television and radios."

"If during a game I just happen to go to a restaurant that has those televisions hanging from the ceiling, or if there's a game on the radio while I'm riding in my car..."

"Isn't that cheating?"

He shrugged. "Sure, but overall I believe in the Plain ways. I can't see giving up the Plain Mennonite faith just because I enjoy an occasional spectator sport."

"I guess having an area like that might help build a rapport with clients who aren't Plain."

"You know, that's a really good excuse." His smile spoke of jest, and she knew his quiet, respectful, noncooperation ways were showing again. He interlaced his fingers, staring at his hands. "I would have told you about this secret love, but I didn't want to scare you away by telling you too soon."

"Uh-huh. And does Dorcas know about this vice?"

"She thinks I've given it up."

"I see. Afraid you'll scare her off too?"

"Nah, she—"

"Women's work." Luke rounded the side of the house, carrying a tray of mugs with steam rising from them. "How do I always get roped into doing women's work?"

Matthew followed, carrying a huge bowl of popcorn, while Kathryn toted the napkins and paper plates. Mary was last, carrying spoons.

The most genuine smile Hannah had seen yet revealed itself in Paul's eyes and slowly edged his lips. Freedom to embrace life anew had taken place for him too. Closure between them mattered to him, and she knew it always would. She lifted a mug of hot chocolate from the tray.

She'd stay as long tonight as her brother wanted her to. They'd all play cards, and she'd probably end up laughing until her sides hurt, but she longed to return to her life in Ohio: the birthing clinic, nursing school and clinical rotations, and the two children who needed the home life she craved to give them.

And Martin. Her heart skipped a beat, and she could see him in her mind's eye and feel inside her the warmth of who they were. Always. Always. Martin.

$\mathcal{M}$ ist rose from the valley where the creek ran, and the new day's sunlight skimmed the tops of the trees. Pulling her sweater around her a little tighter, Hannah leaned against her car, sipping a cup of coffee and waiting for Sarah to grab something from inside the house.

The trees swayed in the morning air, bearing leaves from light yellows to deep golds, from bright reds to sharp maroons. The movement seemed to beg Hannah to linger and watch. She loved Owl's Perch, always had. And now, with healing running through most of the relationships she'd once left behind, the beauty of the place strengthened her. Zabeth would be so pleased for her, and that brought even more comfort.

In jeans and a sweater, Lissa played in the soft dirt near the edge of the garden. She seemed to love the feel and aroma of tilled soil as much as Hannah.

Sarah tapped on an upstairs window, signaling that she'd be down in a minute. She barely looked like the young adult who less than a month ago had poured gasoline around her and threatened to strike a match. She'd needed medication to help, but it seemed to Hannah that, more than meds, she'd needed to find forgiveness and have a sense of power over her life.

Without any doubt, Paul had done a great job of helping her find much of what she needed. His ability to help Sarah seemed more connected to who he was than to his degree. Hannah knew little of psychologists as a whole, but this one used his education as a tool for offering insights and wisdom for living.

Sarah still easily lapsed into talking like a baby and continued with some very odd behaviors, but she was making good progress.

She bounded out the back door, carrying a package wrapped in brown paper with an arrangement of fall leaves on the top for a bow. "Here." She held the gift toward Hannah.

Tears welling in her eyes, Hannah accepted it. They'd come such a long way, and like a garden in spring, Sarah's heart was being cultivated, making all they'd been through worthwhile. She removed the wrapping to find the "Past and Future" quilt. "Sarah, this was on loan to you. It can't be given to me."

Sarah pouted. "He gave it to me." It was a few seconds before she seemed to regain her thoughts. "Besides, I asked Mary. So listen up and hush up." She cleared her throat. "You saw to it that the quilt was made from patches of cloth from family and friends as well as every Amish household in our community. We are a part of your past, and we'll always be a part of your future. I want you to have it so you'll always remember who you are."

In spite of the childlike voice her sister spoke with, it seemed to Hannah that she saw deeply. There were many days Hannah wasn't at all sure who she was. Memories of her Amish childhood swirled like falling leaves. She slid her hand across the quilt. "Thank you. I'll cherish it always." She drew a sharp breath, trying not to cry.

"Mary gave this to Paul to keep him warm while he waited for you to return." She picked imaginary lint off the quilt.

Wishing Sarah hadn't reminded her about Paul waiting, Hannah simply nodded. It was frustrating and embarrassing that part of her wanted to know how long he'd waited. "I'm grateful you're better, and it means a lot to know you're doing well enough to want to give this to me."

Sarah gazed at the sky, growing distracted. "Before we started having trouble getting along, we used to lie in bed each night and talk. Remember?"

"Yes."

"You used to say the hardest thing in life was that no one understood you or helped you find yourself."

Hannah cupped her sister's cold cheek against her palm, causing Sarah to look at her. "Those were childish thoughts. Life is about doing what's right and moving on." But even as she said the words, she knew lives were shaped by kindred spirits and support…or the lack of them. How different would her life be if her father had understood her rather than tried to dictate who she was to become?

Sarah leaned her cheek into Hannah's hand, looking more like a child than an eighteen-year-old. "Paul sees you, Hannah."

The words hit so hard, Hannah fought against tears. It was true. She knew it was, but it didn't matter. Couldn't matter. Surely even Sarah could understand that. Hannah tried to keep that truth from sinking in, but it burned through her, and her heart marched against her chest as if it wanted to get free and run to Paul on its own.

Martin tried to see her. The fact that he didn't sometimes was not his fault. He tried, and that should be enough. No, it had to be enough. What was wrong with her? Was she so weak that her heart wanted the freedom to long for one man when she was committed to another?

She stood straighter. "I have a new family now, dear sister." She pulled Sarah into a hug and held her. "Thank you for the quilt." Hannah kept her in her arms, savoring their newfound victories. Finally she took a step back. "I need to go."

After a few last hugs with Luke and Mary, Hannah and Lissa climbed into the car and headed for Ohio. Fastened into her car seat, Lissa used her CD player and earphones, snacked a little, and slept soundly throughout the trip, leaving Hannah to ponder fairly uninterrupted. Her mind took more twists and turns than the back roads. Soon enough they were on the turnpike, putting mile after mile between them and Owl's Perch.

She rapped her palms against the steering wheel. It'd happened. She'd faced the worst of herself—the horrid, ugly truth—and found peace. Even faced things that couldn't be covered in explanations of events or expressed in a multitude of words, yet Paul seemed to understand every nuance. But that bothered her for reasons she refused to think about.

Martin's two-story stone home came into view, making the drive here feel about two minutes long even though she'd been in the car for hours and it was now past lunchtime.

"Lissa, honey, it's time to wake up."

She began stirring. Hannah reached across to the passenger's seat and stroked the fabric of the "Past and Future" quilt, ready to begin life again, only this time with a serene connectedness to the missing parts of herself. Regrets, yes. They were inevitable, but there wasn't one part of her that was running or hiding or afraid to look in the mirror concerning her past.

She studied the stately house. The immense windows, arched entryway, stacked-stone siding, and meticulous lawns were astoundingly different from the life she'd left behind hours ago.

If it hadn't been for Martin's willingness to barter with her, she wouldn't own a car. But he had done more than help her carry the load of her new life. He became her friend. After parking and cutting off the engine, she got out and opened the door beside Lissa.

She raised her arms, waiting to be unbuckled. "What're you smiling about?"

Hannah lifted the slight kindergartener from the seat, giving her a kiss on the cheek, and settled Lissa on her hip. She then headed for the back door. "I was thinking about your uncle Martin. I have so many things I want to tell him, things he'll want to hear." She closed the car door. "But first I'm sure we need to do damage control to the house. Then we'll unpack, go by your school and pick up any work you've missed, spend at least an hour at the Tuesday quilting, and get groceries.

Next we'll cook a meal, and after dinner we'll get your makeup work all squared away for school tomorrow."

She opened the storm door and twisted the knob to the back door, but the door remained shut. Martin always left the door unlocked and then set the alarm. That way Hannah could get in easily and then turn the alarm off.

"I've got to go potty," Lissa whispered.

"Okay, sweetie, just a minute."

Keeping the storm door open with her backside, she set Lissa's feet on the patio and began digging for her keys. After shoving the house key into the lock, she turned the key. The bolt clicked open. She turned the handle and pushed. The door didn't open.

"Hannah." Lissa sounded desperate. "I need to go."

"Just one more second." Hannah leaned her shoulder into the door. "I know it unlocked. Why isn't it opening?"

"Now." Lissa elongated the word while dancing around, holding her jeans.

Hannah released the storm door and held out her hand. "Let's go to the cottage instead."

While they hurried across the yard, she located the correct key on the ring. After unlocking the deadbolt, she tried turning the doorknob. Someone had flipped the handle lock, and she didn't have a key to that. No one had a key to that. Exasperated, she kept her voice as cheerful as possible. "Lissa, honey, I think you're going to have to use an outhouse like Mammi Annie has, minus the actual house."

Lissa laughed. "I don't think Uncle Martin will like that. He said me and Kevin weren't allowed to do that no more."

Their mother had trained them that when they were outside playing, they weren't to bother her by coming inside to use a bathroom. It was one of many lazy sides to Faye's child-rearing methods that, thankfully, Martin didn't allow. "He'll understand this one time."

While Lissa hid behind the bushes, Hannah called Martin. He

didn't answer his cell phone, so she called his private line at his office. He didn't answer there either. It made no sense for the doors to be locked. She sat on the steps of her cottage, and Lissa soon joined her.

"Hannah?"

"Hmm?"

"I'm hungry."

Suppressing a sigh, Hannah smiled. "Well then, we'll just change plans. How about if we go by the grocery store and get some yogurt and fruit for lunch and then go to your school and get your makeup work? Surely by then we can reach your uncle."

"Can I have an ice cream on a stick?"

"We'll see."

They were halfway out of the subdivision when Hannah's cell phone rang.

"Hi."

"Hey, sweetheart. Sorry I missed your call. I was in the middle of something. So are you home yet?"

"I was, but I couldn't get in."

"Was it locked?"

"From the inside, like someone had latched the keyless deadbolt. And someone had twisted the little lock on the door handle to the cottage too, and we both know no one has a key to that."

The phone line was quiet. "Oh." His voice sounded stilted, and the line went silent again. "It's just a mix-up and no big deal."

"Okay. Did I tax your patience by staying an extra night, and now you've locked me out, or what?"

"No, nothing like that."

"Martin." She crooned his name. "You're acting odd, which is outside of your usual aim to be charming, so what gives?"

"I renegotiated with Laura, and she now works full-time as a nanny and housekeeper. She moved in over the weekend and has a thing about keeping the place locked up." He blurted out the info quickly.

"Oh." She wanted to say more, but the words didn't form. Agreeing to hire Laura part-time had been a concession on her part, not a step plan. He'd been right that they needed her. Hannah would readily admit she'd been wrong to avoid getting help, but to move into having full-time, live-in help and not even talk to her about it?

Phones were ringing in the background at Martin's office, and she could hear him being paged. "She's not there?" he asked.

"Her car isn't. I didn't knock or anything."

"Did you try the front door? She couldn't have used the keyless deadbolt on the front and back doors unless she's inside the house."

Trying to process this from his viewpoint, she still couldn't dispel the disappointment. "No, I didn't think about trying the front door. It didn't occur to me that someone would be in the house." She steered the car to the curb so she wasn't trying to talk on the phone while shifting gears.

"You're upset?"

"I…I'm not sure. If you feel we need her…but to not even talk to me…"

"But you agreed to her being there part-time, and we've both come to like and trust her, so I figured what possible harm could be done? Something came up, and I needed to go in to work on Saturday. When I called to see if she could come over, she'd been out trying to find a more affordable apartment than the one she was living in. Since we have the guest-room suite off of the kitchen…I went for it and asked her spur of the moment. I should've told you."

"Yep." Despite feeling hurt, she kept her tone light and easy. They needed to talk about this, but he meant no harm, and it was his house, his niece and nephew, and his girl who was juggling the typical life of a twenty-year-old—college, work, and family. Still, something about this nagged at her, but she couldn't put her finger on it.

"So you're not going to be angry?"

"Depends. Is that a request or a demand?" she teased. "Just so you know, the answer is request. And because of this, you owe me."

"Yeah?" He sounded more like himself again. "Every time I try to give you anything, you balk, so what could I possibly owe you?"

"Um, I'm off tonight, and there's some peace and quiet for all four of us at a little place up a winding, dirt driveway. Has a wood stove..."

He moaned his disapproval. "I'm going to put that place up for sale if you keep this up."

"Watch it, Palmer. I know where you live...although I can't manage to get in, even with a key."

He chuckled. "Let's not all go tonight, okay? Laura can do everything for Kevin and Lissa—meals, homework, and getting them into bed. That frees us to go somewhere really nice and quiet."

The niggling feeling returned, making her wonder just what it was about Laura's living in the house and taking over full-time that bothered her. Was it her own ego? Did she want to be everything for Martin and this shifted things? At sixty-two years old, Laura wasn't exactly a threat in the attraction department.

"I'm sure Ol' Gert is in need of people attention."

"I contacted the Sawyer family, the ones who live up the road from the cabin. Their oldest boy and his sister are feeding her and riding her regularly. It'll make tending to her during the winter easier now that you're living in the cottage."

Hannah wondered when he'd hired the Sawyer teens to take care of the horse. "But even if we don't go to the cabin, I haven't had any time with Kevin yet."

"Your guilt is working overtime again. He's fine. We had a great weekend, and he didn't miss you anymore than when you pull weekends helping deliver babies."

Torn between what Martin wanted and what she wanted, she said nothing.

"Come on, phone girl," he spoke up. "I deserve a night out with just us. I have the state engineering exams next weekend. I've been studying like crazy, and I want a real date, okay?"

"I did miss being here for your birthday and even for the makeup date for your birthday. We'll go wherever you'd like."

"Well, then I'll make reservations for us and surprise you. I'll also call a locksmith and have him replace the doorknob on the cottage. Hopefully he'll be able to get to it soon." Someone paged him over the intercom again. "I'm looking forward to tonight, but I'm late for a meeting that can't start without me."

"Not a problem. See you tonight."

After grabbing a bite to eat, Hannah and Lissa ran a few errands before returning to Martin's with Lissa's schoolwork in hand. Laura was unloading groceries when they arrived. Martin had been right. Laura had gone out the front door, and Hannah could have entered that way. While Lissa prattled to Laura about the trip, Hannah went into Martin's home office and called the nursing school. She explained to the director of nursing about her family needing her, but she didn't go into detail. Hannah waited while Kim looked up her records. In encouraging tones, Kim told her she had to make up any tests and clinical rotations she'd missed, but she wasn't in danger of not graduating.

The good news coursed through Hannah, bringing her fresh energy. Leaving Lissa to get her makeup work done with Laura's help, she headed to the birthing clinic, ready to see her ever-faithful Tuesday afternoon quilters. She might not get time at Zabeth's cabin tonight, but she'd sneak in a few hours with her Old Order Amish quilting friends.

Hannah turned onto the gravel driveway of the birthing clinic. To her right was the health center. Past that, farther to the right, was the quilting house. The sight of the shop awakened something odd inside her. Horses and buggies were hitched in various places near the quilting house. Smoke rose from the chimney, assuring her the Amish women hoped she would arrive this afternoon. This community of Amish seemed more open to learn and less likely to judge quickly. If there was one thing she would like to take back to her Amish community in

Pennsylvania, it'd be the grace she'd found here—with Zabeth, Dr. Lehman, and these Amish women.

The sprawling branches of the oaks were carrying full-peak colors: gold, orange, yellow, and brick. In a few weeks the leaves would turn brown and fall off, and the subtle beauty of barren branches would replace the intense color.

Hannah entered the small room. A chorus of welcomes hit her so hard her eyes misted.

Sadie rose from the table and engulfed her in a hug, whispering a welcome in Pennsylvania Dutch. *"Kumm, saag uns wege dei Bsuch do yetz."*

Is this what Hannah came for, to tell them about her latest visit with her Amish family? She was here to answer medical questions while they worked on another quilt for charity, wasn't she?

She gazed at the group. Over a dozen women were here. Verna pointed to a metal plate sitting on the wood stove. "Fresh-baked chocolate-chip cookies."

The mist in Hannah's eyes turned to full, brimming tears, but why?

Lois offered a wobbly smile. "They aren't that bad. We promise."

Sadie squeezed Hannah's hand as the room broke into laughter. These women knew what it took to live Old Order Amish, and they understood the pain of breaking away. They'd had loved ones who'd left.

Today she wanted more than just to leave with a sense of peace about her future. None of them would ever prod her to talk, but they were willing to listen, and she wanted to tell them of her past—all of it. And she wanted to share her present, in hopes of never forgetting to carry into her future some part of who she'd once been.

By the time she left the quilting house, it was clear that her emotions had been more raw from her visit back home than she'd realized, but the women's love and acceptance wrapped her in warmth. She hurried to Martin's place, determined to get as much time with Kevin as possible before leaving for the evening. Guilt was already weighing on her, but she and Martin did need an evening to talk. As she climbed out of her car, Kevin barreled out the back door and ran into her arms.

She went to her knees, feeling a thousand hopes and dreams for this child as he held her tight. "Hey, how are you?"

His little face beamed as he released her. "I got something new. Want to see it?"

"Absolutely."

Kevin pulled her into the house.

"Hannah," Laura called.

Almost to the stairway, Hannah and Kevin stopped midstep. "Yes?"

Laura appeared in the doorway of the kitchen. "Martin's secretary called. The locksmith won't be here until after eight."

"Okay. Thanks."

Kevin tugged on her hand, and they went up the stairs and to his room, where he talked nonstop for more than an hour. At some point the doorbell rang, and Laura answered it, apparently receiving a delivery. After Kevin finished talking and was ready to do something besides chat with Hannah, she grabbed her overnight bag out of her car and went to Martin's room to shower and get ready for her date. When she stepped into his bedroom, on his bed was a box with a bright red bow and her name in bold letters across it. This had to be what was delivered.

She opened the card.

Since you're locked out of the cottage, I thought you might need a dress for tonight.

Love you, Martin

The note was personal enough, but it wasn't in his handwriting. She opened the box and lifted out a red, formfitting, silk dress covered with a loose layer of matching chiffon. The dress had ruched cap sleeves, which would show more skin than she was comfortable with. Not at all sure what to think, she held the dress against her body. It was gorgeous, but…

Something inside the box caught her eye, and she moved a layer of tissue to reveal a black silk jacket. She couldn't help but smile. Martin thought of everything all the time. It wasn't the least bit practical, and there was no telling what he'd paid for it, but for his birthday dinner he'd bought her a dress, and she intended to wear it.

Leaving the jacket on the bed, she took the dress and her overnight bag into Martin's bathroom. After a soothing shower and drying her hair for a few minutes, she slid into the red dress.

Red.

She gazed at herself, her long, curly hair draped about her. She didn't look anything like the women she'd grown up with, the ones she'd spent time with over the weekend, or the ones she'd been with this afternoon. But Martin would definitely be pleased. She paused, looking into her eyes. Yet she had to admit that being Plain was more than just a part of who she'd once been, as hidden as that seemed while wearing a red silk and chiffon dress.

She grabbed the pins and began winding her hair into a bun. A rap at the bedroom door caused her to peer out of the bathroom.

Martin leaned against the doorframe, smiling and looking as confident as ever. "I think I like your being locked out of the cottage and forced to wear something different."

She slid the last hairpin into place and stepped across the threshold before turning a complete circle.

"Oh yeah." He nodded his approval, his eyes fixed. "Definitely. Amy clearly has great taste."

"You hadn't seen it before now?"

"Too swamped. Amy Clarke picked it out and then called me with a description. I made sure she bought a jacket, just in case it showed too much skin for your liking."

"Well, according to the look in your eye, you're pleased with the outcome of your joint effort with Amy."

"We've teamed up on projects for years, but we've never yet produced anything near this gorgeous."

She crossed the room. When Martin opened his arms, thoughts of Paul popped into her mind, as if he had his arms open for her. Suddenly a bit shaken and weak-kneed, she snuggled into Martin's embrace.

He held her for a moment before shifting and planting a kiss on her lips. Then he put a bit of space between them, keeping her face inches from his. "How's Paul?"

Slipping from his embrace, she stared at him. "What?"

"Lissa was just telling me that he was injured and you helped him."

"Oh...yeah..." She adjusted the sleeve of her dress, unsure how to explain what'd taken place, really taken place. "A lot of good things happened for me, and I'd planned on our talking about the whole trip later tonight."

"I'm not interested in the whole trip, just the parts that go down memory lane with an ex-fiancé." His eyes and his tone held the intensity of an owner of a thriving engineering firm.

She knew right then that trying to explain what she and Paul had experienced this past weekend was a really bad plan. Martin had been her closest ally since she'd landed here, broken and friendless. But she'd become the woman he was in love with, the one he intended to marry. And maybe, inside of that relationship, full disclosure of every feeling wasn't a wise move, at least until she understood them herself.

Placing her hand in the center of his chest, she studied his handsome face, remembering dozens of parts of the journey that had bonded them in ways no one else could understand. "Paul and I found some closure, and now I own parts of myself that were stolen from me years ago. I came home ready to tell you what went on, feeling like I can begin life anew and having a peace with my ghosts that I never expected. And I don't deserve the tone in your voice."

Do I?

The sensation of Paul opening his arms and her slipping into them had been an unwelcome thought, one that had to be more symbolic than evidence of hidden desires. Her love for and connection to Martin completely outweighed all else. He and the children were her future, her freedom, her strength.

Martin eased his arms around her. "I didn't mean to have a tone."

She dipped her chin, allowing him to kiss her forehead. "You're honest and to the point about whatever is on your mind. I love that about you, even if you ruined a good moment."

He took her left hand and cradled it in his, running his finger over the ring he'd given her. Turning her hand over, palm up, he eased her fingers open. "My heart is right here." He lifted her hand and kissed the center of her palm. "Have I ruined this greeting completely, or can I get it back?"

"Wow," she whispered. "I'd say it's definitely not ruined."

From the roof of the building, Matthew anchored his foot on the top of the ladder as Luke passed him another heavy piece of decking. *"An drei. Eens. Zwee. Drei."*

On *three*, Luke hoisted the wood upward, and Matthew heaved it toward himself at the same time. They moved the last piece of decking into place and hammered it down before taking a seat. His back was completely healed, and except for scarring, he had no signs of ever having been injured.

Luke removed his work gloves and looked at his aching hands. *"Die Arewet iss net zu hatt."*

Matthew chuckled. Both of them were worn out and beat up. "Ya, not *too* difficult." They sat in silence for a bit, resting, the cold air making every breath visible. "Phase two of getting the roof on is complete. Do we have the energy for phase three?"

"Not at this very minute, no." Luke cleared his throat. "So you wanna tell me what the bishop said when he came to visit yesterday?"

"At the next communion, I may not be allowed to participate. He's frownin' really hard about me goin' to the city to stay with a woman." Matthew shrugged. "And he said I had no right to be engaged to an Englischer. Of course I reminded him that it wasn't an official engagement and that her own bishop had been convinced she intended to join the church. He then began talking about the sin of being with a woman before marriage, like going to Baltimore for those two weeks meant I shared a bed with Elle. It wasn't like that."

"I believe you. Never doubted it. But what does Kathryn think happened between you and Elle?"

"I haven't talked to her since she left for home two weeks ago, but she never spoke of it. You think she may be holdin' on to that quiet-like?"

"Seems to me women are hard to figure. What might make one as difficult as a stinging nettle barely seems annoying to another."

The bell rang, signaling lunch was ready.

Luke motioned. "Come on. Let's eat and rest for a spell, then we'll get back at it. I'd like to get the felt laid and half the roofing on by sundown.

"Sure." Matthew wasn't really all that hungry, but he'd go inside and eat. It was easier than seeing the lines of concern across his mother's face.

Once they were on the ground, Luke placed his hand on Matthew's shoulder. "Two weeks and no word from Kathryn, right?"

Matthew nodded.

"Well, for better or worse, I do believe you're about to get a word." Luke pointed at a car pulling into the driveway.

Kathryn sat in the front passenger's seat, her head tilted down as the car pulled to a stop.

Luke smacked him on the back. "I'll tell your Mamm you're busy."

"Thanks." Matthew went to the driver's side of the car, pulling his billfold out of his pocket. How had he managed to only have two girls in his life and both lived far enough away they had to travel by driver in order to see him?

The woman driver rolled down the window, told him the price, and took the money.

"If you'll pop the trunk, I'll grab her bags."

"She doesn't have bags in the trunk."

Matthew glanced up, trying to catch Kathryn's eye, but she was looking at the shop. No bags wasn't good news. The driver left, and Matthew wasn't sure how to begin the conversation.

Kathryn walked toward the shop. "It's coming right along, ya?"

"Ya." Matthew followed her.

The young woman had a head for business, a heart for people, and moods as steady as the passing of time. He only hoped she saw half as much in him as he saw in her.

She stepped through the framing and into the shop area. "I didn't think you'd have the decking on already."

"The aim was to have the roof up by the first of November. In spite of two days of rain when we could do nothin', we're still a couple of days ahead of schedule."

"If I'd stayed and had things organized like you wanted, you could have worked in the barn, filling an order during those rain days."

"I wanted you to stay. That part's true enough. But I'm not all that interested in what buggy-building work could've been done." He grabbed one suspender. "I take it you're not stayin'."

She tightened her black shawl around her shoulders. "I didn't tell Joseph about you wanting us to see each other."

"And you didn't bring any luggage, so I guess I've hit the top prize, messing up our working relationship too." He hadn't really banked on the complications that could come out of this, but he was far more disappointed in losing her than losing a worker, albeit a really fantastic one. He figured she must care for Joseph a whole lot more than it appeared when he saw them together, but the truth was, none of it was his business.

She placed her hands on the framing, as if testing its strength. He studied the delicate lines across the backs of her hands, wondering what all she'd accomplish over the coming years. Like him, she was goal minded. Unlike him, she brought a sense of order to the chaos of each workday. He'd probably not even have the burned-out building removed by now if it wasn't for her skill at organizing.

Kathryn turned to face him. "I didn't tell Joseph because my reasons for not seeing him anymore aren't because of us. He's…safe, and as much as part of me wants that, it's not good enough anymore."

"But you're not staying?"

"Your Mamm's up to running her own household now. We dropped my luggage off at the Bylers' before coming here."

"This is sounding much better as we go along."

"You're not safe, and I find that scary."

Matthew chuckled. "Joseph is, and it seems that's not what you're lookin' for either—whatever 'safe' means." He stepped in closer. "Explain this safe thing."

She shrugged. "I can't, not really. I just know Joseph is and you're not. You want to be. I believe that, but I'm not sure wanting to be is enough."

"Safe." Matthew gazed into her eyes, seeing a beautiful, steady woman, one whose friendship gave him strength. Elle used to drive him crazy with her passionate decisions that she put no thought into. Then when the emotion faded, she had no reason to follow through. "Does this feeling that I'm not safe have anything to do with me going to Baltimore with Elle?"

Her brown eyes studied him. "Should it?" The question wasn't an accusation and didn't hint of jealousy or insecurity.

"No. But the bishop's got me on probation over it. If you're willing for us to court, it'll have to be kept private, real private."

Her brows knit. "I don't understand."

"He'd forget the trip thing if he thought I was seeing a baptized member, and I'll not use you to get out of trouble with the bishop. And I'll not drag your name through the gossip that will take place if he doesn't allow me to take communion."

The lines of concern faded, and a beautiful smile moved clear up to her eyes. "A few years back, when the rumors about Hannah started, it wasn't long before you became a part of them too. You and she were friends. She was pretty far along being pregnant, and you stuck by her—disobeyed the bishop about going to see her. You even stayed overnight with her when you took her to the train depot. That about right?"

"Yes."

"When I heard the rumors, I hurt for Hannah—whether it was her doing for being pregnant or not. But as to your part…" Clearly hesitant, she paused. "It won't make any sense. I mean, it's just strange."

"Strange? That can't be the right word when talkin' about me."

She laughed softly. "My opinions are the strange thing, not you. See, I thought you *had* to be worth getting to know if you disobeyed the bishop to help her and yet were willing to return and take whatever correction he was gonna give."

He stopped all movement, waiting to be able to breathe again.

"The idea of who you were had me curious." She shrugged. "This current problem with the bishop is because you needed time away. You came back with your head on straight. I won't hold going to Baltimore against you."

She made him feel as if what they had could not ever belong to anyone else, and he wanted a name for her that no one else used. "Katie." He said it softly, and the slow, warm smile that crossed her face said she liked it. Matthew lifted the strings to her Kapp and gave them a little tug. "Just where were you when I was going to every singing lookin' for…for you?"

"In Snow Shoe, staying safe."

The back door to the house slammed, and Matthew took a step back. "Are you willing for us to court?"

She nodded. "I am."

Matthew glanced up, seeing Peter walking toward them. He moved his body slightly, brushing his fingers along Kathryn's hand. "Then we keep it a secret for now, ya?"

She lifted her hand that he'd just stroked and stared at it. "Ya."

He'd had no words to express his grief. Now he lacked them to convey his hope.

*H*oping Mary would return her call before time to leave for school, Hannah patiently pointed to an equation at the top of Kevin's math sheet. He sat at the kitchen table, pencil in hand, frown in place, and she stood beside him.

She had an idea to share with Mary about what Sarah could do as a job—rescuing dogs or maybe training them. Her sister seemed to have a lot of misdirected feelings of affection. Maybe working with animals would harness those emotions in a positive way, but Hannah needed feedback from Mary and Luke. If Luke thought it was reasonable, he could talk to Paul about it.

Hannah placed her thumb near the equation Kevin had just worked. "If you have no apples, can you take five apples away?"

He pointed to the paper. "But if you have five and you take zero away…"

"You have zero and need to take five away. You subtract the bottom numbers from the top numbers."

"Oh yeah, I forgot." He studied the paper for a second. "Wait. I think I got it." He lowered his head, writing on his paper.

Hannah ruffled his hair and kissed the top of his head before glancing at the work in front of Lissa. Mary should have received her message by now. It'd been two days, but it was possible no one had checked the answering machine in the phone shanty, and since the cold November weather had set in, they probably hadn't heard it ring.

Laura was out running a few errands, picking up items Kevin needed for a science project he'd forgotten to mention was due tomorrow. After three weeks of Laura's working full-time, the edge of impatience in Martin's voice had faded.

Hannah grabbed the potholders and opened the oven. The back door swung open, and a cold blast of early November air swept through the room as Martin walked inside, looking every bit the executive. Like rockets taking off, Kevin and Lissa jumped up from their seats. Martin lifted Lissa into his arms and kissed her cheek before she wrapped her arms around his neck and stayed there.

Kevin leaned in and hugged Martin around the waist. "I saw a Porsche today on the way to school."

"You did?" Martin gave him a one-arm hug, patting his back while his gaze met Hannah's.

The image of the children clinging to him warmed her. When Faye first left, Kevin and Lissa were most comforted by Hannah's presence, but over the months they'd grown to love him, and he'd gone from tolerating them to loving them as if they were his own, which said a lot since he'd never wanted children.

Kevin nodded. "And on the way home I saw a convertible, a Corvette."

Hannah took the lasagna out of the oven. "How does he know that stuff?" Closing the oven door with her hip, she glanced his way before setting the hot dish on the stove.

"It's guy stuff." Martin raised his eyebrows, teasing her. He put Lissa's feet on the floor and came up behind Hannah, resting his chin on her shoulder. "Smells good."

From his college years on, Martin had avoided eating at home, but with a new family underfoot, he conceded to the routine without complaint.

Hannah glanced at the clock. "Laura ran to the store. I need to leave for class in forty minutes. Let's clear the homework off the table and eat. Kevin, you get each of us a bottle of water and set it on the table."

Martin slid out of his winter coat and hung it on a peg just inside the back door before he grabbed Lissa's papers and backpack off the table. "Only six more weeks of nursing school left, not that I'm counting or anything."

Hannah laughed softly while passing four plates to Lissa. The way he said it, mixed with the look in his eyes, made her realize he'd been counting for a long time. "Yep, I graduate on the Friday before we leave for…" She stopped herself. Just the mention of the two-week Hawaiian trip over the Christmas holidays made Kevin and Lissa spiral out of control with excitement.

He caught her eye, assuring her he knew what she meant. He'd been right that all of them flying to Hawaii, along with his top employees and a couple of friends, would distract Kevin and Lissa from missing their mother over the holidays. He continued clearing off the table while she placed rolls in a basket. The kids were eager, but Martin seemed to long for this trip more than anyone.

"Oh, Dr. Lehman asked if I'd join him full-time at the clinic after the first of the year."

His face twisted with displeasure.

Holding a handful of flatware, Hannah stopped directly in front of him. "Actually, I'm thinking about it."

"Come on, Hannah. Working more hours for him means being on call more. We can't schedule a life around on-call hours." Martin took the utensils from her.

"I would only be on call eight days a month. Four of those days would be every other weekend, and four would be on Tuesdays and Wednesdays, and I'm there every Tuesday anyway. It's quite doable."

He placed the flatware in the wrong spots near the plates. "You make nearly nothing there."

Lissa went behind him, straightening them.

Hannah grabbed a spatula and began cutting the lasagna. "But this is really important to me."

The phone rang, and Hannah glanced at the caller ID. *Mary. Or maybe Luke.*

"Sorry, but I've been waiting two days to hear back from Mary."

He shrugged. "As long as no one expects you to drop everything and blast off to Owl's Perch, Pennsylvania."

She grabbed the phone. "Hello?"

"Hannah." Mary sounded a little breathless.

"Hey, Mary, it's about time you returned my call."

"Your call? I didn't know you called. How…how are you?" Mary's voice sounded hollow.

Trying to hear over the clatter of plates and the conversation between Martin and the children, Hannah motioned for them to begin without her, and she took the cordless into the other room. "I'm fine. We're about to eat dinner, and then I'm off to school. A better question is how are you? Did you like the obstetrician Dr. Lehman found for you?"

"She seems okay. I had an ultrasound yesterday, and I'm scheduled for the C-section on Monday."

Where is the excitement at having seen the baby?

"Monday? Your doctor must think you're a few weeks further along than you figured."

"Ya, that's sort of what she said."

Sort of?

"You okay?" The silence that followed answered Hannah's question. "Mary, what's on your mind?"

"Nothing…"

Searching for the right words, she took into account all she knew of Mary, being Amish, and what Dr. Lehman had taught her, before she started talking in Pennsylvania Dutch. It wasn't long before Mary was telling her what truly was on her mind—the odd sensations in her body, the fears about Monday, and the fact that Luke wasn't home.

Every symptom Mary was hem-hawing about indicated she might

be in labor. "Mary, is there someone within sight? Someone you could holler for to come to the phone?"

"No, but I think Jacob and Mammi Annie are on the property somewhere."

Unwilling for Mary to tread up and down hills looking for someone, Hannah's mind jammed with a dozen possible ways to handle this. "Mary, listen to me." She kept control of her voice, trying to sound authoritative and reassuring at the same time. "I need you to hang up and dial 911. Tell them you need an ambulance. Then slowly make your way inside and lie down until it arrives."

"That's silly. I'm going in for a C-section on Monday. I…I'm fine until then."

"Everything you just described means you could be in early labor."

Mary began sobbing. "I can't… Luke's not here, and—"

"I'll get hold of Paul and send him to find Luke for you. They'll meet you at the hospital."

"No…please. I…I don't want to do this."

"But you *can* do it, and you will for both the baby's sake and yours."

"Will the lady doctor be there?"

"I don't know, and I don't want you staying on your feet long enough to find out. I'll call Dr. Lehman and get him to do what he can, but if she's not there, another surgeon will be."

"I'm so scared."

Hannah's insides quaked. "It'll be fine. Just do as I'm telling you."

"What if you're wrong? What if I'm not in labor or anything?" Mary echoed Hannah's own thoughts.

She could be overreacting, and the ambulance trip and Mary being admitted into the hospital would not only cost Luke a fortune but would cause a lot of distrust and anger against Hannah. Again. But she couldn't take a chance. "I'm not wrong." What else could she say? If she left Mary with any doubts, her friend would ignore the symptoms, maybe until it was too late.

Mary broke into sobs.

In spite of wanting to join her, Hannah remained outwardly calm. "You're going to be fine, and you'll have that baby in your arms even sooner than Monday."

"This is so scary."

Hearing the desperation in Mary's voice and the giggles of the children as they talked to Martin over dinner, she felt the knot in her stomach tighten. The pull to go to Owl's Perch and the desire to be here weighed on her. "You do what needs to be done. I'll come visit as soon as I can and hold this niece or nephew, okay?"

"Ya, okay." Mary sounded calmer now. "You'll find Luke?"

"He's never far, and Paul will find him. Depending on how much time has passed, he'll either bring Luke to the house or take him straight to the hospital. Now do as I said and get off your feet. I'll see you soon." Hannah disconnected the call and phoned Dr. Lehman.

He agreed to try to reach the doctor and at least see if she was on call tonight and, if she wasn't, to explain the circumstances to whoever was on call. He then relayed all the numbers the clinic had given him for reaching Paul. If Paul wasn't on call, he wouldn't have one of two cells provided by the clinic. Wondering if that was part of his decision to stick to the Plain lifestyle or if money was the issue, Hannah said her good-byes.

She pressed the numbers for each cell, but no one answered.

Martin ambled out of the kitchen. "What's up this time?"

"I think Mary's in labor." She held up her index finger for him to give her a minute. After dialing the Better Path, she listened to a message about the office being closed and reopening in the morning. Before it finished telling her how to reach someone in case of an emergency, she hung up. "I told her to call for an ambulance, and now I'm trying to locate Paul so he can find Luke and get him to the hospital."

She had the number for two other places he could be, Gram's and his apartment. She called his apartment first.

Martin's eyes narrowed, and he stepped closer. "You're shaking. You okay?"

"This isn't good news, Martin. Could be really bad news. I won't know for a while." After twenty rings and no one picking up, she disconnected the call and dialed Gram's. "I don't know how long she's been in labor…" Someone answered at Gram's house.

"Hello."

Great. She'd finally reached someone, and it sounded like the same young woman who'd answered the phone the two times Hannah had tried to reach Paul years ago. "This is Hannah Lawson. I need to speak with Paul."

"I, uh…he's…he's…not here… At least…I, uh—"

It was definitely the same person, and she had no doubt it was Dorcas. Hannah's blood turned hot. "Let me interrupt this little spell of confusion for you, Dorcas." She began pacing the floors. "I want to speak to Paul. Now." She measured each word distinctly, softly demanding respect. "And if you don't want him to know about any other times I've called and not gotten through, I highly recommend you find him ASAP."

"Hold on." Dorcas's voice wavered more than Mary's had.

Hannah turned to find Martin studying her.

"What?"

He shook his head. "Nothing." But his eyes were glued to her, perplexed.

"Hannah, what's up?" Paul's voice held that steady calmness she'd come to expect over the last six weeks.

"I received a call from Mary. I think she's in labor, and I told her to call for an ambulance. Luke's not at home, and she's not sure where he is. Can you find him for her?"

"I'll certainly try, but would you rather me get Mary and take her to the hospital?"

"I thought of that and decided against it. If she's in labor, her best option is to be in an ambulance with medical assistance."

"Okay, I trust your judgment. You stick to trusting it. I'll find Luke and call you as soon as I know something. Are you on your way?"

"I'm not sure. I have class. Do you have my cell?"

"I have it. Bye."

She closed her phone and her eyes, praying silently.

Martin slid his arms around her. "Can't they take care of themselves?"

Clueless as to how to share the complexities of her roots, she said nothing.

He held her tighter. "Can I do something for you?"

With her head against his chest, she took a deep breath. "I want to be there."

"It's more than four hours away. Whatever is going to take place will be over before you could arrive."

"I know."

He placed his hands on her shoulders, backing her up and gazing into her eyes. "You can't miss another class."

"I'm not going to be able to concentrate anyway."

"Hannah," he snapped, "the answer is no. I'm not budging on this one." He pulled her back into his arms. "Just wait, and I'll drive you there myself on Saturday as soon as your clinical rotation shift is over. That's just the day after tomorrow. She'll probably still be in the hospital, right?"

"Since she's having a C-section, yes."

he teacher scribbled some type of equation on the board, but Hannah kept fiddling with her cell phone lying on her desk.

When her phone vibrated, she jerked it up, opened it, and pressed the green icon while walking out of the room. "Hannah Lawson." She spoke softly as she stepped into the hallway of North Lincoln Educational Center. Then she tried again, louder. "Hello?"

"I found Luke," Paul stated calmly. "And we're at the Holy Spirit Hospital in Camp Hill. Mary's in—"

Paul's voice stopped.

"Hello?" Hannah thundered into the phone but heard nothing back. "Hello? No!" She slammed the phone shut, reopened it, and punched the call-back button. "Come on."

A rapid busy signal meant something was keeping her from getting a connection. She hurried down the hall to the office. No one was inside, but the door was unlocked. She went behind the desk, tapped a letter on the keyboard to wake the computer, and then connected to the Internet. Within seconds she had a phone number to the maternity division of the hospital.

Using the landline phone on the desk, she made the call. All her hours of working for different hospitals during clinical rotations were paying off in a way she'd never expected. She knew whom to talk to and how to word her request so they'd be willing to locate Paul and give him the landline number where she could be reached.

She sat by the phone, holding a silent prayer vigil. One thing about being raised Amish—faith in silent prayers was as much a part of each day as chores, sweat, and laughter.

The office phone rang, and Hannah jerked it up. "Hannah Lawson."

"Hey, I tried calling you back on your cell. There's no news yet. The nurse said they wheeled Mary into surgery the minute she arrived. We've been here about ten minutes."

"C-sections are fast. You should hear something soon. Just stay on the line with me, okay?"

"Yeah, sure. But don't you need to be in class or something?"

"I'm here. Technically that's all that matters. I'll get the notes off the board and see the teacher before I leave."

"Did you take a course out there in Englischer land on how to track down people via phone or what?"

"I have a little savvy, but mostly I don't take no for an answer anymore, especially when it comes to reaching people. Oh, I thought of an idea about Sarah. It has all sorts of issues for you to work through."

Paul laughed. "And you just happen to tell me that on the heels of saying you don't take no for an answer. What's the idea?"

She began telling him, and within twenty minutes they'd plotted a half-dozen ways Sarah could work with a dog-rescue-and-placement group, maybe even learn how to train dogs for specific jobs.

"This is really good, Hannah. I never would've thought of it."

"Hey." Luke's muffled voice sounded like he was beside Paul. "Is that my sister?"

"Yeah. Hannah, Luke wants to talk to you."

"Perfect. Thanks."

"Mary's in recovery, waking up." Luke sounded thrilled. "The doctor said she did beautifully and that getting to the hospital that quick may've saved her life."

Hannah drew several deep breaths. "Oh, Luke, I'm so grateful."

His boisterous laugh made chills run through her. "I told him my sister's a nurse and knew what to do. We have a girl! Mary's going to want to see you soon. The doc's gonna keep her a few days, maybe run a CT scan before letting her go home." Her brother's fast-paced, excited speech was a bit hard to decipher, but she caught it all.

"I'll be in Saturday evening, around eight or so."

"Around eight?"

"It's the earliest I can make it. I have a work shift first."

"Okay, we'll be here. You and Paul make a good team. You know that?"

Hannah didn't answer. She'd seen inklings of it long ago. "I'll see you on Saturday. Congratulations, Luke."

"Thanks, Hannah. Bye."

She hung up the phone and went back to her classroom, but she was too thrilled and relieved to concentrate.

Hannah rode with her eyes closed and her head against the backrest, glad Martin was driving. His sports car handled the curves and bumps more fluidly than her Honda. He kept a variety of music playing while Hannah rested. Between school, studying, clinical rotations, working for Dr. Lehman, and juggling her ready-made family, she needed the rest.

The night Mary gave birth Hannah didn't sleep. Adrenaline had pumped through her for hours. Memories of her childhood with Mary filtered through her mind as if she were reliving them.

Martin scrolled through the song list on his iPod. "I really don't get why this trip is necessary. I mean, you lived without talking to Mary, without sending much in the way of letters for more than two years, and now you act as if your world will fall apart if you don't get time with her."

"I didn't have contact with her for that time, but then her life was in danger, and now we have a baby to celebrate."

He shrugged. "Seems like a phone call should have been plenty."

"Maybe we should do the band gathering by phone next time, okay?"

"Totally different." He turned up the music.

She settled back and closed her eyes again. From nowhere, thoughts of Paul demanded her attention. Refusing to indulge them, she shifted in her seat and opened her eyes. "How's work?"

"We never talk about my work."

"Maybe we should."

He glanced from the road to her several times. "Nah, if I do that, then I have to hear about babies being born and about events in the lives of those women who come for the Tuesday quiltings."

When silence fell between them, recent snapshot images of Paul ran through her mind. The first glimpse she caught of him at Gram's—his honesty and patience in the face of her anger. Hours later—his gentleness and wisdom with Sarah. In the barn as they talked afterward—his calm but unyielding insistence that she speak to him with civility. Later that same day in the kitchen at the Better Path preparing food. He could have eaten at Gram's, but he'd fixed omelets at the clinic. Had he done that for her?

She turned off the music. "Talk to me. Find something and talk."

"Would you relax?" Martin grabbed his leather CD wallet and pulled out a fresh disc. "I haven't loaded this onto my iPod yet, but I've been wanting you to listen to a couple of songs on my newest album so we can talk about which ones to add to the band's list."

"Meaning some of the words are controversial."

"Not by most people's standards, but, yes, that's what I mean."

Hannah nodded and tried to focus on the songs. Against her will, thoughts of Paul pushed forward again, recounting conversations that had passed between them since she'd returned. As the memories circled, she picked up on nuances of who he was that she hadn't noticed before. More than ever she understood that it hadn't been his apathy that had let her go. It was his patience. When he was hurt at Matthew's, he'd seemed standoffish for a bit, and she thought he was trying to avoid being affected by her proverbial scarlet letter. Clearly there were times when she misunderstood his quiet demeanor.

"Hello?" Martin's sarcastic tone catapulted her back to the present.

She turned toward him. "Yeah?"

Under the glow of streetlights, she saw a lopsided smile ease across his lips. He moved his hand to the back of her neck, rubbing it gently. "I'm going to assume you heard none of the songs."

"Sorry."

He gestured out the window. "It's spitting sleet, and we're pulling into the parking lot. I'll drop you off and then park the car."

"Okay."

She went into the hospital. Paul was in a seat some twenty feet away. She started to go to him but decided maybe she should keep her distance and wait for Martin. It'd be rude to be with Paul when Martin came in. She glanced in the direction he was looking.

Television.

Deciding she couldn't pass up harassing him, she smiled and walked over to him. "Sports-bar restaurants and hospitals?"

Paul rose to his feet. "Hi, Hannah. Someone needed a lift to the hospital, so while I was here…"

"If I had a picture phone, I'd send a snapshot of this to your bishop."

"You think he has a picture phone to receive it?"

She laughed and he joined her.

"Besides, it's Penn State and Michigan. His disapproval would fall on deaf ears."

"I get the distinct impression you'd not repent one bit, Paul Waddell."

"In the words of Hannah Lawson, 'You think?'" His eyes sparkled with mischief. "You handled this with Mary right. There is only good news to celebrate."

He motioned to the chair beside him, and they both took a seat. "Your Daed's in the waiting room. Luke told him you were coming in, and he asked me to bring him here so he could see you."

She quirked an eyebrow. "Didn't you just say there was only good news?"

Paul looked at his folded hands, focused on them while a smile covered his face. "I never pegged you for a legalist, Hannah." Slowly his eyes moved to hers, looking at her the same way he did years ago when he walked so lightly, so carefully with a young girl's heart, never asking for even a kiss though he was in the midst of the lure of college life.

But they did kiss…

Bombarded with memories, Hannah couldn't seem to breathe. She remembered standing in the November rain, wishing all of life were different and their love wasn't forbidden. Through the misting night, she spotted his old truck. He'd come to Owl's Perch, trying to catch a few minutes with her after being separated for months with no contact. The door opened, and Paul jumped out. Ignoring all sense of protocol, she ran down the hill and embraced him. He nuzzled against her neck, even daring to plant a kiss on her cold, damp skin. Her arms tightened, and she remembered fearing it might be just a dream. But his warm, caring hands moved to her face, cradling it, and slowly a smile eased his tense features as he lowered his face until his lips touched hers. Warmth and power swept through her. Her first kiss. So powerful—

"Hannah." Martin's voice drew her back.

She jumped to her feet. "Hi." She slid her hand into his, dismissing romantic thoughts of Paul. Her life, her family, her dreams were with the man beside her.

Paul rose.

Martin's eyes flicked over him before he focused on Hannah.

"Problem?" Smoothly he pulled his hand free from hers and ran his arm behind her, placing his palm on the small of her back. A reminder of her real life. The one she'd built despite everything. The one he'd helped her attain.

"No, not at all." She smiled, offering an unspoken apology.

His professional demeanor seemed to be in place, and his features didn't return an ounce of warmth.

Trying to dispel the tension, she motioned toward Paul. "Paul, I'd like you to meet Martin Palmer. Martin, this is Paul Waddell."

Martin's green eyes flashed with annoyance for a moment before he gave a nod. "Paul." With his left hand still on Hannah's back, he held out the other.

Paul shook his hand. "Have any trouble finding the place?"

"No, but I get the feeling it'll be hard finding a topnotch hotel." Martin's features edged with tautness as he checked his watch. "Why don't we go upstairs so you can see Mary before it gets too late?"

Paul gestured down the hallway. On their way to the elevator, they passed a few groups of people, their voices hushed as they headed for the exit.

Keeping one hand on Hannah's back, Martin punched the elevator button. "It's nearly nine. I'm sure visiting hours are over, so we need to wrap this up quickly." He spoke softly, and she knew he expected a nod.

She didn't respond.

Her dearest childhood friend and her closest sibling had a baby girl. Hannah wanted to celebrate, to watch the joy on their faces as they held this little girl. It meant so much more than the fact they were her family and she'd known what to do to help them. It meant finding strength and tucking it away for days that carried no hope. And she didn't want to be rushed through it.

Only the three of them stepped onto the elevator. Paul pushed the button with the number four on it and the doors closed.

Martin leaned against the wall, eying Paul with disdain. "So, how's the shoulder?"

Paul's expression seemed rigid. "Healed."

Martin rolled his eyes. "I'm sure."

Hannah looked from one man to the other. The gentlemanly welcomes had faded. Martin's thinly veiled manners didn't fool her. He could not care any less about Paul's arm. He wanted Paul to know he knew—everything. And Paul's one-word answer drew a distinct boundary—around what she wasn't sure—but she was becoming familiar with this in-your-face, unmovable side of him.

She knit her brows slightly, trying to pass Martin a silent message to be nice, but he acted indifferent to her subtle messages. "Paul said that my Daed is here."

Martin gave half a nod. The doors opened, and she stepped off with Martin right behind her. While Paul went on ahead, Martin tugged on her hand, and she stopped.

"Do you think maybe you could not flirt with him while I'm here?" His words were but a whisper, his anger deep.

She shook her head. "I...I..."

"I know what I saw in the lobby, Hannah—your eyes locked on his."

What was she going to say to him? Tell him the truth, that sometimes being near Paul was just too much?

Martin started walking in the same direction Paul had, but he was not within sight. They'd only gone a short way when she realized she didn't have a room number for Mary. Turning to go back to the nurses' station, she spotted her father walking toward her.

"Daed..." She pressed her hand down the front of her dress. "I'd like you to meet Martin Palmer. Martin, this is my father, Zeb Lapp."

"Hi." Martin's tone was neither warm nor cold. He had little respect, if any, for her father, the man who'd given Zabeth a difficult time when she chose to leave the church after becoming a baptized member.

Without any appearance of anger or resentment, her father studied Martin before he shook his hand. "Hello." He had no idea who Martin was, no clue that his sister, Zabeth, had spent her adult life helping raise him.

A grin caused lines to crease around her father's mouth. "It's been a couple of days, and Luke's still about to burst he's so excited about being a Daed, but he says no one but him and Mary can hold the baby until you and that Mennonite..." He let the sentence drop, dipped his head apologetically, before looking her in the eye again. "Until you and Paul do."

"What? I had no idea."

"Since most don't come to the hospital for such things anyway, it doesn't matter much. They'll wait until Luke and Mary are home to go by and see the baby." He tilted his head, studying his daughter. "You told Mary to call an ambulance and come here?"

Hannah froze, her mind running a thousand miles a second. He seemed to be asking sincerely and was clearly confused by the contradictions of what'd taken place two nights ago—the ambulance, the surgery, Luke and Mary not allowing anyone in until Hannah and Paul went in. Yet in spite of the confusion and mystery, he didn't seem to be accusing her of any misdeed.

"I did."

Daed adjusted his black winter hat. "You have no more to say than that?"

She shook her head. "No."

Her father's eyes stayed hard on her. "You're a tough one to figure, child. When you were a little girl,"—he held his hand two feet off the ground—"just a tiny thing, you were more independent than half the men I knew. And smart." He scoffed. "You scared me. You should have seen yourself. It was something to behold. I wavered during your whole childhood between being proud of you and fearing you'd turn against God." He rubbed his rough, dry hands together. " 'Do by self.' That was one of the first things you ever learned to say, and say it you did, all the time." He paused, pain reflected in his eyes. "I never once intended to be a cause for you to turn against Him. I thought I was holding you in place, keeping you submissive to a higher calling."

"There is no higher calling than freedom in Christ."

"But I'm your father. I had the right to decide where you should be, how you should dress and act." He lowered his eyes. "And who you should be with."

Determined to share her mind without sounding harsh, Hannah set her will to speaking softly. "Then when is it a parent's responsibility to let go and let their offspring find the path God has for them?"

Her father sighed and removed his hat. "I got some things to say, and I don't mind saying them right now, unless you got a problem with that."

"Go ahead."

"When I insisted on you talking to the church leaders before I'd let you move back home from Mary's, I thought I was helping clear your name. I was sure they'd hear you out and say you were innocent of any real wrongdoing, but then during the meeting I learned that you'd been sneaking around behind my back with Paul and that you'd been keeping all sorts of secrets from me. I got so mad when I learned that, I was convinced you'd lied to me about everything, including the night of the unmentionable. It made sense to think you'd had a fight with him that night and while running home you'd fallen headlong, cutting your palms. And I figured all those tears and rough times you went through were because you was pining over him. Those sorts of conclusions happen when a parent learns a child's been lying." He drew a long breath, twisting the hat in his hand around and around. "But bringing you before the church leaders turned out to be unjust. I just wanted you to tell the truth so we didn't look like heathens with you needing a place to raise your child outside of wedlock, but I never once thought you'd up and leave before we worked everything out."

There she stood, needing to forgive a man whose hand in dishing out misery to her was every bit as real as her attacker's. The second hand on the wall clock made its little *tick, tick, tick.* Words didn't form in her mind. Among the Plain, withholding forgiveness was cause for losing all chance of salvation. The words *I forgive* had to be spoken, and then the person could wrestle with any lingering resentments on their own.

Still, she said nothing.

She could feel Martin's hand on her back, nudging her. He wanted her to speak. Flashing him a look to stop, she sidestepped him.

"That's all I needed to say. Maybe you can think on it a spell, and we'll talk later."

Her father wasn't going to lecture her that her salvation was at stake?

"I…I'd like that." As wobbly as a new calf, she gave him a kiss on the cheek.

His eyes misted. "Go on, now." He pointed down the hall.

She glanced to Martin.

"I'm fine. Go do whatever it is Luke wants. I'll sit with your dad." Her Daed took a seat.

Martin pulled change from his pocket and moved to the vending machine. "Care for a drink, Mr. Lapp?"

Their voices faded as Hannah entered the hallway. Farther down the corridor, she spotted Paul outside one of the rooms, waiting on her. When she came close, he put his hand on the door as if he was going to open it, but then he paused. "Hannah, in spite of any problems this caused you, Luke and Mary are very grateful you came."

She understood. He was giving assurance that whatever price he thought she was paying with Martin was worth it because of Luke and Mary's gratefulness. But Martin wasn't who he appeared to be to Paul. He was deep and wonderful, but if she defended him right now, Paul wouldn't believe her anyway.

Without answering him, she pushed the door open herself. Mary was propped up in bed, her prayer Kapp in place and a tiny infant in her arms. She smiled broadly, radiating joy so strong Hannah basked in the strength of it.

Luke crossed the room and hugged Hannah, almost stealing her breath. "How can I thank you?"

She held on to him. "Oh, I'll have to think that over and come up with a way here or there, regularly for decades."

Luke chuckled. "You do that."

"Look." Mary's raspy voice was barely recognizable. She fidgeted with the blankets surrounding the tiny bundle in her arms.

Hannah moved to one side of the bed and Paul to the other, each looking at the new life in Mary's arms. She lifted her daughter toward Hannah, which made the baby start crying.

Hannah eased the infant from her mother's arms. *"Shh, Liewi, Ich denk nix iss letz. Ya?"* She bounced her gently, assuring her that nothing was wrong, and the newborn became quiet.

Looking like his shirt was entirely too small for his swollen chest, Luke smiled. "We thought about naming her Hannah."

Hannah froze. "What? No. Don't—"

"But we decided to name her after someone easier to raise than you," Mary teased.

"Than me?" Hannah quipped. "What about you?"

Mary giggled and then grabbed her stomach and moaned. "Oh, don't make me laugh. It hurts."

Luke moved to Hannah's side and placed his finger against the palm of his daughter's hand. "We'll do our best to guide her, but as far as who she is or becomes—what will be, will be. And she'll be my daughter the same as she's His daughter, no matter what she chooses. We named her Amanda. It means 'worthy to be loved.' "

"Perfect," Hannah whispered, marveling at the little girl in her arms. An ache tugged at her for all the babies she'd never have and even for the lifetime of holidays and birthdays of her nieces and nephews that she'd miss. Mary and she gushed over the baby for quite a spell before she walked around the bed and gently laid the tiny infant in Paul's arms.

Paul held the girl as if he'd held newborns many times before, and Hannah was sure he had. His sister had children, and no telling how many other relatives and friends had babies. His tall, muscular body appeared gigantic next to the tiny newborn.

She turned to Luke. "If you want to do something nice for me, I'd like for you and Mary to meet Martin."

The newborn started fussing again, and Paul eased her back into her mother's arms.

Luke glanced to Paul before nodding. "Sure, go get him."

When she stepped into the hallway, she spotted Martin leaning against a wall. She motioned for him. When he was toe to toe with her, she stayed put, looking him in the eye. "About Paul in the lobby, I should've been more aware, more careful. I'm really sorry."

He started to brush the backs of his fingers down her arm but lowered his hand.

What had she done to them?

Martin sighed. "I know." Unlike other arguments, this time she received no understanding smile or kiss on the forehead. "Can we get out of here now?"

"Soon. I want you to meet Luke and Mary first." She wrapped one arm through his and kissed his cheek. He remained unmoved, staring at her. Then he slowly turned her hand palm up and eased his finger across the center of it, telling her his heart was hers. Closing her hand around his, she returned his message. She didn't want his heart anywhere else.

He finally drew a deep breath, and she saw a hint of a smile.

Hannah held his hand as they began walking. "They named the baby Amanda, and she's absolutely perfect."

I nside Dr. Lehman's office with the door closed, Hannah bolted to her feet and began pacing. "I don't want to know this."

Dr. Lehman pressed the ends of his fingers together. "That's not the reaction I expected."

"You told me when I woke from that coma that I couldn't have babies."

"No, I said you were unlikely to, and I had no idea you thought 'unlikely' meant no chance. Although looking back at how young and confused you were, I guess I should've clarified it long before now." He tapped the latest edition of a medical journal that lay open in front of him. "There's an article in here that says after a few years of healing, women who were in your situation and your age bracket conceived again without medical intervention."

"Why are you telling me this now?"

"Because I thought you'd be glad to know, and if you're not, then you definitely need to know, don't you?"

His reasoning was sound, but this information would only complicate things between her and Martin. She plunked into a chair.

Dr. Lehman propped his elbows on his desk. "Want to talk about why you're reacting like this?"

Hannah shook her head, wishing the news meant life and love and joy. Instead it meant confusion and…probably arguments and compromises.

"Hannah, I really thought you'd be encouraged by the news."

"One would think." She ran her fingers across her forehead. "Martin's asked me to marry him, and he doesn't want children. I'll have to agree to use birth control when the time comes. Do you know how difficult that is for someone who's been raised Amish?"

"As a delivery doc for the Plain community, I've got a strong idea. It crosses a moral line for most, and in spite of being such a practical group, their love of family outweighs all else."

"I didn't want to know this." Her eyes met his.

He closed the journal. "I can tell. Need to go for a walk or something?"

She wanted to go spend time with Martin and hope he had something wise to say that could make this news work for both of them. He had his usual pre-Thanksgiving entourage at his house right now, playing music and enjoying the day without her.

Hannah glanced at her watch. "How close do you think Elsie is to delivering?"

"With it being her first, a while yet. I suspect at least five hours."

"Can I go to Martin's and you call me when her time is closer?"

"You've been with her, answering her questions, since before she was married. She'll be upset if you're not here."

"I know. I'll be back." She needed to sort through this, and seeing Martin always helped.

"Be back here in two hours."

With her head spinning, Hannah drove to Martin's house, wondering how she'd tell him. He'd probably tell her not to worry about it, that he'd have a vasectomy or she could have her tubes tied or something. Not being able to conceive was one thing, but trying to prevent it? That was an issue she hadn't worked through. The idea of birth control was disconcerting to the very center of who she was. And if she could possibly conceive, she'd need birth control for decades, not just a few years.

Deciding that after their trip to Hawaii was probably a better time to share her newfound info, Hannah felt a little peace wash over her. It seemed that in nothing flat she was parking at the front curb of Martin's house. One glimpse of the place made her wonder just how many extra people he'd invited for this year's pre-Thanksgiving blowout. The driveway and turnaround were packed with cars, and she couldn't afford to get blocked in.

When she opened the front door, she heard Martin singing with the band. Newly hung Christmas lights surrounded doorframes, wound up the staircase, and outlined the windows. Unfamiliar voices echoed throughout as loud laughter greeted her. Hannah slid out of her coat and hung it in the hall closet. She spoke to various people she knew as she went to check on Lissa and Kevin. The children were surrounded by other kids, all of whom barely glanced up from their video games. She refused to go look at the cover of the game. Her vote was to limit their watching television or playing video games to G-rated ones and only once a week, but she stayed out of Martin's decisions on such matters.

Content that things were running smoothly, albeit not in a manner she would have chosen, Hannah went to the kitchen to check on Laura and found her restocking a platter of food. "Hey, you're back. How was it?"

Hannah popped a grape into her mouth. "A young woman I've worked with for a long time is in the early stages of labor in her first pregnancy."

Laura threw an empty plastic platter in the trash. "Don't you usually stay when you're on call and someone's in labor?"

Feeling the familiar pull of her many worlds, she aimed not to let her voice share too much. "Yeah, but Martin forgot I was on call, so I hated to be gone the whole evening." The music came to a stop, and she nodded to the other room. "Speaking of which, it sounds like they're taking a break, so I'm going to let him know I'm here." Hannah weaved her way through the crowd of mostly strangers until she met up with Martin. "Hi."

He smiled. "Well, hello. Fancy meeting you here."

"Uh, yeah, it's fancy all right."

He held up his hands in surrender. "Laura's doing. She put up the lights before anyone arrived today." Placing his hand on her back, he directed her toward the kitchen. "But it does look good."

Hannah noticed a petite woman with shoulder-length blond hair watching them. The woman stepped forward, wearing shiny high heels, a gently molded, knee-length skirt, and matching cashmere sweater. It was the type of outfit Martin would like to see Hannah wearing, modest with a twist of alluring. But it wasn't modest by Plain standards, and she didn't think she could ever dress in that manner on a regular basis. Wearing fancy clothes was hard enough on very special occasions, although she'd have no problem wearing something alluring in the privacy of their home once they were married and the children were down for the night.

Martin paused and gestured toward the blond woman. "Hannah, I'd like you to meet Amy Clarke. Amy, this is Hannah Lawson."

Hannah shook her hand. "Hi, Amy, it's nice to finally meet you. You own the landscape architect business in the same building as Martin, right?"

"Yes, my mom owned it originally, but after I graduated from college, she trained me and then took an early retirement. Martin and I have worked together for a lot of years." She tilted her head and looked at Martin with obvious admiration. "I've been interested in meeting you. Since you've been on the scene, he's easier to convince when he's wrong and he refuses to work too much."

"Don't give her too much credit, Aim. She's known to bring out the worst in me too."

Amy shifted her stance. "So, Hannah, are you counting the days until vacation?"

Martin ran his hand up and down Hannah's back. "She graduates the Friday night before we leave. She can't help but tally each day."

Amy laughed.

Martin opened his mouth to say something else, but the phone in Hannah's pocket rang loudly.

She slid it from her pocket. "Excuse me."

Martin rolled his eyes. "Speaking of bringing out the worst in me..."

She smiled at him before she pressed the green button. She listened as Dr. Lehman's answering service told her to come in right away. She said she'd be there as soon as possible and then ended the call. "I'm sorry. I have to go."

Martin sighed. "Of course you have to leave, because working for no money while disrupting our lives is just right up your ever-altruistic alley."

The sting of embarrassment was complete. If his aim was to make her pay for having to work today, he'd accomplished it.

"Amy, it was nice to meet you, but I think Martin's right. I just brought out the worst in him. If you'll excuse us for a minute, please."

She took Martin by the hand. They stopped by the closet, and she grabbed her coat before they went out the front door. She closed the door behind them, confident her cheeks were still red with anger. "I'm not the one who forgot I was on call. It's only reasonable for me to work this holiday weekend if I'm off during Christmas. And if you'd shared your *extravagant* plans concerning today with me, I'd have reminded you about my schedule." She jerked her coat on.

"You say the word 'extravagant' like this party is something to endure." He shoved his hands into his pockets and moved to stand at the top of the porch steps. "You know, it'd be really nice if just once you did more than tolerate what I have to offer. Just once, Hannah."

"And could that be followed up by you not making plans first and telling me second?"

Martin said nothing, and she hated that they'd had so much trouble communicating lately. They'd once shared everything, and when they first started dating...well, actually, they argued and almost broke up before the very first date, but then they talked things out, and she saw a deeper part of who he was. They became closer that night. That's what they needed—to talk like they used to.

She forced a smile, aching with the things that tore at them. Since the night he'd gone to the hospital with her three weeks ago and had seen her being more than civil with Paul, there had been more stress between them. She'd blown it and done damage, but she would not accept defeat. They'd get past this as well as the news Dr. Lehman had shared, but it wasn't the right time to tell Martin about that.

He kissed her forehead. "Look, we've stumbled on a gap that needs a bridge. You're right. I am guilty of making decisions first and telling you second. It's a habit that needs breaking now that I'm part of being a couple. But if I didn't push, you'd still be living in that cabin, avoiding the lifestyle of the professional and modern world around you. Are you ever going to be ready to let go of the Plain ways and enjoy what's right in front of you?" He kissed her cheek. "Come on, phone girl, make a choice for us."

Hannah slid her arms around him, remembering their first kiss. With one connection of their lips, he'd swept loneliness from her, an isolation that was colder than the Arctic and just as secluded. She loved him more than he probably realized, but was the next great movie, blowout party, gaming station, or extravagant vacation so very important?

She kissed his cheek before taking a step back. "Look, I've gotta run—should have left fifteen minutes ago. Let's talk about this later." She didn't wait for another kiss as she hurried down the steps. "Bye."

"Drive safe." He waited until she was sliding behind the wheel to wave, and then he went inside.

Restless beyond his own tolerance, Paul stood in the backyard of his parents' home, splitting firewood. The day before Thanksgiving was always difficult. The sky hung low with gray clouds, matching his mood. Regardless of how much life had separated Hannah and him, each year they'd had this one day to visit from early morn to almost sunset. The day had demanded little but provided time for talking and playing games while baking foods at Gram's in preparation for Thanksgiving.

With the Better Path closed, and in need of a diversion, he'd come to Maryland to spend time with his family. It wasn't helping. He grabbed a two-foot-long, unsplit log. After setting the round upright on the tree stump, he took the ax in hand and slammed it into the wood, splitting the log from end to end. It seemed that a distraction from Hannah didn't exist. Anywhere.

Over and over again he chopped, tossed, and grabbed another piece. When she'd first arrived back in Owl's Perch and he'd thought she was married, he convinced himself that he had waited for her out of guilt. Even if that'd been true, after being around her for just a few days, he was captivated again. Now everything about Hannah beckoned him, and he felt miserably cantankerous. With everything they'd resolved between them, only one thing kept them apart—her being in love with someone else.

He slung another piece of split wood onto the growing pile, and a thought of Dorcas pushed its way forward in his mind. He felt so bad for her. Not only was he falling deeper in love with Hannah every time he saw her, but his tolerance for Dorcas was becoming thinner. In an effort to be reasonably up-front with her, he told her Hannah wasn't married, and for his effort, Dorcas's health took a turn for the worse.

Mutilating another piece of wood with the ax gave no release from the turmoil inside him. He'd wanted to tell Dorcas there was no way he could court her. Ever. For both their sakes, he wished he was at least attracted to her. After two and a half years, he'd come close to having a few feelings for her, but that was before Hannah drove back into his life. Because of Dorcas's health, he didn't dare tell her how he really felt, so she continued to wait in hopes of a true courtship.

"Paul?" His sister spoke loudly.

He glanced up, surprised Carol was standing near him, looking perplexed.

She stomped the ground and wrapped her black wool coat tighter around her. "You don't even have on sleeves."

"I'm fine."

"Only because you've been out for hours working like a sled dog. What gives?"

"Nothing."

She didn't budge.

Paul motioned toward the house. "Space would be really nice, okay?"

She shook her head. "I don't understand. Dorcas is finally diagnosed. Lyme disease isn't easy to cure, but she's not dying and stands a good chance of eventually having a full recovery."

Guilt smothered him. "How's she feeling today?"

"She's inside, arrived about an hour ago. Why don't you come sit with her?"

He shook his head. "Not now."

Looking resigned, Carol folded her arms tightly across her waist. "She's relieved to have a diagnosis that isn't terminal. Scared at how difficult it's going to be to recover. In pain from what the illness has done to her body."

He set an unsplit round on the stump. "I'll come in and see her after a while." If Dorcas felt decent enough today, she'd have come outside to be with him. Regardless of the reason, the space was welcome. It wasn't her fault that his attraction to her barely registered on any scale during their best days together.

"If I guess at what's eating you, will you nod if I hit it?"

Swinging the ax, he landed the cutting edge on the top of the round, splitting it partially. "Leave it alone, Carol. Just go inside and pretend that if you ignore how I really feel, it'll all go away. That's what you and Mom and Dad have done for years, isn't it?"

Carol stared at the ground. "Yes, we have, but it hasn't changed the truth, and I'm ready to admit that." She lifted her eyes to him. "Tell me what to do."

Paul set the ax to the side. "It's too late. There's nothing to do. Hasn't been since the night I left Hannah."

"Oh, Paul." She sat on the huge stump he'd been using to split the wood. "Is that what's eating you? Are you still in love with her after all this time?"

Hearing the sincerity in her voice, he sensed his restlessness ease a notch. "Sounds crazy, I know."

"Dorcas said Hannah's been in and out of Owl's Perch and that she's not married. So now what?"

"Nothing. She's in love with someone else. The man has a young niece and nephew they're raising. Life keeps moving."

"Paul, maybe you're better—"

"Don't." He pointed at her. "Don't say that maybe I'm better off. It's not true, and if you knew her, you'd know that too."

She shook her head. "I can't believe this is happening to our family again. First, Uncle Samuel living all his days unmarried because of one girl, and now you. Why do you have to care for someone outside your reach?"

"But Hannah wasn't out of reach for me, and I wasn't for her. We had family things to work through, and we could have, if only..."

If only.

The list that could finish that phrase was so long he couldn't make himself admit even half of it. If only he'd followed her home in his truck each time, the attack would never have happened. If only he'd listened to her that night, she'd never have left Owl's Perch without him. If only he'd received a call from her, he'd have left everything and gone to her. If only...she wasn't in love with another man.

It was enough to make him think he might spontaneously combust.

Carol touched his shoulder. "I'm sorry. Sorry I ever argued with you about her. Sorry Dorcas is sick and you can't get free to look for someone better suited to you."

His sister's empathy surprised him completely.

He decided to tell her some of his quieter thoughts. "I'm considering doing volunteer work with our service this coming summer, maybe even something overseas. I just need to make things right with Dorcas first."

"Maybe you'll find someone through missions and service, although when Dorcas can tolerate hearing such a plan is anybody's guess."

He nodded. "I know, but it's also wrong not to tell her."

She sighed. "It's my fault that Dorcas has been invited to hang around all the time. Between my inviting her and her being the daughter of Mom's best friend, we've thrown you two together. I was just sure you'd come to care for her if given time. I never realized it might take a millennium."

"I won't spend my life pining for what could have been with Hannah. It's just that being with her again and seeing her with Martin will take awhile to shake free of. I...I'm..." He shook his head, deciding not to tell her he had concerns whether Martin was the best person for Hannah. His snippet view of the man did nothing to boost his confidence in Martin Palmer. "Anyway, after Dorcas is better, I'll make my plans clear, and then I'll...I'll move on."

That was the only thing that made sense. His phone rang, startling his sister.

"Sorry." He dusted off his hands. "I started carrying one of the clinic's phones…" Since the night Hannah had to call too many places trying to reach him.

"Hello?"

"Listen, I'm on my way back to you."

Warm goose bumps ran up and down his body as Hannah spoke the words.

She drew a breath. "I got caught at Martin's, and now I'm hung up in traffic, some sort of horrific, heart-wrenching mess that I have to break free of before I can get moving, but I'll be there. Assure Elsie of that, even if she delivers before I arrive. How far apart are her contractions now?"

"Hannah?" He knew who it was and wondered why he'd made it sound like a question.

The line went completely silent. "Paul?" She laughed, a warm, beautiful, robust laugh—the kind that haunted his dreams and woke him with a longing to hold her. "You're not in labor, are you?"

"I've chopped over a half cord of wood so far today. That's definitely labor."

"Well, I'm not catching each piece of wood, bathing it, and wrapping it in a blanket. You can bank on that one, bud."

"Bud?" he teased.

"It's a word."

Realizing they'd said the phrase 'it's a word' to each other while playing Scrabble on numerous occasions over the years, he ached anew for the friendship they'd lost. He decided to keep this conversation going as long as possible, much as he had all those board games they used to play. "Yeah, but it's not worth any points since it's a name."

"Wouldn't matter. You'd find a way to rip off any points I came up with anyway."

She'd answered him without hesitating, as if the memories were never far from her either. Was he imagining that? "I never cheated."

"Ah, but did you play fair?"

The cool air whipped through his short-sleeved shirt, and he felt the coldness for the first time today. "Define 'fair.'"

"Ewww, I tend to forget how good you are at wordplay," she scoffed mockingly. "You win this round. I only have four numbers stored in my cell phone, and I was only half watching while scrolling for Dr. Lehman's number."

With emotions pouring into him at the speed of Niagara Falls, he sat down on the stump Carol had abandoned. "Only half watching what: the phone or the road while driving?"

"Yes." She paused. "I'm now a regular statistic—young women in their cars on their cell phones while driving—but I did not cause the accident."

"Says the girl who's on her cell phone, laughing and chatting feverishly."

She broke into laughter again. "Shut up, Waddell."

"You don't sound the least bit displeased about being an Englischer statistic."

"There are things I like about the Englischer life."

Wanting more time, Paul challenged her. "Name them, all of them."

His sister held up a coat for him that she'd apparently retrieved from the house. Holding it out so he could slide one arm in, she offered a concerned smile. He shifted the phone to his other hand and finished putting on the jacket.

"Thanks." He mouthed the word to her. "Hellooooo?" he called to Hannah.

"Paul?"

His name came out broken, and he knew they were losing the connection. Then the line went silent. He closed the phone and paced the yard, thoughts coming at him faster than he could process. *Listen, I'm on my way back to you.*

Carol cocked her head. "She called you?"

"By accident. She was trying to reach Dr. Lehman at the birthing clinic where she works."

"But you immediately began a really friendly conversation with her." Carol sighed, looking unsure of what was taking place. "How are you ever going to move on if you keep having contact?"

"Well, so much for deciding to support me."

"Just don't set yourself up for another hard fall, okay?"

His phone rang, and he jerked it open, taking a second to glance at the caller ID. Her name wasn't logged in this phone's memory, but he knew her number by heart. "We lost the connection."

"Alliance is hilly with dips. Plus we have the Allegheny Mountains between us."

That wasn't all they had between them, but he didn't want to think about that right now. In spite of a niggling sensation that he was involved in something closer to an affair than a friendship, he wanted more. "So, can you tell me that list now?"

He had no intention of asking why she'd called him again or of turning the conversation into something that would make her back off. It was their day, the day before Thanksgiving, and she'd called—by accident—but still his Lion-heart was on the other end of the phone.

"Paul, I didn't mean to call you the first time, and I...I called back because...well, follow-through is important, but I should let you go."

Follow-through?

If she'd had some of that a few years ago, they wouldn't be in this fix. "Come on, Hannah. How great can your relationship with Martin be if it can't handle your talking to me for ten minutes?" He regretted the jab at their relationship the second he said it. "I'm sorry. I shouldn't have said that."

"It's okay. I understand. I'm sure Martin looked like a jerk the other night, but you don't know him. What you and I do know is there's too much between us sometimes. Martin saw proof of it the last time I was there, and he lost his temper." She paused. "Not one second of this is right or fair to him."

More clearly than ever, Paul heard just how completely forthright she'd become while living in Ohio. Unfortunately, a little less frankness would give them some cover to act like their feelings didn't run so deep, to behave like all they had was friendship and no threat to Martin. "Maybe I'm wrong, but I'm not all that concerned about what's fair for Martin. You landed there devastated, and I bet he's stuck like superglue. But because of him, you can't give us a few minutes to just chat?"

"Paul." She spoke softly, as if she understood all too well the truth of his words. "I won't do anything to hurt Martin. Ever. And if he knew I called you by accident, he'd be fine. If he knew I called you back and we chatted about fun things, it'd undermine who we've become. I won't do that. And we have Kevin and Lissa too. But…"

"Well, don't stop now."

"Can you deal with me saying something completely honest?"

"More honest than you've already been? Will I survive it?"

She didn't respond to his jesting. Whatever was on her mind was more serious than the information on Martin.

"Go ahead, Hannah."

"There's something I've wanted to share since the workday at Matthew's. Something I knew I would eventually have to say, okay?"

"Sure."

"I'm not sure Dorcas is… Well, I think you need to be careful, make sure you really know her."

Wondering what would make her say that, he answered, "There's nothing between Dorcas and me. It'd make my life easier if there were."

"You're not courting her, not engaged, not anything?"

"Nothing."

"I'm really relieved to know that. You can trust me that caring for her would not make your life easier. Not ever."

She sounded so sure of knowing Dorcas and seemed deeply relieved he wasn't involved with her. Why?

"Okay, but isn't that the same as my deciding what Martin's like based on seeing him once for a few minutes?"

"No, it's not. Martin's a truly great guy who sometimes has a short fuse. Dorcas is…" She cleared her throat. "As much as I'm tempted to say more, I've said plenty. Look, I need to go. You have a good Thanksgiving and no fudging at Scrabble."

"Bye, Hannah." Paul closed his phone, with armies of thoughts marching through him.

Her words reverberated through him over and over again—*Listen, I'm on my way back to you.* He looked to the heavens, wanting to believe what had just happened was some type of message and all he needed to do was hold on.

And she was worth years of waiting if he could have her love. But why was she so relieved he wasn't involved with Dorcas?

He tumbled that thought around, but then another one came front and center, screaming in his face, making all others disappear. Had she just admitted to caring for him and Martin knew it? Hope rocketed through him. Whatever she carried for him was strong enough for Martin to see it and be angry with her at the hospital. But even if she cared, she'd just said that they'd ruined their chance and she was with Martin now. The blast of hope faded some but far from completely.

Too many things about their past and present just didn't add up. Like how did Hannah return knowing about certain areas of his life? Had Gram told her during their short visit before Paul and Dorcas arrived—the day Hannah had the flat tire in Gram's driveway? It wasn't like Gram to be so open. She was awful tight-lipped about family stuff. But no one outside his immediate family knew about the disapproval he'd been under with his church leaders after Hannah first left.

Except Dorcas.

At the thought the muscles down Paul's back stiffened, and the view around him became invisible. The dark roller coaster his mind had been on came to a screeching halt.

When Hannah called him just now and the call dropped, she called him back just to say a proper good-bye. Yet when she left Owl's Perch for good, she didn't call? She said she'd called at some point, but when?

Suspicion clung to him, begging to be explored.

Until this moment he thought the intensity of her anger with him when she returned to Owl's Perch was to be expected, but that day in Gram's driveway, she'd made a sarcastic remark about how little effort he'd put into talking with her, as if he'd had chances somewhere along the line that he never pursued.

But how?

When she left over two years ago, she had three phone numbers to reach him: Gram's, his on-campus apartment's, and his parents'. He knew for sure now what he thought he knew then—that Hannah had a deeper sense of justness than to hold everything against him for his reaction the night he discovered she was round with pregnancy and he left.

But then why had she not called him?

Paul grabbed the ax and slammed the blade of it into a round. The sound of splitting wood echoed against the silence. He continued working, hoping for a revelation.

Mostly I don't take no for an answer anymore, especially when it comes to reaching people.

The words she'd spoken to him only weeks ago echoed inside him. She said when she'd called his apartment, a girl answered. He'd assumed she'd called on one of the many nights between their last good visit and when he left her, but did she? As he worked, thoughts fell into place that turned his stomach. His suspicions grew like billows of smoke and were just as impossible to pin down.

But one word kept coming to him over and over again.

Deceit.

$\mathcal{J}$n the middle of another song, Martin saw Lissa come to the door, tears streaming down her face. He moved out from behind the keyboard, and she ran to him.

He lifted her. "What's wrong?"

"I hurt my knee, and the other kids laughed."

"Oh, so it's a double whammy, eh? So, which hurts worse, your knee or your feelings?"

Lissa wiped at her tears and hugged him tight. "My knee."

"Well, let's go take a look." He carried her down the steps into the kitchen and set her on the island near the refrigerator. "Let's see if we can roll your pant leg up, okay?"

She nodded while rubbing her eyes. More than anything she looked tired, and he might need Laura to take her out to the cottage to sleep before the party ended. He managed to get the corduroy pant leg up high enough to see her knee. "It's only red. I thought maybe it'd be green or orange polka-dotted."

Lissa giggled. He kissed the top of her head before grabbing a bag of green peas out of the freezer. "Let's use these." He lowered her pant leg and placed the frozen bag over her knee.

"I love you, Uncle Martin."

"Yeah, you're not so bad yourself, kiddo." He winked. The thing was, he had a love for Lissa and Kevin he hadn't known existed inside of people. As frustrated as he'd been with Hannah of late, Amy was right, she had opened his eyes and heart to life beyond work and to these children. It'd taken an Old Order Amish girl to make him reach deep inside and connect with God in a way that'd changed everything about him. And now they were griping and snapping at each other regularly. There was no way he could really tell Hannah what he was thinking. He loved her, which meant a lot since he'd never been in love before, but sometimes he was torn between wanting to direct her steps and accepting that their ideals for how to live rammed against each other.

"Uncle Martin." Lissa patted his face. He looked up. Amy had entered the room. Doug walked in right behind her.

He removed the bag of peas from Lissa's knee. "All better?"

"Yep."

He helped her down. "Hey, Aim, Doug. Care for something to eat or drink?" He motioned to the other island where the food was spread out.

Doug took a paper plate and began putting a variety of snacks on it. "Great gathering."

"Glad you like it."

Amy grabbed a bottle of water out of the open cooler. "Are you and Hannah taking Laura with you to Hawaii?"

He tossed the peas back into the freezer. "No, she wasn't hired full-time when we planned the trip, and it's impossible now to get her a ticket to fly out that close to Christmas." He slid onto the island. "I shouldn't have talked to Hannah the way I did."

Amy leaned against the bar. "You were pretty bad, Martin, but the one you need to apologize to is her."

"I will. The pressure we've been under will melt once she graduates and we go on vacation. We both know that. This year's been too long with too many things to adjust to."

"Hey, does Hannah golf?" Amy asked.

"No, but while we're in Hawaii, that's not a bad idea. It's got all the right earmarks of something she might just enjoy—games and being outside are definitely high on her list of fun things. How long has it been since the three of us and Alex have been part of a foursome?"

"It's been a couple of years, I think."

Doug licked barbecue sauce from his fingers. "News update. I gave up golfing. It's expensive, and I'm horrible at it."

Martin's and Amy's eyes met for a moment as they suppressed a laugh. How poorly Doug played golf was not news, but he was a lot of fun on the course anyway, so no one cared.

Amy took a sip of water. "My dad's a great golfer, and he's my *significant other* for the trip."

"Maybe the four of us can play a few rounds—you, me, Hannah, and your dad."

"Sounds great. I bet you have no clue how much I'm looking forward to this trip. I haven't been in over a decade. I'm doing every luau I can manage."

"I've never been." And he wondered if Hannah would go to a luau. She might not, with girls in skimpy outfits dancing around, but they'd have fun anyway.

"Really? You did such a fantastic job of planning this trip. I just assumed you knew what you were doing."

And for the first time in a very long time, he felt something other than the need to compromise. He felt respected for decisions he'd made.

With the word *deceit* rolling through his head, Paul strode across the yard and went inside.

The aromas for tomorrow's Thanksgiving feast filled the air as Gram and his mother baked a lot of things ahead of time. He wasn't sure where Carol and her husband, William, were, or Dorcas, but his dad was at the kitchen table reading a newspaper.

"Hey, Gram, something's nagging at me."

"I'm listening," Gram called over her shoulder as she loaded the sink with several messy pans.

"I was wondering about the day Hannah came to visit you. Did you tell her about my change of careers or that after she left, I was in trouble with the church leaders over some of my decisions?"

"Of course not." Gram flicked the hot water on and poured dish-washing liquid into the sink. "That's personal family happenings. Besides, I was afraid if I mentioned anything personal about you, she'd up and leave before we had a chance to visit."

Paul figured Gram was right about that. Hannah had returned wanting nothing to do with him, and he was reminded just how far they'd come since then.

"Well, she knows."

"Maybe that friend of yours, her brother, told her," Dad offered.

Paul shook his head. "I don't think he knows."

Piling mounds of baked cornbread into a huge bowl, his mother arched an eyebrow. "I trust we can find a better topic than that girl during our holiday."

Paul straightened, looking directly at his mother. No one seemed more set against Hannah and him than his mother. "Mom, have you ever talked to Hannah?"

"What?" The lines across her face revealed her shock. "Never. And I thought you were over this."

"Dad?"

Glancing to his wife, he looked a bit uncomfortable. Gray colored most of his once-blond hair, but he still managed to look more than a decade younger than his wife. "Your mother and I don't agree on this subject. As badly as you needed to see that girl again, I'd have given about anything to see it work out."

His always faithful and calm dad said what Paul already knew. He'd never betray his son. Paul looked up to see Carol and William now standing in the threshold of the double-wide doorway. "Carol?"

She shook her head. "No. I thought she was a huge mistake on your part, but I'd not withhold that from you."

He nodded, catching a glimpse of the hem of Dorcas's dress around the corner, near the entryway of the makeshift nursery for his sister's baby. Was she eavesdropping?

Dorcas's behavior pricked him.

Something Hannah had said about two months ago returned to him: *"When I did manage to call your apartment, a girl answered."* He'd assumed Hannah was talking about calling him any night but the one, the only one, when he'd asked his sister and Dorcas to man the phones while he looked for Hannah.

"Dorcas, come on out."

She eased out from behind the wall, facing him, looking too frail to be questioned.

Guilt defined her features. Surely it couldn't be true. She'd been his ally, giving him advice, helping him cope. He wasn't in love with her, but he counted her as a friend. "Did you ever answer a call from Hannah?"

"Paul!" his mother called. "Stop this. That Amish girl nearly ripped us apart when we found out about her, and you're going to help her do it again?"

He pointed at his mother. "That 'Amish girl' did no such thing. Your own anger that I'd have a girl you hadn't approved did that. Nothing else." He returned his focus to Dorcas.

She stepped out of the hallway and toward the kitchen, shaking her head. "I wouldn't...I wouldn't do anything to hurt you."

Paul wasn't sure she'd actually answered his question. "Hannah called me a little bit ago by mistake. The call was dropped, and she called me back to say a proper good-bye. She didn't want to say anything else but bye. Now why would someone like that not call after leaving Owl's Perch in such a rush?"

"Maybe she changed over the last few years," his brother-in-law offered. "She was a teen and returned as an adult. That makes a difference, you know."

Paul didn't move his gaze from Dorcas, who was avoiding looking at him. "Or maybe she called and someone's not telling me."

Dorcas stared at a group of photos on the wall that showed Paul at various stages of his life.

Paul's fist came down hard on the countertop. "Answer me, Dorcas."

Her chin quivered. "She told you." The words were barely audible.

Hannah knew?

Tempted to lie, he stayed the course. "I want to hear it from you."

She shook her head, tears trailing her face.

"What, you can bulldoze my life, but you can't admit to it?"

Dorcas looked to each person, as if searching for support. "She was pregnant. We all knew it wasn't Paul's because he never once hesitated to consider that it might be his. Every one of us thought the same thing about her."

Carol stepped forward. "We *thought* a lot of things. What did you do?"

"I… She called. Only twice, Paul. I swear it."

"Only twice? Do you have any idea what you've done?" Paul measured his tone, refusing to yield to the rage inside him. "Tell me when, Dorcas."

Tears ran down her cheeks. "The first time she called, we all thought she was guilty of cheating on you. All of us. Even you thought that for a few days. Then the next time you were beginning to get over her, and…"

Carol looked horrified. "Oh, please say that she didn't call Paul while he had us at his apartment waiting to hear from her."

Dorcas covered her face with her hands, sobbing. "I'm sorry."

Paul couldn't budge, afraid if he did, he might hurt her. "The night she was staying at a hotel, waiting for her train to leave? It didn't leave until early afternoon the next day! I could have gone to her and stopped her from going!" Paul clenched his fists. "Are you crazy? Or just flat-out mean?"

Dorcas lowered her hands, her eyes begging him to understand. "I…I thought she'd been lying to you."

"And the next time, what did you think then?"

"You were beginning to care for me…I could tell, and everyone wanted us to be together."

Paul looked at his mother and gestured at Dorcas. "This is your choice over Hannah?" He clutched his head, total disbelief rocking his world. "How could you, Dorcas? I trusted you. You encouraged me to let her make the first move, to return on her own, but you kept her from reaching me." He took several deep breaths, trying desperately to see the room around him as his vision went red. "It's your fault she's with someone else. And the truth is we'll never know all the hurt and damage you've caused to Hannah…all the lives you've altered along the way, but as long as you got what you wanted, right?"

Needing to get some air, he turned to leave, but then a thought hit, and he turned to face her. "Did you remove the money from our account?"

Dorcas gaped at him, and she looked as if she might keel over. His dad went to her side, and William grabbed a kitchen chair and ran it over to her.

Paul took a step closer. "The bank showed me photos of someone wearing Amish clothing—someone pretending to be Hannah. The bank officials and I figured her rapist stole her bankbook and emptied the account. But you could have taken my bankbook. You have Amish relatives and knew enough to pull that off. Did you take our money?"

She dropped into the chair. "No, I'd never steal from you. I'll put my hand on the Bible if you need me to."

"Never steal from me? What do you think you've done?"

Dorcas broke into fresh sobs, and his dad passed her a box of tissues. While Paul stood there watching her, a memory hooked on to something inside him, and he tugged at it, like reeling in a fishing line.

The day after he'd asked Hannah to marry him, he was here in his parents' home, writing her a letter, when his sister and Dorcas came into his room and interrupted him. He'd penned the fullness of his heart in those pages, and receiving it would have meant so much to Hannah. Those days had been unbelievably trying, nearly impossible to make contact and keep up with each other's life. What were the odds of the only letter his sister and Dorcas knew about being the one that disappeared?

"Did you steal the letter?"

Dorcas's hands fell limp to her side, and her head remained bowed. "Yes."

His sister stepped forward. "Paul, you know enough of the truth. Please stop."

Disgusted with Dorcas, he turned and walked out of the house. He got in his car and started driving. He hadn't started out trusting Dorcas. The whole time they went to middle and high school together, he thought she was selfish and manipulative, but when she was receptive about Hannah, he convinced himself she was a decent and honest person. He should have trusted his gut.

The years of betrayal played through his mind; the ache over all he'd lost by trusting Dorcas seemed to circle endlessly inside him. More than two hours later he pulled into Gram's driveway. He walked across the dark yard, through the pasture, and into the patch of woods. He didn't stop until he was at the footbridge that crossed the creek. This was where he'd asked Hannah to marry him. The place where everything he'd ever wanted seemed to become possible. As clearly as if it'd happened yesterday, he remembered Hannah whispering yes to his proposal. It'd taken a few minutes to convince her that he was serious, that he had no one else on campus, and that they would find a way to win her father's approval.

He'd lost everything he'd ever hoped for due to a violent man, his own knee-jerk reaction, and Dorcas's manipulation. What Dorcas had done under the guise of friendship and warmth was unbelievable.

The price he'd paid—incomprehensible.

Even now, hours later, his hands shook. Looking down at the creek bed, watching the dark water ripple along its winding, twisting path, his thoughts turned to all the things this liquid would do before most of it flowed into the ocean: provide nutrition for the tiny creatures that lived in it, supply water for nearby trees, cattle, and wildlife. It'd smooth stones and bear life. Some of it would evaporate and sprinkle down no telling where in the world.

God had ways that couldn't be seen or calculated from a small bridge while watching the beauty of dark waters pass under his feet. Everything in life carried more, accomplished more than could be seen with the naked eye or even imagined.

He prayed that both Hannah and he would accomplish more than either of them could see or imagine. But their courses had been altered. His was still free enough he would welcome—no, he'd be ecstatic to have her back every second of every day for as long as they lived. But she would have to have her heart ripped out again to return to him.

*I*nside Alliance Community Hospital, Hannah shoved her timecard into the slot and punched out, ending her last round of clinical rotations for nursing school. The Saturday shift ended two hours earlier than usual for the students, and ideas of trying to squeeze in a visit to Mary pulled on her. Hannah needed to talk to someone who would understand her feelings about Martin and babies and birth control. Mary would get it.

Hannah wanted perspective before mentioning the *news* to Martin. It'd been ten days since Dr. Lehman told her she might not be as infertile as she'd thought. Martin had to know, but first, Hannah needed to figure out her own thoughts and feelings about it. She and Martin were having enough trouble communicating of late. The last thing she needed to do was start a difficult conversation without knowing her own mind and heart.

Talking to Mary was the answer. Hannah was sure of it, but she couldn't do it over the phone. The girl would freeze to death in the phone shanty before Hannah finished explaining the mess. Besides, Mary had a baby to tend to. But what about Martin? She'd been at work or school so much lately that they'd had no time together. Still, she needed to find some answers to help strengthen their relationship. Finding peace on this birth-control topic was more important for Martin and her than having a date night.

Confident of what she needed to do, Hannah unlocked her car door and called Martin.

"Hey, sweetheart, I'm on the other line. Can you hang on a minute?"

"Sure." Hannah turned the engine, warming the car while waiting. About the time warm air started to flow, Martin came back on the line.

"Hey, I'm back. What are you doing calling at this time of day?"

"I got off early."

"Good. That works even better. Vance Clarke...I don't think you've met him yet. He's Amy's dad, and he's passed us four TobyMac and Jeremy Camp concert tickets. Kevin and Lissa are psyched. It's at the Canton Civic Center tomorrow, and I was on the other line making reservations at a hotel, so—"

"At a hotel?" Hannah interrupted him. "Canton is what, thirty to forty minutes from your place?" She laughed, trying not to sound like a wet blanket.

"It's an adventure, Hannah. The kids get it. Try to keep up," Martin teased.

"Am I familiar with TobyMac's and Jeremy Camp's music?"

"Sure you are. We sing a couple of their songs. Remember the—" His voice cut out, letting her know he had another incoming call. "Hey, Amy's dad is on the other line. He probably wants to know if we're able to use the tickets."

"Martin, you guys go, but I want to slip to Owl's Perch and see Mary. I'll be back to your place before you are tomorrow."

"What? No," he snapped. "Hold on."

The line went silent for a minute or two.

"You still there?" Martin's voice said it all. She'd ruined the fun.

"Yeah, I'm here."

"Since when did you decide traveling four hours one way is *slipping* to your friend's house? And why are you letting all these visits come ahead of us?"

"It's not like that. I just need to talk to her about some things."

"Then call her. Come on, Hannah. The concert will be fun."

She'd never been to a concert. She imagined booming music, multicolored electric lights flashing everywhere, and people center stage enjoying the limelight, like the concerts Martin had on DVD that he liked to watch. It was so far removed from the Plain life that she wouldn't be able to enjoy it. Besides she really wanted time with Mary.

"Fun for who?"

"For whom," he corrected, "and obviously not for you."

"You have four tickets. Let Laura use mine. And I'll see you as soon as you get home tomorrow."

"Laura's over sixty. She wouldn't want to go."

"She's a well-paid nanny, and she'll help with the children."

"This stinks. I've already told the kids and made reservations. I can't back out."

"And you shouldn't. You want to go to the concert, and I want to see Mary."

"Hannah." He said her name like he was scolding a dog. "For once, could you—".

"You know," she interrupted him, "it's not my fault you made the plans and told the children *before* talking to me. But if you had, I'd say the same thing: go, have fun. I'll go to Mary's, and we'll meet back at your place before sundown. What time is the concert?"

"Six."

"Oh, well then, I'll meet you back at your place *after* the kids' bedtime on a school night."

"There's no need for that tone. They'll be fine. Laura can take them to school an hour or so late if need be."

"And you'll be fine going without me, okay?"

The phone was silent again.

"It was my last clinical rotation. I only have one more full week of school and then one day of finals the following week. Then I'm through. Yay! I'm even thinking of breaking out the pompoms for this."

"You don't own any pompoms." The frustration in his voice faded into jesting. "But I'll buy you some…and maybe a cheerleading outfit to boot."

She laughed. "I'd really like to see Mary before we leave for Hawaii, and making a quick trip this weekend is my only chance."

"Yeah, okay." He sighed. "I figured you'd balk at going."

Which probably explained why he made so many plans first and then told her. She wondered how often that worked in his favor without her realizing what he'd done.

"Are we good?" she asked.

"As good as we get, I suppose. I'll see you tomorrow night."

"Martin, wait." She couldn't stand the idea of them arguing like this. "I know it seems like I'm being unfair, but just give me this last spur-of-the-moment trip, okay? I'll do better. We'll start everything fresh beginning the night I graduate."

"Seeing her is that important?"

"Yeah, we'll talk about why in a few weeks. It's sort of prewedding planning stuff."

"As in our wedding, the one you haven't said yes to yet?"

"That'd be the one."

He chuckled. "Suddenly I like this conversation. Try saying the good stuff up-front next time."

"Sorry, I'm still new to this argue-as-you-go plan."

"Yeah, we've got a few things to work out."

"But you know we'll work them out, right?"

"Yeah, I know. Bye, sweetheart."

"Make sure Lissa and Kevin wear hats so they don't get an earache, okay?"

"Will do. See you tomorrow night."

"Yes you will. Bye."

The night skies threatened snow as Hannah pulled out of Mary's driveway. Without being asked, Mammi Annie had given them privacy to talk all morning. She had left the Daadi Haus where she, Luke, and Mary resided and had gone to the main house with Mary's mother.

Mary had listened and understood in ways no one else could. Unfortunately, she didn't have much in the way of advice—except to keep it honest between Martin and her and to think in terms of what her decisions would mean over the long haul of life.

Mary and Luke didn't know what they'd do from here on out, but no matter what they decided, it wasn't going to be easy. If Mary conceived often, she'd end up needing a C-section every year or two, possibly causing other health-related issues over the course of years. If they chose to avoid that, Luke would be unable to share the marriage bed with her. Neither would ever consider using birth control.

The electric lights shone bright from Gram's kitchen, tempting Hannah to pull into her driveway and visit for a few minutes. She checked the clock. Five thirty. Hannah had plenty of time to visit and still get home before Martin and the children.

She rapped on Gram's door and waited. The thump of her cane against the floor grew louder. The porch light came on.

With the chain lock in place, Gram opened the door to peer out. "Hannah." She slammed the door, unhooked the chain, and swung the door open wide, motioning Hannah inside. "Why, I've done near wore the phone plain out picking it up to call you. I asked God to give me a sign if I was to tell you, and here you are."

"Tell me what?"

Gram hesitated, looking like she might cry. "Dorcas has been sick for some time, and maybe because of this extra stress and maybe not, she's in the hospital, not doing well at all. They can't get her heartbeat regular, and she's in and out of consciousness." Gram clutched her chest.

"Gram, let's get you to a chair." Hannah supported Gram by her free arm and helped her to the couch.

After sitting, she shooed Hannah back. "I'm fine. My chest aches when I get all nervous, has since I was a young woman. Don't worry none about me."

"Gram." Hannah sat on the edge of the couch beside her. "What's wrong with Dorcas?"

"Lyme disease. She had it nearly three years without being diagnosed."

"Why would you want to call me about Dorcas being sick? I know nothing as a nursing student that could help her."

Gram placed her knobby hand over Hannah's and patted it. "I wasn't going to call about Dorcas." She sighed. "I thought I was doing the right thing when I stopped letting you and Paul use my mailbox to write each other."

A little concerned as to why Gram's conversation was rambling all over the place, Hannah decided she would stay awhile. "It's okay, Gram. You were doing what you thought was right. I'll not put blame on anyone for that."

"But what Dorcas has done to Paul by pretending to be his friend when she didn't tell him about your calls…"

Hannah's breath caught. "He knows?"

Gram's eyes misted. "I can't stand watching what's happening with Paul, and I don't know how much more he can take."

"Paul's tough. I see a power and strength in his eyes that can't be damaged even by what Dorcas has done."

Gram squeezed the handle of her cane. "Right now that power and strength Paul has is dead set against Dorcas. Go, look him in the eye, and see if Dorcas's deceit isn't eating him into bitterness. He doesn't care if she dies, and she just might."

"She's that bad?"

Gram nodded.

"I…I didn't know Lyme disease could do that, but I'm not sure I can help anybody deal with forgiveness."

"He'll listen to you… Please, Hannah."

She knew so little about forgiveness it scared her. Every time she thought she had it covered, anger seemed to blindside her. She checked her watch. Almost six o'clock. If she went an hour out of the way to see Paul, she might not arrive at the house before Martin and the children. Guilt nibbled at her. Even if she was able to get there before him, she wouldn't like Martin going to see an old girlfriend like this.

But part of this mess was her fault. She knew the same girl took both messages she left for Paul. She could've tried to reach him again or called Gram and left a message with her, but she didn't. And he needed to know and understand why.

"Do you have his street address?"

Gram wrote the directions to Paul's place, and Hannah went to her car. Concern for Paul weighed on her as she drove mile after mile. Snow flurries swirled through the dark skies. An hour after leaving Owl's Perch, she was pulling into the parking lot of his apartment. She stopped at the curb of what she hoped was Paul's building. Once at the door that matched the info Gram gave her, she heard the muffled voices of several men. She knocked.

"Enter," a male voice boomed.

She knocked again.

"Yeah, yeah, yeah, come in already!"

Whoever said the words, it wasn't Paul. She eased the door open and stepped inside, seeing no one.

"Just leave the pizza on the counter and take the money."

In spite of the one voice that was doing all the talking, in the background the voices of several men vibrated the room—Paul's being one of them. She closed the door and walked in that direction. He was at a table with three other guys, playing cards.

He slapped a card faceup on the table. "If you can't win..."

"You lose." Two men repeated the words loudly, making the third guy throw his cards onto the table. A round of laughter pealed from all of them.

Gram was mistaken. Paul was fine, and he looked good too, tilted back on two legs of his chair, smiling.

"Excuse me."

Paul jolted, losing his balance. He jumped to his feet as the chair fell over backward. The men broke into laughter. "Man, Waddell, with half the decent single women chasing you, one would think you wouldn't lose it over one saying 'excuse me.'" A man with jet-black hair and a five o'clock shadow spoke the words and then turned to look at her. "Then again…" He slapped a card onto the table, staring at her.

Paul's eyes didn't move from her. The hardwood floor was covered in chunks of mud and debris. Every one of the men still had on the messy boots.

Bachelors all of them. Probably. Hannah suppressed a smile.

The guy with the five o'clock shadow looked from Paul to Hannah, while the other two kept talking. "Whoa, idiots."

Movement stopped.

The guy moved toward her. "I'm Marcus King."

She knew his name well. He'd been best friends with Paul since they were kids and one of Paul's college roommates. She guessed the other two were Ryan and Taylor.

"I'm Hannah."

He smiled, shaking her hand as if he already knew her and liked her. "It's good to finally meet you." He turned back to the table. "Guys, we're leaving. Now."

The doorbell rang.

"That'd be the pizza." Marcus went to the door.

Each of the other two men dipped his head as a silent hello while heading for the door. Shock faded from Paul's face. He picked up his chair and ran his hands through his disheveled hair.

"Hey, Paul," Marcus called, stepping back into view. He held up one of three pizza boxes. "I'll leave this one on the counter."

Marcus closed the front door behind him, and the only sounds left were the ticking of a clock and the bubbling of water. Hannah looked around, spotting the source of the trickling sound. An aquarium, every bit as large as Martin's fifty-something-inch, HD, flat-screen TV. Colorful, graceful fish swam about, giving the whole room a peaceful feel. Five feet away, a recliner with a reading lamp behind it faced the tank. Lines of twine ran a foot above her, running from one end of the room to the other, with dozens of Christmas cards straddling the cords.

She closed her eyes, feeling the…quiet of the Plain traditions. No television, gaming stations, or blasting stereos. No Christmas trees or lights or fancy decorations. Opening her eyes, she saw a stack of Christmas presents in the corner, some already wrapped, some not. Christmas celebration was certainly looked forward to, but keeping life simple all year long was the Plain way.

Not better. Not worse. Just one of the many ways believers honored God. A way she understood and respected, even if it wasn't what she had ended up choosing.

She went closer to the aquarium, trying to think of something to say to break the sudden awkwardness. "I like your place."

He came up behind her. "It serves its purpose."

She shifted, looking straight at him, and suddenly the current between them seemed as powerful and tumultuous as the Susquehanna during the spring thaw. Feeling naive for not realizing the upheaval coming here would cause her, she cleared her throat and moved to the strings of cards. "You must have a lot of friends."

"I have a lot of people who send Christmas cards. Whether they're friends or not, there's no real way to know, is there?"

The taint in his voice was distressing. Unable to face him, she continued looking at the cards.

"Hannah." Paul's voice was barely above a whisper.

She turned.

His eyes searched hers, clearly looking for answers. "What are you doing here?"

"I heard about… Well, Dorcas was wrong, and you have every right to be angry."

"Thanks, I'll keep that in mind."

His tone held the quiet anger of a man lied to by too many women, and she hated herself for her part in it.

"Gram said…" She ran her fingers through fallen wisps of hair, trying to push them back into place. "Here's the thing, Paul. I'm the one who chose to only call twice. I could've called again and made sure to leave a message with Gram. But like I told you before, I really didn't believe you wanted me, and even if you'd told me otherwise, I never would have believed you. Never. I would've spent the rest of my life feeling like a charity case, and as badly as I wanted you to make everything better, I knew my lack of self-esteem would grow to rock-hard self-hatred if I didn't start fresh. Those things aren't Dorcas's fault."

"So you're here to set me straight so Dorcas doesn't pay any penalty for her wrong?"

"I'm here because we're friends, because no one understands the frustration, the deep-seated anger, the complications of all we've been through more than we do. Your other friends will try to get it. Martin tries, Dr. Lehman tries, Zabeth tried." She shook her head and sighed. "I get it, Paul, and I guess I thought maybe you needed that."

"What I needed passed me by long ago. The thanks for that go to Dorcas. I know that our Plain ways say we have to forgive immediately, right then, but she carried out her deceit for years. I may pay the price forever for what she's done. Do you honestly think I'm wrong in this?"

The heaviness of his words settled on her like a cloak, and she took a seat on the couch, unable to respond for a while. "Is it possible faith in God over our future must outweigh our feelings in the things of today? And maybe there are lots of types of forgiveness just like there are lots of kinds of love."

"There is no way to forgive what she's done. None. She used her free will to remove mine in a sneaky, underhanded way. Don't talk to me about reaching out to offer her *any* type of forgiveness. Even if you needed that time in Ohio, all of it, I had the right to receive your calls—a God-given right. Of course you were feeling unworthy and having second thoughts after you made those calls, but you reached out. I'll bet you had a ton of conflicting emotions and plans, right?"

Remembering one of her reasons for changing her last name, she nodded. "Yes." She knew she would always hope he'd come looking for her if she kept her last name. Oh, she'd also wanted to keep Daed from finding her, but more than that, she needed to free herself of always hoping Paul might show up for her one day.

"My Daed wants forgiveness."

Paul's stiff-legged stance slowly relaxed, and he sat on the edge of his recliner near her. The arm of her couch and the arm of his chair sat at a right angle, mere inches apart.

"He asked me for it the night we all went to the hospital for Mary. I just stood there, Martin's hand on my back, nudging me to say what should be said. And I couldn't. I didn't come here because I think I have answers to offer. I guess there are times when it's easier to forgive strangers than our own."

Paul placed his forearms on his legs, leaning in.

The aroma of fresh outdoors clung to him, reminding her of when she used to consider the scent of him equal to what integrity would smell like if it carried a fragrance, and in spite of herself, she took a deep breath. "I can't figure out how to connect with forgiveness sometimes. I understand that when we forgive, we're saying what was done to us is not more powerful than God's ability to redeem us from it, and sometimes I'm able, and sometimes I just wish no one asked, no one made me face what's inside."

With his elbows on his knees, Paul cupped his hands together and rested his chin on them. "I hate…this."

"I find it comforting that God hates things too."

"Yeah, I guess He does." He paused, and they remained silent for over a minute before he placed one hand over hers. "She doesn't deserve forgiveness."

Hannah nodded. "Nevertheless."

He rubbed his hand back and forth over hers, and she wished the pull to him would give her a break.

"My fiancée once wrote a letter to me, and I have every word memorized. It got me through…a lot. One of my favorite parts reads, 'Someone did not place his desires under God's authority—nevertheless, God's power over my life is stronger than that event.'" He paused, gently holding her hands in his. "Come back to me, Hannah."

Tears filled her eyes. "You know I can't."

His eyes bored into her, and she was sure he knew much more about her heart than he should.

She slid her hands from his and wiped tears from her cheeks. "He's a good man, and we have Kevin and Lissa."

Paul stood, rubbing the back of his neck while he walked to the far side of the room. He turned. "So that settles it?"

"Yes."

After holding her gaze, Paul gave one nod of his head. "Dorcas is in a hospital less than ten miles from here. I'll go see her tonight. But I will not let her back in my life. She's proven who she is."

"I'm not sure, but I don't think forgiveness means you have to open your life up to them again."

"Maybe you should rethink taking care of things with your dad as soon as you can."

Fighting to stay composed, she stood. "Okay." She glanced at her watch. "I…I need to go."

Paul walked her out to her car and opened the door. "You drive safe and take care of yourself."

"I will." Trembling, she turned the key, waved, and left the parking lot, unable to look back. She began the drive back to Ohio, hoping the pain would ease.

atthew slid the hand plane across what would eventually be the dash of a buggy, shaving off enough wood to make it fit in its designated spot. Across the room Luke pulled, tucked, and fitted the last corner of black leather over the frame of a buggy's bench seat.

At the sound of the clanging bell, he glanced out the window. Kathryn stood on the front porch of his home, sliding the striker onto the triangle dinner bell. With only one shop built and no room designed just for painting, the windows had to stay open for cross ventilation. December's freezing temperatures had forced Kathryn to move into a makeshift office inside his home.

Matthew laid the plane and dashboard on the workbench and removed his tool belt. He stepped outside for a moment, catching Kathryn's eye and motioning for her to come to the shop.

Luke tapped the nail in place before looking up. "I think I'll go home for lunch today."

"You do that." Matthew headed out the side door to the spot where he and Kathryn met when they wanted a minute of privacy.

She'd returned six weeks ago, and they'd been secretly going places together since. Grief over the loss of his brother still clung to him, but Kathryn's presence brought him a deep, satisfying peace with life. He did, however, wish he knew a little better what her feelings were toward him. They had fun, no doubt. Talked often and about everything. Laughed and played even during work-hours. For him, the bond grew deeper each day. But for her? He wasn't sure.

The deal with the bishop hadn't rattled her, even though he was checking up on Matthew regularly. The more he knew her, the more he enjoyed life. He believed with Elle he *could* have enjoyed life if…if she were different, if she had a clue about keeping her word, if she understood any aspect of balancing desires with reality.

She walked toward him and stopped in the yard for a moment to scoop up a mewling kitten. With Kathryn, he *did* enjoy life, even in the midst of grief, because of who she was and what she brought with her naturally as she went throughout her day.

They came toe to toe. Matthew's eyes met hers as he scratched the kitten's head. "How's it goin'?"

She snuggled the kitten deeper in her arms. "It's even colder out here than in the shop, you know?"

He laughed. "Didn't we discuss this once?"

"I'm allowed in the house, but the kitten isn't."

Matthew mocked a sigh. "Fine. Put the cat's bed near the wood stove in the shop, but if she gets stepped on…"

Kathryn giggled. "She won't. She'll stay right up under the bench until she's old enough to climb up high on the rafters." She stroked the kitten. "Oh, I forgot to tell you that I got a letter from my Daed yesterday, and I'm expected to spend Christmas Eve and Day there."

"I guess there's no excuse we could give that would allow me to show up at your house on Christmas without people realizing what was going on." He'd long ago adjusted to not having someone special near him on a holiday, so although this was disappointing, being alone for only a day or two was a nice change.

He tugged on one string of her prayer Kapp. "I guess it's reasonable enough since we did get Thanksgiving together…in a house full of umpteen relatives. Can you be back the day after Christmas? I'll take off."

Her eyes danced. "Oh." She stretched out the word, letting him know she had ideas about that. "With last weekend's snow, if we get another layer in the next two and a half weeks, it'll be perfect for sledding."

Aching to kiss her, Matthew continued playing with the string of her Kapp. "I could enjoy sledding."

"Maybe we could race."

"Two sleds instead of sharing one? Not what I had in mind."

She shook her finger at him, teasing before her expression changed. "The bishop came by earlier."

"Yeah, he came into the shop and spoke with me before he left. Didn't ask too many questions though. Maybe he's decided to give me a break."

She smiled, petting the kitten. "Soon you'll be in his good graces again, then I can quit being just hired help. Ya?"

"Does playing the part of just employee make you uncomfortable?"

She leaned her back against the outer wall of the shop. "Nah, I'm enjoying it. A bit of sneaking around is good for the soul."

"Is it now? Your preacher at home must teach somethin' awful different from mine."

Standing up straight, Kathryn chuckled. "I better go."

Matthew placed his hand on the wall in front of her, stopping her from leaving. She dipped her chin, scratching the kitten's head. "You know how I feel about…"

She let the sentence drop, but he knew the rest of her thought. She'd made herself clear on this subject before their first outing. She was convinced every relationship should be a no-handholding deal unless the couple intended to marry.

He moved in closer. "I do."

She lowered her eyes, and the set of her stare said she was thinking. When she raised her head, he was sure he saw a hint of invitation inside the sparkle.

"Katie, ya know"—Matthew tried to sound casual—"there's nothing wrong with giving me an early Christmas present."

She pursed her lips, mocking frustration as she stared into his eyes. "Are you taking advantage of my pleasure in this secret-keeping thing, Matthew Esh?"

"Trying to, yes."

With an adorable smile in place, she shook her head and went to step around him. He moved directly in front of her. Since he was convinced she was the one for him, all this courting and no kissing was simply too much, but until today she'd not given any signal that he should press the matter. She stopped, seemingly waiting on him to step aside. He leaned in, and she backed up.

"I don't intend to be an Amish housewife."

Matthew's heart skipped. "You don't? Do you want to be an Amish husband instead?"

She laughed. "I'm trying to be serious."

"Then try makin' sense."

"I don't want to give up working beside you in order to have your babies."

"Mmm." Matthew nodded. He had the sneaking suspicion that Kathryn Glick was ready for the first kiss of her life. "You gonna set up baby beds and playpens in the shops?"

"And under the trees in warm weather. Near the garden during planting. And…"

Matthew wrapped the strings to her prayer Kapp around his fingers. "Your need for plannin' and organizin' is steppin' all over my spontaneous moment."

"If you want a housewife, I need to know now. That's not who I am, but your Mamm would be willing to help and love every minute of it."

"Glad you have it all planned out," Matthew whispered. "I got no objections to your plans." He mumbled the words and brushed his lips across hers.

Taking several steps back, she bumped against the wall, staring at him. Reeling from the connection, Matthew drew a breath. She'd just talked about marrying him without his even asking. He was fully satisfied in this moment.

She ran her fingers over her lips before pouting. "Is that all the present I get to give?"

Taking his cue, he wrapped his arms around her. "I didn't want to be greedy."

"I could tolerate a little selfishness now and then."

"That's good to know." He kissed her, feeling confident that nothing would ever come between them.

Mamm called their names, and Kathryn slowly pulled away.

Matthew put a few inches between them, noticing the cat was still sleeping undisturbed in the crook of her arm.

Kathryn smiled up at him. "I like this secret-keeping thing."

"Not too much, I hope. I want to tell everyone when the dust settles with the bishop."

She squared her shoulders, mocking smugness. "Oh, we'll tell *everyone,* all right."

It was her first hint that she wanted Elle to know. He didn't blame her.

Kathryn passed him the kitten and slipped out from between him and the wall. "But until then"—she pointed for him to stay—"we'll enjoy this little mandate of yours."

Enjoy it? It was something he insisted on, and now she was making the boundaries of his decision not only comfortable, but fun.

"Put her somewhere cozy, count to forty, and then come inside, okay?"

She started to walk away, and he pulled her back to him, kissing her again. She wiggled free, her laughter filling the air as she took off running, turning twice to glance back at him, a flirtatious smile across her face.

So Kathryn had a romantic side to her well-rounded way of dealing with life. He should have figured on that. He could still feel her lips on his. Catching one of her glances, he winked, realizing anew that everything he'd ever wanted was right here on the land that'd belonged to his great-grandfather and with a woman whose roots were as true to the Old Ways as his were.

*H*annah unlocked the cabin door and shoved it open. The December cold inside Zabeth's cabin was as unyielding as the loneliness inside her. Silvery moonbeams stretched across the floor, and she moved to the piano without turning on the light. She plunked a few keys. It needed tuning, but she remembered the wonderful songs Zabeth played while Hannah sat beside her, watching.

As a baptized member of the Amish faith, Zabeth had broken ties with every relative to pursue her love of music. Martin carried that kind of passion for music. Hannah enjoyed it, but it didn't reside in her like it did in them.

She walked to the window and looked out back. It was there on the bench she'd first met Martin.

Inside this cabin they formed a friendship and fell in love.

If he'd just come to the cabin...

But he wouldn't. He wanted to sell it. Worse, she'd given in.

Everything between them began to change once this was no longer their haven. This is who she was, and he'd come here over and over again and embraced that part of her.

One lone light bulb hung from the ceiling. She went to the light switch and flipped it on and then off and then on. It was the first place she lived that had electricity...and freedom. Zabeth had supported her every dream, and she'd loved and accepted everything about Hannah.

Still wearing her coat, Hannah flicked the light off and lay on the couch. She needed to leave in just a minute. It was Tuesday, her night off, and Martin was expecting her.

His words beckoned to her—*"Come on, phone girl, make a choice for us."*

She had chosen. The decision was made.

Her future was with him.

After the children were in bed Sunday night, she'd told Martin about seeing Paul earlier that evening. The anger he'd expressed still made her shudder. She rushed through her explanation for going to Owl's Perch—that she needed to talk to Mary because Dr. Lehman had said Hannah might be able to have children. Anger drained from his face, and the conversation shifted. By the time she went to the cottage, she'd agreed to his having a vasectomy.

Lying on her back staring at the ceiling, warm tears trickled down the sides of her face, and she closed her eyes.

Her phone rang, and she jerked. Fishing it out of her coat pocket, she sat up. "Hi."

"Hey, where are you?"

Hannah blinked. "I…I must have fallen asleep."

"You're at the clinic then, and someone is in labor? I thought you were off tonight."

"I am. I…I'm at the cabin."

Silence.

It seemed to define their relationship more than anything else of late.

"I'm leaving right now."

"It's ten thirty, and you're there while I'm here waiting. Didn't you hear your phone ring half a dozen times tonight?"

"This is the first time it's rung."

"It is so time for you to get a new phone."

"I just wanted to see the place, Martin. You used to like it, remember?"

"You used to live there, and what I liked about it was you."

He'd never understand why she didn't fully appreciate his guiding her toward change for the better. And she'd never understand why he couldn't enjoy and appreciate the simplicity of a single light bulb hanging from a ceiling or the pleasure of warm soil under her bare feet as she tended her garden.

But he'd taught her how to navigate the Englischer world. They'd laughed and bonded and fallen in love. He'd healed her broken heart and made it possible for her to slip into a new life. And she loved him. They'd get through this transition. He was right; the cabin needed to be sold, and she needed to move on.

"I'm leaving right now."

She went to her car, barely paying attention to the roads as she drove to Martin's. It was after eleven when she pulled into his driveway. Carrying an armload of books and dry cleaning, Hannah pushed her hip against the car door, closing it. Streams of yellow gold light shone through the huge arched window of the main house onto the sparse layer of snow across the backyard. Martin stood at the second-story window, looking down.

The constant ache that'd taken up residence inside her increased. If they could just talk about what was happening to them, maybe they'd find their way back to each other again.

They'd tried. Both of them.

He'd told her that she needed to finish letting go of the Plain life. They'd sell the cabin, but she could take the on-call hours Dr. Lehman offered. Martin would have a vasectomy, but she could continue with her nursing school.

The concessions he wanted were great.

With the eyes of two young children staring at her even in her sleep, she would become whatever he needed her to be. If she thought about it the right way, the compromises were rational. He was asking her to adjust better to the Englischer life. He wasn't wrong in wanting that.

In spite of her full arms, she managed a wave. Martin raised his hand slowly, returning the gesture. Hoping desperately that the trip to Hawaii would be all they needed it to be, she went to the cottage.

If she could just get Paul out of her mind, many of their other issues would fall to the wayside. Wouldn't they? Balancing all the stuff in her arms, she struggled to open the unlocked door to her cottage. Without flipping on a light, she walked through the dark room and plunked everything onto the small, round kitchen table.

Her cell phone rang, and she dug through her coat pocket to locate it. "Hi."

"Hey, phone girl." Martin sounded sleepy or maybe just tired.

"Hey, yourself." She wrestled to find words and not to sound as empty as she felt. "How was your day?"

"Usual. Yours?"

"Normal stuff, except we delivered a set of twins. The Fishers now have two sets of twins in their brood of nine children."

"Fascinating I'm sure. Can you imagine what the day is like for those parents?"

She flicked on a light. "How one feels about that depends on what their goals in life are." Taking her dry-cleaned uniform with her, she walked into the bedroom and hung it in the closet before returning to the kitchen.

"Yeah, I guess so. I've been meaning to ask about Friday night's graduation. Did you need to do something about a cap and gown?"

Spotting a large envelope on the table under the books she'd piled there, she slid it free. "No, all I need is my nurse's uniform. I actually sent it to the dry cleaner so it'd look its best. I picked it up earlier today."

It was addressed to Hannah Lapp Lawson, but it had no return address. It must have come in the mail today and Laura brought it to the cottage and left it on the table. Maybe her Daed had responded to the letter she sent him. It'd been a very short note—*Dear Daed, all is forgiven. I love you, Hannah.*

It'd taken her hours to write those simple words, but by the time she wrote them, she meant every one. She opened the envelope and shook the contents onto the table. A letter on green stationery and one very thick white envelope slid onto the table. She flipped the white envelope over and stopped cold.

Her first name was written across it in Paul's handwriting.

"Helloooooo?" Martin called.

"I…I need to tend to some things. How about if we talk tomorrow?" Martin said something she didn't really hear before she said goodbye and disconnected the call.

She unfolded the green stationery first and glanced to the end.

From Dorcas?

She returned to the top of the page and began reading.

Hannah,

You cannot imagine how much I do not want to write this letter. I've wished you weren't in Paul's life since the day I learned of you. I wanted Paul to feel toward me the things he wrote in this letter to you. But if love never fails, it seems self-interest is doomed to fail—and now I hold less of his heart than I thought possible.

When you left, he debated over what to do and decided to give you time to return on your own. Whenever he wavered in that decision, I encouraged him to stay the course. He waited for you. And I never told him you called. He waited until he saw you in Ohio with a man he thought to be your husband. And a week later you returned, and he began falling for you again. Perhaps you've truly moved on and I'm only making things worse, but I felt I had to make sure you knew everything, which is what I should have done for both of you to begin with.

Please forgive me,
Dorcas

With temptation to read his letter pounding, she felt guilt close in around her. Reading Paul's letter would do nothing but cause her mayhem. In the tumultuous quiet, an image of Kevin and Lissa filled her, and she was absolutely confident what had to be done. She put Dorcas's letter with Paul's and slid them back into the larger envelope. With her voice screaming inside her, she ignored the desire to read his letter and walked to the trash can. But her fingers wouldn't let it go.

He'd written to her in love and waited more than two years for her to return. Was she really going to throw all the sincerity he'd poured onto paper into the garbage?

"God, help me."

But He didn't. She felt no added strength to release the letter and no freedom to read it. Paul's words from two weeks ago rang inside her head: *Come on, Hannah. How great can your relationship with Martin be if...*

Her need to protect herself from Paul wasn't just about Martin and her. It was about Kevin and Lissa. She wouldn't abandon them. Couldn't. Their dad had, and a few months later their mother had too. Hannah wouldn't add to that rejection. Besides, Martin wasn't likely even to have Kevin and Lissa if she hadn't pushed and prodded him. She couldn't ever turn her back on any of them and still be able to find any part of herself. Dropping the letter into the trash can, she felt her chest constrict. Ignoring the feeling, she went into the bedroom. The mirror that hung on the back of the door caught her eye, and she gazed at herself. The only thing she'd ever wanted was a life with Paul Waddell. That's all. Tears stung her eyes, and without changing clothes, she flicked off the light and crawled into bed.

All Dorcas had managed to do was make the hurt worse. Willing herself to sleep, Hannah closed her eyes. Hours passed, and her desire to read the letter only grew. The temptation to feel some part of what she would have felt then embarrassed her. Disgusted with herself, she eased her legs over the side of the bed and sat up.

She could tear it up or burn it, but she figured that would only cause the longing to mutate into a regret she could never undo. She swallowed hard. This was ridiculous. There was no way she could ignore the letter. If it lay in the trash for a thousand years, she'd still know he'd written it and waited for her.

Wasn't her fear of facing the truth most of what had destroyed them to begin with?

She'd feared what he'd think of her if he learned she'd been raped and later was pregnant, so she tried to hide both. She'd feared watching him fall in love with someone else and have children with her, so she ran. She'd feared if she stood before him vulnerable, he'd reach out to her in pity, so she didn't give him the chance. She'd feared if they worked through everything else, she'd tear him from his family, and his life would never be healed again.

Darkness cloaked the room, and she longed for rays of the new day to come, but there were still two hours of nighttime ahead. Sick of how she'd let fear rule her, she went to the kitchen, flicked on the light, and moved to the trash can. She lifted the envelope from the trash bag, noticing it was wet from sharing space with a used coffee filter. She pulled the white envelope from the manila one. It was slightly damp, and the color of the wet coffee grounds had seeped through. Dorcas had kept it pristine for more than three years, but Hannah had already managed to stain it.

Feeling as if she messed up everything she touched, she sat down, slid the letter out, and opened it.

Dear Hannah,

I've waited so long to get to share how I really feel. My heart is so full now that you've agreed to be my wife. Tonight my family had a party, and I could only dream of having you by my side. Sharing your love and laughter is my deepest desire, and I can't wait for the many gatherings of friends and family in the future when we can be together as man and wife.

I know you are worried about your family and what will happen, but I'm convinced we can work through any struggle and overcome anything or anyone that would separate us. I will do everything I can to win them over.

There are so many unique parts to you, my Lion-heart. I know you can't see it and don't even want me saying it, but I realized it the first day I saw you at Gram's, tending to all the meals for the workers. Just a thought of you brings back a dozen memories of who you are and who we are together. And I don't want you to bury your gifts and talents to be only a helpmate to me. My dream is that we both aim to be exactly who God called us to be. I don't think He stocked you with talents so they would rust or get buried while you play a dutiful wife.

We can't know what life will hold, but I have no preset desires of who I want us to be or what I want, except I want you, Lion-heart, just you, wherever that may lead us.

Unable to read any further through her tears, she lowered the letter and folded it.

Reading it was a mistake. Knowing he'd waited for her and was still in love with her was too much. Now she'd hear his voice inside her all the rest of her days.

She'd fought so hard to let him go because of reasons that now were as lifeless as last year's garden. Nauseous and tired, she went to take a shower.

It was just as over today as it was six months or two years ago, only now her heart was too vested in Paul to be fair to Martin, and she had no idea how to untie her heart from Paul's. She soaked under a hot shower until it started running cool. Longing pulled at her, and there was no ignoring it.

She dried off and slid into her thick cotton bathrobe.

The feelings tore at her. How had Paul handled waiting for her all that time?

The sun was rising, dispelling the darkness. Funny how the smallest light could dispel darkness, but light was never dismissed that easily.

She went into the kitchen and fixed a pot of coffee.

There was a tap at her front door. Closing her eyes for a moment, she drew a deep breath and hoped Martin didn't notice how stressed she was. It wasn't like him to stop in before work.

She opened the door and stepped back. "Hi."

He came inside and closed the door. "I saw the light on."

"Care for some coffee?" She lifted the decanter.

"No thanks."

He sounded different, milder and not agitated at all.

Pouring herself another cup, she tried not to respond to the stare she could feel coming from him. "What's on your agenda for today?"

"The usual. Yours?"

Feeling tears sting, she took a seat, staying focused on the counter, the mug, anything but looking at him. "Not as much to do with school over. I thought about going shopping for clothes for the trip. Maybe begin packing for Lissa and Kevin."

He pulled out a chair and sat. "Before I met your Daed and heard what he had to say, I would have told you to wash your hands of them and *never* look back."

She plunked sugar into her cup and watched the black liquid swirl as she stirred it. "But we both know that somewhere between being done wrong and *never*, people change."

The hum of the furnace and the various soft noises of the electric coffeepot hung in the air, but neither Martin nor she spoke for more than five minutes.

He finally reached across the table and took her hand in his. "Hannah, sweetheart, could you look at me, please?"

She slowly looked up, surprised not to see anger in his eyes.

Martin let out a long, slow breath. "There she is. That's the girl I used to see when we first met, only then she was in love with *what's his name.*" Martin kissed the back of her hand. "He didn't turn his back on you like you thought, did he?"

Hannah swallowed and shook her head. "How…" She choked back a sob and couldn't finish her sentence.

"When Mary was in labor and you were trying to find Paul, you said something to Dorcas about the times you'd called and she hadn't told him." Martin rubbed her hand gently. "When did you find out?"

"The second time I went back." Tears worked their way free. "I've not handled this with Paul right. I'm so sorry."

"I promised Zabeth I'd let you go, help you go, if you ever seemed interested in returning to your community—unless we were married by then." Martin shook his head. "I know you love me, and I know you don't want to leave Kevin and Lissa, but the problems go deep into who we are. We want to be right for each other." He cursed softly. "We tried to be and almost convinced ourselves we could do it, but I don't think we can. Not in all the ways that make a marriage good most of the time."

Through blurry vision she watched him.

"I want someone who wants me, phone girl. I deserve that, and Zabeth would want—no, she'd demand that for me too, just as she'd demand it for you. I haven't waited this long to settle for someone who is in love with me and someone else at the same time. You don't even love anything about my lifestyle—not my house, my hobbies, or my dreams for the future."

"But Kevin and Lissa—they are our dreams and future too. They need us. Please, Martin."

He held up his hand, trying to make her hush.

Hannah searched his face. "They need both of us. I'll try hard—"

He smacked the tabletop, stopping her midsentence. "No more, Hannah. The decision is made." His booming voice made the room vibrate. He closed his eyes and sucked in a ragged breath. "Do you hear yourself? Everything about staying with me is based on Kevin and Lissa!"

Her hands were shaking as he spoke a truth she didn't want him to know.

"You're twenty years old, and they aren't yours. You do know Faye could return, right? I won't give them to her unless she spends time here and goes through drug testing to prove herself, but I will make room for her in their lives and on my property."

Hannah withdrew her hands, placing her palms over her moist eyes.

Martin tugged at her wrist, waiting on her to look at him again. "Could you just think about something for a minute? If you stayed because of Kevin and Lissa, you'd be saying you don't believe God can provide anyone else for them. Or for me." Martin gave a confident smile. "Trust me, there are other women out there who would love to step into your shoes. Some of them are even worth having."

"This can't be happening."

"I always knew there was a chance I'd lose you to the Plain ways and maybe even to what's his name. The moment you got that call from Sarah…from home, I think I knew I had begun to lose you. I just didn't want to admit it."

A sob broke from her, and she covered her face.

"Look, we'll do graduation with Kevin and Lissa, and afterward we'll do a going-away party with the band so the kids get closure. You can invite…"

He let the sentence trail. She didn't have any friends, not in Ohio. She had Dr. Lehman, maybe the Plain women from the Tuesday quiltings, but they'd never come here for a party. She only had Martin, Kevin, and Lissa. All the people who kept Martin's home a buzz of activity were his friends, ones she never managed to truly connect to. Maybe if she'd tried harder…

"I'll transfer your ticket to Hawaii into Laura's name, and we'll explain to the kids that you've decided to move home. I don't want to wait until after Christmas. Between school, work, and returning to Owl's Perch, they've adjusted to you being gone a lot already. The trip to Hawaii will be a good transition time for them." His speech was slow and methodical, as if he'd memorized what he'd say and the tone he'd keep while saying it, but the hurt and anger behind his well-behaved exterior was deep.

Breathing seemed almost impossible as she fought against the tears. In spite of crying, she lowered her hands and looked him in the face. "I'm so, so sorry. This is all my fault."

"Your fault?"

"I pushed you to stop dating others and date me."

"Get real, Hannah. I've never been pushed by any girl into anything I didn't want to begin with. And that includes you."

His words came out as arrogant and condescending as the first time they'd met, and he must have realized it, because he sighed, and then his countenance became more gentle.

"You've changed me, Hannah. Without you, Kevin and Lissa would be in foster care, and I'd be a scrooge in the making, torn between wanting my own way and feeling guilty for abandoning the two most precious things I could imagine. You were here for Zabeth when I was so overwhelmed I was beginning to hate life."

"You never told me that."

He took her hand and turned it palm up. "My heart landed right here because you earned it, but maybe we tried to turn the love we have for each other into something it wasn't supposed to be. As just a friend and the niece of Zabeth—that's a relationship we could've made work for a lifetime. I want someone who can't live without music. Someone who takes pleasure in the same things I do, including my kind of church, the band, friends, movies, fine restaurants, vacations, and swimming, and golfing—"

She held her hand up to stop him. "I get the idea. Thanks."

"We tried, phone girl. We really did. But I don't like who I'd turned into lately in order to try to hold on to you. I didn't sleep last night, trying to think this through. You don't look like you slept much either."

She shook her head.

He stood. "I need to go."

She gazed into his eyes, clueless how to express all she was feeling. "You're a remarkable man, Martin Palmer."

His green eyes held a hardness she knew he was capable of, but Zabeth would be proud of the gentlemanly way in which he was handling himself.

"We'll finish this out amicably, Hannah. I promise." And with that he left.

She went to the door and closed it, then slumped against the frame and sobbed.

The December chill went right through Hannah as she knelt in front of Lissa and Kevin. Since this was the meeting place for everyone who was going to Hawaii, Martin's driveway was a bustle of activity as luggage was moved into the vehicles that would caravan to Cleveland. Christmas was in three days, and the whole gang would be on the island before bedtime tonight by Hawaii's time zone.

Hannah buttoned Lissa's coat. "You have lots of fun and eat fruits and vegetables, okay?" She tugged at Kevin's winter cap, making sure it covered his ears better. "And don't forget to use that digital camera to take photos. Laura said she'll help you e-mail them to me."

They each held a carry-on that Hannah had loaded with things to help keep them busy during the fourteen-hour flight.

Kevin held up the new camera Martin had given him for the trip. "It's gonna be so much fun! You'll be sorry you let Laura take your ticket and didn't wait to move back home until after the vacation."

"I'll be with my brother and niece over the holidays while you're with your uncle and sister. It just makes sense."

"I get it." Kevin shrugged. "Uncle Martin said you're moving, not leaving. We'll see you some, right?"

She nodded, unsure how much contact Martin would allow. He wasn't willing to discuss it.

Lissa hugged her. "Laura said I can have a meal and a Coke and choose my own snack when we're on the plane."

"Oh that'll be fun." Hannah held the little girl close, memorizing the warmth of her. When Hannah and Martin had explained to them she was moving back home, they'd accepted it with only a few tears.

Martin was really good at knowing how to divert the children's attention while they adjusted to new facts in their lives.

He clapped his hands. "Okay, guys, you're in the vehicle with me and three other adults. Go."

They took off running, squealing with laughter. The heavy silence between her and Martin bore the weight of shattered hopes.

Graduation had come and gone. Dr. Lehman and the nurses from the clinic had attended, each carrying a carload of Plain women from the Tuesday quiltings. Laura and the children came. Martin said he needed to work, but they both knew that work had nothing to do with why he hadn't come. Hannah even wondered if he was already dating again. But true to his word, he'd been amicable to the very end.

Since graduation Hannah had logged a lot of work hours, getting the clinic as ready for her departure as she could. Dr. Lehman hadn't come to the going-away party, saying he wanted her to come see him at least once every two months. Whether she did or didn't, he'd come see her every time he went to Lancaster to visit his mother. So they'd made a pact.

Martin pulled his gaze from the van to her. "So, this is it." He paused, looking as if he felt sorry for her. "I'll let Laura help Kevin and Lissa call you whenever they want to, but other than that I could use some distance."

"I understand."

"You're all packed?"

"Almost."

"If you need anything…"

"Thank you."

He pulled some papers from his pocket and held them out to her. "The cabin, as well as about thirty thousand dollars, are yours on your twenty-first birthday—a gift from Zabeth that she wanted you to have when the time came. She had a small life-insurance policy, and you were the beneficiary. Just contact the lawyer who's listed."

She eased it from him, wishing this wasn't happening and yet knowing they had no choice. Tears burned her skin, and she tried to swallow the ache in her throat.

He shrugged. "I sold Ol' Gert to the Sawyer family a few days ago. It's going to be a Christmas present for their children. I didn't figure you'd mind."

She shook her head. "That's fine." Except as things dragged on, this felt more like a divorce than a breakup of two people who'd dated for nine months. But she hadn't run out in spite of how painful the last two weeks had been. The adjustment Kevin and Lissa had made during that time was surprising, like she was a sibling going off to college.

"Take care, phone girl." He wrapped his arms around her, the first truly kind gesture he'd made since he'd ended things between them. She broke into tears. "Sh." He kissed the top of her head before taking a step back. "Don't work too hard."

Laura was in the front passenger's seat but facing the back as she spoke to the other adults in the rented van. She acted more like a grandmother than a nanny, and that seemed to fit both Martin's and her needs. Amy Clarke was in the backseat, helping Lissa get buckled in.

After Martin left, Hannah would leave. That's what they'd agreed to, for the children's sake. They'd also agreed she'd keep the ring, because it'd become clear during this lengthy departure time that wearing Kevin's and Lissa's birthstones was a heart connection for them.

The van backed out. Kevin and Lissa were smiling and waving. Hannah put a smile on her face as she waved until they were out of sight. Martin never glanced back. She slowly walked to the cottage. After crying for quite a while, she took a long, hot shower and finished packing. It was past lunchtime when she left her house keys on the table of the cottage and locked the door behind her.

Barely able to see for the tears, she slid behind the wheel. The pain of leaving seemed just as horrid as the pain she'd carried when she'd arrived in Ohio. But in spite of her heartache and guilt, she didn't regret her time with Martin. Still, he was right; he deserved someone to love and enjoy all of who he was and what he had to offer.

The tears eased some, and she began to pray for him. As the hours passed and darkness took over the winter skies, a bit of hope replaced her anguish, and she began to sense that he'd eventually be happier without her than with her. That meant the children would be too.

As peace began to warm her, thoughts of Paul seeped in again. It was too soon to contact him, to even hint at what was going on in her life, so she drove toward Luke's place. There would be time for her and Paul to talk later. He'd waited for her for nearly three years. Surely she could wait a few more weeks to finish giving her relationship with Martin a decent grieving time. No one knew she was coming, but she figured she could stay with Naomi Esh or Luke and Mary until she found a place of her own.

She reached over to the seat next to hers and ran her fingers across the gift-wrapped present for Paul. In spite of her sense of disloyalty toward Martin, she'd reopened Paul's letter before daylight today and read all of it for the first time. Paul's ability to understand and accept her just as she was had washed over her anew as she read the words he'd written so long ago. Afterward, she wrapped the "Past and Future" quilt for him. She wasn't sure when she'd give it to him, but she knew it'd be soon enough—sometime next month, for his birthday this summer? When was soon enough too soon?

The pastures on each side of her were covered by a blanket of snow, and the clear skies had a purple hue under the quarter moon. From the opposite side of the road, a horse and buggy came toward her. As they passed each other, the rhythmic clopping of the horse's hoofs unleashed dozens of emotions within her. Unlike witnessing horses and buggies in Ohio, Hannah felt she was home. The snow glittered like shards of glass under the moon's glow, enveloping her with an odd yet familiar sense that she couldn't define. She pulled her car off the side of the road and got out. White fields spread out before her with barren trees lining the horizon.

"Hannah."

A whisper swooshed across the field with the winter wind, rustling a few dead leaves with it. Eeriness ran over her, reminding her of the whisper that had called her from Owl's Perch years ago. Now it returned? Just as familiar, just as indefinable.

"Kumm raus."

Almost overwhelmed, her legs wobbled. She knew that voice. Didn't she? Chills ran wild, and she felt so strange. Years ago she couldn't place the voice.

Today she could.

"Oh, Father, was it Paul all along?" Inside her coat pocket, she clutched the letter he'd written to her. She backed against the car for support as epiphanies poured into her. He'd not just come back for *her.* He'd returned willing to marry her and take on the child she carried. Barely able to remain on her feet, she drew cold air into her lungs.

The first time she'd heard the voice to *Kumm raus*—to come out— she'd stood by her infant's grave, yet it came with a multitude of sentiments: hope, longing, freedom…and love so deep she'd thought maybe it was God Himself. And part of it had to have been God. He'd certainly stayed with her through her journey, giving her all the things she sensed inside that whisper—hope and a future.

"God?"

Knowing more pieces to the puzzle than ever before, she sensed that leaving to find Zabeth had not been a mistake. And she could never regret knowing Martin—even if dating him should not have been part of their relationship.

Unable to let go of the whisper, she stayed, but the desire to see Paul grew with every minute. He'd waited so long, so patiently, as if "Kumm raus" didn't mean coming to him—not immediately. If it had been

Paul's voice beckoning to her, he'd called her to come out from under her father's rule, her community's gossip, and the brokenness that was heaped upon her. But he'd been willing to wait until she was also free from the pain.

Because she couldn't reach him, she became entangled in new things that kept her in Ohio.

The need to see Paul intensified. Surely if she handled herself right and kept a careful watch over her actions, it wouldn't be dishonorable to go to him, to give him the quilt and let him know she was…home.

She got into her car and headed for the clinic. If he wasn't there, she'd go to Luke's. Maybe. She glanced at the clock. It was almost seven. She drew close to the four-way stop near the Better Path. The parking lot was empty except for Paul's car.

She shifted gears, pulling into the parking lot. Through a second-story window of the Better Path, she saw Paul in a room that wasn't his office. He appeared to be reading something in his hand. She flipped open her phone and scrolled to the number she'd logged as Paul's—the number she'd accidentally called four weeks ago.

"Hannah," Paul answered, "what's up?"

She tried to find her voice.

"Hannah?"

"Yeah." She managed a whisper.

"Are you okay?"

"Could you look out the window?"

He walked closer and peered down. The surprise on his face made her smile.

"What are you doing here?"

"I…I brought you something."

Through the window he held her gaze for a few seconds. "I'll be right there."

She closed her phone and got out of the car. By the time she'd walked to the passenger's side and lifted the gift from the seat, he was on the front porch, wearing only short sleeves. His gorgeous eyes spoke of love so deep she almost couldn't bear to look. Physical strength radiated from him. She moved to the foot of the steps with the gift.

"Making a quick visit home before flying out, eh?"

That was Paul. Unassuming. Upbeat. And careful in his tone and words to honor the decision she'd given him concerning Martin.

She held the gift toward him, and he lifted it from her. It was wrapped, but it wasn't inside a box.

He removed the gold wrapping paper easily, letting it fall to the ground. "The 'Past and Future' quilt."

"It seems it came full circle back to me, and now..." She choked back the tears.

"Hannah, what's going on?"

She pulled the letter he'd written three years ago out of her coat pocket and held it up to him.

He'd barely looked at it when recognition registered on his face. "Dorcas shouldn't have sent that."

"It was the right thing to do." She slid it back into her pocket. "Paul, I was a part of your past, and I want to always be a part of your future."

"Hannah?"

"I...I'm not sure I should have stopped by here. It's too soon."

He stepped closer, and the rush of power she felt from being near him was something she experienced nowhere else.

"Martin and I...aren't together anymore."

With the gentle movements that so defined him, Paul caressed her cheek with one hand and held her gaze, saying so many things neither of them could voice—not yet, not for a while. "I'm not going anywhere."

"I...I may not be able to have children."

He shifted the blanket to her arms and cradled her face, his hands trembling. "I want you. That's all. Surely you know that by now." He eased his arms around her, holding her tight while resting his head on hers. "You're home," he whispered, his voice hoarse.

Hannah had ached for a moment like this for so long, dreamed of it even before he'd asked her to marry him and oh so long after she thought she'd lost his love completely. With the quilt between them, she wrapped her arms around him.

After long minutes of holding her, he took her by the hand. "I have something I want to show you." They went inside and up the stairs to the room he'd been in when she arrived. Documents were scattered everywhere, and a set of plans were spread out on the table.

Paul held up a finger. "While you look at that and figure out what I'm working on, I need to get something from my office." He stopped at the door and then returned to her. Lifting her face toward his, he studied her. "You're here."

She nodded, choking on fresh tears.

"You're really here."

Tears spilled down her cheeks. He placed his hands on her shoulders, his eyes glistening and a gentle smile covering his face. "I'll be back…"

She looked over the papers, chills covering her as she realized what he was up to. He came back into the office with a shirt box and set it to the side.

Had he been expecting her?

He couldn't have, so how did he have a gift for her?

She studied the info spread out in front of her.

"Do you know what you're looking at?"

"Plans for a clinic."

"Not just a clinic. One that will be designed and staffed as an Amish and Plain facility."

Her heart was pounding so hard she could hear it echoing against her eardrums.

Paul pulled out a chair for her. "It'll take a couple of years, but the board has already voted to turn the guesthouse into an Amish clinic. We have few patients who need to stay there, so allocating that building for housing isn't the best use of it. When you returned in September, my eyes began to be opened to the difference a medical facility for the Plain community would make, more so for the local Amish than Mennonite. I'm not sure how we'll staff it with a doctor and all, but we have plenty of time to work on filling each position."

Remembering years back, before Paul or anyone but her parents knew her secret, she'd felt as if she'd become an empty kerosene lamp, the outward part of no use without its fuel. Oh, how she'd longed for Paul to know everything about her and still love her. How she'd desperately needed to find one thing she was good at and hold on to it. And now all those things were hers. Was this really happening?

"I want to get a bachelor's of science degree in nursing. I just need to know all I can in that field and mix it with all we know of being Plain."

"The board will want you to become a member and use your knowledge and influence, if you will."

"Of course I will."

"Then we'll begin raising money. By the time the clinic is ready to open with all the equipment and supplies purchased, staff hired, and licenses acquired, you'll have your degree."

Paul shifted the box he'd brought in, placing it in front of her, but she couldn't move. He lifted the lid off the box. "Remember House of Grace?"

Powerless to answer, she watched as he picked up photos of a little girl.

"We've been her sponsor for nearly three years now. Look." Paul took out a couple of handmade cloth pouches with cross-stitching around the border.

After running her fingers across the fabric in his hand, she reached into the box and pulled out a large stack of drawings on colored paper.

"She creates pictures from the markers, crayons, watercolors, and stacks of paper we send."

"We?" Hannah choked.

Paul sifted through some of the items in the box until he pulled out one beige paper, a letter from Global Servants. It had Paul Waddell and Hannah Lapp listed as the sponsors.

Hannah closed her eyes, trying to absorb it all. He'd not only waited, but he'd remained faithful to the things they'd begun. Speechless, she returned to looking at the girl's handiwork. The young girl had amazing talent for drawing and painting. Absolute giftedness. Hannah laid one aside and looked at another until she came to a card the girl had made. She'd drawn a beautiful picture of a home with yellow light streaming from the windows. It said:

I love you.
    A-Yom

"We'll have children, Hannah. Maybe never our own, but this earth isn't lacking for those who need someone to love them."

Hannah stood. "Am I dreaming?"

Paul moved in close, staring into her eyes as if he was unsure too. "I keep thinking the same thing. It may take years of waking to find you near to convince me it's all real." He wound around his fingers the wisps of her curls that had broken free of their confines. "You're here. It's a gift that came with a high price. I'll never forget that."

She couldn't tell him she loved him, not yet, probably not until Martin was past being so angry with her and had moved on. But she didn't have to. He got it. Just as Sarah had said, Paul saw her.

He studied her. "When you said 'too soon,' you meant we can spend time together as friends but nothing too serious for now, right?"

In every way he understood her. "Yes."

"Good. This will be a holiday like no other."

~~⁓ᘯᕈ⁓~~

Removing a loaf of bread from the oven, Hannah could feel Paul's eyes on her. Laughter and voices gently roamed through Gram's kitchen from the living room, where the group played board games. Friday nights seemed to bring a new tradition for Paul and her—dinner and games with friends.

Luke and Mary were here with Amanda. Sarah had come with them. Matthew and Kathryn wandered in an hour ago. Unlike the gatherings with the band, Hannah connected here—even when the guests were Paul's friends whom she barely knew. She glanced his way. With his shoulder resting against the doorframe, he watched her, saying everything she wanted to hear.

Since Hannah had arrived two months ago, she'd fallen so deep for Paul her mind couldn't comprehend it. The first few nights she was back, they'd stayed near the roaring fire here at Gram's, talking until Hannah fell asleep on the couch. More than once she'd awakened to find Paul sitting in a chair, sipping coffee and watching her.

She had hundreds of memories packed inside these past two months. She'd taken and passed her state board exams. But she'd missed the application deadline for entering nursing school this winter, so she and Paul were putting their free time to good use.

In spite of the cold weather, they'd gone to the beach, and for the first time in her life she saw the ocean. They'd gone sledding with Matthew and Kathryn, spent time with their friends and family, and shared quiet evenings talking. They'd driven to what had once been his college campus and might become hers too. She'd enjoyed the state museum in Harrisburg so much they'd been three times already, and they'd also gone to City Island. They took a trip to Alliance's train depot, her beloved cabin, and Dr. Lehman's clinic. Paul had met all the women from the Tuesday quiltings. The women were beside themselves to learn she'd returned to the Plain sect, even if it wasn't Old Order Amish. They'd spent time in old town Alliance, hoping to find Kendrick, the young man who'd kept her from freezing to death when she'd landed in Ohio nearly three years ago in the dead of winter. She'd been so busy trying to survive and to put the past behind her that she'd given little thought to Kendrick over the years. But Paul wanted to find him, to thank him and to see if there was anything they could do for him.

Each outing caused the gaping hole of their time apart to close a little more, and now it seemed as thin as a hairline fracture. Paul had asked nothing of her emotionally—not for commitments, or plans, or words of love. But no one read her heart more than Paul, and he had to know she loved him completely. Out of respect for Martin, she'd kept herself in check and not kissed Paul, but her desire to marry him grew by the day.

The first visit to his parents' home started out awkwardly, but clearly she was welcomed by his dad, sister, and brother-in-law. His uncle Samuel came by just to meet her, and he'd more than made up for the hint of standoffishness that Paul's mother, Hazel, gave off. By the end of the evening, his mother was warming up a bit, and Hannah was fairly confident they would eventually become friends on some level. Whatever vibes Hazel gave off, they were friendlier than what Paul was likely to ever receive from her Daed. But Paul and she were together, and aside from the ache harbored in her heart concerning Kevin and Lissa and the regret she held for the hurt she'd caused Martin, no one else's likes or dislikes regarding this relationship mattered.

As amazing and healing as the last two months with Paul had been, she wanted to know how Martin was doing. Kevin and Lissa called her from Laura's or Martin's cell regularly, and she shared in a few minutes of their lives each time. With Laura's help, they e-mailed her photos and called to talk to her about them.

Paul strolled into the kitchen. "What do you think about getting a rescued pup from Sarah after she's done some training and she's ready to put the first ones up for adoption?"

Her cell phone rang, and she pulled it from her dress pocket. The caller ID said it was Martin's phone. "It's Kevin or Lissa."

Paul nodded. "Absolutely. Answer it."

"Hello?"

"Hey, it's me. Got a minute?"

Martin sounded upbeat, and hope that he'd weathered the worst spread throughout her. "Sure. Give me a few seconds." She hit the Mute button. "It's Martin."

"You'll want somewhere quiet." Paul motioned to the back door and helped her slip into her coat.

Walking across the back porch, she took the phone off mute and put it to her ear. Solid white lay across the fields, the night silent as new snow fell from the black sky. "I'm here." Snow crunched under her feet as she went into the yard. She waited for him to speak, praying he'd forgiven her and was ready to embrace happiness again.

"We're gearing up here for a musical blowout. It's a celebration because I received notice earlier today that I passed my engineering exams."

"Congratulations! Although I never doubted you would. Was Hawaii every bit as glorious as you'd hoped?"

"It was even better."

"I'm glad you weren't disappointed. Kevin and Lissa haven't stopped talking about it yet."

Silence hung, and she waited.

"I, uh, I get it, Hannah. I mean, I'm the one who ended things, and I understood even before that, but now all of it makes sense. I'd always banked that with enough time and gentle pressure, you'd become a perfect fit. When I talked you into moving out of the cabin or the dozens of other things I was always pushing you to do, my hope was to get you comfortable in my world."

She figured this was his way of telling her she was right to return to Paul and he was ready to move on. Relief eased its way through her, and tears blurred her vision.

A knock on a door filtered through the line.

"It's open," Martin said.

Hannah couldn't hear all the words being spoken to him, but it sounded like Amy Clarke's voice, telling him where she'd be when he was off the phone.

"Okay, I'll be there in a minute. Listen, Hannah, Kevin and Lissa are asking a lot about seeing you. They're off next Thursday and Friday. You could take them through the weekend too, unless you're schedule isn't free."

"Really?" Her resolve broke, and she sobbed.

He had to be doing a lot better. Before he left for Hawaii, he wouldn't even hint that he might let her see Kevin and Lissa again, but now, if they wanted to see her, he'd allow it. The plan would need to fit around his schedule, which seemed more than fair, and exhilaration danced within her.

"You know, if you could stop crying…"

She wiped her tears, trying to contain her excitement and relief. "Sorry. Go ahead."

"I just figured you needed to know I'm fine." He paused. "No, I'm better than fine now. I know we're both right where we're supposed to be."

As if boulders were being removed, guilt lifted, and she couldn't find her voice.

"Nothing meant more to Zabeth than keeping the Palmer family together as much as possible. She grew too weak and died before that happened, but you came in, and…well, you finished what she began, and now Kevin, Lissa, and I are a family. If it took falling for you for that to happen, I'd do it again."

"Thank you, Martin."

"Just give Laura a call next week, and she'll meet you with the children at the cabin or the clinic or wherever. Okay?"

"I'll be grateful for this forever."

"Back at you. Bye."

Closing her eyes, she shut her phone. Like the snowfall around her, memories seemed to swirl and land gently in random places. As much as she grieved for the pain she'd caused Martin, she could never regret the privilege of being by Zabeth's side—a dying, shunned woman, desperate to hold together whatever could be salvaged in the Palmer family.

Maybe Martin was right; she'd helped change him, and because of that, he was firmly rooted in Kevin's and Lissa's lives.

God was able to bring good out of tragedy, missteps, and even stupid mistakes. Gazing into the snowy dark sky, she trusted God more than ever. "Nevertheless."

Wanting to see Paul alone for a minute before joining the others, she opened her cell phone and called him.

"Hey, you can't win if you're not in here to play."

"Meaning you're losing for the both of us."

The back door opened, and Paul walked across the porch and into the yard. "Something like that, yeah." With one look at her, a smile crossed his handsome face. He tucked his phone back into his pocket. "That was a good call."

She stretched her arms out and twirled around before she ran to him and threw her arms around his neck, laughing.

He held her so very gently with her feet dangling off the ground. "I love you, Hannah. Always have. Always will."

He set her feet on the ground, staring into her eyes. Leaning down, he brought his lips to hers, and the power of every once-forbidden hope and dream danced as a reality within her. He kissed across her cheek and down her neck.

Her knees gave way a bit, and she backed away.

"Hannah?"

"I just need to sit." She sank onto the cold snow. Tilting her head, she looked into his eyes. "Talk about sweeping a girl off her feet."

Clearly the reason for her needing to sit began to dawn on him, and he chuckled. "You had me worried for a minute. Are you sure—"

"I'm sure."

Paul offered her a hand, but the gesture was more than a moment of help. Everything she had ever wanted or would ever want stood with open arms—just waiting for her. She slid into his embrace, wrapping her arms around him and resting the side of her face against his chest. "I love you, Paul." Her voice cracked, and tears threatened. "I love you."

The warmth of waking with Paul's arms around her caused gratefulness to work through her. The first rays of light waited just below the horizon to stretch across the land, dispelling the dark that filled every corner of the room. Enjoying the rumble of the attic fan as it drew in mixed fragrances through the opened window—fresh-cut hay, their vegetable garden, and hints of the patch of woods surrounding the creek—Hannah relished the start of a new day. Life itself stirred her, making her feel as if she were soaring over fields like an eagle. The feeling had become a permanent part of her as she watched Paul build this home during their engagement. The house sat on the ten acres of land that Gram gave them, but the porch, with its ceiling fan for summer and outdoor fireplace for winter, was their favorite spot. It overlooked the footbridge where he had proposed.

The "Past and Future" quilt lay across the foot of their bed, waiting patiently for cold weather to arrive. Her Mennonite prayer Kapp rested on the nightstand beside her. Next to it sat the hand-carved box Paul had made for her, one that held years of letters from people she loved—Paul, Daed, Mamm, Lissa, and Kevin, even a rare note from Martin or Amy, telling her when and where they were traveling so she or Paul could make plans to pick the children up from Laura.

The letters were a reminder that love didn't have to be perfect when forgiveness was applied. That truth guided her through each part of life—even though her father had not yet allowed her in his home. Accepting her Daed for who he was kept hurt from stealing from her when he hadn't attended her wedding. She found that same understanding was able to strengthen her when it came to dealing with difficult people from all walks of life.

Her mother came to visit her on at least one nonchurch Sunday a month. Although Hannah saw her Daed here and there when moving about the community and he always spoke to her, she was more grateful that he wrote to her a few times each year and came by her clinic on occasion just to see her. He had come to their home to eat with Paul and her once, but the idea of his daughter having electrical and phone lines coming into her house worried him. In spite of his unbending beliefs, he tried to open his mind and heart to her. And she, in turn, tried to identify with him. The reality of forgiveness planted and growing in her daily life amazed her. She couldn't claim to understand how it worked, but the freedom it brought was undeniable. And when she got it wrong—overreacted, underreacted, or flared with an incorrect response—forgiveness waited to be embraced.

Running her fingers over the honorary mother's ring that now hung on a necklace she hid under her Plain clothing during the day, Hannah could hardly believe the children were on the brink of becoming teens and that Martin and Amy would soon celebrate five years of marriage. The former Amy Clarke not only filled everything Martin had been looking for in Hannah, but she adored and respected him deeply, bringing a sense of well-being to him that he richly deserved. As much as it grieved Hannah, Faye had never returned, and Hannah doubted that she was still alive. Thankfully, Kevin and Lissa seemed to be doing well, gleaning life lessons from the two households—Palmer and Waddell—that loved them unconditionally.

Zabeth's cabin was a second home to Paul and her. During the school year Hannah worked for Dr. Lehman's clinic one weekend a month, leading a quilting Q and A on Saturday. In the summer she worked at the clinic twice a month. Each time, Paul and she stayed at the cabin. Kevin and Lissa would often stay with them, and in the spring of each year, Paul helped them plant a garden. Kevin chose to grow only watermelons that he sold door to door in Martin's neighborhood. Lissa never wanted to sell anything from her garden. She wanted her produce used for their meals, or she'd have Paul drive her to the local mission, where she could give the food away.

Hannah arched her back ever so slightly, stretching just a little, but she felt Paul stir.

He planted a kiss on her shoulder and rubbed across her rounded stomach. "Sleep, Lion-heart, it's still dark."

But she couldn't will herself back to sleep. Didn't want to, really. The love that ran between them and the love they gave away to others kept life renewed and exciting. For six years Paul and she had contentedly accepted being without children, enjoying every part of the life they'd been blessed with. Always proud of her work and school accomplishments, Paul took satisfaction in their busy schedules, and they continually grew in finding pleasure in each other's arms—unlike anything they'd expected. And now…she could feel their child moving within her.

After attending the deliveries of so many babies, she was even more amazed by the miracle of what was taking place inside her. At twenty-seven years old and with her master's in nursing, she was expecting their first child in mid-December.

Although she worked at the Plain Ways clinic just behind the Better Path, she spent much of her time going to Amish homes and visiting. She met resistance from some, especially the men, but she applied respect and forgiveness and continued to make headway talking with the families about women's health issues.

When it suited Paul, he'd come to the birthing clinic during the long nights and stay in the sleeping room with her. When they were off, they had treasured friends to enjoy—some Amish, some Plain Mennonite, and some Englischers.

Hannah's thoughts continued to roam. Thankfully for Mary's

health, she didn't conceive too often. She and Luke had one more child thus far, a son. In the years since Matthew and Kathryn had married, they'd had three children. Kathryn loved organizing her household and working beside Matthew. They'd built a small home near the shops, and Kathryn brought more joy to Matthew than could be measured in a lifetime.

Hannah believed Dorcas's regret for what she'd done was real and her repentance complete, but the heartache of losing Paul still seemed to cling to her. The battle to keep Lyme disease from ravaging her body was a long one, taking years of medicine and physical therapy to regain her health. She was now overseas, doing missions.

Gracie, Paul and Hannah's Australian Shepherd, came to the side of the bed. Hannah scratched her head, thinking of all the dogs Sarah had trained and sold over the years. Sarah was still single, not yet trusting her stability enough to marry and have children. She remained on her medicine and in counseling. Moreover she trusted Paul's and Hannah's word against any lies her emotions or mind conjured up. In spite of her times of struggling with mental health issues, she continued on, being as productive as possible, sheltering rescued Australian Shepherds. The community had helped fence three acres surrounding Luke's old place for her dogs, and she trained Aussies for all kinds of jobs—from herding sheep to herding Canada geese to helping farmers guard their crops from deer. She also trained dogs to become working companions for several physically handicapped children. Giving Gracie a final pat, Hannah said a quick prayer of thanks for Sarah. God continued to bring healing in her sister's life and ways for Sarah to use her gifts to help others.

Paul brushed locks of hair off Hannah's neck and kissed it, causing goose flesh to run down her. He drew a sleepy breath. "I love you, Hannah." He planted another kiss on her neck. "Are we up for the day?"

"The joys and victories and challenges of the day are calling. Can you hear them?" She put his hand over the left side of her stomach.

"And your son seems to be up for a while too. You don't have to be." But she knew he would. They seemed unable to take the other one's presence for granted.

"It's not even daylight...again. He's taking after his mother already?" he teased.

She sat up, smacking him in the face with a pillow.

He laughed, deflecting the bombardment before he pulled her into his arms, and she snuggled against his bare chest. Throughout their years together, the laughter that rang through their small home as they juggled work with play continued to bring healing to both of them.

They worked with healthy people to keep them healthy and with the unhealthy of mind or body to help them find or regain their health. Life didn't always go the way the suffering ones wanted, but Hannah and Paul drew their strength and peace from things they could never fully understand, that inside the God of *nevertheless,* abundant life could always be found—even on a fallen planet.

"Nevertheless," she whispered.

Paul's warm hand gently moved to hers, and he interlaced their fingers. "Nevertheless."

Acknowledgments

To those who believed, helped, and encouraged—your faithfulness made this novel, as well as this series, possible. Thank you!

Shannon Hill, my editor and mentor at WaterBrook Multnomah. Marci Burke, my critique partner and dear friend. You two are amazing.

Miriam Flaud, my Old Order Amish friend. Your companionship alone has made this journey worthwhile.

Steve Laube, my agent. I stand amazed—from handling stress for me to helping me get a handle on a new project.

Eldo and Dorcas Miller, whose expertise and insights about the Plain Mennonite kept my course steady throughout this journey. Your prayers have sustained me over and over again.

Joan Kunaniec, whose wisdom in the ways of the Plain Mennonite life has been a blessing beyond words. Your knowledge, deep. Your willingness to share, complete.

Jeffry J. Bizon, MD, OB/GYN, whose medical knowledge and energy for this three-book project have been greater than my gratitude can cover. Kathy Bizon, whose friendship, encouragement, and brainstorming help keep me focused.

Vicki Cato, RN, outpatient surgery Northeast Georgia Health System, who's always willing to answer medical questions.

Terry Stucky, whose time and insights into the story and character arc of this three-book series were very beneficial.

Rhonda Shonk, Office Manager, Alliance City Schools Career Centre and the Robert T. White School of Practical Nursing, whose knowledge continued to keep Hannah's schooling experiences accurate.

Carol Bartley, my line editor, whose gentle but thorough edits are trustworthy and absolute as we turn each final manuscript into as seamless a story as possible. I would not have wanted to do this without you!

And a special thank-you to everyone on the WaterBrook team—sales, marketing, publicity, and cover art. I'll never know how I managed to get to work with such a gifted group, but I'm deeply grateful.

Glossary

aa—also, too

an—on

Arewet—word

bin—am

bin kumme—have come

bis—until

bischt—are

Bobbeli—baby

Bsuch—visit

bsuche—to visit

da—the

Daadi Haus—grandfather's house. Generally this refers to a house that is attached to or is near the main house and belongs to a grandparent. Many times the main house belonged to the grandparents when they were raising their family. The main house is usually passed down to a son, who takes over the responsibilities his parents once had. The grandparents then move into the smaller place and usually have fewer responsibilities.

Daed—dad or father

dei—your

denk—think

denki—thank you

die—the

do—here

do yetz—recently

draus—out

drei—three

du—you [singular]

eens—one

Englischer—a non-Amish person. Mennonite sects whose women wear the prayer Kapps are not considered Englischers and are often referred to as Plain Mennonites.

es—it

ganz—quite

genunk—enough

glei—soon

Grossmammi—grandmother

gut—good

hab—have

hatt—difficult or hard

Hatzer—hearts

helfe—help
ich—I
in—in
iss—is
kann—can
Kapp—a prayer covering or cap
kumm—come
letz—wrong
Liewer—dear (used when addressing males past preschool age)
Liewi—dear (used when addressing females and young children)
loss uns blaudere—let's talk
Mamm—mom or mother
Mammi—shortened term of endearment for grandmother
mei—my
mitgebrocht—brought
net—not
nix—nothing
Pennsylvania Dutch—Pennsylvania German. The word *Dutch* in this phrase has nothing to do with the Netherlands. The original word was *Deutsch,* which means "German." The Amish speak some High German (used in church services) and Pennsylvania German (Pennsylvania Dutch), and after a certain age, they are taught English.
raus—out
rumschpringe—running around
saag—tell
uns—us
unsrer—our
verbinne—unite
viel—much
was—what
wege—about
Welt—world
wunderbaar—wonderful
ya—yes (pronounced *jah*)
zu—too
zwee—two

---

* Glossary taken from Eugene S. Stine, *Pennsylvania German Dictionary* (Birdsboro, PA: Pennsylvania German Society, 1996), and the usage confirmed by an instructor of the Pennsylvania Dutch language.